P9-DUM-252

The Negotiator

"Solid storytelling, compelling characters, and the promise of more O'Malleys make Henderson a name to watch. Highly recommended with a cross-genre appeal."—*LIBRARY JOURNAL*

"Dee Henderson brings a refreshing voice to Christian fiction. Her characters are lovable, sweet, and emotionally install themselves into your heart. This is a book you'll want to read time and time again."—SUITE101.COM

"This is a stunning book, which aptly showcases Ms. Henderson's talent."
—PAINTED ROCK REVIEWS

The Guardian

"Henderson is an expert in romance."—*PUBLISHERS WEEKLY*

"This series is definitely habit forming. I find myself anxiously awaiting the next book to find out what is happening with this compelling family.... Don't miss this utterly satisfying book. It's a winner!"— BOOKDRAGON REVIEW

"Dee Henderson has outdone herself yet again. *The Guardian* is dramatic, emotionally intense, yet spiritually uplifting, and should definitely be labeled with a Kleenex warning. Marcus O'Malley is truly a remarkable hero."
— ROMANCE READER ON THE RUN

The Truth Seeker

"The name Dee Henderson is synonymous with authenticity. Her books shine with believable facts and descriptions while her characters think and act like the professionals they are. *The Truth Seeker* delivers another engrossing, enjoyable read."—*ROMANTIC TIMES* MAGAZINE

"This is an interesting book, giving a glimpse of the inner workings of crime scenes, investigative work, and suspense as Lisa O'Malley's life becomes endangered.... If you want a book with depth and intelligent, human characters, this book is for you."—ROMANCECENTRAL.COM

"*The Truth Seeker* is a well-written, fast, and fun read. The characters were very sympathetic, the plot was absorbing, and the emotions felt real."—ALL ABOUT ROMANCE

Novels by Dee Henderson

THE O'MALLEY SERIES:
Danger in the Shadows (prequel)
The Negotiator
The Guardian
The Truth Seeker
The Protector
The Healer
The Rescuer

UNCOMMON HEROES SERIES:
True Devotion
True Valor
True Honor
True Courage

DEE HENDERSON

THE O'MALLEY CHRONICLES

VOLUME 1

The Negotiator

The Guardian

The Truth Seeker

Multnomah® Publishers *Sisters, Oregon*

This is a work of fiction. The characters, incidents, and dialogues are products of the author's imagination and are not to be construed as real. Any resemblance to actual events or persons, living or dead, is entirely coincidental.

O'MALLEY CHRONICLES, VOLUME I
published by Multnomah Publishers, Inc.

International Standard Book Number: 1-59052-429-2

Cover design by Kirk DouPonce/UDG DesignWorks
Compilation of:
The Negotiator

ISBN: 1-57673-819-1
The Guardian

ISBN: 1-57673-642-3
The Truth Seeker

ISBN: 1-5763-753-5

Printed in the United States of America

For information:
MULTNOMAH PUBLISHERS, INC.
POST OFFICE BOX 1720
SISTERS, OREGON 97759

04 05 06 07 08 09 10—10 9 8 7 6 5 4 3 2 1 0

The O'Malley Family Album

The O'Malleys are a close-knit clan of seven men and women, who as children living in an orphanage formed an alliance, adopted each other, and took the surname O'Malley. For over two decades they've held together against all obstacles by depending on one another.

Jennifer, the youngest O'Malley, is a pediatrician in Dallas. When she brings the family together to inform them that she has cancer, she's concerned about how her brothers and sisters will react...and whether she will live long enough to share with them her newfound passion and faith in Jesus Christ.

Each of the O'Malleys has successfully taken on the challenge of a high-risk profession, heroically dealing with life-and-death situations every day. But can the family survive when crisis strikes one of their own?

Kate O'Malley decided at age nine, when she was taken from her abusive family, that someone had to kick death in the teeth for the sake of justice. At thirty-six, Kate is now a hostage negotiator for the Chicago Police Department, a legend in the force, willing to walk into any situation. Kate would rather say there is no God than accept that He would allow the ugliness she has seen man do to man. When her sister's life is in jeopardy, can she trust Jennifer's God to be merciful?

Marcus O'Malley grew up watching his mother pray faithfully, but she died when he was eight years old. Now Marcus is a thirty-eight-year-old U.S. Marshal who thinks prayers are answered as much by chance as by a caring God. When he finds out Jennifer is a Christian, as the guardian of the O'Malley clan, he doesn't want her to get hurt by believing in a God who will only let her down. Can Marcus wrestle with the demons of his past to trust a sovereign God again?

Lisa O'Malley was abandoned at birth and lived in seven foster homes before arriving at Trevor House, with a lizard peeking out of her backpack. At thirty-five, Lisa is now a forensic pathologist who is closer to her pets than to people outside her family. She knows more about death than anyone should, yet she doesn't understand how Jennifer can be so confident that God will heal her. Can Lisa overcome her scientific logic to believe in miracles?

Jack O'Malley was eleven when he lost his parents. He learned early on not to waste time worrying about things he couldn't change. Now Jack is a thirty-four-year-old firefighter who likes to make people laugh and takes unreasonable risks to protect those in trouble. Christmas is one of Jack's favorite childhood memories, yet he believes Jesus is a myth, just like Santa Claus. While Jennifer's life hangs in the balance, can Jack discover the real Jesus—that the baby in a manger is also Jennifer's ultimate Protector?

Rachel O'Malley was a child of divorce. Neither parent wanted her, so nine-year-old Rachel arrived at Trevor House broken and alone. Thirty-five-year-old Rachel is a trauma psychologist, whose gift is helping children survive crises. She sees so many lives ravaged by tragedy that she longs for the heaven Jennifer believes in—where illness, evil, and suffering don't exist. Will Rachel come to trust the true Healer before the worry of losing her sister buries her?

Stephen O'Malley was nine when his sister, Peg, drowned and eleven when his parents died in a car crash. Now thirty-five-year-old Stephen is a paramedic who deals with tragedies every day. But Stephen's on the run—from the burden of his profession, from the grief over his sister's illness, and from a God he doesn't want to trust. Will Stephen be able to relax his grip on life and let God be God, knowing that Jesus is the one person he'll never have to rescue?

book one

THE NEGOTIATOR

"For the Son of man came to seek and to save the lost."

Luke 19:10

PROLOGUE

Dynamite.

Where had he put the dynamite? He shoved aside cobwebs striking his face, moving deeper on his belly into a crawl space that only rats should inhabit. His flashlight lit the area like a Roman candle: It had come from the construction site and could illuminate half a mile. Twenty-eight years of hard work had come down to a pink slip, an insincere "I'm sorry" from the young brat, and a flashlight. He was apologizing to no one for taking the flashlight.

That young brat of a boss would have his own trouble soon. Even a blue-collar guy like himself could figure that out. Some guy tells him to look the other way when he was doing his nightly rounds; something was getting planned.

But the bank manager…he would have to take care of that problem himself. The bank manager was going to be more than just sorry.

The rage ate inside him like the cancer did, and he felt no remorse for deciding he had been pushed around long enough. To take a man's job, to take a man's home, was to take the last of his dignity. If he let them get away with it, he would die a coward. He would rather die a man.

There it was. He pulled the wooden crate toward him, pushed aside the dust, popped the lid with a screwdriver, and looked inside. The sticks of dynamite lay in neat rows. Plenty. They were old, but they would still go boom.

ONE

Kate O'Malley had been in the dungeon since dawn.

The members of the emergency response group comprising the SWAT and hostage-rescue teams had been relegated to the basement of the county building during the last department reorganization. The metal desks were crammed together; the concrete walls needed repainting; the old case files made the room smell musty; and the hot and cold water pipes coming from the boiler room rumbled overhead.

The team was proud of its little hovel even if the plants did die within days. The location allowed for relaxed rules. The only evidence of bureaucracy was a time clock by the steel door so those not on salary could get paid for all their overtime.

Despite the dirt on her tennis shoes, Kate had her feet propped up on the corner of her desk, her fingers steepled, her eyes half closed, as she listened to the sound of her own voice over the headphones, careful not to let the turmoil of her thoughts reflect in her expression. She was reviewing the last of four negotiation tapes. Case 2214 from last week haunted her. A domestic violence call with shots fired. It had taken six hours to negotiate a peaceful conclusion. Six agonizing hours for the mother and two children held in the house. Had there been any way to end it earlier?

As Kate listened to the husband's drunken threats and her own calm replies, she automatically slowed her breathing to suppress her rising emotions. She hated domestic violence cases. They revived unwanted memories…memories Kate had buried away from the light of day.

The cassette tape reversed sides. She sipped her hot coffee and grimaced. Graham must have made this pot. She didn't mind strong coffee, but this was Navy coffee. Kate tugged open her middle desk drawer and pushed aside chocolate bars and two heavy silver medals for bravery to find sugar packets.

She found it odd to be considered something of a legend on the force at the age of thirty-six, but she understood it. She was a negotiator known for one thing—being willing to walk into any situation. Domestic violence, botched robberies, kidnappings, even airline hijackings—she had worked them all.

Kate let people see what she wanted them to see. She could sit in the middle of a crisis for hours or days if that's what it took to negotiate a peace. She could do it with a relaxed demeanor. Detached. Most often, apparently bored.

It worked. Her apparent boredom in a crisis kept people alive. She dealt with the emotions later, after the situation was over—and far away from work. She played a lot of basketball, using the game to cultivate her focus, let go of the tension.

This was her fourth review of the tapes. Her case notes appeared complete. Kate didn't hear anything she could have done differently. She stopped the tape playback, relieved to have the review done. She pushed back the headphones and ran her hand through her ruffled hair.

"O'Malley."

She turned to see Graham holding up his phone.

"Line three. Your brother."

"Which one?"

"The paramedic."

She punched the blinking light. "Hi, Stephen."

"Let me guess; you're screening your calls."

She was, but it was an amusing first observation. "I'm ducking the media for a few days. Are you off duty?"

"Just wrapping up. Had breakfast yet?"

Kate picked up the tension in his voice. "I could go for some good coffee and a stack of pancakes."

"I'll meet you across the street at Quinn's."

"Deal."

Kate glanced at her pager, confirming she was on group call. She slid her cellular phone into her shirt pocket as she stood. "I'm heading to breakfast. Anyone want a Danish brought back?" Quinn's was a popular stopping point for all of them.

Requests came in from all over the room. Her tally ended with three raspberry, four cherry, and two apple Danishes. "Page me if you need me."

The stairs out of the dungeon were concrete and hand railed so they could be traversed with speed. Security doors were located at both ends. The stairway opened into the secure access portion of the parking garage. The team's specially equipped communications vans gleamed. They'd just been polished yesterday.

Kate slid on her sunglasses. June had begun as a month of glaring sun and little rain. It parched even the downtown Chicago concrete, coating the ground with crumbling dust. Traffic was heavy in this tight narrow corridor. She crossed against the traffic light.

Quinn's was a mix of new interior and old building, the restaurant able to comfortably seat seventy. Kate waved to the owner, took two menus, and headed to her usual table at the back of the restaurant, choosing the chair that put her back to the wall. It was always an amusing dance when there were two or more cops coming to Quinn's. No cop liked to sit with his back to an open room.

She accepted a cup of coffee, skimming the menu though she knew it by heart. Blueberry pancakes. She was a lady of habit. That decision made, she relaxed back in her seat to enjoy the coffee and tune into the conversations going on around her. The ladies by the window were talking about a baby shower. The businessmen to her left were discussing a fishing trip. Two teenagers were debating where to begin their shopping excursion.

Kate stirred two sugar packets into her coffee. Normal life. After ten years as a negotiator, there wasn't much normalcy left in her own life. The mundane details that most people cared about had ceased to cause the slightest blip on her radar screen. Normal people cared about clothes, vacations, holidays. Kate cared about staying alive. If it weren't such a stark dichotomy, it would be amusing.

Stephen arrived as she was nursing her second cup of coffee. Kate smiled when she saw the interest he attracted as he came to join her. She couldn't blame the ladies. His sports jacket and blue jeans didn't hide his muscles. He could walk off the cover of nearly any men's fashion magazine. Not bad for someone who spent his days dealing with car accidents, fire victims, gang shootings, and drug overdoses.

He wouldn't stay in this city forever—he talked occasionally about moving northwest to some small town with a lake, good fishing, and a job where he would finally get to treat more heart attacks than gunshot victims—but for now he stayed. Kate knew it was primarily because of her. Stephen had designated himself her watchdog. He had never asked; he'd just taken the role. She loved him for it, even if she did tease him on occasion about it.

He pulled out the chair across from her. "Thanks for making time, Kate."

"Mention food and you've got my attention." She pushed over the second cup of coffee the waitress had filled, not commenting on the strain in his eyes despite his smile. That look hadn't been there yesterday when he'd joined her for a one-on-one basketball game. She hoped it was only the aftereffects of a hard shift. He would tell her if he needed to. Within the O'Malley family, secrets were rare.

At the orphanage—Trevor House—where family was nonexistent, the seven of them had chosen to become their own family, had chosen the last name O'Malley. Stephen was one of the three special ones in the family: a true orphan, not one of the abandoned or abused.

They might not share a blood connection, but that didn't matter; what they did share was far stronger. They were loyal, faithful, and committed to each other. Some twenty-two years after their decision, the group was as unified and strong as ever.

They had, in a sense, adopted each other.

"Did you see the news?" Stephen asked once the waitress had taken their orders.

Kate shook her head. She had left early for the gym and then gone straight to the office.

"There was a five-car pileup on the tollway. A three-year-old was in the front seat of a sedan. He died en route to County General Hospital."

Kids. The toughest victims for any O'Malley to deal with. "I'm sorry, Stephen." He decompressed like she did. Slowly. After he left work.

"So am I." He set aside his coffee cup. "But that's not why I called you. Jennifer's coming to town."

Jennifer O'Malley was the youngest in the family, everyone's favorite. She was a pediatrician in Dallas. "Oh?"

"I got a call from her this morning. She's got a Sunday flight into O'Hare."

Kate frowned. It wasn't easy for any doctor to leave her practice on such short notice. "Did she say what it was about?"

"No. Just asked which day I was off. She was trying to set up a family gathering. There's probably a message on your answering machine."

Kate didn't wait to find out. She picked up her cellular phone and called her home number, listening to the ring; then the answering machine kicked on. She punched a button to override, added her code, and listened as the messages began to play.

Their breakfasts arrived.

Jennifer had left a message. It didn't say much. Dinner Sunday evening at Lisa's. Kate closed her phone. "I don't like this."

"It gets worse. Marcus is flying back from Washington for the gathering."

Kate let that information sink in as she started on her hot blueberry pancakes. Their oldest brother, a U.S. Marshal, was interrupting his schedule to fly back to Chicago. "Jennifer is one step away from saying it's a family emergency." Let any member of the family say those words and the others dropped everything and came.

Stephen reached for his orange juice. "That's how I would read it."

"Any ideas?"

"None. I talked to Jennifer last Friday. She didn't say anything."

"Did she sound tense?"

"Tired maybe; unusual for her, but given the schedule she keeps, not unexpected."

Kate's pager went off. She glanced at the return number and grimaced. One of these days she was actually going to get to finish a meal. She set down her linen napkin as she got to her feet. "Work is calling. Can you join me for dinner? I'm off at six. I was planning to grill steaks."

"Glad to. Stay safe, Kate."

She grinned. "Always, Stephen. Put breakfast on my tab."

"I've got it covered."

She didn't have time to protest. It was an old debate. She smiled and let him win this round. "See you at six."

FBI special agent Dave Richman dealt with crises every day of his life. However, being a customer when a bank holdup went down was not one he would recommend.

His heart pounding, he rested his back against the reception desk and prayed the gunman stayed on the other side of the room.

The man had come in through the front door, shot four holes in the ceiling with a handgun, and ordered some of the customers and staff to leave, specific others to stay.

Dave had nearly shot him in the first few seconds of the assault, but the dynamite around the man's chest had halted that idea. The FBI playbook was simple: When facing dynamite, a loaded gun, and a lot of frightened people—don't get anyone killed.

In the initial commotion, Dave had managed to drop to the floor and get out of sight. He had about six feet of customer counter space that ended in an *L* that made up the reception desk he was hiding behind. So far, it was sufficient. The gunman had the hostages clustered together on the other side of the open room. He hadn't bothered to search the offices or the rest of the room. That most likely meant he was proceeding on emotion—and that, Dave knew, made him more dangerous than ever.

Dave would give anything to have his FBI team on-site. When the local cops surrounding the building ran the license plates for the cars in the parking lot, the trace on his own blue sedan would raise a flag at the FBI office. His team would be deployed because he was present. He had trusted his life to their actions in the past; it looked like he would be doing so again. The sound of sirens and the commotion outside had died down; by now he was sure they had the perimeter formed.

He leaned his head back. This was not exactly how he had planned to spend his birthday. His sister, Sara, was expecting him for lunch. When he didn't show up, she was going to start to worry.

There would be no simple solution to this crisis.

He was grateful God was sovereign.

From the tirade going on behind him, it was obvious this man had not come to rob the bank.

They had a bank robber that had not bothered to get any money. Kate was already assuming the worst.

The security camera video feeds had just been tapped and routed to the communications van. Four different camera angles. Two were static pictures of empty areas, the front glass doors, and the teller area for the drive up. One was focused high, covering the front windows, but it did show the hostages: five men and four women seated against the wall.

The fourth camera held Kate's attention. The man paced the center of the room. He was big and burly, his stride impatient.

The dynamite trigger held in his right hand worried her. It looked like a compression switch. Let go, and the bomb went off. There was no audio, but he was clearly in a tirade about something. His focus seemed to be on one of the nine hostages in particular, the third man from the end.

This man had come with a purpose. Since it apparently wasn't to rob the bank, that left more ugly possibilities.

He wasn't answering the phone.

Kate looked over at her boss, Jim Walker. She had worked for him for eight years. He trusted her judgment; she trusted him to keep her alive if things went south. "Jim, we've got to calm this situation down quickly. If he won't answer the phone, then we'll have to talk the old-fashioned way."

He studied the monitors. "Agreed."

Kate looked at the building blueprints. The entrance was a double set of glass doors with about six feet in between them. They were designed to be energy efficient in both winter and summer. Kate wished the architects had thought about security first. She had already marked those double doors and those six feet of open space as her worst headache. A no-man's-land. Six feet without cover.

"Graham, if I stay here—" she pointed just inside the double glass doors—"can you keep me in line of sight?" He was one of the few people she would trust to take a shot over her shoulder if it were required.

He studied the blueprint. "Yes."

"Have Olsen and Franklin set up to cover here and here." She marked two sweeps of the interior. It would be enough. If they had to take the gunman down, there would be limited ways to do it without blowing up a city block in the process.

Kate turned up the sleeves of her flannel shirt. Her working wardrobe at a scene was casual. She did not wear a bulletproof vest; she didn't even carry a gun. The last thing she wanted was to look or sound like a cop. Her gender, size, and clothing were designed to keep her from being perceived as one more threat. In reality, she was the worst threat the gunman had. The snipers were under her control. To save lives, she would take one if necessary.

Kate glanced again at the security monitors. There was a lot of the bank floor plan not covered by the cameras. There might be another gunman, more hostages—both were slim but potential realities. The risks were inevitable.

"Ian, try the phones one more time."

Kate watched the gunman's reaction. He turned to glare at the ringing phone, paced toward it, but didn't answer. Okay. It wouldn't get him to answer, but it did capture his attention. That might be useful.

It was time to go.

"Stay safe, Kate."

She smiled. "Always, Jim."

The parking lot had been paved recently; spots on the asphalt were sticky under her tennis shoes. Kate assessed the cops in the perimeter as she walked around the squad cars toward the bank entrance. Some of the rookies looked nervous. A few veterans she recognized had been through this with her before.

Her focus turned to the glass doors. The bank name was done in a bold white stencil on the clear glass; a smaller sign below listed the lobby and drive-up teller hours. Kate put her hand on the glass door and smoothly pulled it open, prepared sometime in the next six feet to get shot.

Dave saw the woman as she reached the front doors of the bank and couldn't believe what he was seeing. She came in, no bulletproof vest, apparently no gun, not even a radio. She just walked in.

God, have mercy. He had never prayed so intently for someone in his life, not counting his sister. Absolutely nothing was preventing that gunman from shooting her.

He pulled back from the end of the desk, knowing that if she saw him, her surprise would give away his presence. He moved rapidly toward the other end of the counter, his hand tight around his gun, knowing he was likely going to have to intervene.

"Stay there!" The gunman's voice had just jumped an octave.

She had certainly gotten the man's attention.

If she had followed protocol and worn a vest, Dave could have taken the gunman down while his attention was diverted. Instead, she had walked in without following the basic rules of safety, and his opportunity filtered away in the process. He silently chewed out the local scene commander. The city cops should have waited for the professional negotiators to arrive instead of overreacting and sending in a plainclothes cop, creating more of a problem than they solved.

Lady, don't you dare make things worse! Listen, say little, and at the first opportunity: Get out of here!

"You didn't answer the phone. Jim Walker would like to know what it is you want."

She had a calm, unhurried, Southern voice. Not what Dave was expecting. His initial assessment had certainly not fit his image of a hostage negotiator, but that calmness didn't sound forced. His attention sharpened. The negotiators he had worked with in the past had been focused, intense, purposeful men. This lady looked like everything about her was fluid. Tall. Slender. A nice tan. Long, auburn hair. Casual clothes. Too exotically beautiful to ever make it in undercover work, she wasn't someone you would forget meeting. She even stood relaxed. That convinced him. She had to be a negotiator; either that or a fool. Since his life was in her hands, he preferred to be optimistic.

"I've got exactly what I want. You can turn around and go back the way you came."

"Of course. But would you mind if I just sat right here for a few minutes first? If I come right back out, my boss will get ticked off."

It was how she said it. She actually made the guy laugh. "Sit down but shut up."

"Glad to."

Dave breathed a silent sigh of relief and eased his finger off the trigger. They wouldn't send a rookie into a situation like this, but who was she? Not FBI, that much was certain.

Kate sat down where she stood in one graceful move and rested her head against the glass doors. Her heart rate slowly decelerated. She hadn't gotten herself shot in the first minute. That was always a good sign.

She scanned the faces of the hostages. They were all nervous, three of the women crying. The gunman was probably not enjoying that. The man the gunman was focused on looked about ready to have a coronary.

At least there were no heroics going on here. These nine folks were scared, nervous, ordinary people. Seeing it on the monitor had been one thing, confirming it directly was a relief. No athletes. No military types. She had lost hostages before who acted on their own.

She wished she could tell them to stay put, but the only communication she could make with them was in her actions. The more bored she appeared with the situation, the better. The goal was to get the gunman to relax a little. His barked humor had been a minor, very good sign. She would take it and every other one she could get.

Kate studied the bomb as the gunman paced. It was everything she had feared. Manning, her counterpart on the bomb squad, was going to have a challenge.

It was a pity God didn't exist. Someone, God if no one else, should have solved this man's problems before he decided to walk into this bank with dynamite and a gun. The gunman wouldn't agree with her, but options now were limited—he would end up in jail or dead. Not exactly happy alternatives. She had to make sure he didn't take nine innocent lives along with him.

Ten, counting hers.

She couldn't have the guy shot; his hand would come off the bomb trigger. She couldn't rush the guy; she would get herself shot. If she got shot, her family would descend on her like a ton of bricks for being so stupid. As she knew from firsthand experience, it was difficult enough recovering from an injury without having the entire O'Malley clan breathing down her neck as she did so.

Negotiating to get the hostages released was going to be a challenge. He didn't appear to want anything beyond control of the bank manager's fate—

and he had that. Releasing hostages took something to exchange. She could go for sympathy for the crying women, but that would probably get her tossed out as well.

As time wore on, bargaining chips would appear she could use—food, water, the practical reality of how he would handle controlling this many people when faced with the need for restroom visits.

She could wait the situation out indefinitely, and slowly it would turn in her favor. But would he let that much time pass? Or would he escalate before then?

Dave had a difficult decision to make. Did he alert the cop of his presence and risk her giving away his position with her expression, or did he stay silent and watch the situation develop? He finally accepted that he had no choice. It would take more than one person to end this standoff. That was the reality. He eased his badge out of his pocket and flipped it open.

He moved forward, leaning around the end of the desk.

There was not even a twitch to indicate her surprise. No emotion across her face, no movement of her head, no quick glance in his direction. She flicked her index finger at him, just like she would strike an agate in a game of marbles.

An irritated flick at that, ordering him back.

Dave sat back on his heels. He would have been amused at her reaction had the situation been different. That total control of her emotions, her facial expression, her demeanor was a two-edged sword—it would keep his location safe, but it also meant it would be very hard to judge what she was thinking.

Her response told him a lot about her though. That silent flick of her finger had conveyed a definite order—one she expected to be obeyed without question. She knew how to get her point across. He felt sorry for anyone who would ever question her in a court of law. She must give defense attorneys fits.

He had to find some way to talk to her.

He opened the receptionist's desk drawer a fraction at a time and peered inside. He found what he hoped for—paper. He silently slid out several sheets and took out his pen. He had to make the message simple and the letters large and dark enough so she could read them with a mere glance.

What did he say first?

4 SHOTS. 2 LEFT.

She adjusted her sunglasses.

Okay, message received.

The best way to take this gunman down was from behind, by surprise. But the gunman would need to be close so that Dave could put his hand around that bomb trigger.

MOVE HIM TO ME.

She read the message. Several moments passed. When the gunman paced away from her, she shook her head ever so slightly.

Why not? His frustration was acute. There was no way for her to answer that.

RELEASE HOSTAGES.

She gave no response.

Dave grimaced. This was the equivalent of passing notes in high school, and he had done all of that he would ever like to do when he was a teen. Why had she not even tried to start a dialogue with the man?

TALK TO HIM!

Her fingers curled into a fist.

Dave backed off. Whatever she was considering, at the moment she didn't want to take suggestions. Frustration and annoyance competed for dominance within him. She had better have a great plan in mind. His life was in her hands.

He had no choice but to settle back and wait.

Kate flexed her fingers, forced to bury all her emotions into that one gesture. She would give her next paycheck to be able to go outside for about ten minutes and pound something. She not only had a cop in her midst, she had a would-be hero who wanted to give her backseat advice!

Someone had a federal badge; he thought he understood how to deal with any crisis he faced. That suggestion she move the gunman toward him had been truly stupid: Before any negotiations had been tried, he wanted to force a tactical conclusion. There was one word that defined her job: patience. This cop didn't have any, and he was going to get them all killed.

She had two people to keep calm: the gunman and the Fed. Right now it looked like the FBI agent was going to be the bigger problem. If he got it in his head to act, some innocent person was going to get killed, and she was the one sitting in the direct line of fire.

She never should have gotten up this morning.

Deal with it. Do the job.

Kate drew a quiet breath and turned her full attention to the man pacing away from her.

Dave shifted to ease a leg cramp as he listened to the conversation between the negotiator and the gunman. He knew her name now. Kate O'Malley. A nice Irish name for someone who didn't sound Irish.

The conversation had begun slowly, but over the last hour it had become a running dialogue. So far the topics had touched on nothing of significance to the situation. It was all small talk, and she had that down to an art form. It was too well controlled for it to be an accident. Dave wondered how long she could talk about nothing before she drove herself crazy. He knew very few cops who could tolerate such small talk. They were too factual, cut to the bottom line, take-charge people.

The gunman was still pacing, but his stride had slowed. Her constant soft cadence was beginning to work. Dave knew what she was doing, but he could still feel himself responding to that calm, quiet voice as well, his own tension easing. The stress of the situation was giving way to the fatigue that came from an overload of adrenaline fading from his system. He could only imagine how she was managing that energy drain. The last hour and a half felt like the longest day of his life.

He no longer wondered if she was the right person for this task; she had convinced him. She had a voice that could mesmerize a man. Soft, Southern, smooth. Dave enjoyed the sound. It conjured up images of candlelight dinners and intimate conversations.

This lady was controlling events with just her voice; it was something impressive to observe. Part of her plan was obvious. Wear the other side down; remove the sense of threat; build some equity that could be used later when it would matter.

He was learning a lot of minor information about her. She loved the Cubs. Disliked sitcoms. Thought the potholes in the neighborhood were atrocious. When she went for takeout, her first choice was spicy Chinese.

The topic shifted to which local restaurant made the best pizza. Dave knew what she was doing, trying to convince the gunman to request food be sent in. It would probably be laced with something designed to calm the man down. He had to admire how she was working toward even that minor objective with patience. He reached for his pen again. She was making him hungry, if not the gunman. He had been trying to figure out what he could do to help her out. This kind of negotiation was tiring work. He might as well make this a three-way conversation.

YOU FORGOT THE MUSHROOMS.

She never dropped the conversational ball as she smoothly mentioned what exactly was inside a mushroom cap, if anyone wanted to know.

Dave smiled.

Since her plan was to sit there and talk, he could think of a few more questions for her. She had to be running out of topics. He was more than a little curious to learn about Kate O'Malley. She had him fascinated. She was sitting in the midst of a stressful situation, accomplishing a nearly impossible task, and yet looking and sounding like she didn't have a care in the world. Her conversation was casual, her smile quick to appear. If this was what she was like on the job, what was she like off duty?

FAVORITE MOVIE.

His query was met with the glimmer of a smile. Minutes later, she smoothly changed the subject of the conversation to movies.

He had to stifle a laugh when she said her favorite movie was *Bugs Bunny's Great Adventure.* It didn't matter if she actually meant it or was simply showing an exquisitely refined sense of humor. It was the perfect answer.

IS THIS OUR GREAT ADVENTURE?

High Noon.

Dave leaned his head back, not sure how to top that one. Kate O'Malley was apparently a movie buff. It was nice to know they had something in common. If she could get them out of this safely, he would buy the tickets and popcorn to whatever movie she wanted to see. He was certainly going to owe her. The idea was enough to bring a smile. It was one debt he would enjoy paying.

TWO

Kate watched the gunman pace away. Henry Lott was divorced, fighting cancer, had recently lost his job, and the bank manager had foreclosed on his home Monday. In the hour since she had convinced him to release the four women hostages, his anger had repeatedly flared, volatile and unpredictable. Wilshire Construction and First Union Bank were getting equal amounts of his hate.

She watched, her face impassive, as he waved the bomb trigger in front of the bank manager's face and peeled back one finger, then another, threatening to let go. One of these times it was not going to be an act. Henry would blow that dynamite.

Every couple months there was a case like this, one that actually scared her. She prepared for them, but she was never really ready. Going up against someone who was dying, who wanted to end his life by making a statement, left her little room to maneuver. She knew that. She didn't have to like it, but she did have to accept it.

She had bought them five hours and four hostages. If they were going to get the remaining hostages out alive, they would have to do it by force. The decision didn't come easy, for it was failure on her part, but protecting her pride wasn't part of her job. Henry Lott had finished talking, and it was time she made the recommendation. The bank manager whimpered, and the sound made her want to flinch.

The growing tension in the room had seeped into her muscles and bones; no matter how she tried to mentally divert for a moment and visualize herself somewhere else to get back a sense of distance and calm, the pressure inside didn't abate. Was this the day her family got the phone call they dreaded? Kate closed her eyes for a moment, took a deep breath, and accepted what was going to happen was going to happen.

I'm sorry, guys. I did my best.

She rested her weight back against her hand and tapped her finger twice.

A red dot blinked on the top of her left tennis shoe. She had been talking with Graham most of the day. Morse code was low tech, but it let them pass information back and forth. She tapped out a terse message for Jim.

The present assault plan called for a breach that would come from two directions—they'd blow the steel security door by the teller windows; two seconds later they'd shatter the front glass doors. Flash grenades would come in to freeze the situation. She would have two seconds to clear the glass doors, reach Henry Lott, and close her hands around the bomb trigger.

High risk. She could get shot. She could fail, which was worse.

Her peripheral vision scanned the place where the FBI agent hid. What was he thinking? The notes had ceased during the last twenty minutes. The risk of his being discovered increased with the passing of time; another good reason they should act sooner versus later. She wished she had a way to coordinate with him, warn him. He had turned out to be surprisingly good company during the last few hours. She wanted a chance to say thanks for the notes. His humor was sharp and dry; it came across even in his two- or three-word shorthand. He had stayed relaxed in this tense situation, a fact she appreciated.

It didn't take long for her boss to reach a decision. The teams were moving into position.

She needed Henry Lott to be within five feet. She planned to hit him and take him down, pinning the trigger between them. He had seventy pounds on her; she was going to have a fight on her hands in the few moments before her team could reach them. The frustration of not being able to talk him into giving up would solve some of that disparity. The FBI agent should be able to close the distance to help. She would do whatever it took to win.

She got the signal from Graham. The teams were in position, ready for her mark.

She knew exactly where she would like Henry to be when she made her move. She tapped out another request: Ring the phone.

Henry started across the room toward the ringing phone on the receptionist desk. Kate toned out his words, looking only at the distance. Eight feet, seven feet, six feet…in range. Her fingers began to fold one by one, controlling the first blast. Three. Two. One. Fist.

The steel door blew apart.

Kate surged forward, ignoring the gun, going down with the man, her fore-arm across his windpipe. Her hand closed around his on the trigger release.

They hit the marble floor hard, pelted by exploding glass.

Henry tried to toss her off him. Her shin took a kick from a steel-tipped boot. She felt her wrist going around and fought back with desperate energy. With both hands around his to keep the bomb trigger down, her face was exposed. She saw his left hand coming around and braced for the broken nose. It wouldn't be the first punch she had taken. His blow connected, but it wasn't with her. The FBI agent grunted in pain, threw a short jab back.

She forgave the agent the elbow to her ribs. It was a fight between two equals with her sandwiched between them. She did her best to keep her head down. Wires slid up around her fingers; dynamite wedged against her abdomen.

Henry Lott stopped moving.

She hung suspended in time for a moment, wondering if it was over, waiting for Henry to move. Then she was hearing again, feeling again. The rushing sound of the assault teams, of hostages being pulled clear, made it into her consciousness; muscles quivered from the sudden stress release; forming bruises demanded attention.

"Do you have it?" The FBI agent demanded, his weight still sandwiching her.

"Got it." She was literally curled around the bomb trigger, clutching it like a treasure. Her hands were slick with sweat, and her fingers were cramping, but she had it.

"Don't move."

What did he think she was going to do? Get up and dance? Something sharp was digging into her chest, and she could feel wires pinching her fingers. "Fine. I won't move. But you could," she replied, letting her tone of voice carry a fine bite to it for the first time since she had entered the bank.

He shifted to the side, and she got her first full breath since the fight had begun. She closed her eyes to enjoy it. She was quivering with the fatigue. A wave of nausea swept over her as her body literally shook off the stress. The entire situation had been too close for comfort.

Teammates crowded around, surrounding them, her boss in the front of the group. "Franklin, get that syringe from the doc; make sure this guy stays out. Let's get bomb disposal in here."

"Hostages?" Kate asked, forcing her head to clear and her voice to firm.

"All fine." Jim was looking at the device. "Can you hold that trigger for a few minutes while Manning takes this apart?"

"I'm not planning to let go."

Somebody laughed.

"Okay," Jim said. "Let's clear this place of nonessential personnel. Good job, Kate. I'll see you again in a few minutes. Dave, your team is waiting for you outside."

The FBI agent shook his head. "I'll be out with Kate."

Her boss considered him for a moment, then nodded. He got to his feet. The room began to clear.

Kate was not so willing to concede the point. "I appreciate the thought. Now would you get out of here?"

He sat on the floor beside Henry, breathing hard, looking at her. She frankly enjoyed looking back; he was a good-looking man. His sandy hair was ruffled and the split lip had to hurt. He had the sleek look of an athlete, and she had learned firsthand that his bulk was well-conditioned muscle. This was not an FBI agent who spent his days behind a desk.

"What's the matter? Tired of my company?" The twinkle in his eyes said he was humoring her. She had no hope of getting him to leave. The fact he told her no with a smile didn't lessen her irritation with his answer; it increased it. He was cocky and wrong again. He didn't belong in here. She sighed silently. That was the problem with guys; they always had to be heroes.

The only danger for him at the moment was if she let go of the bomb trigger; the realization made her silently chuckle. She wondered if he had given more than a passing thought to the fact she was the one still protecting him as he sat there keeping her company.

Accents were a hobby, and his was a delight. He was British. Her sister Jennifer was going to be so jealous. If he insisted on staying, then she was going to enjoy it. "Keep talking."

"About what?"

"Anything. I like your accent."

His grin was quick. "Don't knock yours, Southern. I could listen to you all day."

"You have."

"I enjoyed it, too, despite the circumstances." He reached over and feathered a hand through her hair. "You've got glass slivers in your hair."

His touch made her freeze. In any other situation, she would have slapped his hand away, but she couldn't move, and she was suddenly glad she had to remain motionless. She had already shown this man too much of herself in the past hours of conversation, letting him know how prickly she was about being touched by any man other than her brothers would have been humiliating. As his fingers brushed through her hair, she took a deep breath and unexpectedly felt herself relax; it was a comforting touch. "I'm sure I sparkle."

He chuckled. "Actually, you do." He leaned over to brush glass fragments from her shoulder and tensed. "I should have hit the guy harder. You're bleeding."

"It was quite a shower of glass. A few cuts were inevitable." Kate could feel them across her shoulders, her arms. They were beginning to sting.

"You've got more than a few." He moved to let Manning take his place and came around to her side. "Don't lean back." He brushed aside the glass fragments on her shirt with care.

"The cuts are not that big a deal." He ignored her comment. "You never did tell me your name."

"Dave Richman."

"Cute notes."

He leaned over to see her face. "Nice small talk."

She narrowed her gaze but found nothing in his expression to contradict his words. The last Fed she had worked with had panned what she did as being trivial chitchat. Dave had just moved a step out of the hole he had dug for himself with that MOVE HIM TO ME ridiculous note. "It's my specialty."

"It saved lives, including mine. I owe you."

She scowled at the idea. "Don't get too grateful. It was my job. I didn't do it specifically for you."

He laughed, and it was a nice sound. Kate let herself smile. With all Dave's notes asking questions, she might have been chatting more than usual; it was hard to tell after the fact. Her abused muscles cramped. She closed her eyes against the pain, walling it off.

"Another minute and the paramedics will be in here."

"Manning, is Stephen out there?"

"Pacing."

Anticipating the lecture, she winced. "Don't hurry." She saw Dave's look of curiosity. "My brother is one of those paramedics you mentioned."

"Ahh. Be glad you've got family to get on your case."

He had no idea. "Three brothers, three sisters. I'm going to get killed." She had given them cause to worry, which was what annoyed her the most.

"It should be an interesting evening."

"You have a knack for understatements." Remaining motionless was hard work. "You know what I would really like right now?" She knew she was starting to ramble, but the fatigue felt like a heavy blanket, and words had always been her first defense.

"What?"

"A good steak, a cold drink, and a nap, not necessarily in that order."

"Sorry, but what I think you're going to get is an ambulance ride, a couple needles, and some stitches."

Great. Just how she wanted to spend her evening. "What an unappealing thought."

Manning set aside the wire clippers. "You can let go, Kate; it's defused."

The sense of relief was intense but not quite complete. "You're sure?" She wasn't passing judgment, but she was the one holding the trigger.

"It won't go boom," Manning promised.

She eased open her grip on the trigger, heard the faint click of open contacts.

Now she felt the relief. She gladly moved away from Henry Lott. Manning started moving the dynamite to an explosive ordinance box. As soon as it was clear, cops were waiting to handcuff Henry and carry him outside.

Kate sat on the marble floor, content to wait for Manning to finish. It felt better than just good to have this situation over with. She didn't even cringe as she thought about all the paperwork the tactical response would demand. For the moment she was just going to savor the fact it had ended with the gunman and all the hostages still alive.

She draped her arms across her knees and looked around at all the damage. "What a mess."

Dave nodded. "Looks like a bomb went off. Doors blown in, a couple ceiling tiles down, glass everywhere."

She looked over at him. "You have a wicked sense of humor."

"Thanks."

"Don't mention it."

Humor was too rare a commodity in this business not to pause and enjoy having found it in an unexpected place. She could really get to like this guy, despite his charge-right-in attitude and his annoying habit of not listening to her when she was right. They were grinning at each other when they were interrupted. "This is not a good way to start the weekend, Kate."

"Stephen, it's a great way to start the weekend. Go away."

Beside her, Dave choked back a laugh. "Behave."

She reluctantly turned her attention to her brother. "I'm only banged up, I promise."

Stephen set down the case he carried and surveyed her. "At least you didn't get yourself shot. What did you do, go swimming in the broken glass?"

"It's not as bad as it looks."

He gave her a skeptical look. "What else hurts besides the cuts?" He used sterile gauze to wipe away the blood so he could look at the cut on her right arm.

"My tailbone. I've been sitting on this marble floor all day."

"Seriously."

"My left shoulder. I hit the marble floor hard. And my headache is a killer."

Because she had no choice, she sat still as he and his partner dealt with the cuts; she winced when gentle hands hit bruises. Stephen frowned as he touched the back of her head. "Nice goose egg."

"He got in a lucky blow."

"How's the vision?"

"Fine."

"Hmm."

She looked at the gurney that was wheeled in with suspicion. "Stephen, I'm walking out of here."

"If you want to pass out in front of your team, you can. Your blood pressure is low even for you."

"Fading adrenaline. Give me a break."

He accepted something from his partner. "Close your eyes; you don't like needles."

"Stick me with that and you'll be fixing your own steak tonight."

"Would you rather me do it or a nurse you don't know?"

"You play dirty." She turned her head and squeezed her eyes closed.

"It's done." He taped down the IV line. "You want a grape or cherry lollipop?"

She considered hitting him. She plucked a cherry one from his pocket. "You know the only reason I let you get away with the needle is so I can get one of these."

"Jennifer bribes her patients with them."

"Her patients are two years old. I don't like the inference."

"You're the one who made it."

She retrieved the grape one and handed it to Dave. "Eat this and be quiet." She had heard his stifled chuckle.

"Stephen," Dave interceded as he unwrapped the sucker, "you'd better quit while you're ahead."

Her brother looked over at him. "Probably. Would you?"

Dave considered the question for a moment. "No. She's too cute when she's annoyed."

"I knew I would like you."

Kate scowled. "Gentlemen, now that you've bonded, can we go?"

"Sure. But you're taking the gurney." Stephen moved it beside her and grinned. "Just sit on it, Kate. I won't make you go out with the straps and the blanket."

She knew it was going to be a rough afternoon when getting up to move to the stretcher made her light-headed. Dave didn't release his grip on her arm until she was seated and her legs were up.

She saw his concern despite their lighthearted banter, and it bothered her. She didn't want his final impression of her to be one of weakness. It wasn't pride; it was the reality of her job. Managing impressions was critical to keeping her reputation intact—a reputation that insured her voice carried weight when she was called into a crisis situation. If the consensus about her around the FBI offices six months from now was *got hurt* rather than *solved it,* the next time she worked a case with them she would be playing from a weak hand.

Stephen squeezed her hand. She returned the pressure. She knew what he had been doing, the cad. He'd raised her blood sugar level, got an IV line in place, stopped the bleeding, and kept her mind off what he and his partner were doing. He had always been excellent at his job. Stephen was born to the role of rescuer.

There were days she would give anything to trade in her role of negotiator for something more along Stephen's role of white knight. She had to live and work with gray, in the middle of the violence, right at the edge of the grim reaper's hand of death. Getting banged up occasionally in the process just went with her territory.

"Dave, there's room if you want to ride along," Stephen offered.

"I'll take it."

"There's no need," Kate protested, not liking the idea.

Dave's frown silenced her. Having been silenced by a look from some of the best, she changed her profile of him, privately amused. He could simply cool his eyes to convey he didn't like your answer as easily as he could warm them to share humor. It was a trait a good leader perfected.

"Kate, the media is all over this. Be prepared." Stephen warned.

The media would likely make her life miserable for days to come. The two newspapers, not to mention the local newscasts, vied with each other for the most dramatic presentation of a crisis like this. Ignoring the press was becoming her second occupation. "Let's see how many pictures they can take of your back," she suggested to Stephen. That solution to the problem was one of her favorites.

"My pleasure. The squad will love the publicity."

~

"This is not a steak." Kate used the plastic fork to check the suspicious entree. It was bad enough she had lost the debate and been admitted to the hospital for the night; meatloaf for dinner was adding insult to injury.

Stephen got to his feet. "Want me to go get you a cheeseburger?"

"Make it two and a vanilla shake."

"Eat your salad."

She poked at the limp lettuce. "It's dead." She reached for the sealed pudding cup. "At least they can't ruin dessert."

Stephen tweaked her foot. "I'll be back shortly. Behave yourself while I'm gone."

"You want good behavior, too?" She grinned. "You're pushing it, Stephen. You already overruled me on staying here for the night."

"I managed to stop the family from descending on you, so we're even."

She opened the pudding cup. "It's a brief reprieve and you know it," she countered. "Sunday's dinner is going to be interesting. I sure hope Jennifer has earth-shaking news to share or I'm going to be toast."

Stephen laughed. "You walked into it. I'll head the family off for a few days, but after that you're on your own." They had been calling from the moment she reached the hospital.

"I hate being the center of attention."

"Next time don't get hurt."

She couldn't exactly argue that point.

There was a tap on the door. "May I come in?"

"Hi, Dave. Sure." Kate pushed away the tray. "Stephen's smuggling in real food. You want something?"

Stephen paused by the door as he reached Dave. "Cheeseburger, Polish, chili? I'm heading across the street."

"A Polish with the works would be great."

Stephen nodded. "I'll be back in a few minutes. She's getting feisty, so watch yourself."

"Thanks a lot, Stephen." Kate settled back on the pillows and watched Dave take a seat. He looked tired. She wasn't surprised. It was after 7 P.M., and his afternoon must have been much like hers, full of doctors and official statements. She hadn't seen him since she had entered the ER and the medical community had surrounded her.

He stretched his legs out. "You look better than I expected."

"Feisty." She shook her head. "Stephen needs to work on his adjectives."

"I don't know. It fits," he replied easily, taking Stephen's side, probably just because he could. He glanced around at all the flowers. "It looks like you have had some company."

Kate looked at the bouquets, embarrassed at all the attention they represented. "I was just doing my job. You would think I got shot or something."

"The cops like you. It's not like they can bring flowers when one of the guys gets hurt."

"Your sister sent me a bouquet—the orchids."

"Did she?" Dave grinned. "You mean she limited it just to flowers? I was afraid she was going to drown you in gifts, she was so relieved to get my phone call."

"This is so embarrassing. I even got flowers from the owner of the bank."

Dave looked over the arrangements. "Which one?"

"Care to guess?"

He thought about it. "Zealous mortgage management. Rather stale donuts for 9 A.M. We have an owner who doesn't like to spend his money on others. The wildflower bouquet."

"You're good."

"I'm right?" He got up to retrieve the card and grinned as he read it. "Nathan Young. Owner, First Union Bank."

He put down the card, gestured to the two dozen red roses. "Who's your beau?"

She wondered if it was his British side that made the abrupt question come out sounding so stiff. Or was he just irked? She buried the smile fighting to be released. "Marcus. Check out the card."

He hesitated.

"Go ahead. You'll appreciate it."

"'Lecture to come, Ladybug.'" He tapped the card. "Sounds like family."

He did sound relieved. Kate stored that pleasure away to enjoy later. She didn't want him to be interested in her, but she had to admit it felt good to know he was. "Oldest brother. And no, I don't want to explain the nickname." The roses were just like Marcus. Extravagant. Unnecessary. Wonderfully sweet. He knew her too well. She would look at them all night and know if he was not a thousand miles away, he would be sprawled in that chair for the night. The friendship went so deep she wondered at times if Marcus could read her mind. Today had shaken her up more than she cared to admit.

Dave settled back in the chair and stretched his legs out. "You've got a great family."

"Yes, I do." It was a subject that could make her sappy when she was tired. "I heard a rumor it's your birthday today."

"I couldn't think of a nicer person to spend it with."

She couldn't prevent the smile. He was smooth. "Seriously, I'm sorry your plans for the day got so messed up."

He shrugged. "I'm alive to enjoy it, mainly thanks to you. Have they told you how long you will be here?"

"I've been promised I can leave tomorrow morning." She held up the hand with the IV. "The antibiotics will be done in another hour; the doctors are just being cautious. All that glass was covered with flash grenade residue."

"How often do days like this happen?"

Why did he want to know? Concern was nice; worry was another way of smothering. She gave him the benefit of the doubt for now. "Days when you wonder if you will walk away in one piece?"

"Something like that."

"Nothing is routine, but every couple months there's a case like this one that tests the edge."

"That often?"

Definitely a frown. She sighed. Next he was going to be critiquing how she did her job. She couldn't prevent it from being dangerous, but someone had to do it. "In the decade I've been doing this, I've seen it change for the worse. People choose violence as their first course of action these days."

The door pushed open as Stephen backed in, carrying a sack and a cardboard container holding three drinks, rescuing her from telling Dave, *Thank you, but I know how to do my job.* Stephen sat on the edge of the bed and distributed the food. "Two cheeseburgers, Kate. I loaded them with hot stuff for you."

"This is great. Thanks." Her interrupted breakfast had been a long time ago. She listened to the guys talk while she focused on her dinner.

Stephen caught her in a yawn as she finished the second sandwich. "Ready to call it a day?"

Stiff, sore, and feeling every minute of the very long day, she reluctantly admitted the obvious. "Getting there. Are you picking me up tomorrow morning?"

"Ten o'clock, unless you page me earlier," he confirmed.

"Make it nine."

"Okay, nine."

She wasn't sure what to say to Dave. She wasn't interested in saying good-bye and yet to suggest something else…this was awkward. "Thanks for your help today."

She held still as his hand brushed down her cheek, and she saw her surprise briefly reflected on his own face. Clearly he hadn't thought before he made the gesture, had startled himself as much as her. It was nice to know she wasn't the only one feeling off balance at the moment. They were work acquaintances, and yet it kept jumping across to something more personal.

She had little experience deciphering the emotions reflected in his blue eyes; gentleness wasn't common in her world.

"It was my pleasure. Maybe next time we can meet by simply saying hello?" Dave said softly.

"I would like that."

His eyes held hers, searching for something. When he moved his hand to his back pocket and broke eye contact to look at his wallet, she blinked at the abrupt loss she felt. "Good. Give me a call, let me know how you're doing." He put a business card by the phone. "My cellular phone number is on the back."

Kate nodded, well aware of Stephen's speculation. "Good night, guys."

The FBI regional offices were on the eighteenth floor of the east tower in the business complex. Dave tossed his keys on his desk and went to brew a pot of coffee. It was 8:45 P.M. He had some questions regarding Henry Lott that needed answers. He was too on edge to consider going home.

There was such a contradiction in Kate. Who was the real Kate—the cop who had been coolly assessing the situation, prepared if necessary to call for a sniper shot? Or the woman who had been defusing the situation with her chatter—who liked pepperoni pizza, her steak cooked to just a hint of pink, mystery novels, basketball, marathon races, and chocolate chip ice cream?

The two images didn't mix.

He stirred sugar into his coffee and half smiled. He liked her. Despite the contradiction, he really liked her. She could keep her sense of humor in a crisis.

She was going to be hard to get to really know. One moment she was open and easy to read, the next impossible to fathom. Given the nature of her job, he should have expected that. He had crossed a line in those last few moments at the hospital, sensing an unexpected loneliness in her, wanting to comfort and not knowing how to reach her with words. He owed her. He couldn't dismiss that fact even if it did annoy her when he expressed it.

At least they had both come out of the day relatively unhurt. He touched his split lip and grimaced. It stung—he could only imagine what she must be feeling about now. He walked back to his office, set down his coffee cup, and turned on his desk lamp.

It didn't take a name on the door for the office to be recognizable as his. He liked a clear desk, organized files, large white boards, and space to pace and think. The whimsical sketches on the wall, done by his sister, were worth a minor fortune. A signed football from his brother-in-law was under glass on the credenza.

He did not appreciate almost getting killed on his thirty-seventh birthday. The situation had scared his sister. Sara, having been stalked for years by a man trying to kill her, had already taken enough scares in her lifetime. He wanted a few questions answered. He would start with Henry Lott's former employer, Wilshire Construction, then take a look at First Union Bank.

Night had descended. The shadows around the hospital room had finally disappeared into true darkness. Kate preferred the night over dusk. There was a little more truth in the darkness; it at least didn't pretend to hide danger. She reached over and turned on the bedside light.

It was after ten. Her shoulder ached. She was tired of staring at the ceiling. Fatigue had crossed into the zone where it now denied sleep. Normally after a crisis, she would go shoot baskets for a while, bleed off the stress. Denied the release, it was hard to settle for the night.

Accustomed to thinking in the quiet of the night, she reached for the pad of paper Stephen had brought her.

Why was Jennifer coming to town?

Kate wrote the question on the pad of paper and flared several lines out. Work opportunity? Boyfriend? Problem in the practice? Someone giving her trouble? Someone she wants us to help?

It could be practically anything. Kate didn't like not knowing. She couldn't fix it until she knew the problem. Family mattered. Intensely. She looked across the room at the roses. She was glad Marcus was coming.

Staring at the phone, she considered calling him. It was late on the East Coast, but Marcus never cared what time she called. If she woke him up, she'd hear the amused, warm sleepy tone in his voice that someday would delight a wife. He would talk for as long as she liked. She let down her guard with him. He knew it. They were the oldest two of the O'Malley clan and had been friends a very long time. In the quiet of the night they had talked about many things. He worried about her just like she worried about him. It went with the jobs they had.

If she called tonight, he would know she couldn't unwind. It would be better to call tomorrow.

She wished she knew how the case investigation was going. Her teammates were busy while she sat in a hospital. She had never been one to enjoy sitting on the sidelines of an investigation. They had to find the source of the dynamite, how Henry had procured it, where he had built the device. There was a good chance there were more explosives than the amount he had used. If she called the office at this time of night, from the hospital, she would never hear the end of it.

Kate dropped the pad of paper back on the table, causing Dave's business card to flutter to the floor. It took some careful maneuvering to pick it up. She didn't want to lose it.

She turned the business card over in her hand. Bothering him at home was not an option, but the card gave his direct number at work. What were the odds she was not the only one with questions?

The phone call surprised him. Dave glanced up from the printout he held and considered letting his voice mail answer it. His sister Sara would have called his cellular number.

It was his private line. He reached over and took the call. "Dave Richman."

"I hoped you would be at the office."

The sound of her voice was unexpected. "Kate. What's wrong?"

"Relax. I just can't sleep."

Some of his tension faded but not the concern. "The cuts bothering you?"

"They are itching like mad. Listen, can you pull the EOC records for Wilshire Construction?"

"Kate, come on. You're in the hospital. What are you doing working?"

"I need the overtime," she replied dryly. "I bet the data is somewhere on your desk."

Dave shifted printouts even as he smiled. "What are you looking for?"

"Was his termination from Wilshire Construction with cause, or was it age discrimination?"

He flipped through the Equal Opportunity Commission records. "Henry didn't file a formal complaint, but several others from the company have in the last six months. It's possible."

"I thought so. Have you looked at the mortgage?"

She was asking the same questions he was. It was nice to know they worked a case the same way. "Not yet. I'm still checking out the bank."

"Anything interesting?"

"Possibly. First Union's foreclosure rate is about triple that of last year. The bank is one of several owned by Nathan Young. He has a group here in Chicago, another group in New York, and recently bought his first one in Denver. It looks like the same trend is in place at all the banks."

"He's building up cash," Kate concluded.

"It looks that way."

"So Henry's complaint might have some basis in fact."

"We'll keep digging," Dave agreed. "His financial records should be available tomorrow. If there was something irregular in his foreclosure, we'll find it."

"Thanks for starting the search."

"We both want the answers. ATF is working on tracing the explosives. An initial search of his home did not reveal where the device had been built. They sealed the place to do a more thorough search tomorrow."

"Good. I'll touch base with Manning."

She was decompressing. He should have realized it earlier. "I wish I had more to offer."

"This helps."

The silence on the phone crossed the subtle line from a pause to being too long. "Kate, you did a good job today."

"Maybe. At least everyone walked away alive."

"Ease up on yourself. Some situations don't lend themselves to peaceful endings."

"I know. Ignore the whining. I don't normally second-guess myself." He heard her muffle the phone and speak to someone. "The nurse is here."

"I'll hold on."

"Oh. Okay, thanks."

His answer had thrown her. Studying the sketch on the wall across from him, Dave smiled as he waited for her to return.

"I'm back."

"What else do you want to talk about?"

"It's late. I ought to let you go."

He wasn't going to let her go that easily. He enjoyed talking with her. "We're both old enough not to have curfews. Enough about work. Tell me about where you lived to acquire that accent."

"I've heard it sounds good over the phone."

"Quit flirting." He meant it, but still he smiled. She would thank him in the morning. She was tired, on painkillers, and it had been an emotional day for them both; another day, a better time, and his answer would be different.

Her laugh was as nice as her voice. "You know when you dream as a kid about what you want to be?"

"Sure. I wanted to be a pilot, fly fighter jets off an aircraft carrier."

"You would. I just wanted to be different than everyone around me. The South seems as different as you could get. So I decided to change even my voice."

"You grew up here in Chicago?"

"Elm and Forty-seventh."

"You're serious."

"It's hard not to have the accent." She had turned it off like a switch.

"You're good."

"I'll take that as a compliment. So, did you ever learn to fly?"

Why had she wanted to change everything about herself? He let her change the subject rather than ask the question. He had a feeling it would stir painful memories. "As a matter of fact, yes. It's the best place to be in the world, the open sky."

"How so?"

"Freedom, speed, control of an intricate machine."

"You're a good pilot?"

"Yes. Would you like to go up sometime? The jet is at O'Hare."

"Just like that, the jet is at O'Hare."

"I have to fly something. I outgrew the piper cub when I was in high school."

"Maybe I'll take you up on that."

"You should." He didn't like the image of her awake, alone, in a hospital room. "Would you like me to come over? We could watch an old movie; I could smuggle in dessert." He never would have made the suggestion under ordinary circumstances, preferring to keep his work and private life separate, but the events of the afternoon had shredded that normal reticence, left him feeling very protective about her. She mattered to him.

"Tempting."

"But you are passing." The disappointment was intense.

"Taking a rain check. It's late. You need to go home."

Truth or politeness? He wasn't sure. He'd have to make sure she didn't politely file and forget about that rain check. "What time will you be at your office tomorrow?" If she were working from her hospital room, she would not be taking the day off, not with the open questions in this case.

"Ten."

"Call me then, and I'll fill you in on anything else I've found. I'm meeting my sister and her husband for a late lunch, but I'll be here in the morning."

"I'll call you. Go home."

The order made him smile. Normally only his sister bothered to fuss about such things. "Soon. Good night, Kate."

THREE

There was no place like home. Kate walked in the front door of her apartment Wednesday night, kicked it shut, and gave a welcome sigh of relief. A long day at work had resulted in more questions than answers. Nothing about this case with Henry Lott was proving simple to solve. She had tossed in the towel half an hour ago, shoved work in her briefcase, and said good night to Graham. The second day soreness made movement painful and nagged a headache to life.

The rich smell of flowers lingered heavy in the still air in the apartment. Stephen had brought the flowers over after he dropped her off at work. The window air-conditioner unit in the bedroom rumbled to life, breaking the silence and stirring the air. Kate found the sound comforting.

The apartment was not large, but it was sufficient for her needs. She had taken her time to make it her own space, create herself a much-needed haven. The place was warm, comfortable, cozy. Her sister Lisa called it beautiful. Kate had tried. Hardwood floors. Plush furniture. Bold fabric on wingback chairs. She needed someplace in her life where she could relax.

Kate dropped her gym bag by her bedroom door and nudged off her tennis shoes. She went looking for dinner, too tired to really care what she found.

A new note under the smile face magnet on the refrigerator caught her attention. "Ice cream in the freezer, caramel sauce in the refrigerator." *Bless you, Lisa.*

Dessert sounded good.

She fixed a sundae, licking the spoon as she walked back to the living room. She pushed the play button on her answering machine as she walked by.

Reporter. Reporter. Yet another reporter. It was time to change her unlisted number again; it always managed to eventually leak. She was faintly surprised they hadn't staked out her apartment.

She flipped through two days worth of mail—bills, magazines, junk mail. The bills she dropped on the small desk, the magazines went on the coffee table, and the rest she tossed without opening.

Marcus.

Kate paused to listen. Good, his flight was due in Sunday afternoon.

Reporter.

The next message stopped her in her tracks. "Hello, Kate O'Malley. I've been looking for you, and what do I see—you made the news last night. We'll have to meet soon."

It was not a voice she recognized. Puzzled, she played the message again. The words were innocuous, but the tone wasn't. She did not want to meet this guy. His voice had a sinister edge. Probably someone recently released from jail. She sighed and ejected the cassette. She would make a copy of the tape, as she did with all questionable calls. There were several dozen in the archives.

It fit the kind of day it had been.

She opened her briefcase on the coffee table and pulled out the work she had brought home. Henry Lott's financial records. Dave had sent copies over that morning. She closed the briefcase so she didn't have to look at the copies of the negotiation tapes. Listening to hours of dialogue, knowing she had failed to resolve the situation short of a tactical conclusion, was not something she wanted to face tonight.

She turned on the television to catch the late news.

The third news story was another segment on the bank incident yesterday. She had hoped it would have a one-day shelf life.

Kate watched tonight's clip, knowing in advance that it was going to make her mad. Reporter Floyd Tucker and the police department mixed together like oil and water. This was one of his more blatant accusations of police incompetence. Two of the hostages claimed the police had put their lives at risk. A former member of the National Association of Hostage Negotiators critiqued what was known about the case and declared the tactical conclusion to be a use of excessive force.

She shut off the television and tossed the remote control on the table. "Floyd, your expert lost 28 percent of his hostages during the three years he worked in Georgia." She wished Floyd would become some other city's menace, but no one else would hire him.

The police PR department declared the case under review. Floyd made a big deal of that fact. Kate wished he were at least an accurate reporter. A review was always done when a tactical response was taken. She wasn't looking at spending her weekend working for the pleasure of it.

She had dreamed about the bank last night, had watched the bomb go off in her hands. She didn't need the news to remind her. The news story would create more work for her. Case notes were never easy to write when a tactical conclusion was required. It became a psychological assessment of Henry Lott—observations, rationale, an after-the-fact review of the tapes. She would be questioned on her decision; and the more complete she could make her case notes, the less time she would be under scrutiny. These notes would be read more widely than most. The bank's insurance company was already hounding her boss to produce the report.

The phone rang.

She considered ignoring it, then realized she had failed to replace the cassette in the answering machine.

"Hello?"

"I guess I don't need to ask if you saw the news."

Kate relaxed. Dave. "Floyd Tucker is not on my Christmas card list."

"I can see why. It was a very unflattering piece. Ignore him."

She wedged the phone against her shoulder as she got up and rummaged through the desk drawer to find another tape for the answering machine. "With pleasure. How was lunch with your sister?"

"Considering the shock I gave her yesterday, not bad."

"It's always hard on those who have to wait and worry, who can't affect the outcome."

"Yes. Sara has been there before. She's tough. I think you would like her."

"Probably. I like her brother."

"Flirting, now flattery. You're good for my ego."

She could hear the amusement in Dave's voice. This was the third time he had deflected a comment rather than follow up on it. She was glad he wasn't taking her too seriously. He was too much a threat to her peace of mind, and she didn't have time for a relationship. But an interaction like this—lighthearted, fun—was okay. She could live with the line he was drawing. Her heart had been mangled enough in the past. She settled back on the couch. "I think I had best change the subject. Thanks for sending over the information this morning."

"I hope some of it will be useful. I hear Manning found more dynamite."

"A partially filled crate in the crawl space under Henry's home. ATF has the crate numbers to trace, but the markings are old. It will take them some time."

She had spent the day working with Manning trying to figure out where it had come from. Henry wasn't talking. Wilshire Construction, the most obvious place it could have been obtained, claimed nothing was missing from its inventory. Did Henry have help obtaining the explosives? It was a critical question to get answered. She hoped she would find a clue in the financial data spread out before her.

"Did you see his correspondence with the bank?" She pushed the papers around until she found copies of the letters she sought.

The letters found in his home were enlightening. The correspondence stretched back about eight months and had gone as high as the bank owner, Nathan Young, although it was doubtful Mr. Young had ever seen the letter. The reply to that letter had come from a vice president, Mr. Peter Devlon.

The correspondence on one hand suggested a willingness by the bank to work with Henry, and on the other hand took a very hard-line stance. It looked like First Union Bank and the corporate offices had been acting at cross-purposes. It was clear Henry had felt he was being jerked around.

"They were faxed over a short time ago. Henry had been building toward the crisis for some time."

Because of the damage to the bank, employees had not been allowed back inside the building yet. Kate still hadn't seen the bank's version of the mortgage dispute. "I'm thinking about paying the bank president, Nathan Young, a visit. Ask him about the letters, follow up on that foreclosure rate trend you noticed."

"I would enjoy tagging along for that visit."

"I'll give you a call."

"Did you work all day?"

"Yes." She stretched out on the couch and leaned her head back against the padded armrest. Talking to Dave at the end of the day was a nice way to end the evening.

"Want to cash in that rain check? I'll bring over a pizza."

She looked at the bowl of ice cream and smiled. She was not going to feel guilty. "I'm lousy company at the moment. I've still got work to do."

"All the more reason to accept. If you're going to work on at home, you should at least have company. I'm a good sounding board."

After telling Stephen and Lisa she was looking forward to a quiet evening, the realization she didn't want to spend the evening alone surprised her. "What do you like on your pizza? I'll order one from Carla's down the street."

"Make it with onions so I'll only be tempted to kiss you good night."

Her heart fluttered hard, then settled. She couldn't prevent the soft laugh at his rueful tone and carefully chosen words. "You would have to disarm me first anyway. I don't date cops."

"And here I thought that was my line."

Her amusement deepened. "Do you have my address?"

"And your phone number."

"Cute. Come over and I'll put you to work."

"Expect me in twenty-five minutes."

Kate called Carla's and placed an order for a large supreme pizza.

She had a cop coming over to share a pizza. Not exactly a common occurrence.

She had her Cliff's Notes reasons for why she didn't date cops: two people with pagers, long uncontrollable work hours, the dangers in each job. She didn't need to be smothered by someone trying to keep her safe. She had also learned with time that while it was wonderful to have someone available to talk with who understood her job, that also meant there was no place to escape work. And underneath those answers was the real reason she rarely shared—she wanted to date someone safe. Cops were interesting, made good friends, but were far from safe. Cops brought the stress of their jobs home with them. She certainly did. That was a bad recipe for a good marriage.

She looked around the room, tired enough she was going to ignore the urge to straighten the clutter. It probably wouldn't hurt to change though. The jeans and top she wore had been pulled from her gym bag this morning. Groaning at the pain in her shoulder, Kate pushed herself off the couch. She was avoiding taking a painkiller and was paying for that stubbornness.

Her bedroom looked Southern, from the rich rose pattern in the wallpaper to the thick cream carpet under her bare feet. The bed was made; the sheets turned down over the comforter.

She found a white button-down shirt in the closet. She had probably swiped it from either Stephen or Marcus; it was several sizes too big. She slipped it on over a blue T-shirt and turned up the sleeves to above the elbows. There was little that could be done with her hair. She ran a brush through it and clicked off the bathroom light.

She was searching out plates and napkins in the kitchen when there was a knock on the door. After checking that Dave was alone, she turned the locks and opened the door. "What's this?" She grinned. He came bearing gifts.

"A hostess gift, so I'll get invited back."

She untied the ribbon on the sack. Red cherries. Hershey's Kisses. A paperback mystery she had mentioned yesterday. They weren't expensive gifts, but it had taken thought to make the purchases. She sampled one of the cherries, closing her eyes to savor the taste. It was sweet, juicy—delicious. "You'll get invited back."

He rocked back on his heels and chuckled. "Good."

She waved her hand. "Go on into the living room; make yourself at home. Can I get you something to drink? Soda? Iced tea?"

"Tea would be great."

Nodding, she put the gifts on the kitchen counter and opened the refrigerator to pour him a glass of tea.

Hostess gifts. The guy had class. She slid a finger over the cover of the book, reading the jacket text. She was already looking forward to reading the book.

"Here you go." She carried his glass of iced tea as well as the bag of Hershey's Kisses into the living room.

"Thanks. You have a beautiful home."

"I like it. It's my own little peaceful world." She had turned on the stereo shortly before he arrived; music filled the room. The roses from Marcus were prominently displayed on the end table. She filled the candy dish with the chocolates. "Thanks again for the gifts."

He smiled. "I wanted something as a thank-you, and you were already swimming in flowers." He settled comfortably on the couch. Picking up her bowl from the table, he raised his brow and gave her a wicked grin. "Ice cream, Kate?"

She had forgotten to return the bowl to the kitchen. She took it from him, feeling the blush his comment generated heat her face. "Guilty. I started with dessert."

"A great way to break the stress of the day."

A knock on the door saved her from having to come up with a comeback. "Pizza, coming up."

The pizza was fresh from the oven, piping hot, and the cheese still bubbling.

She made a place for it on the coffee table. Choosing to leave the couch to Dave, she settled into the wingback chair across from him.

The pizza tasted great. She had been hungrier than she realized.

"This is excellent," Dave commented after a few bites.

"I've settled more than one dispute in the neighborhood over a pizza from Carla's."

"I can see why." He reached for a second piece. "Why don't you take something to kill that headache?"

That sharp eye made her uncomfortable. "I will if it lasts."

"Were you born stubborn?"

It was a teasing question, but the memories of voices from the past made her headache jump in intensity. "Probably."

He studied her thoughtfully, nodded, then turned his attention to the papers beside the pizza box. "Tell me what you're working on."

She was grateful for the change in subject. "I'm still trying to get a handle on the explosives, the detonator, any of the components. Henry had to get them somewhere. We need to know where and if he had help."

Dave scanned the printouts, set down his plate, and wiped his hands. He moved from the couch to the floor; pushed the coffee table down another foot. He started laying out the reports by date in a semicircle around him. "Let's see if we can track his movements, find out if Henry traveled."

It was a good approach. Kate wished she had thought of it. She reached for the stack of pages Dave offered, then looked at him when she realized he wasn't letting go.

"Add hard on herself to stubborn." He smiled. "Would you relax and let others help? Piecing together puzzles is my full-time job."

"You're right. I'm sorry."

He released the papers and frowned. "This case really shook you up, didn't it?"

"I don't like the ones that I dream about."

"How bad?"

She shook her head, declining to answer. "Anything in particular I should be looking for?"

"The general pattern first; did he travel much, where to."

Kate settled back in the chair and started to work. The quietness was broken only by the sound of pages turning. It was a comfortable silence. She looked up after a bit to watch Dave, focused on the task in front of him. He had been serious about coming over to help.

The phone rang. Dave looked up.

"The machine will get it; I'm screening calls."

He nodded and resumed turning pages.

She heard her own voice end and the beep that followed it. "Hello, Kate. I taped the news tonight."

Her hand curled the paper she held; she had heard that voice earlier in the evening. She took a deep breath, and the calm, detached front that hallmarked her work slid into place. *Give me a clue I can work with.*

"Sounds like you have trouble coming your way. Soon it will be more than you can handle."

The tape clicked off on an amused, deep laugh.

She forced herself to mark her place with a pen, set down the printouts, and not let that voice invading her home get to her. It went with her job. The courts had reversed the truth-in-sentencing law, and the number of inmates being released swelled daily. This sounded like another one determined to harass her.

"I can see why you screen calls."

She could tell from Dave's expression that he was concerned. Having someone else showing a protective streak put her in an uncomfortable position. "Once a month on average, someone I need to avoid finds the number."

"That's a very high incident rate."

She bit her tongue not to reply it wasn't his concern. He didn't mean to step on a sore spot. She changed out the tape as she had done with the first one. She would keep screening calls. When she never answered, most callers stopped harassing her machine after a week. If this caller persisted, it would not be the first time she had requested a tap on her own phone line. "Most call just to show they can find the number," she finally replied. "The persistent callers get traced and dealt with. If there's an obvious threat, it bumps to my boss to decide how to handle it. Those are rare."

"When did you last change your phone number?"

"Dave—"

He held up his hand. "Sorry, consider it unasked. But if you do want some suggestions someday, I could probably make a few. Protecting people is what I do for a living."

"Really?"

"Yes."

"The offer is appreciated, but another time, okay?" She ran her hand through her hair. "I think I will take something to kill this headache." It was a retreat, but a needed one. She found the painkillers the doctor had prescribed that morning, knowing she needed something powerful enough to deal with the aching muscles as well as the headache.

Returning to the living room, she found she simply could not face another moment of work. She settled on the couch.

"Stretch out, get comfortable."

She hesitated, then did as he suggested.

"Kate, why do you do it, your job I mean? You live with so much risk."

He asked it without turning around, continuing to work, but she could tell it was not a throwaway question.

"I was nine when I decided that someone had to kick death in the teeth for the sake of justice."

He glanced back at her. "That's quite a descriptive phrase. You really decided to become a cop when you were nine?"

"Around then."

"What happened?"

Kate hesitated. "It's a long story, for another time."

"Okay. Why become a negotiator?" She was relieved he didn't pursue his previous question.

"It's the center of the action, and I've got the patience and control necessary to do the job well."

"I should have guessed that. You are good at the job, don't get me wrong, but I wish you wouldn't take quite so many risks doing it. When you came through those bank doors not wearing a vest, I was sure you were going to get shot. I was praying harder than I can remember doing in the recent past."

He believed in God? She might not, but she respected people who did. At least they had hope, misplaced she thought, but there. She was always curious. "Do you think it helped?"

He turned around at that question, resting his elbows on his knees as he considered her. "Yes, I do. You don't believe?"

"Does it seem logical to pray for God to stop a crisis when, if He existed, He should have never let it begin?"

He didn't give her an immediate answer, and that had her intrigued.

"Interesting observation."

"Since you believe, thank you for praying."

"You're welcome." He turned back to the paperwork.

Kate didn't raise an eyebrow, but she wanted to. He was letting her close the subject if she chose to without getting uptight about it. From her experience, that suggested three things: He read people well; he was very comfortable with what he believed; and he didn't preach when he talked about religion.

To some people who said they believed, religion was a word; to others, it defined who they were. She had a feeling Dave was in that second group. To understand him, she would have to eventually understand his religion. The fact it bothered him that she didn't believe was kind of nice. People that stood for something made the best friends.

She felt the need to offer a reassurance she rarely made. "Dave, the situation has to be pretty extreme for me to take the risk I did yesterday."

He glanced back at her. "I'm glad to hear that. You're not ready to die."

"Because I don't believe?" She spent the time on her job making small talk. She preferred to avoid it in friendships. And she didn't mind talking about religion when it wasn't going to get shoved down her throat.

He turned, and the concern in his eyes was very personal. "Yes."

His look was patient. He wanted to understand. "It's no secret why I don't believe." She shrugged, wondering if her answer would sound overly simplistic. "My job is to restore justice to an unjust situation. To stand between danger and innocent victims. If your God existed, my job should not."

"He should prevent situations like Tuesday's holdup."

"Yes." She could feel the painkiller kicking in. She braced her hand on his shoulder as she shifted to get a pillow behind her bruised shoulder.

"So where should His interference with free will end?"

"Graham and I debate that question occasionally, and I have a hard time accepting the answer that anything goes. If God is not big enough to figure out a way around free will, He's pretty much left our fates up to chance. I see too much evil, Dave. I don't want a God that lets that kind of destruction go on." She stifled a yawn. She was too tired to have this discussion, as fascinating as it might be. Dave didn't push when he talked about God, but it wasn't like he was going to change her opinion. The pain now easing off, she tucked her hand under her chin.

"You've got a large family. Did your parents have large families, too?"

Another subject shift. He would make a good negotiator. Either that, or he read body language very well. "I grew up in an orphanage." Whatever sympathy that word brought, it was easier to deal with than explaining the abuse that had taken her from her parents' home at age nine.

"You've got three brothers and three sisters."

She shook her head. "I was an only child." She knew the confusion that answer brought. "Can you reach the picture in the silver frame?"

He picked it up from the end table.

"The O'Malleys. We sort of adopted each other. Legally changed our last names, became our own family."

He studied the group photo. "I figured this was you hanging out with friends."

"It is. We were friends long before we became family. Stephen, you've met. Marcus, who sent the flowers. Lisa, Rachel, Jennifer. Jack." She looked at the picture and smiled. "We are constantly stepping in and out of each other's lives. An O'Malley can always count on an O'Malley."

"Sara and I are like that, too. I don't know if I should say I'm sorry you lost your parents or that I envy you what you've found."

"Both apply."

"I would like to meet them."

"Stick around and you will."

He draped his arms across his knees. "We've known each other, what, about thirty-six hours?"

Uncertain as to why he asked, she nodded. "Yes."

"That's long enough. It takes me about twenty-four to make a friend. You're stuck with me."

She couldn't stop the chuckle, then got caught by another yawn. "I think it's time I threw you out and went to bed."

"You do need some sleep." He got to his feet and offered her a hand up.

She walked with him to the door. "Thanks for coming over. I enjoyed it."

"So did I." He stopped, one hand on the doorknob. "If you have a bad dream tonight, call me."

"What?"

"You heard me."

"You're as bad as Marcus. I'm not going to call you in the middle of the night."

"Kate, I'm serious. If you need to talk, call. I won't mind if you wake me up."

This was a different Dave, the amusement gone, in its place real concern. She smiled hesitantly. "If I need to."

He squeezed her hand. "Do." He stepped out the door. "Good night, Kate."

"Good night."

She let the door close and turned the locks, leaning back against the wood. She had expected the emotions from yesterday would fade, not grow. She had seen gentleness in Dave's eyes last night, seen kindness tonight. He was an action-oriented cop, yet she had seen him pull back on three occasions tonight rather than push over her: when the phone call came in, when the subject of religion came up, when he asked about the risks she took in her job. He was a hard man to get a handle on; he was certainly not what she was expecting. There was patience when he wanted to show it.

He hadn't said anything about seeing her again. She wasn't ready to set aside her rule of not dating a cop, but she hoped he did call again soon. Her life was certainly more interesting with him in it.

FOUR

The bank assault and its aftermath were playing again on television. "Is that her?"

"Yes."

There was silence in the room as the clip ran to completion. "I think you're crazy to go after a cop." It was a quiet assessment, already made before, and said more for reflection than for discussion.

"I want her father, but he's dead. His two kids will have to do."

"Just killing them would be easier. Certainly less complicated."

"Not as sweet. I want to ruin them first."

The man behind the desk clicked off the television set with the remote. "Understandable. But we're going to have to wait a while longer than planned. They'll be looking at Wilshire Construction as the source of that dynamite. That old man just messed up a year of planning."

The man sprawled comfortably in the seat across from him smiled. "We want them looking at Wilshire Construction—this way they will already be suspicious. Rather than delay, we need to move up our timetable."

"We can't."

"Getting cold feet?"

"Hardly. You want the two Emerson kids; I want your brother. I just don't want to get caught."

"Didn't you say he's got a flight to New York next week?"

"Yes."

"So what's the problem?"

"Is that her?"

Dave glanced up at his sister Sara's question to see Kate's picture on the television screen; the noon newscast had come back from commercial. He closed the newspaper he had been scanning. "Yes, that's Kate." He watched the reporter's story.

Sitting on the couch in her husband's study, Sara leaned forward to look closer at the image. "What's she like?"

Dave searched to find the right word. "Intriguing."

"Really?"

He understood the reason for her interest. "She's not a believer, Sara," he cautioned gently. Those words left a deep void inside; he felt like a prize of great value had been snatched away. He had left Kate's house last night bitterly disappointed. He had never even considered that possibility, an indication of how strongly he had hoped the evening would be a success. As he had put together the hostess gift for Kate, he had been thinking of plans, possibilities, looking forward to getting to know her better. Those ideas had been stillborn with the discovery she was not a Christian. It didn't change the things that had drawn him to her; it only complicated enormously what he could do about that interest.

He liked Kate. He had never even considered there would be such a problem. That fact surprised him, looking back. Faith was not something he normally took for granted.

His sister looked defeated for a moment, then smiled. "Well, at least you didn't say she was married—lack of belief can change."

Dave leaned back his head and roared with laughter. "You're priceless, Sara."

"I'm happily married."

"I've noticed," he replied dryly, "You keep hoping it becomes contagious."

"Well, my best efforts are coming to naught."

Because he loved her and it was the dream of her heart, he offered—"I'll let you introduce me to another one of your friends." He accepted the reality that with Kate, a relationship beyond a friendship was not likely, and he really did want to settle down. Sara still carried the guilt of having tied up so many years of his life with her security needs. He had been focused on finding the man stalking her, the man responsible for killing their sister, Kim. Having a relationship had been far down on his priorities. Now that Sara was safe, married, and blissfully happy, she was determined to see his situation change. Dave was willing to admit it had become one of his priorities. He wanted to share his life with someone.

"I think I would rather meet Kate."

"Friendship evangelism takes time, Sara."

"But she saved your life."

He set aside his paper and sighed. "It's not that simple. You know that." He had thought about it a lot last night, worried about it, the fact Kate didn't believe. She walked into situations where a guy had a bomb. It made him shudder. But after praying a long time, he had accepted the fact there was really very little he could do. With a guy, it was different. He could get close as a friend, understand the issues preventing a decision of faith, talk through them one by one. Friendship evangelism worked if given enough time.

He couldn't do that with Kate. It was one thing to be friends with a woman, another to get close enough to influence her heart. One of them would likely end up with bruised emotions, and he had the gut feeling it would be him. The way she moved, the way she acted…and that voice of hers—that soft, captivating voice…he shook his head. Kate was trouble for him. The emotions she generated would not easily be contained to friendship.

She wouldn't be an easy person to approach with the gospel, either. Her own words told him she already thought enough about the subject to have some deep reservations. To root out why, have the patience to convince her to reconsider, would be a difficult task, and there would be no guarantee of success.

Sara crossed over to take a seat on the armrest of his chair. "Maybe it won't be simple. But you could use a good friend. Unlike my friends, she might be able to understand your job."

Sara understood his job. She had lived under the security, lived in constant fear of a killer. The past had left her with a knowledge about good and evil that had destroyed her sense of innocence. Dave didn't want that to happen to others, so he rarely talked about his job, rarely shared that part of his life. Part of it was security—what he couldn't say—and part of it was his wall—the things he wouldn't say. He wanted a life, and that couldn't happen if work invaded conversations. He appreciated Sara's concerns that it left him lonely, and she was right, but it also gave him a corner of his life that was normal, and he guarded that corner tenaciously.

The fact Kate would understand his job was sad, for it meant she had also lost, like Sara, that freedom not to know what evil was like. Kate lived with the knowledge like he did. It showed in her eyes. Cop's eyes. Despite the humor, the voice, the charm, and the smile, at the back of her eyes was a reflection of what she had seen through the years. Black. Cold. Contained. Wary.

Dave sighed, accepting he was going to have to see Kate soon, if only to try and shake that image. He glanced at Sara and let himself smile. "I thought I was the one who looked out after you."

"You did—magnificently. I think it's time for me to return the favor."

He locked his arms around her waist and tugged her into his lap, triggering a fit of giggles from her. "Listen, Squirt…"

"I thought I heard you two in here."

Dave looked up as his brother-in-law entered the room. "Hi, Adam."

"Dave." Adam smiled and leaned down to kiss his wife, still trapped in Dave's arms. "If you were planning to change before we leave, you've got eight minutes," he mentioned to her, amused.

She scrambled back to her feet. "I'll be ready in four."

Dave watched her go, content in a way he had not been in ages. "She looks happy, Adam. Thanks." There had been years he had wondered if this day would ever come for her.

"It's mutual." His friend took a seat on the couch, leaned back and stretched and grinned. "So—fill me in on this Kate I've been hearing about."

Sara and Adam had so smoothly tag teamed him into talking about Kate that Dave was almost willing to speculate their ambush had been planned. He smiled as he cut across traffic to reach his car. The wind had picked up as the day progressed, but there were only small clouds to be blown across the sky; the hoped-for rain had still not appeared. He was about to do something he might regret in the morning.

He had the preliminary bank report on Henry Lott's mortgage with him. He had called Kate's office to fax her a copy, but Franklin had said she had already left for the day. The report could wait until tomorrow. Dave knew that, but he had decided to seize the moment and see if Kate happened to be home.

As he drove toward Kate's neighborhood, he tried to decide what he would say when he saw her. He wasn't sure how he had left it last night after she said she didn't believe. He thought he had handled it with tact, not shown his disappointment, but he wasn't going to assume that fact; he couldn't. He would soon know, maybe. Given the way Kate could control her voice and expression, clues to what she was thinking could be subtle at best if she decided to play it cool.

Dave ran his hand through his hair, admitting to himself he had no idea why he was doing this. To hear her voice again. Coax out another smile. He groaned at the realization he had just jumped again in his thoughts to something well beyond friendship and seriously considered abandoning this idea. He didn't need this kind of emotional quicksand.

His jaw firmed. He would keep it friendly. Brief.

He liked her, really liked her; he would just have to start treating her like a cousin or something.

Right. That was easier said than done.

Dave turned onto her block and slammed on his brakes.

There were three squad cars, lights flashing, parked at an angle in front her building.

That call. Kate was in trouble.

He should never have let her blow off that threatening phone call. He had known it wasn't something to ignore, and he had backed off when she got annoyed with him. He didn't do that! Evaluating threats, protecting people was his job. Someone's feelings had to be secondary to her safety, and he had overruled that basic mandate because he wanted to stay in her good graces. If Kate was hurt…

Dave pulled in behind a squad car, grabbed his keys, and hit the pavement at a run. Manning was coming down the building's front steps. "What happened?" Dave demanded.

"Kate got a package."

"Inside her apartment?"

Manning shook his head. "Leaning against the front door."

"Where is she?"

"Inside. We're just wrapping up."

Dave stepped past the lab technician dusting the front door. There was barely room to maneuver in the crowded apartment. Dave knew from the normal tones of voice that the immediate crisis was past, but his heart still pounded. Graham, talking to one of the other officers, spotted him, and waved him back into the living room.

Kate was on the other side of the room. Everything else going on slid into the background.

She looked furious.

That realization stunned him. He had been braced for hurt; prepared, if she wasn't hurt, to see rigid control hiding her thoughts. He hadn't anticipated seeing emotions full blown. Halfway across the room he could feel the emotions shimmering off of her. She sizzled. With her arms crossed, attention on her boss, she paced in three feet of open real estate like a caged tiger.

She hadn't seen him yet, and he was momentarily glad for that.

Stephen came up behind him, carrying a cup of hot coffee.

"There was a package delivered, left leaning against her front door," Stephen told him quietly. "We had gone to dinner at the Italian place around the corner; I walked her home. The florist box was leaning against the door. I reached for it, and Kate slammed me onto my back by instinct, nearly gave me a concussion."

"What was in it?"

"A black rose. Her friend is back."

Kate looked over and saw him before he could follow up on Stephen's last comment. Dave watched her expression change, harden, then clear. He buried a sigh. So much for wondering how she would react to seeing him here.

He moved past Graham to join her. "Kate."

"Dave." She didn't look pleased to see him, but he tried not to take it personally. This place had become Grand Central Station, a fact that had to be frustrating for her. She needed some space. As a cop, that would be even more true than for someone else. For the same reason she would sit in a restaurant with her back to the wall to keep people in front of her, she would be looking for space around her now.

Her boss closed his notebook. "The lab will put a rush on this. We should hear from the Indiana PD in a couple hours, find out if your friend has indeed managed to slip out of his supervised release. In the meantime, patrols are shifted for the night."

"He won't be back tonight. His MO looks the same, down to the ribbon used on the gift."

"Assuming it's him," Jim replied. "We should know something by midnight anyway." He lightly squeezed her shoulder. "At least this time it wasn't a gift-wrapped snake."

Kate chuckled softly. "Hey, I've got first-class admirers."

It took about fifteen minutes for the cops and technicians to finish work, pack up their cases. Dave stayed out of their way, watching Stephen and Kate. Stephen was good with her, able to distract her. Or rather she let him distract her, Dave amended. The apartment door closed, leaving just the three of them.

Kate was looking around her apartment, looking unexpectedly lost. Dave crossed the room and placed his hand on her shoulder, felt the tremor. She was still so angry she was quivering.

"Go get your keys. We'll take a walk," he said calmly.

"It's going to rain."

"The forecast was wrong, and even if it did rain, it would just cool off that temper." He chuckled at the look she shot him. "Don't argue, Kate; you'll regret it in the morning." He turned her toward the bedroom. "Better yet, find a hat. It's windy."

She must have bitten her tongue not to argue, but she stalked away toward her bedroom.

"Kate following orders without a debate, that has got to be a first," Stephen commented after Kate's door closed. "Thanks. I'll get this place put back together while you're gone."

"You sure?"

"Once the fingerprint dust is gone from the front door and all the windows they checked, it won't look quite so invaded."

Dave agreed with him. "Sounds like a plan. Now tell me about this friend that likes to leave black roses."

"Bobby Tersh. Five years ago, Kate talked him out of ending his life. He fixated on her when he got out of the hospital a couple weeks later; it escalated through phone calls to the office, gifts, then took a nasty turn when he felt ignored and disintegrated into threats and to black roses being left on her car, and finally at her doorstep. He was eventually committed to a hospital in Indiana by his family. He's been out of the hospital about a year now on supervised release. This is the first indication there might be trouble again."

"Any history of violence in his background?" Dave asked, wishing he had access to the files. Maybe Jim would help him out there.

"No, just words, not that it necessarily means anything. And we're guessing that it is him."

Dave had already factored that in. "Okay."

They heard Kate's door open. She had changed into a gray sweatshirt with a hood. She looked calmer to the extent it was possible to read her.

"Stephen, we won't be gone long. Don't answer the phone; let the machine get it," Kate said, checking her pockets, avoiding looking at Dave.

Stephen crossed over to her and wrapped his arm around her shoulders. "Get out of here. You don't want to see how I clean your place."

"Thanks."

Dave closed the front door behind them and scanned the street before walking down the steps, alert to anything out of place. It looked normal and quiet, but that didn't mean much. "Which way?"

"North."

He fell into step beside her, not bothered by the silence.

"I've had black roses before," she finally said.

"Stephen told me."

"If his MO holds, I won't receive another one for weeks."

She was looking for an excuse to make that assumption; stupid of her, but he wasn't about to argue the point. "Okay."

Kate didn't say anything else. Dave eventually decided she had brooded long enough and changed the subject. "Did you hear about the Cubs game this afternoon?"

"What?"

"The baseball game. It was a perfect game through the eighth inning."

She stopped walking to look at him incredulously. "No comments about that scene back there? No advice?"

"What do you need to know that you haven't already heard?" he asked quietly.

She scowled.

"You just want someone to fight with so you can blow off steam," he said calmly. "Sorry, you'll have to settle for walking it off."

"Thanks a lot."

"My pleasure."

"You are so annoying." She sighed. "Tell me about the game."

Twenty minutes into the walk, Dave reached out and took her hand. Her fingers were cold, and he grasped them reassuringly. It didn't matter what anyone said, or that this situation was one of the realities that came with the job; it was her home that had been invaded. She had needed a night to relax and instead was being thrust back into a situation that must have been a nightmare. He could tell the memories were back by the shuttered weariness in her face and the fact she had responded with so much emotion—it had been anger, but it had been prompted by fear. And there was nothing he could do to make this go away. He hated not being able to help. He talked about the game, his visit with Sara and Adam, plans for the summer, anything but his work or hers.

"You're not that bad at making small talk," she commented.

He took it as a special compliment. "I spent a few hours listening to you."

She rolled her shoulders, and he saw the tension in her finally drain away. "It was a miserable day. I didn't need this on top of it."

"At least you didn't give Stephen a concussion. He would have been giving you grief about that for months."

"Months? It would have entered family lore." She shook her head. "You can't imagine the fear that hit when I saw him reach toward that package. I didn't even realize I had recognized it; I just reacted."

Having more than once taken his sister Sara to the ground in reaction to a threat, Dave knew exactly what that fear tasted like. It was much more powerful than facing a threat to yourself. "I know what that fear is like," he replied but didn't elaborate.

"It makes me *furious.* Someone wants to come after me, fine, but don't mess with my family. I saw Stephen reach for that package, and I had a sudden nasty image of a paramedic suddenly missing a hand." She visibly shuddered at the thought.

"Let it go, Kate. Stephen's fine. It was a false alarm. The adrenaline will eventually fade."

"Yeah."

She pushed her hands into her pockets, walked some more. "You will conveniently forget the fact you saw me lose my temper."

"Why? You're adorable mad."

"Dave—"

He held up his hands. "It's forgotten."

"Thank you. Now, why did you come over?"

She didn't want to talk about what had happened. He tried not to let his disappointment show. She deserved her privacy, but he had hoped they were on level enough ground as friends she would let him help her out. He would like to repay the debt he owed her.

Because he had no real choice, he let her change the subject. "I've got the preliminary bank report on Henry Lott's mortgage for you."

She pulled her hand out of her pocket to run it through her hair. "I had actually forgotten that case for a couple hours. Thanks for bringing it over."

"It was an excuse to see you."

She sneaked a glance at him, gave a small smile. "It's a pretty lame one."

"True." That smile cushioned her change of subject. He relaxed. She'd learn to share eventually; he'd be around until she realized it.

They had been walking for about forty minutes, had circled back around to her block again. "Stephen should be about done," he commented.

"Yes. Are you coming in?"

He wanted to, but she looked exhausted now under that contained front. "No. You need a hot shower and some sleep, not company."

"You just want to go meddle in this case, too."

He didn't bother to contradict her, just smiled. "Go on. I'll talk to you tomorrow."

"The Indiana PD have no leads on Bobby Tersh?" Dave asked, following Graham through the basement concrete hallways in the county building back to the emergency response group offices.

"He hasn't reported in to his release supervisor in five days; he hasn't been at his job in three. Officers interviewing the family reported they were very cooperative but had little to suggest. They haven't heard from Bobby either."

The steel door at the end of the hallway was locked and electronically coded. Graham paused to punch his code, then held open the heavy door for Dave. The quiet and coolness of the hallway disappeared in an assault of sound. The long open room was packed with desks and people. It was a stark contrast to the FBI offices where they had the luxury of individual offices and group conference rooms.

Dave scanned the room, disappointed not to see Kate. Maybe it was for the best. She might not appreciate having the FBI step across jurisdictions. He had called her boss late last night, and hadn't even needed to explain his credentials as a reason for why he was asking to take a look at the files. Her boss had granted his request and sounded relieved to do it. Dave knew that meant Jim was shorthanded or worried about the possible threat to one of his officers—probably both.

"Debbie, have those files on Tersh arrived from archives?" Graham asked.

The secretary working the phones paused the phone conversation she was on and pointed with her red pen to the cart on wheels pushed against a three-drawer file cabinet with a sprawling fern. They had tried to improvise greenhouse lights for the plant, but the fern still looked sick for lack of sunlight.

"Trust something to archives? That disaster waiting to happen? They are two years behind schedule to move and consolidate that warehouse, and it shows. I used my discretion and kept Tersh classified as an active file. It's the two-inch blue file on the left. I pulled it when I got in this morning and heard what had happened."

"What would we do without you?"

"Suffer the wrath of the system," Debbie replied with a smile. "Do you want me to pull her threat file, too?"

"You'd better," Graham picked up the Tersh file, leafed through it, then turned back to Debbie. "Three years ago, last name Edmond? If that's not in the threat file, pull it."

"Dead cat," Debbie said darkly. "It's there."

Graham indicated his desk halfway into the room, and Dave followed him to it. "Kate has a cat?"

Graham took a seat and glanced back up at him. "Not anymore." He gestured to a chair where a jacket and a briefcase were balanced. "Just put the stuff somewhere. Sorry, we're a little chaotic down here still. They haven't installed the lockers they promised us months ago."

Dave moved the jacket and briefcase, then settled down into a chair that was at least comfortable.

"Jim said to give you access to anything we had. I have to tell you, I don't like the idea of someone going after Kate again. Last year turned into a nightmare for her."

"That bad?"

"Kate is hard to read how something is affecting her, but by the end of the year you could see she was paying the price. She didn't want someone else in her building getting hurt if Tersh became confrontational."

"A case where the courts couldn't do anything."

"The DA tried, but it was hard to get more than a slap on the hands, and that wasn't going to do the trick. When Tersh's family committed him, you could see Kate's relief. If it had gone on much longer, she wouldn't have been able to stop her brothers from intervening."

Graham scanned pages. "It's going to be hard finding the guy if he's somewhere back in Chicago. He worked as a transit mechanic, knew the city very well." Graham handed over the file. "The initial report from Kate's intervention is in there, along with excerpts from that conversation. It was taped, so a full transcript is available, just ask Debbie for it. The rest of the files are the various incident reports regarding the gifts and calls."

Debbie joined them carrying two folders stuffed so full they were spilling over. "Kate's threat file." She handed it to Graham. "Anything else you need, just ask."

Dave was stunned at the size of it. "How many years does that encompass?"

"Two? Three? Most all of it is mail. She spends hours with people, they get sent to jail, and they think they know her, so they write—a lot. There is not much else to do in prison."

"And she's the type of lady that would stick in a guy's mind," Dave observed. She was too pretty, had too striking of a voice. He sighed just thinking about it.

"Exactly."

"Who else could this be besides Tersh?"

"At a guess, there are probably another six serious contenders in this stack."

"Where is Kate?"

"I haven't seen her this morning." Graham leaned back to see around him. "No gym bag sticking halfway out into the aisle, so she probably got paged while she was at the gym."

"She's a busy lady."

"Popular. They call her into situations earlier than they used to."

Graham picked up his phone to check the blinking message light. When he hung up a few moments later, he gestured to the files.

"Are you okay with going through this information on your own? I'm due over at the ATF office to talk about Henry's package. It will probably take me an hour."

"There's at least an hour of reading here before I'm ready to start asking questions," Dave agreed.

Graham's pager and two others in the room went off. "Change that," Graham glanced at his pager. "I'll be back whenever. Come on, Olsen."

"Can I drive?"

"Can you remember which streets are one-way?"

"It was an honest mistake."

"Sure it was."

The noise in the room dropped off as the guys headed out. Dave glanced at the open folder in his lap. Before he assumed it was Tersh as the others had, it would be better to know what they did regarding the other threats that had been made. He set the Tersh file on the desk and reached for the first of the threat files.

He looked up the Edmond case as a place to start.

Kate's cat had been shot through her living room window at 5:16 A.M. on a snowy winter day. Walter Edmond had eventually been charged with firearm violations, vandalism, and cruelty to animals. A cat. There was something more than just maliciousness at work when someone killed a pet. Walter's beef with Kate was over the fact she had talked his girlfriend into filing battery charges after he broke her arm. The sentence was not long enough given the threat Edmond represented.

Dave added the name to the list of individuals to check out. He picked up the next item in the file.

Kate, I wanted a chance to get to know you, but not like this. I didn't need more reasons to worry. And why didn't you ever get yourself another cat? You let him win.

"You like to stay out late," Dave said quietly, burying his emotions.

Kate whirled around on him. "Are you trying to get yourself killed?"

He stepped out of the shadows, not liking at all the fact he had been able to surprise her. He had been waiting for Kate to get home since 7 P.M., growing more concerned the later the hour became. The call she had been on had cleared shortly after six; he had heard Debbie take the call that Kate would not be back to the office. Kate was supposed to be going home, and he had left the station to meet her. And he had waited, wondering where she was and what was wrong. The only good thing the time had done was give him an opportunity to see the number of patrols passing by. He had spoken to several of them. Given the news he had received today, he was grateful to see them. "You assumed you would have time to react. You're a better cop than that, Kate."

"Go away. It's been a horrible day." She turned back to the door.

"Hold it. Give me your keys."

"I can check my own home."

"You weren't even looking around as you walked down the block. Keys, Kate."

She handed them to him rather than argue the point. He pushed her back when she would have entered the apartment with him. "Dave—"

"Stay there," he ordered.

It took him four minutes to sweep her apartment, confirm it was empty, quiet, and nothing obvious waiting for her. "Okay. You can come in."

"Thanks," she said sarcastically, brushing past him.

"You're welcome," Dave replied, letting some of his own stress lash out at her. "Why are you here?"

"Bobby Tersh has disappeared."

"So I heard." She collapsed on the couch. "Lock the door on your way out."

He watched her, his anger fading away to sharp concern. "Where were you today? Debbie just said you were out on a call."

"I was backup for a case on the south side."

"The family of four." He had heard about it on the radio. "An uncle barricaded himself with relatives. Shots were heard."

"The mother and two boys were dead before we arrived. He's facing three counts of first-degree murder."

Dave squeezed her shoulder. "I'm sorry."

"So am I. Go away, Dave."

He tossed his suit jacket over a chair, undid his cuff links as he disappeared into her kitchen. It was an organized place, if rather sparse. Given the few choices, it limited what he could make. He brought her a mug of decaf coffee. She hadn't even stirred enough to kick off her shoes. "Don't take the blame for something you couldn't prevent."

She wearily sat up and took the mug. "I hate losing."

"I've figured that out." He watched her sip the drink. "Want to talk about it?"

"No."

"Feel like eating, or would you like to just go ahead and crash?" He asked, changing his plans. He had hoped to take her out to dinner, distract her, while he delivered the bad news about the details they had learned regarding Tersh.

She finished the drink, pushed the cup onto the table, and sank back down into the thick cushions of the couch."I had a sandwich on the way home."

"You ate in the car."

"It's my car," she muttered into the pillow.

"Get to bed then."

"As soon as you're out the door."

Her irritation amused him. "Good night, Kate."

He waited until he heard Kate turn all the locks on her door before he walked down to his car. He was relieved to have her home. He'd been right about one thing: She had too much on her mind to pay adequate attention to her own safety. Given the choice, he supposed he would rather have her relaxed and let others worry about it; she couldn't be objective. Two days, three at the most, and they should have found Bobby Tersh.

After a day reading the files, he had to agree it did look like Bobby Tersh was back. There were too many similarities in the type of gift, how it was left, when, for it to be an accident. Those details were in the public domain, someone willing to go through all the court filings and the newspaper accounts could put it together, but the obvious candidate was Tersh. How much had he changed in a year? That was the tough assessment. Was it going to be roses and phone calls spread out across weeks, or something more aggressive this time?

Dave settled back in his car seat and reached for the thermos of coffee beside him. Kate's bedroom light eventually went out. Watching out for danger was his business, and he was good at the job, even if he had to do it without her full cooperation. Until they had some idea where Bobby Tersh was, he didn't mind killing a few hours outside her place.

If Bobby Tersh broke his MO, it would probably be in the first twenty-four to forty-eight hours. No use taking chances. Nothing was going to bother Kate tonight. In this case it wasn't even entirely personal, he always got ticked off when a cop was getting harassed. At least that's what he tried to tell himself as the clock slipped past midnight.

FIVE

Kate figured whoever was persistently ringing her doorbell at ten o'clock on a Saturday morning could live with the consequences. It wouldn't be an O'Malley. Family knew better. They would just let themselves in and make themselves at home. She flipped the locks and opened the door.

Dave. Smiling. On her doorstep.

"Here. Coffee. It looks like you need it."

She took the mug from his hand with a sigh. "I was asleep."

"I can tell."

He didn't look repentant about it. She continued to stand in the doorway even when he raised one eyebrow. His irresistible smile could probably charm even her elderly neighbor out of a snit. "The morning is half over, and I've got news." He tipped his head to one side. "Bad move?"

"I was asleep," she repeated, "and didn't I just see you?"

His instant grin was covered by a belated attempt to look sorry. He nudged the coffee mug up. "It's really good coffee."

Her lips twitched. It was wonderful coffee, and he knew it. It guaranteed she would not be going back to sleep. "What's your news?"

"Bobby's car was spotted at a rest stop in Indiana, but they didn't manage to take him into custody."

"Graham woke me up to tell me hours ago," she felt compelled to add. "Is that all?"

"It's a beautiful day."

She squinted at the sun. "It's sunny, dry, and hot. It looks like every other day has this month."

"Exactly. So come spend part of it with me."

"Why?"

He nudged the coffee mug up again. "Can we have this conversation inside?"

"No."

His grin widened. "We'll add ornery to that list. And cute. Your hair is a mess."

Kate ran a hand through it. It was going to be a mess to brush out. One foot idly went over the other as she let the doorpost take her weight. The coffee was helping, but not quickly enough. "I plan to spend today writing case notes."

"Let's go walk the beach instead."

"The beach."

"Sand, water, relaxation. I need it, and I bet you do, too. You've got a great tan. It had to be acquired somewhere."

She smirked. "One-on-one basketball with Stephen. The games move outdoors in April. I don't have enough free time to waste a day lazing around on a beach."

"I guess you don't play HORSE."

"No."

"You had a bad dream last night, didn't you?" The sudden change in subject threw her enough she wasn't able to entirely hide the answer that flickered in her eyes. His hand tipped her chin up so she looked directly into his eyes. "Why didn't you call me?"

"It was 4 A.M."

"And you were just getting back to sleep when I rang the doorbell."

She would give the man points for connecting the dots.

"I know what bad dreams are like, Kate. You should have called. It wasn't just a polite offer. Talking about it would have made it easier to get back to sleep."

"You sound pretty certain about that."

He gave a ghost of a smile. "The voice of much experience. Come on, Kate, you'll enjoy it. Shorts. Something loose and long sleeves you can slip on later so you won't burn."

"I'm on call."

"So am I. It will be the day of dueling beepers. I'll have my cellular phone with me, but bring yours along, too, if you'd like."

She gave in gracefully. Work was not exactly on par to spending a day outdoors. "Come in. I'll get changed."

She found blue shorts, a red cotton T-shirt, and matching red socks. The canvas tote of Lisa's was still in her closet. She slipped in a white shirt, tossed in the mystery Dave had given her, added suntan lotion, cash, her pager, and her phone.

"Okay, I'm ready to travel."

Dave turned from looking at the pictures on the bookshelf. "That was fast."

"If you had said wear a dress, I would have made you wait just for spite."

His rich laughter rolled around the quiet apartment. He took the now empty coffee mug she offered and waited as she locked the front door.

"The blue sedan." Dave indicated. He held open the passenger door for her. Kate slid inside with a murmured thanks. The O'Malley men had spoiled her. She had come to expect the old-fashioned courtesies.

"Nice car."

Dave found his sunglasses and slid them on. "Thanks."

Kate glanced through his cassette tapes as he pulled out into traffic. "Do you have anything besides country western?"

"Try the glove box."

She scanned his tapes until she found what she was looking for. This was more like it. She put in a Johnny Mathis tape.

"I thought you said you liked jazz."

"I lied."

"About something trivial?"

She chuckled. "Dave, I tell the bad guys I like them, too. If I don't have common ground with someone, I make it up."

She saw him frown. He obviously didn't like her lying. Why not? She considered it a necessary evil to doing her job. Common ground was critical, even if she had to invent it.

"What else did you make up?"

"In over four hours of small talk? Enough to keep the conversation going."

"You don't have an Aunt Gladys."

"Good guess."

"Now that I think about it, she sounds a little too eccentric to be true."

Kate looked at the Saturday traffic around them. "It's pretty early to be going to the beach."

Dave's lips twitched. "I think I'll feed you first."

"Smart man," she murmured.

"I gather making it a memorable breakfast might be in my best self-interest?"

"I'm hungry."

He glanced over at her and showed that wicked grin again. "That genteel Southern scold must have taken some practice."

The accent disappeared. "David."

He chuckled. "Sorry, it's just Dave. There's a great place in the north suburbs that makes everything from crepes to Belgian waffles. It's worth the time."

She was slightly mollified. "Strawberries?"

"And blueberries, probably even kiwi if you like."

Kate rested her head back and closed her eyes. "Sounds good. Wake me when we get there."

Dave let the waitress refill his coffee. They were lingering over breakfast. They had split a Dutch apple pancake and an order of strawberry crepes. He was full. Kate was still working on the strawberry crepes.

It felt good to be able to relax with her. He took the threat that black rose represented more seriously than she did; the news Bobby's car had been spotted in Indiana was a real relief. Hopefully by the time he took Kate home this afternoon they would have word that Bobby had been picked up. "Like a refill for the coffee?" the waitress asked.

"Please." Kate motioned to the last crepe. "Are you sure you don't want to split this?"

"Go ahead. I'm done."

"It's really good. You didn't answer my question."

"Which one?" The tongue-in-cheek answer earned him a look that made him laugh. "Okay. Why did I just show up on your doorstep this morning? It was a spur-of-the-moment decision, and it's harder to say no when you are asked in person."

"True. But I was annoyed enough I was going to say no."

He shook his head. "You never considered saying no. Slamming the door in my face, maybe. But you never considered saying no."

"What would you have done if I had?"

"Walked back to my car and picked up my cellular phone. You would have had to eventually answer."

"So tell me again why you wanted to spend part of today with me?"

"Besides the fact Bobby is loose and you need someone to watch your back?"

"We'll consider that unsaid," she warned softly.

"Prickly, huh?" He didn't take it personally; he had already figured out she had an independent streak a mile wide. "Okay. You're fascinating company."

"Fascinating…" She considered the word. "Challenging, maybe. Unusual. Annoying. Aggravating. Fun. Why fascinating?"

The sparkle in her eyes made him smile. "Your humor."

His reply amused her. "That's fascinating?"

"It shows up in the midst of crisis. That's unexpected, therefore, fascinating."

"I wouldn't want to be predictable."

"That you will never be."

He watched her finish her coffee. "Ready to go?"

"Yes."

He picked up the bill and left a generous tip on the table.

He chose a stretch of beach near his home in Lake Forest. The wind off the lake made the sunny day comfortable. He dropped the blanket he had retrieved from the trunk at the beginning of the sand. "Come on; let's walk for a while."

The waves broke into white caps about ten feet off shore, rolling in on the sandy beach. Kate tipped her head back to enjoy the sun. "This is rather nice."

"Yes."

They walked the length of the beach and back. Dave enjoyed every minute of it. She was entranced with the birds flying out of the water. She stopped frequently to retrieve shell fragments, gathering them like a child would.

She rubbed the sand off her latest discovery. "Look at this one. It's got a touch of blue in it. It's pretty."

Dave took what she offered and turned it over in his hand. It was pretty. More so because she had noticed it. "Yes."

She took it back from him. "Odd souvenirs, I know."

"You're going to keep them?"

Her laugh was soft, indulgent. "Probably."

"In that case, let me help you look."

"No way. These are my memories. Collect your own."

Her protest amused him. "You like simple things."

She shrugged. "It's the value I place on something that matters, not what it cost. I like collecting memories of good days."

Dave started to smile; then what she had revealed registered. She was reaching for another shell fragment and didn't see his frown. When she stood, his hands settled lightly on her shoulders. "Have good days been rare?"

He was afraid she was going to sidestep the question. She was slow to answer, and when she did, her tone was serious. "I think everyone has stretches where the good days are rare." Her shoulders moved beneath his hands. "There was a bad stretch when I lost my first hostage, another very long one when I lost the first child."

"That's work. What about otherwise?"

She put her hand over his. Her smile was kind. "It's too early for history." She moved toward the water to wash off her shell collection.

"Too early today, or too early in our friendship?"

"Both."

"It doesn't feel like I've only known you five days."

"Check your calendar."

He enjoyed her grin as she came walking back to him. "I'll give you a week."

"To what?"

"Tell me all about yourself."

"That's generous of you."

"I thought so."

She stored her shells in the canvas bag. "I think I've said enough for today."

Dave smiled and changed the subject. "Where do you want the blanket spread out?"

She looked around. "Over there looks pretty level."

He spread it out.

Her laughter had him looking up. "I really don't think we want to be by an anthill. Try it a few more yards that way."

He didn't see what she was referring to, but picked up the blanket and moved it where she indicated.

"No. It's not level. Move it more to the left."

After the fourth move, Dave's eyes narrowed. She was doing this intentionally. He flicked his wrists, watched the blanket settle, and collapsed on it, wrinkles and all. When she sat down beside him, he tweaked her chin. "That was underhanded."

"You were the one buying it."

He buried the answering grin. Not many ladies had the nerve to try a practical joke. It was a shame, too. He was already thinking about how to retaliate.

She dug a book out of her canvas bag.

"Kate?"

"Hmm?"

"Thanks for coming today."

She settled back on her elbows and looked at him. "You're pretty good company."

"Better than good."

She laughed. "We'll have to see."

The sun was warm, Kate was quiet, and it had been a long week. Dave felt himself drifting to sleep and didn't fight it.

The sun was overhead when he awoke. He stretched; every muscle in his body was relaxed. He turned to look at Kate. She was sprawled on the blanket beside him, soaking in the sun. The book was set aside, about half read. Her beauty hit him again like a blow. He felt shaky inside at the suddenness of the emotion. Why did she have to be an unbeliever? A cop? He would love to have the freedom to lean over and kiss her. He looked away, took a deep breath. *Think cousin.* Right. He should have a cousin as good-looking as Kate. He glanced at his watch. It was past 2 P.M.

"We probably need to move into the shade."

"Later."

He chuckled. She was obviously quite comfortable where she was. "Come on, I'll spring for the cold sodas."

She reluctantly opened her eyes and sighed. "You are waking me up again."

He winced. "Sorry."

"That's okay." She glanced at her watch and groaned. "Let's find that cold drink; then I probably need to get home. Work is waiting."

"You're disappointing me, Kate. I hoped I could at least talk you into lunch."

His smile was rewarded with an answering grin. "You must be losing your touch."

"Ouch."

She laughed. "Seriously, I've got an O'Malley family gathering tomorrow. I've got no choice but to at least get started on reviewing the negotiation tapes."

He watched as she got to her feet and stretched. She was moving easier today, the cuts from the bank holdup having finally healed.

"Think you could find an ice-cream cone to go with that cold drink?"

"Probably." He was surprised at her choice and pleased that she had asked. "You're sure you wouldn't like something more exotic?"

"Just an ice-cream cone."

"How about Justin's?" The locally owned ice cream shop was a regular at the Taste of Chicago, and it was near Kate's home.

"Now you're talking."

He looked at his beeper, confirmed again there had been no page. How hard was it to locate one man? Where was Bobby Tersh?

SIX

"You've been distracted all afternoon. Is everything okay?"

Lisa's question made Kate glance up and realize her sister was holding out a glass of lemonade. "Sorry." She reached to accept it. "Everything's fine." Except for the fact Bobby Tersh was still out there somewhere, now in Indianapolis according to the latest sighting; Dave had her flustered with his habit of showing up in her life; and Jennifer had called this gathering without indicating why. Kate shook her head and sipped at the cold drink. Dinner preparations were finished. Jennifer, Marcus, and the rest of the O'Malleys would be here within the hour.

"I tried to call you yesterday, but you weren't answering at home."

"You should have paged me."

"I knew I would see you today."

Kate settled deeper into the cushions of the sofa, resting the cold drink against her jeans. She had spent well into the evening hours yesterday beginning the review of the negotiation tapes from the bank. The tactical outcome had been necessary, but it still felt like a defeat.

"Kate." Lisa waved her hand. "See? Distracted."

Kate groaned. The last thing she wanted was for Lisa to know work was getting to her. The family already worried about her enough. Stephen had been sworn to silence about the black rose. "Sorry." Searching for a distraction, she offered one she knew would get Lisa's interest. "Dave Richman came over for pizza the other night. He seems to be there every time I turn around lately."

Lisa set down the glass she had just picked up. "Really?"

Kate looked over at her sister and half smiled. "Don't sound so surprised."

"You haven't exactly been dating much in the last year."

Lisa was being generous. She didn't think she had been out at all in the last year. "Don't get your hopes up. His interest is work related." She had noticed his frequent glances at his pager yesterday, waiting for the news that Bobby Tersh had been picked up. She had let it go because it was kind of nice to have him care enough to waste a Saturday covering her back. She would be inviting more attention than she wanted if she mentioned that to Lisa. "I think he'll make a good friend."

The doorbell rang and Lisa rose to answer it. "Don't let him slip out of your life, Kate. You need someone who can make you smile like that."

The O'Malleys spilled in through the door, laughing.

Setting her glass on the end table, Kate got to her feet. The energy that came into the room with their arrival was refreshing.

"Kate!"

She laughed as she was lifted off her feet in a hug. "Hi, Jack."

"It's good to see you're still in one piece."

"Rumors of my death were greatly exaggerated."

"Stephen ordered me not to come serenade you to sleep at the hospital."

"The way you sing, I'm grateful. Thanks for the e-mail gift. Manning is jealous. Where did you find the explosive screen saver?" She had laughed when she installed it. If she grabbed the mouse and cut the wires in time, the bomb would not go off.

"I was going to send you one of those electronic greeting cards, but when I saw the screen saver I knew you would appreciate it more."

"Absolutely."

Over Jack's shoulder, Kate saw Jennifer get swallowed up in a hug from Lisa. Jennifer was petite to begin with and appeared to have lost even more weight, but her smile was radiant, her color good. Kate lowered her voice. "Any idea what her news is?"

Jack lowered his head toward hers; the laughter in his voice disappeared as the serious side he so rarely showed came to the forefront. "We couldn't drag a thing out of her. It must be something pretty big."

Kate suppressed the desire to flinch. It was bad news; she just knew it. "Thanks for the warning." She took a deep breath. Whatever was coming couldn't be avoided. But it would help to stay busy. "Would you mind starting the grill? Marinated steaks are in the refrigerator."

"Consider it done. I'm starved."

"Of course you are. You're always hungry. I want mine pink, not dry."

"I notice, despite all the aspersions to my cooking, that you are still asking me to man the grill."

"Jack, you know Stephen will be out there to give you advice as soon as he sees the match in your hand."

"Just because we don't let you play around with the fire—"

She swatted his arm. "Go on." Jack laughed and moved toward the patio. "Stephen, Jack is going for the matches."

Stephen strode across the room, angling after Jack. "I'm on him. There is no way I am letting him burn *my* steak."

Grinning at the fact the two of them were so predictable, Kate turned to look for Rachel.

Her sister was hanging back half a step, observing it all with a smile. Kate headed toward her because her hugs were always the best. "Rachel. How was Florida?" The tan was there, but subtle.

"I went swimming with a porpoise." The quiet pleasure in her voice reflected the memory. She always had the positive to tell, even in a tragedy. She hadn't been in Florida for a vacation.

"Who'd you take?"

"Diane Faber, age ten. She was a much better swimmer."

"Did she lose one or both parents?" The tornado through Florida's Dade County three weeks ago had taken fourteen lives. As a trauma psychologist, Rachel got called in for the tough cases.

"Her father. He had promised her the trip for her birthday."

Rebuilding positive memories, helping the child know life went on. It was Rachel's special gift to children. "Rough."

"Yes. But she'll make it. How are you doing after Tuesday's excitement?"

"A few bad dreams."

"You got off relatively light then."

"I did."

"Hey, Rachel, you've got to come see my new pet," Lisa called. "I got him this last week."

"Does it slither?" Rachel whispered.

Kate grinned, having had the exact same concern when Lisa mentioned the pet to her. With Lisa it was best not to make assumptions. "A sable ferret. He's adorable."

"The fact it has fur is itself a relief. I want to hear about this bank thing later, in all its detail."

"You will." Kate promised, accepting the fact she would have to tell the story at least once tonight. Rachel nodded and crossed to join Lisa.

"The cuts look like they are healing well."

Kate turned to see Jennifer at her side and had to smile at the opening observation. The doctor would always be there in the forefront. "I wish you had been here. I had Stephen doing the needle bit and offering a lollipop."

"I heard. We were chatting on the phone while you were still in the ER. You'll be happy to know I brought him another case of lollipops since he was running short of cherry."

"I'm never going to live this one down, am I?"

Something flickered in Jennifer's eyes. "Not until someone else in the family creates better news to talk about."

Kate searched Jennifer's expression. That flicker, had it been for good news or bad? "Would that by any chance be you?"

Jennifer flashed a knowing smile. "You'll find out after dinner."

"Leaving me the hot seat for a while?"

"You're good cover. I think I'll hide behind you for another hour."

Kate hugged her. "In that case, I think I should hurry along dinner."

Marcus was leaning against the archway to the kitchen. Kate smiled at his quiet scrutiny. His arm came out to encompass her. "I'm glad you're okay."

She drew in a deep breath and let it out with a sigh, safe in the shelter of his arms. She would have to reassure them all, and it felt nice. "I honestly didn't get hurt that badly."

"I talked to your doctors. You weren't a pretty sight."

"It's relative. I nearly had a busted nose, but Dave got in the way of that blow."

"Richman?"

She nodded. "I'd say the fight was interesting for about forty seconds."

"I talked to him on the phone briefly at the hospital. He didn't mention it."

"As it split his lip, probably not." She leaned back and grinned. "Thanks for the roses."

"My pleasure."

"They were extravagant."

"Someone has to spoil you."

"I've really missed you."

"It's mutual." He rubbed her arms. "What else has been happening in your life? Been hiding any good secrets?" She was hiding so many at the moment it made her face tinge pink. One eyebrow raised. "I think you should explain that blush."

"Maybe later. We've got steaks for the grill, as well as Polish and brats. Would you take them out to Stephen and Jack?"

"The longer you duck the question, the more interested I'm going to be in the answer."

"Curiosity is good for you."

He nodded toward the kitchen. "Get the food."

Laughter erupted from the back patio where Lisa and Jennifer had joined Stephen and Jack. Kate grinned, loving the sound. "Try to corral the kids while you are out there."

"This is your jurisdiction, not mine."

"You're the adult here. I'm going to join the fun."

"Thanks a lot."

Kate slipped her arm around his waist and grinned. "Admit it; you like being the one in charge."

"In this family, that means I get all the grief."

"Exactly." It wasn't just the fact that they were the two oldest; it was the past. She and Marcus had been at the group home over two years before the others had begun to arrive. Their history together went deeper, and unlike the others, they had never had a chance to be kids. "I'm going to hate this answer, but when is your flight back?"

"First thing tomorrow morning."

"I was afraid of that."

"Have something in mind?"

"I was looking forward to a basketball game."

He smiled. "You could use a couple more days to recover."

"I'm a little stiff, but I'm ready to play. I figured you could use the handicap."

"Been beating Stephen recently?"

"Frequently. My fadeaway jumper is red hot."

"Let me see what Jack and Stephen are doing. Maybe we can fit in an early morning game."

"Hey, Kate! We're ready for food out here."

Kate gave Marcus an amused look. "Coming, Jack."

Dinner was a riot. Kate ended up seated between Marcus and Lisa. It had been six weeks since the last full gathering. The stories were numerous and hilarious. Kate sat back and enjoyed the shared laughter. There was something about having the whole family together that made everything more meaningful.

As plates were collected so dessert could be brought to the table, Lisa leaned over to whisper, "Are you going to mention seeing Dave?"

Kate hesitated, glancing around at the group. "Do you think I should?"

"What do you think?"

Why not? It was a night for surprises. Kate picked up her fork and tapped on her water glass. "May I have your attention please?"

The family quieted down. "Knowing the grapevine that cements this family together," she smiled at the main culprit sitting beside her as laughter echoed around the room, "allow me to dispel a rumor that I'm sure will soon be making the rounds. Yes, I have seen Dave Richman since Tuesday; it was not a date. I have not changed my policy on dating cops. Now who wants chocolate or raspberry ice cream for dessert?" She got to her feet to bring out dessert. She loved the looks of surprise around the table.

"Kate is seeing someone." Jennifer was delighted. "This is wonderful."

"Absolutely," Rachel joined in. "Come on, Kate. Details!"

"I've only known him a couple days. I think he'll make a good friend."

"We can tell. Nice blush, Kate." Marcus commented. "When do we get to meet him?"

"Check him out you mean?"

"Of course. Invite him to the basketball game tomorrow morning."

"You guys would have him for breakfast."

"Only if we didn't like him," Jack chimed in from the other end of the table.

Kate grinned, knowing it was true. She might as well find out if Dave was going to survive the scrutiny. No one could read a guy better than her brothers.

"I would want an honest opinion," she said softly to Marcus.

"That serious?"

No. And yet…"Maybe someday."

His hand grasped hers. "Bring him around."

Kate helped Lisa bring out dessert.

"Since Kate has broken the ice, I guess it's time for my announcement, too." Jennifer looked…nervous…Kate decided as she resumed her seat. She glanced around the table and saw the same anxiety just under the surface with everyone at the table. To a person, they were braced for bad news.

"I appreciate you all changing your plans and flying here on such short notice. I didn't want to do this over the phone."

Rachel reached over and grasped Jennifer's hand.

"I met someone a few months ago. Tom Peterson is a doctor in my medical office building. I haven't mentioned him because, well, a lot of reasons, but mainly because it was just a really good friendship. It's gotten serious in the last few weeks." She took a deep breath, her smile tremendous. "I'm engaged."

Engaged? And she had never mentioned him? Kate tried to absorb the news, to understand. This was quick, and Jennifer was not impulsive in her actions.

The first engagement in the family. There was a quietness around the room.

"Congratulations, Jen." The first words came from Marcus. Kate glanced over and saw not only a smile, but…relief? Yes. His worry for Jennifer would have been intense. He was the guardian of the family.

"I didn't mean to worry everybody. The engagement just sort of happened."

Kate grinned. Even Jennifer was having a hard time explaining the situation. It had to be love.

"Where's the ring?"

"When's the wedding?"

"Did you at least bring a picture?"

The questions came in a flurry as they crowded around Jennifer to celebrate, to share the joy.

Jennifer took the engagement ring off her necklace and slipped it on her finger. "I want to bring him to the Fourth of July gathering so you can all meet him. Just showing up with Tom didn't sound like a good idea."

"Now, Jen, you know if you said to like him, we automatically would," Jack protested.

"You had better!"

Kate gave Jennifer a hug. "You love him." She needed to hear that reassurance, for this was her baby sister.

"More than I can put into words."

Kate could see the joy. She could also see something she didn't understand. Jennifer glanced at the others and squeezed her hand. "You'll like him, Kate." Whatever else she wanted to say, it was something she wanted to say privately. Kate returned the pressure. Later.

Stepping back and watching Jennifer, Kate felt uneasy beneath her smile—not for Jennifer, but for the rest of them. Within a few months, the family would expand, become different. She tried to imagine it and could not. It had been just the seven of them for over two decades. She felt the unexpected sensation of threatening tears and blinked rapidly not to let them form.

A hand slipped around her waist and she turned. Marcus. "This day was destined to come. It will be different, Kate, but better."

"Reading my mind again?"

"Feeling the same thing."

She leaned her head on his shoulder. "An O'Malley wedding." She chuckled, finding laughter better than tears. "Can you imagine the surprises that will be dreamed up for the big day?"

"Life is not going to be boring." Marcus reassuringly rubbed her back. "Just think, we'll finally be able to play four on four, girls versus guys, with an expanded family."

She elbowed him. "You guys won't have any more excuses when you lose."

He grinned. "There is that."

The party began to break up shortly after 9 P.M. Rachel and Jennifer were staying with Lisa. Kate didn't doubt that they would be up most of the night talking. Marcus was heading out with Jack.

"Six A.M. game time?" Marcus confirmed, giving her a hug good-bye.

"Yes. With Dave if he's interested." How she was going to word that invitation, she had no idea.

"Good."

Jennifer had stepped into the kitchen. It was the first time Kate had been able to catch her alone. "Jen, congratulations again on your good news."

"Thanks." The smile was real, but so were the subtle signs of strain.

There was more news; Kate was sure of it now. She rested her arm around Jennifer's shoulders. "This is not the only reason you came."

"No. Can we meet tomorrow after you get off work?"

"I can get away for lunch."

Jennifer hesitated. "Evening would be better."

"Okay." The swirling reality of bad news was still in the air. "I'll call when I get off, come by and pick you up?"

Jennifer's hug was tight. "Thanks."

"Anytime. You'll call before then if you need me?"

Jennifer nodded.

"Don't let Lisa and Rachel keep you up half the night. They'll have you in Tahiti for your honeymoon if you're not careful."

Jennifer smiled. "They are debating Paris or Rome at the moment."

"The travel hounds have been let loose."

"I forgot how much fun it was to watch them together."

"It is that. Enjoy tonight. And call Tom."

"It's late."

"Trust me; he'll be waiting by the phone, afraid the family talked you into changing your mind."

"True." Jennifer glanced at the clock and grinned. "I think I'll give it another half hour before I call."

Kate laughed.

"Ready to go, Kate?"

"On my way, Stephen." She squeezed Jennifer's hand. "I'll see you tomorrow."

Stephen's car was blocking hers. "Stephen."

He paused halfway down the driveway. "Yes?"

She leaned against her open car door. "Would you mind coming to the gym a few minutes early?"

"Want to shake the rust off before Marcus arrives?"

"I would hate to get embarrassed on the court."

He tossed and caught his keys, considering it. "Will you go shopping with me to find Rachel's birthday present?"

Kate knew a good deal when she heard it. Stephen could carry the packages. "Deal."

She drove home without the radio on, content with her own thoughts. The fatigue that accompanied a day of emotions was beginning to set in. What else did Jennifer have to say? It was private. She had no idea what that meant. The clock on the dash read 9:48. If she waited until she got home, she could avoid a call to Dave by saying it was too late to bother him. The guys would accept that, but it was a weak excuse. She had never been a coward. If Dave said no, he said no.

She reached for the car phone.

Dave picked up his empty bowl. "Sara, you want more popcorn?"

She was stretched out on his couch using her husband Adam's lap for a pillow. "Sure." She handed him her bowl from the floor. "We can pause the movie."

"I've seen this part." Besides, he didn't want to give her a reason to move. He liked seeing her relaxed and content with Adam. They had come out to his house for the afternoon so Sara could look through old family picture albums, then had stayed for dinner and a movie. "I'll be back in a minute."

Dave found himself a cold soda while he waited for the popcorn to finish. When the phone rang, he grabbed it before the second ring.

"Richman."

"Sorry to call so late."

He smiled. "Didn't I say you could wake me up if you wanted to?" Pulling out a chair at the kitchen table, he sat down and stretched his legs out, making himself comfortable.

"It's not that urgent."

"It doesn't have to be." From the background noise he could tell Kate was on the road somewhere. The fatigue in her voice bothered him. "Where are you?"

"I think I'm lost." There was amusement in her voice.

"Want me to come to the rescue? You can send up flares or something."

"One wrong turn in construction, and I can't tell north from south."

"Well, that's easy. Go toward the tall buildings, and you'll eventually hit the lake. It's large. Very hard to miss."

Her chuckle was better than the fatigue he had been hearing. "This is better. I just found Yorkshire." He heard a car horn in the background. "Sorry for the tangent. Why did I call you?"

He laughed softly. "I don't care. I'm just glad you did."

"Tell me what you've been doing today while I try to remember."

"I had a quiet Sunday. Church with Sara and Adam. Shish kebabs for dinner. There are leftovers if you're interested. There's nothing new on Bobby Tersh."

"It's been seventy-two hours; relax, Dave."

"Just be careful when you get home, or I'll come camp out on your doorstep again."

He was expecting a comeback not a quiet sigh. "You can shoot me anytime."

"What did you forget?"

"My sister got engaged."

"Ouch. Okay, you got more than a little distracted. Which sister?"

"Jennifer."

"You must be thrilled."

"I think I am."

"Not sure yet?"

"It will be a big change for the O'Malley clan."

Adam came into the kitchen, and Dave smiled. "Speaking from personal experience, in-laws aren't too bad."

Adam raised an eyebrow. "Kate," Dave whispered. Adam smiled, finished fixing the popcorn, and disappeared with the full bowl.

"I haven't met Jennifer's fiancé yet. He'll be up here for the Fourth of July."

"Sounds like it will be an interesting holiday."

"We'll be nice. Jennifer has already stamped all the votes approved."

"Good for her." He heard a radio turn on. There was a comfortable moment of silence.

"I've got an offer for you."

Dave leaned forward, hearing the awkwardness in Kate's voice. "What's that?"

"We're having a basketball game tomorrow morning before Marcus has to fly out. Would you like to join us?"

"When and where?"

"Six, at the gym on Haverson Street."

He was not a morning person. "I'll be there," he replied without hesitation. The things he did for a friend. There was no way he was going to mention this to Sara.

"Thanks. I told them to be nice to you, by the way."

"Did you?"

"I don't know if this is a good idea, but I would like you to meet them."

"It's a great idea. I'll meet you there."

"Then I'll see you in about eight hours. Thanks, Dave."

"My pleasure. Good night, Kate."

He held onto the receiver for a few moments after the call disconnected before smiling and walking over to hang up the phone.

"Who was that?" Sara glanced up from the movie for a moment as he resumed his seat in the living room.

"A friend."

He was glad the movie had her too preoccupied to follow up. Adam, however, looked over at him, shook his head, and slowly smiled.

SEVEN

The gym echoed with the sound of a one-on-one intense basketball game. The bounce of the ball, the scuff of tennis shoes, an occasional huff of expelled air. The backboard sang with the impact of two hands on the rim.

Dave was immediately impressed with the intensity of the game being played. Kate and Stephen were the two on the court. They had apparently been playing for a while; her jersey was wet with sweat. Dave glanced at his watch and saw he was on time.

"So much for her being rusty."

He looked to his left and recognized from Kate's picture that he had been joined by one of the O'Malleys.

"I'm Jack. You must be Dave?" The man's smile was friendly, his handshake solid.

"Yes."

"Glad you could come." Jack glanced at the court, shook his head. "I'm getting tired of buying her breakfast."

Dave noted the protest was said with a smile. "The price of a loss?"

"Typically." Jack grinned. "But it makes the occasional wins all the sweeter."

Skirting around the game, they walked across to the bleachers and set down their gym bags.

Kate nailed a long two-point shot from the corner. "Yes!"

Stephen laughed and hugged her. "Good game." The two of them came off the court together.

Dave enjoyed the grin Kate turned toward him. "Hi, Dave." She sat down on the bench and picked up her water jug. She was breathing hard, looking pleased with herself for the win.

"You looked good out there," Dave said.

"Just warming up. You've met the other half of the dynamic duo?"

He glanced at Jack. "Yes."

Stephen accepted the second water jug Kate offered. "Jack, we're going to have to do something to earn us a different moniker."

"It would have to be something spectacular. We've been the dynamic duo since we were fourteen."

"How about the 'twin towers'?" Kate offered. Jack dropped a headlock on her, which made her giggle. "Where's Marcus?"

Jack gestured to the door where Marcus paced, talking on his cellular phone. "Washington called."

"Figures."

These were the guys who had shaped Kate's life. That she was comfortable with them was obvious.

Dave leaned over to her and whispered for her ears only, "Anything on our friend Tersh?"

She shook her head. "No word on his location; no more black roses."

Marcus joined them. "Sorry."

"Everything okay?" Kate asked.

"It will wait for another few hours." He smiled and extended his hand. "Nice to meet you in person, Dave."

Dave didn't miss the assessment being done as they shook hands. "Marcus."

"How do you want to play this?" Stephen asked.

Marcus and Kate exchanged a look. "Three on two. Kate and I will take you guys on. It should be about even."

Jack grinned. "Oooh, I think that was a challenge."

Stephen picked up the basketball. "I do believe it was."

Kate dropped her towel and grinned. "Let's talk strategy, Marcus." The two of them moved to the top of the key to huddle.

Dave watched the two of them for a moment, then looked over at Stephen. "Let me take Kate."

"She's good outside, she can jump, and she's fast," Stephen summarized. "You sure?"

Dave smiled. "I'm sure. Besides, it has to be easier than taking on Marcus."

Stephen laughed. "All right. I'll take Marcus, and Jack can cover."

The game was more intense than Dave had expected. They were playing for fun, but they were playing to win. As the score rose, the depth of the talent on the court began to make itself clear. They were all good players, but Kate and Marcus played in a rhythm that suggested years playing together. She was a dynamo on the court, always moving.

He pulled in a deep breath, fighting to get oxygen into his muscles. He was in excellent shape. He had to be in his profession. Playing with this group reminded him why he should not take those occasional days off from his workout routine.

He coiled the speed he had left and cut right, determined to go to the basket. He cleared Kate's leaping block by mere inches and watched his shot bounce around the rim and come back off the left side. Kate grabbed the rebound with elbows out. Dave knew what trouble was. It was Kate smelling victory.

He would make her earn it.

Hands warily out, he watched her eyes. She didn't telegraph her moves. He had never met someone with her skill for concealing her intentions. She could abruptly pull up, cut, then reverse.

She made a pass without looking. He pivoted to see Marcus go to the rim with the ball. How did she do that? Three against two and they were still getting beat.

"One to go." The satisfaction in her voice was clear.

Dave took the ball Stephen tossed him and dried his hands on his shorts. "It won't be easy."

She grinned. "You're stalling."

Dave took the ball to the half court line with a half grunt, half laugh. He touched the line and cut left. Stephen broke free. Dave passed him the ball. Marcus forced Stephen to pass it back. Dave glanced at Jack and then drove for the basket.

Kate stepped in front of him.

The fear was instantaneous. He pivoted hard to avoid the collision but couldn't avoid crashing into her. She slid to a stop on her backside a few feet away.

"Charge."

To hear her, she had just won a crown rather than a bruise. He offered her a hand up. "Kate, winning is not that important!" His voice shook with anger and lingering fear.

She looked at him, puzzled.

Marcus dropped his arm across her shoulders, breathing hard. "Kate, not everyone is used to the way you throw yourself into harm's way for a simple game."

She wiped her face, then nodded. "Sorry, Dave."

He tossed the ball to Stephen, still scowling. "Sure you are. You'd do it again in a heartbeat to block my shot." From her grin, she heard his muttered comment.

"Take the ball out, Marcus."

The last few minutes of the game were played with a little less contact. Jack evened out the score before a blitz by Marcus came back to win the game.

Kate collapsed on the bench. "Who's going to carry me to breakfast?"

Jack tossed a towel over her face. "What happened to being a gracious winner?"

She laughed and tossed it back at him. "I'll let you beat me at a game of tennis."

"I could do that in my sleep."

A pager went off. Dave reached for his and was amused to see everyone else reaching for his or hers.

"It's mine." Jack grabbed his bag. "I'm gone. Nice to have met you, Dave."

"Don't eat too much smoke!" Kate called after him as he ran for the door.

"I'll be careful!"

Puzzled, Dave looked at Kate.

"Fireman."

He nodded. Fireman. Paramedic. U.S. Marshal. Her brothers had interesting careers.

She turned. "Marcus, how are you doing on time?"

Marcus was stretched out, his elbows resting on the bleachers behind him. "A fast shower and I'll need to leave for the airport."

Kate's face grew pensive. "Call me tonight."

Marcus studied her for a moment, then nodded. "Sure."

Watching Kate with her family was watching her with people she loved. She relaxed, laughed, joked, and cared. Dave was glad he had been invited to come. He was getting to see another side of her.

Marcus got to his feet and offered his hand. "I'm glad I got to meet you."

Dave felt he had passed a test. "It's mutual."

"Stephen, how about you dropping me off at the airport? We'll let Kate and Dave get a leisurely breakfast."

Kate blushed. "Marcus O'Malley—" She scrambled to grab her pager. Her look turned to one of intense frustration. "Never mind. I've got to go." She gave Marcus a quick hug.

When she paused beside him, Dave buried his worry to give her a smile. "We'll talk. Go. Be careful."

She nodded and broke for the door at a quick trot.

An hour spent talking to a woman threatening to jump from a fourth floor ledge put Kate in a quiet mood when she eventually got back to the office. In an effort to discourage conversation, she slipped on her headphones but did not touch play. It took forty minutes to complete the case notes from the incident. And when she was done, Kate felt wrung out. She could summarize the woman's problem in two words: *no hope.*

She dropped her case notes on her boss's desk and left to take a ten-minute walk.

There were days the job hit too close to home.

Life had never managed to break her own will to live, but it had scarred her expectations of what life would be like. She had been a wary little fighter when she was nine. With the passing years, she had gained an appreciation of life and the things that were to be treasured, but there remained part of her that listened to "there is no hope" and resonated with it.

For every bright spot, there was a shadow.

She had the O'Malleys and a past so dark it still made her flinch.

She had her job and a life expectancy that insured she would not be issued a life insurance policy.

Would Dave ever understand the somber part of her that looked at life and better understood the shadows than the light? She thought about him as she walked.

She smiled. Her brothers liked him. Even Marcus, the most protective, had signaled a qualified approval. It created a quandary for her: She didn't date cops, and her brothers were going to be asking about Dave in the future.

When she returned to the office, there was a note Dave had called. *Black Rose* was underlined. Something new? She hoped so. He was smothering her about this black rose thing. If he thought having someone leave her a rose was a problem, what was he going to be like when the threat was serious? The man was too good at his job; he didn't know how to ignore a problem around him. Why couldn't she have been stuck in the bank with a desk jock instead of a frontline agent?

She picked up the phone. When she got his voice mail, she rubbed her eyes, debated for a moment, then left a brief message that she was returning his call, was fine, and that she would be working on Henry Lott's case notes that afternoon. She scanned her calendar. "I've also got a meeting set up with Nathan Young for Wednesday, 2 P.M., if you still want to tag along. Let me know."

She hung up the phone and realized she had forgotten to say thanks for playing basketball with them this morning. Call and leave another message? She ran her hand through her hair. No, better to call back later and tell him in person.

"Hey, Kate, who's your contact over in narcotics?"

She glanced over to see Franklin, his hand covering the telephone receiver, leaning far enough back in his chair it was close to tipping over. "Christopher Atkins. Tall, lanky, looks seventeen—the one that broke up that high school track-and-field cocaine ring."

"Our Henry Lott is claiming drug money used to get laundered through Wilshire Construction."

"Why doesn't that surprise me?" She shouldn't be so cynical, but a night watchman at a construction company trying to cut a deal to get time knocked off a certain prison sentence—there were only so many things he could credibly pull out of his hat. "Want me to call over?"

Franklin spoke briefly into the phone, then shook his head. "No need. Graham's on his way over there now. He figured you would know the best person to ask." He spoke for another minute, then hung up the phone.

"Did anything else come out of the interview?"

"No. But ATF called this morning. They traced the explosives to a now defunct subcontractor that did some demolition work for Wilshire Construction ten years ago. We'll be able to put this one to bed, Kate."

She looked at the case notes on her desk. "Yes." Another couple days and the last loose ends would be wrapped up. She almost wished her pager would go off so she could avoid spending the rest of the day doing her final review of the negotiation tapes.

Kate reached over to unlock the passenger door. "Jennifer, I'm sorry to be so late." It was almost 8 P.M. She had completed her review of the Henry Lott negotiation tapes and had been ready to walk out the door when she had been put on standby for a call out that had never come. She still owed Dave a call to say thanks for coming to the game this morning. She had been away from her desk getting a late lunch when he called back to confirm Wednesday's meeting with Nathan Young.

Jennifer slipped into the passenger seat. "Quit apologizing. This is fine. If I slipped out earlier, I would feel guilty about abandoning Lisa and Rachel."

"Do they have your wedding planned?"

"They are having the time of their lives making suggestions. It is wonderful. There is no way I would have the energy to pull off what can be done with their help."

"So it's good? They are not stepping on your toes?"

"I'm enjoying sharing the joy."

Kate relaxed. Jennifer meant it. She looked at her sister, hoping to find she had misread the situation last night. She hadn't. The tension was still there. "What would you like to do?"

The lighthearted few moments changed to quiet resolve. "Let's pick up a soda at the corner store and then go for a walk."

They bought sodas, and Kate stopped at the nearby park. They set out to walk around its oval-shaped pond. It was a beautiful evening, and several people were out walking around the park.

Kate would have liked to break the silence with some light comment but forced herself to stay quiet. The longer they walked in silence, the more concerned she became.

"I didn't come with only good news."

"I know," she said quietly.

"Kate, I'm flying from here to the Mayo clinic."

She didn't make the connection immediately. "Why?"

Jennifer reached over and squeezed her hand. "I've got cancer."

"You've what?"

"The test results came back last week." Jennifer's shoulders hunched. "They were pretty bad. It's one of the reasons Tom refused to postpone his proposal."

"What did the test results say?"

"The cancer is around my spine. It's rare. And it has spread into at least my liver."

No! The emotions screamed to spill out. They turned inward instead, were stuffed deep, defensively blocked. *Keep focused.*

Breathe.

"We have to tell the family."

"No. Not yet. I'll be back for the Fourth of July. By then I will know the scope of what I'm facing. I was only going to tell Marcus, but he can't afford the distraction. Given what happened Tuesday, I couldn't afford to wait another week to tell you."

"How can you sound so calm about this?"

"Oh, Kate, the emotions roil in a thousand directions. But there is a comfort in knowing I'm okay even if the worst happens. Tom introduced me to what faith is. I *have* to talk to you about Jesus. Tuesday scared me to death."

Kate's thoughts were racing with the onslaught of unexpected news. "First Dave, now you," she murmured quietly, not realizing she spoke.

"What?"

"He said nearly the same thing the other night." She took a deep breath and slowly let it out. "What can I do to help?"

Jennifer's arm circled around her shoulders. "I know this is a shock. I know how big of a burden I'm placing on you. The news is going to affect everyone in the family, and they are going to lean heavily on you and Marcus."

"Oh, Jen, the fact it affects us is nothing compared to the reality of what you are dealing with. Is the pain bad?"

"My right side hurts. There is some numbness in my left leg. But there were few warning signs."

"What are you looking at—surgery, chemotherapy, radiation?"

"I'm being sent to Mayo to find out if there are any options. I won't kid you. Whatever they come up with is likely to be experimental."

"There have to be options."

"The doctors have advised it will be a week of long days and a lot of tests. We'll see what they come up with. As a doctor, I can cope better with the details than the speculation." Jennifer hugged Kate. "You asked what you could do. I want to talk with you when I get back about Jesus. I'm afraid for you."

Jen was afraid for *her.* There was such helplessness in being asked something so intangible. "I wish I could promise there would be no more close calls. But it comes with the job."

"I know that. But do you understand why faith has become such an important issue to me? I don't want to pressure you, but if something did happen, I would have a very hard time knowing I had never talked to you. I want you to read the book of Luke and have dinner with me, then tell me honestly what you think about Jesus."

"Jennifer, I'm afraid I'll hurt you."

"You won't. I would rather hear honest reasons for disbelief than never to have had the conversation with you." She took a slim book from her pocket. "I marked the page."

Kate looked awkwardly at the leather book Jennifer handed her. "You want me to read the book of Luke."

"It's written by a doctor. It's one of my favorite gospels." Jennifer tried to offer a reassuring smile. "Kate, if you still say you don't believe, that's okay. I simply need to talk to you about it."

She was supposed to believe in God while her sister was possibly dying? Reeling from a hit against her family she could do nothing to fight, Kate's hand clutched the book. She couldn't say no to Jennifer's request, but how could she calmly discuss something that made her feel so angry? She had no choice. She would do whatever Jennifer asked. "We'll have dinner."

The clock blinked 3:22 A.M. Kate pulled another page off the printer and skimmed the text as she drank her sixth cup of coffee since midnight. The article from the January *Oncology Journal* filled in a few more gaps in her knowledge. There were two new chemotherapy treatments showing promise, both combinations of existing drugs. Her eyes burned as she struggled to focus and read, but at least it was now fatigue and not the salt of tears. She had given up trying to sleep.

She desperately wanted to be able to talk to Marcus, but instead had listened as the answering machine took his call at 11 P.M. If he heard her voice, he would know. She couldn't come up with a convincing lie right now, even to give herself cover so she could talk with him. This was the first crisis in years where she had not been able to lean on him.

Cancer. It was hard to describe the fear the word evoked the more she read. What she had learned from the pages spread out across her desk scared her to death. According to her research, Jennifer could be facing a 2 percent survival rate beyond one year.

Premature death was part of her world, not Jennifer's. That pain seared. Jennifer didn't deserve this.

Kate had to deal with the personal risk of an early death because of her job. The power of attorney, the will, her bank accounts, financial papers, all of it was organized to make it easier on her family should something happen. She held the same documents for Marcus. There was a sense of preparation for the worst when it came to the dangers of their jobs. But she had never thought about Jennifer as being at risk. The news had struck a soft underbelly.

There was nothing she could do. That was what hurt the most.

She set down the coffee cup, pushing back the small leather book with the words *New Testament* across the front. She had promised Jennifer to read Luke, and she eventually would, but at the moment she would like nothing better than for the book to accidentally fall into the trash.

She could understand Jennifer not wanting to mix the good news and the bad Sunday night. She could understand the caution of wanting to wait until she had more details before telling the whole family. But carrying the secret was going to be the toughest thing Kate had faced in years.

EIGHT

Kate shifted through change for toll money, glad she didn't have to make this trip to O'Hare often. Traffic coming out of the city was a mess. Needing to get away from the office, she had offered to take Franklin's place at the monthly check-in with Bob Roberts, head of O'Hare's security. It was a beautiful day out—sunny blue skies, light breeze. She popped another two jelly beans in her mouth. After this meeting, she was going to take a few hours of personal time and get some much needed sleep.

The shock of Jennifer's news had passed. She was thinking now proactively about questions to ask the doctors. This would be a long battle that none of the O'Malleys would accept losing. If the doctors said a 2 percent chance, then Jennifer would be in that 2 percent. They were O'Malleys. They had dealt with long odds before.

She checked her voice mail messages and was relieved to hear one from Jennifer. Her early morning flight had been fine; she was getting ready to take a cab out to the Mayo Clinic. Kate hung up the phone and made a mental note to call in an hour when Jennifer should be checked in.

There was something majestic about coming into O'Hare on I-190 and realizing they had built an airport taxiway over the highway. Kate slowed her speed to match traffic and watched a huge Turkish Airline Airbus cross from the international terminal to the runway. The plane gleamed bright white, its red tail rising like a hawk. Her car passed under the shadow cast by its wing.

She glanced at her watch. 9:20 A.M. She was a few minutes early.

Kate flipped open the incident plan book and found Bob's number. She called him from her cellular phone and arranged to meet him by the United ticket counter in terminal one. She liked Bob Roberts. She had worked with the former DEA agent several times over the years. Her job today would be to listen, make note of the security changes made in the last month, and coordinate any changes he wanted to make to the incident plan book.

With one hundred flights an hour on average and over two hundred thousand passengers a day, Bob Roberts had a massive job on his hands. The security personnel at O'Hare could handle most incidents, but a constant coordination was done with the city police, fire department, bomb squad, and FBI so that when he did need to bring people in, it would happen in a seamless fashion.

Kate slipped a blank cassette into the handheld tape recorder that went everywhere with her and tucked a couple spare cassettes into her pocket. She preferred dictating notes. She walked through the airport at a leisurely pace, scanning the crowds out of habit.

"Good morning, Bob." He was a man in his late forties, perpetually in motion. Meetings with him were walking tours, the best kind of reviews in Kate's opinion. If they swung out to the general aviation terminal, she planned to make a couple inquiries regarding Dave's jet. Assuming Dave was a regular here, Bob would know what he flew.

"Kate. Glad they sent you. I always have to explain everything to Franklin."

"I'll take any excuse to get out of the office." She retrieved her bag of jelly beans and offered to share. She remembered his sweet tooth.

"Thanks." Bob gestured to terminal *C.* "Let's walk."

"There are a couple general changes worth noting. Customs has a new program beginning this month at Cargo City. They are adding five dogs. I expect seizures will be up over the next month.

"We have doubled the number of security personnel walking the terminals for the next month to accommodate the increase in Fourth of July passenger traffic.

"I've also got a new set of contact phone numbers for you. We've finally got the last recommendations of the review panel completed."

They walked the terminal, Kate making notes, laughing frequently as Bob peppered his serious discussion of security changes with some of the more amusing incidents in the last month.

Bob's pager went off.

He glanced at the code. "Kate, we've got an incident. That's the air traffic control tower."

An incident could be anything from a plane in trouble to a terrorist threat. Regardless, it wasn't the kind of information people around them should hear. Bob used his access card to open a side door in the concourse. They hurried down a flight of stairs to the tarmac. The roar of planes taking off, muted inside, now reverberated across concrete. He pointed to one of the shuttle carts. "We'll take it to the tower."

Kate nodded and climbed aboard.

He tuned his radio to a private channel. "Elliot, it's Bob. We're on our way. What are the details?"

"A bomb threat was called in on the regional ATC line. Five words. 'Get ready for a bomb.' Male voice. Not enough to get a good accent. Popping on the line, possibly a cellular phone."

"Handle it Code Two, Elliot."

"Calls are already underway."

Kate knew the procedures, but since she was carrying a copy of the plan book, she flipped it open. "Is it against the tower, a plane, or a terminal?" She was thinking out loud. They didn't have enough information to know. She glanced at her watch and noted the time. 10:48 A.M. This was supposed to be a light duty morning. Two bomb incidents within a week was a toll she didn't need. Every threat was treated as real.

Passengers and flight crews in the terminals would already be seeing a noticeable shift in the intensity of the security. Unattended baggage would be cleared. Dogs would be out working the areas. The visible sweep would begin while behind the scenes the more intense work began. Fire and rescue would be on high alert. Ground crews would be paying special attention as flights were prechecked and turned around for departure. Luggage would be screened again. A search of the grounds would begin.

Kate looked at Bob. "When was the last bomb threat?"

"Sixteen days ago, called into an airline office. A hoax."

The tower handled air traffic within the tightly controlled class B airspace. Outside that zone of class B airspace, the aircraft were handled by the regional air traffic control center. "The call came in on a regional ATC phone number. How well-known is that number?" Kate asked, looking for clues.

Bob skirted around a luggage carrier. "Obviously it is posted in the regional center. Within O'Hare proper, the tower people would know it and the electrical technicians who maintain the tower. It's a restricted line, but the central phone hub for the complex would have it marked."

Kate worked on her list. "So add janitors and maintenance people in general. It's not secure information but limited."

"Yes. We can run the records, see when the phone number was last changed."

Kate nodded, looking at the words of the threat. "'Get ready for a bomb.' No clock, so he either doesn't want to give us the time it will go off, or he doesn't know the exact time it will go off. It sounds like the device is already in place."

The more she looked at the words, the more she disliked them. "Bob, it is too general to be a hoax." Hoaxes were specific. They wanted to arouse a strong reaction without showing evidence. "This is the first warning shot. Why the tower? That's the only clue we really have."

"Rule of thumb, threat calls go to the media to get attention or to the intended target to get a response," Bob replied.

It was a common convention that bombs at airports targeted planes, but it wasn't an absolute. "The tower itself?"

"Possible. At least it's a contained area to search."

The tower sat detached from other buildings, rose high above the passenger concourses, and looked out across seven runways, one of them over two miles long. Kate followed Bob inside the building and showed her badge to clear security. They headed to the observation deck.

The room was crowded with very busy people. From this location, they had a full 360-degree view of the airspace. The windows in the room had been sealed in at a slight angle with the top edge extending farther out. The glare-resistant, thick glass helped keep the controllers from squinting into the sunlight. Kate could see planes out on the taxiways, lined up ten deep to take off. Massive Boeing 747s looked small from this height. In the air, planes were stacked in defined holding patterns waiting for clearance to land. She listened to the terse chatter between air traffic controllers and pilots and understood a word here and there. ORD was the designation for O'Hare.

Elliot waved them over. "We've got three groups working the problem. Concourses, luggage and cargo, and aircraft. All the dogs are deployed."

"Let's get a team sweeping this tower," Bob requested.

Elliot nodded and reached for the radio.

"Can we route this phone line to the command center in the administration building?"

"I've got a technician taking a look. He said it might have to be a hard jumper at the punch-down block since restricted lines were not made part of the main switch."

"What about getting set up to run a trace if we get another call?"

"Working on it."

"Kate, can I borrow the tape recorder? If this is real, I hope we get more than this vague call to work with."

She already had a new tape in place. "Unfortunately, Bob, I think you will." She watched as the men worked, talking with the deployed teams, their calm efficiency reminding her of how many of these incidents they worked in a year.

It was precisely 11:00 A.M. when the regional ATC phone rang again. The mood all around the tower changed. The odds of this one being real and not a hoax had just risen dramatically. Bob took a deep breath, clicked on the recorder, and picked up the phone. "O'Hare tower."

Kate saw the anger cloud his face and caught his startled look in her direction. He apparently was not given the opportunity to ask any questions. He hung up the phone and clicked off the recorder. "Kate, what is going on?"

He rewound the cassette and pressed play.

"The bomb goes off at eleven-fifteen. The plane is talking to the tower. Tell Kate O'Malley I haven't forgotten the past."

Hearing her name was so unexpected that the detachment so necessary when working a crisis broke to show her own disbelief, and for a brief instance, fear. Who knew she was here? "I have no idea. Play it again."

She closed her eyes and listened, expecting to recognize a voice. It was badly distorted, the words understandable but altered; she could not make out any distinctive features. Probably a digital cellular phone, it didn't have static like an analog line as much as it cut in and out. The cadence of speech, the word choices, both were very deliberate. She looked over at Elliot. "Is this the same caller?"

"Yes."

"Bob, the threat sounds very real. I don't know what the reference to me implies." She had to bury the fear; there wasn't time for it. Her control slipped back in place so that only logic ruled. They would figure out the reference later; right now there were more critical decisions to make and not much time to make them. "How many planes are talking to the tower?"

He was already looking at a monitor. "There are eight departing flights still in our airspace. Fourteen incoming flights are under our control. Another sixteen flights are on taxiways queued up to depart."

"The twenty-two planes in the air. How do we get them down?"

"We can't. Not in fifteen minutes. But we can come close." Bob looked at the tower chief, Greg Nace. "Let's get everything in class *B* airspace on the ground. Take an outgoing flight over one inbound. Prioritize for souls on board."

"Agreed." The tower chief looked at the controllers, every one of them tense and awaiting directions. "Alert the pilots in the air of the threat. Tell them to set down fast. We're going to have to ignore FAA regulations for distance to get this many planes down in time. Let regional control know we will not be accepting any more aircraft into the pattern."

Rapid, controlled chatter began around the room. The men and women talking to the pilots began orchestrating a controlled recovery of planes.

Bob turned to his second in command. "Elliot, how many open gates do we have?"

"Eighteen."

"Find us some more to use. Tell maintenance to back empty planes away from gates. Having a plane full of passengers explode on the ground isn't part of the plan. Get security to the gates to keep people calm."

The tower chief interrupted. "Bob, we've got three outbound flights reporting fuel loads above what is safe for an immediate abort. We'll have no choice but to put them to the back of the queue."

Kate picked up binoculars and watched a Boeing 747 touch down on the runway, white puffs of smoke appearing as the plane's tires touched pavement. It had been a long time since she had felt this helpless.

"Tell Kate O'Malley I haven't forgotten the past."

What did that mean? The bomber knew her? How? And why a plane?

She watched the clock, counted the planes touching down, and listened to the air traffic controllers.

11:12 A.M.

There were still nine flights in the air.

11:13.

Eight flights.

11:14.

Six flights.

She heard a controller give MetroAir Flight 714 clearance to land on runway 32*L*.

11:15.

NINE

MetroAir Flight 714 exploded in midair.

The shock wave from the blast reverberated off the tower windows. It hit the building so hard that tables not secured moved a few inches, lights swayed, mugs rattled, and several binders fell from a nearby shelf. Kate instinctively leaned into the counter beside her to keep steady.

She couldn't tear the binoculars away from the horrific sight. Huge sections of the fuselage slammed down onto the runway and were engulfed in burning jet fuel. The rest of the plane came down west of runway *32L*.

A second fireball erupted on the ground as jet fuel erupted. Cargo City—FedEx, UPS, DHL. One of the major shipping company's planes or facilities had just been hit.

Around her was shocked silence.

Bob was the first to move. His hand squeezed the tower chief's shoulder. "Divert the five flights in the air to Midway. Close the airport; helicopter transports are going to own the airspace for the immediate future."

Orders started to flow to the staff around him. "Elliot, get on the hotline. We need every ambulance, every medical helicopter they can find. Jim, send the pager codes, call everyone in. Get the command center open." He looked back at the size of the debris field already apparent. "Frank, get me the Air National Guard CO on the phone. I need his people, and I need him to enforce the closed airspace immediately."

Kate listened to the orders as she watched battalions of fire engines and rescue personnel speed onto the runway to enter a fight that appeared hopelessly one-sided. No one was walking away from the wreckage. With the binoculars she should have seen someone by now. No one was walking away.

"I want someone sitting on this phone in case he decides to remark on his handiwork. There may be a second bomb; I want nothing overlooked in the search. We need all the agencies—FBI, NTSB, ATF, and FAA."

Around the room, people were picking up the phones. "Elliot, pull together the first update meeting at 1 P.M. I'll be with the fire chief. Kate, stay with me."

She nodded, needing to be pitched into the battle for survivors. It was too late, but they had to try. There had to be hope.

In the past hour and a half, Kate had completely shut off her emotions. She was too numb to feel anything anymore. The faces around her were grim. Helicopters waited on the taxiway to take survivors to the hospitals, but there were no survivors.

It had become a massive crime scene.

This section of the fuselage had not burned, but smoke had roiled through it. The heat lingered in the metal, the seats. The plane structure had been destroyed. She crawled past mangled seats, moving aside suitcases, books, briefcases, magazines, letters. Shoes. Shopping bags. Dolls. She tried not to get caught on insulation, wires, or jagged metal.

Her hands were blistered, scraped from previous work in this section of the fuselage as she helped retrieve victims. She had discarded the borrowed fire turnout coat once the threat of the fire had been suppressed.

They had located the flight attendant who had been at the airplane door. MetroAir allowed last minute walk-ons. The passenger and electronic tickets were in the flight attendant's vest pocket. While there were copies at the terminal, knowing who had stepped through the plane door was the most important check they had; records at the terminal could potentially get tampered with. It was difficult to deal with the fact paper was her priority, a passenger list more important than the passengers were.

One of the two firemen reached toward her as soon as she was within reach. It was a tight squeeze with three of them in the collapsed galley area. "Show me."

The fireman lifted the wall.

Kate knelt down and wedged herself into the space. The name tag confirmed her identity. Cynthia Blake. Kate found it painfully hard to handle the fact the flight attendant looked like she was asleep.

Kate gently retrieved the passenger documents. She wanted to apologize to this lady, her family, her friends, all the people her death would touch. It was guilt she didn't know how to process. Because she had seen the explosion, had been unable to prevent it. Because her name had been mentioned in the threat. Somehow, in a way she did not understand, she was involved in this tragedy. The bomber probably felt no guilt. She did.

Kate turned to one of the firemen. "Have the FBI record her location, and you can move her."

She worked her way back outside.

The intensity outside was worse than that inside the fuselage. All the images blurred together. There were so many victims.

Death wasn't new.

Violent death wasn't new.

This many deaths in an instant of time was.

She did not look at the tickets she carried, did not read the names. She needed the distance for another moment.

The sick feeling in the pit of her stomach increased as she walked past the wreckage. She had been trained to put together a life from little pieces of information. The debris around her reflected so many lives. She skirted around rescue personnel working in a burned section of the fuselage where victims were just now being removed.

She had never realized how massive an Illiad 9000 wide-body plane was. The fuselage wreckage, not to mention the wings, dwarfed the vehicles nearby. Over two hundred people had been aboard this flight. None had walked away.

The smell of jet fuel would take days to clear. Most of it had burned, scorching the runway. The firefight had moved from the plane wreckage to the shipping facility where the battle still raged. Thick black smoke billowed into the air. Kate dreaded to hear news of casualities there.

Stephen was here somewhere, and Jack; she had seen both of them from a distance working with others from their units. How were they handling the disaster? Burn victims were horrible, especially for the men and women who daily risked their lives to prevent such deaths. The fuselage pieces were now smoldering remains, covered in foam and water. If only the plane had been on the ground, been on a taxiway, some might have survived.

How was Lisa going to cope with this? As one of the central staff at the state crime lab, a forensic pathologist, she would be one of those called in specifically to help identify the dead, to reconstruct what had happened. Weeks of dealing with this tragedy would haunt her. Kate felt sick just at the thought.

Who had done this?

Why?

She looked to the south. The land had been an open field of wildflowers this morning, the best of summer's beauty. Now the almost half-mile-square area looked like the center of a war zone, the ground marked by twisted metal, personal belongings, and shrouded white sheets covering the dead. National Guard personnel were already beginning the task of turning the field into a large grid.

The bright blue sky, the sunshine, felt like an insult.

Overhead, police and National Guard helicopters enforced the closed airspace, keeping the news media from flying directly overhead. Local stations, national affiliates would have all rushed news crews to the scene. Kate suspected that with the explosion at 11:15 A.M., the news media had been live on the air by 11:18. The satellite dishes were probably already lined up along the 294 Tollway overpass, broadcasting live pictures as they looked down on the crash site.

She could only imagine what it was like inside O'Hare's terminals. A bomb created instant panic. Not just for the families of the victims, desperate for information, but for everyone else who felt the relief and the guilt that they escaped.

She headed to the forward command center rapidly put together on the runway near the crash. It had become the nerve center for ground operations, manned by the fire chief and his support crew, Chicago police, FBI, National Transportation Safety Board, and emergency medical personnel. Radio traffic was heavy as assistants coordinated men from different districts. She handed the documents to the courier waiting for them and found a place out of the way to wait for Bob. He was talking to the National Guard commanding officer about site security.

There were hundreds of O'Hare employees standing together in clusters along the nearest taxiway, looking out at the wreckage, watching events unfold. They were spectators, but quiet ones, their faces still showing the shocked disbelief at what they were witnessing. Kate understood that shock. She ineffectively wiped at the grime on her hands and looked at jeans now ruined and wished she could close her eyes and make this nightmare go away.

She had to watch this tragedy as the others did, but at least she could do something about it. Whoever had set this bomb would pay. Somewhere in that wreckage before her, on the runway, across the field, was the evidence that would convict him. The victims would at least get justice. Someone had made a mistake when they had made this personal with her.

"Someone's targeting her!" Dave stared at the small tape recorder as he listened to the bomb threat again and felt his heart squeeze. The fear was invading. He couldn't let it overwhelm him. Black roses were one thing; this—how many different ways was Kate going to get ripped into? She couldn't go home without having her job invade her life. This threat couldn't even have been graded; it was so malicious. How did he keep her safe when he couldn't even figure out what to protect her from? Her past was a big, black, ugly hole, and it seemed to be leaping at her from every direction.

He looked over at his boss. "Where is she?" The command center outside this small conference room was packed with people, but he had not seen Kate.

"Out at the crash site. She was in the tower with Bob Roberts when this call came in."

"Oh, that's just great. She's out in the open." He pushed away from the table. "Whoever this guy is, he's out for her blood."

"Dave, we don't know. But we need to find out. You know her better than anyone else in the regional office. We need security on her, immediately. Keep her alive long enough for us to figure this out."

Dave glanced around the empty conference room. "I can't let her know I'm formally protecting her."

"Her boss knows, but she's not the type to handle a shadow very well. Keep it low-key."

That was going to make his job difficult if not impossible. So much for throwing her in a safe house far from here. He sighed. She'd never accept that anyway. "I know what you mean." He thought for a moment. "There's still a reason someone targeted a plane."

"Yes. Find out why."

He nodded and picked up his jacket. "I'll go find Kate."

"Dave—"

He turned in the doorway.

"Be careful."

"Count on it," he replied grimly. "Listen—can you track down one of her brothers? He's a U.S. Marshal, Marcus O'Malley. He flew back to Washington early yesterday morning."

"I'll find him for you."

"Thanks."

Dave was not going to let anyone harm her. She was becoming too important to him. Whether she liked it or not, she now had a full-time shadow. At least now he wouldn't have to do it on his own time. He pulled on the FBI blue jacket. He had a feeling before this was over Kate was going to give him gray hair.

A helicopter lifted off from the runway tarmac, causing Kate to shade her eyes. It flew out slowly over the crash scene. Kate had seen several NTSB officials climb aboard; they must be getting a look at the debris field.

"Kate."

She turned, surprised. Dave was here. He wore a lightweight blue jacket even on this hot day, one of dozens around the area wearing the FBI colors. There were others wearing jackets from the FAA, NTSB, Red Cross, each with their own color; the visual affiliation allowing people to find each other rapidly in the crowd of investigators tasked with different assignments.

"I've been looking for you." He looked like a fighter sizing up his opponent; that was her first impression, and she went with it, instinctively shifting her weight back. She looked at him warily, not able to read what he was thinking. His hands settled firmly on her shoulders. "Are you okay?"

The depth of the emotion in his voice made her realize she had made a mistake. He wasn't hiding what he was thinking; he was trying to keep her from seeing how intense it was. She wasn't accustomed to having someone in the middle of a crisis focus on her instead of the victims. It was personal concern for her driving that emotion in him. Unexpected tears pooled in her eyes but were blinked away. Next to having an O'Malley to lean on, Dave would do. "You heard about the call."

"I did." His face was grim.

All the emotion buried from that horrifying moment when she heard her name came roiling back. To feel afraid was the worst of all emotions. It was the helpless fear a victim felt, and Kate would never let herself be a victim again. "I don't know why he used my name." She heard the slight quiver in her voice and pulled in a harsh breath to fight for control.

"We're going to find out why." His words were gentle, a promise. He brushed at her bangs. "You've been out here since it happened, crawling through the wreckage?"

She sighed, then nodded. "The debris field, some of the fuselage sections that didn't burn. We hoped for survivors, but there were none. Even in the sections I was in, the impact, the smoke was too great." She rubbed her arms. "It wasn't the fire crews' fault, they were here before the wreckage stopped tumbling."

He shook her slightly. "It wasn't your fault, either. I don't know what this guy is playing at by mentioning your name, but you are not responsible for this."

She bit her lip and nodded because he was so insistent. She knew she was not to blame but realized she was involved. "I am connected in some way I don't understand. I've been trying to remember past cases, who might have the skills to do this, but the few men I think could do this are still in jail."

"We'll find the connection."

Yes, he would feel that same certainty she did. No one could look at these victims and not proceed until the case was solved. And she already had a taste of what he was like doing his job; she felt sorry for the bomber they were after. It was difficult though, to know she would be in the middle of the investigation for the duration, that she herself would be under scrutiny by people who had never met her before this event. Her life was private and intentionally protected; to have others prying into that past would bring up old wounds she wished would stay buried. "Have you actually heard the tape, what it sounded like?"

"Yes."

"It was too distorted; I couldn't recognize the voice. If it was someone from a past case, chances are I spent hours talking to him. I should be able to recognize the voice." The call was the only known lead they had at the moment, and it galled her that she could do nothing with it.

"The tape is being sent to the forensic lab. I'm sure they will be able to clean it up." He had the luxury of distance from this, could speak calmly and objectively, a role that was normally hers. She felt an irrational irritation at that fact.

"You shouldn't be out here in the open. Come on, let's get you inside."

She gave him a blank stare. She was too tired to understand his words.

"You're a target, Kate," he said quietly. "Until we understand why, it's not a good idea to be out here."

Her jaw tightened, but she didn't protest when he turned her toward one of the O'Hare security cars. There was little more she could do here anyway, and it was about time for the first update meeting. She was about to be smothered with a blanket of protection if Dave had his way, but she didn't have the energy to fight him on it. She slid into the car without further protest.

He paused the car to give emergency vehicles the right of way. "Walk me through your itinerary for today, everything that happened."

The timeline. Yes, it was going to be critical. She took a deep breath and felt the relief of being back in a role she knew how to deal with. She thought about it carefully. "I got to the office at 6:55 A.M. I know because the news at the top of the hour was starting when I went for coffee. Franklin was fixing himself a bagel with cream cheese, and he happened to mention the O'Hare security review was on his schedule for today. I didn't want to spend the day in the office, so I cleared it with my boss and traded with Franklin. Dave, my name went on no schedule. Maybe four to six people inside the office might have known I was coming. I left the office, met Bob Roberts at the United ticket counter here at 9:40 A.M."

"Did you call Bob before you left the office to arrange the time and location? Did someone at his office have advance warning?"

"No. I called from the car when I was a few minutes out. It would have been about 9:20–9:25." She closed her eyes, thinking back. "We got word of the first phone call at 10:48 A.M. It's scrawled on the top of an envelope I was using to make notes. One hour of time in which someone could have seen I was here at the airport and made the decision to mention me. No. It makes more sense that using my name was planned long before today. I don't think my being at the airport had anything to do with it."

"A past case? Someone who wanted you dragged in?"

"I've had several cases with men this vicious, but the problem is finding one who isn't in jail at the moment who might have the knowledge to do it. And why a plane? If someone wanted to come after me, there are much more straightforward ways to do it." She appreciated his grim expression, the fact he didn't like that reality, but it was one she had long ago accepted she would live with. She offered him the other option she had considered. "This may simply be a red herring because my name has been in the news lately."

It was obvious Dave had not thought about that. "That's possible. In fact, it would be a very good tactic. It would divert resources in the early days of the investigation, buy himself time to cover his tracks while we are busy elsewhere. It's going to take time to get through your past cases." He looked at her and frowned. "If you were named as a red herring, I wish he had used my name instead."

Kate wanted to smile at the irritation in his voice. He didn't like the fact she was in the middle of this. Neither did she. The prospect of spending days reviewing hundreds of cases was not a pleasant one.

His hands tightened on the steering wheel. "There's another problem that will have to be dealt with because of this. You had better plan to disappear before your name hits the media. They are going to chew up any tidbit of information they can find, and the tape contents will eventually leak. The information is too explosive and was heard by too many people."

"I'm already thinking about it." She could stay with anyone in the family, and she probably would to avoid the media pressure. It would be nationwide media, not just local. The last thing she needed was Floyd Tucker shadowing her every step. "Back to the timeline. The second call came in at precisely 11:00 A.M. He knew the bomb would go off at 11:15. What does that tell us? It was a device with a timer?"

"Probably. It's doubtful the device could have been remotely detonated over any great distance. The most logical scenario would be a bomb with a timer in the luggage area of the plane."

"So would the calls have been from nearby?"

"It depends on his rationale for going after this particular plane. If he wanted to see the commotion, maybe."

She absently worried at a blister on her hand that had broken while she tried to build a profile in her mind. "The words of the call were very precise, carefully chosen. 'The bomb goes off at 11:15. The plane is talking to the tower.' That's precise, specific. He likes control. That reference to the plane talking to the tower—you're the pilot; could that be literal?"

"You can listen to the radio traffic with the right equipment. But radio traffic is very concise. A normal exchange with the tower is a dozen words. It's not what you would consider a dialogue. If that statement was itself not another red herring, it meant he was referring to having heard an exchange with the plane."

"Is it possible the reference to me *and* the reference to the tower were both extraneous?" Kate considered that, then realized immediately how looking at it that way cut out the complexity. "The simple truth—he set a bomb to go off at eleven-fifteen. The plane's location was irrelevant. If it had been stuck at the terminal gate if the flight was running late, the plane would have blown up there."

"Exactly. As red herrings, those two statements are brilliant. By adding the reference to the tower, he creates churn in the initial moments before the bomb goes off. By mentioning your name, he complicates the initial investigation."

"And at the other extreme, he meant both of them."

"Yes. To speculate they are red herrings, even to believe it is likely, won't change the reality. They have to be ruled out."

Her past. What would Dave think when he learned what that really meant? She backed away from the thought, not willing to borrow trouble. *"Tell Kate O'Malley I haven't forgotten the past"* told her at least one comforting thing. Her name had not always been Kate O'Malley. She wouldn't be dealing with ancient past. "I'm glad you're here." The words were stark, but they were meant from the heart.

Dave's hand covered hers. "So am I."

The quiet interlude lasted only a moment, for they had reached the administration building.

The command center swarmed with people. Leaving Dave talking with one of the other FBI investigators, she went to wash up, doing what she could with soap, hot water, and a towel. The soap stung her hands. She considered the pain a useful thing, confirming to herself that she was getting past the shock.

A table had been set up with cold drinks, and she headed there. The ice water helped ease the burning in her throat from the smoke she had inhaled. She looked around the room, assessing the mood here. It was not unlike the mood among those working out on the runway. Intense, focused on tasks, faces grim.

Bob Roberts had arrived back from the crash site. He looked at her and gestured to the east conference room. She nodded and headed that direction. People were assembling for the first update meeting.

Dave joined her and held out a chair for her at the large oval table. Out of habit, she reached for a pad of paper and a pen, jotting down the date and time. She recognized about a third of the people at the table.

Bob called the meeting to order. "This is the T+2 hour update. Elliot, what's the time frame for the folks out of Washington?"

Kate idly turned the pen in her hand while she listened to the discussion.

"The full NTSB team will be on site by 3 P.M. FAA thirty minutes after that. ATF and FBI will be bringing in people throughout the next twenty-four hours."

"Have there been any further calls?"

"No. Not to us or the media."

"Where are we with the second bomb sweeps?"

"The terminals have been checked, airplanes and luggage/cargo are going to take at least another three hours to complete. Nothing so far."

Bob looked at the airline representative. "Passenger list?"

The young man looked pale and nervous. "Still temporary. At least another couple hours to confirm."

Kate thought that was an optimistic estimate. Someone who was single, older, with no immediate family, would create an identification problem—it could take days to confirm they were actually on the plane. Beat cops loved getting sent out on the 'we think they're dead' assignments. And there was another complication, a bigger one: *MetroAir allows walk-ons.* Kate wrote it on the notepad in front of her and slanted it to Dave.

He wrote below her note—*How many on this flight?*

Gate attendant thinks a dozen. There would be less paperwork available, less information for those passengers. Walk-ons tended to be travelers who had missed their connecting flight with another airline. They were not expected to be on the flight, and so it would take time for people to realize a loved one might have been aboard.

Bob turned to the Red Cross representative. "Who do we have working information with the victims' families?"

"Jenson with the FAA. He's coordinating the Red Cross, the airline, and the media. The eight hundred number for families has been given out to the media."

"Are there enough qualified people on the phones?"

"We've three-tiered it. Information, counselors, and travel support. We've established half-hour status updates for the families and assigned them a primary contact person. We have arranged media-free space in the terminal and the airport hotel for the families."

"Tell Jenson to arrange for a couple floors at the Chesterfield hotel as well. Let's give family members an option of where to stay. Make sure flight arrangements are into Midway or Milwaukee. We don't need relatives flying over the crash scene once this airport reopens."

Bob looked over at Elliot. "Recovery and identification?"

"A temporary morgue has been set up in hangar fourteen. We've got hangar fifteen being cleared as a contingency if they need more room."

"Has Jenson talked to the families about what will help with identification? Jewelry, clothing, dental charts, X rays?"

"He's got Red Cross trauma counselors working with them."

Bob scanned his notes, then looked back at the airline representative. "Tell me about the flight."

"MetroAir Flight 714, departing O'Hare at 10:55 A.M. bound for New York. An Illiad 9000 Series A wide-body, the first crash for this type of aircraft. It was a connecting flight that originated in L.A."

New plane? Dave scrawled.

Kate tried to remember back to Bob's remarks during past security reviews. He commented on new planes, pointing them out like a proud papa. *Put in service last year?*

Possible mechanic failure, not a bomb?

Doubtful. The explosion ripped the plane apart.

"Any threats to the airline recently?" Bob asked.

"No."

"Labor disputes, problems with the carrier management?"

"Nothing known."

The door opened, and Kate's boss entered the room and took a seat against the far wall. She was glad to see him.

"Who worked the flight?"

Elliot scanned his notes, then answered. "The FBI is interviewing the maintenance crew and terminal reps now. We're working on identifying the baggage handlers and the ticket counter personnel."

"What about the previous flight crew?"

"On their way back from St. Louis."

"How are we doing on the phone call?"

"There is a team on it. The tape is with the police forensic lab now. Phone company technicians are pulling the switch logs to try and locate a billing record."

Dave touched her arm, drawing her attention back to the pad of paper. *"Tell Kate I haven't forgotten the past." Exact words?*

Kate O'Malley. It was significant because her legal name had not changed until she was nineteen.

Bob looked at Elliot. "Security camera tapes?"

"All pulled and under seal. The last two weeks of tapes are being pulled as we speak."

"Card key access logs?"

"Being printed now. We've got the handwritten security guard logs together."

"For now, all information goes into the evidence room. I want two guards on the door and only people on the list allowed access," Bob ordered. "We need to know who was on that plane, where the bomb was located, what it was made of, and how it got onto the plane. Let's meet again at 4 P.M."

Simple questions, none of them easy to answer. Chairs pushed back from the table, and the noise level rose. Kate maneuvered through the crowd to join her boss. "You heard the tape?"

"Yes. For whatever reason, he wanted you dragged in. He accomplished it. I've got staff pulling cases you've worked. We need a lead that will help us sort through them. That's now your primary focus. Spend time going through the passenger list. Find us something we can work with, Kate."

She nodded, taking a deep breath, dreading that look into the details of two hundred lives. "Once I get through the passenger list, I'll start looking on past cases. Can you spare Debbie? Having transcribed my tapes and filed cases for the last five years, she knows how they are going to be indexed on-line."

"I'll get her cut free for as long as you need her. Anything you need, ask."

"Thanks, Jim."

"Have a cop pick up whatever you need from your apartment. The media storm has already begun, and you'll eventually be at the center of it when that phone call becomes known. I don't want you back there until I know what we are dealing with."

It was a request, but it could be made an order. She nodded rather than protest. She would be working here through the night, so it made little immediate difference. "I'll do that."

Jim nodded and moved to join Bob.

Kate rubbed her arms, momentarily unsure who in this room to talk to first. Dave touched her hand. "Stick with me. I'll be working the passenger list with you. Even if the bomber knows you, there is still a reason he chose this plane. Someone on board was likely a target. That's my immediate job, so we'll make better progress working together."

She was grateful and not sure how to say that. "Where do you want to set up?"

"Elliot has a conference room upstairs for us. Susan and Ben from my office are already working on the list."

As soon as they reached the hallway, they saw the line by the elevator. Dave gestured to the left. "Come on, let's take the stairs."

They had to wander the halls for a few minutes to find where Susan and Ben had set up shop. The two of them had appropriated a conference room off an unused office. Kate carefully stepped over the power cords and cables strung across the floor to the two computer terminals and printer that had been brought in. The room looked like one she was accustomed to seeing at the precinct. The table was strewn with printouts and handwritten pages of notes. The white board had accumulated a list of names written in different colors. On the right side of the white board was a list of questions they had considered when looking at the names. Kate already felt at home.

Dave pulled out two chairs and introduced her to Susan and Ben. Kate saw their curiosity and wondered if it was from the bank incident last week or if they had heard about the specifics of the phone call. Either way, she had a reputation before she arrived. Dave settled back in his chair. "Where are we?"

"The lists are still tentative." Susan slid across two copies. "We're patched in with the airline group working on the problem, getting real-time updates."

Kate looked at the data, sixteen pages of it. Her face grim, she read the names, the ages. So many families. "Do we have a seating layout for the plane?"

Ben cleared the center of the table to spread out the blown-up diagram. It was the chart the airline used when booking tickets. "Whether someone was in their assigned seat is an open question, but this will correlate to the ticket information listed on the printouts."

"Three sections—first class, business, and coach?"

"Yes."

Kate nodded, checking the seating chart occasionally as she reviewed names. The chance she would find a name she recognized was slim, but it was the obvious place to start. She turned page after page without success.

Dave set down his list and looked at the white board. "You've already researched some interesting questions. Let's start at the top. How many people had tickets, but did not show?"

Susan scanned her notes. "Preliminary, four. We've cleared one. Tim Verrio, a reporter for a New York paper, who took a later flight. He had tickets issued the same day for two carriers. The others, a Glen and Marla Pearse, Chicago address, no information, and a Bobby York, Virginia address, no information."

"Who is working that problem?"

"Travis."

Kate started to write her list on the pad of paper, then realized to bring the names up for discussion it would be better to have the list on the board. "May I?" Susan handed her the marker and eraser. Kate took them to the board along with the printout. "What about the variation—how many people checked baggage but did not board?"

"The checked tags appear to match, but we've got two problems. This was a connecting flight, and most of the luggage is reported to be damaged and or burned; it is going to take time to physically confirm bags and see if an extra one made the trip."

Kate thought about that debris field, how much of the aircraft had burned, and doubted they would ever be able to totally account for the baggage.

"Anyone cancel reservations for the flight?" Dave offered.

"Another open question. The airline is still working the list." Ben searched through the faxes. "Susan, did we get an answer on who bought their tickets for cash?"

"It just came in. There were two. Assuming these are real names, a Mark Wallace, Colorado address, no information; and a Lisa Shelby, Milwaukee address, no information. Travis has the names."

"We need to find out if they were actually on the flight," Dave noted, adding them to his work list.

Kate double-checked the list she had. "Has the airline confirmed how many walk-ons there were?"

Susan checked the terminal screen. "Tentatively, eleven. We're getting updates on those as they confirm the electronic tickets and the matching credit card charges."

Dave leaned back in his chair. "Does anyone on this flight look like a target? Maybe someone in law enforcement? A judge, mayor, city councilman, state representative? What about someone with a criminal record?"

"I'm about a quarter of the way through the list, and I've found a couple possibilities." Ben scrolled back through the names on his terminal screen. He tapped the screen with the cap of his pen. "The most interesting is a retired federal judge. We've also got a VP for an oil company."

"Can we get bio information on them?"

"We should be getting a fax on the oil company VP soon. But I'm having problems getting anything on the retired federal judge. His name is flagging a U.S. Marshal code."

Dave leaned forward in his chair. "Really?"

"What does that mean?" Kate asked as she saw Dave lock in on the news.

"It means his security was unusually high. They are not releasing any data through normal channels." He looked at Ben. "Was he traveling with someone?"

"No."

"Raise the urgency with Washington; we need to know why he had that kind of security."

The terminal Susan was using beeped. She read the latest update. "We've got another confirmation. A late walk-on. Nathan Young. No checked baggage."

Kate looked at Dave.

"Say that again," Dave asked quietly.

"Nathan Young."

Kate closed her eyes. The world had just become a much smaller place. She looked back at Dave and felt as if she had fallen down a spiraling hole. "So much for our Wednesday meeting with him."

TEN

"If we are looking for a connection between me and a passenger, that is an immediate one," Kate commented, "but who would want to kill a bank owner?"

"Good question." Dave looked at her, puzzled. "The only thing I found was an indication he was raising cash. Did anything else show in your search?"

Kate shook her head, but she was running through all kinds of possible connections in her mind. "Henry Lott?"

"He used dynamite, which is not typical for an airline bombing; he didn't expect to be alive past Tuesday, and now he's in jail—but it's a very interesting question." Dave turned to Ben. "We need a list of people who have seen him since he was arrested Tuesday."

Ben reached for the phone. "I'll have it faxed here."

"Dave," Susan flipped to the back of the passenger list, "we've got another Young on the flight. A Mr. Ashcroft Young."

Kate rapidly found the page. "Related?"

"Hold on."

Susan worked rapidly, then nodded. "Brothers."

"Nathan was a walk-on?" Kate leaned across the table to view the seating diagram again. "Where were they seated?"

"Nathan is in the last row of first class, and Ashcroft—coach, seat 22*E.*"

"They weren't traveling together?" Kate looked at Susan. "When and how did Ashcroft purchase his ticket?"

"May 24, credit card."

"So he was planning to fly coach." Kate glanced over at Dave. "Not as wealthy as his brother?"

"From the flowers Nathan sent, I doubt he would volunteer to upgrade his brother's seat. It would be useful to know why they were both heading to New York. Ben, does anything show on Ashcroft Young?"

"Searching. Whoa! Ten years in jail for cocaine distribution. Released eleven months ago."

"Our bank president was related to a drug dealer?" Kate tried to connect the implications of that but couldn't; it was too incredible to believe. "You're sure?"

Susan was already double-checking. "Yes. They're brothers. What an interesting family. I wonder if they were even speaking to each other."

"Somehow I doubt it." Dave replied, running his hand through his hair.

"What a mess. We need full profiles on these two. Susan, send the information to Karen and ask her to put a rush on it. A bank president and a drug dealer certainly raise interesting questions of money laundering. Nothing appeared on the surface with the banks Nathan owned, but it's time to check that out in detail."

Kate looked at the two names, now written on the white board, and shook her head. "This would be a perfect lead if they weren't both dead."

Dave chuckled at the irony. "We solved the case. *He's dead.*"

Kate set down the marker. "Exactly."

"Run with it a minute. Suppose Ashcroft got out of jail and began pressuring Nathan to look the other way while he laundered money. Nathan resisted, and that put Ashcroft in a squeeze with his employers. Drug runners don't like failure. What about someone setting a bomb to kill them both?"

Kate wished she could find a scenario that made that work but finally had to shake her head. "No matter how you look at it, Nathan was a last-minute walk-on. Until the last moment, it wasn't clear he would be taking this particular flight. You don't pull off something this complex without a lot of planning."

"You're right. But they get my early votes." The fax began to hum. Dave reached back for the page. "The oil company VP bio. Interesting. He was responsible for the company's environmental programs, among other things."

Kate smiled. "Would it be against their ethics for an environmentalist to blow up a plane?"

"I guess we're going to find out. Let's add him to the list as well."

Kate picked up the red marker. "That gives us four passengers on the possible list. A retired federal judge, an oil company VP, our Nathan Young, and his brother Ashcroft Young. One of them with an obvious tie to me. What other surprises are buried in this passenger list?"

She needed to call her family. Kate leaned against the wall of the conference room and momentarily tuned out the discussion going on. How was Jennifer doing? It was coming up on the 4 P.M. meeting, and this was the first time Jennifer had crossed her mind, a fact that bothered her. She had no illusions that this disaster could be kept from her sister. By now everyone in the nation had probably heard a plane had blown up. But there was no reason to tell her about the phone call, to add that kind of stress. The others in the family, however, did need to know.

"Kate."

She blinked and looked over at Dave.

"Ready to head downstairs to the update meeting?"

She pushed away from the wall. "Yes."

They had made good progress on the names, and though they were far from done, they had carefully selected a list of seventeen people to check out in more detail. Nathan was the only apparent passenger linked to her, but with the fax from the city jail confirming Henry Lott had spoken only to his lawyer, the obvious connection to last Thursday's incident dwindled.

The east conference room was crowded with the influx of people from Washington. Kate settled into a chair next to Dave at the back of the room as Bob called the meeting to order. Others were running the investigation now, but Bob remained the information coordinator. "This is the T+5 hour update. Where are we on the passenger list?"

The airline representative was better prepared to be the focus of attention now. "It has been 90 percent confirmed; working copies are in front of you. Two hundred and fourteen, nine of them crew."

"Released to the media, when?"

"Tomorrow noon, assuming full confirmation and the notification of the victims' families."

Who is being notified of Nathan and Ashcroft Young's death?

Dave's written question made Kate realize they had missed an interesting avenue of speculation. *Good question. Nathan's wife, obviously. Who else?*

We need to find out.

"What's the status with the victim recovery?"

Elliot leaned back to confer with the pathologist behind him, then answered. "It should be complete by sunset."

"Are we set up to work through the night?"

"Flood lights are being brought in now."

"Good. Have the black boxes been found?"

The National Transportation Safety Board coordinator nodded. "Voice and data recorders from the cockpit have been recovered. Four of the fifteen airframe data boxes have been located."

"Do we have physical evidence to confirm a bomb or its location?"

"From the debris damage pulled into the engines we are focusing on the forward section of the aircraft. We may have the first structural evidence when the cranes are able to lift sections of the fuselage."

Does the luggage area go the length of the plane? Kate wrote down the question, not certain of the answer. Dave was the pilot.

Typically.

Could the bomb have been inside the passenger cabin, not in the luggage compartment?

Suicidal passenger? Dave wrote. *Doubtful. Maybe an airline employee would plant a bomb inside.*

"When will we be able to begin moving wreckage?" Bob asked.

"Another couple hours. Hangars sixteen and seventeen have been set aside for the physical reconstruction."

"Where are we with the phone call?"

"We've confirmed two facts. It was made from a cellular phone, and whoever placed the call clicked on and played a prerecorded tape. That's how they got the voice distortion."

Why? Kate scrawled. *Hide his voice, or allow someone else to place the call?*

He accomplished both. But we're now looking for two people.

Or one trying to confuse the issue. This was another indication he wanted control. Taping what he wanted to say meant he didn't want any unintended words or noise to be heard. He had likely taped the message several times until it was exactly what he wanted. That meant the reference to her had been deliberate, not a spur of the moment opportunity.

Her past cases. When this meeting broke up, that would be their next focus. Debbie and Graham were on their way with the files.

The meeting lasted over an hour, and when it was done, the next meeting was set for 9 P.M. Kate closed the pad in front of her, feeling the weight of everything that had happened. "Dave, give me a few minutes. I need to call the family. I'll meet you back at the conference room."

He hesitated beside her, looking like he wanted to object, then nodded. "Sure. I'll see you upstairs."

Kate watched him leave, relieved. If Dave thought he was hanging around while she made private phone calls, they were going to have an angry heart-to-heart. If this kept up, she was going to be tossing a few figurative elbows. She had to search to find a quiet place in the administration building. She found an empty employee break room and settled at the table with her cellular phone. She hoped Jennifer had been too busy to see a television but suspected that was unlikely. She dialed the hospital. "Jennifer, it's Kate."

"I've been following the news. Where are you?"

She didn't want to give her the full story. "At the airport. I was doing a security review here when the incident happened."

"You've been at the crash site."

"All day. Stephen and Jack are here somewhere. And Lisa."

"It must be horrible."

"There are no survivors. I just wanted to let you know I would be working here the next few days."

"Thanks. I know it must be intense there. Don't forget to get some sleep."

"I'll manage. How did the tests go today?"

"They have run several, but they haven't told me many results yet."

"You're comfortable? They are treating you okay?"

"They are making this as pleasant as they can. Is there anything I can do for you, Kate? Call others in the family? Anything?"

"Give Stephen and Jack a call later and make sure they're okay. Lisa if you can track her down. They have really seen a horrific sight. I'm okay for now; I'm working with Dave."

"I'll call them. I'm glad Dave is there for you."

"He's stuck like glue at the moment." Jennifer laughed, and Kate forced herself to relax. "Do you know what time the tests start tomorrow?"

"Eight o'clock."

"I'll call you first thing in the morning to see how your evening went."

"Thanks. Take care, Kate."

Kate hesitated before making the next call. Marcus. What did she want to tell him? Ask him? She paged him and did something she rarely did. She added her personal emergency code.

He returned the call within a minute. She could hear muffled noise and realized with some surprise that he was calling from an aircraft. "Kate? Are you at the airport?"

"Yes."

"I'm twenty minutes out of Midway."

"You heard about the tape?"

"I heard a plane went down with a federal judge I once protected. And I've got a page I've been trying to return to Dave. What tape?"

"Hold it. You protected retired judge Michael Succalta?"

"Three years ago. A drug money case out of New York."

Marcus O'Malley had a connection to this flight as well.

"Kate, what tape?"

"There were two bomb threats called in. The first one was five words. 'Get ready for a bomb.' The second came at 11 A.M.; we've got it on tape. Marcus, the exact words of that second phone call were: 'The bomb goes off at eleven-fifteen. The plane is talking to the tower. Tell Kate O'Malley I haven't forgotten the past.'"

"Your *name?* Why didn't you page me immediately?"

Kate took his anger for what it was, fear. "I was crawling inside the wreckage for the first couple hours. I've been in meetings and deep in researching the passenger list since then."

"I'll be there as soon as I can. Where are you working in O'Hare?"

"Second floor of the administration building. Bob Roberts in the command center can give you directions. Dave and I are working on the passenger list."

"Stay with him."

She was puzzled at the intensity in the order. "Why? What are you assuming?"

"The politics of the situation are going to be dicey. There are reasons Judge Succalta might have been the target, classified reasons. You don't want to be in the middle of this any more than you already are."

"Wonderful. That gives us two real problems. That bank incident last Thursday? The owner, Nathan Young, sent me flowers at the hospital; I had an appointment with him for Wednesday. He was on the plane, as was his brother."

"The gunman—Henry Lott?"

"He's only spoken with his lawyer since Tuesday." She had a full-blown headache setting in. She so desperately wanted to tell him about Jennifer and couldn't—she had given her word, but it was all coming down on her like a tidal wave. "Hurry, Marcus. I'm in over my head."

"As soon as I can."

She got no answer at Rachel's. Rather than leave a message, she decided to call back later. She wasn't up to another surprise.

Kate took her time walking back to the conference room, trying to sort out this latest wrinkle. Marcus had a tie to a retired judge on the flight. She had a tie to a bank president on the flight. *"Tell Kate O'Malley I haven't forgotten the past."* Could it mean a tie to the O'Malley family past? How many threads were they going to have to chase?

It felt like everything in her life was coming apart at the same time: Jennifer's cancer, her black rose suitor coming back, and now someone determined to drag her through a nightmare. She either needed half a day on a basketball court or somewhere private to cry.

She reached the conference room and took a deep breath before stepping inside. "Dave, we've got another wrinkle."

"Kate, I thought I taught you to duck." Marcus tossed another case file onto the stack of suspects, his annoyance clear.

She looked at the case number and winced. She hadn't told him about that one. At his insistence, they were going through her old cases while others dug into his link with the retired judge. As he had put it quietly when she protested—if someone was targeting her, he wanted to know it sooner versus later. It was classic Marcus, determined to protect her. Dave could give him lessons. She hadn't been able to move today without Dave shadowing her. She let Marcus get away with it because peace in the family often meant accepting a bit of smothering. Dave was a different matter entirely.

It was almost 10 P.M. They had sent Ben to attend the evening update meeting so they could stay here and work. Debbie and Graham from her office had joined them. Even with the extra help, it was slow going. The first pass through her cases had turned up almost sixty of interest. Twenty-three men with violent pasts released in the last two years. Three cases involving airlines. Thirty-two cases where explosives had been used. It felt like they were being dragged into a quagmire with no end in sight.

"Holding up?"

She looked up at Dave's quiet question, then nodded. He obviously didn't agree because he closed the file he was reading and dropped it back on the stack. "Let's take a short break and see about getting something to eat. Ben may have something from the update meeting that will help us focus this search."

When no one objected, Kate accepted the suggestion gratefully. She walked downstairs with Dave and Marcus. After arranging for dinner to take back, they found a corner of the break room where cold drinks had been set up. Leaning against the counter, Kate opened a soda, needing the sugar and caffeine. Just walking away from the problem was giving her a different perspective on it. "Why didn't he call back?"

Dave looked over. "What?"

"He blew up a plane, and he doesn't want to comment on it? Why not a call back to the tower, the media? Somebody?"

"It may not be a true terrorist incident," Dave replied.

Kate nodded. "That's my point. We have been assuming one person was the target. But if one person was the target, this was overkill."

Marcus frowned. "Enormous overkill."

"Is your retired judge worth this kind of collateral damage?"

Marcus thought about it. "He has some intense enemies, but I would have expected them to hire a hit man, not a bomber."

"Exactly. The same with our bank president. If someone wanted him out of the way, why not take a shot at him? The bomber has put himself at the top of every most wanted list."

"He's into looking for glory."

"Or power," Dave offered. "This is quite a statement of capability."

Kate crinkled the can in her hand and watched the metal flex. The leads were fragmenting in too many directions—the passengers on board, ties to Marcus, her past cases. Which was the right direction? Soon they were going to have to list all the leads, prioritize them, and hope they didn't go after the wrong one. Facts would be nice. She hated working with only speculation.

She changed the subject. "What's happening with your case in Washington, Marcus?"

"We're close to an arrest, maybe another ten days. It's formality now, waiting for sign-off by the deputy attorney general."

"You won't be needed back there?"

Marcus shook his head. "Quinn's got it covered."

"How is your partner? Will he be coming out for the Fourth of July festivities next month?"

Marcus shared a private smile. "Now why would he want to do that?"

Kate smiled back. They both knew Quinn had a habit of tracking where Lisa O'Malley was and what she was doing. "Someday Lisa will notice him."

"Maybe," Marcus replied, noncommittal. "I managed to catch her for a few minutes on my way in. She's going to be working in the temporary morgue tonight, then will be downtown tomorrow if you need her."

"How's she coping?"

"Worried about you."

Kate grimaced at that. She was now safely behind the distance of papers; Lisa was still in the middle of the tragedy. "Someone needs to worry about her."

"I paged Rachel and asked her to touch base later tonight."

"Thanks."

"Lisa will be okay. She's strong and angry that somebody did this. It will get her through the next few days."

"Sometimes I wish she wasn't so good at her job; then she wouldn't constantly get the tough assignments."

"I imagine she wishes the same about you at times."

Dinner arrived, and they took it upstairs for the group. The conference room had acquired more equipment during their absence. Kate set the food on the credenza. "What do we have, Ben?"

"Copies of the security camera video from the gate terminal. And from a variety of sources—driver's licenses, passports, family photos—pictures of the passengers."

"Facts. I love them."

Susan sorted through the pictures. "Here are the two brothers."

Kate studied the driver's license photographs. They didn't look alike, but then one man had been leading a very hard life, while the other had been living in comfort. "Do we have a photo of the retired judge or the oil executive?"

"Here."

Kate laid the four photos side by side on the table and studied them. Was one of these four pictures the intended victim?

"Let's see the video, Ben."

It was two hours of tape, and they paused it frequently, linking pictures to the video. The retired judge and Ashcroft Young arrived early and took seats in the waiting area. Both had brought newspapers to read. The plane arrived from L.A., several passengers got off with Chicago as their final stop. Over time, the area filled with passengers crowding around the check-in counter. There was no audio, but it was clear when the flight attendant began with preboarding announcements. People gathered together carry-on luggage, threw away coffee cups, and businessmen shut down laptops and closed briefcases. The area cleared in an orderly fashion as the plane began to load.

"There's our late walk-on, Nathan Young," Graham pointed him out. A tall man, wearing a suit and tie, carrying a briefcase. Two more passengers entered the walkway after him, and the door closed.

Ben stopped the tape. The room was quiet. So many people, gone forever.

"Did anyone see anything that looked suspicious?" Dave finally asked.

No one had.

Ben removed the tape. "I'll go through it again, Dave, pull stills of faces we haven't identified."

"Thanks, Ben. As you do it, pull the time each passenger arrived for the flight as well as what time they boarded the plane; the information may be useful later."

"No problem."

Dave glanced at his watch. "It's past midnight. Do we keep working, or do we resume tomorrow morning?"

Kate looked at the case files, the names on the white board, then sighed. "Time is not on our side. Let's work another hour."

"No." Marcus interjected quietly. "We'll start missing information. They are setting up cots in a couple of the business lounges. Let's get six hours of sleep and begin again at dawn."

She knew he was right, but it felt wrong to consider ending the day with so little progress. "Is there a safe place we can lock these files for the night?"

Debbie picked up the lid of the nearest box. "Elliot made arrangements for the boxes to be sealed and stored in the evidence room. Graham, you, or I will be the only ones authorized to retrieve them."

Kate nodded. They efficiently packed the boxes and moved them to the cart. Dave retrieved the overnight bag that had been brought from her apartment and his own gym bag. He turned out the conference room lights.

Marcus stopped her downstairs by the command center for a brief hug. "I'm going to see what has turned up on the judge. Let Dave walk you over to the terminal."

"Don't stay too long."

"I won't."

She squeezed his hand. "Good night, Marcus."

Dave held the door for her. The night had turned cool. She took a deep breath and tried to purge the memory of so many cases briefly relived.

"We can take one of the shuttles," Dave said.

"I would rather walk."

Dave nodded and reached for her hand. She was weary to her soul, and it helped at this moment knowing she was not alone. His hand was firm, strong, and she had to stop herself from leaning into him. It was depressing, looking over the airstrip and seeing the debris highlighted in the bright lights. Activity had not slacked off with the coming of night; the men in orange and white jumpsuits were busy moving around the wreckage. The airport would reopen tomorrow if work tonight went as planned.

"Are Stephen and Jack still out there?"

"I hope not, but it's possible. I've seen the disaster plans. The fire crews are the ones given the grim reality of removing the fire victims; they've got the extraction equipment. I saw both of them out there earlier today. It depends on which crews were released." Over two hundred deaths, most of them by fire or smoke; it would haunt her brothers. And Lisa having to deal with the victims' remains…She wanted to cry. There was no other way to describe the emotion as she looked at the burned-out wreckage. "So many children died."

"I know."

"There can't be mercy in this case. Whoever did this deserves to die."

"He'll face the courts and whatever the law decides."

"How can you sound so calm about it?" Her emotions had been stuck between shock and horror the entire day.

"There's a verse in the Bible where the Lord says, 'vengeance is mine.' I have to believe God can deal with this. It's too big an atrocity otherwise."

"Your God let this happen," she replied bitterly.

He squeezed her hand but didn't say anything.

She sighed. "I'm sorry. I didn't mean to attack you."

"It's okay, Kate. I understand the emotion," he said gently.

"Will the bomber be found?"

"You know he will be, Kate."

She needed to explain. "I'm scared that it really is someone who knows me."

"One of these cases you have worked?"

"I don't like the idea of someone who just killed 214 people focusing on me."

"I would say that is a healthy fear. Would it help to know you'd have a hard time getting more than a few steps away from either Marcus or me?"

She smiled, too tired at the moment to register more than a token protest. "Gee, I would have never guessed. I've got bodyguards, huh?"

He shrugged, but she saw the fire in his eyes and had a healthy respect for what that intensity meant. "Someone miscalculated. By going after you, they tweaked the tail of a tiger."

"Marcus?"

"Actually, I was referring to me." He shot her a wry grin. "Marcus is more like a silent black panther. He's even a little more protective of you than I am."

She stopped walking for a moment, let the words sink in. She squeezed his hand. "Thanks. I needed that image. Because of the circumstances, I'll let you tread on my independence for a few days. Please note the word *few.*" She started walking again. "We're assuming the past refers to my days as a cop. What if the reference is older than that?"

"You've got enemies that far back in time?"

Her father, but he was dead.

"Kate?"

She shrugged her shoulder. "I don't like making assumptions. 'I haven't forgotten the past' could be anything. What past is he remembering? It may not be significant to me while being very significant to him. Something he considers a slight might be enough to create a fixation."

"Someone who takes a grudge out of proportion would probably not have the skill to pull off this kind of blast," Dave reassured.

"He put a bomb on board the plane—why?"

"To kill someone."

Kate shook her head. "We're back to that problem of overkill. It doesn't make sense to kill 214 people in order to kill one. Buy a gun."

"To kill more than one person?"

"Possibly, there were families traveling together. But what's the motive? Insurance? Inheritance?"

"Money is always a big motivator," Dave pointed out.

"It's still a problem with overkill. And most cases that target relatives occur at the home or office. Comfortable ground for the killer as well as the victims."

"It would still be worth looking at who inherits what as a result of this crash."

Kate was quiet for a while, then speculated, "If Nathan Young and Ashcroft Young had not both been killed, I could see that kind of animosity in their family. Bad brother kills good brother for having all the money."

"Or good brother kills bad brother for ruining the family reputation."

Kate sighed. "What other reasons could lead to a bomb?"

"It's a strike against the airline. It could put the company out of business."

"Do you think there might be someone who hates the company that much?"

Dave reached around her to open the door. "I know there is a team of agents at the airline headquarters digging to find that out."

They cleared security and entered the terminal, found it was quiet and almost deserted, with police walking the corridor. One of the airport employees quietly gave them directions. The area was roped off from the media, and general passengers had been turned into a Red Cross support area. The business club they were directed to had become a sea of cots. Kate chose an open one and sank down, weary beyond words.

Dave pulled off her shoes. "I'll wake you at six o'clock."

"Unfortunately, yes. When this is over, I'm going to need a month of sleep." She buried her face in the pillow. "Thanks."

"For what?"

"Not telling me not to dream."

"Today qualifies for a bad dream or two. I'll be over there." He pointed to an open cot.

"Okay."

He hesitated. She saw something in his changing expression, as the work focus slipped away and she got a glimpse of his thoughts, which made her catch her breath.

"What?" She struggled to get her eyes open again. She saw him start to say something and suddenly felt afraid. *Dave, not now. I can barely think straight. If you say something nice, I'm going to cry.*

He brushed his hand across her hair as his face softened in a half smile. "It will keep. Good night, Kate."

Dave shifted the small pillow again. There was no way to get comfortable on one of these cots. Kate must have really been exhausted to fall asleep as soon as she was down. He stared at the ceiling, listening to the quiet sounds around him as people slipped in and out of the room, taking turns catching a few hours of sleep.

Hearing that tape had changed things. He couldn't deny the truth any longer. He cared about Kate. More than as a friend. More than as a woman in trouble. He wanted to protect her, keep her safe, to see her laugh and smile...to free her from the shadows he saw behind her eyes. Kate tried to hide the intense emotions trapped inside her, to show only logic and unshakable control, but the emotions showed through on occasion in breathtaking fashion. She so easily pulled the oxygen in a room toward her, having the confidence, the presence, to make a lasting impression on the people she met. Unfortunately, in her job, she had been making that impression on both the good and the bad guys.

He was finally beginning to understand her. Reading the cases she had worked had been informative, tense reading, but informative. Most of the files had partial negotiation transcripts attached. Kate's ability to deal calmly with violent men surprised him, even though he'd seen her do it. It was as though she became someone else in those moments of time. He had read the cases and seen a remarkable similarity. Nothing seemed to ruffle her. There was an extra terseness in her case notes when it was a domestic violence incident, but it was the only change he had been able to find.

Her unflinching ability not to step away made it possible for her to resolve situations no one else would go near. He saw in those case notes a cop whose compassion made her long for justice.

He closed his eyes, fighting the emotion stirring within him. If he had intentionally defined the traits he hoped to find in a woman—in the woman he would love—he could not have done better.

But she didn't believe. Might never believe after this.

Lord, why this? How do I explain to Kate a plane blowing up? I saw it in her eyes, the image of every victim. How does she ever believe when this is what You ask her to accept?

He'd thought often about her comments about God, trying to find the right words to deal with her questions. Kate had a *reasoned* disbelief, and he felt helpless to overcome it, especially now. Her own statements showed more careful thought than most people gave to God: *"Does it seem logical to pray for God to stop a crisis that, if He existed, He never should have let begin?*

"My job is to restore justice to an unjust situation. If your God existed, my job should not.

"I see too much evil. I don't want a God that lets that kind of destruction go on."

They were good questions.

It took a strong faith to face the violence and still believe the sovereign hand of God had allowed it for a reason—a reason the human mind might never comprehend—not as a capricious act of fate.

Lord, couldn't You have stopped this? So many families are grieving tonight. How am I to understand this? How am I to explain it to Kate? It's as though You're pushing her away rather than drawing her closer to You. It makes no sense. She may close the door to considering the gospel because of this, and I don't know what to do. This situation has become a turning point.

Words flowed through his mind then, but not what he'd expected.

"O the depth of the riches and wisdom and knowledge of God! How unsearchable are his judgments and how inscrutable his ways! 'For who has known the mind of the Lord, or who has been his counselor?'"

Being reminded God didn't often explain himself didn't help. Dave sighed and punched the pillow into a ball. He was drawn to Kate, and it was an uncomfortable reality. He did not want this kind of complication in his life. He simply wanted a chance to be her friend, present the gospel, and keep his heart intact in the process; instead, he had someone threatening her, his protective instincts humming, and his emotions entering a freefall.

Lord, if someone gets to her before she believes...

ELEVEN

"Sleep well?" Dave was leaning against a support post when she came back from washing her face. Kate looked at his alert face and sighed. She borrowed his cup of coffee.

"That bad?" He dug sugar packets out of his pocket and smiled. "Finish that and I'll get you its cousin."

"You better find its double cousin. I need a transfusion of caffeine."

"Bad dream?"

She shook her head. "My couch is more comfortable." The bad dreams had been there in full force last night. It had been the bomb in her hands exploding, becoming the plane exploding—then a scramble to pull out victims at the bank, pull victims out of the wreckage.

Dave turned her around and set about rubbing the kinks out of her neck. She leaned into the warmth of his hands, sighing with relief. "Better?"

She rolled her neck and for once it didn't pop. "Much."

"They've moved the update meeting in the east conference room to 7 A.M.; Marcus said he would meet us there."

"They made progress last night."

"Sounds that way."

They walked to the administration building. Kate stared across the tarmac. The water used the day before had created an area of low rising fog that shrouded the wreckage. It was an eerie white cloud given what she knew was behind it.

"I'm sorry you had to see it happen."

"It's hard to brace for something like that. I was watching the clock, knew something might happen, but I never imagined it would be the plane landing." She worked on the coffee. "It was a bright orange flash in front of the wing, and then it seemed to walk back to the engine and the big explosion hit; the plane ripped apart. It shook the tower."

"Are you going to be able to forget it?"

"You know, I probably will. It's too hard to retain an image that shocking. The image of the kid that gets shot is harder to erase."

"How are you holding up?"

"No better or worse than anyone else here. What about you?"

"A bit terrified when I heard you were mentioned on the tape."

"Why?"

"My experience with situations like that means someone has you in his crosshairs for a rifle shot."

"You've protected people like Marcus does?"

"Occasionally. Any of that coffee left?"

She slowly offered his coffee back.

Dave grinned at her reluctance, then tasted the brew. He promptly grimaced. "You like it *really* sweet."

She chuckled. "Sugar helps the caffeine."

"Remind me to buy you some gum so the sugar doesn't rot your teeth."

"If it's not sweet coffee, it's candy. Sorry, I live on sugar."

"And you're not hyper?"

"Not that anyone has been willing to tell me."

"This explains why you never stop on the basketball court."

"Are you going to make excuses for losing like the rest of the guys?"

An easy smile played at the corners of his mouth at her mock outrage. "They do, huh?"

"They don't want to beat a girl.... I was born a jumping bean.... I have home court advantage—they get more creative as time passes."

"Did you play in high school?"

She went cold. "No, I never did."

He rubbed her arm. "Touch a nerve?"

"Yeah." She shook her head. "I played some in college though."

"How many times did you foul out?" A soft laugh underscored his words.

She knew her look was defensive and couldn't help it. "I was used to playing with the guys."

"Uh-huh."

"Listen, buddy, don't knock my game."

"It's a compliment. The way you can take a charge I'm surprised you haven't busted that pretty nose." He quirked an eyebrow. "You have?"

"Jack. Then Stephen had to pack it while he was doing his best not to laugh. It wasn't amusing."

"Who won the game?"

"It's one of the few we've suspended."

"I like that about your family. They can put up with you."

"Hey!" She shoved his chest for that remark, even as she grinned.

He caught her hand and tugged her back. "Face it, you would terrify most guys."

"Why?"

"You like to play on their turf."

"Does it bother you?"

He looked at her, amusement making his blue eyes sparkle. "Why should it?"

"Someone needs to deflate that ego a bit."

"You can try," he offered, his look daring her to accept.

She wasn't going to give him the satisfaction of a laugh but it bubbled inside. "You're worse than an O'Malley."

"I'll take that as a compliment."

"It probably was, but I didn't intend it to be."

"Indian giver."

"Give me back the coffee."

"Greedy, too."

"No, just not awake."

He gave the coffee back. "I think I like you when you haven't had enough sleep."

"Gee, thanks."

"Don't mention it." He held open the glass door to the administration building. "After you."

She sighed and pushed aside their banter to face the work of the day. They were a few minutes early, but the conference room was filling up fast. Dave went to get them two Danishes and more coffee for breakfast.

"Food. Maybe it will help you wake up."

She took the coffee he held instead. "Where's the sugar?" He chuckled and tossed her several packets. "Thanks. Now I'll take the food."

He held out the Danish. "Apple or cherry?"

She lowered the coffee cup long enough to consider the options. "Apple."

Bob called the meeting to order. "This is the T+20 hour update. I understand there is now physical evidence it was a bomb. What do we know?"

"We know it went off inside the first class cabin, not the baggage storage. That it went off under a seat, probably in row three or four; that's still being worked on," the NTSB representative replied.

She scrambled for a pen. *Nathan Young. Row four.*

The judge was in row two.

"Components?"

"Not yet. The airframe metal gave us the first class area and the seats the blast pattern."

Bob looked over to Elliot. "Have we identified everyone who worked this plane?"

"The people inside—maintenance, food service, preflight, mechanics—we're at thirty-nine. The interviews will be complete by midafternoon. Baggage handlers, fuel, et cetera, give us seventeen more."

"Do we know if the device was brought on board the plane here?"

"It may have been taped under the seat during the flight from L.A.; one theory is the bomber arms it just before he gets off the plane here."

Dave frowned. *Big hole. We didn't look at who got off the plane.*

Ben will have their pictures. We saw them get off in that video clip we watched.

Bob glanced around the table. "Anything on how it could have gotten through security?"

Elliot shook his head. "We're working on it."

"What about the phone call?"

The FBI representative spoke up. "Three cellular towers in this vicinity picked up the call at different levels of power. The cloverleaf of coverage extends about two miles. A series of tests this afternoon to duplicate the power levels should give us the precise location."

Kate started playing with scenarios. They had a call made from this area at 11 A.M. It was a small fact, but a useful one. If they could pin it down to inside a terminal at O'Hare, they would be able to focus on the security tapes.

The meeting was brief, with the next one set for 7 P.M., pending additional news. Kate stayed seated as she finished her list. "Dave, if the bomb is inside the cabin, that puts at the top of the list—airport personnel with access to the plane, passengers that got off the plane, and possible targets in first class, two of them being Nathan Young and the retired judge."

"Agreed."

"I vote we take a hard look at the people who got off the plane, then we focus on background checks of everyone in first class."

Marcus leaned against the table beside her. "What are you thinking?"

"A bomb inside the plane, under a seat, small enough not to be noticed by passengers as they settled in, suggests it might not have been designed to bring down the plane. The fact the plane was landing at 11:15 could not have been planned. Maybe the bomb was only intended for someone in first class. That implies the bomber knew where his target would be sitting. Nathan Young was a last-minute walk-on. His seat assignment was not known until minutes before the flight."

"So of the two on the list in first class, the judge becomes the more likely target, and we lose the connection to you."

"Which is why we had better take another look at who was seated in first class."

Marcus nodded. "Run with it."

Kate handed Dave back his pen. He accepted it and tilted his head toward the door. "Why don't you head on up to the workroom? I'll meet you there in a few minutes."

Kate glanced at Dave, then Marcus, and got to her feet. "Don't be long." They were conferring without her, which meant she was the likely topic of conversation. If she didn't know the details, she could avoid having to get mad at them. It was an amusing reality, but it had kept the peace in the family for decades. Marcus squeezed her hand and let her slip past.

The workroom looked much as it had the day before. Case files surrounded

Susan, Ben, Graham, and Debbie. They were deep in a debate over the list of names on the board. Graham smiled when he saw her and pulled out a chair. "Welcome to the war room."

"Making progress?"

"We've been able to eliminate about a third of the suspicious cases so far. What's the latest?"

"Evidence suggests the bomb went off under a seat in the first-class cabin, possibly row three or four." That news got everyone's attention.

"Interesting." Ben reached for the seating chart. "Only twenty-four people in first class. Susan, where's the latest updated list of passengers?"

"Here." She handed over the printout. "They've confirmed another nine names."

"Who was around Nathan Young?"

Susan penciled in names on the chart. "He was here, in seat 4*C.* Across the aisle to his left was the oil company VP. Directly in front of him, two sales reps from a pharmaceutical company—Vicki Marstone and Peter Alton. Judge Succalta is here, in 2*D.*"

Kate frowned. "A nice cluster. Put the bomb under seat 3*C* and they are all possible targets."

"Do they know anything else?"

"Not yet. Can we set up that videotape again? I want to look at who got off the plane."

"Sure, it will just take a couple seconds to rewind." Ben handed over a red folder. "These are the still photos you can use as a reference. I counted nineteen people who got off the plane, three of them crew."

"Is there any way to find out which of them might have been seated in first class?"

Susan found a faxed printout. "This is the L.A. seat assignments."

"Thanks. Any chance we could get a copy of the security tape from L.A.? I would love to know if someone had carry-on luggage there and left the plane here with nothing in his hands."

"I'll put a call through to the agent working the L.A. connection."

"This is briefing T+32 hour update." Bob called the evening meeting to order. "What do we know about the bomb?"

Kate hoped they had something. It had been a long, grueling day with little forward progress given how promising the day had begun. A look at the people getting off the plane, the first-class passengers, had revealed nothing new. They had spent hours in the old case files, and it felt like she had been reliving them all. It was frustrating to know they were this close and not have someone to focus on.

The NTSB coordinator got to his feet and turned on the overhead projector. "It was under seat 4*C* in first class. That makes it under the seat of a Mr. Nathan Young."

Kate let out the breath she had been holding. They were going to be able to explain the reference to her name, not have to dig through her ancient past.

"We'll come back to Mr. Young," Bob decided. "Tell me about the bomb. Components?"

A transparency went down onto the overhead. "We've got a seared briefcase that appears to have been punched from the inside out; a laptop appears to have been carrying the device."

A briefcase? Dave scrawled. *Someone would notice if a briefcase were left on the plane.*

Nathan was carrying a briefcase. She hesitated. *Suicide?*

No. Someone wanted him to carry the bomb that would kill him.

Revenge with malice.

Yes. Someone consumed with anger. Dave paused. *And he's angry with you, too.*

Thanks for the reminder.

Another slide. "The bomb appears to have been inside the battery pack. Note the way it blew. There were metal plates at the back of the battery pack to send the explosion out through the briefcase instead of into the laptop. The machine itself is remarkably intact for the nature of the blast, considering it was found embedded in the airframe."

"What type of explosive was used?" Bob asked.

"Chemical analysis has just begun. Based on the size of the device, it was probably C-4, not quite a quarter of a brick."

"How was it triggered? Was it set to go off at a specific time, or did someone have to arm it?"

"We're still looking for components to determine that."

Bob nodded. "Tell me about Mr. Nathan Young."

Dave referred to the bio they had assembled to answer that question. "Forty-seven. Caucasian. Married eight years, no children. His second, her first. MBA Harvard. He owns four banks in Chicago, six in New York, and recently bought one in Denver."

"The obvious question: Did Mr. Nathan Young know there was a bomb in his briefcase? Was the laptop his? If it was, who had access to it recently? Who would have reason to target him? We'll meet again tomorrow, 9 A.M."

The meeting broke up into smaller clusters of people.

"A bank president killed by a bomb he may have unknowingly carried on board, a brother who was a drug dealer killed on the same plane. Henry Lott angry enough last week that he planned to blow up one of Nathan's banks," Kate summarized. "We've got a lot of questions to answer."

Dave exchanged a glance with Marcus, then looked back at her. "I'll have Ben follow up on Henry Lott again. Why don't we focus on Nathan's schedule and appointments?"

Kate was well aware the two of them were arranging what she did, keeping her away from the one person they knew was dangerous, Henry Lott, but she let it go. She had enough to worry about without trying to figure out how to get around the protective net they were throwing up around her. She'd ignore it unless it got in the way of what she wanted to do. And she wanted to go after those bomb components. Answers could be found there. "His secretary should also be able to help us confirm it was his briefcase and laptop. How early tomorrow morning do you think we can hit their office?"

"The bank headquarters open at 8 A.M. if I remember correctly. We'll be the first ones in the door," Dave assured.

Kate nodded. It would give them a couple hours tonight to plan their questions. "We've got the primary interviews tracking down information on Nathan Young?"

"They're ours," Dave confirmed. "We generate the questions. We can pull in as many people as we need to get the interviews done."

Marcus leaned back against the table. "I'll put someone on the security tapes to track Nathan's movements through O'Hare, see if we can find out how the device got inside the airport. And I'll get the last full audits of the various banks released to see if any accounts were considered suspicious. Anything else you want me to expedite?"

"The brother, Ashcroft Young, can you get his full trial transcript and prison record? The bio we have is pretty thin on details."

Marcus made a note. "Sure."

"Oh, and when you go after the bank records, would you also put someone digging into just how much cash Nathan Young had on hand? Dave noticed his mortgage foreclosure rate was about three times higher than last year, like he was building up cash for some reason. It was one of the reasons we had an appointment with him today."

"Anything else?" Marcus asked.

Dave reached over and closed Kate's folder. "Yes. Dinner. It's almost nine o'clock and I'm starved. This can wait an hour."

Kate leaned back in her chair, twirled her pen, shot Marcus a private glance, and then looked back at Dave to give him a wicked grin. "Are you always like this in the middle of a hunt? Ready to take a break when things get on a roll?"

Dave's eyes narrowed. "Taunting a tiger when he's hungry is a dangerous thing to do, Kate."

She blinked, startled at the comeback. "You mean I've got to find you red meat for dinner, too?"

Marcus stepped back out of the line of fire, stifling a laugh.

Kate giggled as Dave propelled her out of the chair, and it spun around behind her. "Okay, uncle! We'll go eat."

"Good." He knuckled her head. "We'll start with you eating crow."

Her giggles blossomed into laughter. "Your puns are awful when you're tired."

"You ought to hear yours."

The three of them ended up walking down to the airport employee cafeteria, appropriating a table near the dessert bar, and for the next hour left behind the work upstairs.

After two nights on a cot, Kate felt like a pretzel. If Dave didn't let her move back to her own bed for tonight, she was going to be tempted to think about murder. She propped her elbows on the cafeteria table, cradled her cup of coffee in her hands, and did her best to ignore the commotion around her. Dave was finishing an omelette, and she wondered how he could eat breakfast with such apparent enjoyment. Her system wasn't even sure what day it was anymore, let alone what time it was.

Marcus reached over to check the number on her pager. "New York said they would have the bank audit information here sometime this morning. I'll page you as it comes in."

Kate nodded and finished her coffee. She should be looking forward to getting out of the airport and hitting the road, finding some answers. She was, but it was buried under the fatigue. She had dreamed about the passengers last night. They had never said this job would be easy, but how many people was she expected to see die in her lifetime?

Dave reached over and gripped her arm. "Are you okay?"

Startled, she wiped her expression clear of emotion. "Fine."

He scowled at her. "I wish you wouldn't do that."

"What?"

"Pretend you don't feel anything."

She wanted to swear at him for going under her guard. "I'm sorry I don't bleed to your ideal specification," she bit out tersely, pushing back her chair, knowing she had better step back before the anger she felt flared toward him because he was handy.

Dave looked shocked; that made her feel like a heel.

Marcus gripped her wrist, stopping her movement. "Don't go far."

She looked at him, holding back a flare of anger at him as well. She wasn't going to have free movement again until this case was solved and the use of her name during that bomb threat had been explained. "I'll find a phone and check my messages," she finally replied.

Marcus released her wrist. "Thank you."

"Sure." She glanced at Dave, offered an oblique apology. "I won't be long."

Dave was waiting for her by the stairway when she got off the phone, his attention focused on a coin he was turning over in his hand. She could read his frustration in the way he stood, his concentration on a coin. "Ready to go?" she asked.

He glanced at her, then pushed the coin back in his pocket as he straightened. "Sure."

His abrupt answer made her sigh. "I apologize for that."

Dave gestured to the stairs. "You're predictable. You don't like someone to get in your way. Where do you want to start?"

So much for restoring the peace between them. Kate turned her attention to work. "Let's go pay a visit to Nathan's office, then visit his wife."

"We'll take my car." They headed toward the secure back parking lot.

Kate had expected the press to be out in numbers. She did not anticipate that the police would have to open a corridor on the other side of the security gate for them to be able to get past. "There are almost sixty people here, and it's only a parking lot gate."

"Welcome to the age of instant news."

Kate sighed, looking back at the reporters. "I've been intentionally avoiding the television monitors."

"Probably a wise idea. You don't need any more bad news."

He didn't even know of the worst of it for her—Jennifer's cancer. "It's been a horrible week."

"You're holding up pretty well."

"Only because I'm not stopping to think about it." She looked down at her notes. "Let's run through this from the top."

"Start with the bank."

She nodded. "A week ago last Tuesday, Henry Lott shows up at the bank with dynamite and a gun, in a tirade at First Union for foreclosing on his house. He is arrested, denied bail, and has apparently only talked with his lawyer since that time. Tuesday this week, at 9:40 A.M., I meet Bob Richards for a walking security review. At 10:48, the first bomb threat is called in. 10:52, Nathan Young boards Flight 714 as a late walk-on; he is carrying a briefcase. At 11 A.M., the second bomb threat is called in. The message is prerecorded and mentions my name. The bomb goes off at 11:15."

"How does Henry Lott pull it off?"

"Clearly, he can't. Not alone."

"Does he have any family?"

"No. That was what made him so difficult to deal with at the bank. He had no reason not to die."

"Could he have paid someone to kill Nathan Young?"

Kate tried to imagine that scenario. "Three problems. It would have had to be arranged before he walked into the bank. Once Henry was dead or arrested, the guy hired to do it would simply walk away. Second, no money. That was why the foreclosure occurred. Third, it's the overkill problem again. A gun would have done the job. If Henry had been out of jail, maybe his personal motivation would be intense enough to make it a bomb, but a third party would have gone for expediency."

Dave nodded. "Then who else might want to kill Nathan Young?"

"Probably his brother. But he's dead."

"What about his wife?"

"Maybe. We need to see if she inherits everything. But if she did it herself, a woman rarely uses explosives. And if she had help, why use a bomb that had to be smuggled past O'Hare security?"

"Okay. Someone at his office?"

"Interesting." Kate jotted down that possibility. "They would have access to Nathan's itinerary and to his briefcase. But what's the gain?"

"Promotion?"

"It's probably governed by an outside board, but if enough groundwork had already been laid to guarantee confirmation, it's worth looking at. Promotion…what else?"

"Employee rage? Someone decides to kill the boss?"

"Why not a bomb in his car? Or a package bomb?" She sighed. "Dave, why put a bomb on a plane? There has to be a reason."

They pulled into the parking lot of the bank corporate offices. Kate released her seat belt. "Let's go prove Nathan carried that bomb on board the plane."

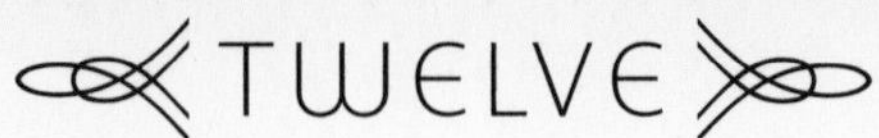

TWELVE

The corporate offices for First Union Bank left an impression of old wealth with the classic elegance, marble, and turn-of-the-century paintings. A brief check with the receptionist and Dave and Kate were invited to the executive floor.

Kate hung back a step and intentionally let Dave do the talking. The office doors behind the secretary opened just as he established the lady was merely a temp for the day, taking the place of Nathan Young's secretary. The man who emerged came forward with the stride of someone accustomed to power. Kate caught a glimpse of a very large room with large glass windows before the door closed. "May I be of help? I'm Peter Devlon, the vice president of Union Group."

The VP who had answered Henry's letter.

Dave brought out his badge again. "Could we speak with you privately?"

"Certainly. Please, come into my office." He gestured to an office on the other side of the hallway. Curious, Kate glanced back at the office he had been in. The discrete gold nameplate said Mr. Nathan Young.

She took a seat as Dave smoothly dealt with the pleasantries. "I'm sorry for your loss."

"It's been a very emotional day here. How can I help you?"

"We have a few questions regarding Mr. Young's itinerary," Dave replied, setting the tone for the interview. They had agreed last night Dave would pursue the questions while Kate waited, ready to step in on inconsistencies she heard.

"Of course." Mr. Devlon leaned against his desk rather than walk around to sit behind it.

"He was traveling to New York on business?"

Mr. Devlon nodded. "He was going out for a 5 P.M. meeting, planning to fly back this morning."

"He was a walk-on for the MetroAir flight. Was it an unexpected meeting?"

"No, it had been on the calendar for about a month. Nathan would have normally taken the company jet." Mr. Devlon grimaced. "His decision to take MetroAir was truly a fluke. We had just concluded a meeting in the business lounge by the MetroAir gate; the flight was boarding, and it would cut an hour off his travel time. He needed to work during the flight, and frankly, that would have been difficult to do on the company plane. His wife Emily had decided at the last minute to fly out with him and stay at their New York penthouse through the weekend. Nathan asked me to fly to New York on the company jet with her as originally planned, get her settled at the penthouse, and then meet him at the office."

Dave waited a moment before asking the next question. "Whom did he meet with at the airport?"

"There were two meetings actually. One with Mr. William Phillips, the prior owner of First Federal Bank of Denver, and the other with the owner of Wilshire Construction."

Kate remained still even though her heart raced as the company name registered. *Wilshire Construction. Henry Lott's former employer.* It couldn't be coincidence that all the threads were running back together: Henry Lott, Nathan Young, Wilshire Construction.

"Why at the airport?"

Mr. Devlon spread his hands. "Mr. Phillips was on a layover, flying on to Washington; this was the only time in their schedules they could meet. Nathan has been looking at who to put in charge of the Denver bank, and he wanted to speak with Mr. Phillips before making that decision."

"Isn't that a little unusual?"

"Not when one of the candidates was Mr. Phillips's son."

"Was he offered the position?" Dave asked.

"No. The meeting was to smooth ruffled feathers only, let him know his son would be considered for the position in a few years if he proved capable."

"Why was the bank sold if the son wanted to run it?"

Mr. Devlon smiled. "Mr. Phillips had nearly run it into insolvency. It was sell or face a lot of bad press if news got out as to the bank's real condition." Kate narrowed her eyes as she heard the satisfaction in Mr. Devlon's voice. He liked that, the misfortune of others. No wonder Henry Lott had felt like he was getting squeezed. Mr. Devlon had written that letter refusing to stop the mortgage foreclosure.

"The second meeting?" Dave's voice had cooled, Kate noted; he had read the same thing in Mr. Devlon's reply.

"Wilshire Construction. It was fit in because there were a few minutes in Nathan's schedule and there was some urgency to the problem."

"What type of problem?"

"The company was having some cash flow problems and wanted to extend their loans, but we had floated them too much as it was."

"What's the status of Wilshire Construction now?" Dave asked, probing.

"We are in the process of terminating their line of credit. They have another ten days to restore enough liquidity to make payroll and buy another thirty days with us, but I doubt they'll survive. Construction can be a ruthless business."

Money trouble. Kate could feel that new thread tying the others together. Henry Lott was having money troubles; his former employer was having money troubles.

"Have they been customers for a while?" Dave asked.

Mr. Devlon folded his arms. "Actually, yes. Almost twenty years. But the son runs the business now, and he's young, inexperienced."

"His name?"

"Tony Emerson."

Kate absorbed the shock as she would a sudden act of violence, not letting the emotions register. *Emerson.* She stopped following the conversation as her thoughts began to race. This was the link to her past. Her distant past.

How many Emersons could there be in this area? Surely enough to give her some cover, at least until she knew the truth. She forced her breathing to go calm. Yes. Deal with the facts. It was a name. One she had reason to hate, to fear, but it still was just a name. There didn't necessarily have to be a connection between it and the bomb threat.

They are connected. You know it. What are you going to do when you have proof?

She wasn't some helpless kid anymore. Even if this pulled her deeper into the crisis, left her vulnerable to people who didn't know her speculating on what it meant. Tony Emerson Sr. was dead. She knew that, had once tossed a rock at his gravestone. She knew he was buried under six feet of ground.

Get through this interview. Get back to the airport. Get the facts. Then do whatever you have to.... She tuned back in to the conversation.

"Were you present for both meetings?" Dave asked.

"I was in the business lounge, yes. I was making a few calls, following up on some business we had discussed on the drive to the airport. I sat in on the second meeting to take notes," Mr. Devlon replied.

"Did anyone else attend these meetings? Associates of Mr. Phillips? Mr. Emerson?"

"I believe Mr. Phillips had his lawyer and his secretary traveling with him. They were working at one of the tables across the room."

Dave turned the page in his notepad. "Do you remember their names?"

"Sorry, no."

"Mr. Emerson?"

"He was alone," Mr. Devlon replied.

"How long did the meetings last?"

Mr. Devlon thought about it for a few moments. "We got to the airport about 9:15 A.M., and I called in a few minutes late for a 10:45 conference call after I left Nathan at the MetroAir gate, so, I'd guess about an hour."

"You said you made notes of the second meeting?"

"Yes."

"Would you mind if I see them?" Dave asked it idly, but Kate heard his interest. He had latched on to that money trouble theory as well.

"They were on Nathan's laptop, I'm afraid. I did e-mail a copy to the branch manager if you would like me to have them forwarded to you."

"The business lounge has power outlets and phone lines for laptops?" Kate broke in to ask.

Peter Devlon was surprised by the question, but answered it. "It's fully equipped as an office away from home."

"You didn't need to use a battery pack?" Kate pushed.

Now he looked puzzled. "No. It was fully charged for his trip to New York."

Kate wondered how this bit of news was going to go over back at the airport. The investigators, having reached the conclusion the bomb was in Nathan's laptop, were going to love being told the laptop had been used just before the flight, and inside terminal security at that.

"Do you have an inventory system for insurance purposes that would allow us to identify that laptop? Its serial numbers or the like?" Dave asked.

"Sure, if you need it."

"It would help."

Mr. Devlon nodded, picked up the phone, and called someone in the bank, passing along the request. "Scott will leave the printout at the main desk for you to pick up."

"What about his briefcase? Anything that might help identify it?"

"That is simple. It was handmade for him last year as a gift from the board. Scrolled leather tooling, a custom-designed handle with, how would you describe it, a form-fit grip?"

"Molded?" Dave asked.

"Yes."

Dave changed the subject. "Would it be possible to get a copy of his calendar for the last few weeks?"

"The secretary can copy whatever you need."

"Thanks, I appreciate that. Do you happen to know why Ashcroft Young was traveling to New York?"

"I'm sorry, no. I was as surprised as everyone else to find he was on the flight," Mr. Devlon replied.

"How would you characterize the relationship between the two brothers?" Kate asked, wondering how much he knew about the brothers. They were going to have to find a handle into the reality they had brothers, a bank president and a drug dealer, both killed on the same flight.

"Strained would be a safe characterization. I assume you know about Ashcroft's past record?"

She nodded. "Yes."

"It caused Nathan some grief during the audit before his purchase of the Denver bank. To the best of my knowledge, they were not on speaking terms."

Kate wasn't surprised at that news, but she was disappointed. If Nathan hadn't told his second in command much about his brother, they were going to have a hard time getting a handle on the relationship.

"I understand Nathan had no children?" Dave asked.

"That's correct."

"So his wife inherits everything?"

"I have no direct knowledge of his will, but yes; it was always assumed controlling interest would pass to Emily should something happen to Nathan. She is already a minority owner, occasionally sitting in on board meetings," Mr. Devlon replied.

Kate was surprised at that news, and from her glance at Dave, he was, too.

"Will she be active in running the banks?" Dave asked.

"I hope so," Mr. Devlon replied. "She's got the talent for it. She headed one of the small New York community banks Nathan acquired—that's how they met. If not, the banks have strong managers, and I can deal with the day-to-day management of the corporate group. We'll adjust to whatever she wants."

Dave nodded and got to his feet. "Thank you for your time, Mr. Devlon."

Kate saw the movement and closed her notepad, glad to have this interview done. Nothing had prepared her for having this case go to the heart of her past. *Tony Emerson.* She had thought she would never have to hear that name again during her lifetime.

She forced herself to wait patiently beside Dave as the secretary copied Nathan's calendar for them going back four weeks. Dave handed the pages to her, and Kate glanced at the pages briefly before indicating it was what they needed. They paused in the lobby to get the inventory list.

Stepping from the chill of air-conditioning to the dry heat of outdoors was a shock.

Dave pulled out his car keys. "Three new players on the table, all with access. Mr. Peter Devlon, the VP orchestrating things; Mr. William Phillips, former bank owner whose bank got gobbled up and his son shafted; and Tony Emerson of Wilshire Construction, about to go out of business." He held open the passenger door. "Kate."

"Sorry."

"What are you thinking about so intently?"

"I'm not sure yet."

He shot her a curious glance as he started the car. "Give me a hint?"

She forced a smile, then shook her head. "We need to see the security videotapes from the business lounge. Do we head back to the airport?" She desperately needed access to a terminal to check out a name.

"Let's see if Nathan's widow is available first, while we are still downtown."

Kate had no choice but to nod. There was no way she could mention her fear.

THIRTEEN

According to the maid that answered Dave's call, Emily Young was sleeping under doctor-prescribed sedation. With that stop delayed, Kate got her wish, and they headed back to the airport. Dave's pager went off fifteen minutes into their trip. He looked at the number, then reached for the car phone. "Richman. I got a page."

He glanced over at her. "Hi, Marcus."

Surprise jolted Kate out of her thoughts.

"Are you sure you want to handle it that way?" He nodded. "All right. We'll be expecting you." He hung up the phone.

"What?" Kate already knew she wasn't going to like it. The fact Marcus had called Dave and her was a pretty big clue.

"The bomb threat phone call contents just leaked to the press."

"Wonderful." She squeezed the bridge of her nose. "That guarantees a fun afternoon."

"Kate, the passenger list was released an hour ago."

When she didn't immediately connect the dots, he did it for her. "Nathan Young was listed. The media is already running with the connection to the bank incident last week. Your boss wants you to lay low, doesn't want you back at the airport. To quote Marcus, it's become a firestorm."

She had to get to a computer terminal. This was atrocious timing. Why couldn't it have held another few hours? "I can't exactly step back from this investigation; I'm in the middle of it." She rubbed at her headache. "Take me to the office then, I guess. I'll work from there and stay with Lisa tonight since my apartment has already been ruled out." She saw the expression on his face. "What?"

"Marcus suggested a more secure place was in order, both for you to work and to stay."

"Why? The press is aggravating and to be avoided but hardly dangerous."

"Because you are a target. Someone who killed 214 people wanted to see you squirm under this media onslaught."

"What's his suggestion?"

"You stay at my place."

Stay with Dave. Of course. It was just like Marcus. Protect her twenty-four hours a day. And Dave had probably been the one to plant the suggestion with him on the assumption this situation might develop; the two of them had been thick as thieves the last couple days. *Stephen, where are you? They are smothering me. I need to be rescued from all these good intentions!* "That is a little overblown." There was a niggling doubt that it might not be, but she was not letting ghosts chase her until she had her hands around the evidence.

"No, it's not. Right now the media is your enemy, not just a nuisance. If they tell where you are, this guy can come knock on your door. Do you want that to be Lisa's door?"

That thought was chilling. "No."

"There is room to work at my place; the security is good, and I won't have to wonder where you are."

"You have access to the files from home?"

"Basically anything I can do at the office downtown, I can do from home."

It wasn't worth the fight. She was losing precious time. "Fine. Let's go to your place."

Dave watched for a moment from the doorway as Kate read through a fax. She had been holed up here in his office for the last half hour. "Finding anything useful?" The fact she about jumped out of the seat made Dave strongly suspect his guess was right. When she reached to blank the computer screen even as she swiveled in his office chair toward him, she confirmed it. Whatever lead she was puzzling over, it worried her.

Something from her past.

He had put that much together. It concerned the case, and she didn't want to talk about it. He set down the cold drink on a coaster by the keyboard. "Sorry I startled you. Are you okay?"

She swallowed hard. "Yes."

He could feel her nervousness, worse, could see almost panic in her eyes. The mask she so easily wore was in shreds. "Susan called," he said quietly, choosing his words carefully so as to give her room to settle down, "the briefcase and laptop both match the information Peter provided."

"Oh...good."

He frowned. Very distracted. What information had her coiled tense like this? He had seen her calmly face down a man with a bomb. This change was alarming.

She had been distracted when they left the bank. What had he missed? He thought back through the information Peter Devlon had provided. It was useful, but nothing to result in this kind of response.

He was not going to crowd her, not when he needed her above all else to trust him. He settled his hand on her shoulder. "Can I get you something to eat?"

"Maybe later."

He squeezed her shoulder gently and stepped away. "I'm going to check security for the house. If you hear the door, it's me."

She nodded. "Thanks."

He closed the door to the office to give her the privacy she clearly wanted.

Whether she realized it or not, this house had just become a formal safe house again. There were already 214 victims. There would not be 215. She was spooked. That was sufficient warning for him.

He would have to explain the security grid to her soon, show her how the grids inside the house turned off and on in zones, but for now he would get the overall security tightened. He called Ben from his cellular phone as he circled the estate grounds, not needing Kate to hear the call just yet. A few minutes later, he closed the phone, satisfied. Travis and Susan were both on their way.

On the drive out here he had wondered what Kate would think of his home. The estate had been in his family a long time, and one person got lost in its spaciousness; it needed a family. Sara had shared the place with him until she married Adam. Kate had simply looked across the well-kept grounds and shown her cop's priorities by asking first about security, then commenting that the landscaped grounds were beautiful.

Satisfied eventually that everything was in order, he reentered the house, reset the security grid for the grounds. It beeped as he was turning away. Thinking he had made an error, he turned and saw a car had pulled to the gate. Surprised, he lowered the grid and cleared the car past the gates.

He was waiting at the door when Marcus got out of the car. "I didn't expect you this soon. Come on in."

"I asked Ben to cover the afternoon update meeting." Marcus offered the sealed box he was carrying. "Those should be copies of all the security tapes of the business lounge." He looked around, curious. "Nice place. Where's Kate?"

"She's working in my office." Dave hesitated. "Marcus, something is wrong."

"Oh?"

"She's been distracted ever since we left the bank."

"Where's your office?"

"Down the hall, second door on your left."

Marcus nodded. "Sort those tapes into some sort of order, and I'll be back to watch them with you." He moved down the hall toward Dave's office.

Dave could see the wall Kate still had up with him—her family could get answers where he could not. How long was it going to be before she trusted him? He hated being left on the periphery of her life, and that realization troubled him. This friendship had been subtly morphing into a relationship even though he knew how dangerous that was for him.

Lord, Kate is invading my heart. She's so determined not to be dependent on others. I want to be in that circle of people she trusts and turns to when life is tough. I want her safe—physically, emotionally—and it's becoming intensely personal with me.

Hearing the knock, Kate instinctively moved her hand over the keyboard, prepared to clear the screen. "Kate."

Marcus. The relief was incredible. "Come in."

Her brother pushed open the door. He looked at her, turned, and made sure the door was closed.

"Did you say anything to Dave?"

"No. He thinks I came to bring the security tapes." He took the second seat and wrapped his arm around her shoulders. "Twenty-two years, and you've never sent a drop everything page before. What's wrong?"

She took a deep breath, not sure how to prepare him for what she had found. It terrified her. "Mr. Nathan Young had a meeting at the airport with his VP Peter Devlon and the owner of Wilshire Construction." She turned the screen toward him. "Check out the incorporation papers for the company."

Moments later, Marcus stilled. "When was this filed?"

"A change of registered agent to this name and address was made four years ago."

His hand started rubbing her arm even as he continued to read. "Who has this information?"

"I'm not volunteering anything, but it's only a matter of time."

"Is your name change part of your personnel file?"

She shook her head. It was the only faint piece of good news there was. "No. But neither were the court records sealed. If it's not on a piece of paper in the stacks of data being looked through, it will be soon."

"What about the address?"

"That is sealed as is all information regarding the case filed by the DA against my parents. My past goes back to Trevor House, and there it ends. But with my real name and my real birthdate, they will eventually match the address. Two Emersons in a bomb case, one of whom changed her last name? Instant conflagration."

He tightened his arm. "How do you want to play this?"

"I want to know if I've really got a brother, first of all. Then I want to know if he blew up a plane with 214 people on board. If he did, I may just kill him myself."

Marcus winced. "Have you pulled his birth certificate? He's not a cousin, another relative?"

"Tony Emerson Jr., named for Dad no doubt," she said bitterly. She flipped back a screen to show him the birth certificate. "He's twenty-six. It fits. He would have been born the year after I was removed from the home." Her hand shook as she blanked that screen. The pain she had been forced to endure because she was not a son...the courts called it child abuse, but that was too polite a word for what had happened. The shaking was anger, rage, and pure fear.

Marcus's hand grasped her chin and turned her to look at him. "Let it go.

Come on, Ladybug. Let it go." He tore her out of the memories by the force of his will.

The cop she was pushed the rage back, the rage at feeling helpless and defenseless. "I have to know."

"Yes." His hand brushed down her cheek. "Stay here. Let me check it out."

"I need to go with you."

He looked at her for a long moment. "No."

"Marcus—"

"You'll kill him," he said simply. "His name is Tony Emerson; he probably resembles your father, and you will kill him. It wouldn't have anything to do with this case."

She closed her eyes. She didn't dare wonder if it were true.

He buried her head into his shoulder. "You don't need the memories. Stay here. If you think you can handle seeing him, go through the security tapes with Dave and make your first look a distant one."

She took a deep breath and nodded. "What do I tell Dave?"

"As little or as much as you want. It's going to take me some time, Kate. I'll call as soon as I can, but you need to keep yourself occupied."

"Be careful."

"You have my promise."

With a final hug, he was on his feet and moving.

Kate watched the door close and slowly uncurled her fist. The O'Malleys were her family. Not someone named Tony Emerson Jr. Not someone born to the man who had nearly destroyed her life. She wanted to run; it was the strongest emotion of all the conflicting ones. Hide. Get away from this reality. She had a brother. How was she going to deal with that if it were true?

She would have given anything in her life to have a real brother when she was young. Now, she could only hope it wasn't true.

FOURTEEN

"Kate, come sit down," Dave asked. She was pacing the living room, arms crossed, looking once again like she felt caged in. Whatever had her worried, it had been sufficient for Marcus to leave immediately after talking with her. The only thing Marcus had told him was an absolutely firm "don't let her leave" warning.

If she heard his request, she didn't indicate it.

Dave set down the remote control. The last thing Kate was ready to do was look at security videotapes. There would be time when Travis and Susan got here. He got to his feet. She looked startled when he touched her arm. "Let's go for a walk."

She blinked, then nodded.

He changed the security grid so they could walk the grounds. They walked the path around the flower gardens in silence. Dave knew she wasn't seeing the beautiful day around them.

"I never said thanks for offering me a place to stay."

She was thanking him for something a few hours ago she had been protesting? Dave felt a cold sensation brush across his spine. He reached over for Kate's hand. "I don't mind the company, and the security fits what you need. This place served as a safe house for my sister. No one will get on the grounds easily."

"What do you mean, it was a safe house for your sister?"

"Maybe you know her as Sara Walsh."

She stopped walking. "Oh." Obviously, she remembered when the case had made news. "You were part of her detail?"

"Head of security for a good part of her life. She was an endearing little brat when she chose to be." He tried to distract her. "You remind me a lot of her."

"How? She's rich and beautiful and…" She sputtered to a stop.

"She has a whimsical sense of humor like you."

"I've seen her children's books." She shook her head and frowned at him. "This is just great. Can't you have a normal family?"

Laughter felt good. "Me? What about the O'Malleys? Sara wants to meet you, by the way."

"You've told her about me?"

"You've been all over the news, remember?"

They had reached the back of the grounds where a small bench was tucked beside a reflecting pool. Dave steered her toward it.

"Do you think we will find out who did this?"

"I think the answer is on the security tapes in the living room."

He was surprised that she looked distressed at the thought. The first inkling of understanding came. "Do you know one of the people Peter Devlon mentioned?"

"No!" It was so sharp, her face so pale, that his hand caught hers to keep her from bolting. Fear. It flashed across her face and then blanked away as she took a breath, buried behind the curtain that dropped across her expression. "No, I've never met either one of them."

That was the truth, he was certain of it, but she had heard of at least one of them. How? She was not someone who gave in to fear easily.

"Did you ever get another call like that one the night we had pizza?" He asked the first thing that came to mind as something to distract her again, and then he realized what he had said. He blinked. *The call.*

"Sounds like you have trouble coming your way. Soon it will be more than you can handle." He distinctly remembered the laugh.

Whoever had made that call knew what was coming.

Kate's eyes were wide, bright. "Dave, I *need* those answering machine tapes. They are in my briefcase at the office."

"How many calls were there?"

"Three. No, four." She shook her head. "I don't know if the third one was the same person. But the others definitely were. The last one was Monday morning."

"They are all on tape?"

"Yes."

He wanted to sweep out an arm and hug her, for he shared the sense of relief; instead he held out his hand and pulled her to her feet. "Come on. We can be to your office and back in a little over an hour."

She started with him toward the house, then stopped. "No. I have to wait for Marcus. That's more important."

Dave watched her bite her lip, obviously torn as to what to do. "Who else can access your briefcase for us?"

"Anyone on the team could get the tapes. And we would need a similar model answering machine."

"Call your boss; ask him to send someone to bring what you need out here. I'll see about getting us a cleaned-up copy of the call to the tower."

She nodded, and once in the house, went immediately to pick up her cellular phone.

"Kate." She paused her dialing. "Have him send an officer to your apartment to retrieve that answering machine tape, and make sure the officer puts in a new one. You haven't been home since this blast occurred. What if that follow-up call we expected was made to your home?"

Nodding, she punched in numbers and was soon in a detailed conversation with her boss.

Dave left her to make his own call. He was relieved to find the lab had been able to remove most of the distortion from the voice. A copy of the cleaned-up tape was on the way. His call finished, he went to join her.

"Do you really think there's a chance my harassing caller is the bomber?"

"I've never been one to believe in coincidences." She looked...pleased...at the idea someone who knew her phone number might be the bomber. He wondered if her need for justice made her blind to the risks she accepted. She scared him; she really scared him. "It will be a while before the tapes arrive. How about dinner?"

"Food?"

"Unless you would like to look at the security tapes first."

"Tell me what I can help fix." She followed him into the kitchen.

Watching Dave sort through cupboards was an interesting distraction. Kate settled against the counter and worked on a piece of celery as she watched.

"Spaghetti?" Dave asked.

"Can we have garlic bread?"

"Do you treat garlic the same way you do sugar?"

"Wimp."

"Hey, if I ever did want to risk an emotional firestorm and kiss you good night, I would prefer that one kiss not taste like garlic."

She moved away from the counter and leaned past him to pluck a glass jar of homemade sauce from the shelf, realizing he had apparently decided to break his own rules about this friendship. "If, huh? Of course, you're assuming I would let you."

His hands spanned her waist and lifted her back slowly. She couldn't explain why, but she could sense there was a struggle going on behind his teasing words. "It's called self-preservation. If we were...involved—" He paused, then cleared his throat and went on. "Then *one* kiss good night would go a long way to insuring I keep my hands to myself the rest of the day."

She blinked at the impact of that smile and knew she would be a goner if he ever intentionally turned that charm her way. This was just the moment, pure and simple, he'd be back to keeping his distance soon, but still...she grinned. "Hands."

He dropped her to her feet, and the emotion—the regret—in his eyes troubled her. "I didn't mean it literally."

She patted his arm, forcing a light tone to her words. "Fine. But I still want garlic bread if I'm eating Italian."

"Then I'll fix it."

"Under the broiler? Nicely toasted, not dark?"

"Whatever happened to the benefit of the doubt? I can cook."

"O'Malley men. They say the same thing."

He grinned. "They can't cook?"

"Not if it involves fire."

He found her a pan for the sauce. "I feel duty bound to defend them as they are not here to defend themselves."

"Don't bother. Once you've eaten one of Jack's charred delights, you'll learn that the best defense is a good offense."

"So who's cooking for the Fourth of July?"

"Jack."

"Really?"

She smiled at his amusement. "We give him the matches. He's happy. Then Stephen guards the food like a pit bull. When it's time to come off, there's this little signal that goes to Lisa, and she distracts Jack while I go steal the food. We've got it down to a science." His laughter made her grin. "I know. But it's Jack. We wouldn't want to hurt his feelings."

"Can I come watch this adventure?"

She blinked. "I guess so, if you want to."

"Trust me, Kate. I do. Hand me the bread knife."

Dinner made it to the table in a companionable fashion.

"Pretty decent," Kate allowed as she bit into the hot garlic bread.

"It's great and you know it," Dave countered. "What did you do to this salad?"

"I'm not telling."

"My sister will kill for a good recipe. I owe her. Come on, give."

"You'll have to ask Lisa. She has sworn me to secrecy."

"Over a recipe?"

"Hey, we know what is valuable in life."

He ate another bite and sighed. "How much to bribe it out of you?"

She grinned. "It would be cheaper to beg it off Lisa."

"Really?"

"Really."

"Now you've piqued my interest. What would it cost?"

"A chance to read that first edition Mark Twain you have in your living room."

"The frog story?"

"That's the one."

"Good taste."

"I know good literature."

He chuckled. "I knew your sense of humor came from a master."

"Twain was a step above comic books."

"You were a reader as a kid?"

Her laughter disappeared. "I don't think I was ever a kid."

The silence drifted a few moments. "I step across that line before I realize I'm even near it. I'm sorry."

She tried to make the shrug casual. "You get too far under my guard. Normally a comment like that wouldn't hit me by surprise."

"I gather the orphanage was rough."

"I had Marcus."

"I wondered. You two appear to almost read each other's minds."

"Considering I knocked him flat the first half dozen times we met, we were destined to be either friends or enemies for life." She smiled at the memory.

"He let you?"

"Hardly. I was a fierce little fighter when I was nine. He didn't think he was supposed to hit girls back, so I sat him in the mud a few times to make my point."

"What did he call you?"

"Nothing. He was the one trying to be nice."

"Oh."

She looked at him. "Don't give me that painfully understanding look. I was an angry little kid, and he wanted to butt into my business. I didn't like it."

"So you hit him."

"It seemed like the thing to do at the time."

Dave leaned back in his chair with his coffee. "What changed your mind?"

"He gave me a puppy."

He choked on his coffee.

She looked at him, daring him to say a word. His eyes narrowed, but he kept silent. "It was this black fuzz ball that had sharp teeth and an attitude, and it tried to bite me every time I tried to pet it, feed it, or work the tangles out of its mangy fur. Marcus just walked by, dumped it in my lap, and said *here.* I was too busy trying to keep the thing hidden from the staff to wonder why Marcus was so determined to pick on me. Every time that dog would get away, Marcus would have to go canvas the neighborhood and bring him back in a box."

"How long did this go on?"

"Probably six months. Then the dog got hit by a car, and I think I nearly pulverized Marcus for not finding him alive. That sort of ended the hostilities on my side."

"I'm sorry about your dog."

"You know, I never called him *my dog* until after he was dead? I always dumped him back on Marcus with all this 'you know what your dog did today' outrage."

"How old was Marcus?"

Kate pulled herself back from the memories. "What?"

"How old was Marcus?"

"Oh," she thought about it a moment. "Eleven."

"That qualifies as a friend for life."

"Probably." She grinned. "I'm going to have to repay him for that dog bite one of these days though. Maybe I'll get him one of those yappy terriers."

"You are dangerous, lady."

"I've got a long memory. Did I hear you say something about dessert?"

"Want something for that sweet tooth?"

"Got the fixings for a sundae?"

"Sure."

"That would be perfect."

He went to the freezer to find their options. "Ice cream appears to be your favorite."

It took her three drawers to find the ice cream scoop. "I'm a creature of habit."

"That's good to know."

"Why?"

"I'll only have to learn everything about you once."

"Dream on." She pulled open the refrigerator. "Do you want caramel or hot fudge?"

"Fudge."

She pulled out the glass jar and put it into the microwave to warm. "Does this qualify as having dinner together?"

He looked over at her, surprised. "I would think so. Why?"

"That's what I was afraid of. Lisa will be expecting a verbatim rundown on the conversation."

He grinned. "Will she?"

"She also wants to know if you've got a cousin or something."

"Lisa doesn't need help in the dating department. Trust me."

"Oh? What have you heard that I haven't?"

"You didn't see that ER doc hanging around her when you were at the hospital?"

"Kevin?"

"I think that's his name."

"She dumped him six months ago."

"Well, he wants another chance."

"Not with my sister. I'll flatten him first."

"What did he do?"

"Made her cry."

"Over what?"

"How should I know? She won't tell anyone. But she was crying, and he's a creep."

Dave passed her a spoon to lick. "Make an O'Malley cry, and you're in mortal danger?"

"Exactly."

"Nice to know you are all such diplomats."

"Simple rules work best."

"That one is simple enough. What's another one?"

She looked at the jar he was holding. "Don't hog the chocolate."

He passed it over with a chuckle. "You're predictable."

"Thank you. I'll take that as a compliment."

They settled at the kitchen table to eat dessert.

Kate worked through half of the ice cream in silence. It was almost time to face those security tapes. The thought made her light mood turn dark again.

"Kate, what's wrong?"

She looked over at him for a moment, then back at the ice cream. "Stuff I can't talk about." She would love to tell him all of it—Jennifer's cancer, the fear the name Emerson generated, but couldn't do it. It was more than just her at this point, it was others in the O'Malley family, and they had to be protected whatever the cost. She didn't need reporters digging into the story of their family history.

"You're sure?"

He sounded disappointed, and she regretted that. "Yes." She caught the red flash from the security grid out of the corner of her eye and turned.

Dave got up to check and looked frustrated at the interruption. "It's Susan and Travis."

She picked up their two bowls and stacked them. "Go meet them."

He looked at her and hesitated.

She smiled, touching his arm. "Dave, I'm not trying to shut you out. I'm just not at liberty to talk about some issues yet. I'm sorry. I may be able to tell you later."

He squeezed her hand. "Just don't keep secrets that are going to affect your safety, okay?"

She couldn't answer that; she wasn't going to lie to him.

He went to meet Susan and Travis.

The patrol officer arrived with the tapes as Travis and Susan walked the grounds with Dave. Kate set up the answering machine on the coffee table in the living room. Why Dave felt the need to have two agents on the grounds tonight she didn't understand, but trying to change his mind about something he had settled on was a hopeless cause.

She heard the front door close and glanced up as Dave came back into the living room. "Which one do we start with?"

He settled in the chair across from the couch. "The one that just came from your machine. I want to know if he called back after the bomb went off."

Nodding, she found the tape. It was a full tape of calls; the point in time that her name was leaked to the media was obvious by the immediate bombardment of the media. Nothing useful.

Kate put in the first tape with the call from Wednesday afternoon and picked up a pad of paper and pen to make sure she transcribed it word for word.

"Hello, Kate O'Malley. I've been looking for you, and what do I see—you made the news last night. We'll have to meet soon."

"Have to meet soon? The guy is stalking you!"

She had heard too many of them over the years to give it that kind of weight. She had known they were going to disagree on this; she tried to placate Dave's concern. "The call talks about the bank holdup. Yes, it sounds like a convict from a case I've worked, but that doesn't mean he has me located yet." She ignored his frown. "Here's the one you heard."

"Hello, Kate. I taped the news tonight. Sounds like you have trouble coming your way. Soon it will be more than you can handle."

The laugh made her shiver. "If that is the bomber, the words could be interpreted as a reference to the plane."

She looked at the jotted notes on the cassettes. "This one would have been—Saturday afternoon."

"I think you've given up trying to catch me. Does that mean I win?"

"Different voice," Dave said immediately.

"Yes. We've already got an idea who this guy is. There's an outstanding warrant for his arrest on an unrelated matter." Kate drew a line through the words she had written. She changed the tapes. "Last one. Monday morning."

"Did you enjoy your weekend? It will be the last one for a while."

"That sounds like another reference to the plane."

She frowned, looking at the words. "Maybe."

"Let's hear the cleaned up tape from the tower."

She found her pocket recorder, inserted the tape, and pressed the play button.

"The bomb goes off at eleven-fifteen. The plane is talking to the tower. Tell Kate O'Malley I haven't forgotten the past."

"The same voice," Dave said grimly.

Her hand shaking slightly, Kate rewound the tape to play it again. It was the same voice. "Call Jim, tell him to pull my phone records." *The bomber had been calling her.* The fear was overwhelming. Could she have prevented all of this? The crash? Her stomach roiled at the thought.

Dave was already dialing. "You are not going back to your apartment till we find this guy, Kate." For once she totally agreed with him; changing cities sounded like a good option right now. Someone wanted her dead. He was toying with her, mocking her, and warning her he was coming. *The black rose of death.* She had probably totally misjudged that "gift" as well as the calls.

Dave got her boss on the line and explained what they had found and arranged to send the tapes to the lab. He hung up the phone.

"Kate!" Dave's hand closed around the back of her neck and pushed her head down. "Don't you dare pass out."

She needed that stinging voice to pull her back from the brink. "Sorry," she mumbled, feeling the rush of blood returning to her face.

He briskly rubbed her back. "Don't do that! You scared me," he complained.

She pushed his hands away, sitting back up. She took a deep breath to push away the tremors. "The rose, Dave. It's not Tersh, it's the bomber. It's a black rose of death."

Dave paled. "He was at your apartment?"

"Yeah. I think so. It's too coincidental that Bobby Tersh would appear within days of that call and the message 'we'll have to meet soon.'"

"Did the black roses make the papers five years ago?"

"They were mentioned when Tersh was arrested, then committed."

She looked at him, hoping he would contradict her interpretation. He didn't. "Bobby's car was never seen in Illinois."

"The bomber borrowed his MO," she agreed, feeling cold.

Set it aside, she demanded of herself. *There was more information about this guy available now that they knew he was making the calls. Don't you dare overreact to this threat! You've vowed never to let someone else dictate, control your life by fear. You're letting him win!*

The reminder settled the emotions, shoved them aside, and calmed her inside. *That's better. Control the situation; don't let it control you.*

She got up to pace. "They were running the tests this afternoon to find out where the bomb threat call originated. What did they find out?"

"Hold on." He called Bob Roberts and asked the question. "How certain are they about that?" He scrawled something on the pad of paper. "Okay. Thanks." He hung up the phone.

"Bob says they've determined the call was not made from inside any of the terminals. The power levels drop way off inside the building. Outside, the area is harder to pinpoint. The power levels were consistent along a strip of ground that goes from the general aviation terminal to the long-term parking lot. They found one area of elevated ground by the parking area that would let you look down onto the runways. If you wanted to watch what happened, that would be a good location."

Kate nodded at the news, but her focus had already shifted. Had she ever heard this voice before? When? Where? The bomb threat was as clear as the lab would be able to get it. She closed her eyes as she listened to it, again, and then again.

Come on. She could nail this guy if she could just remember the voice....

She paced over to the window, holding the recorder to her ear as she played it again. Likely a bomb case...one by one she went through the list of names they had focused on from her past cases, and one by one she eliminated them. They would do it officially at the lab with the tapes on file, but she didn't forget faces or voices.

She felt like throwing the recorder but instead dropped herself down on the couch. "I don't know the voice."

"It was a long shot that you would."

She shook her head. "I don't forget voices, and if I haven't met him, then we've got real trouble." She got up to pace back to the window. "How are we going to catch a ghost?" She saw a car pull up to the distant security gate and heard Dave move to check the monitor.

"Marcus is here."

Kate rather numbly gathered up the evidence that would need to go to the police lab. She sealed the tapes and marked the evidence bag. Marcus was back. He hadn't called. There were several ways to interpret that, and she didn't know which one to prepare for.

Marcus paused just inside the doorway. She had never seen that look before on her brother's face. He held out his hand. "Kate, let's take a walk."

She set down the pad of paper without a word and joined him. The sun was low in the sky now, and the breeze from earlier in the day had died down. She had been through so much with Marcus. He didn't want to hurt her; she could see it in his face. She was braced for the bad news long before he spoke.

"No one has seen him since the blast. He's gone underground."

He had run. If there had been doubts about Tony Jr.'s involvement, hope that somehow she was wrong, they crumbled in the dust. "There was no one at his home?"

"His wife, Marla. Clearly frightened, nervous, but I think telling the truth. She hasn't seen him since Tuesday morning."

Tony was married. She hadn't considered that possibility. If he had a good life, why destroy it? Did he hate Nathan so much? Was losing the business so impossible to live with that he took it out on innocent people?

"There are men watching his house. This is being kept very close to the vest as the facts are checked out—it's high priority, getting a lot of resources, but need-to-know for now."

She nodded, knowing they had to move quickly.

"We should have a good bio on him in the next couple hours. But I've already learned one fact you need to know. He worked as a baggage handler at O'Hare several years ago. He was dismissed under suspicious circumstances. There wasn't enough to charge him, but eight others in his section went to jail for moving drugs."

"So he knows both security procedures and people who still work there."

"That's a safe assumption."

She shuddered at the pieces of this puzzle. "You're saying he did it."

"I don't know. Marla went pale as a ghost at the suggestion. She clearly believes he had nothing to do with it. I asked if she knew anything about the meeting with Nathan, and while she didn't know specifics, she surprised me by offering us access to the company books. It's possible the threat of losing the company was sufficient motive. He probably had access to the explosives. We'll have to find out."

There wasn't much doubt really. He had the means and the motive; he had the opportunity. "He's disappeared."

"Not a good reality, but if he thought there was enough circumstantial evidence to make him look guilty? Maybe he panicked. It wouldn't be the first time we've seen that."

"Did Marla know Tony had a sister?"

"No. He's never mentioned you."

They walked in silence. She tried to absorb the news he had given her but was too tired now to do more than nod. "Get me another place to stay."

"What? Why?"

"I don't want to be here when the word gets out. You know what the media is going to be like. 'Cop's Brother Prime Suspect in Bombing.' I don't want Dave pulled into the middle of this." She didn't want to be near him twenty-four hours a day when the doubts, the suspicions, tore apart what might have become a good friendship.

"Kate, I wish you would reconsider. I think you need Dave's help. He's good at his job."

"I know he is, but I don't want him in the middle of this. Please."

Marcus sighed. "Think about it, in light of what we now know. If Tony is the man responsible, look at what he has done. He killed Nathan not caring how many others he killed. He pulled you directly into it by putting your name in the bomb threat. He's striking out at those who he thinks are responsible for his problems."

"He doesn't know me."

"He probably thinks he does. I'm sure your father had you as the person responsible for all his problems. I'm sure Tony Jr. thinks all the grief he endured in that household was because of you. When he snaps, he goes after Nathan and he goes after you."

"How did he find out who I am?"

"Can you imagine how the bank incident played in the old neighborhood? Some of those folks have lived there forty years. Someone would have remembered what happened to little Kate Emerson."

"I haven't thought about the name Emerson for a decade, and now it's back to ruin my life."

"Kate—"

"Okay, maybe during domestic violence cases. But I closed it off and left it behind." She sighed. "Find me somewhere else to stay. I need some space, and Dave is already beginning to subtly push. He knows something is wrong."

"The news will hold for the night. Give me a day."

She reluctantly agreed.

"Stephen, Jack, Lisa—they will be by later."

"You've already told them?" At his look, she gave an apologetic smile. "Sorry." Tony was her embarrassment, but Marcus was right; it was a family problem.

His arm around her shoulders tightened. "You should be. We stick together, Kate. It will help to have real family around you."

"Marcus, thanks for the thought, but not tonight. Let me get some sleep. Come pick me up tomorrow morning."

"You're sure?"

She forced a smile. "I'm sure."

They walked back to the house in silence. He gave her a long hug before he let go. "I'll see you first thing in the morning."

She nodded and watched until he had made the turn in the drive before closing the door and walking back to the living room. Dave was fast-forwarding through the security tapes. He looked up, got to his feet, and came to meet her. She could only imagine what she looked like to put that expression on his face. "Kate—"

She simply couldn't face telling him. She wanted it all to go away. Did that make her a coward? She didn't care. "Would you mind if I looked at the security tapes tomorrow? I need a few hours sleep."

He hesitated, then nodded. "Sure. Come on. I'll show you to one of the guest rooms."

She retrieved her bag, and he showed her to the guest room at the top of the stairs, gave her a fast review of the security panel if she was up during the night, then laid out fresh towels and got her a new toothbrush.

"Thanks."

The back of his hand brushed down her cheek. "Get some sleep."

When he left, she looked at the wide bed and didn't even bother to pull back all the covers. She collapsed on them, caught a corner of the quilt, and brought it up around her shoulders. The way life was going, she wanted simply to shut it out for a few hours.

FIFTEEN

The page woke her up. It was dark outside, and she came awake, momentarily confused before locating her pager on the nightstand. She pushed back the blanket draped over her; Dave must have tucked her in at some point in the night. She looked at the numbers, saw the area code, and let her heart rate settle. It wasn't the dispatcher. The area code made it Jennifer.

She looked around for her phone, then remembered she had called her boss last. She had probably left the phone in the living room. Moving quietly, she left the bedroom, changed the security grid as Dave had shown her, and went downstairs. She didn't turn on the lights; the cast of moonlight was enough light to move around by. She curled up in a corner of the couch, drew up her knees, then stared at the glowing numbers on the phone. She had to pull in a deep breath before she began to dial. If this was more bad news, she was going to shatter.

"Hi, Jennifer."

"Kate, I just got the message Marcus left with my answering service. I've got reservations for the first flight out in the morning. I should be there by six."

Kate leaned her head down against her knees and started crying. "Jennifer—"

"I can come sit in a hospital and be poked anytime. I'd rather come hang out with you."

She laughed around the tears. "You guys are priceless, you know that?"

"We're family."

"Yes." It felt so good to hear that reassurance. She drew a deep breath and smiled. "We'll talk about your coming back early in a minute. First, tell me how the tests you've had are going."

Dave heard Kate moving around shortly before eleven, heard the stairs creak as she went downstairs. Restless? Dealing with bad dreams? Either case, he didn't like it. He frowned and pulled a pillow over to ease the strain on his neck. She had looked almost deathly gray when she had come back from talking with Marcus, and he had been hoping she would sleep through the night. He hated the strain he didn't understand, the fact she didn't trust him enough to tell him what was wrong even more. He waited, wondering if she had slipped downstairs to the kitchen to get a drink, but he heard nothing. And when she didn't return, he quietly got up and got dressed.

He kept a hand on the banister as he walked downstairs, wondering what he would find.

Kate was curled up on the couch, knees drawn up, her phone dangling in one hand. He could hear the muted tone of an off-hook signal. She had apparently finished a call but had not yet moved to close the phone.

He crossed the room to join her, clicked on the table lamp, and sank into the couch cushions beside her. She was silently crying. He took the phone from her limp hand. "Who were you talking to?"

"Jennifer. She paged me."

He wanted so badly to wipe away her tears. He let himself wipe at two, which drew a shaky smile from her. She backhanded her sleeve across her face.

"What's wrong, Kate?"

She closed her eyes, then looked over at him. "She's at the Mayo Clinic."

Understanding flickered across his face, and when he pulled her to him, she went willingly. He didn't let go of the hug. He didn't have words to heal the pain he saw.

"She's got cancer. Probably terminal."

She kept her head buried against his shoulder, hiding. He rubbed her back, wishing she would show more than silent tears. It made sense now. It was family, and with Kate that would strike at her very heart.

She pulled back after a few moments, scrubbed a hand across her face. "She hasn't told the others in the family. It makes it hard. There is no one to talk to."

"There's me."

She touched the wet stain on his shirt and gave a rueful smile. "I wish she had let me go with her. I would have been far away from the crash."

"They are running tests?"

"Trying to determine a treatment plan." She bit her bottom lip. "It's around her spine, into her liver. Mortality rates are horrible."

"The engagement?"

"Tom didn't want to wait."

"I can understand that." He looked at the tired circles under her eyes and thought back to the basketball game. "When did she tell you?"

"Monday night."

He rubbed the bridge of his nose. "And the plane exploded Tuesday morning."

She half laughed. "It's been a *really* bad week." She rubbed her arms. "Jennifer wanted to come back early. I told her no."

He hesitated. "Is she a Christian?"

"Yes." She looked over at him, and under the weariness, he saw something approaching defeat. It troubled him more than anything else he had ever seen. "She gave me her Bible; she wants me to read the book of Luke."

He stilled, praying for the right words. "Kate—"

"I don't want to hurt her, Dave, not Jennifer."

There were fresh tears appearing, and he understood better than she could comprehend. "You can't believe just because Jennifer wants you to." It would break her heart to hurt someone in her family. He smiled and gently brushed away one of the tears. She was past the hard part and didn't even realize it—she *wanted* to be able to believe. "Have you read Luke yet?"

"No."

"Set aside your preconceived notions and just read it. I'm sure that's all Jennifer is asking."

He hated the fragileness he saw. She was coming apart at the seams; she was so tired, worried, and given the black rose and phone calls—rightfully scared. And he still didn't think he knew everything she was hiding; he still didn't understand what about the bank interview had troubled her. "Come here." He didn't give her a choice. He simply wrapped her into his arms and tucked her head back against his shoulder. "You'll get through this, Kate."

She sighed. "Sometimes I envy you."

He brushed back her hair. "Why?"

"You can still hope."

She went silent, and he waited, hoping for another glimmer into what she was thinking. After a few minutes passed, he rubbed her arm. "Want some hot chocolate?" She needed a distraction, and it was the only thing he could think of.

"In June?"

He heard the amusement. "Yes, in June. Come on; it will do you some good. You're cold."

She eased herself away from him. "Got marshmallows?"

"Somewhere."

"You need lots of them."

He settled his arm comfortably around her shoulders as she swayed a bit on her feet. "Do you?"

"Of course, but if you don't have many, you can put the mug into the microwave, and they puff up really big so you can make a few seem like a lot."

He buried a smile. Definitely exhausted. "Now why does that sound like an O'Malley guy solution?"

"They never remember to go shopping."

"So you help them out."

"Someone has to."

He turned on the kitchen light, and she winced. "Ouch. Headache coming."

"I'll find you some aspirin."

He settled her onto the kitchen chair and frowned at her bare feet. He disappeared for a moment to come back with clean socks. "Careful you don't go sliding with them on, but at least they're warm."

"Thanks."

"Don't mention it." He found aspirin for her headache, then went to look through the cupboard. "Do you want milk chocolate or dark chocolate?"

"You're making it from scratch?"

"I actually surprised you." He grinned. "Is this a first?"

"Probably. But only because it's late. Dark chocolate."

"Coming up."

He was relieved to see a little life coming back into her eyes.

She idly ate a pretzel from the dish. "I forgot to tell you company would be over early."

"O'Malleys?"

"Marcus, if not the full clan."

"I like your family."

She rested her chin on her hand. "I wish you had met Jennifer."

"Did she always want to be a doctor?"

"As far back as I can remember. You should have seen her playing doctor at Trevor House. It was annoying. She would turn our bedroom into a waiting room for her patients."

"She had a lot of them?"

"Anybody younger than her with a sniffle. I'd have to play the receptionist to protect my stuff."

"Sounds like a rough time."

"I especially liked it when the boys would come to have their scrapes patched over. If you went to the house mom, you got grounded for fighting, so there was an underground black market for Band-Aids."

"Did Jennifer know?"

"I didn't tell her." She shrugged. "Hey, it was free enterprise. They were the ones who got into the fights."

"How many did you get into?"

"With a budding doctor as a roommate? If I showed up with a scraped knuckle from a fight, she would take a strip off my hide. Why do you think I became a negotiator? It was pure self-preservation."

He brought over two mugs of hot chocolate. "Enough marshmallows?"

"Yes. Thanks."

He sank into the chair beside her. "My pleasure."

"Are you always this mellow?"

He quirked an eyebrow, amused. "I don't think I've ever been called that before."

"You're like one of those cuddle bears, kind of soft and spongy."

"Kate, you need some more sleep."

"Are you blushing?" She pushed herself up in her seat. "You are!"

"I'm opinionated and stubborn, and I have that on good authority."

"Whose?"

"Sara's."

"What were you playing heavy-handed brother about when she told you that?"

He frowned at her. "Why do you assume I was at fault?"

"Three brothers. I have experience."

"I'm not heavy-handed."

"You admitted someone could tweak your tiger tail, so fess up."

He scowled. "I am not tattling. And don't try to pester it out of me, either. You and Sara are cut from the same cloth. It won't work."

She grinned and dunked a marshmallow with her spoon. "Your roar is really cute with that British accent."

He closed his eyes. "Drink your chocolate."

"Tired?"

"Are you sure you weren't raiding the sugar stash before I came down?"

"When I'm tired, I talk. It's how you stay awake during a long negotiation."

He looked over at her and felt something remarkably like love. Every one of her defenses was down. This was the real Kate under all the layers, and he was falling in love with her. The problems of that reality he would deal with in the light of day. "Then keep talking," he said gently.

She nibbled on a pretzel. "Believe it or not, I'm running out of subjects."

He grinned. "You?"

"I didn't figure you would want any Aunt Gladys stories."

"Have a repertoire, do you?"

"She's a spunky lady. She's done everything from skiing to skydiving."

"Of course. She was created by an O'Malley."

"You've got it." She tipped her mug and frowned. "Got any more hot chocolate? I've hit empty."

"Of course." Her aim was a little off when she handed him the mug. He looked at her more sharply. Past exhausted, getting punchy. Convincing her to go back to bed soon moved up a notch on his priority list. He brought the bag of marshmallows with him back to the table.

She speared one with a pretzel and spun it like a top. "We used to feed these to the squirrels."

He grinned. "Quit playing with your food."

She grinned back. "Have you ever seen a squirrel try to eat one of these? They're sticky inside, and they have to sit and clean their paws forever."

"We get raccoons around here occasionally. They like them."

"I watched a snake eat one once. Lisa came in and shrieked."

"You smuggled a snake into her room?"

She frowned at him. "It was her snake. She thought he had eaten Rachel's hamster."

"Let me get this right—Trevor House, which does not allow pets, had you hiding a dog, Lisa hiding a snake, and Rachel hiding a hamster?"

"Well, kind of. There were the other pets we hid in the garden shed, but that didn't really count because the groundskeeper smuggled in the food. Besides, Lisa arrived at Trevor House with a lizard in her backpack. It wasn't fair not to let her keep it. And once we hid the lizard, it just kind of got easier to, well, *add* things."

"Why do I get the feeling you were the chief instigator of this endeavor?"

Her smile was touched with seriousness. "It was important that the place feel something like home. Everyone should have a pet."

He cradled his mug, liking her all the more. "Marcus protected the O'Malleys, and you watched out for them." She shrugged, not admitting to it. She didn't have to. It was in practically every story she told. From protecting Jack's feelings about his cooking, to guarding Jennifer's dream of becoming a doctor. "I think I like you, Kate."

She grinned. "You're not sure?"

"Pushing for a compliment?"

She laughed and ate the marshmallow.

"Come on. You need to go back to bed."

"I'm too tired to go to sleep."

"Then let's at least move you away from the sugar."

She wrinkled her nose at him but finished the hot chocolate. "That really was good. You didn't scorch it like I sometimes do."

He took her mug to the sink. "Nothing is worse than scorched milk in the middle of the night."

"Tell me about it."

"Buy instant. It will make your life easier." His hands on her shoulders, he turned her back to the living room. "You're going to have a rat's tail to brush out tomorrow."

"Thanks for noticing."

"Don't mention it." He tugged her down on the couch beside him. "Feet."

She frowned at him but picked up her feet. He tucked the throw cover firmly around them, then made her comfortable against his shoulder. "If you're not going to sleep, at least close your eyes."

"What are you planning to watch?"

He flipped the remote over a couple channels. "The replay of the Cubs game."

"They lose."

"How do you know?"

She tilted her head back. "Because they were playing Milwaukee."

"That insures they were going to lose?"

She sighed and gave him a long-suffering look that said he didn't understand baseball. "They were going to lose. Check the scores showing on ESPN News if you don't believe me."

She was so certain she was right he flipped the channels to prove her wrong. She was right. The Cubs lost by three runs.

"See. I told you."

He turned back to the Cubs game, scoreless in the first inning, set down the remote, and slouched down on the couch to get comfortable.

"We're still going to watch it?"

"It's even better when you know the outcome. You don't have to waste all that energy wondering who wins."

"You and Stephen will get along great. He always has to watch from first pitch to last."

"You can either go to sleep or watch it with me. Take your pick."

"Give me the pillow." He reached for the throw pillow to give her. She mashed it into a lump before settling back against his shoulder, her feet tucked up on the couch. He smiled at her. "Comfortable?"

A yawn popped her jaw. "Not entirely, but you're better than that cot last night."

"You're welcome to go back to bed."

"I'll watch a while."

She made it until the third inning. She didn't snore, but she went limp as a dishrag. Her shoulder dug into his arm. Afraid both of them were going to end up feeling bruised, he woke her up. "You need to go to bed."

"Yeah."

She got up but nearly fell over. He grabbed her arm. "Okay?"

She rubbed blurry eyes and nodded. "Good night."

He smiled as he watched her head for the stairs.

Lord, what am I going to do? You know my heart, and it just landed somewhere at that lady's feet. Come tomorrow I'm going to have to scramble like mad to get some distance back so that every time she smiles my heart doesn't stop. But for the record—she's got beautiful eyes, a grin I adore, and I could see myself flirting with her for about the next fifty years.

Wooing someone to faith is what You do best. Please, I'd rather not get my heart broken.

SIXTEEN

Dawn was still an hour away, but the sky was beginning to tinge pink. Kate lay back against the pillows and watched the colors change. Today was irreversibly going to change her life. She knew it. The news about Tony Emerson Jr., if it all checked out, could not be contained more than a day. By nightfall the press would be looking for her.

She picked up the small book she had found in the side pocket of her gym bag and gave a rueful smile. Jennifer's New Testament. The officer who had packed for her must have thought it was important.

She needed to do this, for Jennifer would be here soon, and there was no predicting when the next calm moment would appear in her schedule. *"Just read it without preconceived notions."* That was so easy for Dave to say.

She retrieved the notepad and pen from her bag and opened the book to the bookmark. If Jennifer wanted to talk about the book of Luke, then they would talk about the book of Luke. Her sister was more important than her own unease with the choice of subject. The notepad was habit. Writing questions, notes, and observations would keep her focused. She started reading.

It was a struggle to get through the first three chapters. History had never been one of her better subjects. She was glad reading documents without having the full context was part of her job. Floundering a bit but determined to get through it, she kept reading.

Finally, she wrote on the pad of paper—3:38. Son of God.

Over an hour later she turned the last page in the book of Luke and clicked her pen. It was a relief to close burning eyes for a moment.

She read the four pages of concise notes.

Setting aside the questions, she focused on summarizing what she had read, consolidating the observations. The sketch she drew of Jesus made her hesitate because it was so unlike any other sketch of a man she had ever done.

He was not an ambitious man seeking power. He had power in Himself. People around Him, both supporters and enemies, acknowledged that He spoke as one having authority. He was a man that attracted crowds, but did not seek them out. Departing for a lonely place seemed to be His preference.

He was a man of compassion, gentle, kind, and liked children. He spent Sabbaths teaching. He traveled. There was never a question or hesitation on His part. No doubt. One insight in Gethsemane of a man facing an enormous coming burden.

He healed. The accounts were astounding. They were accounts of immediate, complete healing. A high fever seemed the most minor. Lepers. Paralytics. He raised the dead.

He claimed to have the ability to forgive sins, was personally a forgiving man.

She brought her summary to a conclusion with a stark observation—*Jesus did not receive justice.* He was the Son of God. He was innocent. And He was crucified. She had turned the last pages in Luke and read of the Resurrection on the third day, hard to believe, but at least it gave some justice. Jesus should be alive; He had done nothing to deserve death.

He said the Father was merciful.

Why had He not said the Father was just?

The book she had just read showed within it a culture divided over the issue of Jesus. Betrayal. Plots. Conspiracies. Adoring crowds. Power brokers. Politics.

People had died because they believed this book.

If someone had written Luke as a hoax, they had done a compelling piece of work. She had spent a lifetime studying people. People by nature wanted to lie in a way they would be believed. As a hoax, the book would have been written less grandiose, so that it would be accepted, not scoffed at. To dismiss this as a lie, she had to accept someone had written such a masterful forgery. It was harder to imagine that than it was to at least wonder if it could actually be true.

Jennifer believed, as did Dave. That was also not easy to dismiss.

Troubled, wanting to ignore the topic but unable now to do so, she stared at the ceiling and wondered.

If Jesus were real, the Bible were true, why doesn't He heal Jennifer?

Great. Telling Jennifer that would be just wonderful.

She had to get out of here, do something. Dave would protest, but Marcus would understand. If nothing else, she would go shoot hoops at the gym for an hour. She reached for her phone and paged Marcus. He could tell her the news from overnight while he drove her to the gym.

Any more body blows like she had taken lately, and she didn't think her composure would hold. She really didn't want Dave to see that. The tears last night had been embarrassing enough. She was glad she had told him about Jennifer, but it was hard to envision what it was going to be like when he found out Tony Jr. was her brother. Hopefully, Marcus had been able to make other arrangements for where she could stay. She was realistic enough to know the news would hit like a lead balloon, and she wanted to be far away from here before the fallout hit.

Dave bounced a tennis ball with one hand while he watched the second hand sweep around the face of the hall clock. Kate had barely said hello this morning before she had made a hurried excuse and left with Marcus. If he didn't know better, he would say she was running. She had refused to meet his eyes, mumbled something about needing to shoot some baskets, and swept Marcus out the door. He glanced at his watch to make sure the hall clock was right and knew that if she didn't get back soon, he would have to leave for the morning update meeting without her.

His hand clenched around the tennis ball, then he sighed and tossed it back into his gym bag. He had wanted to wrap his arms around her and give her a hug, nudge her chin up and get her to smile at him; instead, he'd shoved his hands in his pockets and watched her leave.

He was falling in love with her, and it was one of the scariest propositions he had ever faced. He was desperately afraid he was going to end up in a situation where the one thing he wanted most, he couldn't have.

"I envy you. You can still hope."

Remembering her words from the night before, he half smiled. Did hope born out of desperation count?

He was taking every grain of evidence that she was inching toward considering faith and hoping it would actually mean something. And yet, he knew he was blowing the evidence he had out of proportion. Kate was moving toward a decision, but she was still far from it. And his hands were tied until she did. *"You can't believe just because Jennifer wants you to."* He would give anything to be able to take back those words from last night. He wanted desperately to be able to say, *"Believe because I want you to."*

It didn't help that he had no idea what she was thinking—if she even thought about having a relationship that was more than a friendship. He'd deflected her early comments, and she had taken the hint. She was treating him like one of her brothers. Well, almost—she didn't trust him enough to tell him why she was scared.

And she *was* scared. That fact haunted him. He'd already asked Ben to look into it, to see if he could uncover why. There was little he could do about the pressures hitting her, but at least he could look into that. Maybe if he could simply make her feel safe, she would finally begin to trust....

The alert from the front gate security pushed him to his feet. She was back.

He checked the monitor and his disappointment was acute. "Come on up, Ben." He met him at the door.

"I've got some information I think you need to see."

"Sure." Dave glanced at the folder in Ben's hand and gestured to the formal dining room table where there was room to work. "Can I get you some coffee?"

"I'm fine."

Dave looked over at Ben, and something in his voice warned him. "What have you found?" he asked quietly.

There was a rare hesitation from his friend before Ben opened the file folder and laid down several pieces of paper. "Tony Emerson is her brother."

Dave lowered himself into the chair he had pulled out, shocked. "Her brother."

"We had to go back into the juvenile court records to find all the pieces. She changed her name at age nineteen to Kate O'Malley. Before that it was Kate Emerson."

Dave pulled over the indicated piece of paper. "It's not a coincidence?"

"No. Once we were into the court records, we got access to birth certificates." Ben handed him the photocopies. "She was made a ward of the state when she was nine. You really don't want to read the court record," Dave raised one eyebrow at that comment. "Suffice it to say there was sufficient reason for parental rights to be terminated. She was taken from the home a year before Tony Emerson was born. Dave, I don't think she knows."

"She knows," he said wearily. "I'll lay odds she found out yesterday." He rubbed his eyes. "I think Marcus has been checking into it, so he's probably told some of the Washington guys, her boss. Who else knows?"

"Susan. It wasn't easy to find, Dave. If you hadn't told me to look for a connection between Tony Emerson Jr. and Kate O'Malley, I doubt I would have found it. I did some checking. They put a watch on Emerson's house last night; there are patrols looking for him, so the information is getting acted on. Somebody high up must have made the call to keep this close to the vest."

Tony Emerson Jr. was her brother. "Can you cover the morning update meeting? She's at the gym with Marcus. I'm going to head over there."

"Sure. I'm sorry, Dave."

He slowly nodded, and even after Ben left, he sat motionless, staring at the folder. *Why not just rip out my heart, Kate? You could have at least trusted me.*

Marcus was alone at the gym, shooting hoops when Dave strode in. "I've been waiting for you."

Dave felt more than fear at the realization Kate was not here; he felt betrayed. "Where is she?"

"Safe."

"Marcus, don't give me that. She's a material witness to this, a target, something; she's so far into the middle of it I can't figure out which way is up."

The basketball came his way hard enough to sting his hands as he caught it. "And she's my sister."

They stared at each other, both breathing hard, emotions roiling. They were one wrong word away from a fight. "You're sure she's safe?"

"She's with Stephen."

Dave tossed the ball back without the stinging speed. "And that's shorthand for safe."

"In this case—yes. The media will have this information today; we both know it. She doesn't want it landing in your lap. She's somewhere safe, and hopefully distracted."

She didn't want it landing in his lap—great—she really was running. She had run to her brothers, at least there was some comfort in that. But having her somewhere else was only going to make it worse for him. "I want to talk to her."

Marcus considered him for a moment, then turned back to shooting baskets. "I don't think that's a good idea."

"I didn't ask for your opinion."

Marcus froze, then looked over at him. Dave almost backed down…almost. He could still remember Kate sitting at his kitchen table spinning a marshmallow on a pretzel stick, too tired to see straight. He wasn't backing down.

"She said you wouldn't take no for an answer."

The mild answer surprised him, then amused him. "Did she?"

Marcus walked over to the bench and picked up his towel. "Get your car; I'm parked in the side lot. You can follow me."

Marcus led him to a nice neighborhood north of the loop where trees shaded the streets and older homes showed the impact of new money restoration. He stopped in front of a brick, two-story home that was undergoing major reconstruction. Dave spotted two surveillance cars keeping watch on the house.

Marcus led the way up the walk. "Stephen is always restoring something. It's his escape as much as his hobby."

"What's Kate's?"

"Sports."

That made sense.

Marcus unlocked the front door and stepped inside.

The hallway was torn down to open studs and new drywall waited to be hung. The home smelled of fresh paint and new plaster. Dave looked around with interest. A couple walls had been taken down, opening up the rooms on the main floor. Empty of furniture, the potential was obvious to see.

Stephen came down the stairs, wiping his hands on a rag. "You're back soon."

"Where is she?" Marcus asked, glancing around.

"The back bedroom. I pulled the carpeting last night and found hardwood flooring."

"Really?"

"It's in great shape, too."

Marcus moved upstairs, and Dave decided to stay put. Stephen was blocking his way, and it wasn't accidental.

They waited in silence.

Kate finally appeared, coming down the stairs. Any fragileness he had sensed yesterday was nowhere in evidence. When she got near him, the fire in her eyes cautioned him he had better be careful. She was cornered, by the situation, now by him, and she was going to come out fighting.

"Stephen."

Dave gave Marcus points for tact. He waited until Stephen disappeared up the stairs. "Why didn't you tell me yesterday? Trust me?"

"Tell you what? That I might have a brother who is possibly a murderer?" Kate swung away from him into the living room. "I've never even met this Tony Emerson. Until twenty-four hours ago, I didn't even have a suspicion that he existed."

"Kate, he's targeting you."

"Then let him find me."

"You don't mean that."

"There is no reason for him to have blown up a plane just to get at me, to get at some banker. We're never going to know the truth unless someone can grab him; and if he gets cornered by a bunch of cops, he'll either kill himself or be killed in a shootout. It would be easier all around if he did come after me."

"Stop thinking with your emotions and use your head." Dave shot back. "What we need to do is to solve this case. That's how we'll find out the answers and ultimately find him."

"Then you go tear through the piles of data. I don't want to have anything to do with it. Don't you understand that? I don't want to be the one who puts the pieces together. Yesterday was like getting stuck in the gut with a hot poker."

He understood it, could feel the pain flowing from her. "Fine. Stay here for a day, get your feet back under you. Then get back in the game and stop acting like you're the only one this is hurting. Or have you forgotten all the people that died?" He saw the sharp pain flash in her eyes before they went cold, and he regretted his words.

"That was a low blow and you know it."

"Kate—"

"I can't offer anything to the investigation, don't you understand that? I don't *know* anything. I've been trying to erase the name Emerson all my life. I don't know him."

"Well, he knows you. And if you walk away from this now, you're going to feel like a coward. Just what are you so afraid of?"

He could see it in her, a fear so deep it shimmered in her eyes and pooled them black, and he remembered Ben's comment that he probably didn't want to read the court record. His eyes narrowed and his voice softened. "Are you sure you don't remember him?"

She broke eye contact, and it felt like a blow because he knew that at this moment he was the one hurting her. "If you need to get away for twenty-four hours, do it; just don't run because you're afraid. You'll never forgive yourself."

"Marcus wouldn't let me go check out the data because he was afraid I would kill Tony."

Her words rocked him back on his heels. "What?"

"Tony Emerson Jr. If he's my father all over again, I'd probably kill him."

He closed the distance between them, and for the first time since this morning began, actually felt something like relief. He rested his hands calmly on her shoulders. "No you wouldn't. You're too good a cop."

She blinked.

"I almost died with you, remember?" He smiled. "I've seen you under pressure." His thumb rubbed along her jaw. "Come on, Kate. Come back with me to the house, and let's get back to work. The media wouldn't get near you, I promise."

Marcus and Stephen came back down the stairs, but Kate didn't look around; she just kept studying Dave. She finally turned and looked at her brother. "Marcus, I'm going back to Dave's."

"I thought you were. I repacked your bag for you."

Dave found his keys and listened with some amusement as Kate turned on Marcus for making that assumption. Marcus was a pretty good guy, all things considered. Dave dropped his hand firmly on Kate's shoulder and turned her toward the door, cutting her off in midsentence. "Stephen, you'll bring out to the house anything Marcus missed?"

"Sure."

"Thanks. Let's go, Ladybug."

Kate swung back to Marcus. "Great, now you've got Dave calling me that. Did you even tell him what it means?" she demanded.

Marcus rocked on heels, arms folded. "That you're either a lady or a bug depending on how annoying you are? Sure, I told him. You're buzzing like a mosquito at the moment."

"Try a bee. You are about to get stung."

Marcus just grinned. "Nice to have you out of your funk. Go get back to work, Kate."

SEVENTEEN

"Let's solve this case. The answer has to be somewhere in these piles of data." Dave heard Lisa from his vantage point at the base of the stairs where he was waiting for Kate to appear and wondered with some amusement how he had managed to miss the fact Lisa was the bulldog of the O'Malley clan. It was Saturday morning; the case had become stuck, and Marcus had recommended last night that it was time they shook things up—hence the invasion.

Dave's formal dining room had become a mini war room.

Marcus apparently had some serious strings he could pull, for seven large boxes of files now sat against one of the dining room walls—copies of everything that could be found on Wilshire Construction, Tony Emerson Jr., Nathan Young, Ashcroft Young, and Henry Lott.

Lisa, Jack, and Stephen had trailed Marcus in the door, helping him carry the boxes. How Marcus had managed to get clearance for them to see the files, Dave didn't want to know and wasn't going to ask. He had thought it was a full house only to have Franklin and Graham appear next from Kate's office, and then Susan and Ben from his. He was beginning to feel like a poorly paid doorman. If the ten of them couldn't make sense of the data, it wasn't there to be found.

Dave paced at the base of the stairs, beginning to think Kate was intentionally stalling.

Grinning, Marcus leaned against the doorpost beside him. "Waiting on a woman is a very bad sign."

He had to smile. "Lay off, Marcus. If Kate figures that out, my goose is going to be royally cooked."

Marcus laughed. "Lisa sent me for Post-it notes and masking tape."

"Do I dare ask what for?"

"Probably not."

Dave thought for a moment. "Try the top left drawer of my desk."

He sipped his coffee and wondered what it took to get out of this family once you were in. It didn't take much effort to realize the crowd now plotting strategy in his dining room had adopted him. No, maybe it would be better to make this a permanent arrangement. With Jennifer getting married, the family would balance out four girls, four guys. But if he dated Kate, the numbers would tip five to four in the guys' favor. His grin widened. Kate would be ticked.

"What are you grinning at?" She stopped one step up from him.

"Nothing." He let her take his coffee. "Sleep okay?"

"Fine."

He wondered how true that was but didn't push it. "Good."

She tilted her head. "Where is everyone?"

He turned her toward the dining room. "There."

"Then I guess I had better get to work."

"I noticed you're stealing my coffee again, but I'll let you get away with it this time."

"It needs more sugar."

"Why do you think I let you have mine rather than let you fix your own?"

She disappeared into the dining room with a laugh.

"There is nothing on this security tape that shows Tony Emerson messing with that laptop." Jack set the tape on the dining room table and dropped back into a chair.

Lisa, on the other side of the table, looked up from her printouts. "You're sure?"

Dave looked up from the case file he had been reading to listen to Jack's conclusion.

"I've been through it three times. There is a total of eight minutes and fifty seconds where the laptop is not in view; six minutes of that was when it was with Peter Devlon, so I can't rule out that Tony didn't touch it. But there is nothing here that proves he did, only that he did meet with Nathan Young."

Dave watched Lisa scan the large pieces of easel paper taped to his dining room wall, find the right purple Post-it note, and remove it. A yellow Post-it note went up in its place. Lisa was playing colors. Every piece of data was labeled—red for guilty, green for innocent, and yellow for inconclusive. It was a crazy way to work a case, but he had found after an hour her visual system worked. At the moment, with half the questions eliminated, Tony looked circumstantially guilty.

"So we still don't know how the bomb got into the briefcase," Dave observed.

"It's circumstantial that it was Tony Jr. It could just as easily have been Peter Devlon," Jack replied.

Lisa looked over the unresolved Post-it notes. "Okay. What about Wilshire Construction? Do we have any leads on why Tony's company was having such serious cash flow problems?"

"Stress *serious,*" Marcus added from the other end of the table. "From the bank records on the line of credit, it looks like he lost almost a quarter of a million dollars in the last year. I'm surprised the bank didn't pull the plug on him months ago."

"The records I've got make it pretty clear his suppliers were beginning to demand cash on delivery, no longer willing to extend even thirty days of credit," Susan offered.

"You ought to read the union contracts," Stephen added. "Two months ago they forced Tony to renegotiate the contracts so that medical insurance and retirement payments would be made weekly, concurrent with paychecks."

"Had he ever missed those payments?" Lisa asked.

"No."

"Then the unions either knew or suspected something," Lisa concluded.

Stephen nodded. "Looks that way."

"So what was going wrong? Lack of business? Cost overruns?"

"He's busy, and I have yet to find any particular job that is hemorrhaging red ink," Ben noted.

"But he was laying off people," Lisa interjected. "Correct?"

Franklin nodded. "Seventeen in the last three months alone. This business was running on fumes, and he was juggling every week to keep it floating."

"I think Tony was paying off someone." Kate dropped that fact into the room, and it landed like a bombshell.

Dave studied her pensive face for a moment. "What did you find?"

She set down the company books she had been paging through, looking at her notes. "I'm honestly not sure. It looks like nothing at first, just another subcontractor. But it's odd. There aren't invoices for materials on file as there are with every other subcontractor, just reimbursements. It's like the subcontractor doesn't really exist. And when I dig deeper, the payments each month keep adding together into nice round numbers. Five thousand, ten thousand, spread across a few checks. This last month for example: two checks, the first $2,046.11 for cement; the second, $2,953.89 marked lumber."

"Five thousand dollars. Pretty convenient."

"Exactly." She turned pages in the registry. "It's been going on for months."

Jack walked a nickel through his fingers, thinking. "I don't get it—if someone was bleeding Tony dry, wouldn't he get angry at the person squeezing him, not the banker holding his line of credit?"

"You would think so," Lisa agreed.

"Unless they were one and the same," Marcus said quietly. He looked over at Dave. "Can we get the canceled checks for those last payments, see how they were endorsed?"

Dave nodded and reached for the phone. "I think we had better. Kate, what are the check numbers?"

She wrote the numbers and amounts down, then slid her notebook over to him.

A red note went on the board. Blackmail was a pretty good reason for murder.

"Okay, we've got two new stickers to resolve—who was blackmailing him, and why?" Lisa commented.

"Kate, when did the payments start?" Marcus asked, reaching for the blue binder that was the last bank audit for the First Union Bank.

She hunched over the table, paging back through the check registry. It took her several minutes to find it. "Nine months ago. It looks like October 15 is the first payment for $9,500."

"And you think he paid out how much? Roughly?"

Kate did some quick calculations. "Maybe two hundred thousand, give or take."

"And all the checks below the federal notification amount of ten thousand dollars—so even if they were converted and deposited as cash, there would be no immediate trail," Marcus both stated and asked.

Her eyes narrowed. "Yes. Banker knowledge. Or someone who launders drug money."

"Exactly." Marcus started thumbing through the accounts.

Kate glanced at Graham. "Didn't Henry Lott claim in his interview that he suspected Wilshire Construction had been used in the past to launder drug money?"

"Yes, but I talked to narcotics, and it was old news. They've checked periodically, and the business has been clean ever since the kid took over."

Marcus marked a page in the printout. "I think I've found the account. The first deposit is right—$9,500, October 18. There is over a hundred fifty thousand still in the account."

"Who was Tony paying off?"

Marcus double-checked the account numbers. "Nathan. It looks like it might have been routed through another account first, but the money was definitely ending up in Nathan's account."

Stephen set aside what he was reading. "What did Nathan have on Tony to be able to blackmail him like that? And why so much blackmail he put the company out of business as a result?"

"He knew something about Wilshire Construction?" Lisa offered.

"Even if he did, why would Nathan risk it?" Jack asked. "Wasn't this guy supposed to be lily-white—head of some big banking conglomerate?"

Kate nodded. "We thought so."

Marcus tapped the printout. "We've definitely found a money trail. Who could explain the reason?"

Kate rubbed her eyes. "Nathan—he's dead. Tony—he's on the run." She sighed. "Marla."

"Yes." Marcus reached for the phone. "If there is a third person who would know, his wife Marla is a good bet. She got along well with Linda; let's see if she wants to add anything to what she said."

Jack scanned the notes and shook his head. "It's got to be drug related. Nothing else makes sense. Everywhere you look there's a tag that somehow leads back to drugs."

Lisa lined up those notes, and there were a lot of them. "I agree, it's there, but it's too nebulous."

"All we've really got so far is Nathan blackmailing Tony, and Tony killing him," Dave concluded.

Kate closed the Wilshire books and slid them back to the center of the table. "Dave, let me see that transcript from Ashcroft Young's trial."

He found the gray trial transcript binder and passed it to her. "Still think there is some link between both Nathan and Ashcroft getting killed?"

"I just can't buy the fact it was a fluke he was killed, too. Did we ever sit down and plot out a list of Ashcroft's enemies?"

"It is awfully convenient that the blackmail began a few months after Ashcroft was released from prison," Marcus agreed.

Dave glanced between the two of them. "You really think someone planned for Nathan to walk on that flight at the last minute?"

Marcus shrugged one shoulder. "I don't know what I think. It's simply...interesting...that a man who probably had a lot of enemies ended up dead."

Dave looked over at Ben, then Susan. "What do you think?"

"I agree with Marcus," Ben replied after a moment. "Ashcroft—if he came out of prison looking for trouble, he's the type that could find it in a hurry." Ben leaned forward in his chair and started turning down fingers one by one. "We know Ashcroft dealt drugs and at one time had a network operating through O'Hare. We know the blackmail started soon after he was released from prison. His brother is a banker. Even if we can't prove money laundering, the situation smells like it."

Dave thought about it. "So was Ashcroft the intended victim?"

Marcus smiled. "Good question. I bet we could find a long list of motives for killing him."

Kate tossed her pen on the table. "With Ashcroft as the target, we have known criminal activity, an unknown but probably long list of enemies, and a very big problem in the timeline. There's just no getting around the fact Nathan was a last minute walk-on for the MetroAir flight."

She then gave the other scenario. "With Tony going after Nathan, we've got means—he had access to explosives; motive—he was being blackmailed; and opportunity—he's on tape as one of the last two people to see Nathan."

"He's also disappeared," Lisa added.

Kate nodded. "He's also disappeared. But it's still an enormous amount of overkill and a big risk that doesn't make sense."

"Hold it, Kate." Dave rapidly flipped back in his notes. "Nathan wasn't supposed to take that MetroAir flight. Remember what Devlon said?" He found his notes from that meeting. "Nathan was scheduled to take the private company jet to New York. It wasn't until after the meeting with Tony that he changed his mind, decided at the last minute to take the MetroAir flight."

"So Tony never intended the overkill," Kate speculated.

"Exactly."

"And the risk of planting a bomb—play your cards right and if those security tapes don't convict you, they create reasonable doubt."

Dave nodded. "So the risk might actually have been a good gamble."

Kate finally shook her head. "I don't know. We're making this kid out to be a very well-planned, shrewd, no-nerves-showing type of guy. But he doesn't have a serious criminal record; his wife is shaking in her shoes, and Henry Lott called him *that young brat.* It still doesn't compute." She pushed back her chair with a sigh. "I need a walk and some more caffeine."

The news that Tony Jr. was her brother broke in the media just before 7 P.M. Kate watched the first five minutes of the special news report, then retreated as far as the rose garden and sat with her cold soda resting against her jeans.

They had called it a day shortly after 5 P.M. so Marcus, Ben, and Graham could get to the evening update meeting. Marcus was going to fill the other investigators in on what they had so far. Kate was relieved in a way that the family wasn't here. This was a private grief, a private pain, and it cut deep.

"Are you okay?" Dave asked quietly, settling into a seat nearby.

She didn't have words, simply shook her head. She was related to a man who had blown up a plane. She couldn't even put into words what it felt like.

"Kate, it's still speculation. We are so far from knowing everything that happened. You have to know we're barely past the beginning of this investigation."

It was nice that he was trying to offer the reassurance, but its impact was muted by the reality. The press was screaming the news: *Bombing Suspect Related to Investigating Cop.* The assumptions in the story didn't matter. "Are you sure you can keep the press away?" She asked, keeping her focus on work.

"Yes."

"It's going to get rough."

"I've dealt with worse. Kate, look at me."

She reluctantly turned her head.

"It's okay to explode. You're worrying me."

Kate fought back the desire to cry. "I can't change any of this."

"No. But you're giving up. I can see it happening."

She reached over to squeeze his hand, hearing how badly he wanted to help her; she deeply appreciated that fact. "I'm temporarily retreating, Dave. Don't worry. I'll find my sea legs again. I just *hate* having my name plastered all over the news." She didn't want to talk about it anymore, didn't want to *think* about it. Tony Emerson Jr. was going to destroy her life before this was over. She was surprised Dave was not backing away from her; she didn't have years of experience with him to generate the kind of loyalty he was showing to her.

She entwined her fingers with his. "They are going to put me on administrative leave, move me out of this job, something," she said quietly, admitting her biggest fear. "The pressure created by the media attention will demand it."

"I've met your boss. There is no way Jim will let that happen."

"He'll try to protect me. It may be taken out of his hands."

Dave squeezed her hand. "If the worst case happens, and they do? How are you going to cope?"

Kate closed her eyes, relieved he wasn't trying to pretend it couldn't happen. "I've endured worse."

"The O'Malleys will be there for you. I'll be here, too."

"I appreciate that."

Dave hesitated. "You should have more than your job at the center of your life, Kate. Put God in the center. He won't shift even if everything else gets taken away."

Dave, if your God were there, if He cared, why is He letting my life be shaken apart? She was wrestling to understand how what she had read in Luke fit with what was going on, but she wasn't ready to talk about it. She certainly wasn't ready to believe. She bit her lip, not wanting to be rude but knowing she couldn't deal with this subject tonight. She looked over at him, hoping he would understand. "Change the subject, Dave? It's not that I want to knock what you believe, but your God is already supposed to be in the center of this, and I don't like what I see. I'm just not up to a discussion about it tonight." She saw him pull back as if slapped, his expression showing his hurt before it went carefully neutral. She tightened her hand to apologize even as he released her hand.

"Sure. Better yet, I'd better go check security on the grounds for the night." He got to his feet, his voice tight. "I'll be a few minutes."

Kate watched him walk away, then raised her hand and squeezed the bridge of her nose, wanting desperately to throw something, anything, for being such a jerk. She knew how important the subject of religion was to Dave. It wasn't like she hadn't been thinking about what she had read in the book of Luke during the quiet moments of the last two days. She owed him the freedom to mention the subject without having her bite his head off. He'd been listening to all her problems since this disaster began, had been trying to help, and she'd just shown him she didn't have room for his priorities.

There were days she was a fool.

She might as well have never gone to bed. Kate lay staring at the ceiling, watching the moonlight paint shadows around the room. The depression was heavy.

Dave was a nice guy, and instead of being able to have something with him, she was in a situation where they were both getting hurt. She should have stayed with Stephen and not come back here despite the media risk and the threat it would mean to be out in the open. She didn't want to look like a coward, but she didn't have the strength to deal with this. Dave deserved better, and she'd managed knowingly to hurt him this afternoon.

She was running, mentally, emotionally. She just didn't want to deal with the past, and every time he got close, she felt it clawing back at her. The survival instinct of her childhood was back center stage—run away before she got hurt.

She rubbed her hand across her face, looked again at the clock. Two minutes had passed since she had last looked. At this rate she was going to count the seconds until dawn.

Wondering if insomnia was going to be a permanent reality, she rose and quietly dressed in jeans and a sweatshirt. It would help to get out of the closed four walls. The night looked quiet and calm; she might as well sit outside and enjoy the stars.

She turned off the alarm as Dave had shown her and descended the stairs. Two steps from the bottom, the world around her erupted. The lights snapped on, a piercing alarm sounded.

Dave was at the top of the stairs, breathing hard, before she had oriented herself in the confusion. "I didn't set it off, I swear."

He hurried down the stairs past her, pulling on his shirt. He silenced the audible alarm on the pad by the front door. "Grab your phone and get back upstairs. There's a second sidearm in the safe in my room. I left it open." He was already moving to the back of the house, keying the radio he carried. "Ben, what's on the video?"

She nodded and bolted back upstairs. She hadn't set it off, she knew she hadn't.

The picture over his dresser had been set with a hinge and was moved to the side, leaving visible an open safe. She reached for the Glock inside and fitted a clip. She felt marginally safer just carrying the weapon although it came with a sense of dread for the possibility of ever having to use it. A reporter? Please let it be something innocent. She moved to her bedroom, scanned the front grounds and saw nothing moving.

She moved downstairs to rejoin Dave. This was a big estate; even with one other agent stationed at the guardhouse, Dave would need the help doing the search.

The sliding glass doors to the back were open an inch. She stepped outside. "Dave?"

"Here, Kate." He was crossing the grounds to the south of the rose gardens. She moved to join him.

"You two can relax. I've got the culprit," Ben radioed. "Our prowler is back, Dave."

Dave visibly relaxed. He flipped on his flashlight and directed her toward his partner coming around the house.

"Who?" Kate asked, confused.

"Marvel. We thought he had found a new home; it's been a couple months since he last put in an appearance. But I should have planned for him."

Ben was carrying a fat, yellow tabby.

"He's named Marvel because it's such a marvel he's still alive. He must be the dumbest cat in the city," Dave remarked, smiling. "For some reason he likes to warm himself on top of one of the sensor posts. He has to climb a tree to get up there and dangle himself in the air to drop down on the camera perch, but he keeps doing it. The only thing we can figure is it's warm and it feels good on his old bones." Dave took the hissing cat from Ben and gave him a good-natured rub behind the ears. "You just like to cause us all kinds of trouble, don't you?"

"I'll reset the grid," Ben said, slipping his radio back on his belt.

"Thanks, Ben. And you might as well kill the camera feeds, just leave the infrared hot for the night. I'm sure he'll be back to his old habits as soon as we set him down."

"Will do."

Dave glanced speculatively at Kate. "Want to carry him? He's your typical tomcat. Bad mannered. Likes to eat."

She laughed softly, well able to see the two of them had nevertheless reached an understanding. She bet the cat set off the security alarm just so he would guarantee he got a meal out of the deal. "Sure, give him here."

She let out a small huff as the cat became hers to hold. "This isn't a cat; it's a small beast covered in fur."

"It would be nice if he got too fat to climb that tree."

"You could move the camera you know."

"He'd just get more creative."

She rubbed the cat's ears, ignoring the rumble. She somehow figured it was as close to a purr as this cat could get. "What are we going to offer him to eat?"

"There's some grilled fish left."

"That sounds like a four-star feast."

"He'll have it on the back patio. I made the mistake of letting him inside once. A house cat Marvel is not."

Already becoming attached to the heavy cat in her arms, she found the idea amusing. "Well, while you fix him some baked fish for his delight, fix me a milkshake, and Marvel and I will share some dessert."

"Deal. Now hand me that Glock. I'm more comfortable without my guests being armed."

"Gladly." She handed it over, and he removed the clip.

They walked back to the back patio. The earlier depression was gone, and in its place were a few moments on the back patio entertaining a cat with an attitude.

She fell in love.

When Dave brought out the dish with fish, the cat attacked it.

Dave handed her a tall glass. She had learned early on that milkshakes were one of his specialties. "Thank you."

"My pleasure." He settled on the chair beside her with a tall glass of his own. "Greedy little devil."

"He's hungry."

"Somehow I think he's always hungry."

When the bowl was empty, Kate filled it with a little of the milkshake. Marvel wasn't sure what to think about it, was tentative about getting his nose close to it, then began to cautiously lick it.

She was surprised when the cat stepped back from the dish and hissed.

"What?"

"He's got an ice cream headache," Dave explained.

"Oh, you poor darling." She felt horrible. She scooped the cat up to rub its head while Dave laughed.

"The cat will live. I promise you."

"You could have warned me."

"Why? You would not have given him the ice cream, and he loves it."

She shot Dave a skeptical look, but the cat was trying to get out of her hands. She let him, and he returned to the dish, showing a little more caution this time.

"What were you doing up when the alarm went off?"

She had hoped to avoid the question. "I just couldn't sleep."

"Anything you want to talk about?"

"No."

He was quiet for a moment. "Fair enough. We're taking tomorrow off."

"What?"

"We're taking a break. No case files, no notes, no interviews. We both need a break."

She thought about it. The idea felt wonderful. Maybe she'd be able to sleep again. "Deal." The cat finished licking the bowl clean and walked, tail swishing, over to the next empty chair, leaped up, and promptly began to groom his coat, pausing occasionally to stare at them.

"Think he'll stick around?"

"Probably."

"That would be nice."

Dave winced as the cat jumped across into his lap, dug in his claws, and tried to get near the tall glass he held. "It depends on your perspective."

She laughed.

"If he sticks, he's yours."

"Marcus gave me a dog with an attitude; you're giving me a beat-up tomcat. Should I see a pattern in this?"

"Absolutely." He scooped the cat from his lap and held him out. "Marvel, if you're smart, you'll be nice to her. She's the one who thinks you're adorable."

Kate had to hold him still while he thought about bolting, then he malevolently stretched out across her lap.

"Looks like you've got a cat."

Kate looked over, hearing the satisfaction in Dave's voice. "And here I don't have anything to give you," she said tongue in cheek.

"Just make very sure it's something that doesn't breathe, okay?"

"Come on, Kate, the day is wasting," Dave called from downstairs.

She hurried to get her hair brushed. "I'm coming. Hold on."

He had gone to church on his own, leaving her to sleep in, and she was grateful in a way that he had backed off what had been such a painful collision of values the day before. He'd come home, brought lunch with him, and announced they were going out for the day. He'd proceeded to inform her there was a motorcycle in back that qualified as his pride and joy, and she had ten minutes to get ready to go.

She'd scrambled. She loved the idea. She grabbed her leather jacket, knowing regardless of the temperature she would need the protection. She trusted Dave; she didn't trust the other drivers. She joined him downstairs.

"Where are we going?"

"Wisconsin, a quiet out-of-the-way lake. And if you're really good, I'll even bring you home."

She wrinkled her nose at him. "Where's this second helmet you said you had?"

He handed it over. "It's Sara's, so it should fit you."

She tried it on, slipped down the visor, and glanced in the hallway mirror. "I look dangerous."

"Anonymous at least. Come on. Let's hit the road before traffic flowing downtown to the Cubs game picks up."

He had brought the bike around to the front of the house, and it was obvious it was something he took considerable pride in—the motorcycle gleamed. He tucked water bottles in the carrying case.

"You've ridden before?"

"Jack has a bike." She saw his expression and grinned. "My brother," she pointed out. "I ride with him frequently."

"Just remember to sit straight, and let me be the one to shift my weight in a turn."

She slid on the bike and adjusted the footrests to a comfortable distance. "Drive. I want some wind in my face."

Dave slid onto the seat and kicked the ignition.

Two hours later, tired, content, and smiling, she slid off the bike at a gas and grocery corner store miles into Wisconsin.

"Enjoying yourself?"

"Immensely." She took off her jacket and draped it over the seat, grateful for the chance to enjoy the breeze. "How far is the lake?"

"Five minutes. I figured if we get ice cream here, there's a chance it won't melt until we get there."

"I'll get it. What do you want?"

He handed her a twenty. "Whatever you're having."

Kate nodded and headed for the store. She felt the attention that came her way from others at the store, the kind of open curiosity natural between travelers in a new environment. She looked like a casual biker. It created a reaction she didn't normally get. When people looked twice, it was typically because she was a cop, not because they were quietly wondering why she and Dave traveled by motorcycle rather than car.

She wandered through the aisles to the back of the store and the glass door freezers and took her time considering options. She bought strawberry ice cream and added a box of plastic spoons. It was fun doing this for a day instead of working. She didn't goof off nearly enough.

"Give me the twenty."

This wasn't happening. She felt the knife tip prick her ribs from behind at the same instant her peripheral vision caught the stockroom door swinging back the other way and saw in the small pane of glass the kid who had made the threat. It was a teen, barely fifteen, sweating—she could smell the desperation. Clearly the crack problem was as bad in Wisconsin as it was in her Chicago neighborhood; she'd seen that look of desperation too many times. He'd stepped out of the stockroom and was probably planning to retreat the same way.

She shifted the twenty dollars from the palm of her hand to between her middle fingers, extending it to him without saying a word. What a mess. It wasn't even her twenty bucks. And he was going to use it to get high.

He grabbed the bill, stepped back, and she turned and rammed the open flat of her hand under his nose. If she broke his nose it was incidental, she just wanted to guarantee he dropped the knife. If he used the knife once, he would use it again, next time on someone he might hurt. The teen howled, the knife dropped, and the boy made the mistake of reaching down for it. She hooked a foot behind his and put him on his back.

Dave laid a cautious hand on her shoulder, and she about hit him, too. He had seen enough to get the drift. "I've got him, Kate."

She stepped back while he hauled the teen to his feet.

"Buy a box of plastic sandwich bags and get that knife in evidence. You ever testify in the Wisconsin courts?"

"Once."

"Fastest courts for juvenile cases I've ever seen." He looked her over. "You just couldn't take a day off, could you?"

It was said with humor, and she let herself smile in return even though what she wanted to do was hit something to get rid of the fright. "If I were working today, I would have wasted time trying to convince him he really didn't want the twenty bucks before I just took the knife away."

Dave laughed. He got a good hold of the back of the boy's collar and steered him toward the front of the store. "Okay, son. Lesson one. Next time, you really don't want to try and rob a cop."

By the time the local cops had taken statements, reports had been filed, and they were officially free to go, it was almost 5 P.M. Dave slid the paperwork into the bike satchel, glanced over at her, and straightened. "What?"

"I'm sorry about all this."

"Why? You didn't cause it."

"I was looking forward to a day off."

"The sun hasn't set yet, has it?"

"No."

"Then give me a chance to get creative here. I'd like to think I could make some of this up to you."

"Make it up to me?"

He nodded and handed her the jacket. "I chose the place to stop, remember?"

"Now that you mention it…"

"What do you think about ostentatious displays of wealth?"

"What?"

"Just answer the question."

"Tacky."

"I figured that would be your answer." A long stretch limousine tried to maneuver into the parking lot never designed for a car of its length. "So I asked for your basic black instead of your more flashy white."

"You did what—"

She had to laugh as he walked over and held open the limousine door. "Two hours on a bike when you're tired is not fun. Kevin volunteered to drive the bike home. We'll make the trip in a little more comfort."

Kate vaguely remembered Kevin when he got out of the passenger front seat as one of the men who did landscape work for Dave. "I can't believe you did this."

"Two phone calls. The second was for the order of Chinese take-out. I believe someone mentioned you like wontons?"

"I'm sold." She slid into the backseat of the limousine and felt her body sink into the plush leather. The car was huge. With the facing seat it would allow four people to travel in comfort with their legs stretched out. Dave joined her.

"This is really ridiculous. Do you know what my family will say when they hear how I got home?"

"Don't tell them." Dave made himself comfortable as the car pulled out of the parking lot. "It's got a TV, too. We've got food, entertainment, tinted windows. I'd call it a date, but you're still in jeans."

She was too amused by how pleased he looked with himself to do anything but laugh. They were stuck in traffic for an extra hour during the drive home. It was the first time she had never cared.

"Canceled checks confirmed what we suspected. Nathan was apparently blackmailing Tony. One hundred and eighty thousand was paid to the fictional subcontractor, and it all ended up in Nathan's private account. Whatever Nathan knew, Tony was willing to pay handsomely to keep it quiet. Do we have any idea what it was?" Dave asked, looking around the table. The group had reassembled early Monday morning, picking up where they had left off in the work; already the first pot of coffee was gone, and they were well into the second.

"I still think it's drug related," Jack offered, looking at the Post-it notes. "We know Tony was fired from O'Hare under the suspicion that he was moving drugs. Eight of his coworkers went to jail, but the cops didn't have enough evidence to charge Tony. What if Nathan had that evidence?"

"Assuming it exists—how would Nathan have acquired it? Do we have any indication Nathan was involved in drug activities?"

"Nathan—no, but his brother Ashcroft? According to this—" Kate tapped the Ashcroft trial transcript binder on her lap before reaching over for another doughnut—"we know Ashcroft once moved drugs through O'Hare. What if Tony worked for Ashcroft and there was proof of that, could Nathan have gotten hold of it?"

"Ashcroft went to jail for a decade. Someone had to store his stuff, settle his affairs. It would have fallen to Nathan," Graham offered. "A notebook, a tape, it's possible."

"Tony Jr. didn't start to work at O'Hare until after Ashcroft went to jail," Marcus cautioned, looking at the easel sheet with the master timeline.

"Ashcroft could have continued to run his business from inside prison," Graham offered.

"So in order to explain Nathan's blackmail, we need to find a link between Tony Jr. and Ashcroft," Dave proposed, glancing around the table.

Marcus nodded. "Yes."

"This is like looking for a needle in a sprawling haystack," Susan commented, opening a box they had yet to go through. "Dave, which do you want? Tony's O'Hare personnel records or the investigative notes for the charges that weren't filed?"

"Personnel records."

The room was quiet but for the turning of pages.

"Marcus, didn't you say Tony's wife was named Marla?" Susan asked.

"Yes."

"She also worked at O'Hare in the baggage department, the same time as Tony. They must have met there."

"Really? Anything in the cops' investigation about her?"

Susan checked the records. "No."

"The background check we did showed only two parking tickets for her, nothing else, so I guess that's not surprising."

"Found it." Dave pulled out three blue pieces of paper. "Guess who wrote a recommendation for Tony to work at O'Hare? None other than Ashcroft Young."

"You're kidding." Kate reached for the pages Dave offered.

"Didn't they bother to check who his references were from?" Graham asked, astounded.

Dave tapped the top of the sheet. *"Business owner.* Isn't that novel?"

Marcus looked at the timeline. "Ashcroft made the recommendation from jail?"

"Bold fellow, isn't he?" Dave checked the dates. "He would have been three years into his ten-year sentence."

"So he was trying to run his operation from jail." Marcus said.

"Yes."

"That explains the what of the blackmail. Tony worked for Ashcroft moving drugs, and somehow Nathan learned about it," Lisa concluded.

"It's a reasonable hunch. So where's the evidence now? Nathan's dead. At Nathan's home? His office? Tucked away somewhere never to be found?" Graham wanted to know.

"It's going to be rather hard to get a search warrant for a victim's home with what we've got," Dave remarked.

"We can put cars watching both places. If the evidence exists, Tony may try to retrieve and destroy it," Susan suggested.

"Good idea." Ben reached for the phone.

Kate got up to pace the room. "Is it worth killing for? Even if convicted, Tony was looking at what—ten years in jail, out on parole in seven? A decent plea bargain, he's out in five. Why pay almost two hundred thousand and then commit murder to stop that kind of possible conviction?"

Marcus shook his head. "It doesn't add up."

"Exactly. We're missing something. Something big. We just scooped up a little minnow, and a catfish is still lurking in this muck."

"Of all the..." Kate nearly exploded out of her chair a short time later.

Everyone around the table looked up. "What?" Dave asked, speaking for all of them.

She looked at the trial binder as if it would strike out and bite her. "Ashcroft went to jail for a decade for distributing cocaine. Would you like to guess who his partner was?"

Dave could see the anger in her eyes, glowing hot.

"Tony Emerson Sr.," she bit out tersely.

"Your father was dealing drugs?" Dave said slowly.

"He cut a deal with the DA; he got five years' suspended time and three years probation for testifying against Ashcroft. The judge apparently tossed part of the search warrant evidence against him on a technicality, and the DA decided that his testimony against Ashcroft was worth the deal. I don't believe this. Talk about a pot calling the kettle black. They should have put him in jail and thrown away the key."

Stephen offered a slight whistle. "Ashcroft would have been out for Tony Sr.'s blood."

"Put someone in jail for ten years, yeah, he'd hold a grudge. Tony Sr. was lucky; he died in a car accident while Ashcroft was still in jail," Kate concluded.

"Anything suspicious about the accident?" Dave asked.

"He was driving drunk, and he put his car into the side of a tree."

Dave nodded. "It's an interesting link. Does it tell us anything?"

"Just personal family history," Kate replied grimly.

Dave dug his fingers into the back of his neck. Kate didn't look surprised her father had been mixed up in dealing drugs. It was a hard image of her past.

"Do you want me to finish the transcript?" he asked, not sure how to deal with the anger, justified anger, she was feeling.

"No." She pulled her chair back to the table with a sigh. "I've got it."

Twenty minutes later he saw her sit up straighter and pull the trial binder toward her. "Now this is interesting...."

"Got something?"

"Yeah. Ashcroft's bank accounts were frozen—pretty standard stuff, but the guy who originally fingered the accounts and actually triggered the entire investigation? It was Nathan."

"Nathan turned his brother in as a suspected drug dealer?" Dave asked.

Kate nodded. "He sent a letter to the DEA showing a list of suspicious deposits into one of his brother's accounts. It's what triggered the investigation that eventually sent Ashcroft to jail. Tony Sr.'s testimony was used so they could raise the charges to cocaine distribution, not just money laundering."

"So Nathan is into blackmail but won't touch drug money."

"Protecting his banks?" Lisa asked.

"Or kicking his brother where it hurts," Marcus remarked.

It was shortly after 5 P.M. when the last of the folders were closed.

"So what do we think happened?" Lisa asked finally, looking around the room. Dave could tell no one wanted to say what was clear to all of them.

Marcus looked over at Kate, his expression one of quiet sympathy. "Tony Jr. was being blackmailed, forced out of business. That's motive. He used explosives from his own company. He met Nathan at the airport and was able to plant the bomb. That's means and opportunity. Tony Jr. thought Nathan would be taking the private jet, he never intended to kill all those people. That removes the overkill. He's disappeared, not normally the act of an innocent man. That's what the evidence suggests. It may be wrong, but that's what is here. The feud between Ashcroft and his brother is also there, but I think it's unrelated to the events that happened on Tuesday—it was an ongoing family feud, and they are both dead. It's Tony."

Dave listened to him quietly summarize what would go to the DA and knew the case was there. There were still problems. How Tony Jr. knew what type of laptop Nathan carried. Why he had placed the calls to the tower if his intended target was a private jet. But the case was there. He watched Kate drop her head into her hands. She had to hate this job about now.

He kept hoping something would break in her favor, and yet every day that passed, the situation just got worse for Tony Emerson Jr. and therefore her. How long before the stress she was under broke her? She didn't have God to lean on. She was trying to get through this on her own strength, and he knew it couldn't be done.

Dave just hoped she didn't push him away before that crunch time came. He needed to be there for her. It was the one point in time her need for the gospel might overcome her resistance to it.

Lord, please, help her yield. She needs You. She's just too stubborn to realize it. It's breaking my heart to watch her go through this and know I haven't been able to reach her with the gospel. What am I doing wrong? Why can't I get her to listen?

Dave looked over at Kate as she wearily ran her hands through her hair and then began packing away the files in front of her, and he suddenly realized just how badly he had handled the entire problem of faith.

He had been pushing too hard.

He had seen so much emotion in Kate during the last few days he had assumed her decision about God would be an emotional one. It wouldn't be. That wasn't Kate. It would be a decision made with her heart *and* her head. Rather than give her the time she needed to ask questions at her own pace, he had been pressing for the decision. *"Put God at the center of your life."* It had been the totally wrong way to handle that moment of vulnerability on her part, and he had lost an opportunity to simply tell her God cared.

In wanting everything at once, he risked losing everything—that was the bottom line. It was time to back off and get his own act together. Kate needed a friend. It wasn't his job to convince her to believe. God knew best how to draw her to Him. Dave knew that.

It was painful to wait. He wanted the freedom to circle around the table, draw Kate into a hug, and let her rest against him until that strained look on her face disappeared. He could physically keep her safe despite her protests, but at the moment there was little he could do to keep her emotionally safe.

Lord, give me patience with her, please. I need more of it than I have. Her own pace, Yours, not mine, because I can't handle a failure...not on something so important to the rest of my life.

EIGHTEEN

Her family thought Tony Jr. had done it. Somewhere inside there had still been the glimmer of hope that the O'Malley clan would look at the data and find something to change that initial hypothesis; instead, they had found proof to confirm it. Kate accepted it because she had no choice.

Jennifer was due into town tomorrow afternoon. Kate was glad now that Dave had convinced her to invite Jennifer to stay at his house. She talked to Jennifer every day, but it wasn't the same. She wanted the excuse to put her time and energy into Jennifer instead of this case, to be useful to someone instead of being the focus of pity. The O'Malleys didn't mean it, but they were drowning her trying to fix the problem. Kate needed to hear Jennifer's perspective.

"Kate."

The back patio overlooking the rose garden had become her favorite retreat, her spot of territory in Dave's domain that she had appropriated as her own. Kate didn't have to think here, didn't have to consider what was going on in the investigation. At least for a few moments she could forget. She turned her head with some reluctance at Dave's interruption.

He took a seat beside her on the lounge chair. "You once said you wanted a good steak, a cold drink, and a nap, not necessarily in that order. You still interested?"

She saw something in his expression she had not seen before, a deep sympathy, a heartfelt wish to share the pain and take it away, and she drew a deep breath as she felt his words penetrate her sadness. He had remembered, practically word for word. She didn't think she would ever smile again, but this one reached her eyes. "Yes."

His hand brushed down her cheek. "Close your eyes and start on that nap. I'll wake you for dinner in about an hour."

It was a quiet dinner, eaten on the back patio, finished as the stars began to shine. Kate carried their dishes into the kitchen while he closed the grill; then she slipped upstairs for a moment. She owed Dave something, owed herself something.

When she returned to the patio, he handed her a bowl of ice cream.

"Thanks."

"Sure"

She ate half of the ice cream before she opened the topic she was still uncertain about raising with him. "I read the book of Luke the other morning."

"Did you?" He sounded pleased but continued to eat his ice cream, didn't leap all over the comment as she had been slightly afraid he would do. Maybe they had both learned something from that last aborted conversation. "What did you think?"

"The crucifixion was gruesome."

He was silent for several moments. "A cop using the word *gruesome.* It helps to see that scene with fresh eyes. As time goes by, it becomes easy to say He was crucified and immediately go on."

She set aside her ice cream. "I've got some questions I need answered before I talk to Jennifer."

"Sure." He opened the top of the carafe to see how much coffee was left, refilled his, and after a nod from her, refilled hers.

"It might be a long conversation."

"Discussions about Christianity should never be sound bites. I've got as much time as you want to spend."

"When it is over, I still won't believe." She felt compelled to warn him.

"You don't now, and I still like you." He smiled over at her, and he actually sounded relieved. "Would you relax? I don't mind questions, Kate."

She realized her shoulder muscles were bunched and forced herself to let go of the tension. The fact she could talk about a crime easier than she could this subject annoyed her. "That's one thing that struck me early on about you; you're comfortable with what you believe."

"I am. Jesus encouraged honest questions. In Job, God says, 'come, let us reason together.' What do you need to ask?"

She appreciated the simplicity of what he offered. Not a lecture, not pressure. A sounding board. She so desperately needed that tonight. She flipped through her notes for a moment in the light from the kitchen, then closed the spiral pad and set it aside. "I need some context. You believe Jesus really lived."

"I do. Roman historians of the time wrote about Him. Agnostics will argue over who He was, but even they concede there was a man named Jesus."

She thought about what she had read that morning, then slowly began to think out loud. "If I accept the premise that God exists and that He created everything, it is logical to infer He would be able to do what He liked with His creation—heal someone who was sick, still a storm, raise the dead—the things I read about in Luke. The power to create grants the power to control."

"You surprise me."

"Why?"

"You easily accept the premise that God could exist and do what the Bible claims He did. Most people want to say there is a God and yet dismiss the miracles as something that didn't occur."

"The Bible has to be all true or all false. Otherwise, it would be everyone's interpretation. There is no logic to that."

"It's all true."

"If it is, then I have three initial problems with what I've read."

"What are they?"

"God should be just. Yet Jesus did not receive justice. He was innocent and God allowed Him to die. God should be consistent. Jesus healed in Scripture every time He was asked; yet Jennifer believes, prays, and is dealing with cancer. God should care. From what I've seen during my life, He does nothing to intervene and stop violence. Either God is not involved, or He has an ugly side."

"The mysterious plan of salvation, unanswered prayer, and the character of God. Not a bad threesome. Most theology students would have a hard time articulating a better list." Dave sipped at his coffee.

"To answer your first question about justice, you have to understand God's mercy. He is both just and merciful in equal measure. Why did Jesus say He came?"

She flipped through her notes. "That story with—" she hesitated on the name—"Zacchaeus? Jesus said He came to seek and save the lost."

"Part of the mystery of salvation is that to save the lost, us, Jesus had to die in our place."

"That doesn't make sense."

"The people that killed Jesus, what would justice say they deserved?"

"To die."

Dave nodded. "Yet Jesus chose to forgive them. Why?"

"He was showing mercy."

"You don't like that word."

She rolled one shoulder. "It denies justice."

"You instinctively feel the great quandary. How can justice and mercy exist in equal measure? To ignore the penalty, justice is shortchanged. To ignore mercy, people have no hope once they have done wrong—and we have all sinned."

"They can't exist together as equals."

"Kate, God didn't shortchange justice to grant mercy. He paid the full price Himself."

She thought that through. "He was innocent when He died."

"Exactly. Jesus can forgive sins; He can extend mercy because He already paid the full price justice demanded. He took our punishment."

"If He paid the price for everyone, a blanket forgiveness, then mercy is larger than justice. They aren't equal."

"Earlier in Luke, Jesus warns—unless you repent, you will perish. God's wrath against those who reject the sacrifice His Son made will be fierce. There is restraint now, to see who will accept, but on the day Jesus returns, the judgment will be final. Those that haven't accepted the mercy extended to us by Christ's sacrifice will face justice."

"Is that restraint total? God allows anything to happen now, regardless of how innocent the victim?"

"I can understand why you feel God is too hands-off. The plane is a pretty vivid example of the violence man can do to man. God really meant it when He gave man free will to do either good or evil. He allows sin because He allows our choice. But He is not standing back, uninvolved. I know prayer makes a difference."

"Then why hasn't it made a difference for Jennifer? According to Luke, Jesus healed everyone who asked Him."

"Do you remember the parable of the widow and the judge?"

"The only person who could help her was the judge, so she pestered him until he gave her justice."

"Jesus told the parable because He wanted to remind us to pray and never lose heart. He knew we would wrestle with unanswered prayer. If God decides no, or not now, does it mean He is not loving? He does not care? He is not capable? Jesus knew we would not always understand God's plans. He simply assured us not to be discouraged but to keep praying."

"Jennifer having cancer, that is supposed to have a noble end?"

"God is allowing it today for a reason. He may tomorrow decide to cure her."

"Then how do you know He is loving?"

"Because the Bible says God is love. You take Him at his word, even if you don't understand the circumstances. It's called faith."

Kate tried to wrestle through the conflicting emotions. "There is nothing easy or simple about being a Christian."

"No, there isn't." Dave ran his hand through his hair. "I believe, and I still wrestle with the questions you ask. The bank holdup, it had the effect of pushing me closer to God. Is that a sufficient reason to explain why God allowed it to happen? Probably not. Is the fact we met that day a sufficient reason? If Henry Lott had not come into the bank, would he have committed suicide instead? We don't know what God sees in a situation, why He allows something to happen. The bomb on the plane—only God can understand tragedies like that. You learn to trust Him, even when you don't understand."

"'I don't understand' describes exactly where I am."

"You ask good questions. It's the place to begin."

"You would like me to believe."

He looked over at her, and his half smile was rueful. "More than you will ever know."

"I can't believe just because you want me to or Jennifer wants me to."

"I know. Faith is the ultimate personal decision. No one else can make it for you. That is all the more reason to ask the questions."

Kate leaned her head back. The night sky was spread out as a shimmering layer of stars. So much power, so far away. Was God near or far?

She was grateful Dave didn't try to break the silence. The questions lingered, unsettled. From her perspective, belief looked like stepping off a cliff, and she didn't want to get any closer to the edge.

NINETEEN

Jennifer pulled out a kitchen chair, having finished a quick phone call, leaving a message with her fiancé Tom's answering service so he would know she had arrived safely. "I like your friend Dave."

Kate smiled back at her sister, pushing the glass of lemonade toward her. "So do I."

There was an inevitability now about the case against Tony Jr., a matter of waiting for him to be found. Kate had spent today pacing, expecting at any time to hear her pager go off. Having Jennifer arrive late in the afternoon had been a relief, had changed the entire tone of the day for the better.

It wasn't apparent when she looked at Jennifer that anything was wrong. Even the strain of the long trip back was not obvious. Stephen and Jack had brought her out to the estate, and the three of them had been laughing as they came in. Kate was sure neither of her brothers suspected anything. Jennifer had explained the trip as a consult on a case. She hadn't mentioned the fact she was the patient.

"You didn't mention he was British."

"I thought you would enjoy that."

"He reminds me of that singer I had a crush on when I was…sixteen?"

"About that."

"I thought so. I still love the accent. So—" Jennifer twirled the glass; her eyes twinkled—"this is your childhood roommate talking. How serious is it between the two of you?"

Kate grinned. "Good friends, Jennifer. Just good friends." If her life ever settled down again, she might get the perspective she needed to decide if it could ever be anything more. Dave didn't fit the mold of any cop she had ever met. She was learning to her surprise that protection also felt a lot like care. She would be disappointed now if Dave didn't care enough to know where she was and what she was doing. She found she kind of liked that attention.

"Given the fact I've heard rumors on the grapevine that Marcus approves, I thought it might be more serious."

"Marcus is weighing in?" Kate was stunned. He did not normally weigh in on the family grapevine chatter.

"He decided to let Dave protect you. I guess he felt that deserved an explanation."

"This place served as a safe house in the past; it's simply a logical place to stay."

Jennifer smiled. "You don't have to explain it to me."

Kate rested her chin on her hand and looked at Jennifer. "Dave *is* good-looking."

Jennifer grinned back. "He is that."

They looked at each other with the history of two decades spent together and shared a laugh. "We always said we should get boyfriends at the same time," Jennifer reminded her.

"I'm just glad we didn't actually plan this. It was one thing when we were in high school, another when we are supposed to be adults." Kate used her spoon to fish a lemon slice from her glass. "So tell me, how is Tom? Is he still planning to come up for the Fourth?"

"He'll fly in Sunday night and stay through Wednesday. I've booked a couple of rooms downtown at the Hyatt since he's not been to Chicago beyond the occasional convention. I thought I would show him the sights, take him to the Taste of Chicago."

"How did you manage to get rooms at this time of year? They book six months in advance."

Jennifer touched the locket she wore and smiled. "I prayed. And there were two cancellations."

Kate saw the peace on Jennifer's face and wished she understood it. "Tell me about how the tests went."

"I know now why I like to be the doctor, not the patient. Blood work, CAT scans, a biopsy, more blood work, the tests were like a parade. Bottom line—I'm in great shape for someone who has cancer."

"Do they have a plan to suggest?"

"An aggressive cocktail of chemotherapy and radiation. Surgery is a nonstarter."

"When do you begin?"

"It depends if Tom wants to have a bride that has hair or not."

"Jen—"

"That was a joke, Kate. Seriously, sometime in the next three weeks. The radiation comes first, and they may send me to Johns Hopkins for the first round to try to spot target the cancer around my spine."

"Did they tell you what to expect as a prognosis?"

"Kate, it might buy me an additional year."

"That's all?"

"I pulled that guess out of them. They don't like such numbers because they're afraid patients will stop fighting."

"They haven't met an O'Malley."

"Exactly. I'll fight this cancer for every minute I can get. But I may scrap the idea of a wedding and suggest a nice elopement instead."

"The family will understand that once you tell them."

Jennifer drew a circle on the table with her glass. "I'm going to tell Marcus next."

"He needs to know; I hate keeping the secret from him."

"I'll tell him after the Fourth, then let the two of you help me tell the others."

"Okay."

"Enough about my health. What's happening regarding Tony Jr.?"

"There is an APB out on him. Officers are combing his friends and associates to find out who might have seen him. There is no indication he has left the area, but assuming he was well prepared and is traveling with cash, he's probably far away; it could be some time before they locate him."

"I'm sorry for what is happening."

"It's not the shock that I have a brother I never knew about; it's not even the fact he apparently hates me having never met me; it's the reality that he could have done something this horrific. I don't know how to deal with it." She sighed. "Jennifer, how do you deal with the fact Jesus said love your enemies?" She saw her sister's surprise. "I read Luke."

"I wasn't going to ask because I knew how chaotic your time has been." Jennifer studied her. "That is the one thing I thought might be the hardest problem for you in the book; for all the O'Malleys when it comes to that. How do you deal with *God is loving* when you consider the past horrors in each of our lives. I don't know how you are supposed to love Tony Jr., how that applies to this situation."

"I wanted to kill him when I first realized what the evidence showed."

"So many innocent people are dead."

"That, but also just the fact he was there, someone I could hate, with a name I hate, when my father has been dead so many years."

"What do you think now that it's been a couple days?"

"I just want him brought in to face the courts. I want that sense of distance that he is just another suspect in a case. But it's personal, even though I've never met him, and I can't figure out how to get that distance. I'm either angry or sad." Kate studied the water beading on the outside of her glass. "Mainly angry."

"I can understand that. I don't know how the anger changes. I know Jesus has the ability to love the just and the unjust. I guess that is where the change of heart comes from. He does it for us."

"Have you forgiven that drunk driver that killed your parents, Jennifer?"

"Yes. I'm still glad he is doing time, but the hate is gone."

Kate nodded, glad in a way her sister had been able to leave that behind. "I can't undo the fact this guy's my brother, much as I would want to."

Jennifer sighed. "Tony Jr. did a good job messing up your life."

"That he did."

"What else did you think about what you've read?"

"Do you find it easy to do what the Bible says?"

"Not easy, no. But possible. It's different than reading a how-to book and struggling to figure out how. I've found Jesus is much more personal. That prayer makes those directions real for my situation. That tough one, love your enemies, comes with names, things I am supposed to do."

"Give me an example."

"Alisha Wilks."

"You're supposed to love the nurse working pediatrics who doesn't *like* kids?"

Jennifer nodded. "Stop and chat for a few minutes when I make rounds. Smile pleasantly when she complains about their noisy play. I even got reminded to take her cookies on her birthday."

Kate winced. "I bet she complained about the crumbs."

"She did. She's still a terror for the kids, but at least she's a little nicer to mine."

"Loving her means letting her stay in the wrong job?"

"Hardly. I've practically got ordered to stop complaining about it in my prayers and do something about it."

"You've been trying for six months."

"Well, now I've been trying harder. I've met with her supervisor, the head nurse, the chief of pediatrics, and the hospital administrator himself."

"Going to the top?"

Jennifer nodded. "Rocking the boat. The other doctors are shaking their heads, hoping I succeed, but not going near it."

"What happens now that you're going to be off full-time practice for a while?"

"The partners are closing ranks to cover my patients, and Tom has a doctor friend out East who's a great pediatrician. He's agreed to come out for six months, get a feel for my patients, the practice."

Kate knew that had to be killing Jennifer. She had always wanted one thing: to be a doctor practicing medicine.

Jennifer's hand covered hers. "Don't, Kate. I'm okay with it. I'll still be able to do as much as I have energy for; there will just be someone there to help and do what I can't."

"Do you understand why God has not healed you?"

"Kate, it is a complete mystery to me—I don't know. The Bible is clear and pretty blunt: God hears and answers prayer. I don't understand why there has been no improvement. People at church give lots of confusing justifications for why I haven't been healed, but frankly they sound like excuses.

"I do believe God heals people as a result of prayer. In the years I have been a doctor, I have seen a lot of kids get well when all my scientific knowledge said it couldn't happen. I'm convinced now that I was seeing the power of prayer. Why He doesn't act in my case is a mystery to me, only He knows.

"There has been some good come out of the cancer. I'm certainly going to better understand my patients—being a patient is the pits. And you have to admit, it's changed my priorities in life."

Kate grinned. "Married. It's going to be great."

"I can't wait."

"If you elope, none of us will get to be bridesmaids."

"You do realize being a bridesmaid means wearing a dress."

She winced at the thought. "Maybe you can half elope. Just show up at an O'Malley dinner with Tom and a minister and get married right then."

Jennifer smiled. "I think Dave would prefer to see you in a dress at least once."

"He would." Kate turned to see Dave leaning against the doorjamb, smiling at her. "Does she even own anything but jeans?" he asked Jennifer.

Jennifer grinned back. "Not that you would know it."

Kate scowled at them both. "I'm on call. I can't afford to be caught wearing something I can't live in for a while if I had to."

Jennifer chuckled. "She's good at excuses."

"I bet she would look fabulous in blue."

Jennifer quirked an eyebrow at him. "Want to help pick out bridesmaid dresses?"

Dave slowly grinned. "She'd have to model them?"

"Every one of them."

"There would be worse ways to spend a few hours."

Kate, thoroughly embarrassed, slipped from her chair to get out of the line of fire. Dave took two strides over and caught her hands. "We were just teasing."

"Did I say anything?"

"Your face says it all. You look nice in jeans, especially that old pair with the heart patch on the back pocket." He grinned. "They've shrunk just about perfectly. It's just that you would look fabulous in a dress."

She let a smile slip through. "I'll have you know I look better than fabulous."

"Then how about an expensive date somewhere so you can show me?"

"Wear that teal dress you got in Paris, Kate," Jennifer suggested, smiling as she watched them.

"Paris?"

Kate smiled and nodded. Paris, Illinois, but he could live with the mistaken assumption. Rachel, Lisa, and Jennifer had ganged up on her to celebrate her last promotion and had convinced her to spend almost a month's pay on one single dress. Kate glanced at Jennifer. "Do you think Marcus would approve?"

Jennifer winced. "Dave, how's your health insurance?"

His gaze lazily appraised Kate; then he flashed Jennifer a wicked grin. "She looks that good in it?"

"Yes. Just tread lightly if Marcus sees you together. Protective big brother will have something to say."

"When?"

Kate slipped her hands free of his, then grinned. "I'll think about it."

"Kate—"

"Jennifer and I are going to watch a movie tonight. Do you want to join us?"

"Is it going to be mushy?"

Kate looked at Jennifer. "We'll compromise with a comedy. We girls get the couch, you get a chair."

Dave waved them on. "Go pick it out; I'll make the popcorn."

Kate slouched on the couch to finish the popcorn in the bowl on her lap as the movie tape rewound. Jennifer had just gone up to bed. It was still early, and Kate was toying with the idea of raiding Dave's collection for another movie. The first movie had been great. It had been good to sit with Jennifer, share laughter—be reminded that all the good times with her sister had not suddenly disappeared.

"What would you like to watch next?"

She tilted her head back to look at Dave. "You're game for another?"

"Sure." He opened the cabinet that held the movies.

She scanned his selections. "How about *Apollo 13?*"

"You like the classics."

"Love them."

Dave put in the tape. "Should I make more popcorn?"

She considered what she had left, then grinned. "This should get me to *'Houston, we have a problem.'*"

He chuckled as he took a seat on the floor, using the couch as a backrest. "Just let me know. I'll pause the movie. Is that what you remember from your favorites, the dialogue?"

She nodded. "Occupational hazard. Voices are my thing. I can pretty much give you word for word my favorite movies."

"I remember the music."

"Do you?"

"*Magnificent Seven* is the best."

"The guys wanted to make that our theme song. We shot down the idea."

"It would have been a great choice."

"But it had one flaw: It only allowed for seven."

"True."

The opening movie credits began.

Kate glanced toward Dave a few times during the movie. He was absorbed in the story even though he must have seen it numerous times. She liked that about him; he focused on what he was doing. It was a long movie, and by mutual consent they paused it halfway through.

"This was a good choice."

Kate trailed him into the kitchen with the popcorn bowls. "Very."

"Join me for some coffee?"

"Sure."

He set about fixing it. "Can I ask you a serious question?"

She tilted her head. "Sure."

"Why don't you date cops?"

"Wow, you don't mind tossing a tough one."

"It's late. I'm curious."

"Have a reason behind the question?" She laughed at his look.

"I'll take the fifth for now."

She nodded and decided he deserved a serious answer. "You haven't been around for the 2 A.M. pages; watched me walk out of back-to-back crises; seen me focused on a case to the point I forget to eat. I don't like to explain my actions, talk about me, plan for the future. All those things put together are tough on a relationship." The deeper reason, concern that she would choose the wrong man and walk into a stress-filled marriage was private. She had seen Dave under the stress, and he handled it well.

"Was there someone?"

"A few years ago, a friend of Stephen's. He's in Atlanta now."

"Were you close?"

She shrugged.

"I'm sorry."

"So was I at the time." She smiled. "It's easier now simply not to date cops."

He nodded, handed her a cup of coffee, and slid over the sugar. "Like kids?"

"Who doesn't?" She heard the wistfulness behind the amusement in her own voice. He was broaching a subject pretty dear to her heart.

"Think you will like being a mom someday?"

"Not as long as I'm a cop."

"The two can't go together?"

"No child should have to wonder if his mom is coming home from work."

"Can you imagine a kid having to deal with two cops for parents?"

She was grateful he shifted the topic slightly. "It's not the kid, it's the parents. Even the most rebellious teen would not be able to dream up what cops would wonder about."

"I can just see it—late at night, the kid out with the car, and he's past curfew. Are you the type who would pace or go look for him?"

"I'd be calling the car phone, paging him, and checking with his friends. *Then* I would get serious."

He laughed at the image. "You'd make a great mom."

"Maybe."

He smiled. "You're comfortable hanging out with me."

"Fishing for a compliment?"

"Just checking. Come on; let's finish the movie."

Kate nodded, appreciating the fact he was closing the conversation for now. She was coming to respect that about him. The things he cared the most about were the topics he was the most careful with. She had seen it when he talked about faith, and he had just shown it again. It was a rare trait for most people—patience. As a negotiator she could deeply appreciate it. While she had learned the skill, she sensed something different with Dave. He had the patience inside him.

She knew how much he wanted her to believe. It was probably the only thing stopping that date question he skirted around. There had been numerous friends who had never asked her out because of her job, a few who met her family and chose not to ask, but Dave was one of the first to do so because of principle. It said something about his priorities that she admired.

It was also frustrating her—this was one evening where she would like to be sharing the couch with him rather than have him apparently content sitting in a chair several feet away.

Kate went no farther than the patio chairs, settled down, and made herself comfortable. The movie was over. She had convinced Dave to go ahead and turn in. She would be up in a while and would set the security grid.

The stars were bright tonight. She rested her head back, studying them overhead. It had been a day of great emotional swings, and this pause, this solitude was desperately needed.

She was falling in love with him.

She was emotionally vulnerable right now. She knew it, and she tried to remind herself of that as she felt her heart softening. Jennifer's cancer, learning she had a brother.... Other than Jennifer's engagement, Dave was the only good thing that had happened recently. That's why his steady support was making a big difference in her life right now.

But no matter how hard she tried to explain away her emotions, she knew she was denying the truth. She was falling in love with him.

It was scary. She didn't want to risk getting her heart mangled again in a relationship that could go nowhere. It wasn't only the question of faith; she had only to look around Dave's home to see how different their respective backgrounds were.

The idea of sharing the depth of her past with anyone, let alone someone she wanted to think well of her, petrified her. And as much as Dave knew, he knew only the tip of what he would eventually learn if it did get serious between them. She poured herself single-mindedly into her job because she knew how risky it would be to open up the rest of her life. Would Dave understand the things that gave her nightmares? The underlying reasons the O'Malleys were so important to her?

She would love to be able to rest the weight of what was happening on Dave, curl up in the protection he offered, and find a safe haven here. It wasn't fair to him. She had to consider the reality of her family, his.

What would his family think of her? She hadn't met his sister Sara, but Kate knew how close Dave and Sara were. How would Sara feel about having her brother involved with a cop? Sara had seen enough violence in her life already; somehow Kate didn't think it would be easy for her to have another cop in the family.

She sighed and forced herself away from it. Love just wasn't a good idea. Not with the two of them. They were destined to be only friends. And there were other questions she had to decide tonight. She couldn't afford to think about it.

She turned her attention away from the emotions that confused her to the reality she had to accept and find a way to live with.

She had a brother.

Did she want justice or mercy? It was a hard decision to make, but it was time to make it. Tony Jr. was her brother. She wanted to deny the ties, keep away from the hurt, but she couldn't any longer.

The circumstantial evidence strongly suggested he was guilty.

When he was located, did she want to meet him? He was family. Yet to get to know him in these circumstances would only make the hurt go deeper.

Did she want to distance herself from the case, from him, or did she want to seek some form of mercy from the courts? Did she owe him that because he was her brother? Did she owe herself that?

She needed there to be mercy, she had to have justice. Both now strained inside in equal measure. She could feel the paradox that Dave described existed in God—justice and mercy in equal measure. God might be able to create a situation that had both, but she didn't have that ability.

She looked at the expanse of stars.

"Jesus, I'm not sure yet what I believe, but I'm trying to understand. You said You hear and answer prayer. If You do exist, I know You'd understand the struggle I'm facing. You're bigger than I am. You make decisions I will never understand. If there is a way out of this dilemma, will You show me?"

Prove he's innocent.

It was such a soft reassurance; it was the peace she felt first, then the reality of the words. Yes, that was the only way out of this problem. It would be mercy for Tony and justice for the families.

Evidence pointed to Tony being guilty. To prove he was innocent…could it be done?

She pushed out of the chair with new resolve. There was only one way to find out.

TWENTY

He had called in a bomb warning. If he weren't already dead, he would have killed him just for that.

Where were the videotapes? Three hours of looking had led to nothing. He knew they were here somewhere.

If that call led back to here and they started digging into the past, his perfect alibi would be destroyed. All because that stupid fool had to go and taunt the cop.

He was glad he was dead. He had made the decision in the spur of the moment. No more than twenty seconds to see the opportunity and take it. He was glad he had taken it. But where were those videotapes?

He had thoroughly searched the apartment, a long tedious job when he had to make sure everything went back neatly in its place, and the tapes weren't here. Short of tearing out a wall, there was little else he could do. If the videotapes hadn't already been destroyed, they had to be tucked somewhere.

Probably a safe-deposit box...but he had found no key.

Maybe they were lost forever now.

Maybe.

Maybe not.

They would make no sense to just anybody glancing at them. They were simply old security tapes after all—over a decade old, and the company that made the machine required to play them didn't even exist anymore.

Even if they were found and turned into the cops, they would be of very little use unless someone actually explained where they had been taken and what they captured.

There was only one other person still alive who knew the videotapes existed and what they meant.

He could kill him, too.

He lingered on that thought, considering it, tasting it, evaluating the risk.

Yes. If he had the chance, he would kill him. Then this conspiracy would be down to one, with no witnesses left. The future he had dreamed about for years was his, and he was not going to let anyone take it from him now.

Yes. Best to kill him.

TWENTY-ONE

Dave tucked the cordless phone tight against his shoulder as he wrestled on his shoes. Sara's call had woke him up, and he realized with some dismay that he had slept through his alarm. The house was quiet, and that had him concerned. Jennifer normally slept late, but Kate—if she was out wandering the grounds it wasn't going to be good.

"How is Kate doing?"

"I'm worried about her," he replied, understating the reality. He was afraid for her, and how she was coping. He was having to stand back and watch the situation tear her apart, and it was killing him. Several times in the last few days he had found her sitting on the back patio, staring off into space, not hearing him join her. For a cop trained to react to her environment it was a disturbing thing to see. About the only thing that drew a smile from her these days was that fat tabby cat, and Dave found it annoying to be jealous of a cat.

"I have to imagine it will take a while to get over the shock of learning she not only has a brother, but that he's probably responsible for the bombing."

"Shock I could handle. Something else is going on." What, exactly, was hard to figure out. Kate was ignoring the manhunt to find Tony Jr., something he had expected her to want to be very involved with. She had instead been going back through the files for the last several days with an intensity that had him worried. Dave had no idea what she hoped to find. She wasn't saying, and his offers to help her had been dismissed with an absentminded thanks but no.

"Would it help if I came over?"

He brightened at the idea. "Actually, yes. I would like you to meet her, and it would be a good distraction for an afternoon. And I think you'll like Jennifer; I'd like you to meet her while she is here."

"Why don't Adam and I join you for lunch after church tomorrow?"

"That would be wonderful. And I want to hear all about your trip to New York. You didn't call me nearly often enough."

"It was an adventure. I spent too much money. Adam had me walking until I thought I would collapse. Lunch with my editor went well. I'm frankly relieved to be back home."

"Shall I plan to put something on the grill? The weather should be nice."

"Please. I'll put together a salad and bring dessert."

Dave slipped on his watch as he said good-bye to Sara. He set the phone back on the night table. It would be good having them over; he had missed her the last couple weeks. And he really wanted Sara and Adam to meet Kate.

He headed downstairs to start breakfast and get himself some coffee. If he didn't strongly suggest breakfast, Kate tended to bypass the meal. Dave stopped, surprised, and backed up. Kate was in the living room, comfortably slouched in a chair, feet propped up on the coffee table, folders stacked around her on the floor, a notepad in her lap. It looked like she had been there for a considerable amount of time. "Have you been up all night?"

She looked at her watch and grimaced. "Yes."

Diverted from his plans to get coffee, he crossed the room to join her. Unable to resist, he ran his fingers lightly through her hair. "What are you doing?"

She leaned her head back against his hand. "Now I know why a cat enjoys that so much."

Her sleepy smile was adorable, and he wanted to lean down and kiss her, but wisely smiled instead and let his hands slide down to her shoulders and gently squeeze. "You're punch-drunk tired."

"Probably. I've got an idea."

Curious, he took the seat across from her. "Tell me."

"It untangles if you look at the fact Ashcroft wanted to kill Nathan."

"Ashcroft is dead."

"Ignore that for a moment."

Ignore that for a moment. Right.

The focused grim stress from the last few days had disappeared, and he wasn't about to say something to bring it back. Realizing he was humoring her, he nevertheless settled down to listen, relieved to have her at least willing to discuss what she had been doing. "Go on."

"This was more than a family feud. Ashcroft wanted to kill Nathan because he was the one who turned him in and sent him to prison for ten years. He was bitter and angry and out for revenge. Ashcroft wanted his brother to suffer.

"Next, look who cut a deal with the DA to provide evidence against Ashcroft. Tony Emerson Sr. So if you buy the fact Ashcroft would go after his brother for writing that letter to the DEA and starting the drug investigation, he would certainly like to go after the man who testified against him. But since Tony Sr. is dead, that leaves Tony Jr. and, through a twist of fate, me."

Dave stopped thinking about humoring her and started seeing the connection she was making. It was curious. "Where does that lead?"

"What if it was Ashcroft blackmailing Tony, not Nathan? Ashcroft might be able to implicate Tony as one of those who had moved drugs for him at O'Hare. So Tony was paying off Ashcroft. It makes more sense than Tony paying off Nathan. That never did feel right."

"Then how did the money get into Nathan's account?"

"Someone put it there to make Nathan look less than lily-white. I haven't figured that out entirely, but it's logical. If Ashcroft hated his brother enough to kill him, he would certainly like to destroy his reputation in the process."

"A lot of assumptions."

"It's there and plausible. Ashcroft planned to kill his brother and frame Tony. He was laughing at me when he made that Wednesday call because he could do it and drag me down at the same time."

Dave nodded. Someone had gone directly after Kate by using her name in the bomb threat, by sending the black rose, by making the calls. He could see Ashcroft doing that.

"Tony is being blackmailed, and he's running out of money. Ashcroft puts the pressure on, blackmails Tony to kill Nathan. Then Tony gets lucky when Nathan decides to take the MetroAir flight and the bomb kills Ashcroft as well."

"Tony is still guilty."

She tossed her pen across the room.

Startled, he looked at the pen buried in the dirt of a fern and thought the flash of temper was a pretty healthy sign. Her aim was good, even upset; he'd have to remember that. He looked back at her, seeing the frustration. "It's a good theory, Kate. It just doesn't clear Tony."

"Well, I hate the current theory."

"We watched Ashcroft Young on videotape. He was at the gate terminal reading a newspaper. He could not have planted the bomb. We know from the security tapes that the laptop was checked by security; the bomb was not in the laptop when Nathan arrived at the airport. So even if Ashcroft did plan to have his brother killed, he still had to have help. Tony is still a coconspirator."

She groaned and rubbed her eyes.

"You think he might be innocent?" That realization surprised him. He knew she would like him to be, but the evidence was overwhelming that Tony was involved.

"I would prefer it." She sighed and looked over at him. "I want to go to First Union Bank today."

He hesitated. "Okay. May I ask why?"

"We go back to the beginning. I want to know about that foreclosure rate increase. The bank manager might give us a straight answer."

"You're sure?"

"Yes."

He offered his hand. "The bank opens at 8 A.M. We can have breakfast before we leave."

"Good. Jennifer was going to sleep in, but I'd like to be back early."

"I'll leave her a note as to our plans."

"Okay." She walked over to retrieve the pen. "Sorry for throwing stuff."

She sounded so sheepish about it that his chest rumbled with laughter when he hugged her. "With that aim, at least I won't have to wonder if I get hit by accident."

⁂

The glass doors to the bank had been replaced. The walk across the parking lot to the doors was very much a repeat of the time weeks before, down to the asphalt sticking to her tennis shoes. Staff at the bank looked startled when they walked in and were recognized. The bank manager came to meet them, his smile profuse. "Thank you for what you did that day."

Kate remembered him. He had done pretty well for the pressure he had been under. She smiled in return, liking him. "You're welcome, Mr. Tanner. I was wondering, could you answer a couple of questions for us?"

"I would be glad to. Please, come into my office; have a seat."

Looking around the bank, the evidence of what had happened had been erased. Kate followed him to his office and took a seat.

"We noticed the mortgage foreclosure rate was unusually high this year, like Nathan was raising cash. Would you have any idea why?" Dave asked.

"Actually, I would say it's more like Peter Devlon was the one raising cash. If someone with a loan problem could get past Peter to see Nathan Young and have a reasonable case, the loan would be extended. I was getting faxes from him all the time directing action to be delayed on certain loans."

Dave glanced at his notes. "Was there any such arrangement for Wilshire Construction? I understand Tony had a meeting with Nathan, and the notes were e-mailed here."

"Let me check the business loan files." The manager moved to the file cabinets and came back a few minutes later with a thick blue file. "Yes, here are the meeting notes." He scanned them, then frowned. "They are from Peter Devlon in regards to the meeting, basically say no change is to be made, and to proceed with terminating the line of credit." He set aside the page, looked at the next one, and smiled. "Here's what you are looking for. Nathan faxed this to us shortly after the meeting. Tony asked for a ninety-day extension so he could complete the Bedford site, and he was willing to put up his home as collateral. Nathan said to accept the offer."

"Such a dichotomy in instructions was common?"

He waffled his hand in the air as he smiled. "There were meetings, and there were meetings. Peter is very much by the book, and Nathan didn't like to meddle in what were day-to-day decisions. Since Nathan married, the banks had become more and more Peter's to run. But on the side, when it wouldn't rock the boat—yes, this was common."

"How did Peter typically react when he found out?" Dave asked.

"Furious, of course. He'd rant on about his authority and order us not to follow such substandard practices, but there was little he could do to enforce that edict. Nathan was *the* boss, after all."

"And Nathan made the banks more human," Kate observed.

"Not always good business, I know. But the personal touches were Nathan's way of doing business."

"Is there a time stamp on the fax, when it was sent?" She asked.

Mr. Tanner scanned the document. "Tuesday, 10:48 A.M."

"Where does Wilshire Construction stand now?" Dave followed up.

"We put through the ninety-day extension when we received the fax Tuesday morning."

"Would you know why Nathan and/or Devlon was raising money?" Dave asked.

"It's not exactly hidden knowledge that Devlon would have liked Nathan to take the Union Group's banks public. The stock he hopes to receive in such a situation would be worth millions. Every few years he was able to convince Nathan to tighten policies, raise more cash, to get the banks ready for such a move."

"Nathan used the cash to go buy another bank instead?"

The manager smiled. "Exactly. Nathan was content to keep the banks under private ownership."

"Thank you, Mr. Tanner. You've been very helpful."

Kate waited until they were back in the car. "Tony didn't have a reason to kill Nathan Young; the loan had been extended."

"He was still being blackmailed, and he couldn't make those payoffs even with a loan extension," Dave pointed out.

"True," Kate conceded, "but who was really blackmailing him? Nathan or Ashcroft? And what do you want to bet Devlon now convinces the widow she would be better off a multimillionaire, that it's time to take the banks public?"

"Probably. But how does that relate to Tony? He's the one getting blackmailed."

Kate sighed. "I don't know."

"Where to now?"

"Back to your place. I want to look at the files again. I missed something; I know it."

"Kate, you need to get some sleep."

"Later."

"Try now. Lean your seat back; you can get a thirty-minute nap on the way back to the house."

"Seriously?"

"Kate, go to sleep."

It was his look as much as his words that made her chuckle and recline her seat.

"Good night."

Kate sorted through the boxes in the formal dining room and pulled out two to take over to the table, following a hunch.

Dave leaned against the dining room table beside her. "What are you looking for?"

"I don't know. I'll know when I see it."

"I'll get you an early lunch."

"Thanks." She barely noticed when he ruffled her hair before he walked away.

He came back with two plates, sandwiches and fruit, and took a seat beside her.

"The explosives." She took a bite of the sandwich he had brought her as she paged through the file. "These are Wilshire Construction's invoices. There should be something here."

"How does that help Tony? Proving the explosives used in the bombing were shipped to Wilshire Construction just tightens the case against him."

"Only if he took them."

She pulled some paperwork from the file with a frown. "They bought two lots of explosives for the same demolition. That's interesting. Look at the dates and project codes."

It took Dave time to trace through the paperwork. "It looks like one shipment went to the subcontractor doing the work; the other appears to have disappeared. It's not in the inventory or the shipment log as being returned. There is a receiving slip for the shipment on April 5; we've got an inventory audit on…April 8. The lot is missing."

"Any signatures?"

"The receiving clerk and the supply manager, nothing unusual. Those signatures are on 80 percent of the paperwork here."

She looked over at the boxes. "Dave, hand me that top far left box. Henry Lott kept all his old timecards."

"You don't think…"

"April 5 to April 8."

They split the stack and thumbed through the timecards looking for the right dates. Dave found two, she found one. "He worked security those three nights."

Dave got to his feet. "Come on, Kate, let's go see Henry."

Kate leaned against the one-way glass as she watched Henry Lott. They had decided it was best if Graham did the interview. Henry still looked angry, bitter, much as he had at the bank. Kate was grateful she didn't have to hide what she was thinking and pretend to like him at the moment.

"Henry, we know the explosives that brought down the plane came from Wilshire Construction. We know you worked security the three nights when they were taken. Do you really want to be an accessory to 214 murders? Who was around the site those nights, Henry?" Graham's voice sounded slightly hollow through the audio feed.

"He told me to look the other way. Paid me a grand. Cash."

"Who, Henry? Who told you to look the other way?"

"Ashcroft."

"Blame a dead guy. That's real smart, Henry."

"I'm telling you the truth. Ashcroft shows up, tells me to look the other way, mind my own business, and he pays me a grand to do it. I don't want the grand, but I don't want the trouble either. He's a mean one, Ashcroft. So I looked the other way."

"Just like you used to do in the old days, huh, Henry? Turn your head and mind your own business? Is that how you knew they were moving drug money back before Ashcroft went to jail?"

Kate glanced at Dave. It was enough. "Ashcroft taking the explosives puts him deeply involved."

"He's still dead, Kate."

They had enough for a warrant to search Ashcroft's home. Kate didn't know what she hoped to find. Evidence being used to blackmail Tony, something to suggest where it was.

What they found was an apartment of a man who had thought he was traveling to New York for a few days. The place was neat, orderly. The draperies had been closed; the refrigerator had been emptied of perishables and the trash taken out.

The answering machine flashed several times showing messages.

A dead man's home always felt slightly...wrong.

She played the answering machine messages, found nothing there, and then played the introduction message, hoping to find she recognized Ashcroft's voice. To her profound disappointment, there was no introduction message recorded, just the recorder beep.

She followed Dave through the rooms as they decided where to begin.

Within an hour, Kate stopped expecting they would find anything. Ashcroft didn't keep even general financial records such as cable bills, magazine subscriptions, and ATM slips. There was no trace of a safe-deposit box key, anything to indicate other places he might store records.

There were no address or appointment books, no calendars. It was possible they had been with him on the plane, but Kate figured it was more likely Ashcroft's habit to write nothing down.

"Anything?"

She looked up from the last drawer in the desk. "No. You?" Dave had begun in the living room, then moved to the bedroom.

"No."

Kate sighed and looked around the room for anything she might have missed. "We've got another dead end."

"The press will show up here soon; we should go. The guys from downtown can finish this."

She nodded, knowing Dave was right. She walked back with him to the car. "This is getting depressing."

"We know a little more. Ashcroft was expecting to go to New York for a few days."

"It's as good an alibi as any. If Nathan had gotten on his private jet carrying that briefcase, he, his wife, and Devlon would have been killed, and we would have naturally been looking at Ashcroft, only to find we had him on security tapes sitting at the MetroAir gate."

"Exactly. I'm sorry, but none of this really helps Tony."

"I know." She sighed. "We've got to explain what happened without Tony being part of the story. I really do think it's there. I just don't see it."

He put his arm around her shoulders and gave her a hug. "You're trying, Kate. That's what matters. I'm proud of you."

She really hated the fact she blushed. "Really?"

"You're acting on the hope he's innocent. That can't be easy given how much the evidence suggests otherwise."

"He's family, Dave. Not the kind of relative I would have chosen, but he's family. He's going to get every benefit of the doubt I can give him."

"Jennifer, if you're going to prune my roses for me, at least cut yourself a couple bouquets to take inside. You're embarrassing me." Dave handed her a glass of ice tea as he joined her.

Jennifer smiled. "They are so beautiful. I'm just enjoying the chance to work with them. This is pure therapy. Where's Kate?"

"I hope she's taking a nap, but I somehow doubt it. She's probably back in the files again. I wish I had something to offer her, but I'm just as stumped as she is."

"She's like this when something about a case is bugging her. Don't worry about it. She can conserve energy better than anyone I have ever met."

Dave cut her one of the American Beauty roses. "I'm glad you agreed to stay here. Kate needs the diversion. She literally lit up when she saw you arrive."

"I'm the favorite of all the O'Malleys, didn't you know that?"

He laughed at her tongue-in-cheek reply. "I think you might be, if only because they're relieved you are the youngest, not them."

"Do you have any idea what it was like to have six guardians?"

"Stephen wouldn't be so bad. And having Kate for a roommate had to be an adventure. But Marcus? How did you ever get a date past him?"

"Put them all together and they were pretty intimidating." Jennifer smiled and turned her attention to the white roses. "Could I tag along with you to church in the morning?"

"Sure. Services are at ten o'clock."

"Thanks."

Dave crouched down beside her to gather up the cuttings. "How do you think Kate will react if I invite her to come?" It was a casual question, but one he carefully weighed asking. He was aware Jennifer paused, studying him a moment before answering.

"She's the type who will invite herself if she's interested. But I'm planning to ask her."

"I don't mean to ask behind her back, but is she interested in Jesus, Jennifer? Or has the bombing pushed away that interest?"

Jennifer rocked back on her heels. "Dave, she has to get to the point she can trust Him. She's not there yet. It's not just the confusing realities such as why God allowed the plane to be bombed, or the difficulty in following commands like 'love your enemies.' Those are there, but ultimately, with Kate, it's personal. She has rarely heard 'I love you' where it was meant without strings. Give her some time to realize Jesus means it."

"Her childhood."

"Exactly. It was pretty rough."

"I've been figuring that out."

"There's hope for her. The Lord won't change what He means with 'I love you.' Kate's the type that will keep testing it until she figures that out."

"I had figured it would be understanding justice, mercy, and the rest."

Jennifer chuckled. "Oh, she'll challenge you for answers and explanations on all kinds of tough questions. She's nothing if not logical, and she expects to find out answers to questions or at least understand the theological knot. Giving her a simplistic answer is the worst thing you can do. But the bottom line with Kate is whether someone really is who he presents himself to be."

"I'm sorry God used something so difficult as your cancer to push Kate to look at the gospel."

"You noticed that, too? I didn't mention it to her."

"I noticed. What do you want me to pray for, Jennifer?"

"That God gives me enough time to complete this mission."

He understood it, what would be closest to her heart. "To lead all the O'Malleys to Jesus."

"Yes. Kate's the first nick in the wall. When she comes around, there will be two of us to convince the third. When the third believes, the fourth becomes easier to convince."

Dave chuckled. "And here I thought Kate was the plotter."

"I'm the youngest one in the family, remember? I know how to get things done."

"Here you two are. I wondered where you had disappeared."

Dave turned to see Kate crossing the patio. "Come convince Jennifer to cut herself a bouquet of flowers."

"How about a bouquet of pink ones, Jen? They would look great in the living room."

Jennifer nodded and began to cut the bouquet. "They would."

"Sara and Adam are planning to come over for lunch tomorrow. Anything in particular you two would like fixed on the grill? Ribs? Pork chops?"

"You're brave enough to fix ribs?" Jennifer asked, glancing up.

"Sure. Think Marcus and rest of the family would be willing to join us?"

"Jack and Stephen are off duty; Lisa would be the only question mark," Jennifer said.

"I'll ask them," Kate offered.

Dave heard the pager. It startled him, and he tensed as he realized it was Kate's pager going off.

She reached down and shut it off, reading the number as she reached for her cellular phone. She dialed. "Yes, Jim."

Dave watched her eyes shadow. "Of course. I'm on my way."

She closed the phone and studied it for a moment before looking up at him. "Can I borrow your car?"

"About this case?"

"No. It's unrelated. They've got a standoff, and I'm the closest." She looked at him quietly, waiting.

She couldn't tell him details; he knew that from dozens of his own cases. He wasn't ready for this, but he had to be. She was going back into danger because it was her job to do so. It was a test, not one she had asked to create, but one that was suddenly there between them. "Can you duck the press?"

"Jim said he would make sure my name stays off the radio."

He reached in his pocket, found the keys, and handed them to her. "Switch the radio to your department frequency. It's set to ours. Be careful."

"I will. I may be late for dinner."

He watched her leave and wanted to swear at her for making her last words such a casual comment. If something happened to her…

Jennifer slipped her hand into his. "Relax. She doesn't take unnecessary chances."

"Jennifer, she'd step in front of a bullet if it were necessary, the same way she would step in front of someone going for a basket and take the charge. She would never think about the risk to herself; she'd just act."

"You're in love with her."

His frustration over the situation was intense. "And it's the most miserable reality of my life. My hands are tied."

"She'll believe, Dave. She has to."

"I just hope it's sooner rather than later." He sighed. "She's going to be annoyed, but it will be easier to wait where she is than here. Would you like to come along?"

Jennifer smiled. "No. I've got more practice at this than you have. But call me when you know something, please?"

"I will."

Kate leaned her head back to catch the breeze coming along the side of the brick apartment building, tired but content after two hours spent settling a violent quarrel that had begun over the simple reality of melted ice cream. She wondered how many cases this made that she had resolved peacefully. It was an idle thought since she only counted the ones that had failed. A win was simply to be enjoyed.

Dave sat down beside her on the metal stairs of the fire escape. She was too tired to be surprised that he had found her. She gratefully took the water jug he offered her, drinking half the quart of ice water before pausing. "It was hot up there." She looked over at him. "Any word on Tony?"

He shook his head. "No."

She nodded. "It would have been too good to hope for."

"You settled this one peacefully?"

"Yes."

She finished the ice water. He handed her an apple. She smiled. "I prefer junk food. This is marginally healthy." She took a big bite anyway and wiped away juice running down her chin with the back of her hand.

"Natural sugar. You'll get used to it."

Her smile broadened. "You're trying to change me."

"If I didn't meddle, you wouldn't have anything to complain about."

She grinned and toasted him with the apple. "True."

Her shoulders were stiff, and she rubbed the right one, hoping to relax.

"Let me."

He started to work out the kinks. "Lower to the left." She relaxed. "Right there."

"What were you leaning against? You've got a rust streak down your back."

"Do I look like a skunk?" She tried to twist and see, finding the idea amusing.

"Maybe a red one." He dumped some water on a towel and wiped off the worst of it. "Would you like to go chase the sunset?"

She was working on the apple and wasn't sure she had heard him correctly. "Do what?"

"The sunset is beautiful from the plane. And the weather is perfect. The case investigation won't slow down if you take a couple hours off. It would do you some good to get away from it for a while."

"Tonight?"

"Yes. We can catch it if we hurry."

"I thought we needed to stay away from O'Hare."

"Sara and Adam took the jet to New York. I had them route it back to Milwaukee. It's not too far a drive."

She was ready for a nap, but she could sleep anytime. She looked at him, trying to decide if it was love or just affection that made his face so endearing to her. "What about Jennifer?"

"Lisa came over. They were making brownies and talking about Fourth of July plans when I called."

Kate nodded. Jennifer was in good hands. "I need to change."

"I'll buy you a tourist T-shirt at the airport."

"I could use something for the baseball game." She saw the question in his look.

"The O'Malleys have a game on the Fourth, and my lucky shirt died last year."

"Really?"

"I did this slide into home, and Marcus didn't move out of my way. I need a better shirt."

Dave grinned at the image. "Something that will make him move?"

"Exactly." She tossed the apple core into the trashcan by the house. "Can you afford me?"

"Probably." He held out his hands. "Come on, let's go."

TWENTY-TWO

Compared to the complexity of O'Hare, the Milwaukee airport was a breeze. They parked in the lot across from the terminal, then browsed in the tourist shops. They passed through security and walked out to the private hangars.

"There she is." Dave pointed to a plane by the third hangar.

Kate stopped, stunned. The plane was a gleaming, midnight blue Eagle IV. "It's beautiful."

"She. This lady has her own personality."

The pride in Dave's voice was obvious. Kate looked at the jet, then back at him. "This is what you fly for fun?"

"Yes. Though I do use it frequently for work. It makes it easier for the team to get around. Come on; let's get you settled inside. My flight plan is already filed. Give me twenty minutes to complete the preflight, and we'll be ready to get in the air."

She reached up to slide her hand across the smooth, gleaming metal of the wing. "It's such a sleek, beautiful plane." Not small either. It would take some walking to circle this plane.

"One of the best." He brought down the stairs and offered her a hand.

"Oh, my." Kate had expected nice, but this was *really* nice. No crammed-together seats or lack of legroom here. It had been configured with plush leather seats and mahogany side tables, and honest-to-goodness wallpaper and blue carpet. There were even two sketches carefully mounted on the cabin wall. "This is great."

"The cockpit has windows that come all the way down to your elbows. You'll see what I mean about a great view."

"I can join you up front?"

"I can even teach you to fly it if you would like."

"Don't you have to be certified to instruct?"

He smiled. "Yes. I'm a good teacher, too. Care to find out?"

She let that settle in. He wasn't joking. "I'll think about it."

He ruffled her hair. "Do. Dan said he would stock the refrigerator for us. Make yourself at home. The walk around won't take long." He stepped into the cockpit, came back with a flight log and checklist, and disappeared back down the stairs.

Kate picked up her bag and moved to the back of the plane. She was going to have a hard time flying on a commercial aircraft after seeing this luxury. The lavatory was full cabin width, with marble counters and matching hand towels. In the drawer she found a sewing kit and small scissors and cut the tag off her new T-shirt.

The evidence that the plane was someone's home in the air began to be apparent as she took Dave at his word and looked around. In the cupboard next to the refrigerator was someone's idea of snacks. Not a small bag of peanuts, but a full can of cashews, half a package of pecans and hazel nuts still in their shell waiting to be cracked. They were bracketed by a bag of Oreos and peanut M&Ms.

A sketchpad was tucked in with the magazines, well-worn playing cards in the pocket beside the table, and three paperbacks beside a stack of CDs. There were feather pillows and blankets, even a teddy bear in the back closet. Kate smiled at the whimsical bear before closing the door. They were touches of people's lives. Neat, orderly, but personal. Touches of Sara by the look of them.

Kate laughed when she stumbled upon the stash of sports equipment. Besides the golf clubs, there were very well broken-in baseball gloves, a couple scuffed baseballs, a Frisbee, even a Chinese box kite. She could just see Dave taking off for a weekend and flying somewhere to join friends for a game of golf. With this plane, it could easily become commonplace.

"Been up to see the cockpit yet?"

She turned and smiled. "Not yet."

"Grab us a couple cold sodas and come join me. You'll enjoy it."

The electronics were not what she had expected to see based on the movies she could remember. Like the plane itself, the electronics were sleek, modern, well designed, and colorful. "Where did all the knobs and dials go?"

Dave smiled. "I know. The dash looks like a nice piece of sound equipment, doesn't it?"

"Built-in radar?"

"Yes. Come on; buckle into the copilot seat. You won't disturb anything."

She slid into the seat carefully, not sure she was ready to have pedals at her feet and a wheel in front of her. You could fly the plane from this seat, and it was intimidating. She carefully put her soda into a holder, fastened on the spill guard top, and quietly watched Dave methodically check settings and work down the checklist on his knee. She recognized comfortable movements that came from thousands of repetitions.

"There are headphones behind you on the right."

She looked around and found them. He showed her the toggle for voice.

She heard him speak briefly with someone over the radio, and a crewman appeared before them on the tarmac. On the signal all was clear, Dave touched one red button, then another, and the two jet engines came to life with smooth, steady power.

He finished working down the preflight checklist, then turned the brace board on his knee and held up his hand to the crewman. He got a smile and wave toward the taxi line with the batons. "We're all set to travel."

She listened as he slipped easily into the tower radio traffic. She wasn't able to understand what was said even though she heard the words, recognized his repeat of the instructions and his acknowledgment. The plane began to roll. Fascinated, she watched him handle it with ease, his hands light on the wheel, and his feet in motion. He took it directly down the centerline of the taxiway and into the queue behind two other planes waiting to turn onto the runway and into the wind for takeoff.

"You use your feet as well as your hands?"

"Rudder and brakes are at your feet. Use the brakes right, and you can turn this plane on a dime."

Minutes later he got clearance for the runway.

It was everything she had hoped for and yet so much more. The plane had much better speed than Kate expected, and Dave handled her with finesse, bringing the nose up and guiding the plane smoothly into a climb.

"I filed a flight plan for us to cruise at thirty thousand feet. Airlines don't usually fly at that altitude. We'll head west toward Denver and be traveling with the sunset for almost an hour, depending on the cloud cover."

He spoke briefly with the tower and moments later reached down and retracted the landing gear. Noise inside the airplane diminished. They traveled through the first cloud bank, coming out above it. The sun was shining on the top of the clouds. "One more cloud bank, and then we'll be leveling off."

Kate yawned to clear her ears as she watched the display climb through twenty-eight thousand feet.

Dave reached down and adjusted the trim, eased forward the nose, then leveled off at thirty thousand feet. "And that's how this baby cruises."

The beauty entranced her. She was looking close up at the top of clouds, not through the scratched Plexiglas windows on a commercial plane. "I can see why you love it."

The top of the clouds came up toward them looking like billowing cotton balls, the high altitude winds tugging wisps of white. She watched new clouds build ahead of them, exploding into the clear air as growing mushroom clouds. "What's it like when these are thunderstorm clouds?"

"If you're high enough to be above the storms, they are a spectacular display. Most of the lightning actually happens up in the cloud, and it will light up like a Christmas tree. The clouds will form very rapidly, shooting thousands of feet into the sky."

"This is already spectacular."

"Just wait. It gets better."

When the sun slipped to the right angle, the clouds suddenly became a blanket of pink below them. "Wow. Have you ever taken a picture of this?"

"A few. But even film can't do the breathtaking color justice."

"How long will this last?"

"We'll be able to stay in this zone of color for probably half an hour. You'll see it paint the canopy of clouds high above us here in a few minutes."

Kate saw the colors of the sky in all their brilliance, from the blanket of pink, to the deep caps of red, and then the deep streaks of blue and gray as the sun slipped lower on the horizon. Dave banked them south, showing her the color gradients appearing. "If we were closer to the Rockies, you would see the snow-covered mountaintops being touched with the color as well."

"Has Sara ever tried to capture it on canvas?"

Dave smiled. "A few times."

"Thank you for showing me this."

"It was my pleasure." He brought the plane back around on a return heading. "Would you like to fly her? Now's a perfect time and place for a lesson."

"What would I have to do?"

"Just put your feet lightly on the pedals and your hands on the wheel. You'll barely have to touch either to keep her on this heading. There's no major crosswind to deal with."

"Are you sure you trust me with your toy?"

Dave chuckled. "I won't let you fall out of the sky."

Tentatively she reached forward to take it.

"Good. Relax your grip a little more on the wheel; hold it like a feather you don't want to crush."

It was as easy as he had described to keep it level; the plane barely seemed to move even though the readout showed them doing over three hundred knots.

"Try a gentle turn, say about ten degrees to the right."

Beginning to anticipate the responsiveness, she brought the plane into a bank to the right, coming out at exactly ten degrees and holding it there.

He chuckled. "I already see a budding perfectionist. Good. Level it out and we'll try a climb."

Kate grinned and smoothly came back level. The fact his hands were comfortably folded across his chest said he either had confidence or strong nerves. Either way, she appreciated the compliment. "I think I could get to love this."

"Hang around, and we'll be dancing around the sky frequently. Bring the nose up in a climb and watch how it changes your airspeed."

She did and easily saw the correlation. "Is this how they do a hammerhead? Go into a pure vertical climb and stall out their airspeed?"

"Yes."

Growing more comfortable by the minute with the fact she was playing with a multimillion-dollar toy, Kate smiled over at him. "Show me how the rudders are used."

Dave grinned, scanned the skies and the radar, then took the controls and slipped the plane left. "Feel how I'm moving them?"

She could, and she memorized the sensation. It was the same light touch as with the turns. "Yes."

"Try it."

The lessons continued until the light was totally gone, and then Dave took over, flying by instruments the remaining distance into the airport. When the plane set down with a smooth, rolling flair, Kate was already regretting they were on the ground. "That was really fun."

He smiled. "Don't worry. You'll get a second invitation."

He taxied from the runway back to the hangar, following the directions given by the crewman with the glowing red batons. When the engines shut down, the still, quietness of the night reclaimed them.

In the glow of the one interior light turned on, Dave completed the flight logbook and slipped it back in the map case.

Kate unbuckled her seat belt, loath to call it a day. Dave stopped her move to slide from the seat with a gentle hand on her arm. "Kate." She looked over at him and saw the smile. "You'll make a great pilot. You really should keep taking lessons."

"You're a good teacher."

"I'm also willing to work for free. How about it? Want to hire me?"

His hesitation, so rare in him, made her smile. "You're hired." She wasn't going to let an offer like that pass by.

She watched as Dave completed his walk around the plane, speaking with the crewman. He stepped back on board for a moment, then came off carrying something white. He joined her as the crewman moved the plane into the hangar.

"What's this?" She was amused to realize he was carrying a pillow.

"You're getting some sleep on the trip back."

"I can't stay up and talk?"

He caught her hand in his. "Not tonight."

They walked together to the car. Kate settled with the pillow, reclining her seat back, turning so she could look at Dave. Would this be the norm for days spent with him if they did try to make a relationship work? Frustrating moments when a case had no apparent solution, tense moments when her pager went off, quiet moments ultimately relaxing together? The idea was getting easier to accept. It was hard to imagine not being with Dave in the middle of a day.

"What are you thinking about?" Dave asked.

"Today."

He glanced over and smiled. "I heard a yawn under that word."

"My eyes are tired." She snuggled into the pillow. "It was a nice evening."

"Yes, I was thinking the same thing. Sleep, Kate."

Her eyes were already sliding closed. "If I don't remember to say good night later, consider it said."

He chuckled lightly and brushed his hand along her cheek. "Sweet dreams."

TWENTY-THREE

Dave stopped at the bottom of the stairs and frowned, then headed down the hall toward the dining room and the smell of coffee. Kate was there, a stack of empty candy wrappers beside her, sipping a cup of coffee, studying the notes on the wall.

"I didn't hear you get up. How long have you been down here?"

She looked over and smiled. "Since about 2 A.M., I guess. I've got something to show you."

She looked...pleased. He pulled out a chair, intrigued.

"Devlon did it."

Where has she gone this time?

She laughed at his skeptical look. "It's all there." She gestured to the wall. "I was almost right yesterday. Ashcroft is the one who started it all. But it was Devlon that helped him, not Tony."

Dave settled down in the chair, willing to give her room to explore ideas. She'd been up most of the night again. She probably had found something. Not what she hoped for but something. "Explain what you've found."

"Ashcroft wanted to kill Nathan because he turned him in and sent him to prison for ten years. He wanted to go after the man who turned evidence against him, Tony Sr., but since he was dead, Ashcroft had to settle for framing Tony Jr. and dragging me down instead. But Ashcroft also wanted to rebuild his drug operation, and that meant the one person he didn't go after was his inside man at the bank." The look that entered her eyes was one Dave had never seen before: fierce, cold, calculating. "Devlon."

She tapped the audit book beside her. "Ashcroft was blackmailing Tony, but Devlon moved that blackmail money to Nathan's account so Nathan would look less than lily-white."

"That makes him a bomber?"

"Yes. Because it means he was doing Ashcroft's bidding. And the evidence suggests he had been doing it for years. With the attempt to convince Nathan to take the banks public, Devlon couldn't afford a whiff of that becoming public."

She tapped the top Post-it note. She had taped up a new easel sheet and done her own Post-it notes. Dave noted her handwriting was atrocious and wondered if she had been filling them out while they were stuck on his wall. He buried a grin; he didn't think he'd win points for asking.

"Are you paying attention?"

"Yes."

She frowned at him. "Pay close attention, buddy; I've been up for hours to figure this out."

"I could use some coffee if this is going to be a long explanation."

She handed him hers without even a comeback, and Dave started paying serious attention. She didn't relinquish coffee easily.

"Nathan turned Ashcroft in, got him sent to jail because of a suspicious account. Guess who brought that account to Nathan's attention?" She tapped a note. "Devlon. He'd probably been handling Ashcroft's drug money for years. When the auditors got too close, he covered his own back."

She tapped the second note. "Ashcroft gets out of jail a decade later and starts blackmailing Tony Jr., squeezing him hard enough he's running out of money. Tony Jr. needs to get the bank to ease up, give him time, but there's Devlon, insuring it's going to play by the book. Tony's looking at bankruptcy, and he can't make the next payment. Ashcroft then moves to pressure Tony Jr. into planting the bomb."

"Which the evidence suggests Tony Jr. did."

Kate shook her head, and Dave was startled at her confidence. "Tony Jr. said no; I'm certain of it.

She walked him through what she thought had happened. "That left Ashcroft with everything arranged, the money moved, Tony Jr. set up to take the fall, the calls made, his alibi established, the perfect opportunity to act, and no one to plant the bomb. But he's got a card with Devlon. So he uses it. Think about it. Ashcroft had enough evidence to push Devlon into moving money around. One step further is planting the bomb in Nathan's laptop. We know Devlon had access; he was the one using it that morning.

"And in the end we get a classic double cross," she continued. "Devlon doesn't like the fact Ashcroft has him over a barrel. But it's pretty easy for Devlon to take care of Ashcroft, he just does some fast talking and puts Nathan on the MetroAir flight as a last-minute walk-on. Good-bye Ashcroft. Good-bye Nathan. Devlon has a nice alibi; he was supposed to fly to New York with Nathan until the last-second change in plans. Tony Jr. looks guilty; Ashcroft who could implicate him is dead; and he walks away running First Union Group, with the prospect of the banks going public now that Nathan is no longer there to resist the idea."

"So he gets everything but the girl."

Kate smiled. "He could be seeing Nathan's wife, Emily, on the side for all I know."

She looked at the board, then back at him. "Do you see any holes? Because I don't."

"The phone calls."

"We still need to track down the voice on the tape, but I now think it's going to prove to be Ashcroft's. And the location the bomb threat call originated from—I'll lay money when they did the tests, they didn't check the power levels from inside a plane parked at the gate. They'll match the footprint we have."

"And the calls to your apartment? The black rose?"

"Both were Ashcroft. If Ashcroft was smart, and I'm willing to bet he was, the calls would have been made from a pay phone somewhere. We might find a florist who remembers him buying the rose."

"How do we prove this?"

Kate began to pace. "Devlon strikes me as arrogant. What do you want to bet he's already moving some of Ashcroft's secret accounts to his own?"

"We go after Devlon's financial records?"

"I would. And what do you want to bet he's already tried to get his hands on the evidence Ashcroft was using to blackmail Tony with? He's going to have problems if Tony starts to talk."

Dave leaned forward and slowly set down the coffee mug. "Kate, if you're right, Devlon is vulnerable to Tony talking—214 deaths vulnerable. He's not going to hesitate to make it 215."

He watched her literally pale in a heartbeat.

"Call Jim. We've *got* to find Tony."

Dave shook his head, dialing Marcus instead. "We've got to pick up Devlon first."

"Call Marla, too. If she knows what's going on, she may be able to convince Tony to turn himself in if he calls her."

He nodded, agreeing, even as he gently pushed her back into a chair.

He had always admired Marcus's ability to absorb information. His questions were brief, pointed, and he went to the bottom line much faster than Dave. Marcus would take care of getting Devlon brought in for questioning.

Closing the cellular phone, Dave called Jim next. The cops were already looking hard for Tony, but at least they would know now he was as much at risk of being a victim as he was a possible bomb suspect. The calls made, Dave closed the cellular phone, set it back on the table, and took a hard look at Kate. He crouched down to get at eye level with her. "It's going to be okay. We'll find Tony."

"I'm scared to death something will happen to him before we find him." Their gazes met. "He's innocent. I've got a brother, and he didn't do any of this."

He wrapped his arms firmly around her. "Sometimes there is something wonderful besides mercy and justice."

"What's that?"

"The truth."

Her smile wobbled a bit. She hugged him, hard. "Could we go to church?"

"Really?"

She nodded against his shirt.

"Why?" He didn't want to push too hard, but it desperately mattered.

Her hand settled over his. "Call it curiosity." Her hand tightened at the look of disappointment he quickly tried to mask. "I'm cautious, Dave, despite all that you see in my job. I'm not going to risk my heart without understanding much better who I am giving it to. That direction in Luke of 'follow me' requires a lot of blind faith in who you follow. Give me some credit for wanting to go forward with my eyes open and not half closed."

"I keep hoping faith will be easy."

She smiled. "Give me time. I make it hard because I have a hard time trusting."

"He's trustworthy."

"Yes, I am beginning to think so." She released his hands and got up. "Let me go check on Jennifer."

Kate was glad she had Dave on one side and Jennifer on the other as they walked through the lobby of the church toward the sanctuary. Ben was trailing them half a step back. Dave diverted them to the balcony where fewer people could approach and start a conversation. Kate wondered if it was to make it easier on her or for security reasons. When Ben took up a position at the stairway exit, she figured it was probably some of both. Dave had been edgy this morning as they left the house. As he had quietly reminded her, the only time Devlon had met her, she had been with him.

The music started, and Kate set aside the problem to focus on the service. She had been truthful with Dave; it was curiosity that made her ask to come. Jesus had heard her first prayer and helped her figure out a way for there to be both mercy and justice. She was curious why He had done that. She owed Him something in return, and if it couldn't as yet be an agreement to follow, she could at least say thank you.

Dave settled his hand comfortably around her waist, sharing his bulletin with the words for the songs. Kate knew how important this was to him, how proud he was to at least have her with him. It was Independence Day weekend, and the choruses were about freedom. Freedom in Christ. Was that what Dave and Jennifer had found? Freedom?

She was beginning to understand the distinction between "follow me" and "follow these rules." Jesus was the person who made it all fit together. Mercy, justice, loving others. Jesus had shown her love when He answered that first prayer. There was no reason to do that on His part. Except maybe the desire for her to notice and say thanks.

One of the stories from Luke came back to mind; it had been on the lower left-hand side of a page, toward the back of the book. A story of ten lepers. They had all asked for mercy, and Jesus had healed them all. Only one had returned to say thanks.

Thank You, Jesus.

You're welcome. The soft reassurance was gentle; it felt warm inside like a smile. She let out a soft sigh of relief; at least one instinctive step toward Jesus had mirrored that of another fellow searcher long ago.

The songs ended, and they took their seats again.

Was she ready to take the step she knew was next? She had reached the point it no longer felt like stepping over a cliff to trust God with her future. But was she really ready to answer "follow me" no matter where it might lead? She had been wrestling with it since reading Luke. Some of the pages were now worn with her notes. Knowledge was no longer the issue. Trust was.

Dave had shown her in his life a peace that came from inside, and she knew after weeks of observation that the peace came because of his faith. She wanted to enjoy that peace, but it was a very big step.

She had never been one to step back out of timidity. Her life, certainly her job, would be easier with that resurrection promise to cling to, a guarantee of eternal life. Even a possible future with Dave rested on this decision.

Kate shut out all the pluses and minuses, closed her eyes, and took a slow breath, retreating as she did when in a crisis to the quiet place inside where she could listen to her own heart. Trust. It was there.

Jesus, I'll follow. It's a choice I make, knowing what that means. I will follow where You lead, and do what You teach. I do believe Your love explains Your mercy. I choose to believe it will never waver or burn low, that Your love will be there for me for an eternity. Forgive me for a lifetime of saying not now. Forgive my doubts, my sins, and my stubborn heart. And please, make me a better cop when You place me at the crossroads of another person's life.

If there had been a sparkle of warmth before, now the joy was so intense it felt almost hard to breathe.

"*...for there is joy before the angels of heaven when one sinner repents....*"

She wanted to laugh as she realized the Scriptures had already recorded her journey. She had heard the Bible referred to as a living book, and now she understood. Her journey was one others had taken, yet also uniquely hers, and uniquely understood. The book had been written in preparation not only for others, but also for her.

She felt Dave's arm tighten around her waist, realized there were tears on her cheeks, and reached blindly into her pocket for a tissue.

Lord, I need to find Tony. He's my brother. I would like to say hello. Will You help me?

"Kate, what's wrong?" Jennifer asked softly.

She shook her head, not wanting to disturb the service with a whisper that might travel given they were seated in the balcony.

Dave's arm slid around her and turned her gently into his shoulder. His strength felt so good. She rested her head into that hollow he offered and let the last few moments of emotions be absorbed into the comfort of his embrace.

Was this, too, what it meant to be in love? An embrace that didn't need words to explain the commitment? She knew, in the same way she knew with the O'Malleys, that she could ask Dave for anything she needed, and if it was in his power to do it, he would.

She could do the same with Jesus. He wasn't going to let her down. She took a deep breath, for the realization touched deep.

Thank You, Jesus. I'm going to enjoy meeting my brother. She felt the humor come back as the stress dropped away, and she smiled slightly. *But, Jesus, please, we're going to have to do something about that name. Tony brings back too many memories, and going with simply Jr. is not much better.*

As the sermon drew to an end, she began to pull back from Dave, mop up her eyes. She hoped her face had the same peace she had seen on Jennifer's but was afraid her eyes only looked red. There was more to do. She wanted to talk to Jennifer to be sure she understood what baptism meant. The reason for the urgency Jennifer felt to share what she had discovered was plain. The rest of the O'Malleys had to believe; they couldn't afford the delay.

She turned to Dave as the service concluded and saw the worry on his face. She squeezed his hand. She didn't want to explain until she had a few moments to regain her composure. The crowd in the balcony began to disperse.

Ben stepped aside to let a couple coming toward them through. Kate hurriedly wiped her eyes one last time. Dave's sister Sara trailed closely by her husband; Kate knew them instantly from the pictures around Dave's home. This was so embarrassing.

"Sara." Dave stepped forward and enveloped his sister in a hug. "Come meet Kate," he said turning to make the introductions.

Kate liked the lady at first sight. Beautiful, the pictures had not done her justice; petite, and with an open inquisitive gaze that made Kate aware of just how closed her own expression must be. She had instinctively retreated to the impassive mode of observing as soon as she saw them. She could feel the nerves taking over as she said hello and shook hands.

Jennifer stepped forward, and the awkward moment passed. Jennifer could charm anyone with her smile and her calm manner. It let Kate take a half step back and simply follow the conversation as Jennifer and Sara talked about New York.

Dave touched her arm. "I'm going to bring the car around. Come down the back stairs; Ben knows the way. Sara and Adam are going to follow us."

She nodded.

Two minutes later she was following Ben through the relative quiet of the back stairways, Adam beside her. Kate found Sara's husband to be a confident man, charming, and from his attention to his wife a couple steps ahead of them, very much focused on those he loved. They reached the lower landing.

"Let Ben check for reporters before we go out," Adam suggested when she would have opened the door to the step outside.

"I'm never going to get used to this," she remarked, dropping her hand.

"With time it will become second nature. It's part of the reality of being news."

"Outside of a church?"

"If they had a lead on your location, absolutely." He glanced over at his wife, who was still in a discussion with Jennifer, then turned back to Kate. He rested his shoulder against the wall, relaxed, watchful, sharing a smile. "Dave managed to forget to mention you were from the South."

"He's been talking about me." She didn't know whether to be secretly thrilled or embarrassed.

"Not enough to satisfy Sara."

Kate glanced over at her. "Your wife is lovely."

Adam chuckled. "You should see the disaster that is our bedroom. She had absolutely nothing to wear suitable for this occasion. You make her nervous, Kate. Hence the fact she's hiding behind your sister at the moment."

Kate blinked, just once. "I do?"

"You do; so relax. The nerves are mutual." He was making a well-educated guess; there was no way she appeared nervous. She knew how hard the disciplined control had clamped down on her expression. If anything, she appeared distant and aloof.

"I don't have to see them to know they are there. Was that you Saturday afternoon? The early evening news reported the standoff in progress."

She rested her back against the wall, unconsciously positioning herself as a cop would to keep the world in front of her. She decided she liked Adam. "Yes."

"I'm glad you were able to settle it peacefully."

"Almost all situations have peaceful conclusions if there is enough time." She glanced again at Dave's sister and decided it was easier to ask Adam than to try to broach the subject with Sara later. "Is Sara okay with what happened at the bank? I know it had to have been a hard day for her, waiting so long for news. And with her past—"

"A few nightmares, a few old memories, she's dealt with it."

"I wish it hadn't happened." She grimaced. "I never did send a thank-you for the flowers. I honestly meant to."

He flashed her a grin that made her blink for its warmth. "You're forgiven."

Ben came back inside, held open the door, and gave the all clear. Adam moved to rejoin his wife. "We'll see you at the house in about twenty minutes."

Kate nodded and went with Jennifer to Dave's car.

Dave had stepped out to hold the car doors for them. "Thanks, Dave." She slid into the front seat and reached automatically for the seat belt.

Traffic was beginning to build as they drove back to his home. They had just reached the Lake Forest town boundaries when he looked down, startled, his hand going to his waist. His pager set on vibrate mode had gone off, Kate realized.

He pulled it from his belt and looked at the number, immediately reaching for the phone. He punched in the number as he drove.

"This is Richman."

He listened and his expression became grim. "We're on the way."

"They've found Tony. He's holding Devlon at the bank corporate headquarters."

Her throat closed. *Tony had taken the situation into his own hands.* She had found her brother only to lose him. Her face cleared of the churning emotions. She couldn't afford to give in to them. Tony had managed to get himself cornered with the one person who would want to make sure he didn't come out alive. "Is the situation contained?"

"Sealed off to the top floor. Jim wants you there."

"Marcus?"

"On his way."

He started dialing again, glancing back in the rearview mirror to her sister. "Jennifer, I can have Adam and Sara take you back to the house."

"No, I'm coming along. It might be useful to have a doctor on-site."

Kate knew if a doctor were needed it would be one accustomed to digging bullets out of people rather than a pediatrician, but she would never say as much. She wanted Jennifer there simply because she was an O'Malley.

Dave reluctantly nodded. His attention turned to the phone call he had placed. "Adam? We've got a change of plans." He explained what was happening.

Kate tried to suppress the impact of what was happening, found it difficult to do.

Dave hung up the phone.

Kate asked the question that was bothering her the most. "How did Tony get into the corporate bank offices on a weekend?"

"At a guess, Devlon let him in, thinking to resolve the problem. He's arrogant enough he probably thought he could kill Tony and then claim self-defense."

She cringed having Dave confirm her worst fear. "Yes. It's been all over the news that we have been looking for him. Devlon would have seen that as a way to excuse his actions."

She rapidly dug out a pen from her bag and flipped open the pad of paper she had left in the car the day before, forcing herself to action, to the work that she could do. "Do you remember the bank? The layout of that executive level?"

"Two elevators opening onto a wide east-west corridor. Two secretary stations, the one guarding the east wing was Nathan's secretary. Three doors behind her. A conference room, Nathan's office at the end, Devlon's office."

"Who worked in the west wing?"

"I didn't see the nameplates. But it was the same layout. Two offices and a conference room."

"I'm guessing the corridor was about fourteen feet wide?"

"Yes."

"Were the emergency stairs to the left or the right when we stepped off the elevators?"

"Right. There was a large fern, restroom, and then the emergency stairs."

"The offices are on the top floor, so we may be able to get good use of the roof of the building. It's ten floors, and there are taller buildings on all sides, so line of sight will favor us. Which room is the most likely for them to be in?"

"If it's just Tony and Devlon, Tony would likely have pushed the confrontation into Devlon's office."

"Even though the room has full windows?"

"He'd pull the blinds but not realize he's still vulnerable. Safer would be to move to the interior conference room."

"Okay. He'll have line of sight down the corridors, but that's also a problem for him. He can't really eliminate a threat to his back, even if he moves into one of the end offices. There are still the windows." Kate could see the situation and knew how good the SWAT team was. They would be able to breach the floor if it was required. "Did you notice the ceilings?"

"Plaster."

"The rooms are large, not much furniture. An assault team would be able to come in with clear lines of fire."

"Kate, a peaceful conclusion will be found. Trust that."

"I'm praying Jim lets me do the talking."

"You're too deeply involved in this case. Don't get your hopes up. You're going to be on the sidelines for this one."

"You're relieved at that fact."

"Are you going to hate me if I say yes? Devlon isn't exactly a friendly hostage to protect."

"How are they going to handle this? That the one being held hostage is the one probably responsible for blowing up the plane?"

"*Probably* is the operative word. We've got a theory, but not airtight proof against Devlon. And he *is* the hostage."

"Tony is in deep trouble."

He didn't respond. He didn't have to.

TWENTY-FOUR

The block around the bank had been sealed off. Media vans and their journalist teams were along the perimeter, trying to get the best vantage point or interview. From the numbers present, word must have leaked that this standoff was related to the airline bombing. Police had to control the crowd of spectators at the barricades. Overhead, the steady thumping beat of police helicopters guarded the scene. Kate scrambled for her badge and hurried through the crowd of cops to the forward command post, Dave jogging along beside her. There were so many different agencies here, men from her unit, the FBI, some of the ATF people. The task force had descended. It was a noisy, busy environment. Exactly what she expected.

"Jim."

He broke free from the cluster of men to join her. "I'm sorry it's going down like this, Kate."

She kept her voice cool. "I've never met him." She had to keep her distance if she was going to have any hope of being involved before this was over. "Where are things?"

"Come take a look at the blueprints. I could use your firsthand knowledge, both of the environment and the two men." She followed, well aware of the less-than-comfortable looks coming from others in the command center. As far as most of them were concerned, she was related to a suspect and therefore a security risk. She was grateful to have Dave beside her. She sensed when someone else joined them and saw the men around the room abruptly shift their gaze away. Kate glanced back. Marcus. Between Dave and Marcus there was an implicit warning being issued to others in the room. It felt nice to know they were protecting her back.

She turned to look at the blueprints as Jim identified locations. "We've got the elevators shut down, Graham and a team in position on the stairs, more on the roof. It appears to be only Tony Jr. and Devlon on the tenth floor. Shades are drawn, lights are off, but snipers in the surrounding buildings have picked up movement—" he tapped a location—"here."

"Devlon's office."

"Yes. The security guard downstairs said Devlon cleared Tony Jr. to come into the building. Franklin and Olsen are working to get us video optics snaked in through the ductwork along here so we can see what is happening. Phones have been isolated; we've already shut down the air-conditioning, and we're preparing to shut down electricity and water."

Kate nodded, having expected all of those steps. "Tony Jr. arrives at the bank, and Devlon clears him to come up. What happened when he got up there? Were shots fired? How did we get word about what was going on?"

"That's what's so puzzling. Fifteen minutes after Tony Jr. went upstairs, Devlon called the security guard to say he was being held hostage and told him to call the police."

"Tony Jr. *wanted* us brought in?"

"Yes."

"Have you made contact?"

"Christopher. He's gotten through by phone. Tony Jr. wasn't in the mood to talk, said to call back in an hour. We're still twenty minutes away from that time."

If Kate had to pick someone to handle the negotiations in her place, Christopher would have been her choice. "Is everyone aware Devlon is a suspect in the bombing?"

"They know. But Tony Jr. is not making this easier for his own defense."

"If Tony Jr. dies, the ability to prove it was Devlon who planted that bomb gets more difficult."

"I know that, too." Her boss looked at her. "I can clear you to work with Christopher, but as much as I'd like to, I can't give you the phone."

It was more access than she thought she would get. "I'll take it."

"Get him up to speed. You've got about fifteen minutes before that next call."

Kate nodded and turned to scan the room. She spotted Ian in the corner, and he waved her over. Leaving Dave and Marcus talking over the tactics of the situation with Jim, she crossed the room; where Ian was, Christopher would be. She was right. Christopher had made a private corner for himself tucked behind the communication gear. He was lighting his pipe, ignoring the commotion. It was so traditionally Christopher that she couldn't help but smile.

He spun around a chair for her. "Nice mess this one is, lass."

"How much do you know?"

"Not nearly enough. The FBI profile," he lifted the pages from his lap, "is worthless. It assumes Tony is the bomber, something I understand you doubt; therefore, its conclusions are probably wildly wrong. From that kid's shaky voice it is clear he's petrified."

She let out a deep breath. "Innocent, but so terrified he's going to get himself killed by doing something dumb."

"Lass, you and I are going to make sure that doesn't happen. Tell me everything you think happened."

Since she didn't have much time, she sketched in the case. The facts did look incriminating. There had to be a reason to look deeper and see that Devlon was the one who had actually helped Ashcroft. Tony was her brother. No one was going to get away with framing him for something he didn't do. "Tony probably went after Devlon thinking the only way to clear his name was to make the man confess."

"Rather naive of him."

"Yes."

It was time to make the call. Ian set it up for those in the room to hear it. Kate wished she were the one reaching for the phone instead of Christopher.

Come on, Tony, pick up.

"Hello, Tony, it's Chris again."

"Why did you shut off the electricity?"

To keep you from seeking safety in the restroom, maybe get you to crack a window blind. That wouldn't be said of course. Christopher was right. Tony sounded young...and frustrated. Frustrated was not good.

"The alarm inside the bank was ready to sound, and we knew that would be rather distressing for you to hear. We didn't have the codes, so we shut down the system the only way we could."

There was a pause. "I want to speak with Marla."

Wife. Kate scrawled the word for Christopher. He nodded. "We can try to arrange something."

"When she gets here, call me. In the meantime, start looking for the combination to Devlon's office safe."

"What are you looking for?"

"Just get me the combination." Tony slammed down the phone.

Kate winced. "An hour hasn't eased that sound of panic."

Christopher reached over to replay the conversation. "He gave himself an hour to search the place, and he didn't find whatever he expected. What's he looking for? And what happens if he doesn't get it?"

She ran her hand through her hair. "He was being blackmailed. Maybe he is looking for something he thinks Devlon acquired."

"I'm surprised he wasn't pleading his innocence."

She looked at Christopher and saw it was an observation, nothing more, and agreed with him. "I think he's given up believing someone will listen."

Christopher nodded. "Then we'll just have to convince him otherwise."

"We've got video," one of the technicians across the room announced.

Kate pushed back her chair so both she and Christopher could see the screens being turned on. They had one camera with a view of the corridor, another that had been lowered into the corner of Devlon's office.

"Are the tactical teams getting this?" Marcus asked.

"Yes."

Devlon sat in a chair that had been pulled to the center of his office.

Kate leaned toward the screen. "What's that around Devlon's wrist?"

"Looks like he's handcuffed to the chair," Christopher speculated.

"Tony made a mistake leaving Devlon in a chair with rollers. If things get interesting, his hostage can move on him. And he left the other hand free."

"He should have used a phone cord, an electrical cord, something," Christopher agreed. "The kid's not thinking things through."

Tony stood in the doorway of the office, trying to watch both directions of the corridor, a gun in his right hand. He had made a few changes to the furniture arrangements. One of the secretary's desks had been pulled over to give him access to the phone. The other desk had been moved in front of the stairway door.

The two men were arguing about something, Kate could see Tony's growing anger and Devlon's belligerence.

"Can we get audio?" Kate asked.

"Franklin is laying down the relays. You'll have it in another minute," Olsen promised.

Dave rested his hand against her shoulder. Kate appreciated the silent support. Tony was pacing. Having seen too many situations like this, she could read the growing storm. Audio sputtered on, the first words broken by static. "...you framed me with that meeting! Now I want those tapes you took from Ashcroft's apartment."

"What tapes? I was never near Ashcroft's apartment."

"I saw you coming out! Now where are the tapes?!"

Kate flinched an instant before Tony fired the handgun wildly over Devlon's head.

The chatter over the secure mikes was instantaneous as the SWAT teams positioned to swarm in.

"No! Everyone stay in place. Do not breach! Repeat, do not breach!" It took shouts from the team leader to get over the vocal traffic and freeze them from moving. "We're still secure!"

Christopher had his hand on the phone. Jim nodded at him. It rang for almost a minute before Tony stormed back across the room to pick it up.

"Tony, what's going on up there? Is anyone hurt?"

"Everything is just fine. Just keep away from me and get me what I want!" In the monitors, Kate could see him still pointing the gun at Devlon.

"You've got a lot of nervous cops around you. It's not a good thing to fire a gun in this situation."

"Where's the combination?"

"We're still checking, Tony."

"I want that combination!"

Kate watched the monitor, worried at the agitation. Was he on something? The situation would be impossible to stabilize if he was.

"Calm down. If we can't locate it, we can drill the safe for you."

Kate wrote. *Tell him we know it's Devlon.*

"Tony, we know you are innocent. We know that Devlon is the one who planted the bomb."

"He's trying to frame me for it."

Ashcroft.

"We know Ashcroft planned this entire thing, that he and Devlon set you up to take the blame." Christopher looked over at her. "Tony, he framed your sister, too. Come out peacefully and let us sort this out."

"I don't have a sister."

"She's sitting right here. Kate Emerson, thirty-six—although she doesn't look it, a decent cop for someone who no longer walks the beat. You want chapter and verse on your parents? The house where you grew up?"

There was silence. "She died years ago."

"Hardly. She changed her name, but she's been here in town all her life. Her name is Kate O'Malley. Maybe you saw her on the news lately."

"I don't believe you."

Christopher covered the phone. "Kate, I need you up there."

Thank you, Christopher. His word was gold unless they went tactical. She looked at Jim for agreement. "Go. Join Graham on the stairs."

The gear was ready. She shoved her feet into the boots.

"What are you doing?"

She didn't spare the seconds to look up at Dave. "My job." Olsen handed her the vest. She pulled in a deep breath to snug down the straps. The gear was custom designed for her, and she got it on fast.

"Ian, audio check."

She nodded as she got a good clear signal through her earpiece.

"You're going to negotiate this?"

"Christopher is. But I'm the proof."

"Give me a minute. I'm coming with you."

She could argue with him, but it would take time she didn't have. "Hurry." She saw Christopher hang up the phone.

"Kate, get in position. Marla is about five minutes out. I'll put her on the phone with Tony, then try to work it so you can open that stairway door and chat with him."

"Can we do anything on the safe combination?"

"Even if we could, the risk is too great that it's empty. If Devlon did ever get his hands on evidence that somehow could incriminate him, you can bet it's long since been destroyed."

Kate knew he was right, but it would be so much easier to have something in hand to convince Tony he could safely end this standoff.

Marcus touched her shoulder as she went past. The pressure was a silent message of support. He was listening in to the same tactical chatter she was. She squeezed his hand in return and moved to the door. She was about to meet her brother for the first time. She could think of much easier places to do it.

She looked over at Dave as they entered the building. He had borrowed gear, was decked out much as she was. His face was grim, and she didn't need that additional stress. He had volunteered to come along. She didn't mind him protecting her back, but added pressure was not something she welcomed or needed. A cop stationed in the bank building lobby pointed toward the stairwell.

Kate glanced over at Dave as they entered the stairwell. "Ten flights. Bet I beat you to the top."

"This is hardly a race."

She took the first flight, going up two stairs at a time. "It's not a major war either. He's not going to shoot his sister."

"Really? You know that for a fact?"

He was afraid for her. How was she supposed to deal with that? She didn't want to deal with it. He shouldn't be putting her in a situation she had to deal with it. "Didn't you say prayer made a difference?"

"Yes."

"Well then quit raining on my prayer. I intend to meet my brother and get him out of this mess." She turned the corner and sprinted up the next flight. "It's just like a kid brother, digging a hole I have to get him out of."

"That's what this morning at church was about?"

"Part of it. I'm okay if something happens. Quit stressing out, or you're going to be worthless to me if this does go bad."

"You believe?"

She took a moment in the turn at floor five to look over at him. "You don't have to sound so skeptical about it."

"Sorry. You took me by surprise."

She took a deep breath and sprinted up the sixth flight. "You get what you wished for and you're surprised. Where's the logic in that?"

He grinned at her. "There is none. It's pure relief."

"Then catch up. You're slowing me down."

She slowed as they reached the eighth floor, and by the turn into the tenth walked the last flight to eliminate the noise. Graham had six men with him. They had taken positions away from the door, against the concrete wall. Graham smiled when he saw her and whispered over his mike, "Good to see you. No real change. Thompson has the video feed."

She nodded and stopped beside Thompson to get a look. The situation looked much as she had left it. Except now Tony was fifteen feet away on the other side of this door. The nervousness had as much to do with the uncertainty of meeting him as with the danger in the situation.

Christopher's voice came over the command circuit. "Kate, Marla is here. I'm going to patch the conversation onto channel three."

"Switching to three," Kate acknowledged. She leaned against the concrete wall beside Graham. He wordlessly handed her a piece of gum. She smiled and accepted it. She knew even as she unwrapped it that it would be Juicy Fruit. Graham was accustomed to long waits.

Marla's voice came over the channel, strained and worried. "Tony, the building is surrounded with cops. Give yourself up before you get hurt. Please."

"It doesn't matter. I've got Devlon, and one way or another he is going to pay." Kate frowned at Tony Jr.'s choice of words. They were definitely running out of time.

"Tony, Marcus O'Malley is down here. He's with the U.S. Marshals, and he knows about Ashcroft and Devlon. You can trust him."

"If they know what happened, how come I'm the one being hunted? No, Devlon is going to confess. He's going to tell them what he did."

"Tony, please."

"Did you meet this sister that I've supposedly got?"

"No, she's not here. But they tell me she's the one who actually figured out what happened."

"Put Chris back on the line."

"Here he is."

"Marla says this Kate isn't there. Are you lying to me? You said she was beside you. If she's real, put her on the phone."

"Better yet, why don't you meet her? She's at the stairway door."

"I'm not opening any door to the cops! What do you think I am, a fool?"

Kate folded the gum wrapper into a nice foil square.

"Tony, she really did figure out what was going on. I've got one of the calls Ashcroft made to her right here. Hold on, I'm going to play it."

"Hello, Kate O'Malley. I've been looking for you, and what do I see—you made the news last night. We'll have to meet soon."

"That's her answering machine tape, Tony. That's Ashcroft's voice, isn't it?"

"Yes."

"He was dragging her into this. Besides this tape, we've got others. He used her name in the bomb threat. Kate O'Malley is very real; she's a cop, and she's your sister. When she says it was Devlon and Ashcroft, she knows what she's talking about."

"I open this door, the only person I want to see on the other side of it is her. Her hands better be in the air, and she better be motionless. I see anyone else and I'm going to shoot."

Kate flipped back to the command channel. "Got it, Chris."

The others with Graham had been listening in. Given the way the door would swing open, they didn't have to shift far to be out of the line of sight. Dave put himself within reach of her.

She calmly took a breath and keyed her mike. "I'm in position."

The doorknob turned with a sound as if it needed to be oiled. Thompson held the small display so she could see Tony stepping back to the center of the room, gun raised, pointed at the door. Chris gave the green light. "Any time you're ready, Kate."

She opened the steel door with her left hand, as it would let her right hand be in the air when he first saw her.

He took another step back, both hands coming up to grip the gun. "So you're my sister."

"I don't know if it's a pleasure to meet you or not, but yes, I'm your sister."

Her calm words surprised him. When she said nothing else, she saw a puzzled look and his hands adjust themselves on the gun grip. He could only keep the gun sighted like that thirty to forty seconds before the fatigue would force him to either get mad and create some more adrenaline or lower his arms and the gun. His body couldn't produce more adrenaline, a simple fact of how long the crisis had been going on. She waited him out.

"How come you never came back home and bothered to tell anyone you were alive?" The gun lowered a fraction as his arms began to tire.

"I hated our dad. And no one bothered to tell me about you." She looked past him into Devlon's office and nodded toward Devlon. "Would you believe he was the one to first mention your name? That was not a pleasant experience, thank you very much."

"You really are my sister?"

"Yes. I haven't been called Emerson since going on forever. My name is legally Kate O'Malley, but I'm not dead, despite what Tony Sr. said."

He pulled the desk forward several inches, keeping the gun aimed at her. She watched him and made a simple decision. She took one step inside the room.

"Kate, get back here!" The words were hissed at her over the earpiece.

She moved to the left, past the desk, and sat down against the wall. "Close the door, Tony. I think it's time you and I talked."

"Kate, when you get out of this—" Dave sounded more than just angry.

"What are you smiling at?" Tony demanded, nervously shutting the door.

"My boyfriend is yelling in my ear."

"Take that mike off."

"No."

He stared at her. Kate calmly stared back.

"Tony, sit down," she said mildly, just to give him the means to save face. She leaned her head back against the wall, relaxing to make herself comfortable for what might be a long day. "I hate that name, by the way. You got a nickname?"

"What?"

"I have no intention of calling you Tony."

"Junior."

"Get real. You're related to an O'Malley. Have some class." Marcus tried to cover his laugh with a cough and nearly made her deaf. She turned down the volume on the command circuit with her thumb.

"Mom used to call me Will."

"Will." She tried it on for size and found she liked it. "Not bad. Okay, Will.

Rule one in the O'Malley world: Don't mess with your older sister."

"That's you."

"Since I'm the one who believes you're innocent, lose the sarcasm. Why did you run? It made you look guilty."

"I didn't. I heard about the bomb, and I went to Ashcroft's to try and recover the video he had. Only Devlon here got there first. I couldn't come forward after that because everything I needed to prove Devlon was Ashcroft's partner was on that video."

"So you came here today to get it."

"He has it."

"Tony, Devlon would have destroyed it the same day he got his hands on it."

"Then give me one reason I shouldn't just shoot him now."

"You may have moved drugs because of pressure from our dad; you may have been stupid enough to let Ashcroft blackmail you; and today is going to give a prosecuting attorney a delight, but you have not killed anyone. Devlon in that office has killed 214. I need justice, not your idea of vengeance, thank you very much. He screwed up my life, too, you know."

"I've turned over a new leaf. You can ask Marla. I haven't even had a parking ticket in years. It was just easier back then to do what Dad said than to fight him. And Ashcroft was framing me with it. He stole explosives from the construction site. Everything pointed to me."

"You only look guilty. I figured it out." She looked at him, trying to decide the best tactic. "Ashcroft knew more about O'Hare security than you did. The cops investigating his organization sent eight people to jail, got you and two others fired, but the evidence they have developed suggests Ashcroft was rebuilding his network since he got out of jail. He didn't need you to get the bomb into O'Hare, but you were a great fall guy. He was already blackmailing you; why not frame you, too? Who set up that Tuesday morning appointment at the airport?"

She smiled as she saw his eyes narrow. "Yes, I thought so. Devlon. There will be a phone record of the call he placed to you, showing it was Devlon and not you that set up the meeting at the airport. What about that fax the bank manager received, extending your loan—who stood at the fax machine and sent it, you or Nathan?"

"I did."

"From the business lounge."

"Yes."

"Did you know you are on tape doing so?"

"Security cameras are there?"

"Yes. The fax came through at 10:48 A.M. It's there in black and white on the top of the page. But someone else had just called in the bomb threat, and I wrote down the time we were paged about it. 10:48 A.M. You were busy, Tony, and you're on tape being busy."

"That's not much."

"There are electronic fingerprints on the money Devlon had been handling for Ashcroft. It's pieces of a puzzle, Tony. We've only been looking at Devlon a short time, and we've already turned over some ugly things under the rocks. You'll have to trust me when I say there will be more." She was pleased to see him lean against the desk, relax ever so slightly. "Why were you letting Ashcroft blackmail you? Why were you paying him off?"

"It wasn't for me. It was for Marla. She's on one of the security tapes with Ashcroft. She didn't know. She was just delivering a package. She had no idea what was in it."

"I believe you."

"I couldn't take a chance a jury might not. She's the best thing that ever happened in my life. And once I paid the first blackmail money, Ashcroft had me."

The phone began to ring.

"You had better get that, Tony. And listen to what they have to say, okay?"

Tony took a step toward the phone.

She heard something fall. She came away from the wall and to her feet in less time than it took Tony to turn toward the office, but the error had been made. They had been talking too long without either checking on Devlon, and his chair had been on rollers. She heard a faint whisper in her ear that was someone screaming for her to get down and felt her heart stop. She'd turned her mike down too low for them to warn her when Devlon began to move. Her own instincts now screaming at her, she hit Tony with a blindside tackle just as gunshots split the wood of the desk.

Devlon was shooting at them.

Tony tried to bring his hand up with the gun to return fire, and Kate did the thing that seemed most logical. She hit him.

She knew enough to shut her eyes. The flash grenades went off as brilliant repeating strobes, and the decibel level of their noisemakers made her ears ring. Two figures in black came across the desk still partially blocking the stairway door, took firing positions by Devlon's office, and in went another flash grenade.

The assault was finished before Kate could sort out the players. She sat up, wincing with pain she didn't bother to mask.

Lord, this wasn't in my plans.

She coughed up blood.

"Don't move." Dave's face wavered in and out of focus.

"Broke a rib."

"And a few other things."

"The vest took the hit." She could feel the radiating bruise, had to suck in air to make the world stop swimming. "I told you a younger brother was trouble." She tried to laugh at the observation but couldn't. The vest that had saved her life was too tight. She reached for the straps with hands that didn't seem to want to coordinate their movements.

"Kate."

She looked up. "Marcus, I'm not dead." He was pale as a ghost.

"Get Jennifer up here." The order from Marcus over the command circuit made her grimace.

"I don't need the full family for a busted rib."

"What you're going to get is a doctor, so shut up."

"You may have punctured a lung," Dave said quietly, supporting her against his shoulder.

She was beginning to get her breath back. "I bit my tongue, rather badly, with that blindside tackle. The slug hit nothing but Kevlar, but it packed a punch. I need my ribs strapped and something cold to drink." She saw the relief cross Dave's face. "Remember to tell Jennifer I want the cherry lollipop."

He kissed her forehead. "I'll do that."

"Good." She looked at Tony Jr., now coming around with a groan. "He's got a jaw like a rock. I nearly broke my hand."

"Be glad you did. If he'd had that gun in his hand when the team came through, there would have been little choice."

"I know. I guess I've now officially got more family."

"I know a good lawyer."

"He's going to need one."

"Don't scare me like this again, Kate." Dave ordered. "You weren't supposed to enter the room."

"I don't take chances lightly. I figured this time the stakes were high enough."

Dave brushed back her hair. "Maybe."

"You're just annoyed you couldn't take a bullet for me."

He grinned. "I've already got my scars."

"Do you?"

"Yes."

"Forget to duck?"

"Insuring someone else did."

Jennifer had joined them, and Kate didn't want to lose this moment. "Jennifer, come back in about an hour."

Dave choked back a laugh. "Would you behave? I'm not going anywhere. That's a promise."

TWENTY-FIVE

Kate speared an olive from the dish with her toothpick. They had a beautiful day for their Fourth of July bash. The park pavilion was perfect for the massive spread of food they had brought with them. There was something about a family picnic that restored her faith in the better things about life. She looked over at Jennifer, and then back at the rather brutal game of horseshoes going on. "I really think you should just plan to elope with Tom before the family scares him off."

"No need. He's winning."

Kate turned to pay more attention, her hand cushioning her taped ribs. She had a hairline fracture, a nuisance, but it was going to bench her from the baseball game that afternoon, and that had her really annoyed. In the last decade she had missed only two O'Malley baseball games, and both of them had been due to pages. "Really? No one is throwing the game?"

"Tom just nailed another ringer."

Kate grinned. "I bet that's giving Stephen fits."

It felt good to finally have a day to just hang out with the family and not have to worry about what was going to hit her the next day. Tony Jr. was working on a plea bargain with the DA, and Peter Devlon would eventually be facing one of the biggest trials in U.S. history.

She was still getting used to the reality she had a brother. Will, she refused to think of him as Tony Jr., was still very much of a mystery to her. They had forged a tentative acceptance of the fact they were related, but any sense of a personal relationship was going to take time. She had met Will's wife, Marla, and had liked her immediately. Time. She would need a lot of it, so would Will.

Dave dropped his arm around her shoulders. "Hey, beautiful. What's happening?"

"Just chatting. I thought you were watching Jack and the steaks."

"He's burning them," Dave replied cheerfully.

Jennifer got to her feet with a laugh. "I'll go."

Dave nudged Kate over, and she made room for him on the bench. She smiled at his slight sunburn and feathered her hand through his hair. "Is the day everything you expected?"

He slowly leaned in against her, invading her space, before kissing her, taking his time to purposefully drive her crazy. "Pretty much." He grinned. "What's the blush for?"

"My family is watching." *And you've been driving me crazy the last few days.*

"They've unanimously decided I should stick around."

She grinned. "Have they?"

"Yes." He interlaced his fingers with hers. "What about you?"

"You mean I have a choice?"

"No."

"I didn't think so." She rolled a shoulder, pretended to think about it, and finally caved in. "You can stick around. I've decided I rather like your company. Besides, I know better than to go against the family."

He studied her for a moment, and the smile became tender. "I was thinking along the lines of something serious."

"How serious?"

"How about, for now, a promise that you'll be my girl for at least the next year? The guys think it's a good idea."

"What?"

"Is it the proposal or the fact I asked their permission?"

She blinked, hard. *Jesus, I was expecting this question in a few months, not now. Dating a cop is a big deal.*

Dave was God's man. And she had learned to trust Him.

She knew what she wanted.

She turned toward him and leaned her arm back against the picnic table. "We have an unwritten rule in the family, you know."

"What?"

She smiled. "Never turn down an invitation to an adventure."

He relaxed. "Good. We'll have one."

"That's a guarantee?"

"You can take it to the bank." He looked at her. "Not First Union."

"I already don't know if I can handle your sense of humor."

"You'll learn."

"That's easy for you to say." She leaned her head against his shoulder, made herself comfortable. His arm settled around her shoulders. "You can handle the pages?"

"I've survived three. By my calculations, I've only got about a thousand to go before you retire."

She chuckled. "You're going to count them?"

"Absolutely."

"Do I get keys to the jet?"

"Is it a deal breaker?"

She grinned.

He ruffled her hair. "Okay, they're yours. Along with lessons."

"Thanks." She rested her hands against his chest, watching his eyes as he studied her, as he smiled. "I love you, you know."

His hands cupped her face. "I know." His arms comfortably encircled her waist. "I love you, too."

Hearing the words still made her blink; no man had ever said them to her with that confident certainty. She studied him, feeling for the first time uncertain, and trusting him enough not to mask what she was feeling. His expression softened, and the growing warmth in his gaze flooded over her. He barely had to lean forward to kiss her. "Trust me, Kate. I love you."

His reassurance settled deep inside. She rested her hands against his chest to give a cheeky grin. "Good."

"You haven't actually answered my question yet," he pointed out.

She wanted to laugh. "Yes, I'll be your girl."

"Good."

"That's an awfully smug look."

"Marcus said if I could get you to agree before game time, I could be team captain."

Her elbow caught him in the ribs as she moved back.

"Hey!"

"Where's Marcus?"

He rubbed the sore spot. "Probably getting out of the line of fire."

"He should."

"I'm unofficially part of the family, Kate. Leave your brother alone."

"I don't need him arranging my life."

He caught her as she moved to get up. "As if anyone could. Sit." His arms closed around her ribs below the wrap to make sure she did. "He's got a party planned for tonight for Tom and Jennifer. He thought I might like to come celebrate with you."

She blinked and what had been annoyance changed to a concerted effort not to let a tear fall. "Marcus planned a party?"

Dave gently hugged her. "Yeah. He thought it would be a nice O'Malley tradition." He kissed her softly. "I agree with him."

Kate leaned into the kiss. "There will be fireworks at the party."

He smiled. "I think we've got some fireworks right here."

"Fireworks and love. Nice combination."

"Break it up, you two. It's lunchtime."

Kate leaned back, blinked, and realized the family had joined them. She smiled. "Jack, did you burn my steak?"

"I tried my best."

She laughed. "Dave, are you sure you're ready for this family?"

"I wouldn't miss this adventure for the world."

Dear Reader,

Thank you for reading this book; it was such a pleasure to write. I fell in love with Kate O' Malley. After spending time with Dave in *Danger in the Shadows*, I knew he was one of the few people who could handle Kate! They have a bright future together.

A cop is driven by a need for justice. I was curious to find out which would be more poweful—a need for justice or a need for mercy—if the dilemma became very personal. I sketched a story that let me explore the subject, and found Kate's journey through the questions fascinating. Even I found the solution to her dilemma a surprise. Any time the character of God becomes the basis of a story, I have found it to be a wonderful book to write. I hope you enjoyed the story.

As always, I love to hear from my readers. Feel free to write me at:

Dee Henderson
c/o Multnomah Fiction
P.O. Box 1720
Sisters, Oregon 97759
E-mail: dee@deehenderson.com
Web site: www.deehenderson.com

Thanks again for letting me share Dave and Kate's story.
Sincerely,

Dee Henderson

book two

THE GUARDIAN

But truly God has listened;
he has given heed to the voice of my prayer.
Psalm 66:19

PROLOGUE

"Can I take Mom the flowers?"

They were not allowed inside the ICU, but the nurse who had come out to the waiting room nodded anyway. Janelle knew what the boy did not, and it made her want to cry. His mother was dying. Let him take the flowers.

Marcus was such a polite young man, patiently sitting alone in the ICU waiting room for the brief visits allowed each hour. He had been coming for the last nine days. A neighbor who worked at the hospital brought him in each morning, and each evening took him home.

He had brought roses with him today, three of them, carefully wrapped with a damp paper towel around the stems, foil around that. There were grass stains on the knees of his jeans. He had told her yesterday that he was tending the rose bushes during his mom's absence.

"Can I get you something to eat? A grilled cheese sandwich maybe?"

"No, thank you."

She was positive the boy was hungry, but there had been a tirade the one and only time his father had come to the hospital and found him sharing a sandwich with an orderly. Marcus had politely refused the offers of food ever since.

"The chaplain is with her now," Janelle told him, and the boy's relief was visible.

"He prays good."

"You pray wonderfully too." She had seen him with his mother's Bible, struggling to sound out the words as he read.

"I try."

He pushed off the molded plastic chair, not tall enough for his feet to reach the floor when he was sitting down. "Thanks for coming to get me."

"You're welcome, Marcus."

She watched him walk to the glass door of the ICU, use all of his weight to pull it open.

He hadn't asked her if his mom was getting better. It was the first time he had not asked.

It was hard to breathe; her lungs kept filling up with fluid. She had rallied today, and it was with a sense of urgency she knew she had to see her son. Renee heard

Marcus before she saw him and wiped away any sign of the strain, smiling toward the door. He came in escorted by the supervising nurse, carrying flowers.

Her heart tugged at the sight of him, wearing his favorite baseball shirt, washed but wrinkled, and blue jeans that would need a stain remover. He had asked her yesterday how to do the laundry right.

She hugged him, ignoring the IVs, marshaling her strength to make her grip firm. Her smile came from her heart. "You brought me flowers."

"I picked your roses. Was that okay?"

"Very okay. They're beautiful." She laid them on the blanket at her chest so she could enjoy them.

The chair scraped against the tile floor as Marcus pulled it to the edge of her bed.

He eagerly told her about the kittens at the neighbors and the way the black one with one white paw liked chasing a feather duster. She let him talk, smiling at the right places, watching him, holding his hand. Her son. The joy of her life. The doctor had told him laughter was good medicine, and he had latched on to that and taken it seriously, coming with a story each day to make her laugh.

She would ask about his morning, but in the last couple days he had started to avoid answering that question. It wasn't going well at home, and he wanted to be her guardian and not tell her. She brushed her fingers through his hair; it would need to be cut soon. She hoped he didn't end up having to do it himself. His father would not think of it.

"Mom?"

She had drifted on him; the story was over. She smiled an apology. "I'm laughing inside, honey."

"It wasn't very funny."

That drew a chuckle.

Her strength was fading and she could hear the wheeze returning.

Marcus's hand in hers squeezed tight. "Shall I get the nurse?" he asked, his voice calm but his eyes were anxious.

Two minutes with him. It wasn't enough. But the reality could not be denied. "Yes." He moved to slip his hand from hers, and instead she tightened her hold. "Before…you do. I want my kiss."

He grinned. He was a boy again instead of the solemn young man. He leaned across the railing to rub his nose against hers, then kissed both cheeks European style. "Love you, Mom."

"I love you too." She held him tight. "And Jesus loves you."

"I know."

He went to get the nurse.

The simple faith of a child. She was grateful. He had found something strong enough to get him through what was coming.

She panted for breath. They would clear her lungs again, and soon would have no choice but to put her on to the respirator. She feared she would never come off it. The doctor's reassuring words could not change what she knew in her spirit was coming. She gripped the roses and a thorn pierced her finger. Despite the fever she was shivering again.

She would be leaving Marcus with only his father. It was a heavy burden to place on an eight-year-old's faith. A single tear escaped to slide down her cheek. She had already cried for her husband and her son, for everything lost that could have been. Tears now would literally choke her. *Jesus, be my son's guardian. He needs You.*

Renee closed her eyes and focused on living one more day.

Marcus scuffed his tennis shoe against the tile floor and stared out the waiting room window, wiping furiously at the tears. He had to stop crying; they would see and they wouldn't let him visit anymore. The thought was a panic rising in his chest. He gulped back a sob and worked his jaw.

She wasn't getting better.

He had to pray harder.

ONE

U.S. Marshal Marcus O'Malley tucked the cellular phone tighter against his shoulder as he studied the latest photographs sent by the North Washington district office. Eighteen faxes. The picture quality grainy at best; the information about each individual sketchy. Each had made threats against judges attending this July conference at the Chicago Jefferson Renaissance Hotel. The pages crinkled as only cheap fax paper could as he thumbed through them, memorizing each one.

"Kate, what are you not telling me?" He was trying to have a telephone conversation with his sister while he worked and it was…interesting. He would have said aggravating, but he loved Kate too much to get annoyed with her easily.

His sister Kate O'Malley could be clear or ambiguous at will. As a hostage negotiator she knew how to choose her words, and she was being deliberately obtuse at the moment. It was 7:05 P.M. Friday night; Supreme Court Justice Philip Roosevelt would give the keynote speech at 8:00 P.M. before an audience of over twelve hundred, and Marcus did not have time to read between the lines.

Kate was trying to tell him something without breaking a confidence; that told him it was family related. And it was important enough she was willing to go to the edge of that confidence to let him know about it; that told him it was serious.

"She was supposed to tell you last night…"

Marcus flipped back to the ninth fax and frowned. Something about the picture was triggering a glimmer of a memory. Tom Libour: Caucasian, early forties, clean shaven. It was an old memory, and he could feel it flitting just beyond his recall. He didn't forget cases he had worked. Maybe something his partner had worked? He scrawled a note beside the photo, requesting the incident report be pulled. He passed the stack of faxes back to his deputy. "Who?" Jennifer, Lisa, or Rachel? In a family of seven, Kate had just cut the list in half.

The seven of them were related, but not by blood—by choice. At the orphanage—Trevor House—the decision to become their own family had made a lot of sense; two decades later it still did. As the oldest, thirty-eight, he accepted the guardianship of the group; as the next in line Kate protected it, kept her finger on the family pulse. He didn't mind the responsibility, but it often arrived at inconvenient times. What was going on?

"I've said too much already; forget I called."

"Kate—"

"Marcus." Her own frustration came back at him with the bite in her voice. "I didn't ask to be the one she chose to tell. I'm stuck. I'll push her to tell you; it's the best I can do."

The family was close, but Kate—she was the one he talked with in the middle of the night; they had shared the dark days. They were the oldest, the closest, and there was no one he trusted more than her. "How serious is it?"

He retrieved his black tuxedo jacket from the back of a folding chair. He would be standing behind the Supreme Court justice during the speech doing his best to look interested while he did his real job—decide who in the crowd might want to shoot the old man.

"I'm pacing the floors at night."

Marcus, reaching to straighten the lapel of his jacket, stopped. Kate had the nerve to walk into situations where a guy held a bomb; the last thing she did was overreact. Something that had her that worried—his eyes narrowed. "Who, Kate?" He couldn't take the weight off her shoulders if he didn't know. If Kate had given her word, she would never say, but he couldn't just leave it. He needed to know.

"Can you get free later tonight?"

Time was tight. This was the biggest judicial conference of the year, but he wasn't about to say no. Quinn would do him a favor.... "The banquet and its aftermath should be wrapped up by ten-thirty. I can meet you after that."

"We'll join you even if I have to drag her there," Kate replied grimly.

"Deal. And even if it's just you, come over."

"I'll be there. Besides, it's probably the only way I'll get to see Dave."

Marcus spotted FBI Special Agent Dave Richman on the other side of the room, deep in a discussion with the hotel security chief.

This conference had attracted explosive media attention. The Supreme Court was about to go conservative. With the announcement by the president of a nominee to replace retiring Justice Luke Blackwood, the landscape of the law across the nation would forever change. Most of the judges on the president's short list were in attendance. Dave had drawn the unenviable job of trying to figure out how to control and manage the media access.

"He's here. Do you want to talk to him?" Dave and Kate were dating. Dave having even gone so far as to formally ask all the guys in the family for permission. It was serious on her side too—Kate didn't let just anybody outside of the family get close to her heart.

"No, I know you're swamped. I just miss him."

She was in love. Everyone in the family knew that. Her face brightened when she saw Dave, and that impassive control she kept around her emotions, so necessary for her job, disappeared. Even her Southern accent intensified. Marcus kidded her about being love struck and she teased him back about hovering. That was okay; she needed a big brother watching out for her. "Then you definitely need to come over tonight. I'll tell Dave to expect you."

"Let me surprise him. Besides, knowing my job, I'll probably get yanked by a page on my way over there."

She sounded irked, and he enjoyed that. "Love can be so rough."

"Just wait; your turn is coming."

He wasn't seeing anyone now, and short of someone colliding with him, at the moment he didn't have time to notice anyone. His hands were full with his job and the O'Malley clan. But knowing Kate, she would probably try to set him up the first chance she got. She loved to meddle in his life, just like he did in hers.

And he knew if she did he'd have to grouse about it just for the principle of it, but he wouldn't really mind. There was never going to be time to date in his schedule; it would simply have to be found. "Good-bye, Kate. I'll see you later."

He closed the cellular phone and his amusement faded. What was wrong? Jennifer O'Malley had just gotten engaged; he didn't think it was her. That left Lisa or Rachel. Lisa was always getting into trouble with that curiosity of hers, but if he had to place a bet he would guess it was Rachel. She had been unusually quiet during the Fourth of July family gathering only days before.

Marcus had no choice but to set aside the problem for the moment. He joined his partner Quinn. "Are we ready?"

"I think so." Quinn looked like he hadn't slept in the last couple days, but then he normally looked that way so it was hard to tell. Quinn had general hotel security: 37 floors; 1,012 rooms; and 50 meeting rooms to cover—it was like trying to plug a leaking dam with cotton balls. Unlike a federal court building where they could screen who entered or left the building, what they carried, this hotel was wide open to the public.

"I got the hotel to agree to close delivery access to the kitchens for the evening; it freed up another three men for ballroom security," Quinn noted. "And I moved Deputy Ellis to Judge Blake. Ellis has covered the Fourth Circuit in the past, maybe he'll be able to talk the judge into following basic security guidelines."

"Thanks. Nelson was showing the strain."

"I can't blame him. Blake is by far the most difficult of the judges on the president's short list." Quinn closed the folder of assignments and tossed it on the cluttered desk. Neatness had disappeared under the churn of numerous problems. "Do you think any of them have a chance of getting the nomination?"

To the U.S. Marshals, who knew the judicial personnel across the country better than the president who appointed them and the congress who confirmed them, a Supreme Court nomination was a race they handicapped with the skill of veteran court watchers.

Marcus considered the names for a moment, then shook his head. "No." The names on the list so far were good judges, but not the great ones. They were the political appeasement candidates, on the list until the scrutiny of the press gave the president something he could use as cover for not nominating them. The real candidates would be in the next set of names that surfaced.

Marcus adjusted his jacket around the shoulder holster, checked the microphone at his cuff, then did a communication check on the security net. He tried to get himself mentally prepared for the long coming evening covering the justice. "I swear Deputy Nicholas Drake ate bad sushi for lunch on purpose. Tell me again how I got elected for this honor rather than you?" he asked while he scanned the room, reviewing where they were at with a check of the status boards. As usual, they were having a conversation but their attention was on anything but each other.

"You're better looking."

Marcus grunted. "Sure. That's why I get asked for *your* phone number." His partner Quinn Diamond attracted attention without trying. The man looked like he had just stepped off his Montana ranch. There was something untamed about him and women seemed to know it. His face was weathered by the sun and wind, he could see to the horizon, and his gaze made suspects fidget. He called women ma'am and wore cowboy boots whenever he could get away with it. Marcus enjoyed having him as a partner; life was never dull. They had tracked fugitives together, protected witnesses, and kept each other alive. Quinn didn't flinch when the pressure hit.

"Actually, Marcus—I'm afraid I kind of blew it the other night," Quinn admitted.

Surprised at the sheepish tone of voice, Marcus glanced over at him. "How?"

"Lisa." Quinn reached into his jacket pocket and took out a folded cloth. He flipped back the folded velvet to show a sealed petri dish. "She sent me a petrified squid."

It was so like his sister Lisa, Marcus had to laugh. "Sounds like a no to me," he remarked dryly. Was this what Kate had stumbled into? A tiff between Quinn and Lisa? It didn't fit Kate's reaction, but it was certainly an interesting development.

"Where did she get this thing?"

"A forensic pathologist—I imagine that was one of the more tame replies she considered sending you."

"All I did was ask her out."

"Quinn, it is painfully obvious you did not have sisters." Marcus took a moment to explain reality. "Two years ago you asked out Jennifer—she's now engaged. Last year you asked out Kate—she's now serious with an FBI agent. This year you asked out Lisa. You just told her she's your third choice. Rachel might forgive you; Lisa will never let you forget it."

"Can I help it if you've got an interesting family?"

Even a friend like Quinn wasn't going to be allowed to hurt his sister. "Flowers will not do; you'd better get creative with the apology."

"I'm still going to get her to say yes."

"I wish you luck; you're going to need it." Quinn would be good for Lisa. He was one of the few men Marcus thought would understand her and the trouble she got into because of her curiosity. Marcus was beginning to feel a bit like a matchmaker having just subtly pushed Kate and Dave together less than a month ago. "Tell you what. I need to free some time late tonight to meet with Kate. Swap the time with me and I'll talk to Lisa for you."

"And tell her what?"

"Only your good points."

"Why don't I believe you?"

Marcus grinned. "I've already told her the bad."

The security net gave the five-minute warning to the start of the evening program. Judge Carl Whitmore would speak first, and then it would be his Honor Justice Roosevelt. Marcus would be glad when the evening was over. "Come on, Quinn, we need to talk to Dave about press access to Justice Roosevelt after the keynote speech."

"Please—give me crowd control; anything but his Honor. I love the man, but he likes nothing better than to rile the media for the fun of it."

"He's appointed for life; his life is boring without controversy."

"You mean he's too old to care if someone decides they want to kill him."

"Exactly."

"You're going to owe me for this one. The last time his Honor held one of these media question and answer sessions, I had to expel a heckler and I ended up all over the evening news."

The Jefferson Hotel served chicken kiev, rice pilaf, and steamed asparagus for the main course at the banquet. Judge Carl Whitmore was too nervous to eat. He politely ate a few bites and moved food around on his plate before finally pushing his plate aside.

Soon after the dinner plates were cleared away, the man beside him rose, moved to the podium, and gave a warm welcome to the guests. He began an introduction that Carl knew would take at most two minutes to give. Carl reached for the folder he had forced himself not to open during dinner.

The introduction finished.

Carl took a deep breath and rose to his feet. He shook hands with the man who had introduced him. Polite applause filled the room.

He slipped off his watch and set it down on the edge of the podium, removed the pages of his speech from the folder and arranged them neatly to the left of center on the podium, and then took a final moment to slip on his reading glasses.

Shari had written a note at the top of the first page with a bright pink felt tip pen—*Remember to smile*—and she had dotted the i in her name with a small heart. That fact, as much as her note, made Carl smile as he lifted his head, faced the bright lights, and smoothly began his prepared remarks to the twelve hundred guests in attendance.

Bless her heart. What would he ever do without her?

Carl had been given such loyal friends. He had gone to law school with her father. Shari, her brother Joshua, and her parents William and Beth, had flown out from Virginia to be here for this speech. The hour of his greatest disappointment was also the hour he learned how rich his life really was.

The president's short list of judges had become known Tuesday, and his name had not been on the list. There had been early rumors that he was being considered, and those rumors had taken on substance when the FBI quietly began checking his background. Carl had begun to let himself hope. He was a bachelor, his life was the law, and to serve on the Supreme Court was his lifelong dream. His disappointment was intense. But in the audience were four people who understood, who shared his disappointment, and were determined to lift his spirits. He had been blessed in his friends. He had the important things in life.

He began the speech he had waited his lifetime to give—a perspective of conservative thought in judicial law.

The lights had partially dimmed as the speech began. Shari Hanford was grateful, for it helped hide the fact she had started to twirl her fork, reflecting her nervous energy.

Even though she had not written this speech, she had worked on minor refinements and knew it word for word. Fifteen years in politics, the last ten of them as a speechwriter, and she still couldn't get through listening to a speech without holding her breath. She knew how important this was to Carl. If something she had suggested didn't work…

She gave up trying to hide the obvious and reached for a roll left in the basket on the table and tore it in two. Maybe it would settle her stomach. She regretted eating the chicken kiev; she should have been smart like Carl and waited to order room service later.

She would much rather be the one giving the speech. When she was at the podium, the nerves gave way to the process of connecting with the audience, adjusting the presentation: the inflections, the timing, the emphasis necessary to persuade people to her point of view.

Her brother Joshua looked over at her and gave her a sympathetic smile. Normally he would be kidding her about her nerves, but not tonight.

Carl began page two of his prepared text. His presentation had been flawless so far. Shari rested her elbow on the table, her chin against the knuckles of her right hand, and ate the bread as she watched him, feeling his passion for the law come through in his words. She didn't understand why he was not on the

Supreme Court short list. Someone at the Justice Department had really fumbled the ball in not recommending him.

Lord, I still don't understand why he was passed over. The quiet prayer was a running conversation that had been going on for days. *It's an enormous disappointment. Didn't the hours invested in prayer mean anything? It's not like I expect every prayer to be answered, but the big ones—*

This was the dream of Carl's life. Why build up hope with the FBI background check and then yank it away? Surely there could have been an easier cushion for delivering an answer of no. I have watched this man love and serve You all of my life. He could make a difference to this nation like no one else on the short list. He would be a great justice.

Her pager vibrated, Shari jerked, and her water glass rocked. It was her emergency pager; she had left her general pager upstairs. Her heart pounding, she pulled it from her pocket. Her job demanded the two pagers; prioritizing people clamoring for her attention was a necessary part of her life.

Only the VIPs in her life had this number, and most of them were sitting at the table with her. She read the return number. It was John Palmer, the governor of the Commonwealth of Virginia. Her boss and longtime friend, he was not one to page unless it was urgent. And for him to call, knowing Carl's speech was tonight—

She rubbed her thumb across the pager numbers, feeling torn, then reluctantly acknowledged she couldn't ignore it for twenty minutes. She reached for her handbag and retrieved her cellular phone. "I'll be back in a minute," she whispered to her mom, slipping away to call John back. Her movement attracted notice from the tables nearby and she cringed, hoping Carl hadn't noticed. The last thing she wanted to do was interrupt his speech.

Opening the side door, she slipped out of the ballroom. To her surprise she found herself in what appeared to be a back hallway—across from her was an open door to a utility room. The hallway was empty, narrow, even somewhat dark. She had obviously come out the wrong door. Shari hesitated, then shrugged off her mistake, glad not to have to worry about the press being around. She dialed John's number.

She had worked for him for over ten years. She added elegance to his communications, his message. She was working long hours as his deputy communications director to get him reelected. What was wrong?

Shari paced the hall toward the windows as she waited for the phone to be answered, then paused and closed her eyes as fatigue washed over her. The Fourth of July campaigning had been four days of nonstop travel, crisscrossing Virginia. She had been home a day to pack and then she had met her parents and brother to fly out here to Chicago for the three-day conference. It was supposed to be a rest break for her, but it wasn't happening. Her body clock was off, leaving her wide awake at 2 A.M. and fighting sleep at noon. She struggled to suppress her fatigue so it wouldn't show in her voice.

Her pager went off again. She scowled. There was apparently a crisis breaking in Virginia and she was halfway across the country in Chicago. She had known getting away in the middle of an election was a bad idea.

Normally she thrived on diving into the problems and being in the center of the storm. Joshua called it her hurricane mode: dealing with incomplete information, immediate deadlines, impending catastrophes—she found being in the center of the action a calm place to be when she was the one controlling the response. That wasn't the case tonight, she was too far away. She lifted the pager to look at the number and see who else was demanding her attention.

It was like getting physically battered.

Sam. He hadn't called her directly in almost five months, not since she'd slammed the phone down on him last time. She rarely lost it so eloquently, and she had done it in style that evening.

Sam Black. The man she had let get deep into her soul and curl around her heart; he was like a black mark she couldn't erase. She had loved him so passionately and today just the sight of his number was enough to bring back a flood of emotions to paralyze her. It had not been a gentle breakup between them, for dreams had imploded and expectations had been crushed. It had been intense, painful, and a year later it still haunted her.

Sam was another prayer God had not answered.

She wanted to swear, did slap her hand against the wall and pace away from the windows. She was trying to solve her growing dilemma about prayer while stuck on a phone walking the halls of a hotel in Chicago.

She hated not having her prayers answered.

You're spoiled, she told herself with a wry smile. *And God still loves you anyway.*

She looked again at the pager. Sam had the ability to be cordial, even friendly when they spoke, and the best she could do was chilly politeness as the embarrassment of what could have been washed over her and the sound of his voice brought back all her hopes. She chose to ignore his page even as she wondered why he would feel the need to call.

The phone was finally answered. "Sorry about the delay, Shari. Thanks for calling back so quickly."

She briefly wondered how John had functioned before caller ID. "Not a problem. What's happening?"

"How would you like Christmas about six months early?"

She could hear the smile in his voice. "What?"

"Carl is going to make the short list. Your brief helped, Shari."

Her heart stopped momentarily. "You're serious." She had labored over that brief presenting Carl's qualifications for the court; she knew Carl's past cases better than his own law clerks; she knew the man. It was the best position paper of her life. John had passed it through to Washington—one voice in a sea of voices.

"I just got off the phone with the attorney general. They've recommended Carl to the president. The attorney general expects a positive decision to happen tonight."

She closed her eyes, knowing she needed to apologize to God. "John, you couldn't have given me better news."

"Keep him near the phone tonight?"

"Of course! I'll make sure we're prepared to celebrate when the call comes." She rubbed her forehead, gave a soft laugh. "Talk about a reason for an ulcer—Carl makes the list and then we wait some more. The president makes his choice in ten days."

"At least you'll be pacing for a good reason."

It was a running joke between them, her habit of pacing when she thought, talked, waited. "Any other major issues?"

"Nothing that won't wait another day."

"I'll talk to you tomorrow then." She closed the phone after saying thanks once again.

Carl was going to make the short list. Her high heels sank into the carpet as she spun around, feeling like she would burst keeping such a secret for even a couple hours. *Lord, thank You! And I'm sorry for thinking it didn't matter to You.* She had to at least tell her brother Josh. They could order a special room service dinner for Carl—lobster, maybe. After the call came, they could invite a few of his friends to join them.

Lord, the anticipation is so strong I can taste it.

Carl might actually be sitting on the Supreme Court when it opens its next session. The image of that was incredible.

She pulled open the side door to the ballroom so she could slip back inside.

"Oh. I'm sorry!" Shari pulled up at the sight of men in suits carrying guns. They turned, the three nearest her, blocking her line of sight into the rest of the room. This was definitely not the ballroom.

None of the doors in the back corridor were marked. She had obviously gotten turned around as she paced and talked on the phone. She had walked in on men carrying guns. Her heart rate escalated, about the same instant the three men near her actually relaxed. Their assessment had been swift.

The man on the right removed his hand from inside his jacket. She wanted to give a nervous laugh as she realized he had instinctively put his hand on his gun. This was clearly not turning out to be her night. She had been introduced to foreign dignitaries and hosted senators for dinner and never fumbled as much as she had in this one evening.

"No problem," the man nearest her said as he smiled, disarming her panic with a charm that made her blink. His entire demeanor softened with that smile. Tall, edging over six feet, the seams of the tuxedo strained by muscles, a gaze that pierced. He would have been a threatening figure without that smile, but it changed everything. It was like getting hit with a warm punch when his attention focused on her.

She had come in the side door of what was obviously a security control center, and now stood behind two long tables where cables and power cords from PCs and faxes snaked down to the floor. The room was actually quite busy, at least twenty people present; most had paused what they were doing at her entrance and quiet had washed over the room.

"That door should have been locked; it wasn't entirely your mistake," the man commented, stepping around the tables and over the wires to join her. His black jacket hung open, his shoulder holster visible. She instinctively knew he was one of the men in charge. There was a confident directness to his look and words. His hand settled under her elbow and without being obtrusive about it, steered her back out of the room. She felt the power in that grip checked to be light. "You came two doors beyond the ballroom."

She was acutely embarrassed, but he was being nice about it. "I've always been directionally challenged. I didn't mean to go somewhere I didn't belong."

"No harm done."

She had never been able to shake that one fatal flaw in her makeup—her inability to keep her sense of bearings—and it was her own fault. Frankly, she didn't pay enough attention until it was too late to correct the mistake.

Every year she made a solemn New Year's resolution to try harder, and every year she managed to forget that promise and get herself back into situations like this with painful regularity. And to do it in front of three good-looking guys...there were times she really did want to be able to shrink into the woodwork.

She took a deep breath and let it go; the damage was done and it was time to recover as best she could. The realization touched her smile with humor. "I'm Shari, by the way."

"Shari Hanford. Yes, I know." He firmly closed the door behind him, then released her elbow and offered his hand. "Marcus O'Malley."

She blinked at the fact he knew her name, then realized a man in his position probably knew most everything; a fanciful notion but not one she would bet against. She had attended too many judicial events where men like him melted into the background not to have a healthy respect for what he did. Not that Marcus would ever melt into the background of anything—he'd be the one attracting the attention.

Up close, the reality of his presence was overwhelming, absorbing her senses. Weight lifter, runner, something...he was an athlete and it showed in his build. She looked because she couldn't help herself. Her gaze finally met his and she blushed slightly at the confident directness and quiet amusement she saw in his eyes.

"Marcus. It's nice to meet you." His hand was strong and callused, and when it closed around hers she felt the clasp of warmth through her fingers, palm, and fine bones of her wrist. She wanted to believe it was her imagination that had her hand trapped in his for a beat too long, but then he smiled, still holding her hand, and she realized it was not her imagination. She wanted to blush again but found herself holding his gaze instead.

It had been a long time since someone not associated with work looked at her with that kind of frank appreciation. It did wonders for her sense of morale. She didn't have to worry that he was going to be hitting her in the next moment with a request for a quote from her boss. She knew she looked her best. She had pulled her hair up, chosen gold jewelry, and defined her eyelashes around her blue eyes. In her new white linen suit she looked not only professional but elegant. It was nice to have that fact noticed.

"It's a pleasure to meet you, Shari." He released her hand. "I've got a minute, I'll see you safely back to table six."

"Oh, that's how you knew my name," she remarked and instantly wanted to kick herself. That was a really elegant comment. What would she think of next? The weather? She wanted to impress him not leave a bigger impression of a scatterbrain.

His smile deepened. "Yes." He nodded to the phone and pager in her hand. "You got a page?"

"Yes. And I tend to pace as I talk, hence the total confusion when I finished the call."

"Was it at least good news?"

"Very."

"From that smile, I would think so."

"Are you always this direct?" she asked, both amused and charmed.

"When I'm killing time with a pretty lady."

She would have preferred beautiful, but she could live with pretty.

What he had said registered. Someone was running a security check. She had wondered; they were ten feet from the door to the ballroom and they were standing still. *Josh, I managed to make the U.S. Marshal's security breach logbook.* It was going to be hard to live this one down.

Marcus had to be swamped tonight, and this was taking time from more important duties, but he was not making her feel stupid. The opposite actually. She deeply appreciated his ability to be kind. She grinned. "Should I tell you all my secrets now, or do we wait for someone to find my file and tell you all of them?"

His brown eyes deepened and warmed to gold. "Security precautions are part of a conference like this; it will only take a minute. But if you have some interesting ones...?"

"None that I'm willing to share unilaterally."

There was a beat in time and then he laughed, a delightful sound, warm and rich. "Well said."

She wished she met guys like this more often; politicians rarely had a good sense of humor. She leaned against the wall, letting her shoulder absorb her weight and take the strain off her sore right ankle that she had wrenched earlier in the day playing tennis with Joshua. Marcus looked comfortable in that tuxedo and at home with the authority he wore like a second skin.

"Have you been enjoying the conference?"

She risked showing her interest. "Yes, but it just got much nicer."

His slow grin…she wished she could bottle the warmth it gave so she could enjoy it again later. "I see I'm not the only one who knows how to be direct."

"I have a feeling I'm about out of time. They'll have me cleared soon," she replied easily while her heart thumped a patter she hadn't heard in a year. The guy didn't have a ring on, he was breathtakingly handsome, he could turn her to mush with his smile, and he didn't have a thing to do with politics. She was feeling unusually courageous. Tonight had already been such a roller coaster of emotions that she figured one more would fit right in.

"Why do you dot your i's with a heart?"

She blinked. "How did you know that?"

"They actually cleared you a few moments ago. Among other things, you signed for the table six tickets."

"Marcus."

He didn't look the slightest bit apologetic. "Saying good-bye wasn't at the top of my priorities. Listen, would you be interested in joining me for coffee tomorrow morning? I'm already having a late dinner with my sister tonight."

She didn't know quite what to say. Yes, she did; she just didn't know how to say it. She took a breath and let herself drop into the unknown. "I would love to join you for coffee."

Any question of whether that was a good move or not disappeared when she saw his expression. Knowing she had put that look of satisfaction on his face…it felt good. Very good.

"I'll call you." He gestured toward the ballroom. "Let me see you back."

Shari walked with him, bemused by the turns this evening was bringing.

They had almost reached the correct door when it opened and her brother stepped out. Shari paused, surprised, and Marcus actually drew her back a step behind him. She got the feeling he automatically assumed a threat and quietly put her hand on his forearm, felt his muscles flex under her hand, as she stepped forward and passed him to meet her brother. "Hi, Josh. Did you think I got lost?"

"You have been known to in the past," Josh agreed easily, putting his arm around her shoulders. "Just making sure the page wasn't bad news."

"Some of it was very good." She reached up and comfortably grasped her brother's wrist with her hand. He was assessing the man with her and not being too subtle about the fact. "Joshua, this is Marcus. Marcus, my brother."

His right arm around her shoulders, Josh didn't try to shake hands, he simply nodded politely. "Nice to meet you." The two men looked at each other for a moment, then Josh glanced back at her. "We'd better get back. Carl is just wrapping up his speech."

"Carl!" She had totally forgotten him for a moment. "How's he doing?"

Joshua laughed. "Excellent."

Marcus apparently heard something over his earpiece; his expression became distant as he lifted his hand and replied into the small microphone at his cuff, saying something too soft for her to hear. When he glanced back at her, his gaze was still warm, but it was obvious his attention had been diverted. "It was nice to meet you, Shari. Please excuse me?"

She nodded and watched him walk purposefully away, back the way they had come.

"Security?" Josh asked.

She nodded and didn't bother to explain how they had met or about the invitation to coffee. "Let's catch the end of Carl's speech. I've got some great news to tell you!"

"Pretty lady," Dave commented, his British accent conveying an extra weight to his choice of the word *lady.*

Marcus glanced at his friend as they crossed to the elevator that was reserved for security use this evening. "It took you long enough to confirm it was an honest mistake."

"I noticed you weren't complaining."

Dave was probing and Marcus knew it; he just smiled and ignored the comment. The family grapevine would love to hear news that he had met someone he liked. He didn't intend to feed it even unintentionally.

They wanted him to be happy, and every couple years his social life became a hot topic behind his back on the family grapevine. It would settle down when someone else in the family became more interesting.

Family. He had to love them. Dave was fitting right in.

Shari fit what he was looking for at the moment. She was someone he could relax with for a few minutes in the midst of a pressure-filled weekend. He had learned to seize those unexpected moments in life.

Over the security net came word Justice Roosevelt was ready to come down. Separating the conversation he was having with the security net conversation he was monitoring was habit after all these years. Marcus completed a sentence with Dave and made a request on the security net with barely a pause in between. He got back confirmation from the three agents securing the area into the ballroom that they were ready. Satisfied with his own inspection of the area, he gave the go-ahead. "Send his Honor down."

Dave watched the elevator numbers start down from the nineteenth floor. "Going to find an excuse to meet her again?"

There were some things that couldn't be kept a secret in this tight knit security community and in this instance Marcus didn't even try. "We're having coffee in the morning."

"Can I tell that to Kate?"

If Dave mentioned it tonight, Kate would likely find an excuse to drop by the hotel in the morning. "Save it for when you need to dig yourself out of the doghouse for something," Marcus replied, drawing a laugh from his friend.

Connor Gray sat at table twenty-two and twirled his fork as he listened to Judge Whitmore's speech. He listened and his hate grew; his target was now in sight.

His older brother was dead because of this judge. For twelve years the death penalty appeals had wound through the system and no one had stopped the sentence given by this man. It had been carried out.

Now he would return the favor.

He had thought about it, as he had promised his brother he would do. He had thought about it for nine months. He had almost decided to let it go as Daniel had asked, until rumors of the Supreme Court nomination had surfaced.

Connor had gotten hold of a copy of the brief floating around. It was good. Very good. It laid the road map for a senate confirmation of Judge Whitmore. The president was known to be heavily weighing that reality as he made his decision; it wasn't going to be easy to get a conservative justice confirmed. The brief tipped the ultimate decision strongly in favor of Judge Whitmore. There was no way Connor would allow this judge to sit on the Supreme Court.

He could get away with the murder. He knew what it would take to convict him, and they wouldn't have it. He had planned with a logic his brother would have been proud of. The mistakes others made had been eliminated. Witnesses. Evidence. He knew what it would take to create reasonable doubt. He had more than just alibis in place.

And he knew the value of the character card at trial. He had been forced to become the good son, to pay for the sins of his brother. As a result he was a man who didn't even have so much as a parking ticket to his name. He could claim the best schools; he had a Rolodex of the right friends, a distinguished career.

He was being forced to act sooner than he had planned. Judge Whitmore wasn't on the president's short list yet, but Justice Department sources said the judge's name would be added soon. Once he was on that list, reaching past security to get to him would be impossible.

As it turned out, even that change in timing had worked out to his benefit. He was here, within sight of his target, and no one suspected what he had planned.

Connor excused himself as Judge Whitmore's speech concluded.

TWO

Shari was safely back at table six. Marcus saw her seated there as he scanned the room. He stood behind Justice Roosevelt: listening, watching, attuned to any movement in the crowd, staying relaxed, ready to react. An older couple, a second look confirmed they were her parents, sat to Shari's left. Joshua sat to her right. A nice guy, her brother; young but protective. Not many men would have made that direct a silent challenge to him.

As an older brother himself, he had accepted the silent challenge with more amusement than personal irritation. Shari was frankly too open with strangers; she needed a Joshua in her life watching out for her.

He was going to enjoy having coffee with her. He liked her willingness to admit with self-directed humor to being directionally challenged; he liked the confidence in her gaze when she met his. She carried herself with the ease of someone comfortable with who she was. He smiled just thinking about her comeback regarding sharing secrets unilaterally. Someone who could laugh at herself was rare and very appealing.

She was pretty; not classically beautiful, but pretty. When she'd walked into the Belmont room by mistake he'd captured details out of habit: brunette; blue eyes; five-feet-three; slender; midthirties; a small, white scar on the left corner of her top lip; teeth so straight she had probably worn braces as a child. A few minutes with her and she had his full attention. She reminded him of his sister Jennifer, someone who vibrated with life.

It was such a subtle sign, Shari reaching up to grasp her brother's wrist, but it shouted. In her world, family was close, special, and trusted. She had been given that gift by luck of birth; he had found it with the O'Malleys. They'd share at least one thing in common: love of family.

He wished he had bumped into her under different circumstances. This was bad timing. It wasn't like either one of them lived in Chicago; it wasn't like he would get a chance to see her after this weekend if he wanted to follow up coffee with a more substantive invitation to dinner. Unless…the back of Shari's photograph had given her name, listed her residence as Virginia.

He traveled constantly with work, was based out of Washington, but his apartment was in Arlington, Virginia, just across the Potomac River, north of Arlington National Cemetery. When he was in town, he took advantage of the hiking trails maintained on Roosevelt Island for his morning run. If Shari were interested, if she lived somewhere in his area of Virginia, maybe he wouldn't have to meet her once and then say good-bye…

"Movement on the right, yellow zone, subject unidentified."

Marcus turned his attention toward the threat without appearing to move. If someone unidentified broke the red zone, ten tables from the speakers' table, they would be forcibly stopped. The waiters were not all waiters.

Nothing had happened; it was the best kind of evening. Marcus stretched a cramp out of his right shoulder and rubbed his forearm. Ever since the O'Malley baseball game on the Fourth of July when he'd backhanded a throw to catch Dave out at first base, the muscles had been acting up. He smiled, remembering Kate's outrage when Dave had been called out. A sore arm was worth it.

Chairs fell with a clatter. Marcus turned to see two workers move to pick them up. The hotel crews were beginning to take down the decorations in the ballroom, rearrange the tables. In seven hours this room had to be reconfigured for a breakfast meeting for six hundred.

"Marcus, we've got a problem."

His partner Quinn was striding across the room toward him. "The evening was going so well. Justice Roosevelt?"

"Thank goodness, no. He's safely tucked back in his suite on the secure floor. Washington just called. The president added Judge Whitmore to his short list."

Marcus raised one eyebrow. "The president added him at this time of night?" He shook his head in answer to his own question. The decision had likely been made some time ago and they were only now hearing about it. His frustration showed in his scowl. "When are they going to realize they need to warn us first, *before* they take the names to the president for consideration?"

"Exactly. Be glad they didn't leak the name during his speech."

"Is there a room free on the secure floor?"

"The East Suite."

Marcus glanced at his watch. Kate would be here soon. "Let's go find the judge and get him moved to the nineteen floor. Did you pull his threat file?"

"It's being faxed over now. Apparently it's pretty clean."

"That will change as his name leaks out." They left the ballroom and moved through the lobby, skirting past guests to the private corridor. "Do we have a deputy we can assign?"

"I was thinking about Chuck Nance," Quinn replied. "He's covering the live television interviews in the Ontario Room; he'll be free within the hour."

"He's good; okay, get him assigned. How else is it going?"

"Besides a fender bender, a paparazzi trying to get a photo of Judge Frenston kissing the wife of Judge Burkhaven, and the hotel running out of imported caviar? It's just wonderful. You should have this job."

"Burkhaven's wife?"

"Don't worry. I was tactful when I suggested they might want to find some privacy."

"I wish I had been a fly on the wall."

"This keeps up, I'm going to ask for a reassignment. I hired on to chase bad guys, not be a diplomat."

"But you're so good at it," Marcus protested, chuckling at Quinn's scowl. Marcus saw Dave ahead of them, just stepping into an elevator. "Dave, hold the elevator."

Dave caught the door so they could join him. "What's up?"

"We've got a judge to move to the secure floor. Can you give us a hand?"

"Sure. Who?"

"Whitmore. Room 961," Quinn replied.

Dave pushed the button for the ninth floor of the hotel.

"Shari, you're pacing again." Joshua, stretched out on the couch, waved her out of his way so he could flip through the television channels looking for the late news.

"The phone is never going to ring."

"Would you quit worrying? The call will come. Carl is not even back yet. He was still talking to the conference host when we left to come up."

Shari knew he was right, but still... She walked over to the desk where she had temporarily set up shop for these three days, looking for something to do to keep herself occupied. Patience was a virtue she would one day have to work on. "How long before dinner arrives?" They had settled on ordering Italian, Carl's favorite.

"Fifteen, twenty minutes."

She rummaged to find a pen and pad of paper, deciding she might as well do some work. She was working on a major school reform speech. The same day the speech was given, a detailed position paper would be released. Getting the two to meld together with clarity was a challenge.

The suite she was sharing with her parents was like many hotel rooms she had stayed in over the years, and as usual her things had sprawled. Abandoning the desk since it did not have room for her, she settled in one of the plush wingback chairs, and set her glass of iced tea on the side table.

She had always found it easy to get lost in her work, but tonight it was a struggle. When she realized she'd scrawled the name Marcus in the margin of her note page, she forced herself to turn the page. Marcus was tomorrow morning's distraction, and if it was one thing she prided herself on, it was keeping her focus.

Not that she had heard a word of Supreme Court Justice Roosevelt's speech tonight, not with Marcus standing behind him on the stage. She was almost certain Marcus had looked her way more than necessary during the evening. She would like to imagine he had really winked at her, but she wasn't quite certain enough to risk asking him in the morning. Marcus got better looking the longer she had looked, and she'd sat there bemused for over an hour.

A cop. She was interested in a cop. She gave a silent chuckle. Given her profession, it was probably as good a choice as any. She'd love to have him at her side when the mud started to fly at one of the numerous social gatherings she attended as part of her job. She had a feeling politicians would temper their words around him.

Anne was going to enjoy hearing this news. John's deputy chief of staff, her longtime friend, had been encouraging her to get over Sam for months. Of course, it wasn't exactly going to be easy to find the right words... *Anne, I bumped into this guy with a gun.* She grinned. Yeah. That would work.

She glanced up when the sound of footsteps came her direction. Her dad had changed from his suit.

"Working on John's speech?"

Dad knew her well. "Trying to." He had read the first draft yesterday.

"You've got a challenge making the intricacies of bond refinancing clear."

"Tell me about it. I just keep reminding listeners it's money. Either pay now or pay more later. That always catches attention." A knock on the door interrupted them. Joshua got up to answer it. Room service had arrived with dinner. Shari set aside the work to help Josh clear the table so they could set it out.

"Is Carl back?" her dad asked.

Shari heard something from next door. "There he is now, right on time."

She walked across the suite to the connecting door with the adjoining hotel room, carrying one of the hot cheese-filled breadsticks Josh had ordered for an appetizer. The good news hadn't come yet, but this feast couldn't wait. She tapped on the door. "Carl, dinner's here." The connecting door had never been latched and it swung open under her hand. "Josh thinks your speech—"

The muted sound of a silenced gunshot echoed through Carl's room. Horror swelled inside Shari like a wave as she saw Carl crumble backwards to the floor, his face turning toward her. His eyes showed unspeakable fear, surprise, then a blank nothing. The breadstick dropped from her hand. The shooter stood to her left, less than six feet away. She had surprised him; that fact registered in the brief instant when she simply stood there.

He wore a dark suit, tailored, with a burgundy red tie, a white herringbone shirt, and black shoes polished to a high shine. His face showed angry determination, and his gray eyes as he turned to look at her were filled with intense hatred.

She tried to scream and when it came, it ripped from the back of her throat.

He was already firing as he swung toward her; the first bullet kicked up wood from the door frame inches from her face. Her hand flew up at the sharp sting.

Joshua hit her; it was a full tackle with no finesse, catching her low in the ribs and knocking her out of the doorway. She slammed into the side table, and the lamp crashed down with her as she tumbled over the couch. Her forearm hit hard wood, her right knee twisted, and her chin cracked against the floor, sending shooting pain through her face.

The shots went on and on, emptying into the room, and then it went deathly quiet. Shari could hear nothing but the pounding of her heartbeat. She lifted her head slowly from the carpet abrading her cheek, heard a door slam somewhere in the background, and turned her head, quivering.

"Josh!" He lay partially over her lower legs, crumpled to the floor with his arms outstretched. He wasn't moving. She tried to slip free without her high heels hitting his face.

As soon as she was clear, she turned and scrambled back toward him on her hands and knees, seeing a spreading pool of blood staining his white shirt around his right shoulder and his upper back. The sight terrified her. All her life she had watched him be the adventurous one, the athlete, and now he lay crumbled with his eyes closed as if all the strings had been cut. She turned him awkwardly so he wasn't lying on the wound.

She heard her mother moan and looked around, then froze as she watched her mom try to lift the limp body of her father into her arms. A streak of blood along the wall showed where her father had been flung back by the bullet's impact; he had crumpled there. He couldn't be dead. No! He couldn't be dead.

It registered and yet it didn't; disbelief was overriding what her eyes were telling her. Someone had killed Carl; tried to kill her; and shot her brother and her father.

It hit so hard she couldn't breathe. Couldn't think. Couldn't pray. Words weren't connecting.

Joshua's eyes flickered open: blue, dilated. Almost immediately they began to glaze over. He made no sound, but his eyes…

Her thoughts cleared. Her mind sharpened. The moment crystallized. An icy calmness settled across her.

"Mom, lay Dad flat. Get pressure on the bleeding," she said, hoping it wasn't too late for him.

She pressed her hands tight against Josh's shoulder, feeling them grow slick with his blood. "Hold on, Josh. Just hold on." She could see her hands shaking but couldn't feel it. "You're going to be all right."

He struggled to breathe. It was a frightening sound.

The table was on its side and she yanked the fallen phone toward her by the cord. She had to hang up the receiver to get a dial tone back. She hit zero, leaving a bloody fingerprint.

"There's been a shooting in suite 963. We need medical help." She was stunned at how clear her voice was. She was so tense her muscles were going to break bones, but her voice was calm. Joshua and her dad couldn't afford it if she panicked.

"Ma'am—"

"My name is Shari Hanford. Someone just shot Judge Whitmore. My dad and brother were also hit. I need help, now! Suite 963," she repeated.

"It's on the way." She had rattled the reception desk attendant. "Stay on the line—"

Shari dropped the phone to the carpet, not hanging up, but needing both hands for Joshua. "Mom, how's Dad?" She swiveled around on her heels and saw her mom's face. If she wasn't already having a second heart attack, she was on the verge of one. Her mom was one of the strongest ladies Shari knew, but not in her health. A heart infection after surgery ten years ago had made her vulnerable, and a mild heart attack two years ago had worsened that outlook. A shock like this could kill her. "Mom, where are your pills?" Shari asked urgently.

"I'm okay for now. Stay with Josh."

Shari looked at Josh, then back at her mom, a sense of panic taking hold. Help wasn't going to arrive in time. *Jesus, I need You more now than I've ever needed You before. Please, send help quickly!*

"Shots fired! Suite 963. Repeat, shots fired, suite 963!"

Marcus, Quinn, and Dave flattened against the side walls of the elevator, realizing with a startled and then grim glance between themselves that the elevator doors were opening on floor nine at that very instant. Marcus hit the emergency stop button, relieved they had silenced the alarms during the security preparations. Guns drawn, they moved out of the confined space, covering for each other.

The elevator opened into a small alcove. A gold plaque on the facing corridor wall showed rooms 930 to 949 and stairs to the left, rooms 950 to 969 and vending to the right.

A glance up showed none of the guest elevators were moving. The shooter hadn't gone out this way. "Freeze the southwest elevators," Marcus quietly ordered the control center. "Three officers now on the floor."

Dave slipped a small four-inch mirror from his pocket and used it to check both directions of the corridor. "Empty."

The only sound was the faint one of the ice machine down the hall. It didn't mean much. Marcus knew these hotel rooms were nearly soundproof, having more than once opened the door to his suite to find that Quinn had the television blaring so he could listen to the news as he shaved.

Marcus touched Quinn's shoulder and pointed left toward the stairs.

Quinn nodded and moved that direction.

Marcus tapped Dave to help him investigate suite 963.

The vending area at the end of the hall worried him and he kept his attention on that danger point as they moved down the hall. A guest room door opened and they both pivoted, guns aimed, only to immediately check their movements. Dave waved the horrified guest back inside his room.

Marcus reached the closed door to suite 963, stopped, and Dave slid past him to the other side. Dave removed his master hotel card key and quietly tapped his knee, indicating he would go in low. Marcus nodded.

Dave silently inserted the card key, then pulled it out. The red light flashed green.

Marcus met Dave's gaze and in that intense moment knew Dave was thinking the same thing he was. Kate would kill them both if either one of them got hurt.

Dave pushed open the door.

It caught on the chain.

Marcus, his momentum already taking him forward, barely checked in time to avoid hitting the door. They had the right suite number. A false alarm? No. The smell of gunpowder lingered in the air and it was impossible to miss the smell of blood. Someone had slipped the chain in place out of fear? *Or had the shooter barricaded himself inside?* "Police! Open up!"

Dave prepared to kick the door open. Over the security net Marcus could hear the coordinated response of U.S. Marshals, FBI agents, and uniform cops rushing to close the area. Backup was coming, but they didn't have time to wait.

The door chain jangled as someone tried to open the door.

The door swung open. Marcus and Dave instantly elevated their weapons to the ceiling. It was a lady in her fifties. Her identity registered at first with disbelief. It was Shari's mom, Beth Hanford. Marcus reached out and caught her elbow to keep her from falling. Her face had a distinct pale grayness, and there was blood on her dress.

"I've got her." Dave wrapped his arms around her waist to lower her to the floor. Marcus heard the grimness in Dave's voice, the shared impact this was having on him. They had been talking about this family only a few moments ago.

A scan of the room showed carnage. Shari's father had been shot. Joshua had been shot. Shari turned from where she was kneeling beside Josh, desperation coupled with intense relief in her eyes.

Marcus hated the fact he had no choice but to ignore her. First he had to know the rooms were secure. Dave was moving to the left, checking the suite bedrooms. Marcus moved to the right and the open connecting door.

He drew a deep breath. Judge Carl Whitmore lay on his back, the empty look in his eyes confirming the worst. Marcus had never lost a witness or a judge on his watch and fury washed over him.

He forced himself to take a deep breath before he walked past the judge to check the bathroom, anywhere someone could hide. When he was sure he was alone, he knelt to confirm the judge was dead, careful where he stepped so as to minimize what he disturbed of the crime scene. "Judge Whitmore has been killed." His words over the security net quiet and cold.

Judge Whitmore had died facing into his room. Someone had been inside the room. Waiting. Marcus hadn't known the judge and the Hanfords were friends, but the open connecting door suggested they were. The lock had to be released on both sides. Were the Hanfords just unfortunately in the wrong place at the wrong time, or were they targets as well and the hit had gone bad? It was an ugly thought.

The dead could wait; there were survivors to attend to.

Dave was already working on Shari's father, William. Marcus skirted the overturned furniture to reach Shari and Josh. He closed his hand carefully around Shari's shoulder and looked her over swiftly, trying to tell if she had been hit as well. He had seen victims walking around so deep in shock they didn't even realize they were hit.

There was a nasty gash on her right cheekbone just below her eye and her face had been scuffed, but the blood staining her suit and her hands, some of it dark red, having dried, and other patches bright and wet, didn't appear to be hers.

"I can't get the bleeding to stop."

Her voice was steady but she was quivering under his hand. He wished he had time to wrap his arm around her and hug her, try to stop the shivers. That this should happen to her and her family the same night he had met her…it made him sick at heart. "It's okay, Shari," he said gently. He eased his hands under hers, wedging his fingers under her palm, keeping the pressure on Joshua's shoulder steady. "I've got him."

She was leaning forward over her brother and Marcus was crowding her space now they were so close together. Did she realize her eyes were wide and her breathing fast, that her heart was pounding? He counted five beats in the moment he realized the twitch showing at her throat was her heartbeat. Calm down, he wanted to urge and was helpless to help her do that. She'd just lived through a nightmare. She blinked. *Good girl. Come on, blink again.* She finally did. *Where are those paramedics? I need to get you out of here.*

He turned his attention to her brother. He had to rip Josh's shirt to get a look at the injury. The bullet had hit him in his right shoulder, deflected off his collarbone, and come out at an angle just below it. Nasty, and bleeding heavily. Joshua's pallor was sharp; his eyes were closed and his lips were beginning to turn slightly blue. The young man he had admired earlier that evening was dying Marcus realized with grim resolve, determined not to let that happen. One fatality was more than enough.

"I need to get Mom's heart pills."

Marcus looked toward Beth and saw what Shari had. "Go," he said urgently.

Shari nodded and got to her feet, almost falling, catching herself with a hand on his shoulder. Her hand tightened as she drew a deep breath, took the first step away. His eyes narrowed as he watched her walk toward the bedroom. It looked like she was in danger of folding, but she kept going.

The sound of gunfire and someone tumbling and striking concrete burst over the net. "Shooter on the stairs. He's heading up!"

Marcus jerked. Up toward the secure floor. "Quinn? Come back."

"He winged me. I'm okay," Quinn replied, his breathing ragged. "You guys coming down from nineteen be careful you don't shoot me by mistake and finish the job."

His partner was under fire. Marcus looked over at Dave, desperate to go. They had to be two places at once. Dave, his face taut, shook his head. Marcus hated it but accepted the fact Dave was right. They couldn't leave Joshua and William before help got here. "Where are those paramedics?"

"Coming up under escort. I told them to rush it and get medivac on the way."

"Mom, your pills," Shari said. "I grabbed Dad's prescription bottles too. The paramedics will need to know about the blood pressure medicine."

"I'll tell them. His medical alert tags, they'll need those too."

"Dad's wearing them," Shari said a moment later. "Mom, do you need to lie down? Are you okay?"

"I'm okay. Go, help with Josh. The man needs the extra hands."

He most certainly did. Marcus glanced over, ready to tell Shari to stay with her mom despite that fact, only to meet Beth's firm gaze. The lady might be having a hard time physically coping with the suddenness of the shock, but there was steel in those soft gray eyes looking across the room at him. Beth was a fighter; that boded well. He studied her face for a moment, then gave a slight nod to her and looked over at Shari. He really did need her hands.

Shari rejoined him. She had thought to grab a stack of towels while in the bathroom. "Will these help?"

He took one, grateful. "Absolutely; thanks." He glanced over to see she had already given Dave several.

"He just started shooting."

Marcus looked sharply at Shari. In the back of his mind he had been hoping she had been in the bedroom, somewhere else, at least been spared actually seeing her brother and dad shot. Given what she had just said, he was surprised she had any composure left. "One shooter?"

She nodded and her brow furrowed. "White, late-thirties. Not tall, maybe five-foot-eight—" she visibly struggled with her words as she remembered—"well dressed."

Over the security net he could hear each step of the hunt to pin the shooter down. Men were moving to seal the entire wing of the hotel. "What was he wearing?"

"A dark suit, navy, and a red tie."

He relayed the information as fast as she gave it. "Did you see his face?" When she flinched he momentarily hated himself.

"Gray eyes. They were so violent. And his hair was dark, almost black, really thick."

"Glasses, beard, mustache?"

"A thin mustache, wider than his mouth, no beard or glasses."

"Anything else about him? Did he say anything?"

She shook her head. "I remember thinking 'I surprised him,' then Josh hit me."

Marcus glanced again at the open connecting door, the overturned furniture, and this time he was the one who flinched. Shari must have been the one to open the connecting door. The splintered wood on the door frame was level with that gash on her face. The shooter had tried to kill her. Marcus felt his hands go cold at the realization.

Quinn swore over the security net. "He's out of the stairway. Repeat, the shooter got out of the stairwell. He's somewhere on floors eleven to fifteen!"

"Rule out floor fifteen, we've got the corridors covered," another deputy called.

Several moments later, another voice came across the secure channel. "I'm on fourteen. There's a merger meeting going on in the telecommunication conference center. The security guard says it's been quiet. The shooter's got to be somewhere on floors eleven to thirteen."

Three floors were still an eternity of space. There were service elevators, guest elevators, two sets of stairs, and that didn't even consider the hotel rooms. Marcus broke into the security net traffic. "We need a hostage negotiator located. Now," he ordered. "See if Kate O'Malley is in the hotel."

Dave turned to give him a frustrated glance. "Why does it always have to be Kate who's around when trouble breaks?"

"Tell me about it," Marcus replied, feeling a growing anxiety that this situation was so rapidly spiraling out of control. He knew the risk he had just potentially dropped into his sister's lap. "Nobody handles barricade situations better than Kate, we both know that. The shooter is pinned; he's not likely to give up without a fight when he's got rooms of hostages available to choose from."

"Someone shoot him before then, please," Dave replied tersely.

Marcus silently agreed, knowing if this became a barricade situation, they were facing high odds there would be another innocent victim. Kate had the nasty habit of putting herself between a gunman and a hostage. She was still getting over a hairline rib fracture from the last time she had done it. The Kevlar vest had stopped the bullet and she'd walked away from the situation annoyed with all the fuss he and Dave made. Marcus didn't think she had any idea how much gray hair she had given them in those twenty tense minutes.

He listened as men began to evacuate the hotel rooms one at a time. "How's William doing?"

"Not good," Dave replied. "Joshua?"

"Not much better," Marcus replied grimly. "Shari, keep pressure right here."

He took her hands to show her what he wanted, felt the coldness in her long fingers as he placed them over the towel. "I need to get his feet elevated." Anything to stop Joshua from bleeding out. Over the security net came word the paramedics were passing the seventh floor. Finally.

The bleeding was slowing. "Just keep it steady there, okay?"

She nodded.

They had a shooter loose. Judge Whitmore had died facing into his room. Someone had been inside. And according to Shari, it hadn't been a lady. Marcus broke into the security net traffic again. "The shooter may have a room pass key. Maybe even a master."

"Any other good news?" Quinn asked.

"He likes to wait and take his victim by surprise."

"Wonderful. We'll try to avoid walking into one of his surprises," Quinn promised. "Clearing these rooms is going to be slow work. It would be nice if we could get a sketch of this guy. From the description, it could still be one of many guests. Mustaches are in favor this year."

"It's a priority," Marcus promised. He looked over at Shari. She was biting her bottom lip and her face was pasty white. He hoped she was a fighter like her mom. As soon as they got this situation stabilized, he was going to have to take her through the last twenty minutes in detail. There were times he hated what he had to do in his job. It was not how he had wanted to get to know her.

"Shari." She finally looked up. "The phone call to the desk, helping Josh, describing the shooter—you did good."

Tears flooded her eyes. "Thank you," she whispered.

THREE

The paramedics arrived, and with them came enough help to secure the ninth floor. For Marcus the relief was palpable. The paramedic who joined him lifted the pressure pad from Josh's shoulder to get a quick look. He shook his head. "Jim, get the stretcher over here and get me an ETA on that medivac helicopter."

A paramedic was helping Shari's mom. Two paramedics had begun working on William, their words terse and their actions fast as they worked to get the bleeding stopped and his breathing stabilized. Shari had moved to join them and looked lost as she knelt near her dad and watched them. As soon as Marcus was sure Joshua was taken care of, he moved to her side.

He was finally free to wrap his arm around her and try to stop the shivers. "Hold still." He reached over to the open case the paramedic had brought up and tore open one of the gauze packages. He used it to wipe at the blood on her cheek. Her blue eyes were wet, the pupils very dilated. He changed his mind; she was beautiful. A guy could drown in those eyes. It was a nasty gash. She winced when he taped the bandage in place. "Sorry."

"It's okay."

"We need to get your mom out of here," he said, knowing it was the best way to get her out of here as well.

"I know. But I don't want to leave Josh and Dad."

"They are going to be medivaced to St. Luke's. We'll meet them there," he promised. She didn't protest when he lifted her away from her dad.

Marcus motioned Officer Young over. "Is there an empty hotel room nearby?" Marcus quietly asked the officer.

She checked on the security net, then nodded. "966."

"Shari, I want you to go with Tina and change clothes, wash up, then get together what you think your mom will need."

It wasn't much, but at least the blood on her hands and clothes could be dealt with. She looked down at her hands, turned them palm up, and flexed them as if they hurt. She seemed to be seeing the blood for the first time.

Tina encouraged her to turn toward the back bedroom to get her things. Using a different room was necessary, for this suite was now a crime scene. Marcus watched until they disappeared in the bedroom, and then he had to take a deep breath, letting it out slowly. He'd just watched Shari's life disintegrate. In a few days, his might be the last face in the world she would want to see as he became part of the memory of what had happened tonight.

The paramedic with Shari's mom motioned him over.

"Mrs. Hanford?" Marcus knelt down beside the stretcher to be at her level. The lady was beautiful, but the last half hour had aged her severely. She'd been lying when she told Shari she was okay; it was there in the strain on her face and the faint labor of her breathing. But when his gaze met hers, any suggestion of fragileness disappeared. There was anger there.

"Tell me how Josh is, they won't tell me anything."

"He's not as badly hurt as your husband." It wasn't much, but to a mother it would mean something.

She searched his face, then nodded, relieved. "Thank you." Her eyes closed. He would have moved back but she took a deep breath and opened her eyes, and what he saw in her gaze made him go still.

"Find the man who did this." It was an order.

"We will." It was the one thing he was certain of. They had a judge murdered; they would find the shooter. "Did you see him?"

She shook her head with regret. "I was in the bedroom. I heard Shari scream, and then I saw Bill.... I wish I did have something that could help you."

The paramedic, out of her sight, shook his head and indicated they had to get her out of here. Marcus eased back to disengage, only to stop when Beth's hand closed on his arm, gripping it with surprising strength. She was fighting to keep tears from weakening her voice. "Shari's going to need me tonight and I'm going to be worthless to help her once the doctors get hold of me. Promise me she won't be left on her own while Josh and Bill are in surgery. Promise me."

"Beth, you've got my word," Marcus reassured softly. Shari was a witness; there would be security with her around the clock. But even if that security hadn't been necessary, he would have still stepped in to make arrangements for her. The guilt already hung heavy. There should have been a way to prevent this from ever happening. Shari wasn't going to be left to pace a waiting room alone tonight.

Beth's hand on his arm loosened. She even gave a glimmer of a smile. "Don't let one of the political 'close friends of the family' sit with her either. They'll want to distract her by talking about the governor's race. That's the last thing my daughter needs. Her guy is losing, and she absolutely hates to lose. She'll end up in the hospital bed next to me."

Marcus couldn't help but return her smile. "No politicians, no press." He eased free, aware of how gray her face was even with the oxygen the paramedics now had her on. "They are going to take you to St. Luke's hospital; I'll be bringing Shari there in a few minutes."

Beth nodded, and Marcus rose to let the paramedics take her out. He liked Shari's mom. Stubborn grit, his sister Jennifer would have said, and said it with admiration.

Shari would be a few moments. Marcus moved across the suite to the connecting door, turning his attention back to the victim.

Within the hour, the national news would have the details and this investigation would become a coordination mess. The only way to survive the firestorm was to solve the case fast. When he found the shooter…

"What do you think?" Marcus asked Dave.

"The shooter had the nerve to walk into a place full of cops; the hit was well-planned. He got surprised and didn't finish off the witnesses, so he's not an ice-cold, paid professional. This was personal," Dave replied, thinking out loud.

Marcus began to string together what he saw. "The shooter waits for the judge to enter the room; kills him with three shots to the center of the chest. He's surprised when the connecting door opens. He hits the door frame instead of Shari, and the other shots fired into their suite appear to be scattered, so he's acting panicked. A little more control and all of them would be dead."

"His plan is blown. And for him, the plan was everything."

Marcus went back on the security net. "Quinn?"

"Go ahead."

"This shooter had a plan, a detailed one; it got blown by unexpected witnesses and his reaction shows a distinct lack of control. He's running now without his plan. Anything is possible."

"Permission to give this manhunt back to you?" Quinn asked dryly.

"I'll get you a sketch of the shooter. I've got witnesses to get out of here," Marcus replied. Anything was possible. Including the shooter doubling back to try and eliminate his mistake. Shari might be the only one who had seen his face, and that made Marcus very uneasy. "How bad are you hurt? I can send up a medic."

"The shot grazed my left arm, it can wait."

Marcus had no choice but to accept his word for it. Taking Quinn off the manhunt was the last thing he wanted to do. There were very few marshals with his expertise. "Make sure you get a firewall established below floor nineteen; moving Justice Roosevelt is more dangerous than it's worth. How's the evacuation going?"

"About a third done. We're moving the guests to the Paris conference room, doing interviews there to see if anyone saw or heard anything."

"Has Kate arrived on scene?"

"She's with me now."

"Hi, Marcus. Thanks for the business."

Her voice over the net was her working one: clear, calm, not yet bored. She only sounded bored when she had a gun pointed at her head. "Kate, quit chewing gum on the security net. It's annoying."

"Sorry. Are you under control down there? I could use a look at the scene. I need to know how this guy thinks."

"Emotionally," Marcus summed up in one word. "As soon as the paramedics get done, Dave's going to own the crime scene. He can arrange a walk-through."

"I appreciate it."

"Marcus, it's Quinn again. We're flushing these three floors. We've got this hotel wing secure, but this shooter was moving fast."

"You think he might have slipped through."

"We're coming up on fifteen minutes and I haven't been shot at again."

"Point well taken. Consider this situation no longer contained."

"Got it."

With that simple decision, the response had just leaped from the hotel to six blocks around the hotel and all the airports, train stations, and other means of exiting the city.

Marcus dropped off the security net.

Beth and Joshua were wheeled out. The paramedics moved to transfer William to a stretcher.

"William doesn't have much of a chance. He took two hits to the center of the chest," Dave said softly.

They had a witness to a murder who might lose members of her own family; it complicated matters enormously. If William died—it could either strengthen Shari's resolve to help or create enough fear that her memory would become vague. Marcus had been around witness protection long enough to know there was no way to predict how someone would react to such an event. Shari's world right now was her mother, father, and brother. Getting them somewhere safe was critical.

"I'll stay with them at the hospital, work with Shari," Marcus decided. "You've got this crime scene; tear it apart. And let's hope we've got another witness somewhere on this floor. I don't know how much more Shari will be able to give us."

The paramedics headed out with William. Marcus watched them leave, then turned back to Dave. "Talk to Mike down in the command center. We need the full file on Judge Whitmore: Get men digging into his past cases, and find out *everything* there is to know about who knew he was going to appear on that short list and when they knew it. Then get men working on a profile of William Hanford and his family. They were friends of Carl. The shooter got surprised. I want to rule out any possibility he had them further down on his master plan."

"You've got it, Marcus."

Marcus slapped him on the shoulder, more grateful than he knew how to say that Dave was here. Almost family counted. Six months, he figured, probably less, and Dave and Kate would be engaged.

He picked up one of the extra towels left in the living room to wipe the blood off his hands, pulled his signet ring off to drop it into his pocket until he could clean it. His watchband would need to be soaked to come clean, he recognized with some dispassion.

Officer Tina Young appeared in the suite doorway, and Marcus turned, expecting Shari. The expression on the officer's face had him abandoning his task to cross the room. "She washed up, changed, and then—" The officer stepped aside and pointed to room 966.

Marcus moved to the other hotel room.

Shari was standing by the sink in the bathroom, one hip resting against the marble countertop. She'd changed into jeans and a pink sweater but was still barefoot. She looked painfully young.

The tears were falling unchecked. She wasn't making a sound, but her shoulders were shaking. Her right thumb was rubbing at the remnants of dried blood on her other palm, trying to erase it from the crevices of her hand. She'd washed, but not all the blood had come off.

Even knowing this was inevitable, that the controlled calm during the crisis would give way to the shock, didn't ease the impact seeing it had. Words weren't going to help. Marcus bent and picked up the wet towel she had been using that had dropped to the floor. He slid his hand firmly over the back of her wrist, capturing the offending hand in his, feeling her fluttering pulse under his long fingers. The wet towel had grown cool. He turned on the water faucet, made sure it got no more than moderately warm, and picked up the soap.

It didn't take an expert to know what seeing her brother's blood on her hands was doing to her. He finally got her palm clean. He spread her fingers and washed the faint traces of blood from between them. He could do little about the blood under her nails. Very neat nails with light red polish, two now jaggedly broken.

"The water always stays pink."

"Shari, look at me." He had to repeat it twice before she raised her head. The tears were ending, but behind them was a heavier blackness. "You can't help your family if you fall apart."

He had to stay blunt. She needed a reason to focus and the best thing that could happen would be if this despair could be replaced with anger at the shooter. It would give her the ability to get through the coming hours.

She drew in a deep breath as if he'd slapped her. "I'll be okay."

He squeezed her hands, regretting that he couldn't step in and coddle her. He would love to wrap her in cotton right now and deny the world any chance to get close to her and cause her more pain. That wasn't possible. "I'm going to need your help in the next couple hours."

"I'm having trouble with my own name right now."

"The shock will fade," he calmly replied. Her hands were clean now, her fingertips had even begun to wrinkle. He reached for a dry towel and folded her hands in his, drying them. "Ready to leave?"

The first stark glimmer of a smile appeared. It was a painful reminder that the lady he had met and found so enjoyable earlier that evening was now gone; her smile was fractured. "Absolutely."

"Good." He held her gaze for several moments, wishing he knew how to read what she was thinking. She was looking at him as if she wanted to ask something but was mute. She turned toward the bedroom and the moment was broken.

Tina had found tennis shoes for her. Shari sat on the side of the bed and pulled them on.

"Joshua was airlifted to the hospital about a minute ago. Your father should be airborne in a couple minutes. Your mom is already on the way and I've got a car downstairs for you."

She nodded.

Tina handed Shari a shopping bag. "The clothes for your mom."

"Thanks."

"Come on," Marcus said gently, putting his hand on Shari's back to direct her. He didn't like the fact he was leaving while the hunt for the shooter was still in progress, but he had no choice. In the triad of witness, shooter, and crime scene, they were all critical. He trusted Quinn to handle the shooter, and Dave to handle the crime scene. He would rather have Shari and her family remain his responsibility.

He escorted Shari down the hall to the elevators, keeping his hand under her elbow. She was limping and it looked like she was favoring her knee, not her ankle. He would have to make sure a doctor checked her out when they got to the hospital.

The elevator controls had been overridden so that only the security center could activate them. He asked for the first floor. They were going out a secure entrance on the first floor rather than descend to the lobby where the press could see them. Shari leaned back against the elevator wall as it descended.

Marcus didn't break the ensuing silence. She needed time to collect herself, and he needed time to think. They had contingency plans in place for hospital security, but his first order of business would be to get them strengthened. This shooter had shown no qualms about acting in the midst of heavy security.

The media was going to be a problem as soon as they learned which hospital they should haunt for news. This was not going to be a one day story; he would have to plan security for the duration of the time Joshua and William were in the hospital. And Shari and her mom would eventually need other accommodations—he couldn't risk bringing them back to this hotel; they would need someplace close to the hospital.

"Carl's really dead."

He looked over at Shari, understanding the need to be told what she already knew. "Yes."

"Why did this happen? Why him?"

It was the hardest question to answer about any crime: why. If they caught the shooter and he confessed they would get a definitive answer. Short of that, it would take a long investigation to figure out the motive. "We'll find out."

She rubbed her eyes. "He never knew he was going to make the short list."

His gaze sharpened. "You knew?"

"That page during dinner was John passing on the news. Josh and I had ordered a special dinner to the room to celebrate. Carl hadn't eaten much at the banquet. I should have told Carl rather than wait for him to get the official call, but it was going to be a surprise. He needed some good news. And he died never knowing..."

Her voice drifted off. Marcus waited a moment to see if she would say anything else. "Who's John?"

She took a deep breath. "My boss, the governor of Virginia. I need to call him."

The governor of the Commonwealth of Virginia was her boss. This situation, already highly political, would have the extra dimension of the Hanford family being personal friends of Governor Palmer. "I'll get it arranged," he promised. "Shari, did you tell anyone about the page?"

"Joshua knew, and my parents, but we were waiting for Carl to get the official call before we invited his friends to the suite to help us celebrate. Do you think Carl was killed because he was going on the short list?"

There was no sense trying to keep the obvious from her. She would be in the middle of this investigation until its conclusion. "It's possible." The look of pain that crossed her expression was intense, as if that answer wounded her personally. Why? "Do you think you can help me put together a sketch of the shooter?"

"I'll try." She bit her lip. "I only saw him for a few seconds, Marcus. And after that first moment when I realized what I was seeing...it's scattered."

"Do you think your brother saw him?"

She shook her head. "He was off to my right when the connecting door opened. I was still screaming when that bullet hit the door frame, and Josh hit me in that instant. I don't think the shooter moved beyond the doorway." Her eyes closed, and she shivered. "Josh got shot because of me."

"Shari—" He waited until she looked over at him. "Trust me. Josh is glad he was able to reach you in time. As hard as it is for you to see him hurt, just remember, he would feel worse if you were the one hurt."

She gave a glimmer of a smile. "A guy thing."

"Yes."

"Are they going to be okay? Josh...and Dad?"

"Can you handle the truth?"

"No, but I would prefer it."

The job demanded he keep a professional, impersonal distance. There were times that kind of distance didn't fit the circumstances. He reached over and gripped her hand, having found long ago that bad news delivered with a touch sometimes helped lessen the sting. For both of them. "I think you'd better be prepared for the worst," he answered gently. "Josh is hurt, but he's young. I think he'll make it. But your father…it looks bad. He might not make it through surgery."

She had to know that, had to be prepared, and it would be wrong not to warn her. He felt her flinch, saw her jaw work, then she shuttered her expression. "He'll make it. He has to," she whispered fiercely. "I'll help you however I can with information about the shooter, what happened. But can you wait to talk to Mom until tomorrow? She's already had enough shock for one day."

"I think so. We're going to make this as easy on all of you as we can; that's a promise."

"Will you be staying with us at the hospital?"

She'd just been shot at and she sounded apologetic for asking if he would be around to help as all the churn hit. He knew his life was going to be chaotic in the next few days as he worked the case, but it was nothing compared to what had just hit hers. She was a witness; her family was hurt; within days any secrets she thought she had would be considered fair game for reporters across the country…she'd just lost her life as she knew it although he didn't think she fully realized that yet.

"I'll be watching out for you throughout this," he replied, determined to do what he could to throw a shield around her from the worst of it. "That's a promise, Shari."

He felt it, those words. It was an O'Malley promise. She wouldn't understand what that meant, didn't need to. It was enough for him to realize the line he had crossed. The shooter had made a fatal mistake. He had shot a judge with impunity. He had hurt a lady Marcus knew. He had made the case personal. Marcus would put the weight of the O'Malley family behind solving the case, and together they were a group it was unwise to cross.

She squeezed his hand. "Thank you."

Marcus looked at their linked hands. Her hand not only fit his but looked right there. He rubbed the back of her hand with his thumb. She was strong like her mom. She'd get through this. With a little help from him. He squeezed her hand before releasing it. The elevator doors opened. "Stay close."

Kate O'Malley positioned herself beside Quinn by the door of room 1124. It was one of eleven rooms on this floor where they hadn't been able to get an answer on the phone. They had used the registration information to try and track down the guests in the hotel and failed to do so. They had no choice but to assume the room was a threat situation.

They were using fiber optic cameras under the doors to make a first look, then opening and searching the rooms. Kate leaned her head back against the wall. She was at Quinn's elbow on the distinct probability they might open a door and have a gunman with a hostage waiting for them. Those first seconds would be critical and all hers to deal with.

"What do you think, Kate?"

They had to do these sweeps fast, eliminating rooms; every minute without the gunman found simply spread the threat area. They also had to move with caution. It was the adrenaline draining; the worst kind of search. It didn't help that her gum was getting old. "You're bleeding on the carpet."

Quinn looked and scowled. "A few drops; you would think I was bleeding out the way you keep hassling me. At the price they charge for rooms, the hotel can probably afford to shampoo the carpet."

"Lisa's not here; someone's got to hassle you." Kate rather liked Marcus's partner, and the fact he annoyed her sister Lisa only increased that conclusion. She took another glance at the fiber optic feed. This was a suite of rooms, one of the highest risk entries since they could see only a portion of the rooms. They were at fifty seconds and still no sign of movement. "Open the door."

Quinn popped the lock and they swept into the suite; four men from the SWAT team, Quinn, and Kate following them in.

"Clear."

"Clear."

"Clear!"

The cops were efficient and thorough; all rooms, closets, and other places where someone could conceal himself were methodically checked.

"This is getting old," Kate commented, feeling her heart rate slow down.

"Tell me about it," Quinn replied. "Any ideas?"

"Get a structural engineer up here. I'd love to know what other ways there are off these three floors. Air ducts and the like. We're running out of rooms to check."

Quinn nodded. "Worth trying. There should be an engineer in the Belmont room." He made the call down to the security center, requesting the man be found and brought upstairs.

The guest room door was sealed with police tape to show the room had been swept. They moved to the next room on their list and began the careful process of setting up the fiber optic feed.

"A dead judge; two wounded. Want to lay odds we're going to open a door and find our shooter has killed himself?" Quinn asked.

"Doubtful. He acted in the middle of a hotel full of cops. He had a plan to get away. The mere fact he went up instead of down is striking."

"This guy gets away, life is going to get very ugly until he's caught."

Kate nodded. She was already bracing for the worst. Marcus had always been there for her when she needed him; it looked like she was going to be returning the favor. A U.S. Marshal having a judge killed—someone was going to have to sit on Marcus and remind him to get some sleep occasionally.

She held up a hand, made a fist, and the officer moving the fiber optic lens held steady. Quinn took a look at the small display and agreed with her. Only two feet wearing blue socks were visible, but someone was lying on the bed. He motioned an officer to dial the room phone again; Kate saw no movement. He wasn't moving to answer the ringing phone.

"Room registration?" Quinn asked.

"Kevin McCurry. A judge from the seventh circuit," another officer replied.

Quinn looked at her. "Your call."

"Thanks a lot." Kate considered the situation for a moment. "We've either got another victim, a very heavy sleeping guest, a hostage, or a dead shooter. The room lights are off. We kill the hall lights, unlock the door, open it a fraction, and we slide the fiber optic camera in high, so we can see the room. In the worst case, we risk getting gunfire back at us."

Quinn nodded. "It will work."

Ten minutes later, they were dealing with an irate guest whose hearing aid had been turned off.

She had just gone to bed and her pager was going off. Lisa O'Malley rolled over and squashed it with a forceful hand. Bleary-eyed, she tried to find her shoes. They had been kicked off haphazardly when she collapsed on the bed. Her boss had promised her a weekend off call, but she didn't truly mind, even though it had already been a sixty-hour week. If she slept, she would dream, and thanks to Kevin they had become the kinds of nights she would prefer to forget.

The ER doctor had been a steady date up until six months ago when he'd taken a slap at her profession and she had been stunned to realize he meant it. She had come home, curled up on the couch, and cried, and no guy had done that easily since she was sixteen. She had promised herself to tell Kevin no in the future, but last week he'd caught her at a weak moment and she'd said yes to dinner. It had been a disaster. Would she never learn? He was still a rat.

A squeaking metal wheel broke the silence and she looked across the room at the metal cage with the spinning wheel. Her white mice were awake. "Sorry, guys. I didn't mean the insult."

A page at this time of night could only mean one thing: the lab was dealing with so many homicides they were shorthanded and were calling in other shifts. And since she was one of the few forensic pathologists in the office that enjoyed the on-site work, she would probably be spending the middle of the night in some city alley. She would rather go deal with the dead than with another living person. She turned on the bathroom light and winced. She looked like one of the dead.

She looked like Quinn. That realization didn't improve her mood. She was glad she had said no to Quinn's offer for dinner. Women liked him too much for her to want to compete for his attention. And while she knew she wasn't the most sparkling or witty lady in her family, being asked out third was humiliating. She was the O'Malley that couldn't stay out of trouble and couldn't seem to get her social life together. Quinn had been feeling sorry for her.

Enough. She was off men. They didn't make them as nice as her brothers and there was no use having her heart hurt again. She had been crying on Jennifer's shoulder last night, feeling like a wimp, and she hated that.

Lisa picked up the pager and went to work wondering who had died.

FOUR

"Shari." Marcus held out the Styrofoam cup. It was hot tea, very sweet. She took it from him with a murmured thanks. She was still too shaky on her feet for his comfort. If this didn't get some color back in her face, he was going to insist she accept a sedative. "Are you sure you don't want a doctor to look at that knee? You keep rubbing it." They were the only ones in the hospital waiting room. Security had this section of the hospital floor closed.

She glanced at him. "I'll be okay. I just aggravated an old injury. Josh talked me into skydiving once and I landed hard."

It said a lot about Shari that she would allow her brother to talk her into trying something like skydiving. She was either fearless or brave enough to face a petrifying fear. Stepping out of an airplane took a lot of nerve. "Adventurous."

"A sucker when it comes to family." She leaned her head back against the wall.

"Your mom is settled?"

"In room 841 down the hall. They gave her something to help her sleep. With her history of heart problems, the specialists didn't want to take chances. She was...annoyed at their insistence, but she took it."

"She struck me as strong willed."

"She's never been one to accept without a fight the fact her health is not good."

"The surgeon said it's going to be another hour before there is any news on Joshua and William," he commented, glad now that he had intercepted the doctor coming to see Shari. He left unsaid the grim assessment the doctor had made about her dad. She had enough to deal with at the moment, and nothing the doctor had said would change the outcome.

"Until they are out of surgery, and that will be hours, no news is good news." She sighed. "I should probably get on the phone, begin making some calls."

Her voice was steady; her color was coming back, but he could hear the reluctance. "No reason to rush it." He drank his coffee and waited.

"Has anyone ever told you you're good at being tactful?"

"I'm a cop, Shari, but I've also been in your seat waiting for news about family. I can give you a moment; not much more than that, but at least a moment."

"I appreciate it." She finished her tea. "Open your notebook. I'll give you what answers I can."

Marcus glanced at his watch and noted the time on his notepad. "Walk me through what happened tonight."

"Where do I start?"

"Anywhere safe," Marcus suggested quietly. "How about early this evening when you went down to the banquet?"

"We went down together, Carl and my family, about 5:45 P.M."

Marcus started filling pages as she talked. She thought her family had gotten back to the suite about 9:45. Room service had been delivered. Carl had been shot minutes later. Marcus wrote a note to himself to make sure they immediately interviewed the hotel employee who had delivered that room service. The security net had put out the alert of shots fired at 10:20, so Shari's time estimates sounded accurate.

"When you knocked on the connecting door, it swung open on its own?"

"The latch hadn't caught."

"Where was Carl when you saw him?"

"In front of me, about five feet inside the room." Her voice choked. "He was falling backwards and I knew his head was going to hit the wall. I heard the echo of the shots."

"Where was the gunman?"

"To my—" she looked momentarily confused.

Directionally challenged. "You're facing into the room. Where's he standing?"

She held out her hand, her look grateful. "Here. By the foot of the bed."

"Was there much distance between them?"

"Four feet? Five? Not much more."

The gunman must have stepped out from the bathroom to the end of the bed and fired. "Did you hear Carl say anything? Cry out in alarm?"

"He seemed surprised, startled."

Surprised to find someone in the room, or surprised because he knew the shooter?

"What happened after that?"

She stumbled over the words when she tried to describe the minutes in the suite before he and Dave had arrived. Marcus paused her. "Relax. Take it slow." He had to ask. He needed to know if she had noticed anything else about the shooter after that first shot.

"I'm sorry, Marcus. After Josh hit me…" She shook her head.

"It's okay. Let's change subjects." He picked up the larger pad of paper he'd borrowed from another officer, then removed a second, more expensive fine-lead pencil from his pocket. "Let's try to get a sketch."

"You're an artist?"

"I'm decent at the basics." The importance of faces to his job had given him years of practice. "Close your eyes, think about his face, and just tell me what you see."

Her eyelashes fluttered closed, and she drew and released a deep breath. "Think tough. Intense. He's got wide cheekbones and broad eyebrows. Everything about his appearance is well groomed, except it looks like he has run his hand through his hair."

As he sketched, Marcus paid attention to how she remembered details, listening for when she hesitated. He had worked with a lot of witnesses over the years. Shari had an unusually sharp memory for details; very little of what she said was vague. "What do you do for the governor?" he asked idly.

"I write speeches; I'm working on his reelection campaign."

"You use memory tricks to remember the name and face of everyone you meet." It was more a statement than a question; the answer was pretty obvious. He sketched in the jawline of the suspect.

"Yes. It's instinctive now."

There was something about watching a quarry appear under his pencil that always made an impact on Marcus. It became personal, the attachment of a face to the crime. The face would stay with him for years, would remain vivid until the case was solved. Since most of his cases were tracking down fugitives, he often spent his time traveling modifying sketches of suspects to age them, change their appearance, until he knew their face as well as he knew his own.

"How would you adjust this?" He turned the sketch to her.

"Hey, it's not bad."

He smiled at her surprise.

She took it from him, studied it. He watched her close her eyes, then open them for a brief instant and close them again—it was a memory trick, a way to give her a good comparison. She handed the sketch back and indicated the cheekbones. "Lower the cheekbones just a little, and broaden his eyebrows."

Marcus refined it.

"Better."

Over the next twenty minutes, he changed it until Shari could think of no further adjustments. "That's him."

Marcus studied the face, memorizing it. He added all the specifics Shari had told him about the shooter to the bottom of the page—age, height, weight, clothing. "Let me get people working on this. And I am going to get someone to look at that knee," he warned. "You need an ice pack on that and probably a dozen other bruises."

"Josh hits like a linebacker. And I am starting to feel the effects. My ribs ache."

Shari was just like his four sisters. Downplaying what hurt unless he called them on it. "Then it's definitely time for you to see a doctor."

He glanced at his watch, found it was coming up on midnight. "I won't be long. And I'll have Craig stay with you while I'm gone."

"I'm okay, Marcus."

"I know you are, but humor me." He reached in his pocket. "Until we can get your things cleared at the scene, I got you another phone."

He hesitated, then pulled a blank page from the back of the notebook and wrote down two numbers. "Memorize them," he said quietly. "If you ever need me, for any reason, a problem, a question, just to chat about the weather—" he smiled—"or to share one of those secrets of yours, page me and put in the second number. It's unique. I'll call, no matter where I am."

She looked at it, puzzled.

"You don't need to understand. Just use it if you need it."

"Some kind of secret code."

He smiled faintly. "Something like that. A family one." He picked up his notebook. "I'll try to bring your address book back with me. Should I bring your pager, or would you like me to conveniently lose it?"

"What a tempting thought. But you'd better bring it."

"Will do."

"Marcus, how much can I tell people?"

He hesitated and became serious. "Don't tell people you saw him."

"Do you think that information can be suppressed?"

"The longer it can be kept quiet the better."

He squeezed her shoulder lightly as he rose, reassuring her again that he would be back. He didn't want her feeling abandoned in the middle of the commotion, something that could happen without it being intended as investigators working the case focused on the dead at the expense of the living. "Listen to what the doctors tell you. And if you do need to leave this secure wing for some reason, take Craig for company."

"I've got a baby-sitter."

"Something like that," he replied. "Like I said. Humor me."

"Right. Okay. It's a guy thing."

He chuckled. "A U.S. Marshal one at least. I'll be back."

Shari watched the door close behind him and found it took a few moments for her smile to fade. She really liked that man; he was definitely the right person to have around during a crisis. He was right about her habit of memorizing a face and name, and she had the habit of also remembering first impressions. For Marcus it was an interesting combination of words: tough, strong, kind.

She looked at the numbers on the slip of paper, memorizing them. She had worn her emergency pager far too long not to understand the significance of what he had given her. She was frankly surprised at the scope of what he had just offered.

His hand when he had squeezed her shoulder had been warm and comforting, if impersonal. He thought she could get through this; it came through in his steady gaze and touch. Shari wished she shared his confidence.

She rubbed the back of her neck. She more than just ached; the headache was becoming vicious. The muscles in her back had tightened to the point they would break; her bones refused to unlock. She got to her feet to walk the length of the room, willing to accept the pain from her aching knee to try and get her muscles to relax.

What she needed to do next… Where did she start? There were relatives to call, distant ones, but a lot of them. Shari felt ashamed to realize at that moment she was actually glad her family was in Virginia and wouldn't be able to descend for a few hours. She simply didn't have the means to cope with a crowd right now, and they would want to talk about the details. Aunt Margaret, Mom's sister, would be a great help to have here, but she lived in London. It would take a day for her to make the trip.

Carl's friends. How was she going to break the word Carl was dead? Shari shuddered just at the thought. He'd been in her life since her earliest memories, a friend of the family, the uncle she had never had. How was she supposed to tell his friends he had been murdered?

A heart attack she could have handled, but shot to death—maybe John could make those calls for her. Someone would have to call before they found out from the media.

She knew Dad was executor of Carl's will, and he was in no position to deal with that responsibility. Neither was Josh. That meant Carl's funeral arrangements would fall to her. And she would have to get plans underway quickly or Mom would try to step in. That was the last kind of stress Mom needed right now.

She had never planned a funeral before.

"I need that pad of paper," she murmured. She was starting to think, and she wished she could shut it off for a moment, the assault of things that needed to be done. She didn't want to be the one to handle them, but by default she was elected.

She was thirty-four, and until this point in her life the toughest challenge she had been asked to face was the defeat of legislation she had poured months of effort into, the defeat of a candidate she believed in, and the heartbreak of a relationship gone bad.

The terror she had struggled to push down and contain while Marcus was here broke through, and she leaned her head against the window, her breath fogging the glass.

Jesus, why?

She felt tears sliding down her cheeks as she remembered Carl lying dead, Josh shot, Dad shot.

I've never seen so much blood before. This is my family and it stands on a precipice of being shattered in one night. Carl is dead. Mom is at risk. Josh and Dad are both in surgery. I feel like Job tonight who lost his family in a single day.

She needed her dad and brother to recover; she didn't even want to think about God giving a different answer to her prayer. How was she supposed to pray? She had no eloquence, and not many words, only emotions. *I am so scared, Lord. Did my brief cause this? I prayed so stubbornly for Carl to reach the court and I poured all my skills into writing that brief. Did I walk Carl into getting killed?*

Jesus, I am so scared that I did just that. And now Josh is hurt, and Dad might die too!

It had been unintentional, but the guilt swamped over her like a wave.

It took time for the words memorized long ago to come through the turmoil. When they came, from Psalm 68, they settled over her with softness.

"Blessed be the Lord, who daily bears us up; God is our salvation. Our God is a God of salvation; and to God, the Lord, belongs escape from death."

Jesus had already proven His power over death. *Bear me up, Lord. Hold me tight. And get all of us through this night. Please…*

They should have found the shooter by now; Marcus knew it. He strode into the hotel past the security, past the growing crowd of reporters, his jaw tight. At least with a solid sketch they could turn the tide back in their favor and force the shooter to hole up and thus stay in the area.

The emotions from being with Shari were finally beginning to bleed off. There was no such thing as impassively being around grief; it always rubbed off and had to be dispelled somehow. Some cops dispelled it in morbid humor; others absorbed it and it tore apart their personal lives. Marcus tended to direct the emotions he felt back in intensity toward the case.

He couldn't undo what had happened to her, to her family, but he could help bring her justice. Swift, complete justice. He had never lost a judge before and it stung, viciously.

The security center activity appeared chaotic on the surface, but only until it became apparent how the groups had appropriated space. Mike had overall coordination of the room at the moment, and he was pacing as he talked on a phone.

Marcus held up the sketch and waved Mike toward the east side of the room where Luke was working; he got a nod in reply.

He joined his deputy, Luke. "Shari was able to give us a sketch of the shooter. Put priority on getting copies to Quinn and to hospital security. Then put a rush on getting it run through our databases. I want an ID on this guy."

"Do you want it given out to the media?"

"I want to hear Dave, Quinn, and Mike's opinions first, but probably. I would like to get a name to go with the face first. The media's all over this?"

Luke nodded. "News got out about twenty-five minutes ago. We've made all the networks. The phone lines have been jammed with the volume of TV crews and print reporters. We've implemented our contingency bank of isolated numbers. So far they know it was Judge Whitmore killed; they know there were others hurt. It hasn't leaked yet that there's a witness and so far we've been able to suppress the Hanford name, but I don't expect that to hold."

"Neither do I. Grant is coordinating all press information?"

"Yes."

"Get a copy of the sketch to him as well. And tell him to do what he can to kill the witness information somehow. The shooter knows Shari saw him, but I'd rather not keep reminding him of that fact."

Luke handed over two manila folders. "Carl's threat file and what there is so far on the Hanford family."

Marcus flipped open the file on the Hanfords. They had pulled together a lot in a short time: pictures, bio sketches, newspaper clippings. He focused on Shari's personal friends. She needed someone with her tonight. If he could get it arranged, all the better. "Luke, track down Governor Palmer of Virginia for me. He'll have heard by now, I'm sure. Tell him I want to speak with him about Shari."

"I'll get him for you and forward the call."

The number of newspaper clippings on Shari was thick and this was only a brief set compared to what would come with time. A good rule of thumb: Anyone in the news this often had enemies. "We need someone focused solely on building Shari's file. She's our only known witness and I don't like the look of this file. She is way too public a figure—these are news articles not social page clips. That means trouble. Tell them to pull everything for the last three years and get it to me fast."

"News footage as well as print?"

"Yes."

Marcus opened Judge Whitmore's file. Carl's threat file was indeed slim—twelve threats in five years. Marcus skimmed the codes on the index page. Three death threats, but none of them in the last couple years. He frowned. There wasn't much here to work with. "Anything at all on Whitmore's personal life? Relatives, background, finances, anything?"

"They are digging."

"Have someone track me down as soon as it comes in."

"Will do. There's a growing list of calls coming in for Shari and her family. The hospital knows not to give out information, and the hotel has been instructed to simply take messages. Any change to that?"

"No, keep that blackout in place. I'll ask Shari if there is a family friend she wants to have return calls on their behalf. They are going to need a family spokesperson to deal with the press. Quinn is upstairs?"

"Yes. Nothing turned up in the floor sweeps."

"The shooter's gone." The clock was a harsh master.

"We'll plaster the city with the sketch. You know the local cops will do a full-court press to be the ones to bring him in."

"There is that," Marcus agreed, just wanting the guy found. "I'm going to touch base with Dave and Quinn, then head back to the hospital. Page me if we get anything."

He stepped out of the Belmont Room and literally bumped into his sister Jennifer. He automatically reached out a hand to steady her. "Jen, what are you doing here?" He was surprised, not only that she was here, but that she was inside the security zone.

"I patched up Quinn while he growled at me. Your partner doesn't like doctors. He's as bad as some of my pediatric patients."

"How bad was he hit?"

"Sixteen stitches, but he bled for a good hour and a half before he paused to let me fix him up. And he would have refused the local if I hadn't told him to shut up."

"It sounds just like Quinn."

"He's stubborn as a mule," Jennifer agreed. She took a deep breath. "Actually, Marcus, I'm glad I bumped into you. I've got a 9:00 P.M. flight, and I need to talk to you sometime before then."

He went still. "You came over with Kate for dinner."

"Yes."

"What's wrong?" Kate, who knew what was going on, was very worried. He brushed back her hair, tipped up her chin, and tried to read her expression.

"Nothing that won't keep until later today."

"Jennifer—"

Her hand settled firmly on his forearm. "It will keep; I'm serious." She gave him that tolerant smile he had come to know only too well as she talked people into what they didn't want. "I promise we'll talk before I have to leave."

Trivial things did not have Kate pacing the floor. Marcus was not about to let this be pushed aside. Unfortunately, at the moment Jennifer was right, there were competing demands on his time he couldn't ignore. "You're sure?"

"Yes. Do you need any help at the hospital?"

Given the circumstances, he had to accept the change of subject. "Yes, I think I will. Can I page you? Will you be around the hotel?"

"Yes, I'll be here. Go to work."

Marcus had no choice. "I'll page." He headed to the elevator.

The crime scene had extended to encompass the entire ninth floor. An officer assigned to serve as case scribe recorded Marcus's badge number, name, and time of arrival to the floor. With the guests evacuated, the floor now effectively sealed off, only necessary officers remained.

Two crime scene technicians were taking a powerful light down the hallway, looking for evidence that might have been missed on the first pass.

Dave came to meet him. "How are Josh and William doing?"

"Still in surgery, but holding on. How's it going here?" Two men from the medical examiners office were waiting with a stretcher and a folded body bag; Judge Whitmore hadn't been moved yet.

"It's under control."

Marcus followed him into the Hanfords' suite. The crime scene technician videotaping the scene paused to change cassettes, mark the first one into evidence. It was necessary to walk with care; yellow numbered evidence tags marked items slated to be collected once they were photographed.

He stopped at the connecting door. His sister Lisa was kneeling beside Judge Whitmore's body, studying his left hand. Marcus was surprised to see her, then realized it made sense. This was as high a profile case as you could get. The medical examiner and the state crime lab commissioner would have talked, assigned one of the central staff to coordinate the scene. "Lisa."

She glanced back. "Hi, Marcus."

"What do you see?"

She rocked back on her heels. "Very light powder burns. He tried to block the first shot."

She wore latex gloves but was spinning a gold pen. Marcus had learned to leave her pens alone. She liked gold because the blood would wipe off. On the clipboard tucked under her arm, he could see part of her preliminary scene sketch.

"We've just started to actually process the scene. It will be another hour before we can move his body, probably five or six hours on evidence. Dave said you were the one who entered this room in the initial minutes after the shooting."

"Yes."

"I need your shoes."

His shoes. Of course. "My room is downstairs. Can I get another pair, then bring these back?"

She frowned back at him. "I suppose, seeing as how you've been over to the hospital and back in them."

"There's a hole in my sock."

"Is there?" She was amused at that. She looked back at the area of carpet in front of her. "Thanks for sealing the scene as early as you did. This place is a treasure trove."

"What have you found?"

"Your shooter made a mistake." She gestured with her pen, indicating an oval area to her left. "There's a gun powder residue pattern here, and he walked through it when he crossed over to the connecting door to shoot the Hanfords. And over there—" she pointed to the right—"he put his right foot down on a blood splatter arc. Inside the door he's left the edge of a shoe print with blood on it. We've got blood traces in the hall coming from the sole of his right shoe."

"Can you tell me anything about him?"

"Sure. He's not a very good shot." She indicated the shots that had killed Judge Whitmore. "Look at the spread of these three hits."

Marcus had never figured out how things that made even cops queasy Lisa could work around without a qualm. Death didn't bother her.

"Other than that, not much. Ask me again after I get the autopsy finished and start putting together the forensic data. I'll have to put some geometry into the entry and exit wounds, the blood splatters. Give me enough time and I'll probably be able to give you the shooter's height, weight, and what he ate for dinner."

She wasn't being facetious. In a case last year she had figured out the killer liked clams from a toothpick found at the scene. In a town with one seafood restaurant, it had been useful information. "Shari said his shoes were highly polished," Marcus told her.

"Really? Useful. I may be able to get you a brand name on the shoes. Think she might be able to remember details?"

"I'll ask."

"This is a nice, tight, dense weave carpet. We should be able to get some good images with a high contrast photograph." While she spoke, Lisa collected several samples of Carl's blood, sealing it into vials. It was a harsh reality, but by the time the body reached the morgue to be autopsied, most shooting victims had bled almost totally out.

She got to her feet, careful to step back on the black tape. "If you have to enter the room, stay by the tape," she warned. "We've done a fiber lift from there so we can move around, but the rest of the room is still unprocessed."

She closed the vials in a biohazardous evidence bag, sealed it with a bar code, initialed the tag, and passed the sack to a technician to document. "We should be done with the photographs within the hour, then the real work will begin. Between the fiber evidence and the fingerprints, we'll be here well into the day."

There were shell casings numbered. Holes in the plaster circled with black marker. Mistlike blood splatters typical of gunshot wounds. Marcus saw evidence marker number 74 set beside the overturned phone. "The bloody fingerprint on the phone is likely Shari's. She was the one who called the desk."

"A lady that can keep her cool."

"Yes."

"Whenever you can make the unobtrusive request, I'll need her fingerprints and those of her family."

"I'll arrange it."

"Dave, I'll need fingerprints of everyone who entered the room, including the paramedics."

"I'll get them."

"What's this?" Marcus asked. A black circle had been drawn on the carpet.

"We've got one bullet that ended up in the hotel room one floor below," Dave replied.

"How did that happen?"

"A fluke of bad construction. We were lucky; the room was unoccupied."

"Am I the only one already beginning to think this case is going to be bad luck around every corner?"

"Quinn would agree with you. He's growling."

"He hates getting shot at, not to mention not being able to track his quarry."

The hotel lounge off the sixth floor atrium was abuzz with word that there had been a shooting. Connor sat at a window table, sipping his drink, ignoring the commotion.

The judge was dead. *Retribution* was a beautiful word.

"Did we negotiate a great deal or what? They folded, just like you predicted, more concerned with the size of their own golden parachutes than the final terms of the sale." His partner in the merger talks was in festive spirits. When the formalities concluded tomorrow on the 43 million dollar merger of the two law firms, the man would personally walk away with almost 4 million. "Having the talks under the cover of this conference was a stroke of brilliance. There won't be anyone cutting in to steal this deal away."

Connor turned the glass in his hand, only half listening. The merger could have gone in the trash for all he cared. The discussions had already accomplished what he hoped for—they had given him an alibi that would be very hard to penetrate. He watched the officers down below on the street look for him: a well-dressed man with thick black hair and thin mustache.

His premature gray and receding hair, lack of mustache, dark glasses, and rumpled shirt showing the effects of working marathon sessions for the last three days had not merited him more than a passing glance by the cops moving through the hotel. Even with the sketch he envisioned they would eventually have, they were in for a rude surprise. Tomorrow he would stroll out of the hotel, just another guest. The gun was locked in his room safe. What better way to protect the evidence than to let the hotel do it for him?

Did they realize he was still sitting in their hotel? Personally, he thought that was the most brilliant portion of his plan.

There should not have been a witness to the actual shooting and he scowled again at that memory. Their presence had cut severely into his escape time and had nearly gotten him caught. Now the excitement was over. He had always assumed someone would see him near the judge's room and had used that to his advantage. It was the best principle of deception. They were looking for him, without realizing they were looking for someone who looked only vaguely like him. And a lot like someone else.

And all they needed to do was bring in one suspect, conduct one eyewitness lineup based on that misleading information and he would be able to discredit any eyewitness testimony they tried to use later. Reasonable doubt allowed for so much useful maneuvering.

Only one person had really seen him, and he had seen her. He had tonight to figure out how to deal with that. And he would…he most certainly would. Daniel had warned him it took only one mistake.

His father would be horrified. His good son had just gone irreversibly bad.

Connor smiled at his drink. He'd never wanted to be the good son. By the time Titus realized what he had done, all the loose ends would be wrapped up. Even Titus would not be able to deny him his rightful place in the business then. Connor had earned his place.

He raised his drink and silently drank a toast to his dead brother Daniel. May he now rest in peace.

FIVE

Shari leaned against the wall beside her mom's hospital room window and watched traffic flow on the street below, red taillights breaking the darkness marking outbound traffic. Two A.M., and still the city did not sleep. She had been down in traffic like that before, rushing home only to turn around and come back to work while it was not yet dawn. In the intense last few months of campaigns, life ran at a seven day a week, twenty-four hour a day pace. She wished her life was that simple again, when being rushed for time was the biggest stress in her day.

Someone murdered Carl.

Who? Why?

Her dad and brother being shot were incidental to him. He destroyed her family and it was incidental to him. She wanted this guy. Desperately. And while she knew the marshals would be all over this case because Carl had been killed, she couldn't leave it there.

There was no one who knew Carl better than herself and her dad. She had personally read all of Carl's cases and writings in the last few weeks. Somewhere in her memory, or in her father's, was the person with a motive to kill Carl.

She drank the hot coffee the nurse had gotten for her, pushing back fatigue. Waiting for news was hard. There was no word from the doctors on Joshua or Dad. At least her mom was stable for the moment.

Shari prayed again for her dad and Josh, feeling the heavy weight of guilt knowing they had been hurt because of her. If only she had never written that brief. *Lord, give me strength.* The emotion had run its course and now there was only deep weariness. She prayed for the long night to be over.

Shari turned when the door opened slowly with a soft whoosh of air. In the dim light of the room she recognized Marcus. She didn't envy the man the job he had to do. He paused in the doorway and looked over at her mom, then nodded to the hall.

With a final look to confirm her mom was soundly sleeping, she crossed the room to join him in the hallway.

Marcus weathered better under pressure than she did. His gaze was steady and calm. She knew every bit of the stress from the last hours reflected in her face, and he wasn't missing much of that as he studied her. She hadn't been under this kind of intense scrutiny in a while. He was judging how well she was holding up, gauging what she could handle hearing.

"They've looked at your cheek?"

His question surprised her. She touched the bandage. "Yes, it will heal. Thanks for asking." The doctor had warned there might be a scar, but she didn't care. It was only the outward scar of a much bigger inward wound she would carry forever. "You've got news?"

"They're bringing Joshua down from surgery to the recovery room. He'll be there about an hour before they move him to the ICU, but the surgeon okayed a brief visit now."

Shari hesitated.

His look gentled. "The unknown is always worse than the truth."

"Even when the truth is going to be pretty bad?"

"Even then. Let's go talk to the surgeon."

The surgeon met them outside the recovery room still wearing his scrubs. Shari listened but didn't really hear much of what he was saying, her focus on the marked doors behind him. "Thank you, doctor."

"He came through surgery well, Miss Hanford. Please remember that when you see him." He held the recovery room doors open for her.

Shari followed a nurse, aware of Marcus immediately behind her, glad she wasn't entering this sterile, white place alone. The faint hum of machines was as much a part of the backdrop of sound as the quiet movement of the nurses.

"Joshua." She swallowed hard when she saw him, for most of the right side of his chest and all of his right shoulder were swallowed in bandages. He was breathing on his own and his color was pretty good, but the amount of damage was worse than she had expected.

A warm, firm hand curled over her shoulder and squeezed gently. "It looks worse than it is," Marcus whispered. "Remember what the surgeon said."

Pins in his collarbone. Torn muscles. Ninety percent recoverable. That was all supposed to be positive news. It just didn't change the fact Josh had been shot. She hated hospitals, was afraid of what she saw; it reminded her too much of those long weeks when they had almost lost mom.

Push it away. That's the past. And family needs you now—strong, together. She leaned over and gripped Josh's hand. "Hey, Josh. There's a pretty nurse here you haven't even noticed yet." He didn't stir, wouldn't for hours yet. "You always did like to sleep through the big adventures." She wanted to cry rather than razz him, but she refused to let the tears fall.

"Sit down, Shari," Marcus offered, having retrieved a chair. "You're the best medicine there is for him right now."

She took the seat, grateful, and continued talking to Josh, letting the conversation wander, just wanting him to hear her voice.

Josh was going to have a nasty six months of recovery. There would be months of physical therapy to be able to lift his arm, rotate his shoulder, carry a briefcase. Even writing was going to be a problem in the next few weeks. He had paid that price for her. How was she ever going to repay him?

Marcus pulled over a seat for himself, sat down, and stretched out his legs, steepling his hands. Shari appreciated his quietness. He was a man with stillness inside, not someone in perpetual motion. She wished she could borrow that trait. She burned through energy like a hot candle. At the moment she felt like she was burning down to the end of the wick. "You need to change your shirt." There was dried blood on the white cuff.

"I'm sorry. I didn't notice—"

She stopped him with a hand on his arm. "I didn't mean it that way. You paid a price for tonight as well. I'm sorry about that."

"I would have preferred being able to stop him."

At the disgusted sound in his voice she turned toward Marcus. He really meant it. He would have preferred to be in the middle of an unavoidable shoot-out with the man than to have arrived too late to do anything about it. His job took a courage she would never understand.

As calm and still as he was, she suspected he was actually very much on a hair trigger to react if necessary. He wasn't sitting beside her with his jacket open and a sidearm visible because he had free time. He was beside her because there had been a realistic judgment among the marshals that she needed that kind of protection.

He was responding like a cop. She wished she knew how to tell him thanks. "The shooter nearly destroyed my family and it was entirely incidental to him."

"Trust me, it's not incidental to those of us working the case."

"I wish I had been able to help you more with what happened."

"On the contrary, you gave us a great deal. Focus on your family; we'll find the man responsible."

"I want to help."

"Shari—"

"I know I fell apart on you earlier, but I won't again. You need a motive and there is no one who knows Carl better than myself and Dad."

He didn't say anything for several moments. "Deal."

He attached no strings, but she knew they were there. To get access to the investigation, she would put up with a lot of strings. She hadn't grown up around three lawyers without understanding how a criminal case was built. They would find the shooter, and she would insure they had a conviction. Not to do everything she could would be to let down Carl and the price he had paid.

Jesus, You say not to hate, but the hatred is getting me through this crisis. I can feel it building toward the shooter as I look at Josh and think about Carl, about Dad. I cry like David did—destroy my enemy! Make him pay. Whoever did this, I pray with an intensity that wells from my soul that You will lead the marshals to him. Answer this prayer. Please.

Marcus looked over at her, concerned, and she realized her emotions must have been showing on her face. She forced herself to relax. Josh stirred and she tightened her hand on his. *Get better, Josh. I need you. I don't want to be the strong one in this family.*

After they left the recovery room, Marcus walked Shari back to the waiting room. He watched with concern as she sank down on the couch. "You need to get some sleep." It was coming up on 3 A.M., and her voice was beginning to drift when she spoke.

"I close my eyes and I see it happen," she admitted quietly. "I'll wait a bit longer before I face the dreams."

Marcus took a seat in the chair near the couch and braced his elbows on his knees as he studied her. He felt for her and the reality of what she would go through in the next few weeks. The trauma would show in so many ways: being spooked by sudden sounds, hesitation before walking into a room, fear of the dark, headaches, mood swings—her system would purge the emotions of that memory trapped in a slice of time in numerous ways.

He wasn't a trauma counselor like his sister Rachel, but he knew where the healing had to begin. "When you close your eyes, where does it start?"

"With my hand reaching up to knock on the door. If only I hadn't froze—"

He wasn't surprised at what troubled her the most. "Because you froze in the doorway, it was your fault?"

"It feels like it."

"How long did you freeze? Two seconds? Three? How long before it registered and you got voice to scream?"

"A few seconds."

"If you had been able to scream and distract the gunman, would his shots have missed Carl? Would he still be alive?"

She blinked. "When the door swung open, Carl was already beginning to fall; I heard the echo of the shots."

"So you couldn't have saved Carl," Marcus said quietly. "If you'd been able to scream sooner, would you have been able to save your father?"

"I don't know."

"Shari, your screams saved your family. They flustered the shooter." He had to make her understand the importance of that. "Don't let your emotions believe a lie. They will never heal if you do. You did the only thing you could."

"I'm never going to be able to forget."

"No, but you'll remember the reality, not a distortion. You're dealing with it remarkably well."

"I'm shaking like a leaf."

"But you're not folding. Give yourself credit for that." He wished he could convey to her just how impressed he was with that fact. The strength inside her was showing. "Are you sure you don't want me to get someone to wait with you?

There are a number of people who have asked if they can come up. Friends of your family, of Carl."

She shook her head. "No. I'm hiding; I know it. But at the moment it's easier. The family will be arriving later today, there will be plenty of people then." She looked over at him and there was some ruefulness to her look. "In the meantime, I'll just dump it on you."

"I've got broad shoulders," he replied, willing to take whatever pressure he could off her. She had put up a wall between herself and the rest of the world as a way to deal with the crisis, and he had no desire to push her out of that safe security. "You really do need to get some rest though, at least catnap for a while. I'll wake you the instant there is news."

Since she was yawning, she didn't protest again. She stretched out on the couch, tucked her arm under her head. "Would you pray for my family?"

Her request surprised him, and put him in a hard position. He had believed, a long time ago, but now…

She noticed his hesitation. "You're not a believer."

It was more complex than that, but—"No, I'm not."

"I won't apologize for embarrassing you. You should be."

No apology, no backpedaling. A woman not afraid to keep to her position and believe she was right. He found that frankness refreshing. Even if he knew she was wrong. "I'll be glad to ask those I know who do believe to pray."

"Thank you. I would appreciate it."

He heard the warmth in her reply, she meant that, and he added another nugget to what he knew about her. It didn't bother her when someone didn't agree with her. That was rare.

Lisa was like that. Confident of her positions, willing to swim upstream to defend them. Kate staked a position and frankly didn't care if anyone agreed with her as long as she knew she was right. Jennifer wanted everyone to agree with her but would stand alone if she could convince no one else to stand with her. He smiled. The family never let that happen.

He watched Shari drift to sleep.

The only sound in the room was the muted passing of people in the hall outside. He needed to go talk to Quinn. It was after 3:00 A.M. and the manhunt should have seen some results with the sketch, but he found himself reluctant to move.

He had noticed that when Shari spoke about the terror, she had not mentioned the fact the shooter had tried to kill her. What she had mentioned was that she hadn't done enough to help her family. While he understood that, he would do anything for the O'Malleys, he also knew the silence spoke volumes, for it was signaling that was the one fact she couldn't cope with and so hadn't yet processed.

The harshest night of her life and the only thing he could really do was make sure no one tried to kill her again. It was a bleak assessment to live with.

He hoped she would sleep until morning but knew that was doubtful.

He reached for his phone and punched in the numbers to page Jennifer. It was one thing he could offer Shari. He had seen her reaction to entering the recovery room. He didn't want her facing the maze of medical questions and doctors without someone there to interpret what was said. And no one had a better bedside manner than Jennifer. Having spent a short time with Shari and knowing Jennifer, he suspected the two would strike it off as friends.

"Show me where you lost him, Quinn."

Marcus followed Lisa and Quinn into the stairway. Listening to them when he was functioning almost totally on caffeine was not a smart move. Lisa was peppering Quinn with questions that had no answers.

Marcus had worked cases with Lisa before; he knew how good she was. Not only did she approach cases differently, her mind simply didn't work like most people's. She saw connections others missed. Her curiosity only got her in trouble when someone let her get out into the field without a chaperone. He didn't think Quinn would be letting that happen in this case.

Lisa paused and rubbed her thumb across the scar in the concrete where the bullet had been removed. "You fell down the stairs."

"Guilty," Quinn replied. "I was looking down the stairs thinking he had gone that way when he shot at me from above. I wasn't worried about saving my pride, just getting out of the way."

"I wasn't implying it was funny. I'm glad you didn't break an ankle."

"The last I saw him was…there." Quinn pointed. "After I stopped tumbling and worked my way back up the stairs, he was gone. So where did he go? The agents coming down from above had him pinned below the fourteenth floor."

Lisa walked up the stairs and disappeared from sight. "For him to have gotten a shot off at you—" her face reappeared—"he had to be here. Then he turns…" She hit the wall with her hand. "As soon as I reach for the stairway door, I drop out of your line of sight. He could have gone out of the stairway as soon as he fired."

"Do it. Exit the stairway at the tenth floor and let's see if we can hear you," Marcus asked.

He looked at Quinn as they both heard the metal door close. "I don't know, Marcus. By the time I stopped falling and could hear again, the door could have already clicked closed."

"Could you hear it?" Lisa called down.

"Yes. Go up to eleven and try it there. And run up the stairs."

They could hear her on the stairs. "I'm sure I heard him on the stairs, Marcus. I remember it sounded like a clatter; Lisa is wearing tennis shoes and it was more distinct than that. I don't think he got off on ten," Quinn said.

The sound of a stairway door closing was audible but much fainter. "It could have been eleven," Marcus realized.

"Yes."

They walked up the stairs to join Lisa at the eleventh floor landing. "What do you think?"

"Eleven, twelve, or thirteen," Quinn confirmed.

"You said you heard his shoes?" Lisa asked.

Marcus recognized that vaguely unfocused look on her face. "What?"

She shook her head and looked at the stairs going up. "Start back at ten and look hard at the steps for anything that looks like a print, a scuff. The technicians were through here once but came up blank, and that was a surprise." She started walking up.

Marcus and Quinn shared a look. They had just been dismissed to doing tech work. "You can almost see the idea percolating," Quinn remarked.

"She's a bulldog." They started down the stairs. "Where are we at with the sketch?"

"We're getting decent coverage: the hotel guests and staff; officers throughout the area—the airports, trains, and buses—they're also running it by taxi drivers, giving it to tollbooth attendants. We've got officers canvassing the surrounding six blocks showing it around; we'll repeat that at dawn.

"All flights going out of O'Hare, Midway, Meigs, or Milwaukee before 8 A.M. are being checked. We're also tracking down every vehicle we can place in this area: the parking garage and area parking lots, pulling the drivers licenses.

"The database guys promised to work a few miracles. By morning, several variations of this sketch will be on every law enforcement officer's desk in the nation. I don't think this is his first criminal act. Someone has to have dealt with this guy before."

Quinn's experience showed. All it would take was a nibble somewhere along the line and this manhunt would spring forward. Quinn could be ruthless when he was hunting. "When do you want to release it to the media?"

"Top of the hour. We should be ready to absorb the false leads by then."

"Have there been many claims of responsibility?"

"At last count—nine. The two that seemed credible have already been eliminated. They are working to clear the rest."

"You have enough men?"

"I'm getting whatever I ask for," Quinn assured. "Washington was clear on that. What I need now is some luck."

"You'll get it."

"Or Lisa will create it."

Marcus looked at his partner and smiled. "That she will." He sighed and looked down at the stairs. "You know, it is a lot easier tracking someone outdoors."

"Give me a case that has open air, dirt, and mud any day," Quinn agreed. They spread out to see what they could find.

"Does this look recent to you?" Marcus asked several minutes later. There was a chip in the paint on the wall in the turn to the eleventh floor, about waist high. The gouge was angled, about half an inch long, and deep at one end. Loose plaster fragments were still in the crevices.

"Yes, it does. His gun clipped the wall," Quinn speculated.

"That would be my guess."

"At least we found something. Which is more than Lisa can say."

"I heard that," she called down. "When you get tired talking about a paint chip, you want to get Walter? And tell him to bring his full kit."

Walter was the best crime technician at the scene. Marcus glanced at Quinn, and the two of them moved up the stairs. "What have you found?"

She was sitting on the thirteenth floor landing, in her stockinged feet, having sacrificed one of her tennis shoes to use as a doorstop. She had on latex gloves. She was studying the bottom edge of the door. "Does that look like shoe polish and specks of blood to you? It sure does to me." She glanced up at them, a self-satisfied smile on her face. "Your shooter was in a hurry to open the door. He pulled it open right into his highly polished and bloody shoe. At least I think so. The lab will be able to prove it."

"Very nice."

She narrowed her eyes at Quinn. "You call me ma'am, I'm going to push you down the stairs."

"I wouldn't dare; ma'am."

Marcus put his hand on Lisa's shoulder to keep her seated. Quinn still hadn't learned. Lisa never made an idle threat. "Think you can track where he went once he got out on this floor?" he asked to distract her.

"We'll do a luminol test down the hallway carpet, see if we can pick up any more traces. I'll need you to get the hotel to momentarily shut off the hall lights."

"I'll get it arranged," Marcus agreed. "Okay, half his escape route has been found. Quinn, let's talk about the interviews being done. We need to talk to everyone on this floor. And I want to start a detailed look at those attending this conference or working in this hotel. Whoever did this was comfortable being here. Lisa, what about Carl's hotel room door? Carl had his room key in his hand. So what did the shooter use? Was it a master passkey? A copy? Is there any way we can find out?"

"I'll take a look at the logs and the mechanism."

"I'd appreciate it. Find him for us, Sherlock."

"A guy did this. How hard can it be?"

Marcus laughed.

Quinn held out a hand to help her to her feet. "You solve it, I'll buy you dinner."

"I solve it, I might even accept."

The ICU was silent at 4:00 A.M. Shari leaned back against the wall, watching her brother. She had been able to get an hour of sleep before the dreams came; she supposed she should be grateful. "Jennifer, Marcus mentioned when I first met him that he was planning to have a late dinner with his sister. Was that with you?"

It was nice having Marcus's sister here. Jennifer was comfortable around the ICU; the medical equipment didn't intimidate her. And Shari found it very helpful to just have someone listen.

"Kate and I," Jennifer replied. "You had met Marcus before this happened?"

"Earlier this evening. I got lost in the hotel," Shari replied, feeling like it had been a year ago. A decade ago.

"That was an interesting comment for him to have made."

"We were going to have coffee later this morning," she said quietly.

"Really? I'm sorry events overtook that."

Shari looked over, hearing the interest in Jennifer's voice. "It was just coffee."

"Still, an unusual request on his part."

Beneath the fatigue, Shari felt a glimmer of curiosity. "Marcus doesn't date?"

"No. And Kate, Lisa, Rachel, and I have been trying to change that."

Four sisters? Shari smiled at that, wondering if Marcus felt it was a blessing or a curse. Probably a blessing. "You've got a big family."

"There are seven of us, but it's not exactly a traditional family. We're all orphans. We sort of adopted each other, became our own family. Legally changed our last names."

Shari had heard of many families breaking up but rarely of one so intentionally forming. That must have been a powerful pact. "Seven?"

"It's a great group. We are constantly stepping in and out of each other's lives. Marcus is the oldest."

"A nice older brother to have. He's protective."

"The guardian of the group," Jennifer agreed.

"Which are you?"

"The youngest of the family—" Jennifer smiled—"everyone's favorite."

"An older sister doesn't get the same respect," she replied lightly, amused, thinking about her close relationship with Josh.

Shari crossed back over to a chair. Her body hurt and she eased herself down. Her spirit hurt worse. She could feel the dark depression creeping over her. In the middle of the night it was hard to hold on to optimistic thoughts. "From what you have said, Jennifer, I'm guessing—are you a Christian?"

"Yes. Kate and I are both recent believers."

"I think I embarrassed Marcus when I asked him to pray for my family."

"Don't worry about it. He needs someone to remind him he should reconsider his position. It's hard, after losing parents, to hear Jesus say I love you and know He means it."

Shari could only imagine how hard that must have been, losing the security of loving parents. She also heard the reality—Jennifer hoped to someday change his mind. "Carl was a Christian. Joshua and Dad believe. I'm grateful for that, but it doesn't take away the pain."

"The grief must be huge right now. Carl being in heaven doesn't change the fact he was killed."

"It's never felt this dark," Shari admitted softly.

"Jesus can find you in the darkness."

Those sounded like words from personal experience.

Life had shattered, and none of this made sense anymore. Shari looked at Josh. She let her hand touch the bandage on her cheek. A few more inches and she would be the one in the hospital bed…or dead. *Marcus, please find the shooter. I'm afraid of him.*

SIX

"Joshua, do you remember Carl meeting or calling anyone?" Marcus asked. The sky had begun to lighten outside the ICU window. He had confirmed what he feared, Joshua hadn't seen the shooter. Shari remained the only eyewitness.

"Not that I recall. We had a quiet Thursday and Friday. He was working on his speech with Shari, playing backgammon with Dad." Josh worked his good hand, pain etching his face at the simple movement. "How's Shari?"

"Hopefully still sleeping. She saw you in the recovery room about 3 A.M. You were out of it."

"Not entirely. She's right. The nurses are pretty." He gave a glimmer of a smile, then grimaced. "They told me Dad was in the recovery room. Is there any more news?"

"They'll be bringing him down to ICU soon." Marcus hesitated, but accepted it would be better if the news came from him rather than Shari. "It's not good."

Josh stilled. "What are the surgeons saying?"

"His blood pressure isn't stabilizing."

He was silent for a long time. "He's a fighter, like Mom." He looked over and held Marcus's gaze. "Where are you at in finding the shooter?"

"Shari was able to give us a good sketch."

"I almost wish you hadn't said that. Security is with her?"

"Tight. She doesn't realize she's got a permanent shadow."

Josh nodded. "Thanks. Keep it there, and if she raises a fuss, let me know."

Marcus recognized the worry of not only a brother but an assistant DA. "Will do."

"Has my extended family arrived yet?"

"They should be arriving shortly after 10 A.M. I suggest you get what rest you can before then."

Josh gave a reluctant laugh, then groaned. "The understatement of the year. I love them all, but there are a lot of them."

Josh's expression firmed, and Marcus recognized the burning anger in the man. "I can't protect Shari right now; I can't help her. And she has a nasty habit of assuming she can handle a stressful situation on her own without leaning against someone. Be careful with her. She's had a hard few months and she'll shatter if she gets pushed too hard." He gave an irritated grimace. "And whatever you do, don't let her get near the press. She'll consider it her professional obligation to get out there and answer their questions."

"You can relax a bit, Josh," Marcus replied. "You haven't told me anything I haven't already suspected. And I've read the press clippings on her from the last few years. She's stubborn, but I'm more so. I'm not letting her get in the midst of this press swarm; they would eat her alive. I like her too much for one thing, and second, she happens to be our only witness at the moment. If she gets annoyed with me, it won't change things. I don't plan to budge."

"Good. Let her hit a brick wall. I owe you."

"And I'll collect if I need it," Marcus warned.

"Fair enough."

Shari twisted her wrist, moving the cellular phone receiver away from her mouth so she could sip at the hot coffee. "No, Chris," she interrupted, pulling the phone back down. "There won't be press coverage at Carl's visitation. I want something private and by invitation only."

John's press secretary was a good friend, but she wasn't letting him sway her on this decision. She understood his point of view, but solving the press pressure wasn't her problem. "John is giving the eulogy at the funeral, but there is not going to be press coverage there either. That's assuming we bury Carl at the church next to his parents—we're still talking about Arlington National Cemetery with the military honors he's due as a decorated veteran. It's been offered."

She drank another sip of coffee, feeling much steadier after a second catnap. She had woken up, found a pad of paper, and got to work. She didn't want to grieve yet, and the only way to handle the emotions was to ruthlessly deny them any room to emerge. There would be time to cry later, when she had some privacy. She had the nasty suspicion once she started to cry, she would cry for a long time.

Carl had been a friend, and she was going to make certain what happened in the next days and weeks honored his memory and didn't make a spectacle of the crime.

Dad was in recovery. Get him into ICU, firmly back on the road to recovery, deal with a thousand details from family to press, and after it was all past, then she would stop and let the emotions take over.

"We're going to make the final decision after the family gets here. Call me back about 1 P.M. and I'll let you know details. You can release them then," she offered, giving him at least something to work with.

"In the meantime, could you send me out copies of all the area newspapers? I want to see how this is playing and correct any inaccuracies I can before they spread. And before you release John's itinerary, give me a heads up so I know reporters have it."

"I'll do that. How's your father?" Chris asked.

"Still in recovery. We're not releasing information yet. Anne volunteered to serve as our family spokesperson. I'll let her release a statement once she gets here."

Shari spotted Marcus coming from the ICU and cut Chris off. "I have to go. Call me at one."

The phone closed and tucked in her back pocket, she walked across the hospital hallway to meet Marcus, bringing with her a second cup of coffee she had poured when the nurse told her Marcus was in with Joshua.

He smiled as she drew near. "Your idea of a double hit of caffeine?"

"Double latte this is not," she agreed, longing for a stop at Starbucks for her normal start to the day. "But in this case, I thought you might need it," she offered, holding out the cup. "Black. And strong enough to drop an elephant."

"I'll risk it," Marcus said, accepting the Styrofoam cup.

"You haven't had any sleep yet," she observed, reaching out to touch his forearm.

"Too much to do. I'll get around to it later."

"In that case, I hesitate to ask, but do you have a minute?"

He sipped the coffee, smiled. "Absolutely. What's happening?"

"I've been thinking about who might have had motive to kill Carl."

The humor disappeared from his gaze. "Go on."

"There's a document in my briefcase back at the hotel that I think you should read. It's a brief, recommending Carl for the court."

"You wrote it?"

She nodded. "There's a section that addressed his controversial cases. Some of them sound obscure, but I've read the transcripts. I'd like to sit down and go through them with someone."

"Shari."

"You said I could help."

"We are already looking at his past cases."

"Please. I know them better than his own law clerks. And it would help feeling like I'm doing something. He was a good friend, Marcus."

He rubbed the back of his neck, then finally nodded. "Later today, after your family is here and settled?"

"Thanks."

He nodded toward the officer who had been with her all morning. "Is Craig working out okay?"

"He's been a doll." And never more than a few feet away even on this well-secured hospital wing. Shari found that...interesting. She didn't want to hear why Marcus considered it necessary.

Marcus winced. "Don't tell him that."

She laughed. "I didn't plan to."

The floor nurse came to get her. "Shari, your father is being brought down from the recovery room."

She took a deep breath. The light moment had just been swallowed by reality. She knew seeing her dad was going to be a shock. The surgeon had been down twice to talk with her since Dad had been moved to the recovery room. "Let me get Mom."

"Shari."

She looked back at Marcus.

"He's a fighter. Remember that."

It helped, just hearing Marcus say those words. Dad would get through this. She had to believe that. She nodded her thanks and went to join her family.

The hospital chapel was a small room. Shari came seeking relief from the exhausting pressure. The chapel had padded pews and rich red carpet; a simple layout designed for all faiths. The room lights were muted. Shari walked to the front and slipped halfway into the second pew.

Her hands reached for the back of the pew in front of her and she rested her chin on the wood, looking not at the muted watercolor on the wall before her but back in time at memories, at the days before the shooting had occurred.

She pressed her forehead against the mahogany wood of the pew. Would her dad ever wake up? *Jesus, I can't take much more of this.* The day was creeping by without change and it was killing her slowly. *Please let him wake up and get stronger. I can't lose him. I can't.*

Tears ran down her cheeks and she wiped them away. She couldn't fall apart. Her family was here, and they had enfolded her in warmth, but they also required her to be strong. She didn't have any strength left.

She just wanted God to answer her prayer. She was trying not to let fear get the upper hand. God was in control. But as the day progressed with little change, it became harder and harder to pray without sounding desperate.

Her mom was at peace even in the midst of this uncertainty. Shari knew it came from her mom's own two brushes with death: the heart infection and the mild heart attack. Beth had accepted her life was in God's direct hands. And facing this crisis was her way to say Bill was in God's hands and rest at peace.

Try as she might, Shari couldn't find that same quiet trust and peace. She wanted to wrestle with God like Jacob had done to get the answer she wanted—her father to stabilize. Which was better? The passive, simple trust her mother had, or the intense, this-matters-to-me persistence she felt?

She wished she understood prayer. Two decades as a Christian and she still struggled with it.

Her pager went off. It was her emergency pager; she had shut off her regular one. It was Sam. She waited for the reaction to arrive, the intense emotion at realizing it was him and felt…nothing. The upheaval their relationship represented no longer was the emotional swamp it had been before. It was trivial compared to the reality she now had to deal with.

He had called several times during the night and the course of the morning; she had the message slips but had not returned his calls. She would take this page, she finally decided, knowing she needed to talk to him. But not here. She got to her feet. Craig was standing by the door at the back of the chapel.

"Would it be possible for me to just walk around this hospital floor?"

"Sure. Just give me a minute." He went on the security net and a minute later nodded. "We can circle this concourse, come back around to the waiting room where your family is staying."

"Thanks." She placed the call as they walked. "Sam."

"Shari. Thanks for taking the page."

It was awkward. "You've heard?" She knew he had, but she wanted an excuse not to have to talk about the specifics.

"I'm with John now. How's your dad?"

"Holding his own."

"Josh?"

It brought a tired smile. "Already proving to be a bad patient."

Sam hesitated. "And you?"

Jesus, what do I say? The pain of the past had lost its grip and dropped away. The friendship was still there, under the hurt feelings of the relationship that had failed. And right now she really needed what they had once shared. "It's been a bad weekend, Sam." She wished he were here so she could get a hug. He had always been good for a hug.

Windows overlooked a central courtyard. Shari stopped there, rested her forearms against the oak railings, studied the play of sunlight across the grounds.

"How can I help?"

She had known those would be his next words. He had always been a practical man, never more so than when someone was fighting tears. "I'll need someone at Dad's law office on Monday to help me with his court calendar, let me know what can be postponed and what has to be transferred."

"I'll handle it. What about Josh at the DA's office?"

"Josh spoke to his boss this morning."

Sam knew her; he didn't ask the emotional questions of what had happened. He asked about her family, about things that needed to be done, focusing on the immediate future. They talked for twenty minutes, and it helped more than Sam could ever know.

"It was good to talk to you," she finally said, relieved to have the past finally feel closed.

"The same. I really would like to come out if you'll let me."

"No, it's okay. Family is here. And it's more of a relief to know you have things handled back there."

"If you change your mind, just ask. I'll call later when I've got these details for you. Please tell your family I'm praying for them."

"I'll do that."

After they said good-bye and she hung up, Shari didn't immediately move.

The sadness was intense. It had gone so wrong with Sam. They should have meshed so well, but it had instead come apart in ragged fashion.

He was one of the best state legislators around, and she had liked him from the first moment John had introduced them. When Sam had asked her out, she had felt so special. And the year going out with him had made her life sweep by.

Sam had been supportive of her work, had listened to her dreams. She wanted with a passion to someday be in politics herself, not just working behind the scenes for someone else. And then the day had come that still haunted her.

Sam had proposed marriage with the assumption that she would stay as the person behind his own political career. Maybe it wouldn't have been so hard to accept if he hadn't also said he wanted to postpone having children.

She had looked at being the wife of a politician and she had loved him enough she had almost said yes. But in the end she had turned him down. And over the painful months that followed had come to resent what he had done. There wasn't a place for her dreams in his vision of the future, not for a family, not for a career of her own. She had been honest from the beginning and he had heard what he wanted to hear.

She had pushed to have a relationship and what she had gotten was burned. *Jesus, I don't understand what went wrong. I know I made a mistake in that relationship with Sam. Was this again a case of wanting something so badly I didn't see the problems; I saw only my dreams?*

"What's wrong?"

Marcus had replaced Craig sometime during her reverie. Shari closed her eyes, frustrated. Marcus was seeing her fighting tears again. This was getting embarrassing. She wiped her eyes with her sleeve, then turned. "Ever have something you wish you could go back and undo?"

He rested his arms against the railing beside her, kindly ignoring her tears. "Shall I count them?"

"Mind naming one?"

"I told my sister Kate I liked her broccoli casserole."

Caught off guard by his rueful tone, she had to laugh. "You lied."

"I felt sorry for her. Now I just feel sorry for me. She makes it nearly every time I go over for dinner."

She needed that. A lighthearted moment in the midst of this mess. "Why don't you tell her?"

"I'd hate to hurt her feelings."

"She probably suspects."

"Knowing Kate, that is more than just probable. But as the years pass, there are some secrets that take on a life of their own."

"True."

Shari grew serious and looked at the phone in her hand. "I wish I could change two years ago. Make a yes to a dinner invitation a no. It would have saved so much heartache."

"You were just talking to him?"

Trust him to assume the truth. She nodded. "It's hard, picking up the friendship after the relationship falls apart."

"I know. It can take a lot of apologies on both sides. But it is worth that effort." He held out his hand. "Want some ice cream? I've heard chocolate fixes most problems in life."

He surprised her again. "You brought ice cream." He had arranged lunch to be catered in earlier for her family, as there was a large press presence in the cafeteria.

"Guilty. I promised your young cousins Heather and Tracy."

She took the hand he offered and let him turn her away from the railing and the memories. She would have liked to keep hold of his hand, an embarrassing realization; when he released her hand, she pushed hers into her pocket. "Was this before or after you answered their dozens of questions about being a marshal?"

"I like kids."

"I noticed." She tilted her head to one side and glanced up at him. "I don't suppose you brought cherries to make a sundae." She was craving a sugar fix right now.

"And whipped topping. The good stuff is in the details."

"That's a great line. Could I borrow it and use it someday?"

"Use it? In a speech you mean?"

"Absolutely. Speechwriters love the perfect phrase. Evil empire. Where's the beef? Nixon's checkers speech. Every speechwriter dreams of having something they wrote become part of the national lexicon."

"Anything of yours reach that stature?"

"I'm working on it. I want something funny to be my legacy."

"Not something profound?"

"There are too many boring politicians. Trust me, I listen to the speeches." Her mouth quirked in a grin. "Besides, profound isn't very likely to happen. So I'd rather be remembered for something funny."

"It's good to have a dream in life. Someday you'll figure out that perfect line."

"You seem certain of that."

"Trust me, Shari. You'll think of it." He paused to let a nurse pass in the crowded hallway. "Is there anything else I can do for your extended family here? Anything else you need?"

"Could you get me the national newspapers? I don't want the TV on because they are only able to speculate right now and keep repeating what happened."

"All of the national papers?"

"I'm news starved. I admit it. It's an election year."

"And it's a good distraction for you to have right now."

She appreciated the fact he understood that. She forced herself to turn back to serious matters. "We've got Carl's funeral arrangements decided."

"I spoke with your mom before I came to find you. Don't worry about transportation back to Virginia. There will be assistance for all those kind of details."

"I appreciate that." They turned the corner back to the secure wing of the hospital. He reached around her to open the waiting room door for her. She wanted to keep talking with him—she was enjoying the conversation—but the kids came to join her, reaching for her hands.

"I'll be around, Shari," Marcus reassured. "And if something comes up, just page."

She nodded her thanks and had to leave it with a smile as her good-bye.

SEVEN

"Jennifer."

It was 5:45 P.M. Saturday night, and Marcus had walked out of an update meeting before it concluded, leaving Quinn, Dave, and Mike to handle the last details with Washington. He had to talk to Jennifer before her flight. It was too important a conversation to let this case push it into something done over the phone.

Jennifer turned from where she stood looking at the window display of one of the shops in the hotel main corridor. He could see the fatigue. She had been at the hospital visiting with Shari's family. He had paged her to come over to the hotel but now wished he had arranged to meet her there instead. His tentative idea that they could get a quiet corner of the restaurant and talk changed to something more practical. Room service would do fine. Kate would be joining them soon.

"Do you mind if we talk upstairs? It will be a lot more private than anywhere else. I promised Kate dinner when the meeting she's in finally gets done, and room service sounds like the best option."

"I'd prefer that," Jennifer agreed.

Marcus dug out his room key for the suite on the eighth floor he shared with Quinn and gestured Jennifer to the nearest elevator. "How are things at the hospital? Any change with William?"

"His blood pressure is still fluctuating. That's not a good sign. But he's held on this long."

"Still unconscious?"

Jennifer nodded. "Shari and Beth have been taking turns sitting with him. It's hard on them, the waiting. But at least Joshua appears to be firmly out of the woods. The doctors are talking about moving him from the ICU sometime tomorrow afternoon."

"Good—for more reasons than one. He strikes me as a man able to keep Shari from carrying the weight of the world on her shoulders."

"You don't have to listen to her for long before you realize how close the two of them are. But if you think Josh can keep her in line—"

"Okay, she'll humor him, but she'll listen to him."

"That I buy."

Marcus unlocked the door to room 812 and held it open for Jennifer.

"I can see Quinn is being his normal meticulous housekeeper." Jennifer picked up two shirts tossed across the living room chair and added them to the stack on top of Quinn's open suitcase that was dumped by the door of the suite rather than put away in the bedroom.

"Neatness is a virtue I have yet to instill in him," Marcus replied dryly. With four sisters, he had learned early. "Cut him some slack, his mind has been on other things."

Marcus flipped closed the stack of files on the couch and put them back in his briefcase so he could sit down. He vaguely remembered reading them Friday afternoon before all this had begun.

"Does Quinn travel anywhere without this hat?" Jennifer picked up the cowboy hat tossed onto the side table and tried it on for size, laughing. "This thing needs to be given a decent burial somewhere. It's been beaten. And it smells like a horse."

"Now that I think about it—no. It's his part of home that always comes along."

Jennifer set it back down. She gathered up drinking glasses, disposed of fast food sacks, tossed shoes into the bedroom. Marcus knew better than to suggest she leave it. If he let her deal with clutter for five minutes, she would be able to sit and talk. Make her sit with the room still a mess and she would fidget the entire time.

"Is it the fact Quinn is less than neat about minor things the reason Lisa says no to his dinner invitations?"

Jennifer glanced over at him. "Has Quinn been walking around with a puppy dog face after being turned down?"

"Sadder than a hound dog. What's Lisa's problem?"

"Kevin."

"I thought that was over months ago."

"That's what we all thought. He must have caught her at a weak moment. She said yes to another date and came home with her jaw all rigid and her back up. I spent Thursday night with her and she was positively morose about the entire species of things male."

"I knew I should have paid that guy a visit after last time. I would have if Lisa hadn't insisted I leave it alone."

"Don't worry. Jack was going to say a few words on all the O'Malley's behalf; I told Stephen to go along as Jack was a little hot under the collar. And I told him not to tell Lisa until after the fact."

"Good. Thank you. Lisa doesn't deserve the jerks she gets in her life." Marcus snapped his briefcase shut and moved it to the floor. "She needs Quinn. He will not laugh at or belittle her profession, and he won't hurt her heart. He's a little old for her, but he's a guy with deep roots. She needs that kind of stability behind her. He won't budge when she gets herself in trouble."

"She doesn't want to live in the middle of nowhere."

"That's it? That's honestly why she's been saying no?"

"There's that, and the fact he typically looks good enough to eat and most every woman in the room notices him."

"Minor problems." Marcus understood Lisa. She was the only one in the family who had been cast away at birth, had spent her entire life in foster care. She was the most independent of the group; used to going her own way. She had never locked onto feeling like she belonged, so he and the rest of the O'Malleys had simply swallowed her up and made her a place.

Frankly, if they wanted an adventure, they all knew the best one would be had by joining Lisa for a weekend. She was the fun in the family, and they all loved her. Marcus hated to learn she was hurting. "Think she'll kill me if I send her some flowers?"

"Marcus, haven't you seen her scrapbook? She's got a flower pressed from each bouquet you've ever sent her."

"You're kidding."

Jennifer laughed. "She's sentimental, although she will kill me for saying it. Send her flowers, or better yet, why don't you send her something for her ferret? Lisa had me in stitches Thursday evening laughing at the antics of her latest pet. She's doting on that animal."

"Empty paper towel tubes still his favorite?"

"Yes."

Marcus sank back into the sofa seat, feeling the tension drain away. "Jennifer, what's going on with you? It's been too long since we've really talked. I've missed you with you being all the way down in Texas."

She sank into the plush chair she had cleared and looked at him, her smile fading to be replaced by...sadness; an expression so unusual for her he didn't know what to think. "I've been thinking of how to tell you this and now I don't have words."

"Just tell me, Jennifer," he said gently. Two decades of watching out for this family had taken him through the highs and lows of each of their lives. He didn't know what was wrong, but he would fix it, somehow. It was the one thing he could offer the family that was uniquely his to give. "I think I'm prepared to hear about anything."

She looked across the six feet of the room separating them, and suddenly there was moisture in her eyes. "Marcus, I've got cancer."

He wasn't prepared for that. It stung hard, like a knife in his ribs when his guard was down. He visibly flinched and forced himself to take a breath. "Cancer." She looked fine, but her eyes never wavered from his, and this wasn't something anyone in the family would joke about. A dragon from the past roared toward him and the image of his mom flashed by. No. This couldn't be happening. Not someone else he loved getting sick.

She came over to sit on the couch beside him and he had to force himself to hear her words through the rushing memories. "I'm sorry. I know how hard it is to hear. It's around my spine, has touched my liver. I start radiation Monday morning at Johns Hopkins."

The cold was like a grave opening up. "You told Kate."

"She's the only one that knows," Jennifer said softly.

His hand settled on top of hers and his thumb rubbed the side of her wrist finding the reassurance of her steady pulse. Anger surged over the pain. Anger of a man mixing with anger of a boy—all of it pouring toward God. *Not again. Please, not again.*

"When did you find out?"

"I got the first suspicious test results a month ago. That trip to the Mayo Clinic? It wasn't a consult on a case; I was the patient."

How had the family not clued in to the evidence? A month. The family grapevine normally knew the moment anything of significance happened, and she had been dealing with this for a month without saying anything. Alone in a hospital, without family to visit and keep her company…it broke his heart. "Jen, I wish I had known."

"Kate needed you, Marcus. I couldn't help her in the midst of the toughest month of her life working that airline explosion investigation. What I could do was insure she had your undivided attention. Kate needed you, and I didn't want to distract from that."

"You needed me too."

She squeezed his shoulder. "I knew you were only a phone call away," she reassured. "That was such a comfort to know. They were doing the tests and poking and prodding me; it was still an undefined enemy at that point. I kept hoping that when they gave an answer it would be better news than it turned out to be. This is going to be a terrible, long battle, Marcus. Rest assured, I'm going to lean hard against all of the O'Malleys."

"The engagement."

"Tom didn't want to wait. We're going to postpone the wedding until the immediate course of treatment is past. Hopefully I'll get a period of remission."

She wasn't talking about a cure. "The prognosis is that bad?" he whispered.

"People don't live with this kind of cancer, Marcus."

He'd find a way to help her beat this; it would get every breath of energy he had. "You will." He was the guardian of the O'Malleys—he had to find a way.

She looked at him, and there was compassion there, for him, for what this meant. *She's dying and she is worrying about me.* He forgot sometimes just how stubborn and intense every member of this family was.

He closed his eyes for a moment and forced himself to look forward, to what she was going to need. He wanted to give her a hug and realized he was scared to death he would hurt her. If it was low around her spine, he couldn't even hug her without thinking about it first. His hand settled on her shoulder. "Is Kate going with you to Baltimore?"

"It's not necessary. Tom is flying out to stay with me."

He looked at her and she grimaced. "Sorry."

"The family will be there. I'll declare the emergency if you won't."

"Marcus, I want the family there. I'm going to be leaning on all of you like crazy, but the next few weeks are going to be long days, boring even, and I'm going to be sick for most of them."

"Do you honestly think any one of us would care?"

"I will."

"Tough," Marcus replied, for the first time feeling a glimmer of hope touch his voice. "Are you going to tell them or do you want me to?"

"I've made rather a mess of it I'm afraid. I didn't want to cast a shadow over the Fourth of July festivities and everyone's first chance to meet Tom. And I was going to tell Lisa Thursday night, but she didn't need this kind of news on top of the week she was having. Then when I left her place, it seemed more crucial to tell Jack about what was going on with Lisa than to hit him with my news. I've run out of calendar days."

"Kate and I will solve it. Don't worry about it. Your flight tonight is at nine o'clock?"

"Yes."

"What happens tomorrow?"

"I get admitted at Johns Hopkins, they repeat the blood work, take more X rays. If everything is still a go, they start the radiation treatments Monday morning."

"Family will be there."

"Marcus—Shari really needs you right now. The others have jobs and commitments to keep. I really will be okay. Radiation and chemotherapy are a normal part of life for a cancer patient."

"I hear you, Jennifer. Now hear me—we need you. We're going to be there for every inning, not just the peaks and valleys." He saw her eyes glisten, saw her blink back moisture.

"I knew you would respond this way."

He wiped her eyes dry with the sleeve of his shirt. "You're our favorite. An O'Malley has never lost a fight yet; we're not going to start now. Tell me the details, all of them, everything the tests have shown, what you've read, what the cancer doctors have said."

They talked for half an hour and then Kate came to join them. Marcus understood in one brief look at Kate how relieved she was now that he knew. This secret must have been killing her. He'd seen the strain on occasion and written it off as her adjusting to dating Dave. He could not have been more off target.

The three of them talked until Jennifer said she needed to get to the airport. They walked with her down to the lobby. Marcus was reluctant to see her go. "Is it safe for a hug?"

"Yes. And I'll be bummed if you don't."

He folded her carefully into his arms and buried his head against her hair. "Can I send you flowers?" he whispered, and felt relief as her laughter bubbled from her chest.

"I hope you'll fill the entire hospital room by the time I get released."

"Just the hospital room?" Marcus asked, pulling forth humor he didn't feel. "I'll call you every day and be there as soon as I can."

"I know, Marcus. Please don't worry; I promise no more surprises. You'll know everything going on."

"I'll keep you to that." He reluctantly let her go.

Jennifer hugged Kate.

"Call me when you get in," Kate said.

"I will," Jennifer promised.

Marcus looked over at Kate after Jennifer left and felt a heavy weight settle across his chest. "Kate, I'm so sorry you had to carry this secret alone. I knew you were stressed, but I thought it was everything going on in your own life, never something like this."

"I didn't like keeping the secret from you but didn't feel like I could push Jennifer any harder to tell you. She's still struggling with this, a lot deeper than her words are reflecting."

Marcus wrapped his arm around her shoulders. "Come on, I'll order us room service. We've got to talk."

"Deal."

They returned back to the suite and Marcus glanced at the room service menu but had no interest in eating.

"You have to eat," Kate said, reading his expression. "Order two cheeseburgers. If I'm going to eat, so are you."

She was right. Marcus ordered the two cheeseburgers.

Sharing a dark day and doing it with Kate, there was no one he would prefer to be with. "How many crises have we weathered through the years?"

"Too many. And this one is going to be the toughest." He could hear the tension in her voice, the fear, for her Southern accent she used as a shield shifted to stretch the vowels. It was subtle, not many people would notice, but he could hear the change. The accent was like a cloak she pulled around her when the emotions were high. Language and the tone of words were both her profession and her way of expressing what she felt. And when she dropped that accent and reverted to the Chicago clipped speech she had grown up with…he'd only seen it happen a few times, right before her anger exploded.

"We're not going to lose her," Marcus assured softly, going to the heart of her fear.

"It's going to rip the fabric of this family if we do. I'm so glad she's a fighter."

"Does Dave know?"

"Yes." Kate hesitated. "Did Jennifer tell you she was baptized last month?"

Marcus was startled at the news. "No."

"Tom introduced her to Jesus."

"She's praying to be healed." He said it with dread, knowing how badly she was setting herself up to be hurt.

"Yes."

She'd believe, pray, and when they weren't answered, it would cut like a dagger. Prayers were answered as much by chance as by a caring God. "She's grasping at straws. I don't want her to feel that disappointment if things get as bad as she described it could, if her prayers are not answered."

"Marcus, she's not the only one who made that decision to believe. I did too."

Kate. This couldn't be happening—it was his job to protect his family and they were walking down a road that would hurt them. How had he lost touch so quickly with what was happening in their lives? It had been an extraordinary few weeks with the airline bombing and the discovery Kate had a younger brother, but still, he should have seen what was going on. "Why—"

"I don't think it's false hope. I think Jesus really does care, really is God, and He's powerfully involved in our lives." She stopped him when he would have interrupted. "I know what happened with your mom. You and I both know what it feels like to be abandoned. But I think you're wrong to let that close the door on Jesus. The Bible says He was forsaken too—the day He died on the cross. He understands; He definitely knows what that pain feels like. And if He hadn't been willing to accept the pain of the cross, Jennifer and I wouldn't have the hope we do today."

Her words were calm and sure, and Marcus felt a degree of envy slip in alongside his deep doubts. She was logical, certain, and she had done the one thing he had thought was not possible: find a way to be comfortable with God.

It wasn't a subject he wanted to tackle with her, not when it would mean opening the door of his past with all its pain and disappointment. It was so much more than just God not answering his prayers. It was God abandoning his mom, not answering her prayers. There had been no one more committed and faithful to God than his mom, and she had died in that hospital because she could no longer breathe. He'd traveled this road already and did not want to see Kate and Jennifer hurt.

It wasn't the right time to have the discussion. He shifted the conversation back to Jennifer. "We have to call a family emergency."

It meant tossing Rachel on a plane in the middle of the night to get here, having Stephen and Jack pull in favors to get their shifts covered at the firehouse, have Lisa somehow get her pager reassigned. But if ever this family had had an emergency, they had one now. They had to talk face to face. "I want an O'Malley there with Jennifer on Monday."

"Agreed. I've already been working my schedule so I could go," Kate replied.

"I'm worried about how Rachel will take the news. It will hit her the hardest, I think."

"She empathizes when a moth hits the car window; she feels everyone's pain as her own. It makes her a wonderful trauma psychologist, but when it's family—"

"She'll never be able to find that internal distance. She'll be absorbing the implications of this as deeply as Jennifer."

"She'll want to go out east immediately; that's a given. Do you and Rachel want to go out east first?"

Kate nodded. "We stay through the week, then Stephen and Jack shift their vacation time around and come out next—we can cover the next month without a problem."

"I'll talk to Washington about getting Craig assigned to be primary for Shari and her family."

Kate shook her head. "Don't do that. I understand why you want to, but I don't think you should. Jennifer will accept us being there when we are using vacation time; sliding in visits between assignments. If you step out of an active job it will make her feel guilty, and that is the last thing she needs adding to the pressure she already feels. If Quinn can cover for you briefly, Dave can fly you out and back so you can visit."

"Kate, I need to be there for me; it's not just for Jennifer's benefit."

Jennifer was dying. It suddenly struck him what Shari must be feeling. How was she still able to walk around and function? He felt like someone had just slammed him and ripped apart his world. He faced losing Jennifer and he felt like the walking wounded. For Shari to have lost Carl, now to be watching her dad struggle to hang on…

"We fight, Marcus. I've already got a four-inch binder of information for you to read. We're about to become cancer specialists."

"I never dreamed this would happen. I worry about Stephen and Jack getting disoriented in a fire, of you encountering the one hostage situation that can't be resolved, of Lisa stumbling into someone with a real skeleton in his closet; but when I worried, it was never about Jennifer. She's a pediatrician; she's the safe one."

"You can't protect this family from life."

"It's my job to try."

Kate gave him a look that fell somewhere between pity and loyal admiration. "Page the others. We'll meet as soon as Rachel can get a flight back."

The hotel directly across from the hospital was vintage versus modern, Old World elegance adding to its peaceful charm. Marcus checked one last time with the three men on the security detail watching the floor where Shari and her mom were now staying, then let himself into the adjoining suite to theirs. Her family had been given other rooms on the floor. It was coming up on midnight. They were short staffed everywhere, and Marcus had decided in the end it was best to be near the hospital tonight.

Craig looked up from the paper he was reading.

"All quiet?" Marcus asked it softly, for the connecting door between the suites was open.

"Yes." Craig folded the newspaper. "Do you want me back here in the morning or should I meet you at the hospital?"

Marcus shrugged off his jacket and loosened his tie. "Why don't you report to the hospital about nine; I'll make sure they are covered to there."

"Will do. You've got several messages."

Quinn would have paged with news on the shooter; that was the one message Marcus was waiting for. "I'll get to them. Thanks."

Craig rose with a nod, said good night. Marcus locked the door behind him. He walked through the dark rooms lit only by the moonlight, too restless to settle even though he was exhausted.

Jennifer. He needed to be there at Johns Hopkins, and soon. He had bought coffee for an oncologist at the hospital after talking with Kate, and the medical information swirling around in his head all felt black. Jennifer hadn't been kidding when she said it was going to be a tough fight.

All the O'Malleys had been paged. Rachel was able to grab a cancellation on a late flight and should be halfway back to Chicago by now from her current Red Cross assignment in Florida. She had returned the emergency page and asked only one question. "Where?" It had been the typical response of all the O'Malleys. The number of family emergencies called in over two decades could be counted on one hand. They would meet first thing in the morning, and by then he had to decide how he would break the news.

Faint sounds echoed from the adjoining suite. Marcus walked over to lean against the door frame. "Couldn't sleep?"

His quiet words startled Shari, and she stopped halfway across the living room. "I didn't realize you were here."

"We're trading off shifts for the evening."

She waved her hand toward the minikitchen in their suite. "I was just going for something to drink."

"Want some company?"

"Sure."

He walked toward the minikitchen. "Anything in particular you would like?"

"A glass of milk."

He smiled at her tone. "Don't apologize. It's good for you." He found a glass and opened the refrigerator, knowing from past stays in this hotel that the suites came complete with all the makings for breakfast. "Want something to eat to go with that?"

She declined.

He poured her a glass of milk, then retrieved a piece of cold pizza for himself from the box one of his guys must have ordered. He had, in the end, only pushed around the cheeseburger while watching Kate eat.

"I've eaten a lot of cold pizza in my life, but rarely by choice."

Marcus felt the tension uncoil at finally having something on which the world would not rise or fall to talk about. "Cold pizza is great. It's the best way to eat leftovers. Now Chinese, that is not good cold."

"You live on carryout."

"Travel enough, it's a requirement of life." She settled on the couch and he took the chair by the window. "How's your father?"

"No change. There has been little this entire day."

"I'm sorry about that, Shari. Truly sorry."

"He'll pull through."

He didn't bother to try and temper her hope. He now knew all about hope at any cost, against any odds.

It was late, and he didn't hurry to start a conversation, content to simply share her company. She curled up with her feet against the cushions, her back braced against the side arm of the couch, her hands holding the glass linked across her knees. Her hair was still tousled from restless sleep, and the black college sweatshirt she wore looked beaten up and faded, matching the jeans. It was a far cry from the elegance of the first time he had met her, but Marcus decided he liked this Shari better. She had vibrated with life and energy before; this version was a look inside when the comfortable circumstances were stripped away.

He tucked away another nugget of information about her; she was not troubled by silence, didn't feel a need to fill it with sound. The quietness after the turmoil of the day felt good, and it was nice to share it.

She eventually stirred. "I would like to go to church in the morning. Would that be possible?"

"Would the chapel service at the hospital be okay?"

"Yes."

"I'll be glad to make the arrangements."

"Thank you. I know you don't believe, but it's important to me."

"Shari—trust me, it's not a problem." He should have been more careful in what he said. As many doubts as he personally had, he had a heritage from his mom that respected religion, and Shari didn't need any more sources of turmoil in her life. He changed the subject. "I read your brief recommending Carl for the court."

"Did you?"

"You're good. You certainly convinced me."

"Communication is what I do for a living."

She said it quietly, and it took a moment for the significance of what she had said to register. He'd lived in Virginia for a long time; she worked for the governor, was working now on his reelection campaign. "Modesty doesn't suit you. You're very good at what you do." He smiled. "And despite your protests to the contrary, you can write profound and elegant sound bites. I actually haven't minded listening to the campaign speeches."

She returned his smile. "You're being generous, but thank you. I can write the speech, the brief, just don't ask me to sit through its delivery by someone else. I would much rather be the one giving it."

"So you do have an Achilles heel."

"I've got a couple to go along with those secrets I don't plan to share."

Her dry humor in this moment was deeply appreciated. "Good secrets, are they?"

"I bet you've got a few."

"More than a few," he agreed easily.

"Care to trade one?"

"There's a grapevine in my family, so you'd have to promise to keep it quiet."

His words got her interest, and her curiosity; she sat up straighter. "Okay."

"I know who swiped Rugsby the raccoon, our family mascot. There is about to be a ransom demand made for him."

"Please tell me that's a stuffed animal."

"Jack won him for Kate at a carnival when we were in our teens."

"Who took it?"

"Rachel and Jennifer. They decided to give the others a real puzzle to solve."

She chuckled softly. "Let me guess, you put them up to it."

"Every good plan needs a mastermind. Besides, no one in the family would ever suspect it could have been Rachel and Jen."

"That's good."

"Very. I think I'll stump them. Your turn. Give."

"Josh has been using a marked deck of cards for when we play rummy, and he doesn't realize it."

Marcus choked on his soda.

"One of the kids left the deck of cards at the house, and it got put away on the shelf of games."

"And you feel guilty winning as a result."

"Worse, I'm having to count cards to make sure I lose half the games."

"An honest cheat. You could just tell him."

"Remember when you said there were some secrets that take on a life of their own? This one has."

"You're a card player?"

"Josh is. That and dominoes. I personally prefer Scrabble, but he refuses to play because I wipe the board with him most games. Are you a game player?"

"Within the family, it's Monopoly. There have been a few games that have gone on for days. Personally, my partner Quinn and I play a lot of chess."

"Any good?"

"I haven't beaten him yet."

"How long have you been trying?"

"Oh..." Marcus thought about it, "about five years."

"Years?"

"I'm a slow learner. And the guy is brutal at the game."

"It's the victory you dream about."

"Yes."

The clock chimed another quarter hour gone. Shari got up and carried her glass to the counter. "Thank you, Marcus."

He leaned his head back so he could see her. "For what?"

"Just being here. For providing a distraction and a laugh. I'll see you in the morning." She moved back through the rooms to return to bed.

Marcus watched the door she had left through and smiled. The more time he spent around Shari, the more he liked her. Her habit of falling back on humor in the midst of the crisis told him more about her than she probably realized. She had learned to cope with ongoing crisis and stress from somewhere. Since her family appeared close, it had to be her political job.

Marcus finished his drink, speculating on what was an unusual discovery. He knew what it took to cope with ongoing pressure. She had developed a skill that would not only calm down her own reaction, but also those around her. John had made a good choice when he put her to work on his campaign.

He sighed. This situation was out of her league. They had to find the shooter, and quickly. Asking Shari to cope with this crisis for more than a few days would be asking her to endure a weight that would break her. The intensity of it came back as he thought about how little progress they had made during the course of the day.

Shari needed him. Jennifer needed him. In a few hours all the O'Malleys were going to need him. He had never been one to shy away from responsibility, but this burden he wished he could give to someone else. He got to his feet, weary. A day couldn't get worse than this one.

Marcus woke to the sound of his pager, reached over to check the number, and then picked up the phone. "It's Marcus." He rubbed his eyes at the news he was given. "Five minutes. Have the car brought around to the underground garage." He went to wake up Shari and her mom. William Hanford had just taken a turn for the worse.

William Hanford coded at 3:07 A.M. Sunday morning.

Marcus pulled Shari out of the way as nurses and doctors worked to bring him back from cardiac arrest. They stood on the other side of the glass watching as CPR was done and repeated attempts were made to get his heart started. Beth, her sister Margaret, and a nurse with her stood off to one side inside the room. Marcus had never realized how long doctors would continue the fight. Ten minutes passed, fifteen.

Shari watched it all…silent, still.

He could almost feel the intensity of her prayers.

As a child he had tried so hard to believe enough to have his prayers answered, but one by one they had failed. His mom had died. His dad had continued to drink. And eventually he had been abandoned. It wasn't just family that abandoned him, it was God. For the first time in years, he wished he could pray and know it would be answered. *Shari believes. Please answer her prayers. Please don't abandon her.*

The doctors worked another five minutes. And then the activity slowly ceased.

"No." It was a quiet wail.

Marcus turned Shari into his chest and away from the reality before them. "I am so sorry."

He could feel the pain flow off her in a wave. He tightened his arms, enclosing her in a firm grip, afraid she would fall. And then with a deep gulp of air she turned back into the room. "Mom." She pulled away to join her mom at her father's side.

Marcus had to look away from the grief. Anger flared hot and intense inside: at the shooter, at fate, at a God who didn't care. He was sick and tired of religion that offered false hope.

Shari didn't have the reserves for this kind of emotional hit. God got all the praise and thanks for fortunate coincidences attributed to prayer, while men like himself had to deal with the disappointment, disbelief, and grief when those prayers were not answered. It wasn't right to raise hope and disappoint, and that was what religion did.

And as he watched, fear wrapped itself hard around his heart. This was the face of the pain he would feel if he ever lost Jennifer; this was the pain that would rip apart the O'Malleys, and he didn't know how to brace himself for the possibility the unthinkable would one day happen.

The waiting room had become Shari's private place to grieve. Joshua was awake now, had been told. As she had expected, his reaction had been intense. He'd tried to throw the vase on the bedside table through the wall. And he'd gotten mad at himself for not stopping the shooter, for not yanking the door closed and throwing the lock when he knocked her out of the doorway.

Mom and Aunt Margaret were sitting with him. She had slipped away from the other family. Shari couldn't handle Joshua's grief, her mom's, on top of her own. *If only she hadn't opened that door!* Tears ran down her cheeks and the Kleenex clenched in her fist was worthlessly sodden. She wiped her face with the back of the sleeve.

She was more than just hurt, she was angry, and it was bottled up like an explosion inside. She paced to the window. She, too, felt like throwing the coffee mug she held against the wall, watching it shatter. She could almost taste the fury.

God how could You do this? Mom grieves but says this was Your will. Well it wasn't mine! I want my father back. I want my prayers over something critical to matter to You!

The sobs were wrenching her chest so hard she couldn't breathe. It wasn't the best way to handle this; it wasn't the mature Christian thing to do, but she couldn't stand the stoic acceptance others in her extended family were determined to showcase. If God didn't like her getting angry it was His problem, frankly she didn't care. There wasn't much left in life He could strip away from her.

The anger eventually burned out into exhaustion.

She sank down on the couch and leaned her head back against the fabric, looking up at the ceiling. *I don't like You anymore, God.*

The silence felt sad.

What was this family going to do without Dad?

Shari contemplated the impossible and tried to find a way to accept it.

Someone sat down beside her. She didn't bother to look over. Marcus. She was becoming used to his stillness. She wanted to bury her head against his shoulder and cry until there were no more tears, to take him up on the friendship he offered and pass to him this weight collapsing down on her. But there was only sadness now, too deep for any more tears. She lowered her head and sighed. "Marcus, I want this all to be a bad dream."

He brushed back her hair caught on the bandage on her cheek. "I know."

There was rain hitting the window. A soft rain, leaving drops on the window-pane that eventually joined together and slid down the glass. "The sky is crying," she commented, fatigue making the observation significant.

Marcus's hand closed firmly on her shoulder. "Shari, you're going to get some sleep. You'll deal better with this after you've slept twelve hours."

"It won't change the fact Dad is dead."

"No, it won't."

She wanted time to stop, but life was going on without Carl and her father. "I'm tired."

His other hand hovered and then settled against her back. "Come on, Shari."

Shock best described the O'Malley family reaction as they gathered at the hotel late Sunday morning and heard the news about Jennifer. Stephen and Jack looked grim. Lisa stunned. Rachel wrestling with disbelief. Kate, who already knew, had reached to grip Dave's hand. Marcus looked around the hotel room and felt like his heart was breaking.

"She's already in Baltimore?" Jack asked.

"Her flight was late last night."

Rachel took a deep breath. "What's the plan? We need to be there."

"If we juggle schedules, I think we can cover the full time she is in the hospital."

Every one of them wanted to fly out first. Marcus smiled, for it was the first moment of relief since Jennifer had given him the news. He wasn't carrying this alone. He kept forgetting at times just how powerful this family was when it came to rallying around one of their own. "Get your calendars. Let's figure it out."

Shari woke up late Sunday morning, not certain at first where she was at, vague memories of ugly dreams clouding her thoughts. There was movement in the suite outside her closed door.

It hit her again, the heavy weight of what she had to carry now because of what one man had done. Her eyes were too dry to cry anymore. Dad was dead. So many things pressed against her that had to be done. His funeral arrangements. His law practice.

The door cracked open. She turned her head on the pillow, looked over, expecting her mom, saw it was Marcus.

"Awake?"

"Of sorts." She swung her legs to the side of the bed. The sweats she had worn to the hospital, collapsed in bed wearing, were rumpled but at least warm; her bones were still chilled. "Come on in." The grief was so heavy that she couldn't remember what it had felt like to once smile. "Any news on the shooter?"

"No."

She eased to her feet and crossed over to the chair, sat down to take the weight off her aching knee. She wearily looked at the window and the sunlight streaming in. "I slept a lot longer than I intended."

"Your mom wanted you to sleep."

"Is she here?"

"I just took her back over to the hospital. She's with Joshua."

She should probably join them. She frowned at her shoes, then awkwardly pulled them on. She got to her feet. Her thoughts drifted.

"Are you okay?" He had crossed the room to join her.

She heard the concern in his voice and wanted more than anything to find her composure and not appear like she was going to fall apart on him. "I'm fine." She gave him a polite smile and was totally disconcerted when he lifted his hand to push back the hair on her forehead. Her eyes closed as the pressure of his palm eased her aching headache.

"You've got a slight fever."

An aching headache, a strained voice…she should have known. Add a fever and it was her common pattern for when she got a cold. "Stress reaction. A couple aspirins will knock it down." He looked skeptical but she had weathered this reaction too many times to be worried about it. And at the moment a cold didn't seem like something of much significance.

She ran her hand through her hair. "Let me get my hair brushed. I'll join you in a few minutes."

"I'll find you those aspirins."

"I appreciate it."

In the bathroom she washed her face in cold water, looking in the mirror at eyes that were weary and dull. There was no life left inside. She forced herself to get ready, to brush her teeth, then picked up her hairbrush and ruthlessly tamed the matted hair. She went to join Marcus.

He would have had a great deal less sleep than she had, and yet he looked alert and focused as he stood by the window scanning the street below. Again his stillness struck her. She had met only a few men able to function under stress with that kind of focus.

He turned when she entered the room, and she didn't miss the fact the suit jacket he wore concealed his gun. It was odd, how rarely she thought of him as a cop. It was the memory of their first meeting that prevailed.

He handed her two aspirins. "See if these help." She took them, grateful. He held out a coffee mug. "I promised you coffee. I'm sorry it's under these circumstances."

"So am I. I was rather looking forward to that date."

Her words caused his impersonal, assessing look to disappear momentarily, and she was enveloped once again in the warmth of his smile. "So was I."

Marcus. How I would have preferred this weekend to be different. I would have more than just enjoyed sharing coffee with you; I would have been hoping for your phone number. I don't want to lose this potential friendship to the crisis this has become.

She returned his smile with a brief one of her own, wishing she had more emotion left she could put behind it. She settled down on the couch. The coffee was strong and hot and it helped give her something to focus on.

"I've got something for you." Marcus reached into his pocket. He handed over what looked like a pager, but it had no LED display.

"What is it?"

"A pager with a special frequency. Depress the button and it sounds on our security net. It's a precaution. Get in the habit of wearing it clipped on your jeans. If you get in a situation that makes you uncomfortable for any reason, and I mean any reason, and one of us is not already at your side, press it. Don't think twice about it."

She turned it over in her hand and nodded. It was an indication of what might happen. She was a witness. It was settling in what that meant. It wasn't just testifying one day in the future; it was getting her safely from now to the time the shooter was caught and she could testify.

Just looking at the device strengthened her resolve. "How can I help with the case? This guy killed my father. I need something concrete I can do. I hate feeling this helpless." She could see from his expression that he didn't want to pursue it right now. "Please."

He settled into the chair he had sat in last night, his expression guarded. "You knew Carl well."

She knew how he liked his eggs for breakfast, what his favorite comic strip was, what musicals he enjoyed, what authors he favored… Somehow she doubted that was what Marcus needed to know. "He and Dad went to law school together. I've known him all my life," she replied softly.

"Then help me figure out motive."

I've been thinking about nothing else and I don't know. He was a good man. "What can I answer?"

"Tell me about Carl's family."

"His only family is an aunt on his mother's side. She's eighty-nine, has Alzheimer's, and doesn't recognize anyone. Carl has been her legal guardian for years."

"No one else?"

"Carl was an only child and he never married."

"His estate is large?"

"He was conservative with his money. He didn't travel. Other than upkeep on his estate, books were probably his largest expense. Maybe 8 million?"

Marcus's eyes narrowed at that estimate. "Who benefits?"

"Charities. The house is slated to be sold with the proceeds going into trust to care for his aunt."

"Any business ventures? Active investments that might be having problems?"

She shook her head. "Stock index funds, bond funds, and cash. He didn't want to have to worry about it."

"Anyone in his life? Was he seeing someone?"

"The law was his life. He had a lot of friends, but no one in particular he was seeing."

"That leaves his work."

"The obvious connection, given where he was killed."

"Tell me about his career."

"Going back to the beginning—he was a district attorney, a state judge, a federal judge, then Court of Appeals for his last seven years. In one word, his record is conservative."

"Your brief listed several cases. Which do you think merit attention?"

"Last year on the appeals court, there was a bank fraud case that cost a lot of people their retirement savings. Carl wrote the opinion that upheld the lower courts' finding dismissing the central charge. It was the right legal decision, but not necessarily the right moral one if you wanted justice."

"A judge and jury can't convict if the evidence isn't there."

"I know, but that didn't stop the hate."

"What about your family, Shari? Any enemies?"

His question threw her, and then what he was asking settled in. She felt cold suddenly, very cold. "You think it relates to us? I surprised the shooter."

"Yes. But why didn't he lock the door? I can't dismiss that you might have somehow been a target as well."

"Dad has been in corporate law and estates; there has been no personal threats that I know of. Joshua—he works for the DA, some of his cases are intense." Shari thought about that in detail. "But no, I don't think so. I've been in politics for years. Behind the scenes but definitely in the center of things. I'd be the one with enemies. But they would be political enemies. No one likes to lose, and these races and policy issues can consume a lot of cash."

"Any names keep you up at night?"

"No."

"Think about it."

"You're just trying to scare me."

"Trying to open your eyes," Marcus said soberly.

Connor dropped the newspaper on the park bench, the sketch on the front page below the fold. "We've got a problem."

His cousin Frank didn't look up from the crossword puzzle he was working. "So I saw."

"It's got to be dealt with before Titus gets back from Europe."

"It's going to take some planning. I already checked. She's under tight security."

"And we're only going to get one chance. Contract it out?"

"I can handle it," Frank replied. He turned over the newspaper and tapped the article. "That's where we act."

EIGHT

"Lisa, what do we have?"

Marcus found his sister seated at the round work table in her office, one hand wrapped around a carryout Chinese carton showing two protruding chopsticks, the other around a small cassette recorder being used to record observations as she studied eight-by-ten photos from the crime scene. How she was managing to eat was a mystery.

The lab he had walked through was pristine, her office another matter as she chased every idea that occurred to her. He cleared the spare chair of files to have a place to sit.

"You look horrible," Lisa observed.

"Thanks. Tell me you have something." It had been six days of frustration and he would really like to end this week with some good news. They were chasing leads in four states with nothing substantial to go on.

"Fibers," she replied.

She handed him the Chinese carton. "Eat. You look like you've been skipping meals." Spinning her chair around, she reached for the pale blue folder balanced on top of her phone.

"In your interview with Shari, she said the shooter was well dressed, wearing a navy suit."

Marcus nodded. The chow mein was lukewarm. Lisa must have been holding the carton for the good part of the last hour.

"It's blue-gray actually. European wool, European dye. I doubt it's a suit that comes off the rack. I'm working on getting a manufacturer. That's a freebie. I've got something better." She shifted the photographs on the table to one side and laid out large perspective shots. "Look at where the shell casings fell."

Seven of them were shown in one photograph of the room, four in the other. "Okay. What am I supposed to be seeing?"

"Where was the shooter standing when he shot Carl?"

"Somewhere about here, at the end of the bed," Marcus indicated.

She nodded. "I used Carl's exact height, the entry and exit wounds, and the blood traces and projected those back. The shooter was standing right here." She pointed with a pen. "He shot Carl. That gives us these three shell casings." She indicated the three in a close grouping. "What did he do next?"

"Turned to shoot Shari."

"And hit the door frame kicking up wood. He was firing as he turned." She held out her right hand and swiveled. "Like this?"

It hit him then, what she was showing him. "The bullet should have been buried in the door frame or the wall as his hand came around, not splintered the door frame."

"He's left handed."

Marcus reached over, wrapped his hand behind her neck, tugged her over, and planted a kiss on her forehead. "You angel. Can you prove it?"

She giggled. "What do you think?"

"Show me."

She pointed to the picture. "Okay. That fourth shot, the shell casing is up here; it struck and nicked the side of the dresser. The only way to get it angled in there is if he was firing with the gun in his left hand as he swiveled left to right."

She laid down a close up of the door frame. "See the angle of entry? The way the wood chip was kicked up? Here's the line." She laid down a ruler on the master grid she was using. "Same thing. The only way to generate the chip and throw it out like this is to be at this angle. Either the shooter stepped back before he turned and fired, or the gun was in his left hand."

She pushed aside the photos to lay down one that was a contrast photo. "And look at this. The bright white is the gunpowder residue luminescing. We're looking straight down at the carpet in this photo; this is the edge of the bed. Look at the bright line of the arc."

"It goes left to right relative to the bed."

"And if the gun was in his right hand, the gunpowder residue would have fallen more on the top of the bedspread and it wouldn't have hit the draped portion. Instead it's bright on the falling edge of the bedspread."

"You've convinced me."

Lisa leaned back in her chair. "Good, because that's the most useful news I've got. The rest you're not necessarily going to like."

"What is it?"

She had to search her office to find it. She retrieved a red folder from the floor by the whiteboard. She opened it and handed it to him. He recognized a photo taken from a microscope; the bottom index showing it was taken at 120 times magnification. It was a blowup of a dark, curved fiber.

"See the change in color at the base of the curl?"

Marcus nodded.

"Your shooter doesn't have thick, dark hair. He has a very good hairpiece."

"Our sketch is wrong."

"Distorted. A hairpiece suggests he might actually be bald. This was found lying on a blood splatter, so it's not a historical fiber to the room."

Marcus rubbed his eyes. He did *not* want to have to tell Shari this news. They had begun to suspect something like this as the hours and then days went by without the sketch producing the leads they expected. "Anything else?"

"The shell casings don't match anything in the national databases. But the firing pin impressions on the shell casings do show a unique off-center flaw. We'll be able to get a definite match if we ever get the gun, even if they try to destroy the barrel riflings."

"What about the shoes?"

"He's a size nine and a half. We don't have enough to generate a brand. We do have a wear pattern that we might be able to match if we get the shoes."

"No fingerprints?"

"Actually, forty-three distinct prints, but they are all tracing to people who work in the hotel or who stayed in that room in the past. Dave has the list."

Marcus knew how hard she had been working to get them this much inside of a week. He needed more. The threat to Shari, rather than lessening with time, had only intensified. The shooter was out there, thinking, planning, knowing he had made only one real mistake. Shari. Marcus could feel the danger, and Quinn was coiled tight with the frustration of having nothing but one dead end after another to chase. "What next, Lisa?"

"The scuff mark on the thirteenth floor stairwell door. I want permission to take crime technicians through all those hotel rooms. We never found a trace of where he went once he reached that floor. Maybe he never left it."

Marcus absorbed that observation. "He had one of those hotel rooms."

"He had to dump the disguise somewhere, and if he had yanked it off in the hallway, the search should have found fibers similar to this one. We didn't."

"Thirty-seven rooms? It will take some significant crime technician work and time."

"I'm more worried about the hotel having a fit."

"I can take care of that," Dave said from the doorway.

Marcus swiveled around.

Dave smiled. "Hotels rent rooms. We'll just rent the entire floor. That should keep them happy."

"Your own pocketbook?"

"Consider it a cheap solution to the fact I would like to see Kate this month. A few more weeks of these kind of hours, and she'll forget why she's dating me."

Dave didn't make a big deal about his family's wealth, but he did use it on occasion to move obstacles out of the way. That family wealth had led to the kidnapping and death of Dave's sister Kim. What other people saw as only good, Dave knew for both its good and bad. And having grown up in Britain, he had a cool practicality to his sense of the family fortune. It wasn't something he owned as much as something his family for generations would have. Marcus knew Kate was still struggling to get used to the idea she was going out with a guy who could spend whatever he liked whenever he chose to. Marcus thought about Dave's offer for a moment, accepted the practicality of it, and nodded. "Thanks. Arrange it."

"What are you hoping for, Lisa?" Dave asked.

"That he used a room to change his suit. There should be gunpowder residue on that suit, and very probably blood splatters. If he set it down on the bed, dropped it on the floor, we'll find traces. And we can match fibers. Find the room he used, and maybe we get the grand jewel—that he took off his gloves and left us a few prints."

Marcus trusted her hunches. "Sweep the rooms, Lisa."

It was after 11:00 P.M. Monday; the hospital floor was quiet. Shari took a handful of jellybeans from the dish at the nurses' station and ate them as she walked back to meet Marcus. Over the last nine days, life had fallen into a routine, if it could be called that.

Waiting for leads on the shooter; waiting for Joshua to get back his strength. Adjusting to having security with her at all times...she would be so relieved when this was over. All the family but mom's sister Margaret had returned to Virginia. The funerals were scheduled tentatively for Friday depending on Josh's ability to travel.

She found the extra time on her hands hard to cope with. The two deaths had ripped a void in her life. The hole in her heart regarding God ached. She no longer tried to pray. She was simply too tired to want to risk getting hurt again.

Left unspoken was the fear of what would happen if the shooter was not found soon. Life couldn't go on like this indefinitely. And she didn't want to leave the protection of having Marcus around. He was a strong shelter against the danger.

He was sitting in what she had come to think of as his seat, one of the cushioned chairs in the open area just across from the elevators where he noticed everyone who came and went on the floor. The television was off. She had noticed he preferred not to watch the news, while she was feeling the withdrawal from its absence.

Craig normally had the day shift, but at about 10 P.M. Marcus took over after having spent his day working the case. Shari had to admit she looked forward to the evenings. They talked about the investigation, but they also talked about family, both his and hers. Marcus had been intentionally drawing her out about her dad, Carl, and that helped. He was being the one thing she most needed right now. A friend.

He was reading a book while he waited for her, taking a moment to relax. It was a different one than last night she realized when she saw the spine. She'd read it last month. She was restless. She glanced at the page he was on: 69. "Do you know who did it yet?"

"Davidson, the brother-in-law."

She settled on the arm of the chair near him, hearing the certainty. "You're sure?"

"Yes." He looked over at her, settled the open book on his chest. "Read it?"

She nodded.

"I'm right, aren't I?"

His slow smile caught her attention and she wished she could say no. "Yes, you are."

"The only author I've found that consistently stumps me is H. Q. Victor, but since she's soon to be extended family, that's okay."

The thick crime novels by the British writer were some of her favorite reads. They were so real: stories about children who disappeared, were found murdered, and the hunt to find those responsible. "H. Q. Victor is a lady? You're kidding me, right?"

"Dave's sister, Sara."

She had met Dave a couple days ago, found the man Marcus called a friend charming. He'd kissed her hand while Marcus glared and she'd laughed at that. Shari couldn't decide now if Marcus was serious or not. But H. Q. Victor was British, and the first thing she had noticed about Dave was his delightful accent. "You're joking."

"It's a small world."

"I can't believe you know her. I love reading her mysteries."

"I'll mention she's got another fan when I see her. Ready to go?"

"Yes."

She gathered together her bag and briefcase. He escorted her through corridors the hospital security staff had established as safe corridors, taking her eventually out through the basement to the parking garage, where a car was brought around to meet them.

The press presence around the hospital was intense. So far Shari had chosen not to speak directly with the reporters, encouraged in that action by Joshua and Marcus. Anne released statements on her behalf and handled the press inquiries. Marcus wanted to keep the reporters and cameras a far distance away and Shari had to agree. He did it for security reasons; she did it for privacy reasons. She didn't have much privacy left. What she did have she wanted to protect.

The formal press briefings were held at 2 P.M. at the FBI regional office, and she had been watching them on television, knowing in advance from Marcus what would be discussed but always hoping against hope there would be breaking news to report. This had become an intense, slow, grinding investigation that would eventually find the man who killed Carl and her father, of that she was certain.

She had been in fights like this before in a political sense, when moving legislation required tenacity and hours of hard work in the face of no apparent movement. Then it would suddenly break free and everything would happen swiftly. It took a husbanding of energy to endure events like this. She was slowly accepting that.

They crossed the street to the hotel, using the private underground entrance. The day she could walk across the street was over, Shari realized with grim humor. She wished she could have a moment of normalcy back. She hadn't appreciated it nearly enough until it was stripped away.

She paused with Marcus as he stopped to talk with Luke, confirming security arrangements for the night. Shari had gotten to know most of the security detail by first name, and she was impressed with their focus. They were professionals, but she had also picked up on the fact this particular case was also personal. No one wanted to let Marcus down.

Her mom had come back to the hotel with Aunt Margaret earlier in the evening. Shari unlocked the door to the suite, found a solitary light on and the rooms quiet. They had apparently already turned in for the night.

Marcus crossed over and closed the drapes against the night. "What would you like from room service?"

Shari was getting accustomed to Marcus and his late night snacks. Ever since she had blown off dinner one evening, he had been unobtrusively ensuring she would have to be rude not to eat something. "How about some supreme nachos?"

"Sounds good." He picked up the phone and placed the order. "Ten minutes," he commented, replacing the phone.

She settled on the couch, pushed off her tennis shoes and flexed her stiff knee, relieved to be back at the hotel. "Josh managed to do reps lifting the five-pound dumbbell with his good hand."

"Excellent."

"Yeah. Only then he dropped it on his foot. I laughed and he tossed me out of the room," she added ruefully.

"I would say he's about ready to travel."

"What time is our flight back to Virginia Wednesday?"

"We'll be taking a private flight, so it's at our discretion. We'll probably leave the hotel around 9 A.M."

"It will be good to be home. Being executor of Dad's estate is a lot more complex than I realized. I thought I knew what to expect until I started wading through all the logistics. And since Dad was executor of Carl's estate, both have fallen to me like a tidal wave."

"Take your time. You'll do fine. I'm sure your dad chose you because he knew you would do an excellent job."

She looked over, surprised at the comment. It was nice to hear that confidence expressed.

The food arrived, and Marcus positioned the plate between them.

Shari tugged one tortilla chip free. "I like this quiet time of night. I always used to be a morning lark, but I'm becoming a night owl."

"I figured it was the bad dreams causing you to avoid bed until sleep forced you there," Marcus countered.

He'd noticed, but his response had been to simply adjust his own schedule to spend late evenings with her until she was willing to turn in. She should have realized it. "Some of that is happening too."

"Try reading at night. It will distract you."

"Can I borrow a book?"

"Sure. As long as you don't choose a mystery or suspense."

"You've got something else?"

"I think there's a biography in my briefcase."

His pager went off. Accustomed to the interruptions that were a frequent part of his life, she was surprised at his reaction when he saw the number. Pages related to work often resulted in a look of distance, occasionally she could pick up subtle tenseness, but this—before he even took the call he looked worried. "Excuse me, Shari."

He retrieved his phone and dialed, crossing the room to the windows. Shari tried not to eavesdrop, but since he hadn't left the room she couldn't help but hear. His words startled her.

"Kate, what's happening? What did the doctors say? How is Jennifer doing?" He had been expecting the call hours ago. Kate had been good about calling after each scheduled treatment.

"I walked in on Jennifer crying today, not that soft it-hurts kind, but the bone-wrenching crying that makes you ache because there is nothing you can do. Between the pain of the spreading cancer pressing against her spine and the effects of the radiation that makes her so sick she can't eat—she is being pushed to the literal breaking point."

Marcus closed his eyes, feeling his heart wrench. Jennifer had been lying to him, keeping her voice steady and confident when they talked when she had to be so scared. The distress and tension in Kate's voice was obvious. He needed to be in Baltimore, needed to see them. He was letting them down. His family needed him and he wasn't there.

Just as soon as Shari and her family were back in Virginia and security had been figured out there, he was going to get to Baltimore. "Please tell her I'm thinking about her. I'll call her again in the morning. How's Rachel holding up?"

"Much better than I am," Kate admitted. "She's good in these situations, Marcus. I never realized how good. When Jennifer is resting, I've often found Rachel down one flight on the pediatrics ward, lending her special touch there, bringing smiles to children with not much to smile about. Then she comes back and joins Jennifer and tells her about each one. Rachel knew without being asked the best distraction she could offer was the pediatric patients Jennifer loves."

"I'm glad to hear that."

"Your latest gift of pink roses arrived this afternoon. Jen wouldn't let me read the card, but whatever you wrote, it made her day."

"I intended it to," Marcus replied. "And no, I am not going to tell you what was in the card," he told Kate with a smile. He and Jen were making arrangements for Rugsby to reappear. It was at least one laughter-filled distraction he could offer Jennifer. "I talked to Stephen last night. He said he was flying out in the morning with Jack."

"They get in at ten. Tom is going to meet them at the airport."

"You haven't said how he's doing."

"He's a guy I would have fallen in love with had Jennifer not found him first. You can see it in his eyes, Marcus, the knowledge he has as a doctor of just how grim things are, but he's never beside Jennifer with anything less than optimism."

"He sticks, no matter what the cost. We both knew that the day we met him."

"He loves her so much you can feel it when you see the two of them together. When they are quiet and simply holding hands…I've left the room a few times rather than intrude."

"I'm glad you are there. I'll be out as soon as I can get it arranged."

"Jennifer knows that."

"Please, call me if there is any change."

"Day or night, I'll page."

"Thanks, Kate."

He slowly closed the phone. Jen. He felt tears moisten his eyes. Life wasn't fair. It wasn't fair at all.

"Jennifer is sick?" Shari didn't want to interrupt his thoughts, but she did desperately want to take that look of hopelessness from his face.

Marcus turned, pulled from his thoughts. "Cancer," he replied heavily.

Shari felt shocked. Jennifer had been so nice to her the evening of the shooting; there had been no indication anything was wrong. "She never said anything."

"She just told the family. And it hit like a bombshell. She's at Johns Hopkins, undergoing radiation and chemotherapy."

"It's bad."

"Very."

She ached for him. She thought about commenting on Jennifer's faith, but it would sound like a religious Band-Aid. She had faith and she still felt angry at the platitudes people said as they made their condolences. She missed her dad and Carl so bad it ached. And Marcus was in a harder position, being asked to accept months of knowing the worst might happen. "Marcus, I am so sorry. Please, come sit down. Can you go see her?"

"Once you and your family are back in Virginia and the security is tight, I'll cut away for a day and fly up to see her."

"Is there anything I can do?"

"Pray."

She heard the skepticism, the faint trace of irony...and the agony. He needed hope. She wanted to comfort, not debate, but she simply didn't know what to say. She wrapped her arms around her knees, leaned her chin against the fabric of her jeans.

It's not like I've got a great track record, Lord. You and I are barely talking right now. I prayed intensely for Carl to make the short list, and he ended up dead because that prayer got answered. I prayed with every bit of emotion in my body for Dad to make it, and he died. What am I supposed to tell Marcus?

"Why don't you believe?" she finally asked, not sure if he would answer her.

He sat down heavily. "I did once, as a child, before the orphanage. My mother believed. But her prayers didn't seem to make a difference, and after a while it became easier simply not to hope."

"Hope deferred makes the heart sick," she murmured. "The Bible says that in Proverbs."

"There's truth to that."

"What happened to your mom?"

"She died. Pneumonia."

A terse reply; he would have been young, and she could hear the hurt that still lingered. He had lost his mom just like she had lost her dad. Had prayed, and watched her die. And he had decided as a result not to believe. It hurt, how much she could empathize with him. If she didn't have two decades of faith anchoring her down and causing inertia, she might have broken under this pressure and stopped believing too.

She hugged her knees tighter against her. "What was it like, when you lost your mom?"

He didn't answer her right away. "Like I was the one being put in the grave. The thing I feared most had happened. She was the only light in my world, and it was gone." He looked at her. "Like it must feel with your dad being gone."

She knew exactly what he meant. "I've spent my life with Dad always there as a compass, believing in me, convinced I could succeed, backing my dreams; and now he's gone. It's a horrible void. I find myself going through days waiting, hoping, for something to come along and take away that ache."

"Time fills it. And the good memories return."

"I don't think anything in life is going to be harder than attending the funerals."

"Shari, you'll get through them."

"Because I've got no choice."

"Because you're a survivor," Marcus corrected.

Shari blinked, his assessment catching her off guard. She had only spent a little over a week with him, but he had managed to understand her in a more profound way than Sam ever had. On the surface her life might appear easy, she had the family wealth, the close family, but her professional life was defined by her stubborn ability to fight on against the odds. And in prayer… She wasn't ducking her head and accepting what had happened; she had practically picked a fight. "Yes, I am. And so are you, Marcus."

He gave a rueful smile. "Yet one more thing we have in common."

"I think this one is more important than a love for chocolate ice cream and a habit of keeping humorous secrets."

"Oh, I don't know. It depends on what kind of day it's been."

She laughed. "You're good for me."

"Of course I am." He leaned over to his briefcase and pulled out a biography of Roosevelt. "Take a book and go curl up in bed. You need some sleep."

"Political history. Nice choice."

"Guilty. I thought of you when I picked it up." He quirked an eyebrow. "Don't stay up reading all night."

"Yes, sir."

"Good night, brat."

She tweaked his collar as she passed behind him and said good night.

NINE

Shari didn't think she was going to make it through the eulogy at her dad's funeral. She fought the tears, struggled to keep her voice steady. It was the toughest speech she had ever written, ever tried to give. She had labored for hours to find the right words.

The church was filled to capacity. It was a private service by invitation only, because of security, because so many wanted to attend and the church could only seat three hundred. Her dad had been loved.

Joshua had come up to the stage with her. Her voice broke and she felt his hand come to rest against her back. She couldn't look at the crowd. She raised her eyes desperately to the back of the church instead. Marcus stood at the back of the sanctuary and her gaze caught his.

Marcus, this is so hard.

His gaze was steady as he looked back at her. He believed she could do this. He'd sat up with her for over an hour last night just listening when she hadn't been able to face turning in. He was one of the few men she had met that didn't cringe when someone cried. He'd just pushed over a Kleenex box and stayed, not trying to solve the pain, just sharing it. She took a deep breath, looked down at her notes, and when she resumed, her voice steadied.

Joshua had given his remarks before hers, and when she finished he led her from the stage back to her seat beside their mom. "You did a good job," he whispered, leaning down to hug her. She wanted desperately to give him a full hug in return, but with his arm strapped to his chest she had to accept simply wrapping one arm around his waist. "Thanks," she whispered. "So did you."

The final song began. The service was nearly over and with it part of her life.

Beth took her hand. Her mom was bearing up under this burden so much better than she was. For Shari, it was facing all over again the reality of what had happened two weeks ago. "Honey, this is a day to celebrate, despite the sadness."

Dad was in heaven. Shari forced herself to smile. She wished that fact would take away the pain, but it only made her aware of how long it would be before she saw him again. She focused on the flowers adorning the front of the stage, picking out the beautiful bouquet from the O'Malley family. She wondered if Marcus had any idea how much that gesture had meant to her mother as well as herself.

And what he had done for Josh… She didn't know how to say thanks to

Marcus for what she had only now begun to notice. The one-on-one conversations between the two men, the coordination going on—Marcus had put Josh firmly in the middle of every decision being made.

Marcus's actions had passed on the mantel of head of the family, made it real and concrete. She wasn't surprised by Joshua's maturity and steadiness; under his carefree approach to life he had always been a decisive man like their father. But Marcus had given him the gift of acting on that reality. And it had helped Josh cope with his grief.

The funeral concluded. The organ music resumed as ushers came to escort them from the front pews of the church down the center aisle. The graveside service was being held at the adjacent cemetery. Shari was dreading it. There was a hole dug out there, the dirt turned up, and even the false green carpet of grass laid across that dirt and around the stark evidence would not hide the truth. She was afraid her composure would break.

Carl had been buried early that morning at Arlington National Cemetery. It had been easier to maintain her composure with that very formal ceremony. The honor guard, the folded flag, it represented the tribute of a nation to a good man.

This was the tribute of a family to a husband and father.

Marcus appeared at her elbow as the family prepared to go outside. "There is a canopy set up to provide shelter from the wind, and they have set out chairs for the family. Please stay under the canopy after the short service until Quinn and I join you."

Shari nodded. She was very aware of the fact they were physically keeping her surrounded as she moved around outside. For the first time since the shooting almost two weeks ago, she was not in a protected environment. It had been well advertised in the media where she would be today and when. It would scare her, that realization, if she didn't have so many other emotions absorbing her.

She trusted Marcus to keep her safe.

She was the only witness to the shooting, and the burden of that sat heavily with her. Two men were being laid to rest today and justice for them now rested with her. She knew that, Marcus knew that, and somewhere out there the shooter knew that.

She walked out to the graveside with her mom and Joshua, accompanying the rest of her extended family.

Remarks at the graveside were simple. Their pastor read from Psalm 34, Dad's favorite. A prayer was said. And then two ladies from the choir closed by softly singing *Amazing Grace.* The words rang through the glowing sunset of evening with a sweetness that finally brought peace.

Shari placed the rose she held on the smooth casket. *I'm going to miss you, Dad. Until we meet again in heaven…* Her hand rested one last time on the polished wood and then she stepped away.

A chapter of her life was over.

It was a good night for a sniper, Marcus realized as he checked with the men securing the perimeter of the church property. They were running behind schedule and Marcus could feel the danger of that. Twilight was descending. In the dusk settling in the open areas around the church, around the clusters of towering oak trees, the shadows themselves spoke of hidden dangers.

The perimeter was tight, but there was a lot of open ground around this building. Marcus scanned the area as he headed to the side entrance leading into the sanctuary. With the lights on in the building and dusk turning to darkness outside, Shari was rapidly becoming a clear target. The building had too many glass windows and doors to keep her away from all of them as she mingled with the guests.

It was time to move.

Judging from the cars in the parking lot, there were still about thirty guests present. The governor and his wife had left not quite half an hour ago, and with them most of the remaining VIPs, reducing the security at the church to its lowest point for the day.

The press was being held at a distance at the entrance to the church grounds, but several were still there with their long camera lenses, hoping to get a picture or even a few words from those who had attended the private funeral.

Marcus raised Luke on the security net. "I'm changing the travel plans. We're going to take the family out the back entrance. Cue us up to leave in five minutes."

"Roger."

Shari, her mom, and Joshua were all near the front of the sanctuary talking with the minister and his wife. Marcus had been too occupied during the last hour to really look at Shari, an unfortunate reality that went with the job, it was everyone else who was the threat. He looked now and what he saw concerned him. She was folding. He could see it in the glazed fatigue, the lack of color in her face, the betraying fact Josh had noticed and now had his hand under her arm.

Definitely time to leave.

Marcus moved to join them and relieve Craig.

Shari saw him coming and broke off her conversation to join him. "Marcus, could—"

The window behind her exploded.

Shari heard someone gasp in pain and the next second Marcus swept out his right arm, caught her across the front of her chest at her collarbone, and took her feet right out from under her.

She felt herself falling backwards and it was a petrifying sensation. She couldn't get her hands back in time to break her fall and she hit hard, slamming against the floor, her back and neck taking the brunt of the impact. His arm was pressed tight across her collarbone, his hand gripping her shoulder. He wasn't letting her move even if she could.

"Shari—"

She couldn't respond her head was ringing so badly.

That had been a bullet.

She wheezed at that realization; her lungs feeling like they would explode. Around her people were screaming.

Another window shattered.

Oh, God, I don't want to die. I'm sorry for getting angry with You. Help me!

Marcus yanked her across the floor with him out of the way. "South. Shooter to the south!"

She could hear him hollering on the security net, and it was like listening down a tunnel. Who was bleeding? Someone was bleeding, she could see it on his hand.

He swore. A firm hand settled on her face. She gasped.

His elbow had nearly broken her nose.

It was coming home to her now, very much home. Someone was trying to kill her…again.

"Cover us! We're going out the back."

Shari felt herself being lifted, sandwiched between Quinn on one side, Marcus on the other. "Mom!"

"Craig's got her. Go!"

Quinn grabbed her hand to propel her forward. She knew this church, and as they moved left past the music room she got her bearings well enough to realize where they were going and managed to take the stairs with good speed.

In the back of the church they exited into darkness, surprising Shari because there should be building lights on. A van was waiting. Shari found herself literally lifted inside, after her mom. She was dazed with the speed it was happening. Joshua was helped into the front seat. She hurriedly moved over on the bench as Marcus slid in beside her and the door slammed shut. Quinn stood outside the van and slapped the side door to let the driver know he was clear, and they immediately started to move.

As they turned the corner of the building the streetlight shown through the van windows and Shari saw the bright red blood. It was a brutal flashback. The shakes hit hard. She looked toward Marcus. And she panicked.

"You're hit!"

"It grazed me," Marcus replied forcefully, trying to get a look at her face. His left arm burned with fire as painful as getting hit directly, but he wasn't worried about himself. Shari was bleeding profusely.

She was nearly frantic. "I'm okay, Shari." He wrapped his arm around her and pulled her tight, absorbing the shakes. "I'm okay," he said deliberately. She'd seen enough people bleed.

"Lean her head back," Beth urged. "And get pressure on that bleeding." She passed up what Kleenex she had left. Marcus looked back at Shari's mom, was relieved to see her color was still good.

He turned back to Shari. "Lower your hands, let me see." His own hands were shaking as he worked to stop the bleeding. Thank goodness it didn't look like her nose was broken.

"Was anyone else hurt?" she struggled to ask.

Great question. "Craig?"

Craig was already on the closed circuit radio. It took a minute to get an answer. "No one else was hit. Tactical is moving. They are getting the last guests safely out of the building."

"What about the shooter?" Joshua asked.

"Quinn's working it," Marcus replied, knowing it was too early to get an answer to that. He had seen the cold fury on his partner's face. The shooter would likely be caught; he had to have known that, and still he had made the choice to try and kill Shari. Marcus felt a fear that went deep. They had to stop him tonight. The next time it might have a very different outcome.

They had already worked out contingencies for this; they were heading toward the Hanfords' house. They had established good security there before allowing the Hanfords to land in Virginia, and they didn't need another variable tonight. Marcus looked forward to the driver. "Luke, call ahead and get us a doctor at the house."

"Already done."

"Josh, how's that shoulder?"

"Fine."

Marcus glanced back toward the front of the van again. *Not fine.* If Josh had ripped those stitches…one problem at a time. "The press is going to be heavy at the house. News of what occurred will be out, and I wouldn't be surprised to see a television helicopter show up. So even after we stop, stay put until I clear you to move," he instructed.

It was a brief drive, for the Hanfords lived only a few miles from the church. When the van arrived at the house, Luke pulled through the security perimeter and around to the back of the house.

Marcus pushed open the van door. He counted nine men in the security detail that had assembled to meet them. "Jim?"

"We're secure."

Marcus opened the door for Josh, helped him ease out. "Keep your mom and

Shari in the kitchen for a minute," he asked Josh in a low tone. "And next time lie better. You're pale as a ghost. You nailed that shoulder hard."

"Yeah. But Mom will forgive me, and what Shari doesn't know she won't worry about," Josh replied grimly. "Besides, you don't look too good yourself."

Marcus knew again why he admired this man. "Go."

He slid open the van door. "Beth." He extended his hand and helped her out. Her face was tense, but it was worry for her daughter not for herself. Marcus had come to love this lady, for she reminded him of his own mom. He gave her a brief hug and passed her to Jim. "Into the house." He turned back to the van. "Okay, Shari."

She didn't want to take his hand because of the blood staining hers. He reached in and grasped her forearms, sympathetic to the problem. She was showing definite tremors as adrenaline faded.

He didn't expect her balance to be good, and he didn't intend to risk letting her stumble. He lifted her down, ignoring the pain that tore through his arm. She started to say something, but he shook his head. "Inside." He tucked her close and hurried her toward the house.

When they entered the house the doctor who had been called was waiting and Marcus didn't give Shari a chance to turn her focus on him or her brother. He eased her into a kitchen chair and let the doctor take over. "I'm so sorry about the nose."

She leaned her head back, closed her eyes, and relaxed. "Josh has done worse. He nearly broke it one time. But if you could find a couple aspirins, I would dearly love you."

Dearly love you... In the emotions of the moment, the words first hit his heart and made him blink before his mind sorted out the figure of speech. If she ever said it and meant it...he shook his head as he inwardly smiled at his reaction, part of him still caught off guard. "Not a problem."

He got them for her, then wordlessly handed the bottle to Joshua. Finally admitting to himself how seriously he also was hurting, he swallowed four.

"Marcus, let the doctor take a look at that arm," Beth insisted.

Shari struggled to lean around the doctor to see him. The last thing he needed was Shari seeing the reality of someone else who had been shot. "In a moment," he assured Beth. He stepped out of the kitchen. "Jim, what are you hearing?"

"They got plates on a black SUV. An APB just went out. They're looking. So far—" Jim shook his head.

The shooter had gotten away. It physically hurt. "Are we in a position we can hold here for tonight?"

"Yes."

"Okay. The detail is yours while I get this gash bandaged. After the doctor looks at Joshua's shoulder, send him back to the spare bedroom."

Marcus had not yet unpacked; he wrestled his suitcase open with one hand, found a clean short sleeve shirt. He walked into the adjoining bathroom.

The bullet had scored through his suit jacket and shirt. Marcus sucked in his breath as he eased off the material. The O'Malley clan was going to be all over his case when they heard about this.

The gash wasn't deep, but it was long with very ragged edges, and it burned like fire. Marcus was grateful it hadn't cut deeper into the muscle. Another two inches over and it would have shattered bone and possibly ruined his career. *And if a fluke of glass hadn't deflected the shot, Shari would be dead.*

That was the source of the real fury he felt. He should have overruled them on the funerals and refused to let Shari attend. He should have gotten her out of the area immediately after the graveside service. Regrets didn't change reality.

He hated being shot. He was trying to wipe off the blood when the doctor joined him. "How's Joshua?"

"Bruised, but the stitches held."

The doctor was good, efficient, but did not have the bedside manner of Jennifer. "I can try and butterfly it closed or just stitch it."

Marcus did not like needles any more than Kate did. "Butterfly it."

He let out a deep breath when the doctor finally wrapped gauze around his upper arm.

"Change it tomorrow morning. If the bleeding seeps, we'll have to stitch it."

He nodded and slipped on the clean shirt. "Let Jim get you past the press out there."

"Will do."

Marcus headed back to the kitchen.

Beth had put on coffee. "Let me," she gestured to the collar he was trying to straighten one handed. "Shari went up to change, and Josh is handling the onslaught of phone calls."

"I'm sorry that William's funeral was touched this way. I'm more sorry than I can say."

She looked at the bandage on his arm, then back up at him. "We knew this risk existed, Marcus. We took a gamble and we lost, and it looks to me like you paid the price for our decision."

"It's just a graze."

"Sure it is. I'm grateful for what you did. Thank you for keeping my daughter safe." She reached up and kissed his cheek.

Marcus blushed slightly. "You're welcome." His mom had been like this, always calm despite the circumstances. And those were the best memories he had, of an innocent time before his own life had gone wrong. "I need to head back to the church. Jim will keep security tight here."

"Please be careful."

He gave a rueful smile. "You've got my word, for what it's worth at the moment."

"It is worth a lot. Godspeed, Marcus."

"Let's go back on videotape, Ben," Lisa requested. She broke the seal and entered hotel room 1319, pulling on a fresh set of latex gloves. They were looking for blood, for gunpowder residue, for fibers. With thirty-seven rooms to cover, the process was painfully slow. They had been at it for a week, working late into the evenings. This was the third room she had looked at today, and she was only doing the quick tests, a complete team was coming behind her.

She broke open the tape on a rolled up plastic guard used to give a safe footpath until fiber collection could be done. Every precaution that could be taken to preserve evidence was being made. She just hoped the effort would only be wasted in thirty-six of the thirty-seven rooms.

"Lisa."

She paused and came back to the doorway. "Yes, Walter?"

"You're going to want to see this."

She pulled off her gloves, made sure Ben had her on tape as closing, sealing, and initialing the tag for the room. She was determined to make it hard for a defense attorney to challenge the evidence collection.

She moved to join Walter at the door of room 1323.

Two technicians were working with him, and they had both stepped out into the hallway, leaving the room empty. She scanned the room. It was orderly, the bed made, but she noticed the less than straight way the bedspread draped. Someone had disturbed it since housekeeping had last made up the room. A light gray dust used to raise fingerprints coated the furniture showing the progress the technicians had made.

There were no fingerprints. It hit her like a shock, how even the gray dust was. Not a single tape lift had been made of a print. And that made this room shout like it had been painted red. "No prints at all?" she asked, incredulous.

"Not even on the wooden coat hangers," Walter replied.

It couldn't be this obvious. "Where's the room paperwork?" Walter handed her the clipboard. She flipped through the stack of notes. "This room was not done by housekeeping since the last guest checked out on Saturday?" she asked, one eyebrow raised.

"Maintenance had been pushed off until the conference was over. This was one of a block of rooms marked unavailable so that they could upgrade fixtures in the bathroom, replace the closet doors. They were planning to also replace the shower caulking and the bathroom tile grit. The work order is here; they just hadn't gotten to this room yet. Housekeeping wasn't scheduled until after that work was done."

Lisa looked at Walter, and her friend who rarely reacted to what evidence suggested until the last lab tests were run actually smiled. "We've got the room exactly as he left it."

She looked back at the paperwork. Henry James. He had used a credit card for payment. "Fingerprints, what else?"

"We were just getting ready to luminol for blood."

"Ben, I want both you and Tom videotaping. Mark, go to the highest contrast film you have. We're going to do this room a foot at a time. Expect the traces to be faint."

Fifteen minutes later, with preparations complete, the room lights were shut off. They worked clockwise around the room.

Lisa shifted back on her heels to avoid brushing against the bedspread. Faint places began to glow as Walter sprayed the carpet. "Hold it there," Lisa asked as a streak appeared.

Against the tight weave of the carpet it appeared at first as a quarter inch wide straight line and then the smudge appeared. It rolled to the right. She frowned, studying the surprising pattern. She was expecting something from his shoes or his clothes… "He sat down, took off his shoes, and one rolled on its side."

"Shoe polish?" Walter asked, indicating with his pen dark spots in the pattern.

"I certainly hope so."

She waited until Mark had photos taken, then moved to collect several samples, using a penlight clamped between her teeth for light, sealing the swabs in vials. "I may want to cut out this piece of carpet. Grid it off."

"The hotel will love you."

"And I'm just getting started."

She completed the evidence tags on the vials.

They moved to the bedspread and found nothing. "Give us the room lights," Lisa requested. She blinked as her eyes adjusted. "Fold up the spread, we'll take it to the lab. The same with the sheets. Walter, I'm going to start working fibers on the carpet. See what you can raise in the bathroom. If he washed up—"

"I'll find it."

She used what had once been a lint brush, tape sticky side out to collect the fibers, rolling it on the carpet, then rolling the tape onto evidence strips of paper, documenting where each lift was made. It was slow work, hard on the knees, as the carpet was gone over with care to insure nothing was missed.

This evidence analysis would take hours of microscope work back at the lab. Lisa found the first visually promising fiber an hour into the work. Against the white of the paper strip, the fiber trapped by the tape was dark.

She made a side note to put this fiber strip at the front of the queue to be analyzed.

Having covered the carpet by the bed, she began working toward the wall.

"Lisa, we're negative for blood traces in the bathroom."

With the entire room wiped of fingerprints, the news was disappointing but not surprising. "I don't suppose he left the obvious? Something in the trash can?"

"Not even a gum wrapper."

"I would have preferred he left the gum," Lisa replied with a smile as she carefully lifted another tape. It was rough as she smoothed the tape against the paper. A closer look tilting it to the light showed it glittered. Glass fragments?

She looked with curiosity back at the carpet. A foot from the wall and the carpet was smooth. The shards weren't crushed deep into the fabric as if they had been vacuumed over. It was an odd place to find glass.

"Is there a glass missing from the set on the bathroom counter?"

Walter checked. "All four are here, still wrapped. What do you have?"

"I'm not sure. Do you still carry that jewelers eyepiece?"

"Sure." He passed it to her.

The light refracted through the shards captured under the tape. She looked up at the wall, saw a faint stain on the wallpaper. "Someone got mad and shattered a glass against the wall?" It would take some force to break one of the thick hotel drinking glasses.

"Walter, the housekeeping records for this room—they've got a missing and restocked items checklist on the back of the forms. Did they replace a glass recently? And have we done an inventory of the room? Towels, soaps, those plastic dry cleaning bags, the contents of the minirefrigerator—I'd like to know if anything is missing."

She worked twenty minutes lifting glass, finding nothing larger than slivers. Someone had spent time trying to clean this up. "Let's kill the room lights; I want to look again at this area."

Nothing showed when they sprayed the surface of the carpet. Lisa used a straight ruler edge to rifle the carpet fibers. A few faint glimmers appeared down in the carpet. She nodded, pleased. He'd cut himself picking up the shattered glass, probably no more than a paper cut, but it was there.

"Think there will be enough to test?" Walter asked.

"Doubtful. And it's odd that there isn't a glass missing from the room. This may be old. Mark, give us room lights."

She eased back to her feet. "Check the trash bag for any hint. And swab that stain on the wallpaper. It looks like a liquid splash the way it trails down."

She took a step back trying to get perspective on what she knew from what she suspected. No fingerprints. Everything else maybe. If she made the wrong call…"Walter, I'm going to go give Dave a heads-up. I want the room sealed when we're done and an officer assigned to sit outside the door and make sure it stays that way. Get a forensic team working on the paper trail—the guest signature card that was filled out, anything with room service."

"Will do."

She clipped on the security badge needed to get her past the security one flight up. The command center had moved to the telecommunication conference room on the fourteenth floor, freeing up the Belmont Room for the hotel and letting Dave coordinate easier an investigation now active in four states.

As soon as she entered the room, Lisa knew something was going on. The tension was palpable.

"Any word from Marcus and Quinn?" Dave asked, pacing.

"Not yet," Mike replied. "The situation is still fluid." The large screen at the far end of the room was shifting satellite feeds. "The local television station has a cameraman at the scene; we're tapping into their uplink to get a firsthand look."

It emerged out of the snow on the screen, the picture zooming in on the building, recognizable as a church even in the fading light. The audio was that of the reporter and cameraman talking to the station manager; this feed was not going out to a live audience. When the camera panned left to right, the back of the building appeared dark.

"Tactical is there," Mike observed. "There's Quinn."

"Dave."

"Not now, Lisa. Someone took a shot at Shari."

"We found the room."

"I'll be done—" He spun around. "What did you say?"

Marcus found Quinn walking across the church parking lot. "He got away."

"Left the sandbag he used to brace the rifle and walked away," Quinn replied. There was a touch of admiration in his voice; even the hunter could appreciate when an adversary made a smart move. "Come on, I'll show you."

Quinn led the way from the church grounds across a footpath that ran to the nearby ball diamond into a grove of elm trees. Marcus could hear the faint sound of water in the quiet night. There was a drainage tile forming a narrow ravine. Quinn stepped over it and up a slight rise. Large spotlights had been set up with bright yellow crime scene tape wrapped around a section of tree trunks.

The rifle lay on the ground in the underbrush, the barrel resting on a twelve-inch wide, rough fabric sandbag. Someone would have noticed a guy carrying a rifle, but leaving it and just walking away—it showed cool nerves. And the fact the shooter wasn't worried about it being traceable.

"The clear weather worked in his favor, the sun behind him, the elevation giving line of sight into the sanctuary. It appears he walked out after the shooting by circling around the shed used to hold the groundskeeping equipment for the ball diamonds. The SUV was sighted there."

"Our patrols?"

Quinn tipped his powerful flashlight to the right and luminated a crushed path through the tall grass going through the grove. "Our two man patrol. The guy was fifteen feet away and wasn't seen. He probably had his blind in place before dawn."

Marcus swore.

"We've got an APB out on the black SUV, it had local plates but we don't have the tag numbers. No one apparently saw him but we're canvassing for a mile. And I've got men getting copies of all the video shot by both the news media on the ground and the helicopters flying over this area."

"Is it the same man?"

Quinn handed him a .308 shell casing. "Someone that gets flustered enough to miss at close range and someone skilled enough to miss by an inch at two hundred yards on a windy day through thick glass?"

"Two shooters."

"Two shooters."

Marcus crumpled the soda can in his fist.

"Make them disappear," Quinn advised.

"You have a preference?"

"Both shooters have shown they can blend with the city. Let's get them on our turf."

"Agreed."

"How bad were you hit?"

"It hurts," Marcus replied tersely. "Quinn, I'm tired of being on the receiving end."

"Tell me about it." Quinn rubbed his own arm. "They're two for two, and next time it's not going to be one of us."

"Have we ever had a case where we *both* got winged?"

"No. And it's beginning to make me mad," Quinn replied. "Did you hear the news from Dave? Lisa thinks she found the room."

It was the first good news of the evening. "I knew she would come through."

"Stubborn lady. I'm going to owe her dinner."

"If you're lucky, she'll collect on the debt."

Quinn smiled. "True. Listen, head back to the house and get the Hanfords ready to move at first light. There's not much else to do here. We're going to stay and canvas again at daybreak, but this scene looks contained. We'll start tracing what we've got down to the type of sand used in the bag. The rifle, the bag, even the way he set up to make the shot—something is going to register with an existing MO. This wasn't his first time; it's too high profile an attempt."

"Agreed. Find him, Quinn."

"Between Lisa and me, these two shooters are going to wish they had never thought of reaching out to kill a judge, let alone threaten a lady you like."

Marcus shared a look with his partner, then simply slapped Quinn's shoulder and turned to head back to the van. Quinn knew him. This case had long ago become very personal. He'd like to wring the neck of the man who had gone after Shari. He'd settle for putting him behind bars for life.

Shari carefully lowered herself to the edge of her bed, her back muscles aching. The headache had grown in intensity.

God, I'm sorry. You've got a generous, merciful heart. Forgive me for being a jerk. I'm sorry I turned a cold shoulder to You. Not talking to You only hurt me.

She wrapped her arms around her waist. The man who had killed Carl and her dad had tried again to kill her. That fear made it hard to think. She wished Marcus were here. Even though he had been injured, she knew he wouldn't let that danger push him away. He would know what she needed to do.

She was worried about him, out there tracking the man who had done this. She was only now beginning to appreciate the fury she had sensed in Marcus this evening as events had unfolded. She hoped he wouldn't take any undue risks. She didn't want anyone else hurt because of her.

She couldn't stay here with her family. She was putting Josh and Mom in danger. She didn't know how to deal with that fear.

It was so confusing, everything that had happened. All the way back to Sam. Her life was in tatters. *God, I need time to figure this out and deal with all these emotions. And I need You to keep me safe. I've been hurt and angry, but now I'm scared and I'm rushing back to You because I know You are the One who is my refuge.*

There was a tap on the door. She looked up and smiled slightly. "You look like you feel worse than I do."

Josh crossed the room to join her. "I sometimes think the doctor's help is worse than the injury. And it takes forever for the muscle relaxants to kick in. How are you doing?"

She knew her face was bruised and swollen. And her jarred back and spine made movement come at a high price. "I'll be okay." She looked at her brother as he sat down. "What are we going to do, Josh?"

"First, get that tone of defeat out of your voice. We're okay." He brushed back her hair. "He won't get another chance at you. We'll make certain of that."

"Josh, he almost shot Mom. Another few inches to the left—"

"He didn't."

"I can't take the chance he'll try again." She wanted to run and didn't know how or where.

"We'll let Marcus make the recommendation on what we do next."

Her brother was handling this so much better than she was. He hadn't once complained about the fact he had been shot, and his recovery had been far from easy. She sighed. "Tomorrow, I want you to update my will."

"Shari!"

She shook her head. "It's not morose thinking. I want to know everything is in order. Because Dad's is so out of date it's making dealing with the estate a problem. And he is listed as my executor." Somewhere in the house a phone rang.

"You should probably forward the phone to the answering service again." Their phone number was unlisted, but that hadn't mattered. The press had found it. They had hired a firm to take messages.

"Mom is waiting on a call from Margaret."

"Josh, it's for you," Beth called from downstairs.

He got to his feet. "Come downstairs. It's not good to brood."

She smiled when he ruffled her hair. "In a minute. Thanks, Josh."

"Sure."

Shari was still up. Marcus had been expecting that, even though it was close to midnight. She wouldn't find sleep this evening easy.

"Can I get you some coffee?" she offered, getting up from the kitchen table where she had been sitting, reading a book.

"Please."

Shari poured him a cup.

He hadn't seen her before he left to return to the church; what he saw now made him wince. He had really done a number on her face. "Let me see." He crossed over to her and tipped up her chin. "You need some ice on that cheek." He rubbed his thumb very lightly across the darkening bruise, absorbing the pain of what had happened. He'd hurt her. It left a deep ache inside. If only he had been able to react faster…

"Marcus, don't worry about it. It's like walking away from a car wreck with only a bruise—you definitely don't mind the bruise. You saved my life."

"I think the wind and a thick plate glass window did that. I just helped."

She smiled, reached up, and kissed his cheek. "I'll take helped. And I will let you get me that ice. It's starting to ache again."

He hesitated for a moment, feeling an unexpected warmth roll through his chest. *Shari, you have the habit of slipping under my guard. I don't mind, but I wish I deserved it. I let you and your family down.*

He had been afraid she would come out of this crisis quivering in shock, but she was rolling with it. When it was her family in danger it was one thing, herself another. He felt the same kind of admiration coupled with unease he felt with Kate. His sister never let the danger she was in bother her, and Shari was mirroring that by trying to keep a strong front in place.

He shook off the distracted thoughts and moved to the freezer. He improvised an ice pack with a clean towel. "Try this."

She winced when she touched the cold to the soreness. "It will help." She sat back down at the table and watched him. "This is proving to be a very rough day."

"A terrible, horrible, no good, very bad day," Marcus replied, borrowing a line from the children's story. It was that or apologize again, and he was starting to sound like a broken record.

"No luck with the shooter?"

He shook his head, debating with himself how much to tell her. He wasn't ready yet to tell her they suspected there were two shooters. Not until he had spoken with Josh. "There is a lead on his vehicle. We're looking." He sat down with his coffee. "In the morning we're going to be moving you from this house to a place that is more secure."

"All of us?"

"Yes."

"I would prefer not to be near Josh and Mom."

"I can understand why you feel that way, but I think it's best if you stay together. Once you're tucked somewhere that hasn't been broadcast by the media to the world at large, the situation will be much easier to manage. Your mom needs the rest, and she won't get it if you're someplace else and she's staying here amid the security we would have to bring in. Josh needs to focus on regaining his strength, and being battered by the press isn't going to help him out. Think of it as a much needed family vacation."

He watched her rub her forehead with her hand before she looked up at him. "I don't mean to make this difficult, but how long do we plan for? Days? Weeks? I've got two estates to deal with. My job. The campaign. It's not like I can walk away from all of this and come back later. In an election, every day is critical. I need to give John and Anne some idea of what I can do, what has to be transferred to others."

"When you are out on the campaign trail, you're working by phone, e-mail, and fax. Pack up what you will need and plan to work that way for the next few weeks. You can still work behind the scenes, just not from here."

"I'm going to have to go through all the paperwork here just to know what I need for Dad's estate, the same at Carl's home office."

"Ask your secretary to box it up and we'll arrange to transport it; you and Josh can go through it together."

"Can I at least sleep in tomorrow morning before I have to pack?"

He smiled at that. "Sure, as long as you're packed by seven. This is for the best, Shari. I wouldn't ask it if it wasn't."

"I know. I don't have to like it, but I do believe you."

"You killed a judge! Just like that...*poof.* I will kill a federal judge!"

Connor had walked into the family estate prepared for this explosion from his father. The demand that Connor come had arrived with blunt intensity within minutes of Titus's return from Europe. For ten minutes he had taken it...but no more. "He sent my brother to his death. *Your eldest son.* But you ignore that. You let it pass without reply. Someone has to look at what that means for the family name. You make it weak!"

His father turned at that, swift as a cobra, his voice cold. "Because you are my son I will forget that you said that. But do not push me again. We are not too weak to act…we are too powerful! This family cannot afford the ire of the government, and you have brought it to our front door. This is no longer a business where passion rules but pragmatic power. You learned nothing from what I have spent fifteen years teaching!"

Connor was aware of Anthony, his father's first lieutenant, pacing outside the room, and for the first time he felt the touch of fear cross his spine as he faced his father's anger. For the first time he felt the irreversibility of what he had done. He braced his feet.

He had been in this study since his childhood answering to his father. Anthony would understand why he had acted and killed, Anthony was the old school. But he was left cooling his heels outside, which said his father had already overruled Anthony's suggestion for what should be done.

"Who helped you?"

Connor thought about lying but knew it would be useless. "Frank."

"I'm glad you admit it."

His father tossed the newspaper onto the desk, the hated sketch on the front page below the fold. "You were careless."

"There is no evidence connecting me to the shooting. There is only one witness. The others didn't see me," he replied, willing to placate. "She can be eliminated."

"So I see," Titus replied with great irony. "You did a great job with that too."

"Frank missed. He won't next time."

"Frank has been taken care of."

Connor blinked. Titus had killed his cousin? A chill crossed his spine at the dismissive way his father had said it.

"Did you really think you could set me up, Connor?"

Still feeling the cold of the previous comment, this one caught Connor off guard. "What? I didn't—"

"Because I didn't know what was happening in my own family, I am now liable for conspiracy for the murder of a federal judge. It was my eldest son sentenced to death by Judge Whitmore. Frank worked for me. I paid him while he went on those errands for you. Whether I ordered it or not, as the saying goes, 'the buck stops here.' I can't prove I didn't know what you and Frank were planning. The jury will assume I not only sanctioned it but set it in motion."

"That wasn't—"

Titus waved him to silence. "My interests happen to coincide with yours—for the moment. I solved your problem. I hired Lucas Saracelli. Your witness is as good as dead. But now I ask you. Who's going to solve my problem? You!"

Connor knew he was in trouble as that cold fury hit him. "I have no interest—"

"Shut up. You will go back to your law office, back to your good job, and you will keep your mouth shut. You will toe the line so hard that it squeaks. And to help you out, Joseph is joining your firm tomorrow. He is at your side until I say otherwise. And Connor…I mean it. Keep your mouth shut. Now get out."

Connor wisely left.

TEN

It was a former hunting lodge, now someone's expensive vacation home, with two wings of bedrooms around a central kitchen, den, and living room. It sat a few hundred feet from a sprawling lake. Shari wondered who had owed the marshals a favor; it must have been a big one.

"The town is two miles to the east," Marcus commented, pausing beside her on the spacious porch. "We know all the residents of these homes by sight."

"Would it be too much to ask where we are?"

"The middle of nowhere."

"You are obstinate. How about the state?"

"Area code 502, given you'll find that out when we set up a mirrored e-mail account."

"The western part of Kentucky."

He laughed. "Nice to know you remember the important things in life." The laughter faded and the seriousness returned. "There are ground rules."

Having had them drilled into her by both Marcus and Joshua, she felt like rolling her eyes. "No one is told this location; all phone calls are made on the special cellular phone you got me; all mail is routed through my office."

"And you go nowhere without a shadow."

"I was hoping you had forgotten that one."

"Not likely. Choose your room, I'll bring in your bags. East if you want a sunrise, west if you want to sleep in."

"West," she said decisively. It felt good to make a firm decision for herself. She took one step toward the front door but then paused and came back. She hesitated, then rested her hand on his arm. "We're safe here, Marcus?" *You're safe?* She didn't want anyone else getting shot because of her.

His hand covered hers, linked with her fingers, offering a reassuring grip. "Only two people know where we were heading: Quinn and Dave. I didn't even tell the pilot until we were in the air, and he's got a memory that is notoriously forgetful."

She felt the intensity in his gaze, the strength in this man. She wanted to cling and did tighten her hand in his. "Thank you for this."

He reached up and brushed back her hair, blown by the wind across her face, his gaze holding hers. "I'll do everything I can to keep you and your family safe; that's a promise."

Did he understand what that meant to her, to have a man care that much? He had already demonstrated he'd take a bullet for her. She was growing attached to him in ways that went deep into her heart. She released his hand, placed hers on his chest for a moment and with a quiet nod, turned and wisely went inside.

It was a beautiful home, a place to retreat and let time heal some deep wounds, a place to get her perspective back together. Marcus was sliding into the void left by Sam, and as powerfully beautiful as it was to be cherished by such a man, she knew their futures would eventually diverge. She was sold out to God, and he was still struggling with a difficult past. To face another heartache so soon after Sam... *Jesus, I didn't choose any of this. Don't let me get hurt again. And please, don't let me hurt Marcus. It's the last thing in the world I ever want to happen.*

Marcus dropped his bag by the side of the bed, wearily unfastened his shoulder holster and secured the 9-millimeter Glock and placed it beside the bed. He sank into the pillows face down, let the mattress absorb his weight, felt the sunlight streaming in the west window warm his back. They were safely here; it had been his one focused goal and it had been accomplished. Craig had security for the next few hours. Unpacking could come later.

Marcus fell deeply asleep and didn't waste energy dreaming.

He was pulled awake by a noise he couldn't ignore.

His pager was going off.

He had no idea how much time had passed, five minutes, several hours. All he was certain of was that he had been deeply asleep. His eyes blurred as he read the numbers, and he had to squint. Baltimore. Jennifer.

His hand groped across the bedside table for his cellular phone and he dialed from memory. "Hi, precious. How are you doing?" he asked sleepily.

"Much better for hearing that endearment."

"Tom might be your guy now, but I'm not giving up that title easily. You've been my precious since I chaperoned your first date." He shoved a pillow under his shoulder to make himself more comfortable. "You sound better than you did yesterday."

"I got a reprieve, treatment was moved to this afternoon."

"Did your latest company arrive?"

Jennifer giggled. "No, but I know they are on their way. Stephen has sent a dozen pages tracking their progress across the country. And he's been calling from the plane to tell me these stupid jokes. I keep telling him to stop, and Jack just keeps telling Stephen new ones to pass along. The last call was from the airport here, they were just getting ready to land."

"No wonder you're giggling. Jack's jokes can make your ribs hurt from laughing so hard."

"Exactly, and laughter's good medicine." Her tone became more serious. "I just wanted to call and tell you the Rugsby trail is ready."

The conspiracy had begun. "What did you and Rachel decide on?"

"The Rugsby ransom requires each O'Malley to do something specific. Seven letters are ready to be sent."

"Am I going to groan when I open mine?"

"Yours is the best of all of them."

"Jennifer—"

She laughed. "This is so much fun. Rachel is going to mail them tomorrow."

"I knew I was starting something I would live to regret."

"The only way out of paying the ransom is to figure out who took Rugsby. He's well hidden?"

"Definitely." He'd just arranged for the animal to be shipped back to Rachel; she didn't know it was coming. It would give her a bit of a jolt when the mail arrived. "Lisa might figure it out if you give her enough time to work on it."

"The ransom is payable in a month. We should be okay." Her tone changed; she laughed. "I just got invaded, and Stephen's carrying one of the ugliest wrapped packages I have ever seen."

"Since I know what he's bringing you, you don't know the half of it," Marcus replied with a smile. "Talk to you later, Jen."

"Bye, Marcus."

He hung up the phone, awake now, but not in a hurry to get up. He was glad he had set the entire Rugsby silliness into motion. Jennifer's laughter helped ease at least one source of concern. She was a fighter, his sister, even if she was the soft, gentle one in his family. And he wanted—needed—to see her soon just to share a hug.

Stephen had found Jennifer a truly ugly shirt. It was loud, obnoxious, startling, and just the kind of thing to make her laugh. Knowing Jennifer, she'd wear it too.

Marcus linked his hands behind his head, found his thoughts drifting sharply back to Shari and what had happened.

Two shooters. What did that tell him about the man who had killed Carl? It reaffirmed what shooting Carl had told him—the man would take big risks. Two people involved meant he would risk having someone else who would be able to turn and testify against him. His frustration would be high after this failure. And he would likely try again. Marcus sighed, glad he had been able to get all the Hanfords relocated.

It was going to be a long day.

He picked up the phone. "Dave, where are we at? Do we have anything on the rifle?"

He arrived on a midmorning Tuesday flight into O'Hare from Saudi Arabia and took his leisure checking through customs. His jeans were worn, his blue casual shirt bore the small logo of an oil drilling company, and his boots were scuffed. A man accustomed to working anywhere at short notice, a veteran of worldwide travel, he was relaxed as his one bag was scanned, his passport checked. His passport gave his name as Larry Sanders but his real name was Lucas Saracelli.

His only luggage was the one carry-on bag. Once through customs he stopped at the first shop with newspapers and bought the *Chicago Tribune* and the *Chicago Sun Times.* He was behind on the sports news. At a pay phone he called a private taxi service that came in limousines rather than yellow cabs, then walked down the concourse. He'd get a good steak and fries for dinner he decided and find a bar with a baseball game. It was good to be back in the States.

His ride was pulling up as he exited the terminal. Lucas handed his bag to the driver to stash in the trunk, took a seat in the back of the limousine, and reached for the complimentary soda sitting in ice. "Take me to the Jefferson Renaissance Hotel please." He had long ago learned the easiest place to begin a search was at the beginning.

Shari Hanford.

He thought about the picture he had been sent as he drank the soda, scanned the first newspaper, and occasionally glanced up to watch the towering city skyline grow ever closer.

A witness.

He sighed. He hated going after witnesses.

At least there would be security around her and he wouldn't have to take down someone totally defenseless. He hoped the men on her side were good at their jobs. If this hit turned out to be easy, it would leave a bitter taste for months.

He had to find her first.

It was the part of a contract he enjoyed the most.

Arriving in the middle of the day had shortened the commute time. The driver pulled up to the entryway of the Jefferson Renaissance Hotel before Lucas finished reading the first newspaper. He folded the two papers and tucked them under one arm, gave the driver a generous tip, and entered the foyer of the hotel looking around with interest at the press and the security present.

At the desk he flirted with the receptionist, signed the register, and accepted a room key. He was given a room on the seventh floor and after dropping his bag at the end of the bed, opening the drapes, turning down the air-conditioning to cold, and placing the do not disturb tag on the door, he wandered back down to the bar. "What's all the excitement about?" Within five minutes he had found a reporter eager to be a fountain of knowledge.

ELEVEN

It had rained during the night. Shari sipped her coffee and watched the wind stir the lake waters. The sky was just beginning to lighten as the sun came up, the blue very pale, the one cloud in sight tinged pink. She sat watching from the window seat in the den, the spot she had chosen over the last four days as her favorite in this spacious home. For wanting to sleep in, she had been awake way too early. The bad dreams had been there again, just beyond memory, and the anxious feeling as she awoke was just beginning to fade.

The nearby trees in her line of sight had shed some of their leaves and their trunk and branches were black silhouettes against the lightening sky behind them. Black and stark could be quite beautiful. It was an unexpected observation. There were times when black and stark could be turned into something of great beauty.

Thanks for that reminder, Lord.

She saw Marcus and Quinn reappear from around the boathouse. She braced her chin on her drawn up knee and watched the two men. She had been surprised when she first saw them down at the lake. When did those two sleep? She wondered at times if they did.

Steam was rising off the lake waters behind them. She was beginning to think this was one of the most peaceful, beautiful places she had ever stayed.

It was quiet here. She had been up almost an hour and the phone had not rung. She had her time to think. And over the last few days she had spent a lot of time doing just that.

Having life stop had shown her a pattern to her life that she didn't necessarily like to see. To distract herself from the pain of her breakup with Sam she had turned her focus to work. To distract herself from grieving for Carl and Dad she had been using the long list of funeral and estate details. She had been using anything to push away the confusion over prayer. She had been hiding, and that was for a coward.

Her life wasn't going as she had planned, and she had let anger flare toward God rather than step back and reconsider what was propelling her.

She wanted a life in public service, wanted it with a passion that went back to her teens. It was the noble cause her father had inspired. And she wanted a family. She had defined what those two things looked like, had defined the timetable for them, and for someone who prided herself on her ability to be flexible and compromise to get things done, she had been rigid when they came apart.

She didn't want to rethink her life, but she was getting a chance, tucked away here, stripped of the time demands that drove her schedule when she was working at home.

She wanted another distraction. She *needed* a distraction. And he was walking back to the house right now. Marcus.

What would have happened if they had simply been able to have coffee that Saturday morning? If none of this had happened? She'd never know.

He had gotten shot protecting her. And he was here with her family when she knew he would rather be with his sister. She wished she knew what made him tick. He was a fascinating man, hard to get to know because he was a man with so many deep layers, but a true friend.

If only he hadn't pushed away God.… She sighed and avoided following the thought.

She picked up the pad of paper she had carried downstairs with her. It was time to work out what her priorities had to be for the day. She missed her newspapers. She always started the day with coffee and a stack of newspapers to peruse.

Priorities for today. She wrote down one word with a grimace. *Estate.* The boxes of information had arrived last night. Today she would sort and try to get a handle on what was there to deal with.

"You're up early."

She started. Marcus was going to give her a heart attack with his habit of sneaking up on her. She hadn't heard him enter the house.

"I couldn't sleep." She looked hopefully at him. "I don't suppose the newspapers have come?"

"Sorry. It will be another day before they are being forwarded."

"This is worse than taking the batteries out of my phone."

"Had breakfast yet?"

"The least you could do is sympathize."

He grinned. "That you don't have your dozen newspapers? You need to get a life for a few days."

"It appears I've got no choice. Breakfast—you're not on duty? I saw you walking with Quinn."

"Craig has the detail until noon." He held out his hand.

Shari set aside the pad of paper and let him pull her to her feet.

"So what do you have on your agenda for the day?"

She groaned. "Paperwork."

Shari reached into the cardboard bankers box for another thick file folder. She had always thought of her dad as organized until she sat down to go through all the paperwork. Arrayed around her on the table and floor were various stacks of information—insurance, stocks, car titles, bank statements, tax return information. Her laptop was open and she was trying to complete a spreadsheet of everything the estate would need to have appraised.

"Josh, have you found the paperwork on Grandfather's farmland?"

"Somewhere." Her brother searched through the stacks on the coffee table. "Here it is."

She added it to physical assets.

The folder she had picked up was past brokerage statements. She began putting them into date order. In the back of the folder she stumbled on a set of pictures that must have fallen into the box when it was packed.

The top image brought an instinctive laugh. She must have been about twelve in the picture, Joshua nine. They were both draped around a dog that had earned the name Mutt. She flipped through the others from the camping trip they had taken to the Rockies. "Oh my. Mom, you'll like these."

Beth had the photo albums open around her. Shari handed the pictures over. "We had such fun on this trip. I remember standing on the Great Divide in the snow while Dad took our picture. And the striped chipmunks that would eat peanuts. Oh, and that lake that turned pale pink when the sun set."

"Don't forget the trout," Joshua added.

Shari glanced out the window at the lake. "Do you suppose this lake has good fishing?"

"It's a great lake for bass fishing," Marcus replied from the doorway.

Shari swiveled around. "Really? Could we go fishing sometime?"

"You would have to be willing to get up at dawn."

"I could do that."

"We might be able to some time," Marcus agreed. "Beth, could I speak with you for a moment?"

"Of course. I was just about to get some iced tea. Come join me."

Shari watched her mom take Marcus's arm as they left the room. "What do you suppose those two are up to now?" she asked Josh, slightly envious of her mom for the close relationship she had formed with Marcus.

"They were talking about the nearby town this morning over breakfast. I know Mom would like to visit the local shops," Josh replied, not looking up from the paper he was reading. "What do you want to do about the contents of the safe deposit box? There's a note that the original of this document is there."

Shari turned her attention back to the task that had to be done. "Do you think Dad's secretary can access it for us?"

"I'll write up a limited power of attorney from the estate."

"I can arrange a birthday cake from the local bakery," Marcus suggested once he and Beth were in the kitchen away from Shari's hearing. Finding out Shari's birthday was a week from Saturday had thrown him. It was bad enough she would have to deal with her father and Carl not being present, but to also have to spend her birthday here, away from her friends—it left a bad taste.

Beth poured herself a glass of iced tea. "I've got plenty of time to do some baking. I'd just need you to get my recipe file sent from the house. How about a chocolate cake with a layer of pudding inside?"

"Is chocolate her favorite cake?"

"She's a cupcake person. Don't worry; I'll make her several. She likes lots of icing and those colorful sprinkles on top."

"Does she?" Marcus smiled. "Well, I personally love the idea of a chocolate cake."

"Will we be able to go shopping for gifts?"

"The trip will have to be planned, but it won't be a problem. I'll get you a list of shops that are in town. Getting Shari occupied elsewhere will be the real problem."

"Nonsense. You can take her out to lunch or a movie while Josh and I shop."

"Subtle, Beth."

"I like you. Shari could do far worse."

He looked at her, at this lady he had come to admire, and had to smile. "She's a witness. Please remember that."

"You won't be protecting her forever. You're good for my daughter."

It didn't do any good to point out the problems. The stark difference in backgrounds. The fact he couldn't say he believed. Beth had already heard them and waved them aside. Shari could adjust; he could change. And Marcus was amused to realize he knew better than to assume Beth wouldn't get her way. "And you're the nicest mom I've ever protected."

"The only one."

"Still the nicest." Marcus accepted a glass of iced tea. "You remind me of my own mom."

"One of the highest compliments I think you could give me."

His pager went off. "Excuse me, Beth."

He walked down the hall to get some privacy. "Yes, Dave."

"Washington called. The president has made a choice for the Supreme Court nomination. He's going with Judge Paul Nelcort."

Marcus frowned. "When will it be announced?"

"There will be a White House Rose Garden announcement at 2 P.M."

He moved to where he could see Shari. "The timing could be better."

"I thought you could use a heads-up before they find out the news."

"I appreciate that." This moment had been inevitable, but it was going to cut sharp. When he hung up, Marcus found himself torn over whether to tell them now or wait.

Beth touched his arm. "There's news?" she asked, concerned.

He nodded. Best to do it now rather than wait. "Let's join the others."

He walked back into the room with Beth at his side. Shari was laughing with Josh, and it was a sound Marcus had rarely heard. He didn't want to rob that laughter from her.

Shari's smile slowly faded when his serious expression registered. "Something has happened."

There was no way to cushion this but to simply say it. "The president has decided to nominate Judge Paul Nelcort to the Supreme Court."

It was a shock; there was no other way to describe how she took the news. It brought back that night, that image of seeing Carl die. Marcus saw it happen and willed her to push through that pain. There was nothing he could say that would make that easier to deal with. She just had to accept it.

"He's a good man," she finally said. She got up from her seat, crossed toward Mom, then shook her head. Her fist struck the door frame as she turned toward the stairs. "Excuse me."

"Let her go, Marcus," Beth said, stopping him with a hand on his arm.

"She's feeling this was her fault. That she wrote that brief."

"I know. But telling her it's not true won't change what she's feeling."

Shari pushed the clothes she had tossed on her bed that morning to the floor and sprawled face down on the comforter. The emotions roiled and she grabbed a pillow to silently bury her head against it. She wasn't going to let herself cry. She wasn't!

Jesus, the only thing I can do is pray that the shooter will be found. Please. I lift that prayer to You again. I've been doing my best to quietly trust You like Mom does, but this…my heart fractures. I need there to be justice for Carl. I need the shooter found. It feels like You don't care. I know that isn't true, but the days pass without news. And I'm afraid of him! I need him found.

She rolled over and reached for her Bible on the end table. She turned to the bookmark she had left at Psalm 4 that morning. The first verse had caught her attention.

"Answer me when I call, O God of my right! Thou hast given me room when I was in distress. Be gracious to me, and hear my prayer."

She had hung onto that verse when she found it, for it not only expressed David's own moments of turmoil with God, his distress, but also his similar need to have a prayer answered. She read the words again and clung to them.

Lord, You're a God who loves justice. Bring justice. Swift, complete justice.

She rolled back over and looked up at the ceiling. *And Lord, maybe it's time to also say one other quiet, private prayer. Please let Marcus reconsider believing in You.*

She needed a future, and she wanted him in it. And she needed someone to talk to. It couldn't be family, for they would only be hurt by the questions she'd ask. Marcus could help.

Marcus closed the phone, frustrated. Someone took a shot at Shari and they had no leads. All the evidence they had and right now it led exactly *nowhere.*

"Someone will see him, someone will talk," Quinn observed from his seat at the other end of the front porch. "It will happen. Just because the rifle has led nowhere doesn't mean someone didn't know what was planned. Two people are involved. That's one too many. Somewhere the nibble is going to appear."

"Care to take a trip back to Chicago and help shake that tree?"

Quinn tipped back his hat and glanced over. "If you like."

"I think so. We're secure here." Marcus leaned against the porch railing, studying the trees. There were men watching the road, and three patrols covering the grounds. They knew flights that came in to the small local airport, and guests that checked into the local hotels. This location was secure, but someone determined... They had to find the man who shot Carl soon or he was eventually going to find them and make another attempt.

"Lisa will come up with something from the room."

"Maybe."

"What's with the pessimism? You're normally the optimistic one of the two of us."

Marcus swung his arms in front of him, restless. "This case is different."

"I've noticed," Quinn replied dryly.

"I don't mean Shari, well, not entirely."

"I know, Marcus. Someone killed a judge this time. It's different," Quinn agreed. "At least the Hanfords seem to have settled in here. It's not a bad place to stay if we need it for a few weeks."

"Shari's not sleeping," Marcus said heavily. A glance back at the house showed the den lights were still on. She had settled there after dinner with a pad of paper, working on a speech for John, and she was still there now, long after Beth and Josh had turned in.

"Did you really think it wouldn't be a problem, having been shot at twice?"

"It would help if she would talk about it."

"She will when she's ready."

As the days passed, Marcus wondered if she would ever get to that point. "She needs to blow off some stress."

"See if she likes to play basketball."

"What?"

"She's not the only one who needs to blow off some stress. You're pacing. And you don't pace. If you're not going to open a Bible and start resolving the questions you've been avoiding for years, then at least admit what avoiding them is doing to you. Ever since news of Jennifer's illness broke, you've been building to the point you're going to blow."

"I know you're a Christian, Quinn, but I really don't want to talk about it."

Quinn swung his feet down from the railing. "Good enough. I'll be around when you do. When Josh goes into town for physical therapy, take Shari over to the gym near the hospital. I'm sure it would be possible to reserve some private court time."

Shari playing basketball. It was an interesting idea. And goodness knows he would love to run the court for a while. "I'll think about it."

Quinn scanned the dark night. "When do you want to relieve me?"

"6:00 A.M.?"

"Sounds good. I'll schedule a flight back to Chicago, sleep on the plane."

Marcus straightened from the porch railing. "Say hello to Lisa for me."

"That sounded like a subtle push to me."

"Do you need one?"

"Nope."

"I didn't think so. I'll see you in the morning, Quinn."

His partner nodded.

Marcus opened the door and walked by memory through the dark house to the kitchen. The fatigue was heavy, and normally he would have taken advantage of going off duty to get some sleep. Instead he found himself retrieving two tall glasses, opening the freezer, and finding ice cream. He got out two sodas and set about making two floats.

He walked through to the den.

Shari was curled up in the big leather chair, several pages of a yellow pad of paper turned back. She was spinning a pen between her fingers, lost in thought. Marcus paused in the doorway for a moment just to enjoy the sight.

There were deep stapled stacks of research materials, read and underlined, dropped on the floor around her. He could see her early frustration in the wadded up pages tossed toward the wastebasket. She was struggling to find the words. She started writing, ran out of room at the bottom of the page, and rather than turn to a new page, turned the pad and wrote in the margins.

He waited until she finished writing. "Making progress?"

She glanced over. "Finally. You can't believe how hard it is to make the environmental issues surrounding water resource management something interesting to listen to. John's got a great legislative initiative drafted, but writing a speech that can convince people why it matters to their lives just like taxes and education—even I'm having a problem staying awake."

She accepted the float. "I'm going to get spoiled if you keep this up."

"Sure you are." He settled on the couch across from her. He enjoyed the picture she made, curled up, comfortable.

She set aside the pad of paper to sample the float. "Very nice."

"Drink slow, you'll get an ice cream headache."

"Warning noted."

He reached down, picked up one of the wadded pages, and lofted it toward the basket.

She winced when it went cleanly in. "Ouch."

"I'm a better shot than you."

"True. But I wasn't trying very hard."

"Your competitive streak is showing."

"Good. I would like to think Josh taught me something."

"I saw you working weights with him this afternoon. How's he doing?"

"His good arm is just about back to full strength. He's ready to see the physical therapist."

"It's all arranged. He starts tomorrow afternoon."

She nodded and went quiet.

He settled back, enjoying his float, waiting, wondering what her topic for tonight would be. She always had one. Ever since those early days at the hotel when late night room service had become habit, they had talked late at night after the others had turned in. Marcus enjoyed the time.

"Tell me about your sister."

They had talked a lot about family in the recent weeks. He had been drawing her out about her dad, pulling out the good memories. She in turn was fascinated with his large family, had seen the photos in his wallet and laughed at the humorous stories he told. "Which one?"

"Kate."

Marcus sank down against the back of the couch, feeling the taut fabric give slightly. "My middle of the night phone buddy," he said easily, in simple words encapsulating the heart of his relationship with Kate. She had always been there no matter what the time or reason for the call, and it had been the same going the other direction. Those hours in the middle of the night were priceless to him.

Kate had been kidding him recently about the unusually late hour of his calls. Marcus had not told her they were getting delayed because he was first chatting with Shari. He knew Kate wouldn't mind, but she would find that fact too fascinating for comfort.

To describe Kate…he didn't want to brush off the question with a simplistic answer. It was sometimes hard for people to see the real Kate behind the impassive negotiator wall she presented: polite, nice, but very hard to know what was going on behind her watchful gaze.

"As a negotiator, she's without compare. The higher the pressure, the more bored she appears. Kate is…it's hard to put into words. She's the heart and soul of the O'Malley family. I may be the leader of the group, but Kate is the fighter, the courage, the well of fire that cements us together. She's the passion behind all that we are. When trouble strikes, she jumps in with both feet, plants herself, and takes the battlefield with her elbows out. When she's beside you, it doesn't matter what the odds are, you can relax; she's like a big rock, immovable. She defends the family. I love her for that."

"And you defend Kate."

"When she needs it. I would trust her with my life and have on occasions. Kate's the one who knows my secrets."

"All of them?"

She doesn't know I'm enchanted with you, but she's a very perceptive lady. She's probably already figured that out. Your name has a habit of coming up a lot.

"Almost all of them. She doesn't have to know that I did kind of push her toward Dave, or that I punched the boy harassing her in sixth grade, or once had Jack swipe her car keys so she couldn't go after a fellow cop that blew a negotiation—minor stuff like that."

"For the good of the family kind of secrets."

"Something like that. You still owe me another one of yours. I'm ahead."

"You need to check your tally."

"Scout's honor."

"Were you ever a scout?"

"No."

She wrinkled her nose at him. "I'll give you the benefit of the doubt." She settled more comfortably against the leather chair. "Let's see, another secret..." She smiled suddenly. "I voted for my opponent when I was running for high school senior class president."

"You threw a political race?" He found that idea amusing.

"Just one vote. We had this debate on the small wattage radio station that the high school guys ran. I found my opponent's arguments very persuasive."

"Who won the race?"

"I did. By a landslide," she admitted. "But then I understood the need for a turn-out-the-vote drive the day of the election."

"It sounds to me like you wanted to make sure he got at least one vote."

"Well...maybe that too."

"Was that your first taste of politics?"

"It was running for office. I'd been stuffing envelopes, passing out campaign literature as a volunteer since I was twelve. I fell in love with the idea of campaigns and the intricacies of issues and getting your guy to win."

It was new to him, meeting someone with politics as her passion. He found he enjoyed it. There was depth to her knowledge of issues that he admired, and more than once he had gotten her to debate with equal fervor both sides of the same issue. She worked very hard to understand the point and counterpoints to an issue. It was a work ethic he really admired. "When did you start writing speeches?"

"I'd see campaign flyers, and think they didn't get the message across. So I'd rewrite them. I'd listen to John give speeches; he would ask what I thought, so I'd tell him. I would quote back what worked and what didn't. Anne finally hired me. I fell in love with the job."

"A self-starter."

"Or at least able to indulge a passion."

"You're fortunate. Your passion became your career."

"Yes." Shari agreed, but her eyes shifted away as she said it. Marcus noted the unspoken qualification she made. Something to figure out here, he noted, and tucked it away to think about.

"Do you still enjoy it?"

"Most of the time." She grimaced. "Except when I'm under deadline and the speech isn't working." She held up the pages. "Like this one."

"Keep working on it, you'll get it."

"Or rip it up trying." She held up her float. "Thanks for this."

"You're welcome. Do you have an extra pad of paper? I'll do some work while you finish that speech."

"You've got more confidence than I do." She passed over a blank pad of paper.

Marcus pulled the sketch from his pocket, the one they knew was misleading.

"I'm sorry I got that sketch wrong."

He wasn't letting her take the guilt for that, and it was ground they had been over several times in the last week. "Don't be. It was just one of many ways he arranged to misdirect us." He started modifying the sketch, creating yet another permutation to the dozens he had made in the last few days.

The room became quiet as they both worked. Marcus turned the page to make another sketch. And instead found himself sketching Shari.

She was focused on the speech, lost again in thought. He'd been studying her over the last weeks with more care than he realized. The sketch came together with great detail. He would never be able to capture the quality that most fascinated him, the joy that lit her face when she smiled, but he tried.

Her posture when she worked was atrocious. He smiled as he saw her wiggle down in the leather chair to get more comfortable. She sprawled. Just like her stuff. Between the books, the newspapers, the pages she had printed from Web sites and stapled together, the crumpled pages of rejected words, someone would have to want to invade her domain to get near her.

He wished she wasn't a witness. It made this situation difficult, because one of these days he wouldn't mind invading her space to kiss her good night. She had, after all, spent the last weeks doing a very effective job of invading his heart.

TWELVE

"Haven't you ever heard of the word *sleep?*"

Lisa looked up from the microscope, startled to find someone in the lab at 4:15 A.M., even more surprised to see Quinn. He was supposed to be somewhere in Kentucky with Marcus. He wasn't exactly the person she would have chosen to stop by.

"Don't frown. I come in peace."

He held out a small white sack and she was curious enough to glance inside. "Food is not allowed in the lab."

He shook it slightly, making the M&Ms rattle. "I asked for extra red ones."

She glanced at him, saw the twinkle in his gaze, and took a handful.

He tucked the sack in his jacket pocket. "Tell me what you've got so far."

She sighed. "Not enough." She had been back over the hotel room with a fine tooth comb and it was frustrating her to no end.

"What's the carpet?"

She had cut out two sections of carpet from room 1323, one with the blood and shoe polish trace and the other where the glass fragments had been found. "I found shattered glass fragments on the carpet. Some tested positive for traces of blood so I'm trying to recover enough to get a DNA test."

"Think you'll be able to?"

She held up the thin vial she had worked most of the day to collect. "I'm having to take the carpet weave apart thread by thread to find them. We'll see. It's a long shot."

"I owe you dinner, but would you be willing to change that to breakfast? I'll be glad to feed you while you tell me the details."

Lisa looked at the work left to do.

"It will still be there in a few hours."

"Make it somewhere still serving a cheeseburger and fries at this time of morning and you've got a deal."

"I think I can oblige."

Lisa put the evidence back under lock and key.

"Do you want to walk or take a cab?" Quinn asked as Lisa signed out of the building, and they cleared security.

"Walk," Lisa replied. She found the walk with Quinn helped revive her energy.

She had been practically living at the lab since this case began. "I found—"

Quinn cut her off. "Give yourself five minutes off work."

She was surprised at the stringent tone of the order but nodded. It got very quiet. She didn't know what to say to him if it wasn't about work.

Quinn led the way to a restaurant six blocks away, a hole in the wall that she had heard about but never visited. It catered to taxi drivers and construction workers. It was busy even at a quarter to five in the morning. Quinn steered her to a booth rather than a barstool. The menus were thick, with everything available at all hours.

"Cheeseburger and fries?" Quinn confirmed, Lisa nodded, and he placed an order for both of them. The food arrived within minutes. The fries were thick wedges and the cheeseburger more than a handful, thick and stacked with onion, lettuce, and tomato.

"When was the last time you ate?" he asked as she dug into the fries.

"I don't remember. I think it was a candy bar lunch."

"I'm flush enough to be able to afford a second cheeseburger."

She was finding the food too enjoyable to mind the remark. "I'll accept."

He waited until half the cheeseburger was gone and the sharp edge of her hunger had been satisfied. "Okay, now you can tell me what you have found."

She picked up a fry, grateful to be free to talk about something she was comfortable with. "It's Carl's blood and shoe polish on the carpet. We've got more fibers from the hairpiece the shooter wore. And a few more fibers that match his suit. There was a trace of gun residue in the safe. It's certain now that the shooter used the room. He had the arrogance to store the murder weapon in the room safe. But we've got no fingerprints."

"What about the registration of the room itself? Someone was there."

"It's a block of rooms reserved by the conference. Show up with a conference ticket and they hand you a room key. The credit card that was used for extra charges turned out to be stolen. The name Henry James leads us nowhere. The signature card has only the prints of the hotel reservation clerk. Whoever was in that room used the express checkout and carried the weapon, his disguise, out with him on Saturday."

"Keep looking. He made another mistake."

Lisa wished she had his confidence. "I hope so." She changed the subject. "How's Marcus?"

"His arm is fine. His heart—" Quinn smiled—"that's a different matter."

Lisa paused, intrigued. "Shari?"

"That would be my guess."

She set down her drink and leaned back against the bench. Marcus was getting serious. Well, it was about time. "Shari." Her smile widened. She had met Shari briefly, and Kate and Jennifer had both mentioned her in their calls. There had been speculation, but nothing firm.

"Don't put it on the family grapevine until I am away from here so it won't be obvious I'm the one who passed on the news."

"Quinn, there are times I like how you think." She was feeling very generous at the moment and the normal reserve to her smile dropped away as she beamed at him. "Going to finish your fries?"

He blinked, then smiled back. He slid his plate toward her and handed her the catsup bottle. "Enjoy."

Marcus leaned over Beth's shoulder to watch her ice another cupcake. "Are we ready for tomorrow?" A week had passed since Quinn had left for Chicago to try and move the investigation along. Marcus had turned his impatience with the delay into going overboard with the birthday planning.

"All set. I'll just need you to keep Shari busy for about two hours while I get the decorations put up."

He sneaked a taste of the icing from the mixing bowl. "Not a problem. I'll make sure she comes with me when Josh goes to see the physical therapist."

"You can have a cupcake if you like."

"Better yet, can I have one for tomorrow to soften the blow when I tell Shari she's about to be had?" Shari was so absorbed in work; they had managed to plan what amounted to a small-scale bash without her noticing.

Beth laughed. "Sure."

Marcus squeezed her shoulder. "The gift you asked to have delivered arrived. I put it in your closet upstairs."

"Think she'll like it?"

The dress Beth had bought Shari was gorgeous. Marcus leaned against the counter beside Beth and gave her a knowing smile. "I do."

She didn't bother to hide her humor. "Good."

"Craig has the rounds this evening. I'm going to go find your daughter and convince her to take a walk. Would you like to come along?"

"Thanks, but I'm planning to watch that Columbo movie with Josh at the top of the hour."

"Making popcorn?" he asked, hopeful.

"I'll make extra."

"Thanks. Shari promised me a Scrabble rematch tonight."

"She'll tromp you again."

Marcus chuckled. "Probably. But she feels so bad when she wins it's funny."

"She likes you."

"Think so?"

"Marcus, you're as bad as Shari. Don't you two ever talk?"

"We talk all the time."

She snorted. "Then why are you both asking me the important questions?"

"Good point." He leaned over and kissed her cheek. "Like I said, I'm going to go find your daughter."

As the days passed, security had fallen into a pattern. Marcus was comfortable they had the situation here contained. It didn't lessen his guard, but it did help the coil of fear in his gut relax. Shari was safe here. That was the important fact in life. As restless as he was to be back in Chicago where the action was, to be in Baltimore with Jennifer, here was where he needed to be. Since that was reality, he had let himself seize the moment and enjoy it.

He found Shari in the den. He was becoming accustomed to her work schedule. She worked hard. Too hard, he sometimes wondered, for the motivation to solely be the work that needed to get done. She had something to prove and he was beginning to think it was with herself. She was a lady in a tough profession, very good at what she did, and she didn't cut herself much slack.

She was still in the midst of a phone marathon, working on a speech on fiscal policy. She needed someone to remind her to slow down. When she hung up the phone and before she could dial again, he leaned over the back of the couch and set his hands down on her shoulders. "Slip away and come watch the sunset."

She leaned her head back to look at him. "There are more calls to finish."

"Those will wait. The sunset won't."

She considered for a moment, then set aside the notepad. "Sure, why not. It's not like I'm making much progress. I'm back to negotiating my original language from this morning."

"That just means you were right this morning."

"Well, I'm lousy at convincing people of that."

He came around the couch, offered his hands, and pulled her to her feet.

"I knew John was dumping a hornet's nest in my lap."

"So why did you say yes?"

"Because I like a challenge. But I hate writing a speech by committee."

They stepped outside. The wind had picked up, and Shari reached up, pushing her hair back.

"I found a great place down the beach."

She fell into step beside him. "It's good to get outside."

"You need to take more breaks."

"True. Another good intention I haven't followed through on."

Marcus pointed out a fallen log. Shari sat down, bracing her arms on her knees. A low front had brought in a band of white wispy clouds. The reflections of the clouds glittered on the water. "You're right. This is a great view."

They sat together in silence watching the colors change as the sun set. Marcus felt no need to break the silence.

The colors drifted into darker hues. "Which do you like better, a sunset or a sunrise?" she asked idly.

Marcus glanced at her, considering. "Sunset."

"Why?"

"Because you're never awake to share a sunrise with me."

He watched the startled faint blush spread across her face. "Marcus—"

"You asked."

"Are you flirting?"

"What do you think?"

"I think you are being very nice."

Nice. Marcus buried a sigh. *And I'm trying to get your attention.* Nice *wasn't the word I was hoping for. So much for making the point subtly.*

She leaned her weight back against her hands and turned her attention back to the sunset. "I used to date a guy named Sam."

Marcus went still. He had not been expecting her to come back with an offer for a serious discussion. He turned so he could look at her. Sam. He knew that name from the file developed on her, had seen a couple newspaper clippings, and remembered the conversation she had referred to at the hospital. "What happened?"

"We had different visions of where we would go as a couple."

"Do you regret it now?"

"No. It hurt like crazy, still does at times, but it was the right decision."

Shari looked over and considered him for a moment. "Marcus, are we going to be friends when all this is over? Or is this one of those special friendships that exists for the moment and is one you remember with gratitude when the event is passed?"

"Which do you want?"

"I like you."

He smiled. *Finally.* "It's mutual."

"And you're a complicated man."

She had looked further than the surface. "I'm an O'Malley." He wished he could explain everything that meant, about what it meant to be part of the family he had chosen to lead. He went back to her original question. "As far as I'm concerned, these last couple weeks are an interruption to what will be a very long friendship."

"An interruption? Why?"

"Because I'm working. That changes the situation."

"Constrains it, you mean."

Trust her to be direct. He had always admired that. "If you like."

She was silent for a long time. He would have said something, but her expression had become serious. "I need a friend right now, Marcus." She sighed. "I wish you believed. I really need someone to talk to."

"What about?"

She shrugged her shoulder, didn't answer.

"I may struggle with it and have my doubts, but I've got two sisters convinced the Bible is true. Trust me. I'll do my best to understand."

She gave him a small smile. "I still think you'll eventually come around."

"Don't get your hopes up."

"Jennifer and Kate strike me as being persuasive."

"They can be. Talk to me. What are you wrestling with?"

"Why Dad died."

"Because you prayed for a different outcome?"

She nodded.

"Jennifer is praying to be healed."

"And you're wondering if she has a chance at getting a positive answer."

"I've wondered," he said simply.

"A twenty-year Christian and an unbeliever wrestling over the same question. If you find an answer, I'd appreciate hearing it." She shook her head slightly. "Change of subject. How is Jennifer? You haven't said much in the last few days."

"She says she's fine. She's lying," he replied, weary. It was impossible to imagine what it was going to mean, the radiation and chemotherapy not working.

"Fine can be a matter of perspective. Someone broken of spirit can be worse off than someone physically ill. When do you go see her?"

"If things work out I'll take a predawn flight Tuesday, spend the day, and take a late night flight back."

"I wish you had been able to go last week."

"It couldn't be helped. Jack and Stephen are there. And I've been talking to her every day."

The shadows were beginning to lengthen. Marcus got to his feet and held out his hand. "The sunset is fading; it's time we were inside." Since the church incident, he wasn't taking chances. She slipped her hand into his. "Want to go into town with me tomorrow? I thought I might go play some basketball while Josh is at physical therapy."

"I can get out of the house?"

"Just to the gym. No shopping I'm afraid."

"I'll still take it."

He led the way back down the beach, skirting driftwood.

"Would you teach me how to play?" she asked.

"What?"

"Basketball."

He looked over and caught her half smile. "Now you tell me."

"I'm kind of athletically challenged too."

"You're smart. You can learn."

"Tell me that after you've spent an hour chasing the basketball. What time do we need to leave?"

"Nine o'clock will be early enough."

Time alone with Marcus was worth this. Shari shut off her alarm and crawled out of bed, trying to remind herself of that. It was not yet 7 A.M. She vaguely remembered seeing 2 A.M. This was horrible. And it was her birthday. She considered crawling back in bed and burying her head under a pillow. She would prefer to sleep through this day rather than be up at dawn. No. If she ducked back into bed, she would never hear the end of it.

She staggered downstairs after a hot shower, barefoot, carrying her socks, in desperate need of coffee.

The radio was on in the kitchen. She wasn't surprised to find Marcus working at the counter. He was in jeans, a black T-shirt, and tennis shoes. The casual attire didn't eliminate the obvious signs of his job—the badge, gun, and radio on his belt, the small earpiece he wore to keep him in touch with the other officers.

He set down the spoon he was using to mix muffin batter, wiped his hands on a towel, and gave her a smile, wide and welcoming. "Sit down. I'll fix you breakfast."

He was cheerful at this time of morning. She wanted to groan. If she had to talk coherently, she was in trouble. She took the coffee he offered, retreated to the table, and found the first newspaper, searching through it for the comics page.

He tugged down the newspaper. "Happy birthday."

"Please, don't remind me."

"How old are you today anyway?"

She wrinkled her nose at him.

"That's okay. I already know," he remarked smugly.

"If I have to endure this day, please feed me."

He laughed and returned to the stove. "Do you want hash browns with your omelet?"

"Please."

He was a very good short-order cook and she had long since stopped trying to suggest she should help. Breakfast was his domain. If she wanted to fix and bring him lunch to wherever he was working, that was another matter.

There was quiet for the next several minutes. Shari read the comics, turned to the national news, then moved to the political page.

Marcus set down a plate with a western omelet, toast, hash browns. He set a glass of orange juice beside the plate.

She looked at the orange juice with distaste.

"Eat. And orange juice is good for you."

"I'd rather be told to drink milk. Orange juice is nearly as bad as grapefruit juice."

"Since it's your birthday..." The glass was removed and was replaced with one of milk. "Better?"

"Much. Sorry, I don't mean to be so cranky."

"Sure you do. It's your birthday. It's already started off as a bad day."

"Please don't be cheerful. It's bad for my digestion."

He laughed.

She bit into her toast. "Aren't you going to eat?"

"Already did. I fixed the guys breakfast."

"Well, I hope you're still hungry. If I eat all of this I won't be able to move."

"It's a competitive advantage to have my opponent slow on her feet."

"Well, I think—"

He cut her off with a raised hand. "Yes, Craig."

Shari recognized that distant look as his attention shifted in an instant to work. He was pushing back his chair and heading to the door moments later. "Shari, stay here in the kitchen. Luke will be joining you."

She felt an intense wave of panic. Something was wrong. Her attention immediately swung to windows and she shoved back her chair and moved to the other end of the kitchen away from them. Marcus had said to stay in the kitchen. She wished he would have said for her to go upstairs.

Was someone out here? The shooter?

Josh came into the kitchen carrying his tennis shoes. "Shari, can you—" He saw her face. "What's wrong?"

"I don't know. Marcus just got called; he left in a hurry."

There was a heavy pause as they both considered the implications. Josh reached for a chair, swung it around. He pulled on his shoes with his good hand. "Can you tie my shoelaces?"

"Sure."

"Not knots like you did last time."

He was trying to distract her as well as get ready in case they had to move. She forced herself to smile back. "Me?"

"Yes, you."

She hurriedly tied neat bows.

"Thanks. I'll go see—"

She caught his arm. "No. Stay here."

They heard the front door open. "Miss Hanford?"

"In the kitchen, Luke."

He joined them and held up his hand to stop the questions. "There was a traffic accident up the road. You'll be hearing the police sirens soon."

"Marcus didn't react to an accident."

"Accidents make a good diversion. We're sweeping the grounds as a precaution. Go ahead and get ready to head into town. We're comfortable this was simply a minor traffic accident."

"You're sure?"

"Mrs. Garrett clipped her cousin Joe's truck. We've known both of them for years. This is nothing more serious than a failure-to-stop-in-time fender bender."

But it was a reminder of why she was here. The last time she had gone out in public she had put her family at risk, and Marcus had been shot. "Maybe I shouldn't go—"

Josh settled his hands on her shoulders. "It will do you good to get out of the house for a while. Go finish getting ready. You're not staying behind because of this."

She knew that tone. She wouldn't be winning this discussion.

He turned her toward the door. "It's your birthday. You're getting out of the house."

Shari went upstairs to finish getting dressed. She was looking forward to the day. Her mom was just finishing her makeup. "Good morning, honey. Happy birthday."

Shari stopped to give her a hug. "Thanks, Mom."

Her mom gave her a knowing smile. "Have a good time today."

Shari couldn't help the small blush. "I will."

When she went downstairs half an hour later carrying her gym bag, Marcus stood by the front door talking with Josh. He held out his hand when he saw her. "Ready?"

"Yes."

He stopped her at the door after Josh had stepped out on the porch. "If something doesn't feel right, what do you do?"

"Press the panic button."

"*Before* you try and figure out what it is that bothers you."

"I remember."

"Good. You can leave the rest of the worrying to me. Luke and I have it covered. Deal?"

She squeezed his hand. "Deal."

"Then let's get out of here."

She followed him around the house to the driveway.

"You're in front with me," Marcus directed. "Josh and Luke are in the back."

It felt strange being back in a car. Marcus noticed her tension as they drove along the winding roads toward town. "We're fine. That's Craig in the truck in front of us."

The trip took only ten minutes. Marcus took Josh and Luke to the hospital first, then drove on to the gym. He waited until Craig parked, got out and scanned the area, then signaled it was clear before he shut off the engine. "We'll go in the back entrance. Stay close."

Shari nodded. He circled the car and opened her door.

Marcus paused on the basketball court when Shari joined him from the women's locker room. She had dressed in black shorts and a burgundy T-shirt. Her tennis shoes were so white they had to be brand new. She had pulled her hair back in a ponytail and it bounced as she walked.

"We've got the court to ourselves?"

"For the next hour and an half."

"I wondered." She set her bag down on the bleachers next to his and crossed the gym floor to join him.

"This is a basketball." He bounced it to make his point.

She bit back a quick grin. "I think I remember that part."

"Remember free throws?"

"Just give me the ball."

He tossed it to her and she caught it with a clean slap.

She dribbled twice, then sent it in a clean arc toward the hoop. It was short, coming off the front of the rim, but her shot was good form. Marcus scooped the ball up and with one hand tossed it back to her. "You've played before."

"Ages ago."

She set herself, dribbled twice, and sent up another free throw that hit the backboard and went slightly right.

By the time he had fed her back the ball a dozen times, she had found the basket. "You're a bit too much of a perfectionist. You wince every time you miss."

"I bet you rarely miss free throws."

"Not often," Marcus agreed, "but then I rarely get to shoot them. The family doesn't often call fouls."

"Enough shooting. I want to burn some energy. Let's actually play."

"One-on-one?"

"You don't play girls?"

"Just making sure your ego can handle getting beat." He tossed her the ball.

He was between her and the basket and she came right at him, cutting right as soon as he committed himself to come toward her. No one would mistake the determination on her face. He moved to cut her off and she spun back out to the top of the key. It was a good percentage shot, and she took it, sending up an arc to the basket.

He blocked her shot.

"I see you don't give freebies." She had chased down the ball first, stood dribbling just outside the three-point line.

"Do you want one?"

"Not particularly."

She came in on the baseline, her shot missed, and Marcus recovered it. The basketball was warm, rough in his hand. His first shot hit nothing but net. "What do you want to play to?"

"Twenty-one."

He tried to purposely miss often enough to give her a chance.

"You could at least cheat without making it obvious," she remarked without heat, having chased down one of his misses.

Her shirt was damp with sweat, her breathing rapid. "Want to take a break?"

"Not till the game is over."

He was three baskets away from putting the game away; there was no use leaving her in misery. He put up the next three shots as soon as he touched the ball, made sure they were flawless, hitting nothing but net.

She stood back with her hands on her hips and watched the last one go in. "Ouch."

"I've been playing a long time," he commiserated.

"I would have never guessed," she replied dryly. She sat down on the bench, picked up a towel, and offered him one.

He took a seat beside her, watching her mop her face. "Thanks for playing. You're a good sport."

"I enjoyed it." She tipped her head to glance at him. "Even if you are a poor winner."

"A what?" he asked, laughing.

"You should be celebrating the victory. You finally beat me at something."

"Since it's your birthday, I'm being kind. I'll wait to gloat until later."

"Thanks."

He glanced at the clock on the wall. "We've got another half hour before we pick up Josh."

"Good, I can take a shower."

He nudged her white shoes. "Those need breaking in."

She raised one foot. "I bought them because I had this great New Year's resolution to start running. You can tell how far that idea got."

"You need a running partner to get you in the habit. I go most days I'm home to jog the hiking trails on Roosevelt Island."

"Really?"

"I could probably be talked into buying the coffee if you'd like to join me."

"Run? Early in the morning?"

He buried a grin. "Yes."

"That's brutal."

"You might enjoy it."

"Or I can decide I won't and not bother to try."

"Somehow that doesn't sound like you."

"That's exactly how Josh got me to try skydiving. You'll have to try another tactic."

"Don't worry, I'll come up with one."

"Why do I get the feeling you're going to keep asking until I agree?"

"Who? Me?"

She got up with a laugh and tossed her towel at him. "I'm going to go take that shower."

Shari came out of the locker room, shuffling her gym bag, towel, and tennis shoes and trying to get everything to fit inside the bag. She collided with Marcus, saw the gun in his hand, and froze.

"What happened?" He was propelling her back down the hall and toward the alcove.

"I'm fine." She stammered the words because it was obvious something was wrong. Marcus was tense, terse, and hustling her out of the hallway.

"Then why—" His eyes closed and he took a deep breath, then he shook his head and reached around the gym bag to the pager clipped on her belt. He shut off the panic button. "You nearly gave me a heart attack."

"I'm sorry! I didn't mean—"

He kissed her hard, stopping the apology.

Shari went from being panic stricken to being unable to think bliss in the blink of an eye. This was absolutely heaven. She felt her heart leap in delight and recognized joy. Her hands came up to curl around his forearms and she leaned in against him.

He pulled back half an inch to breathe again. "I do not mind false alarms. Don't get the wrong idea. I was just too far away."

She blinked, still rolling with the shock of that delightful, unexpected kiss. He had such alive brown eyes; she found them absolutely fascinating. She could feel him breathing. She should be feeling embarrassed, but being held in the shelter of his arms was absolutely wonderful. She looked ruefully at the fact but for the gym bag squashed between them, there was no space separating them. She could feel the blush starting. "You're not anymore."

He looked at her for a moment, then dropped the gym bag to the floor. "Come here," he said softly. He gave her a moment to decide and then pulled her close.

This kiss lasted long enough for her to close her eyes and get lost in the wonder of it.

Marcus ended the kiss and rested his forehead against hers. She felt his silent chuckle. "Should I apologize, or just say happy birthday?"

"It is my birthday."

They stood that way, silent, sharing the moment. Shari had no desire at all to come back to reality and deal with what had just happened.

He finally eased back half a step. "I've been wanting to do that for a long time, but I apologize for the timing, and the circumstances."

He was apologizing. She wanted to slap him for that, but he sounded so chagrined she decided to be magnanimous and not take it like the insult it felt like. She glanced around at the potted plants and empty chairs in the alcove. "A public place. You could have chosen worse. And Marcus...I don't kiss and tell."

"Get that look off your face. I enjoyed kissing you tremendously, and if you keeping scowling at me I'm going to do it again." He wrapped his arm around her shoulders, gave her a brief hug, and tugged her ponytail. "And I'm grateful you'll keep this quiet. I'm the one with the active family grapevine."

She relaxed. "Come on—I top that. I've got Mom. Your family is still learning compared to her."

"I'll grant you that one." He turned her toward the hallway. "We need to go meet Josh or he is going to be worried."

She didn't want this moment to end. "Can we talk tonight?"

"Are you going to pretend not to be tired at midnight?"

"I haven't been hiding the yawns," she said, chagrined.

He gave a small smile as he brushed back her bangs. "Not very well."

"Then I'll take a nap."

He laughed. "If you're up, we'll talk," he promised, to her delight.

THIRTEEN

They picked up Josh and Luke at the hospital. Shari was grateful when Marcus engaged Josh in a conversation about how the physical therapy had gone, what the schedule was for the next week. She wasn't sure she could hold a coherent conversation at the moment.

She thought about the kiss, absently touched her lip. Just thinking about it made her heart warm. What had it meant to Marcus? He had been reacting to the emotions of the moment; she had felt that in the kiss. But it went a lot deeper as a possibility of what might come. The ride back to the house was too short; she needed time to think before she accidentally said the wrong thing. Would he feel she was ducking him if she retreated upstairs for a while? At least she had a powerful distraction to get her through her first birthday without her father and Carl.

Marcus pulled around the house and parked.

Josh and Luke got out of the car.

"Shari." Marcus paused her as she would have opened the car door. "Hold on a second."

She looked over at him and was puzzled as he reached around to the backseat, and retrieved a small white bakery box.

"For you." He said simply, holding it out. He quirked a smile. "Happy birthday."

She opened it and grinned when she saw it. He had gotten her a cupcake. "How did you know?" She shook her head. "Mom."

"Yes."

She lifted it from the box, peeling back the wrapper. "Like a bite?"

"This one's yours. I sampled as she baked."

She laughed as she got icing on her fingers. "This is great."

He waited until she finished, then reached over and wiped away a spot of icing she had missed at the corner of her mouth with his thumb. "I know you would have preferred to skip recognition of this day. I know how you miss your dad and Carl, but you need to let those around you celebrate. It helps them have something positive to do."

"What did you guys do?"

He came around and opened her car door, offered his hand.

"Marcus?"

"I figured you should have at least a small warning."

He walked with her to the house, took her gym bag when they reached the porch, and reached around her to open the door for her.

"Surprise!"

Marcus had given her about a minute to adjust and prepare, but it would have been hard to prepare for this no matter how much time she had—the streamers, the balloons, the hand drawn signs done in colorful markers. The dining room table had been set out with a buffet of finger foods. The guys from the security details, those off duty, had joined her family. It was like being fifteen again and finding herself the focus of the extended family. "How did you—" She just shook her head and laughed. "Never mind. I don't think I want to know."

Josh wrapped his good arm around her shoulders. "We had fun."

Shari let herself be tugged into the room. She grinned as she recognized where all the cartoons from her newspapers had been going. They were intermixed among the streamers. "Cute, Josh."

"Get yourself a plate. We'll let you eat while we drown you in presents."

"Impossible. I can never have too many presents."

She hugged her mom. "Thank you," she whispered.

"Your dad would have been proud of you today. Enjoy it."

They had insured it would be impossible not to.

She picked up the first plate and officially opened the party.

Shari was very aware of Marcus through the afternoon, as he slipped in and out of the room, talking on the security net. He had made this possible. She deeply appreciated it.

When Josh insisted, she settled on the couch in the den to open presents. There were videos, and locally made taffy, an engraved watch, and a large puzzle. Small gifts that reflected the circumstances.

Mom had bought her a dress. It was absolutely beautiful. Her gaze caught Marcus's across the room. She looked down with a blush when she saw his smile.

Josh had gotten her a hand-tooled leather briefcase. It was the gift her dad had been threatening to get her for years. She looked at it for several moments, then reached over and wrapped her arm around Josh's neck, hugging him. "Thanks."

"You're welcome."

With a laugh she let him go. The wrapping paper had bunched beside her on the couch. She reached for the trash bag.

"One more."

She leaned her head back at Marcus's words. He was holding out a thick package. It was wrapped in heavy brown shipping paper. She accepted it, curious. "From you?"

"Something to keep you occupied."

It was heavy, and she would have thought it was a book except the package gave and she had to grasp it with both hands to steady it. She set it in her lap and opened the package. "What's this?"

Marcus just looked at her, a slight smile edging up the corners of his mouth. "What's it look like?"

It was well over a ream of loose pages. The top page simply said *Paula*—centered, on the middle of the page. It took her a moment to realize she was holding an H. Q. Victor manuscript. It was…she checked… 728 pages.

"Her next book. I asked Quinn to bring it back with him. It should keep you busy for a few days," he said, satisfied.

She caught his hand when he would have stepped back. "Marcus. Thank you," she whispered.

"My pleasure."

Most of the party banners and streamers had been cleaned up, the party was over. Marcus made his final rounds for the night, then passed off security to Craig. The lights were still on in the den. He had wondered if Shari would turn in early, given how long her day had been. He leaned against the doorpost, delighted to find she had waited up for him.

She was reading the manuscript. She was slouched in the seat with the manuscript in her lap, turning pages with one hand and eating a carrot with the other. He was willing to bet she had been seated just like that for the last several hours. The bag of vegetables left over from this afternoon's tray was almost gone, and about a hundred pages of the manuscript had been set down in a semineat pile on the floor. There was an absorbed expression on her face as she read.

"Is it any good?"

"What?"

He moved into the room. "The story. Is it good?"

She stretched her arms back over her head, arched her back, and smiled. "One of her best."

"Am I going to interrupt if I join you?"

"No, but I'm tossing you out if you yawn so I can keep reading," she replied with a small laugh. She set the manuscript down beside the chair.

He settled down on the couch. "Thanks for being a good sport today. I'm afraid once the planning started, it got out of hand."

"Mom told me you instigated the food."

"Guilty. I enjoy the leftovers."

"Thank you for arranging it. I didn't want to celebrate without Dad, and that would have made the day drag by. With the celebration, the day flew by and it was much easier to handle."

"It's hard to feel sad when Josh is tossing peanut shells at you for flubbing a joke."

"Yeah."

He saw a look of private amusement cross her face. One he had seen in his own family. "What?"

"I short-sheeted his bed."

"You know if you start going tit for tat, it's going to escalate on you fast. There's plenty of time while you are stuck here to dream up the practical jokes."

"I know. And I'm going to enjoy it." Her amusement changed to seriousness. "What do you want to talk about tonight?"

He had thought about that a great deal throughout the afternoon, and he chose to offer a serious, difficult topic, one he knew they needed to talk about. He had made the decision he wanted a lot more with her than just a friendship, and it was going to mean facing some topics that were going to be difficult for both of them. He was a cautious man when it came to introducing something that would hurt a friend, and he knew the risks. He brought up the subject of religion as an indirect observation. "Jennifer is going to want to talk about what she believes."

"Very likely."

"Shari, she's praying to be healed, and instead she's having to face growing worse. I don't understand, and I don't want to say the wrong thing."

Her posture straightened, and her focus narrowed. "Do you really want to know what I've discovered about prayer?"

There was a frank challenge to her words. She didn't think he was going to like her answer. "Yes, Shari, I do."

"To be passive and throw up your hands and say, 'I don't care, whatever You want, Lord,' is as much a cop-out as pushing for only what you want and not being able or willing to accept something different. To deny Him being Lord." She looked across at him moodily. "It hurts to have prayers not answered. The difference is I still believe in the One to whom I pray, whereas you simply stopped praying."

Her warning had been with cause. It was the first time she had shown him the emotion behind what she thought of his disbelief. She didn't temper it, and he had to admit, hearing it stung. It pricked where he was vulnerable, being called a coward.

"We put everything we are into our prayers. What we think about Jesus. What's happening in the world around us. What our dreams are about how life should be. Our sense of hope. Prayer is the ultimate struggle. It can be exquisite joy, and it can also be painful tears.

"I don't want to belittle the pain you felt over what happened to your mom. But you decided through the eyes of a child what the world was like, what God was like. If adults struggle to understand Him and sometimes get it wrong, don't you think a child might too? Jennifer will get through this moment because she knows Jesus. However He decides to answer her prayer, she'll be the strong one. It's you I worry about."

Her words ran out and she flushed, dropped her gaze.

He didn't know what to say. "Ouch."

"You asked. But I didn't mean to say it exactly that way."

"Shari." He waited until she looked back up. "You're direct. I've always admired that. And you are right in one thing. You kept trying to understand, and I gave up." He gave a faint smile. "And you just told me in more eloquent terms than Jennifer ever will what she will be thinking."

He had offered an olive branch to diffuse the tension and he was grateful when she accepted it. "You're forgetting Kate."

He groaned. "Tenacious gets a new definition with Kate."

Her expression became serious. "Marcus, you can trust Jesus with Jennifer. He loves her. I know that."

"I'll think about it."

"Thank you. I know you can't make a decision just to please me, or Jennifer. You're kind enough you would probably try on most subjects to do just that. But this is different. You have to make a decision you can live with."

"No, Shari. I have to make a decision I can live with and one I can defend," he corrected. "I've got O'Malleys to deal with."

"I'd commiserate with you, but I'm secretly delighted they are there pushing you out of your comfort zone. I like your family."

"I've noticed," Marcus replied dryly. "Kate calls me and promptly asks for you."

She gave a small smile. "Like I said, I like your family."

"What do you talk about anyway?"

She laughed, and there was no mistaking that blush. "You."

That blush did it. He got up and invaded her space, resting his hands on the arms of her chair. He leaned down, until he was inches away, then went still, searching her gaze, finding the anticipation waiting there. He had been thinking about the kiss from this morning throughout the day, wondering. Apparently, so had she. He leaned forward and ended the lingering questions.

This kiss was warm and touched with an intriguing sense of mystery. The softness and sweetness pulled him to explore. He angled his head to deepen the kiss as she reached one hand up and slipped it behind his neck.

He forced himself to ease back. He was tangling with her emotions, her heart, and he wasn't going to do that to her, not until he could promise he was going to be a forever part of her life. She'd had enough tears; he wasn't going to be the cause of any more. Her bemused expression made him feel so good. "Finish your book," he whispered. "This is too explosive for tonight."

"Probably." Her hand at the back of his neck tightened gently and then she grinned. "Sweet dreams, Marcus."

"Shari—" He swooped to steal one last kiss. "Good night, minx."

FOURTEEN

Marcus flew to Baltimore on Tuesday, taking a predawn flight. It was going to be a long, hard day, seeing Jennifer, then flying back very late that night. His sleep had been intermittent at best. Shari had accomplished more than she realized with that good night of hers. He had spent most of the night dreaming about what might be. He was almost glad to get the day away. A week ago he had thought it would be a chance to get back his perspective; instead it had become a chance to decide how best to proceed.

He lifted his briefcase to the empty seat beside him and opened it, intending to do some work. There was a small white envelope resting on his planner with his name on it. Surprised, he picked it up. He recognized Shari's handwriting. Under it was one addressed to Jennifer. Curious, he opened the envelope addressed to him and slipped out a piece of stationery.

Marcus, I wanted to say thank you for a wonderful birthday. You helped ease my way through a painful day. That was not only thoughtful, that was very kind. And I loved the gift.

I wish there was something I could do to repay that and help you get through the tough day you now face. I hope that seeing Jennifer will clarify how you can help her and your family.

I am so sorry I was abrupt last night when you asked about prayer. Please let me apologize again. You have become such a good friend, and at times I find the chasm of faith between us so frustrating, but that doesn't excuse "directness" that lacked tact. Forgive me. Hug Jennifer. Because you love her, help her laugh. Because I believe, I'll pray for her. We will both be good medicine.

I'll be thinking about you today, and if you just want to talk, call me. You know my number.

She had dotted the *i* in her name with a small heart.

Shari. The very presence of the note touched his heart.

She cared about his family. He leaned his head back against the seat, his thumb rubbing the edge of the note. He felt a deep sense of relief. He was falling in love with her. And the idea no longer felt like bad timing. He had planned to get the O'Malleys settled first, but Shari was showing him she had room for his family without even realizing she was doing it. She was moving toward his family, inviting him to share them, and showing she wouldn't feel uncomfortable in their circle.

This case could not be resolved soon enough.

He closed his briefcase, putting aside the work, and leaned his head back, closing his eyes. How did he proceed? He had not only Shari and her family to think about, but the O'Malleys. To change the family dynamics in such a fundamental way—this wasn't going to be easy, and the last thing he wanted to do was hurt any of them.

The flight was landing in Baltimore before he had figured out a plan.

Kate met him at the airport. He saw her leaning against a concrete pillar watching the passengers as he entered the concourse from the departure gate. She was in jeans and a blue shirt, arms crossed, and even from this distance he could tell she was letting the post support her. His eyes narrowed at the sight, for to show that exhaustion wasn't like her. Hospitals and doctors had always been a strain for her, and the stress of the situation was now plain to see.

Kate saw him, straightened, and came to meet him. As soon as they were free of the crowds, Marcus wrapped her in a hug. He was going to have to get Dave out here to be with her somehow. Kate wasn't one to let many people support her, but Dave was one person who could get under her guard and take care of her.

"You look tired."

So do you, he thought but didn't say. "A little. Thanks for coming to meet me."

"My pleasure. How's Shari and her family?"

"Recovering. It's been quiet. How's Jennifer?"

"Delighted that you could come."

Marcus left his arm around Kate's shoulder as they walked the concourse. "Have I told you lately how much I appreciate you? You're a trouper to be carrying this for the family."

"I'll take the compliment, but nonsense," Kate replied, lightly slapping his chest. "You need to quit feeling sorry for yourself. No one in the family thinks less of you for not being able to be here. And we'd be kicking you back to work if you tried to come. You've got a case to deal with."

"I'm hoping we can get a break in the case soon. Something has to give."

Kate smiled. "With Dave, Lisa, and Quinn on the job, you've got good help. Tell me about Shari. How did the birthday go?"

"She's a good sport. And she got through it fine."

"I'm glad. Did she like the book?"

"Loved it."

"What else did she love?"

He tweaked her nose and she laughed at him.

He had brought only the one carry-on bag. They headed out to the parking lot. Kate indicated her car.

The trip to the hospital was too short for Marcus to feel mentally prepared to see Jennifer. He was nervous suddenly, that he would say the wrong thing, react the wrong way.

Kate walked with him into the hospital. "Marcus—go up by yourself. She's in room 1310."

He squeezed Kate's hand and moved to the elevator.

Marcus took a deep breath before pushing the partially open door back to Jennifer's private room. Bouquets of flowers lined the window ledge, and there were so many get-well cards, they had been clipped like streamers to a string so they would be visible from the bed. In the chair by the bed sat a big panda bear and a smaller green dragon. Marcus slipped into the room quietly, for Jennifer looked to be asleep.

She had lost most of her hair. A bright rainbow scarf had been tucked around her head to cover the baldness. It was such a visible assault it made him want to cry.

He took the seat beside her bed, hoping not to disturb her, but she stirred.

"Marcus…hi." Her voice was much softer than before, and she looked like a waif for she had lost so much weight, but her smile touched her eyes.

He clasped her hand and leaned over to kiss her cheek. "Hi, precious."

He kept her hand folded in his as he pulled the chair over. She shifted on the bed and couldn't cover the wince. He helped adjust the pillows she used to brace her back. "Better?"

"Much." Her fingers interlaced with his. "It is good to see you. What were you thinking, going and getting yourself shot?"

Marcus closed his eyes, laughed, and leaned forward to rest his chin on the side rail of the bed so their faces were close. Trust Jennifer to get right to the point. "Someone wanted to shoot Shari."

"So you stepped in front of a bullet."

"I would have if I had known it was coming. He missed."

"I'm glad he did."

"So am I."

"You like her?"

He nodded.

Jennifer searched his face, then reached up and brushed back his hair, smiling. "Try—you're falling in love with her."

"Just between you and me—yes, I think I am."

"That scares you."

He nodded again.

"Why?"

"She's a witness, Jen. And I'm afraid I'm going to get my heart broken when this is over and life gets back to normal."

"Nonsense. She's too smart to let go of a good thing."

Family loyalty was such an admirable thing. "Can I show you something?"

"Sure."

He reached for his billfold and withdrew the sketch he had made a few nights before while Shari was working. He unfolded it and smiled as he looked at it. He handed it to his sister. "A pretty typical pose for Shari."

Jen studied it, then laughed. "Oh, this is priceless. Did you show her?"

He shook his head. "She gets so absorbed in her work. She's good at it, Jen. Start her talking about policy and you had better have done your homework. And I'm starting not to wince when she tells whoever answers the phone to tell the governor she'll call him back later."

"An interesting circle of influence."

"Hmm."

"Marcus, we need her in this family," Jennifer said gently. "Someone has to be able to articulate with clarity what makes us unique. Shari would be perfect. We all like her."

"You do?" They had been talking about him on the family grapevine. He shouldn't be surprised, but he was.

"We do. She'd be good for you." Jennifer squeezed his hand. "She's got a good sense of humor. You need that. And she's already proving she can handle the pressures of your job. She's accustomed to traveling at a moment's notice. And she tells these really great stories on the phone that can leave you in absolute stitches. When you're away you can always call home and be cheered up."

"And here I was afraid you would be disappointed in my choice."

"Because her background is so different? Marcus, she likes you, and she really wants to fit in. I think she envies what you have with all of us. Kate likes her, and you know how careful a read of someone's character she is. We're thrilled with Shari."

He was bemused by her answer. "I wish it was as simple as waiting for the day this crisis is past, but it's more than that. Even if you are right, there are obstacles."

"I know. Shari and I have talked."

"It's hard, Jen, not to be skeptical. Shari's prayers for her father were not answered, yours to get well don't appear to be. I don't want to hurt any of you, but it doesn't fit."

Jen looked at him, thoughtful. "She's already felt the hurt that comes from having a relationship unravel over different expectations for the future. She isn't going to walk herself into a similar chasm on something as vital as religion."

"Sam."

Jennifer nodded. She thought for a moment. "I can't answer all your questions, but maybe I can answer one. About me. Try reading John chapter 11 again. When Jesus' good friend Lazarus was ill and dying, Jesus heard the news and He said something very surprising. He said 'This illness is not unto death; it is for the glory of God…' It makes me wonder what He said when cancer struck me.

"Jesus loved Lazarus. Jesus could have said the word and healed him; He had done that with the sick in other situations. But in this instance He chose not to. He wasn't acting callously; it wasn't the fact He didn't care.

"When Jesus went on to say 'Lazarus is dead; and for your sake I am glad that I was not there, so that you may believe,' He was making a profound choice. He loved the men He was with to the point He was willing to let His friend die so that they might be convinced to believe. Then Jesus went and raised Lazarus from the dead."

"Your cancer is to get us to believe?"

"No. My cancer is because sin messed up this world and my body is dying. But the delay in answering my prayer for healing—that might have a silver lining. It got Kate thinking about God. It's thrown you back in turmoil." She squeezed his hand. "You've rejected God for years because of the hurt. Do you think I mind being used to tug you back? Marcus, I want you to have to face the past and deal with it."

She stopped him when he would have spoken. "Just think about it, okay? Shari and I are not going to convince you. You have to convince yourself." She pointed to the stack of magazines on the side table. "Change of subject. I need your opinion on something."

Because she was suddenly trying to sit up, Marcus hurriedly moved to help her. She was visibly weak and she collapsed back on the pillows he put behind her with a grateful smile. She picked up the top magazine and opened it to a turned down page. "So, what do you think about this wedding dress?"

"Jennifer."

She grinned and patted his arm. "A guy's opinion. That's all I want. I've marked five that I really like."

"Lisa, the lab results you were waiting on are in."

Lisa looked up from the arson investigation reference book she was scanning to find the burn point for latex to see Paula coming through the doorway of the lab. Her friend had been working on doing the DNA extraction from the glass fragments. It was after 9 P.M., the labs were quiet, most of the staff gone; they had both stayed late to see the tests finished.

"What's the verdict?" With only enough DNA recovered to do one test, they had rolled the dice on which test to do.

Paula smiled and held out the file. "See for yourself."

Lisa accepted the file, feeling butterflies in her stomach. If they had guessed wrong…

She scanned the printout and the transparency and felt relief deep inside. It wasn't a full panel of markers, but what she was seeing was going to be enough. They had the major markers. "Enough to index."

Paula nodded. "If he's in any of the databases, this should be sufficient to generate a match."

"Thanks, Paula. I owe you one."

"Good. Is your brother Jack seeing anyone these days?"

Amused, Lisa shook her head. "Not since Beth moved to New Hampshire with her new job."

"That's too bad about Beth."

Lisa laughed, knowing where Paula was heading. "I suppose he's on the rebound."

"Next time he stops by, convince him to take you to lunch and then remember you already had arrangements to have lunch with me so he'll do the polite thing and make it a threesome." Paula grinned. "You can get paged or something."

"You know, I could just tell him you're interested in going to lunch with him."

"Better if he thinks it was his idea."

Lisa thought about it for a moment, then decided it would be good for Jack. It was about time he was dating again, and the idea of it being with her friend was...intriguing. "I'll see what I can do."

"Great. I knew I could count on you. I'll catch you later." Her friend headed back upstairs.

It was time to find out if all the painstaking hours of work were going to pay off. Lisa flipped on lights as she walked through the lab carrying the test results. She headed to the secure terminal, where she sat down and began entering logins and passwords, working her way through the layers of security until she finally was able to log into the national crime reference database.

Working slowly to make sure she didn't make an error, she worked down the DNA panel, identifying and entering the marker values used by the national database. She started the search.

The system was slow tonight, hers was one of several indexes being run, and she pushed away from the terminal rather than sit and watch the screen. She went to brew a pot of coffee. What if this didn't pan out? What did she try next? She was tired enough she didn't know. She always tried to have a game plan in mind, an idea of what she would try next if this led nowhere, but this case was running thin on leads to chase.

She took her time fixing the coffee, making it strong, needing the caffeine.

Quit stalling. If nothing matches, waiting here isn't going to change that.

She walked back to the desk. On the terminal an index number had appeared, was blinking red.

She spun around the chair and took a seat, on the verge of having not only an answer for Marcus but the solution of the case. She wrote down the index number, switched databases, and pulled up the details.

Daniel Gray. Age 31. Armed Robbery. Aggravated Assault. Murder in the First Degree.

She scrolled down the screen.

"What the..."

She just looked at it for several moments, stunned.

Deceased. October 27, last year. Lethal injection by the Commonwealth of Virginia.

What in the world did she do with this?

She considered the probability the DNA tests were flawed and finally rejected it. She was not above a mistake, but she knew the care that had been taken with this sample, the safeguards at each step. It was solid.

Could blood on glass fragments survive over nine months in a hotel room? No. She also rejected that. The glass shards had not been scattered over and worn into the carpet, the sharp edges dulled from friction. The glass was recent.

The database used only a subset of the markers in its search. The DNA of the shooter was similar enough to match with a dead man? She had got a mitochondrial match. It could only happen with a close family relative.

She went back to the original database, pulled the full index panel, printed it, and grabbed a red pen. She clicked on the light box and set down the DNA panel she had developed for the shooter next to the one from the national database.

Forty minutes later she knew she was looking at the answer to the case. "Hello, Daniel Gray," she whispered, easing back from the light box. "Let me guess, Judge Whitmore sentenced you to death. So who in your family decided to get revenge? Your father, your brother? Someone did. And I don't have enough DNA markers from the partial test results to tell, so we've got ourselves a nice mystery here."

She reached for the phone...and hesitated. Quinn...if he understood the importance of her telling him before Marcus, then maybe she would start giving him the benefit of the doubt on other things too. She punched in Quinn's pager number and marked it urgent.

Ten minutes later when he still had not returned her page her frustration was intense. Forget it. She picked up the phone to call Marcus. As she punched in the third number, Quinn walked through the door.

"Your page was marked urgent." His cowboy hat and his jacket were wet. It must be raining outside.

"Sit down." She was still annoyed enough at the way her heart had leaped when she saw him that she wasn't feeling particularly friendly. He raised one eyebrow at her brisk tone and pulled over a stool.

She handed over the page. "The DNA test results on the glass shards are back."

He read it, then looked at her. "You're sure?"

"Yes. There's your motive. The shooter is someone in his family."

Quinn checked his watch, then reached for his phone and dialed. "Marcus, we need you in Chicago. Lisa has something you should see." He listened. "See you then," Quinn agreed and closed the phone. Lisa wasn't surprised that Marcus asked no questions. On her word alone, he would come without question.

"He'll divert to O'Hare. Who else do we need?"

"Dave," she decided. "And someone who can get us details of the Daniel Gray case."

Marcus got Quinn's page on the way to the airport. With luck of timing he was able to grab a seat on a United flight bound for Chicago just ready to pull away from the gate.

He walked into Lisa's lab very early Wednesday morning, coming straight from the airport. Her assistant pointed him down to the research library conference center. Dave was there, Quinn, and eight others from the investigative team. They squeezed in another chair for him. He set down his briefcase, accepted the coffee he was handed, and looked across the table at Lisa. "What have you found?"

The sunlight was streaming into the room from the big windows behind her. She was tipped back in her seat with her hands cradling a cup of coffee, and she had the unfocused look of someone who had not yet been to bed. She gave a rueful smile. "The shooter is dead."

He didn't even blink. "So are we looking for a body, a zombie, or a ghost?"

"Trust you to be literal." She leaned forward and handed him a sheet of paper, crumpled from having been passed around. "The DNA I was able to pick up from the shattered glass generated this hit."

"Daniel Gray." Marcus read further down, then looked up abruptly. "Executed?"

"The death sentence was given by Judge Whitmore. The DNA matches to the Gray family. There are subtle differences in the panels when you go beyond the tags used in the database index. The shooter is a close relative of Daniel Gray. A father, brother, cousin, son. But I didn't have enough DNA markers to work with to get it tighter than that."

Marcus felt intense relief. They had the motive. Someone had gone after Judge Whitmore because of the decision he had made in this death penalty case. "Okay, you've been working this all night. How far have you gotten in identifying who in the Gray family is the shooter?"

Dave sorted files in front of him and handed over two. "Daniel Gray's father is one Titus Gray. You'll need a week to read the full file. This is the Cliffs Notes. He's into every racket on the East Coast from drugs to gambling. The FBI has been focusing on his family for years.

"I would make Titus a natural for the shooter except for one thing," Dave continued. "Titus apparently disowned Daniel after he was sent to prison and has had absolutely nothing to do with him since. A search of the prison records has yet to turn up so much as one phone call or one letter, let alone a visit during the twelve years Daniel was incarcerated."

Marcus read again the printout for the executed man. Sentenced to death for the murder of an undercover cop. "Why disown him? I somehow doubt Titus would consider killing a cop offensive."

"As best we can conclude there was a power struggle in the family. The hit wasn't sanctioned."

Marcus nodded. "That I can believe. Okay. Who else?"

"There is one brother. Connor Gray. He was fifteen when Daniel was sentenced. Shortly thereafter, Titus sent Connor to a private school in Europe. From there it was Harvard Law School. Then private law practice. If Connor is involved in the family business, no one can find a trace of it. He's got a clean record, not even a misdemeanor. And he doesn't get along with his father."

"Was he close to his brother?"

"There are records of occasional visits to see Daniel, fourteen over the twelve years. He was not there when his brother was executed."

Dave picked up the last file. "We ran the alias Henry James, used to rent room 1323, through the databases again looking for some link to the Daniel Gray. The alias has been used by a man named Frank Keaton—he's a first cousin, has worked for Titus for fifteen years. He's suspected of two murders and about four assaults."

"A father, a brother, and a cousin."

Dave nodded. "And motive with all of them."

"There's more," Quinn added from where he leaned against the wall by the door. "Connor was at the Renaissance Hotel that weekend."

"You're kidding."

"Room 1317. He was involved in merger discussions being held under cover of the conference."

Three people in the family could have done the shooting; all had reasonable motive. "What about the sketch?"

Lisa silently handed him a file. Marcus opened it and groaned. It took only a glance to know they had a problem with their most powerful evidence. "So Shari saw either Frank or Connor. With the disguise that was used it could easily be either man."

Quinn nodded. "We've shown both Frank's and Connor's pictures at the hotel. The security guard for the fourteenth floor telecommunication center is positive on Connor. And we've got three who have identified Frank as being here the week before the shooting."

Marcus looked across the table at his sister, tapping the file in his hand. "Who's left-handed?" he asked quietly.

She gave a small smile. "Connor," she answered simply. "The one without so much as a parking ticket."

Connor and Frank had to be involved, but the father—had it been a family conspiracy to kill the judge? "The father, Titus. Is there any way he was not involved?" Marcus asked the room at large, looking for their perspective.

"His eldest son was sentenced to death by Judge Whitmore. Frank works for him. The church shooting sounds like Frank," Quinn added. "He's known to brag about his marksmanship."

"Missed at six feet, missed at two hundred feet by a hair. Two shooters. Connor and Frank."

Quinn nodded. "I think so."

"And Titus ordered them both to act," Marcus concluded.

"I don't think Frank would act without Titus's approval," Dave confirmed.

"Is there anything concrete on Titus?"

Dave shook his head. "He was in Europe when the two shootings occurred. Wiretaps that the FBI had in place for other reasons didn't overhear anything. We'll have to get either Connor or Frank to supply that connection. Frank is used to a hard life and jail time. Connor is more likely to turn on Titus if the pressure hits, but he's also his son. I think we'll need to have both Connor and Frank to get leverage to reach Titus."

Marcus ran the three names over again in his mind—father, brother, cousin. "Is there any way Titus and Frank acted alone? Without Connor?"

Lisa shook her head. "Connor probably hoped it would appear to be the case, but he made a fatal mistake. He's the only one who is left-handed. Connor is the shooter."

Marcus would trust that opinion. Connor had shot the judge at the hotel, Frank had shot at Shari at the church, and Titus had set them both in motion. "Where do we find them today?"

FIFTEEN

Marcus shifted in the plane seat to reach up and shut off his reading light. It was late, he was tired, and they were still over an hour from the lake house. Dave and Quinn were flying back with him.

With the reading light off, he was able to see again the view out the small plane window. The blinking light at the end of the plane wing lit the scattered thin clouds around the plane, bathing them in whiteness. Cruising at twenty thousand feet, they were in broken cloud cover with some clouds drifting by below them. When he could see the ground there were clusters of lights marking cities and towns and then black landscape broken only by the occasional line of lights from cars.

Marcus stretched out his legs and considered trying to get some sleep, only to discard the idea. He had never been comfortable sleeping with the low drone of engines as the background.

The plan was in place after a long day of conference calls with Washington.

If Shari could pick out Connor in a lineup of photos, they would move against Connor and Frank. Arresting Titus would have to wait for more evidence. No one wanted him to slip through when they had a chance to send him away on conspiracy to murder a federal judge.

Marcus felt an ache in his heart, knowing the gamble they were taking. The evidence was all circumstantial. But the risk of flight was simply too great to wait—Connor and Frank could disappear anywhere in the world at a moment's notice.

The warrants had to find the direct evidence. The gun used to kill Judge Whitmore, the blood-splattered suit, the gloves, the shoes, the disguise. It was hard to accept the reality that Lisa, by being so thorough with the evidence, had done the defense attorney's job for him.

The evidence pointed to either Frank or to Connor—the partial DNA markers obtained from the shattered glass said it could be either one of them; the sketch Shari had given suggested both; witnesses placed both men at the hotel. The defense attorney would have a credible argument for reasonable doubt regardless of which man they attempted to convict.

They would never get a conviction on Connor if all they had unique to him was the fact he was left-handed. Frank had the criminal record; Connor didn't.

And if they tried to convict Frank, his attorney could reasonably argue the shooter had been Connor.

They had to find direct physical evidence. Or they had to get either Connor or Frank to cut a deal and talk because the option was unacceptable. A conviction would rise or fall on Shari's eyewitness testimony. And that would place Shari's life in grave danger.

Marcus pulled out the sketch he had done from her description of the shooter and turned the reading light back on. A few subtle changes and it matched Frank. A few others, and it was Connor.

What if Shari couldn't pick out the shooter from the photo lineup?

For the sake of the case he hoped she could.

For the sake of her safety, he hoped she couldn't. He wanted her removed as a factor in this case.

He was concerned about how she would react when she heard the news they had a suspect, learned the crushing news they might not have the evidence to convict. If the worst happened—an acquittal, a hung jury—it would destroy her. And he didn't want to see the glimmer of fear in her eyes when she looked at the photo of the man who had tried to kill her.

Put it aside. There is nothing you can do but deal with it as it comes.

He wanted to protect Shari from what was coming and could only ensure he was there when she had to deal with it.

He hesitated for a moment, and reached over to his suit jacket. From the inside pocket he removed the slim book—a New Testament plus Psalms and Proverbs—that Jennifer had given him. He'd read the passage she had marked in Luke on the flight to Chicago, gone on to thumb through the text and read words that were familiar to him from his childhood.

He could remember his mother reading him the stories from Luke.

This was the last moment of quiet he would have for several chaotic days. He owed Shari a decision; he owed himself a decision about Jesus, about prayer. The turmoil he felt didn't set well. And while this issue remained between them, he and Shari would remain at best cautious friends.

He couldn't afford to make the wrong decision. He knew how profound his life would change no matter what he decided. If he chose to again believe, to lay aside the doubts, it might give him a future with Shari, but it would create a sense of turmoil within the family. It would make it very hard for Rachel, Lisa, Jack, and Stephen not to feel a sense of discomfort over the fact they didn't believe.

He had been the leader of the O'Malleys for over two decades. He knew what it meant to look out for the family—be there to comfort, provide for them, support, solve problems, see trouble coming and head it off, bail them out after a mistake, keep the peace, love them. He couldn't afford to make the wrong decision. He couldn't walk them down a road to being hurt. He wouldn't shake that sense of family unity without being absolutely certain it was the right decision to make.

Jesus said He wanted to be Lord. He said, "'Follow Me.'" Marcus could feel the clarion call of that order and its absoluteness. It was one of the unfortunate realities with religion, there was no middle ground. He believed and followed or he didn't.

Marcus had no practice with prayer since he was a child, and it felt awkward.

Jesus, You're asking a lot of me. It would mean trusting the O'Malleys to You. Not to mention Shari.

He could admit to himself he was worried. Who would look out for the O'Malleys if something happened to him? He had no illusions about the coming danger. When Connor knew they were after him, when Titus did—arrests would not be made without risk.

If something happened to him, who would keep Lisa out of trouble?

Who would give Rachel a hug?

Who would talk to Kate in the middle of the night when she carried the weight of the world on her shoulders?

Who would ensure Jennifer got everything possible to help her get well?

Who would be the older brother Stephen and Jack needed behind them?

Jesus, I need You to value what I value. Is it wrong to want that? This family needs a good strong leader. Trusting You for me is one thing, for them is something larger and deeper.

From his childhood came the memories of intense tears, and the unexpected rush of emotions had him clenching his jaw. The pain crashed back with a furor.

Jesus, I've got only one question really. How do You reconcile a child being abandoned by a loving God? I believed in You once, and I got crushed when Mom died. That's the pain You have to deal with if I am to accept again Your statement that You love me. If I'm to trust You.

He wanted to be optimistic. But he wasn't walking into a land mine of disappointment again. The last words his mom had told him from her hospital bed as she held his hand in hers, in a grip so soft his hold on hers had been the stronger one, her last words had been the whispered ones: "Jesus loves you." His mom had died that night. Shari said a child couldn't have the same perspective as an adult. Maybe not. But a child was not as easily fooled by words. They saw actions.

He closed the New Testament and slipped it back into his pocket.

He wasn't sure what he expected, what he wanted to know or see happen to settle his questions. There was an honest willingness to consider believing in God again. But he didn't know what he sought, what the reassurance was he needed to have.

Circumstances demanded that the issue slide to the background for the next several days. He was almost grateful.

The plane touched down in the darkness.

It was a silent drive to the lake house. Marcus saw lights on in the den as the car curved around the drive. Had Shari waited up for them to arrive? It wouldn't surprise him. Marcus retrieved his suit jacket and briefcase but left the one piece of carry-on luggage in the trunk. They would not be here for long, regardless of the outcome of the photograph lineup; the only question was their destination. He didn't want to be away, but Luke could manage security here.

Marcus followed Dave and Quinn around the driveway to the porch and walked into the house as Shari came from the den. It was so good to see her, and her smile…it was like coming home. She didn't hide the fact she was glad to see him, and in another situation, he would have reached out his arm to gather her into a hug. He wished he wasn't going to be erasing that smile with his words.

"I didn't think you would be back tonight. Dave, Quinn—it's great to see you." She looked back at him. "How's Jennifer?"

Her words threw him back a day to the reason he had originally left. It didn't feel like it had been only a day since he had seen Jennifer. "She's doing pretty good, all things considered. She's picked out her wedding dress," he offered with a smile, then turned serious. "Shari, would you wake up your brother?"

She looked from Marcus to the others, her expression growing still. "What is it?"

"After your brother is here."

She hesitated, then nodded and moved upstairs to wake Joshua.

Her brother and mom joined them in the den five minutes later. Shari didn't sit down, stopping instead just inside the door.

"What is it?" Her voice was steady, but she was twisting her fingers together.

"We've got a photo spread for you to look at," Marcus replied, watching her accept the news. He nodded to Dave, who opened the folder he carried and set down the prepared photograph spread on the desk. There were eight pictures in it, all chosen to look similar. Two of them were Frank and Connor.

Shari stepped toward the desk.

Marcus watched her face for a reaction as she looked down; he saw the shock hit. "That's him." She looked up at him, her gaze startled. "How did you—"

"Who, Shari?" Dave prompted.

Without hesitation she put her finger down on Connor. "He lost the hair and mustache."

Quinn looked over at Marcus.

"Call the pilot and tell him we're flying out tonight," Marcus told Quinn. "I want to be in New York by dawn."

Shari turned toward him, and he could see the fire in her eyes. "Who is he?"

"He's just a suspect at this point. It's best you don't know until we investigate further."

"Marcus, I know this is him. Why did he kill Carl? Why did he kill my father?"

Marcus looked at Joshua, at Beth, and then told Shari the basics. "It may have something to do with the Daniel Gray case."

That news rocked her. "The death penalty case. Over a decade ago."

"Yes."

"Not the Supreme Court short list. Not my brief."

He should have realized the relief that would be. He crossed to her side, reached for her hands. "No."

"You're going after him."

She wasn't saying she was afraid for him, but it was written all over her face. "Yes, we are. I don't know how long we will be gone."

Her hands came up to grasp his. "Marcus, be careful."

There were moments where caution didn't fit. He leaned down and kissed her. "I'll be careful. That's a promise."

She leaned against him, hugging him tight, and then she stepped back and looked over at Quinn. "Make him keep his word."

Quinn laughed. "Yes, ma'am."

"We need ideas; that place is a fortress," Marcus observed. Connor's home had full security, roving guards, and driveways leaving from three different sides of the grounds. By the time they served the search warrant, got access, and secured the grounds, Connor could destroy a lot of evidence and possibly even slip the grounds. And that was assuming they were not met with violence. They couldn't predict how the man would react when confronted. He had killed a judge; he didn't have anything to lose.

"We can serve him at his office."

"Walking into a law firm and arresting one of their partners will be like waving a red flag at their profession."

Dave pushed back his chair from the table where Connor's estate blueprints were spread out. "We need to arrest Connor and serve warrants on his home, business, and vehicle at the same time."

"Agreed." Marcus looked at the marshal from the local office. "Gage, any ideas?"

"What about a street stop? Catch him between home and work. He drives himself; we should be able to establish surprise. And we can act with a small enough team we could limit any chance of a leak getting back to him once the warrant has been issued."

Marcus thought about it and nodded. "Have teams ready to move into his office and home as soon as he's been stopped?"

Gage nodded. "We should be able to prevent him from getting word out to anyone."

"Get it set up. Rick, is your team ready to serve on Frank's home?"

In five days they still had not been able to locate Frank. The decision had been made to arrest Connor, serve the search warrants, and hope to pressure Frank out of hiding.

"We're ready," Rick confirmed. "Those watching his house have seen three men present. We'll go in with four teams. There's an officer ready to shut down the security system when we move."

Marcus looked at his watch. "Let's get all the teams in place. We'll act when Connor leaves work."

The group separated to implement the details.

The waiting was over, and Marcus felt the change in focus inside. Five hours, and it would be over one way or another.

He considered calling Shari but didn't want to add to the stress she was carrying. Better to tell her after it was over.

At 4 P.M., Marcus walked with Dave and Quinn to the waiting vehicles, having gone through the plans in detail with Gage.

A street stop was a three vehicle maneuver. They were using an SUV, a blue sedan, and a white delivery van; nothing about them suggesting they were law enforcement vehicles. The nine officers assembled to assist them wore street clothes over the bulletproof vests. They would act somewhere on the drive between Connor's office and home, choosing the location that was most advantageous based on traffic.

They assembled across from Connor's office building where they could see his vehicle. When Connor left the office driving his Lexus, they slipped into traffic behind him.

The SUV, serving as the lead vehicle, eventually passed Connor's car and moved up in front of him. The delivery van and the sedan trailed Connor through town, eventually moving to be the vehicles immediately behind him. Connor's car turned east on Thirty-second street.

Marcus saw the streetlight changing to yellow up ahead. He keyed his radio. "We'll act here. Get ready."

The light turned red. Greg in the lead SUV came to a stop. Connor's Lexus stopped behind him.

"Do it," Marcus ordered.

The SUV suddenly backed up right to Connor's bumper. Connor saw it happening and went to his car horn. Gage whipped the sedan around the van and crowded Connor's driver's door at the same time Bill pulled the delivery van forward to touch the back bumper of the Lexus.

Officers were out with guns drawn at all sides of his car before Connor realized it was more than just someone backing into him. "Keep your hands on the wheel."

Surprise had him obeying.

Marcus let Gage take him from the car, formally making the arrest.

"I'm surprised at the timing of your arrest." Connor smiled as his hands were handcuffed. "You would have been welcome to walk into my office and serve your warrants." He looked around at the slowing traffic, then back at Marcus. "All this street stop buys you is some bad press that you have to explain when I'm eventually released. You don't have enough to hold me. You've got what? That I was in the hotel? It took you long enough to figure that out."

Connor shouldn't be talking, but there was truth to the saying a lawyer who has himself as a client was a fool.

"We've got Frank and an eyewitness," Marcus replied, making a deliberate move to shake the man up.

Connor blinked. His smile disappeared. And then he smiled again. A cold smile, thin, but a smile. "You don't have Frank, and your eyewitness will never testify."

It was a soft, distinct threat.

Marcus slammed Connor back against the car. "Who did you hire?"

Quinn and Dave leaped forward to pull him back. Marcus ignored them. He was looking into the eyes of the man who had killed Carl and Shari's father. Any doubt of that had disappeared.

"*I* didn't hire anyone."

Marcus heard the emphasis. Titus had made the hire.

"And if he doesn't get paid until a year and a day after your witness is dead, you are going to have a hard time linking the two."

Even Quinn paled.

"Dave, get him out of here." Marcus shoved Connor toward the waiting car.

"Marcus."

"I know, Quinn."

Only one man had that unique signature of payment. Lucas Saracelli. He didn't miss at two hundred yards. He didn't miss at four hundred yards. Dark. Wet. City. Country. It didn't matter. He had been on the international law enforcement agencies most wanted lists for the last twelve years.

"We've got to get her out of there. Fast. It's a cover that will never hold. And he's got a big head start."

Marcus could feel the fear; three teams on the ground would never hold. "Agreed. But where?"

"My ranch," Quinn recommended. "We want to avoid a fight with this guy, but if it happens, we had better have every advantage."

Lucas was sharing a beer with a flight attendant from Jamaica when the phone call came. The Washington, D.C., bar was noisy and packed, but he chose to take the call where he was. "They just picked up Connor in New York. The team was led by U.S. Marshal Marcus O'Malley. They flew in on a private jet."

Lucas smiled at the flight attendant. "Fine. Thank you for the call." He hung up and reached for another pretzel. Shari was somewhere in Kentucky, and her escort was now in New York. Interesting.

"Business?"

"Maybe. When's your return flight?"

"Seven."

"Then business can definitely wait until 7:15 P.M. I promised you an escort back to the airport."

She giggled. He liked the giggle. He set down the beer. "Come on. Let's dance."

SIXTEEN

Marcus took the call on the plane. They were on a private flight back to the house by the lake, having pulled together as many men as they could within an hour. "Yes, Dave."

"The search warrants have been served on Connor's office and home. We got some interference from the staff on duty at his home but it's been dealt with. We managed to get the surprise we hoped for, but I'm afraid that is all we've got going in our favor. The crime lab technicians are taking the place apart but so far there is nothing that can be directly linked to the crime. The two house safes are empty; the three weapons registered to him are accounted for and don't match."

"We need something, *anything.*"

"We're working it. Just focus on Shari. I promise you, now that we've got Connor, we are going to turn his life inside out. If there is evidence here we will find it."

"Frank?"

"No sign of him. I've got a bad feeling about him, Marcus."

The reality that he might have already skipped town was very real. "Put the warrant out on the wires so if he is traveling in the U.S. we'll have a chance of learning about it."

"It will be out within the hour," Dave assured. "Stay in touch and let me know when you get in."

"I'll call as soon as we land," Marcus confirmed, and said good-bye. He closed the phone and looked back at Quinn. The lack of evidence was a serious problem he would wrestle with later, they had an even more serious one to deal with. "How do we stop someone who has no stop button? Once a hit is accepted, it can't be withdrawn with this man."

"Do you think Connor could have hired him?"

"No, he doesn't have that kind of money. It had to be his father, Titus."

"Can we crimp Titus to the point he won't be able to pay so the guy will make the decision on his own to back off?"

"We'd have to seize the entire operation. To do that we need inside information. If convicted of the murder of Judge Whitmore, the only way Connor could avoid the death penalty, avoid dying like his brother, would be to cut a deal and talk about his father's business. But he won't talk unless he thinks he will be found guilty, and he's confident Shari will never testify."

"A vicious circle."

"We've got no choice. We'll have to stop Lucas."

Marcus rarely felt fear such as he did now. Lucas could have been in the States looking for Shari for as long as a month. The lake house wasn't safe; nowhere truly would be until Connor, Frank, and Titus were convicted and sentenced. The escalation this represented was horrific.

In all his years as a marshal protecting witnesses he had never faced a challenge like this. That it was affecting the woman he loved…he forced aside the emotion lest it paralyze him. "He could have entered the country anytime since July 8."

"Titus had to get in touch with Lucas somehow in order to establish the terms of the contract. Maybe we can get a lead on him through that."

"If Titus went through his contacts in Europe to make the arrangements we may never find it. We might have a better chance locating Lucas from the sniper rifle he's going to need to acquire once he is here in the States. The one thing we can be certain of is that it will be custom made."

Marcus pulled out a pad of paper. "Walk me through the security arrangements we can make immediately and over the next few weeks at the ranch."

"Assume he learns Shari is at the Montana ranch: He then has to get to the ranch—by air, by car, across country by horse, or walk in by foot. So that's our first line of defense. We'll start with arranging for the county sheriff to close the bridge over the Ledds River. They've been discussing the need for repairs for the last four months, so local residents will not be surprised. That will make any traffic approaching the ranch from the south stand out and give us a chance to track it."

"How do we deploy the security detail?"

By the time the plane touched down at the airport near the lake house, they had worked out a security plan for the next several days. It wasn't sufficient, nothing really would be, but it was a workable plan.

On the drive to the house, Marcus tried to work out what he would say, and how Shari might react to the news. How was he supposed to break the news there was a paid contract out on her?

They arrived back at the lake house at 9:20 P.M. Marcus left the others fanning out behind him to cover the grounds and strode toward the house.

"Marcus!" Shari scrambled from the couch in the den to come and meet him. "He was arrested? You got him?"

"We arrested Connor." The relief that crossed her face was obvious, intense, and complete—and he was going to destroy it. He grasped her hands, cushioned them tight between his own. "Shari, get your things. We need to leave."

Her relief changed to confusion as his expression registered. "What's wrong?"

He stopped her words with fingers across her lips. "I'll explain later. Go. Pack what you can fit in one bag." He had decided the best way to handle it for now was to simply duck the question. Josh came from the kitchen and Marcus took advantage of it. "Josh, we need to talk." He nodded toward the den.

Beth was in the doorway of the den, a book in her hand, listening. Marcus crossed to her side, leaned down, and kissed her cheek. "It's good to see you. Help Shari pack? I'll explain in a few minutes."

She nodded, worried. "Of course, Marcus."

"It will be all right," he reassured her.

He strode through to the privacy of the den, Quinn joining him.

Josh closed the door behind them. "What's going on?"

"There's been a contract put out on your sister."

Josh absorbed that hit, his eyes widened and then hardened. "Can you keep her safe?"

"I won't let someone get to her." Marcus paced the room, anxious to get moving. "We need to get her out of here though. She's been stationary too long and we need someplace more isolated than this."

"You've got to tell her."

"Tell me what?"

Marcus turned, frustrated. Shari had ignored his request. He wanted her packing. And definitely not hearing the details now.

"Marcus, tell me."

He looked at Quinn and realized he had no choice. "Shari, sit down."

She complied only to the extent she perched on the arm of the couch. "What is it?"

He hoped she didn't panic. "Connor's family wants you dead. They've put a contract out on you."

She looked confused. "He's already tried to kill me twice. This is a surprise?"

"This time someone was hired to do it. We need to get you out of here."

"You're afraid."

"I'm…concerned. The man they hired is good."

"You're better," she replied bluntly, catching him by surprise. She surged to her feet. "We split up. I don't want Mom near me."

Josh looked over at him. Marcus had to agree with Shari on this one. They were going to need to move fast, and he was very concerned about Beth's health if things got serious. He couldn't guarantee medical help would be nearby.

It was clear Josh didn't want to leave Shari's side, but he reluctantly nodded. "Aunt Margaret's in London. Can I take Mom there?" Josh offered.

Marcus looked at Quinn. "Safer than staying in the States," Quinn agreed. "By the time their flight lands, we can have security ready."

"Josh, it would probably be best." Marcus paced over to stand beside Shari. "I'm sorry."

She shivered. "He's arrested, and I'm in even more danger."

"He's getting desperate." He wrapped his arm around her shoulders. "Trust me, this is almost over. Now go pack. We've got to go."

"Tell me about the man who was hired."

Marcus looked up from the very old photo of Lucas he was doing his best to absorb and update. The private jet was cruising at thirty thousand feet. Shari had moved back to join him. Her voice was pitched low, for around them the security teams of men were working. It was after midnight. He nodded to the seat beside him. "Have a seat."

He waited until she was seated and strapped in, then slid over the sketch he was working on. "His name is Lucas Saracelli. We don't have anything recent."

"You said he was good. Why? What makes him good?"

"He's a patient man. He doesn't leave a trail behind him. And he doesn't need to shoot twice."

"Then I'm not really safe."

"Not if he can find you, get close. We're going to make sure that doesn't happen." He reached over and squeezed her hand. "We don't want a fight with this guy. We simply want to lay low until the grand jury can be impaneled and you can testify."

"And the trial? It's going to be months away."

"We'll cross one milestone at a time."

"I'm afraid, Marcus."

"I know. It's justified." He ran his fingers through her hair. The fear he felt was intense for her, but he wasn't going to let it show. "I won't let anything happen to you. That's an O'Malley promise. My promise."

She leaned over to rest against him. "Thank you, Marcus." She snuggled her head down against his shoulder. "And to show how much I trust you, I'm going to catch a catnap. Wake me when we get close to wherever we're going."

And I wonder why I love you. He leaned over and kissed her forehead softly. "Sleep well."

He watched her drift to sleep.

Jesus, I wish I could trust You with her safety. She's now as important as any O'Malley to me. She's got a lot of courage, and she's trusting me not to let anything happen to her. Quinn and I know how good Lucas is. I'm going to need help.

That's my reality, Jesus. Are You as invested in my family and Shari as I am? That's my line. It's not one particular prayer, any one answer; it's a settled, absolute bedrock confidence that I can trust You with the people I love.

Show me the way back.

Shari looked down on the ranch as they descended to the private airstrip at dawn. She hadn't asked where they were going; had been surprised when twenty minutes ago Quinn had moved to the seat beside her, pointed out the river below, and indicated it was the start of his ranch land.

"Quinn, how do you ever leave here? It's beautiful." The ranch below was rolling hills, large stretches of timber, and a lot of pastureland. She could see the cattle from the air.

"Someone has to stick with Marcus to keep him out of trouble."

She heard the humor but also a lot not getting said. She liked Marcus's partner, but even after spending weeks with him, she had learned very little about him. Marcus trusted him absolutely and that was enough for her to do the same.

The plane set down on the airstrip and taxied toward an open door hangar with a Cessna inside. They were about a half mile from the ranch house she had seen from the air. When the plane came to a stop, Shari unbuckled her seat belt and gathered up the one bag she had with her and her briefcase.

"Stay inside for a moment," Marcus cautioned.

She waited for them to secure the area.

"Okay, Shari." Quinn offered her a hand down the steps as she left the plane. "Welcome to my home."

She looked around, curious. "Thank you for offering such a wonderful hiding place."

"It's my pleasure. Let's get you under wraps."

The security detail with them had already fanned out.

A truck pulled up. Shari dropped her bag in the back and got into the passenger seat as Marcus traded places with the driver. He turned the truck toward the house. "I need to explain a few things if you're up to it."

She looked over at him, seeing the intensity, and nodded. "Of course."

"Quinn has a number of ranch hands who will be patrolling the boundaries of the ranch, but it's open land. So what we're going to do is establish a very tight perimeter around the house, out at about five hundred yards. Inside of that will be constant patrols. I'm afraid it's going to mean you see a lot of the ranch house and not much of the ranch."

"I'll cope. Just tell me what you need me to do. I don't want any of you getting hurt."

"Trust me. We'll be fine."

They passed several large barns and a stable on the way to the house. She would love it here had she been able to visit under other circumstances. There were horses in the pasture near a barn.

Marcus parked in front of the house and came around to help her down from the truck. Shari walked beside him to the house. The one-story ranch house sprawled, breezeways and vistas connecting together what appeared to be three different wings. Flowers lined the walkway, and hanging plants, spaced between white columns, decorated the porch.

Marcus held the door for her; she stepped inside and stopped. She found herself standing on the threshhold of a great room—open, spacious, gleaming with hardwood floors. It was as modern as any she had ever seen—Western, masculine in tone and furniture, but filled with art, both sculpture and oil paintings, the open room adding an enormous sense of calm coolness, as if the house had seen generations and stood unaffected.

"This is Quinn's home?"

"He can surprise you," Marcus replied. "I'll introduce you to Susan and her husband, Greg, later. They maintain the house and grounds when Quinn is away." He smiled. "Susan's responsible for the order you see. You'll like them, I'm certain."

Marcus gestured to the hallway to the left leading into a wing of the house. "It's best if you take the first guest bedroom. It doesn't have the best view, but in this case that will be an advantage."

Shari nodded and walked through to the room he indicated. There was a Spanish flavor to the decor in its bold color bedspread and the rugs on the hardwood floor; the furniture was heavy mahogany. "It's beautiful, Marcus. I'll be comfortable here."

"Good. Unpack. I'll check with Quinn, then I'll give you a tour."

She nodded and lifted her bag to the bed, opened it, and began putting items away. She was grateful that they had chosen a private home such as this for the next few weeks. The house was beautiful. It conveyed a calm and restful tone—if she had to be housebound, at least it would be restful versus stuck in the impersonal quarters of a hotel somewhere.

Marcus and Quinn hadn't chosen this place at random. They wanted to be on familiar ground they controlled. They were setting up for a siege. She pushed the disquiet of that thought away, stored her empty bag in the closet, and went to find Marcus. She found him in the kitchen, talking on the phone as he poured himself a cup of coffee.

"Shari." Marcus held out the phone. He smiled at her puzzlement. "Your mom."

She whispered a thank-you as she accepted it. It was wonderful to hear her voice. "I'm fine, Mom. It's beautiful here."

She settled into a chair at the table and spent fifteen minutes reassuring herself that Josh and Mom were safe, reassuring her mom of the same with her. When Shari was done, she smiled and held out the phone to Marcus. "Thank you. That was nice, for both of us."

"You're welcome." He hung up the phone. "Are you fine?" he asked quietly.

She took a deep breath and let it out, accepting for the first time since she had been told the news just what was being asked of her. "I'm not letting the man who killed Carl and my father off. I'll testify. Your job is to get me safely there. I'll do whatever you say is necessary. Courage I don't lack. Common sense, yes. Courage, no."

He looked over at her, not saying anything for several moments. "You've got backbone. I admire that. This isn't going to be easy."

She understood that. She knew she didn't understand the risks and danger as he and Quinn did, that he would never reveal most of them, but she understood the fact she would have the best security that could be offered. "No, it's not going to be easy. But it's the right thing to do. I'm stubborn that way."

"We had to rush you away from the lake house. I'm sorry you were not able to have more time with your mom. And Josh is already frustrated with the distance."

"We're a strong family; Josh will get over it, and Mom has every confidence in you, in God. She'll worry about my safety, but she'll cope."

He held out his hand. "Come on. Let me show you your new home."

Shari followed him through the house, taking her time to linger on the art and the books and the photos. "I would never have imagined this to be Quinn's."

"He finds items he likes and sends them back here. Some of the pieces are works of his mom's. She was a gifted sculptor. This house is a memory to her and the love of art she passed to Quinn. He doesn't take enough time off to enjoy this place as he should."

"Why is he a marshal when he has this ranch? Surely it's a profitable enterprise."

"It's one of the best in the state," Marcus replied. "Quinn has good reasons for the choice he made. And the ranch will still be here thriving when he wants to come back to it full time. His ranch manager is an excellent man, dedicated to this land."

Shari was surprised that Marcus chose not to answer her question, then realized Quinn had also made the same evasion earlier. A mystery there. She tucked it away to think about over the next few weeks. Spending time here would probably give her the answer.

"Come on, let me introduce you to Susan."

They found Susan in the kitchen starting breakfast. Marcus introduced her and Shari knew immediately from the warm welcome that she had found another friend. She asked if she could help fix breakfast, and Marcus left her there while he went to touch base with Quinn.

Shari was fighting fatigue by the time Quinn and Marcus came back to the house and breakfast was served. The sleep on the plane had been short and broken. She forced herself to eat something, then listened to Marcus and Quinn as they discussed the plans for the next few days.

She carried her plate back to the kitchen.

"Shari, go ahead and turn in." Marcus paused at her side, his hand rubbing the back of her neck. "I know you're exhausted."

She wanted to lean against him and just accept the strength he offered. She accepted reality. "Yes. But don't let me sleep the entire day away."

"Four hours. Six, if you're deeply asleep," he reassured.

She walked through the house to the guest room. She was surprised to see a large vase of red roses now on the nightstand. Shari crossed over to them and withdrew the card.

You are the best: courageous, brave, and funny. Remember that. Marcus.

She blinked back tears. The tenderness was overwhelming. She pulled one bloom from the vase. He was a wonderful man. Special. And she was in love with him.

She curled up on the bed, holding the rose, and letting the tears she had denied for so long fall, too tired to fight the sadness that welled up inside along with joy. Optimism was breaking against reality and shattering. She was going to get her heart broken again. His doubts would pull her away from her faith if she let her heart become fully attached to him.

Jesus, why does life just keep getting harder? I love Marcus. I want a future with him. She wiped away her tears. She was tired of being afraid. *Protect me. Protect Marcus.*

Was it possible to resurrect her dreams? For a marriage, a future? *Lord, You've instilled them in my heart. Let them come true. I want these tears to turn to joy.*

SEVENTEEN

"Dave, consider something," Marcus directed his request toward the speakerphone on Quinn's desk. "Connor waited nine months after the execution of his brother to kill Judge Whitmore. Why wait? Why wait nine months and then take the risk of shooting him in a place full of potential witnesses and cops?"

"The murder was planned only after Judge Whitmore emerged as a contender for the short list," Dave speculated. "Connor didn't want the judge who sentenced his brother making it to the Supreme Court."

"Exactly. But I think it's even tighter than that. Whitmore's name was floated months before as a potential candidate. Why didn't Connor act then? It makes sense now, knowing that Whitmore didn't make the original short list of names, but how did Connor know he wasn't going to make that list? It wasn't until Shari's brief appeared that the odds became good that Whitmore would be added to the list and have a good chance of being nominated." Marcus tapped his knuckles on the polished wood of the desk. "Connor is a lawyer."

Dave's voice hardened. "He somehow saw a copy of the brief."

Marcus had a sinking feeling that this case was going to link back to Shari's brief after all. "Find out. His law firm has a Washington office so it's not implausible that someone at the firm has a contact inside the Justice Department. Something put this man in motion; I want to know if he saw a copy of the brief or if we can establish someone told him about its existence."

"I'll put a high priority on finding out," Dave agreed.

"That's my one new observation since yesterday. What do you have?"

"Regarding the timeline, we've got a few more pieces filled in. We know Connor took a flight to Chicago the evening of July 5; he booked those tickets on July 1."

Marcus flipped open his notebook on the desk and added the details to the calendar clipped inside. "One day after we know Frank was seen at the hotel."

"It plays. Frank was the advance man; he determined a hit at the hotel would be possible, and Connor booked to come out."

"Connor is going to argue it was the merger discussions suddenly getting serious that caused the abrupt decision to be in Chicago," Marcus replied, thinking as the defense attorney.

"If we can show Connor saw the brief and then sent Frank out to look at the hotel, we can at least establish a pattern of conduct leading up to the hit."

"We've got motive—we have to nail down means. How are we doing at establishing Connor's movements at the hotel the night of the murder?"

"I just talked to Mike. They've found three people who can confirm he was in the banquet room when Judge Whitmore gave his speech, and two that will testify they saw him leave as the speech concluded. That's obviously significant. After that—the security guard confirms Connor was at the merger discussions late that evening. So there's an open three-hour window to nail down."

"What do Connor's hotel room door logs show?"

"They muddy the waters. The door to his hotel room opened and closed with a card key five times during those three hours. He claims to have been discussing merger details on the phone with a partner in New York, that he went to the vending machine, stopped to buy a paper, then set out a room service order for the next day. For all we can tell, it could've been Frank using Connor's hotel room and providing an alibi of activity."

Marcus sighed. "No surprise there; we knew they planned this in detail. He's going to have reasonable doubt alibis in place. Where are we at on locating Frank Keaton? Anything?"

"The last confirmation we have on his location is from an FBI surveillance tape taken at the Potomac Shipping Company. He was seen there on Wednesday, July 19, accompanied by another man who works for Titus."

"Two days before the shooting at the funeral."

"We haven't been able to turn up anything suggesting Frank's whereabouts after that. Assuming we are right and he did make the attempt on Shari at the church, he appears to have fled immediately afterwards."

"Or something happened to him."

"How Titus reacted to the failure is hard to predict. Word is out on the street to see if we can get a clue."

"What was Frank driving?" Marcus asked.

"I checked. It was a light blue sedan, not the SUV we've been looking for."

There was a tap on the door and it opened. Marcus waved Quinn in to join him. "Anything at Frank's home?"

"We could charge him on a few weapons violations; he has a small arsenal that is unregistered—ballistics is checking them against prior unsolved cases—but other than that nothing useful."

"Dave, we know who did it, we know why, there just has to be a way to conclusively prove it. I gather Connor is no longer talking?"

"Titus had a lawyer here shortly after Connor was brought in. Now that guy is someone who is scary. A check of his past cases gives a Rolodex of names for people you do not want to know. Connor has been strikingly silent since having a conversation with his new lawyer."

"Find Frank," Marcus decided. "It's our best hope of breaking this case open. And focus on linking Connor to that brief."

"Will do."

"Have they convened the grand jury?"

"It's set for Saturday, September 2."

Another nine days. Marcus was relieved it wasn't any longer. "We'll arrange to fly out the night before the grand jury testimony. I don't want to leave this secure site before I have to. Could you arrange to come out with Kate and Lisa? I want to review this case from top to bottom one last time. I could use the additional manpower for the flight east."

"Good idea. I'll see what I can arrange and call you back."

Marcus concluded the update call and leaned back against the desk. He was weary to the soul with the twists and turns this case was taking. He looked over at his partner. "It is not supposed to be this way. Someone murders a judge; we're supposed to be able to do something about it. They take out Shari, he gets away with having murdered a judge."

"She'll testify."

"If we can get her there safely," Marcus replied. "What else can we be doing to find Lucas Saracelli? There has to be something."

Quinn tossed his hat on the table. "Good question, Marcus. I wish I had an answer. We have at best an old picture; at worst one that will no longer be close if he's had surgery done. We know the unique signatures of his MO. But the rest is a bunch of maybes—possibly American born and military trained because of the type of rifle and ammunition he favors; a probable residence in Europe as most of his contracts have been there. The few clues from the scenes of his hits show he is a man who plans in great detail, studies the area before each hit, and takes as long as he deems necessary to fulfill a contract."

"I hate this."

"Do you want to move her again before the grand jury convenes?"

Marcus thought about it, then finally shook his head. "No, you're right about this being the safest place to defend. Moving her will only leave another trail that's fresh. I would rather have our trail go very cold on him."

Going over the problem again wouldn't get a different answer. Marcus pushed away from the desk. "It's late. You missed dinner. I'll let you get to it."

"Shari's in the library. You might want to stop by."

Marcus raised an eyebrow. There was an unexpected note of concern in Quinn's voice. "Thanks, I'll do that."

Shari was curled on the couch in the library. Without the lights on. That was a bad sign. Marcus leaned against the door frame, trying to decide what was best. She had become noticeably quiet over the last week and it hadn't been easy to draw her out. "You want company?"

His question startled her. She turned to look back, then reached over to click on the table light. "Sorry. Come on in, Marcus. I was just thinking."

He had misinterpreted the situation. He had been afraid she was fighting tears, but her voice was steady.

"What are you thinking about?"

"How much can change in a short time. A month and a half ago I didn't know you, there wasn't someone trying to kill me, I had a family intact."

Her tone of voice bothered him; it had a bitterness he had never heard before. But he understood her emotions so well, was glad in a way that she was finally letting heaviness bleed off rather than try to accept it. The stress of what had happened was still coming, was going to break her or refine her before it was over. And the fact she was letting him see the emotion was itself a sign of trust that was a gift to him.

"This was a day Carl always celebrated—the anniversary of his first day on the bench."

The memories—he understood so well how they would appear unexpectedly from the past and bring back the pain. "Shari—I'm sorry."

She sighed, rubbing the back of her neck. "Sit down, I could use that company." She tossed the unopened pad of paper and pen she held onto the couch beside her. "You choose the topic tonight. I'm pretty morose."

He chose instead to simply take a seat and share the silence.

"You want to know something funny?" Her voice didn't sound amused.

"Sure," he quietly replied.

"I'm really getting tired of chocolate ice cream."

It took a moment for it to sink in, and then he leaned his head back and burst out laughing. "Oh, Shari."

"What are the odds that you can get some pralines and cream ice cream out here in the middle of nowhere?"

"Are you sure you don't want something easy, like maybe fresh lobster?"

"If that was an offer, I won't turn it down." She turned her head, shared a smile, and then gave a sigh. "I miss my family."

"I know. I miss mine too."

"Did you hear from Jennifer?"

"She sounds very tired. They were doing another round of bone scans today." He reached in his front pocket for a folded envelope. "Here. I think you ought to see this."

She reached over and accepted it. "What is it?"

"Rugsby's ransom demand. My part of it anyway." She unfolded the note, bit back a grin, but not before he saw it. His suspicions had been right. Either Jennifer or Rachel had recruited her. "Now I wonder who gave them that idea?"

"It's just a sketch," she replied.

Marcus folded his hands across his chest and watched her. "Sure it is," he said softly.

"I have to admit, I'm not sure I'm up on my Snow White and the seven dwarfs, but which one does this make you?" She looked at the sketch of the character, then back over at him. "Sleepy?"

"Try Grumpy," he replied with a gentle threat.

She giggled. "So if all the O'Malleys got tagged with a seven dwarf character as their clue, how does this get back Rugsby?"

"Turn it over."

"*'Deliver Snow White to me or Rugsby dies. Signed, The Wicked Witch.'* Ohh, this is good. Who's Snow White?"

"Guess."

She looked at him, then looked back at the note, startled. And then she started laughing as she held up her hands. "No way. I'm not getting in the middle of this. Your family makes jokes an art form."

"You started it. Grumpy indeed."

She passed back the note. "If I'm stuck here, you can hardly be expected to deliver me on the date specified. Who's the Wicked Witch?"

He folded the note and slid it back into his pocket. "At the moment I could label just about any of the O'Malleys with that title," he replied dryly.

She had a hard time stopping the laughter. "Marcus, I needed that."

"We both did."

He relaxed on the couch and simply watched her. "This will eventually be over."

"Not soon enough." Her expression turned sad again, tired. "I've been praying for patience. So far it hasn't worked. Or maybe it has and I'm just having to learn to appreciate the answer."

"Just take it a day at a time, Shari. That's all you can do."

She picked up a document from the stack beside her. He recognized her now dog-eared copy of the brief she had written recommending Carl for the court. "I can understand the hatred that drove Connor to kill. But I don't understand why he followed through with it when he did, where he did."

"Shari, trying to understand Connor's rationale—it will never really make sense."

"Was my family part of his plan?"

"No."

She looked over at him, moodily. "Did he want to make a public statement? Is that why he killed at the conference and not back in Virginia?"

"We don't know," he said quietly.

"Carl was killed because he was going to make the short list. Daniel had been dead nine months. The timing had to be significant."

He wouldn't lie to her, but he wouldn't support a conclusion that was only a speculation, not when it would hurt her. "If he chose the conference for any specific reason, it may simply have been for the confusion and the time it gave him to escape. We have no reason to believe he ever saw your brief, that he had any way to know Carl had made the short list."

"But you're looking for that link."

"We're looking."

Marcus watched with concern as she set aside the brief and leaned her head back to look up at the ceiling. How he wished he could strip away the pressure and give her some peace.

"Marcus, how do you cope with the sense of incompleteness? The sense that their lives were cut short? Both Carl and Dad? Time keeps running across events. It's not just the holidays and birthdays, it's the baseball games we had tickets to go see, weekend vacations we had planned."

"You loved them, Shari. There is no way to remove that void."

"I know God wasn't surprised. But it doesn't feel like there was much preparation beforehand for the shock that hit. I know it wasn't an accident that had you and Dave and Quinn close by to help, but it's so hard to accept I will never see Dad or Carl again. I still wake up of a morning and for a moment think everything's fine, then remember."

"It would worry me most if you didn't have this grief coming through. Do you still dream about that night?"

She grimaced. "I've been shot in my dreams so many times I think it's like a repeating tape."

"I wondered."

"The dreams no longer make me panic. Maybe that's progress."

"It is. Good progress."

"How long will it last?"

"Months, maybe years. I think your prayer for patience is the right one. You need time for the grief to heal, time for the memories to fade in sharpness, time to adjust your expectation for the future. Be gentle with yourself; you'll make it."

She gave a slight smile. "At least here there is plenty of time to pray."

"I envy you your ability to believe," he said abruptly, reopening a subject he had avoided talking about for the last week. He was searching for his way back, but it was hard. He had been rereading Luke. It was so hard to set aside the doubts. He just wanted some peace back in his life.

She looked over at him, curious. "Marcus, why do the O'Malleys trust you?" She let him think about it for a moment, then answered her own rhetorical question. "They chose to trust you. You can lead them into harm's way and they'll charge behind you without question. You know that, which is why you carry your responsibility so seriously. That's all I'm doing, choosing to trust Jesus even if I don't understand what or why something is happening. Jesus wants you to choose to trust Him again. He won't take that trust you place in Him lightly."

"Have you settled your turmoil about prayer?"

"Part of it. I've at least settled my confusion on how to pray. Mom quietly trusts and accepts what God does; I want a specific answer and I pray with passion for that. I always thought my problem was that I had to be like Mom, and I'm not made that way. An issue that matters to me inevitably becomes something I am passionate about."

"What did you learn?"

"Jesus was both. A simple answer, I know, but realizing it was a profound change. Jesus was both trusting and passionate. He brought His petitions with loud groans and tears. He acted like Elijah. 'The prayer of a righteous man has great power in its effects.' Wrestling powerful prayer. And conversely, there was the contentment of knowing He was speaking with the Father who loved Him. *'Father, I thank thee that thou hast heard me. I know that thou hearest me always, but I have said this on account of the people standing by, that they may believe that thou didst send me.'*

"I still don't have contentment over unanswered prayer, but I no longer wonder whether God loves me or if He hears me. If it's a prayer where I speak with passion, God's okay with that, and if it's the quiet trust of a child with a problem, that's good too."

"I'm glad you found some of your answers."

"You'll find your answers too."

"Trust isn't easy."

"Marcus, who's Jesus? What's His character like? Answer that, it will help." She rested her chin on the couch pillow she had picked up. "Can I ask you a personal question?"

Surprised at the change in subject, he nodded. "Sure."

"What do you dream about for your future? The reason I ask—I've had nothing but a lot of time to think in the last few weeks, about what is important, about what I want to do when this is over. Do you ever do that too, when you're stuck on assignments like this?"

What he said was important to her, he could tell from the way she was studying him as she waited for the answer. He hadn't talked about it much outside of the family, occasionally with Quinn. "I want to be director of the marshals one day. Move it forward as an agency, bring more mavericks like Quinn and Lisa in to help rein in the bureaucracy and keep the focus on the nuts and bolts of the investigations."

"You sound very sure of that dream."

"I know where I'm heading."

She glanced away. "What about personally? What about kids? I already know you like them. Do you want a family someday?"

He smiled at the way she tried to make her direct question indirect. *Yes, Shari, I would love to have a family with you.* They weren't at a place where he could say those words. "Absolutely. And I've thought a lot about someday adopting too. The O'Malleys would spoil them rotten."

"Six aunts and uncles. I can see what you mean."

"What about you?"

"I would love kids someday."

He heard the wistfulness. "You'd make a wonderful mom."

"Mom would love to be a grandmother."

She'd walked herself into thinking about her dad. He saw it when it happened. Quietness washed over her. He didn't try to break it. There would be no grandfather for her children.

He finally spoke. "Let it go."

"Yes." She looked across at him and changed the subject again. "I hope you don't lose Jennifer."

He didn't want to think about such a possibility, but he had to. He had to be prepared for it in order to be prepared to help his family. The sadness was overwhelming. And Shari understood it. He looked at her and felt the enormous emotions ease, just for being able to share them. "If the unspeakable ever happens, will you come to the funeral with me?"

She nodded.

"Thank you, friend." He wished he had the right to wrap her in his arms right now. And if he wasn't careful, he was going to say the wrong thing. "Come on, it's time you turned in," he wisely decided. She was not always going to be a witness. And that day was not going to come soon enough.

He walked Shari to her bedroom door and forced himself to simply say good night there. Rather than rejoin Quinn, he walked further down the hall to the guest room he was using. Out of habit he picked up the book on the nightstand, planning to read for a while, then sighed and set it back down.

He reached again for the Bible. Take one step forward, feel out if it was safe, then take another step. He felt like he was crawling back, walking on thin ice.

He was finally beginning to understand part of it. Those who believed, believed completely and trusted with abandon. His mom's happiness that he had basked in as a child had come from God. She had flourished in her faith despite circumstances—her spirit had been trusting, her smile always there. Decades later he was still grieving the loss of his mom. That was the most profound fact he had realized. It wasn't faith as much as it was grief. He had lost so much.

Who was Jesus? What is His character? Shari asked very good questions. He settled on the side of the bed and started reading where he had left off.

There would be a future with Shari, if everything worked out just right—he had to cling to that hope. His emotions were so involved that seeing that sadness in her tonight was overwhelming. He wished he could give her something to make the stay here easier. Missing family was something he understood only too well.

When he said Jennifer was doing as well as could be expected, he had been stretching the truth. Jennifer was in the fight of her life and she was at best only holding her own. It was the unsaid reality in Kate's voice, in Rachel's.

At least this ranch was like an island, an isolated spot.

But were their tracks covered deeply enough?

EIGHTEEN

Marcus let the roan he was riding pick the way down the steep slope to the streambed. Only a thin stream of water snaked down the center of the cracked ground. This tributary to the Ledds River showed the effects of the unusually dry summer.

The sun was hot, and after two hours of riding his body felt the heat down to his bones. Quinn had already crossed the gully. Marcus sent the horse up the far bank, trying to ignore the crumbling dirt making the task difficult. He liked to ride, but he didn't do enough of it to be relaxed like Quinn and was still working out a relationship with this particular mount. Quinn's definition of broke for riding was not necessarily his.

The rolling pastures for most of the ride had given way to steeper hills, and ahead were the bluffs that cut through the south edge of Quinn's land. Bluffs that Marcus had walked with Quinn numerous times in the past.

Bluffs and a grave.

Quinn reined in to wait for him, scanning ahead with binoculars and reaching for the rifle. Marcus drew up beside him.

"There." Quinn pointed.

Marcus took the offered binoculars and followed the indicated direction. There was a faint curl of white smoke lifting on the still air from a small grove of trees in the distance. The daily air surveillance had seen it that morning.

"We'll follow the riverbank to that outcrop of rocks and then approach the grove on foot from the east," Quinn decided.

Marcus nodded and slid out the rifle he carried. Sending one of the ranch hands to check this out hadn't even been considered. The odds that Lucas would give away his position with smoke were slim to none, but an ambush to get information, shake them up—that was possible.

They left the horses and worked slowly to the grove.

Marcus looked over at Quinn, he nodded, and they moved in, rifles ready.

The site was deserted.

It had been a campsite, the crushed grass and holes in the ground showing where a small tent had been pitched, a worn path going west showing the campsite had been active for at least a few days, a crude fire ring of stones held bits of charred wood. A coffee can near the fire ring was the source of the thin, waffling white smoke and it stunk. Marcus approached it cautiously, watching his feet for any trip wire around it. A handmade wick was burning down into something that was a muddy white.

"Someone's homemade bug repellent," Quinn concluded, looking at it.

Quinn walked over the log that must have been used as a bench and spread out a pile of sharp-edged stones beside the log with his foot. "He was cave spelunking. These are the discards he gathered but didn't want to carry out."

"Not Lucas."

"Not unless he was amusing himself by killing time."

Marcus walked around the site. "He didn't want to carry out the smoke pot."

"Not exactly the sweetest smelling thing to carry with him."

"He was here at least two, three days. How did we miss seeing him?"

Quinn snuffed out the bug repellent pot. "You can't see this campsite from the air without the smoke, and someone walking in, we're only going to see him by luck or if he crosses into one of our tightly patrolled areas."

Marcus turned back on his pager and opened his phone, called back to the house, and alerted Luke to what they had found.

"Let's ride back along the bluffs and make sure he's left, not just moved on to a new site," Quinn suggested. Marcus nodded his agreement. He would like to know who this guy was.

They walked back to the horses.

Quinn became grim the closer they came to the bluffs. Marcus didn't break the silence; he knew what this place represented. Quinn's father had been murdered at these bluffs—why, who had done it, those questions had never been answered. They rode for an hour along the bluffs in silence and saw no signs of anyone.

They turned back toward the house.

Marcus finished his third water bottle and tucked it back in the saddlebag. When the situation was different, he would like a chance to bring Shari out riding for a day. He knew she loved to ride, and so far they had been forced to limit her to the immediate area around the ranch house. And now it looked like he had better limit it even more just to be safe.

His pager went off. Marcus reached for it and looked at the number. Dave. Marcus opened the phone, called a secure number, and then called Dave. "Dave, it's Marcus. What do you have?"

"We've found Frank Keaton. He's dead. Two shots to the head, execution style. His body turned up in a landfill this morning, which means he was dropped in a dumpster and hauled out here. Based on location in the landfill and the condition of his body, it's likely he was killed shortly after the shooting at the church."

Marcus drew in the reins of his horse; his attention focused on the news he had already begun to suspect would be the case. "Connor knew Frank was dead when we arrested him."

"That would be my guess as well."

"With Frank dead, splitting Connor and Titus is going to be next to impossible. Do you think there's any hope the ballistics are going to match with the gun that killed Judge Whitmore?"

"Gut feel? No. They look like they are different calibers. I'll know for sure in a day when ballistics is done."

"Pull any resources you need to investigate Frank's death. If the murder case against Connor and Titus for Judge Whitmore's death ends in a hung jury, I want to at least be able to nail them for Frank's death."

"Already working on it," Dave replied. "I'll call with an update this evening."

"Thanks."

"Frank?" Quinn asked when Marcus hung up.

Marcus passed on the grim news. The importance of Shari's testimony had escalated. The remaining week to the grand jury testimony felt like an eternity. Where was Lucas Saracelli?

Marcus nudged his horse forward. "Let's get back to the house."

She had to talk to him. Shari stacked the cookies she had baked and moved them to the glass tray. She was doing her best to fill time and stay busy. Susan had been gracious about turning over the kitchen to her this afternoon.

Her attention was still on the phone call she had had earlier that morning with Jennifer. Tired wasn't adequate to describe the weakness Shari heard in Jennifer's voice. The chemotherapy was taking so much out of her.

The results were in from the bone scans and they weren't good. They showed the radiation had only limited the speed of the cancer growth but had not been able to stop it. Jennifer was in unusually low spirits. Her hope that the hospital stay was coming to an end had been crushed with the latest news.

Shari had to convince Marcus to go back to Baltimore. She knew he wanted to be there, knew as well that he would not easily leave here given the threat Lucas represented. She had to find a way to insist that he go. If she could only think of something in Virginia that would demand his attention—if he was traveling east for the case, he would swing north to see Jennifer.

She wished she could see Jennifer, share more than just a phone call. They had become good friends over the last few weeks. Jennifer was using what energy she had for the best things in her life: time with her fiancé, planning her wedding, her family. Shari hoped she had that same grace should she ever face such an illness.

Shari frowned as she slid another tray of cookies into the oven. Marcus would take this latest news hard. Jennifer had been trying to prepare him for the worse, but Shari knew he was nowhere near being able to accept that he might lose his sister. And if time was measured in months, not years, this time mattered intensely.

She heard Quinn's voice in the hall, talking with Susan.

Shari wiped off her hands, relieved that the guys were back. She didn't know what had called them out early that morning, but she had seen them mount the horses and arrange security so they could be gone for several hours.

"Marcus will be in soon," Quinn reassured her when she joined him.

"Everything is fine?"

"Absolutely. You've been baking?"

She gave a small smile. "Trying to."

"The guys will love you."

Marcus stepped inside the house. Shari could see the fatigue and wished she had better news to welcome him with. She crossed to join him and reached out to softly touch his hand. "Jennifer called."

"When?"

"This morning, about an hour after you left. She'll be in her room for the afternoon."

He nodded, rubbing the back of her neck. "Ice water first, I'm parched, then I'll call her back."

She was surprised when he rested his arm across her shoulders as he walked with her back to the kitchen. Something had happened that morning, enough to make him show the fatigue. "Can I get you something to eat?"

"I'd appreciate a sandwich."

"Roast beef and hot mustard?"

He held up two fingers. "I like your sandwiches."

He sampled one of her cookies as she fixed the sandwiches. "I hate to do this, but would you consider staying inside the house for the next couple days?"

She looked over at him. "Of course. Whatever you need me to do."

"We need to come up with a better plan for covering someone trying to come toward the house from the north."

She nodded. "Then I'll stay in the house."

He picked up the first sandwich and got to his feet. "Let me go call Jennifer back."

Shari thought about warning him to be prepared but didn't have the words.

He paused beside her, rested his hand on her forearm. "I talked to Tom and then her doctors late last night," he said quietly. "It's okay, Shari. I know what she was told this morning."

"You know?"

"One of the specialists from Mayo who first saw her was flying out last night to join her doctors, was due to get there midmorning. They are far from reaching the end of what they are willing to try. This is only a disappointing turn, not an end in the road."

"I wish you could go see her. She sounds really down."

"Shari, she's worried about you and your safety; it's one of her first questions when we talk. We'll be back east soon enough and I'll be able to see her then.

Don't feel guilty about the timing of this. I made the choice to stay with this case. And my family was involved in making that decision. I've accepted that distance from Jennifer for a short time is part of it."

Shari heard the calmness and was surprised at it.

"Part of knowing how to lead the O'Malleys is knowing what to bring to the table that can help them. The doctor from Mayo can help as the next course of action is chosen. There are treatments that will help Jennifer; we'll find those ideas and people." He ran a hand down her cheek. "Trust me, we're only in the first round."

She relaxed. "Call her."

"Are you okay?"

She nodded.

"If you have a few extras, box some cookies. I'll arrange to get a package to her."

"I'd like that."

He selected another one and smiled. "Besides, these are good."

Marcus settled in the den to call Jennifer. He wasn't surprised when Kate answered on her behalf. "Hi, Ladybug."

"Marcus." He heard her smile. "Good timing, as always. Can you do us a favor?"

"Sure. What?"

"Arrange a delivery. We want Chicago-style pizza for dinner tonight. Two of them. Large."

He had to laugh. "I see your solution to this problem is starting with the fundamentals."

"Jen is eating like a bird and pizza sounds good to her. But it has to be good pizza."

"Don't worry, I'm already writing it down. I'll get two sent from Carla's packed in dry ice if you can find a place to bake them out there."

"Not a problem."

"It will have to be a late dinner."

"First flight you can arrange is fine. Jen takes a late evening nap so we can watch the late shows and get a good laugh."

"Ask her if Benny's cheesecake sounds good too."

"Hold on." A muted conversation went on. "Strawberry topped."

"Got it."

"Thanks, I appreciate it. You'll like the new specialist from Mayo Clinic; he joined us during lunch. He's from Louisiana, and he and Jen spent half an hour discussing hot Cajun cooking. Then they started talking about kids and he pulled out his wallet to introduce his favorite patients."

Marcus relaxed; a doctor, but also one comfortable being more than that. "I already like him."

"He spent over an hour with Tom and Jennifer going over the film from the bone scans of her spine." Her voice became serious. "They want to try radiation pellets around her spine."

He knew the details of that option; it wasn't his favorite, but he understood why it would be chosen over another chemotherapy cocktail. Jen would be looking at surgery around her spine, something that made him queasy, and then more radiation. "How did she take the news?"

"A lot of questions; she and Tom are still talking about the risks."

"I can't say I'm thrilled with them either." They would be taking the gamble that the radiation would destroy the cancer before it destroyed her vertebrae.

"I think she's waiting to talk to you before they make a final decision."

"Then pass me over and I'll add my two cents worth to this discussion."

"Coming up."

The phone at their end changed hands. "Hi, Marcus."

Marcus understood immediately why Kate had purposely stayed lighthearted and done the talking. Jennifer's voice was so weak he could hear her breathing easier than he could her words. The doctors had warned him to expect the weakness to continue until they were able to end this round of chemotherapy and give her body time to recover. "Hi, precious." He tried to relax.

"I worried Shari. Sorry."

"Jen, it's good for her to worry about someone else. She's thinking about you, not the mess here."

"Okay." There was a faint smile. "Let her worry."

"She was baking cookies to soften the word that you had called."

"Oh."

He laughed. Not every batch Shari had baked had been a success. "Relax. These were good. She'll send you some."

"Good." Her voice grew serious. "You sent a good doctor."

"A favor from an old friend," Marcus reassured before she could ask. The doctor was one of the best cancer doctors in the country, and his time was at a premium. Marcus had tried to offer compensation and had been turned down. "That bank robbery eight years ago where the kids were killed, I mentioned I got to know the local investigator quite well. Your doctor is his son."

"I liked him when I met him at Mayo; I like him even more now."

"I know he's suggested several options, recommended one. What do you want to do, Jen?"

"The surgery might cripple me."

"I know," Marcus said softly.

"And they'll need to do it in the next couple days. You won't be here."

"I know that too."

The quietness was that of twenty-year friends.

"Have the surgery," he said quietly.

"Will you carry me down the aisle if the worst happens?"

He moved the phone away so he could bite back tears and steady his voice. "Sure."

"I would ask Jack, but he would drop me; fireman that he is notwithstanding," she said with forced lightness.

"I'll walk you down the aisle or carry you. That's a promise."

"Thanks."

"You're welcome."

"No hair, so my wedding pictures will be interesting."

"Rachel will get creative. Trust me, you'll be beautiful."

"Of course. Besides, I've always dreamed about being size six for my wedding."

He had to laugh. The illness had not robbed Jennifer of her essential good humor. "Pick the dress out, and it will be my wedding present to you."

"That's charming of you."

"I'm a charming kind of guy."

Shari knocked softly on the doorjamb. Marcus was relieved to see her. He held out his hand and curled his around hers when she joined him.

"I'll tell the doctor yes."

Marcus's grip tightened on Shari's hand. "Do that, Jen. I'll talk to him in the morning for the schedule details."

"Would you talk to Rachel for me later?" Jennifer asked. "She's been too quiet."

"Sure, Jen."

"Tell Shari hi for me."

"I'll do that."

"Here's Kate back."

"Marcus."

He had to clear his throat. "I'm here."

"Call me after ten, okay?" Kate asked quietly.

"I'll call."

"Good-bye for now."

Marcus closed the phone, stared at it a moment, and took a deep breath. There was some relief just in knowing he didn't have to keep the carefully maintained calm in place for Shari. He had meant what he said earlier, about this being the first round of a long fight, but it was still an intense strain. He rubbed his eyes. "They're going to put radiation pellets in her spine."

Shari tightened her hand around his. "You'll be okay. All of you. How can you not go?"

He shook his head. "The other O'Malleys are there; I'm needed here."

She wanted to argue, then stopped and simply nodded. "Send her some orchids. Those you got for me last week were gorgeous."

He rubbed his hand across hers, then picked up the phone. "First things first. They want two Chicago-style pizzas and a cheesecake sent out for dinner."

"Do they?"

"Hmm." He was amused at Kate's request. "I think I've become their delivery man."

"I think they just want you to feel involved."

"Probably some of that too." He wrote down the number directory assistance gave him for the pizza place near Kate's home, then placed the call.

It never failed to amaze him what mentioning Kate's name could do in her neighborhood. Carla herself came on the phone to get the details and gladly volunteered to take care of the shipping arrangements. A brief second call took care of the cheesecake request.

"Unless you need to rejoin Quinn, why don't you come keep me company," Shari offered, tugging his hand.

"Doing what?"

"I thought I'd ice some of those cookies. You can watch, or do some too if you like. It will give you something mindless to do while you tell me what was going on this morning."

He didn't particularly want to be alone at the moment. He let her pull him to his feet. "Lead the way. As long as you promise not to make blue icing this time."

"But it's a guy color."

"I draw the line at blue food."

Marcus called Kate late that night after his final rounds, spent an hour talking with her about Jennifer's upcoming surgery, the details of the security arrangements he was making with Dave for the grand jury testimony, family schedules for the next two weeks. When he hung up, he walked to the window of his room to look out into the darkness, weary in his heart.

Two days from now his sister would be in surgery. He knew the pellets had a reasonable chance of killing the cancer, but the risks involved—he couldn't do anything to minimize them, that was what made the situation so hard to accept.

"Jesus wants you to choose to trust Him. He won't take that trust you place in Him lightly."

Shari's words echoed again. He wanted to be able to cross the hesitation and trust enough to pray, but he felt mute the closer he came to that line. He had believed and prayed for his mom and she had died. It wasn't logical, but thinking about praying for Jennifer brought a resonating fear that, in doing so, he would lose her too. The emotion wasn't rational. But it was powerful.

He had always thought in the mix of experiences each O'Malley shared from the orphanage that it was Kate who bore the worst scars from the past, that Rachel carried the most pain. He had never dealt with the reality of how strong his own memories still were.

"I miss you, Mom," he whispered as he traced a hand down the windowsill.

Jennifer would come through surgery strong, and this treatment would be effective. Shari was praying for her. That had to make a difference.

Why couldn't he just trust?

Because he'd made a deal with God so that his mom would live, and she had died. And inside his heart he was still an angry little boy.

Marcus sighed and forced himself to turn out the lights and turn in, trying to sleep. It did not come for a long time.

NINETEEN

"She's out of surgery?"

"In recovery," Kate confirmed. "They gave her something to make her woozy and used a local so her system wouldn't have to fight off the heavy sedation. Marcus, she's reacting to it like she's drunk. She's trying to sing nursery rhymes at the moment. They said it would wear off, which is a shame. I would kill to have a tape recorder right now. She's never going to believe me."

"What did they say about the actual surgery? Was it successful?"

"Better than they hoped for. Even Tom was smiling when he saw the film results showing the placements."

Marcus could feel the building relief. "And the risks? Is she moving her toes?"

"The biggest problem at the moment is she wants to get up and go for a walk. The local has removed any concept of pain, and her foggy mind clearly does not remember she's just had surgery. They've got her strapped down to keep her back still."

"Thanks for calling me immediately."

"No problem. Let me call Lisa and Dave. I'll brief you again once she's been moved from the recovery room."

Marcus hung up the phone. Shari was waiting, impatiently. She had been pacing around the house ever since word had come that Jennifer was going into surgery. "She came through just fine," Marcus said, taking away the worry for them both. "She's got good movement in her feet, the pellet locations look good, and she's in recovery."

"I'm glad," Shari said simply, her smile sharing the emotions that were hard to fit into words.

Marcus crossed the room, leaned down, and gently kissed her. "Thank you for praying," he said quietly, from the bottom of his heart. Jennifer was in better shape than he could have hoped for. Shari's prayers had really mattered.

"Marcus," she studied his face, reached up, and cradled it in her hands. "You are very welcome."

Quinn came down the hall and the moment of privacy was lost. Shari tightened her hands around Marcus's as she stepped away, then turned. "Quinn, there's wonderful news regarding Jennifer."

Marcus reread the interviews of those who had seen Connor at the hotel and finally admitted defeat. He had been over these interviews until he could quote them. As much as he wanted to find something the team had missed regarding Connor, it wasn't there. He closed the folder and dropped it on the floor.

"No luck?" Shari asked absently, not looking up from the book she was absorbed in reading.

"No."

He had to smile as he watched her. She was sitting with her legs draped over the side of the deep leather chair, the side table light turned on. He reached down for his sketch pad and pulled out his fine pencil. She looked beautiful tonight, truly relaxed.

He took his time with the sketch. She was inspiring him to improve his art, so he could try to do her justice.

An hour passed as he worked and she turned pages in her book.

"Can I see?"

He glanced up to see she had set aside the book. He didn't want to show her, but only because it would be to admit she had been the subject on more than one occasion.

He closed the sketchbook and handed it to her.

Watching her face to see her reaction, he knew exactly when she turned pages and saw the first portrait. She turned the pages more slowly after that.

She looked up at him. The one time he didn't want her to hide what she thought, she did. She slowly smiled. "I'm flattered, Marcus. You're an unfulfilled artist under that badge and gun."

Come on, Shari…what are you thinking? I've got my heart on my sleeve in those sketches.

"My mom loved to draw." He hadn't told anyone that but family.

She flipped to a blank page. "May I?"

Not sure what she planned, he nodded. She picked up her pen. Her sketch was done fast, with a hand that didn't stop, her confidence showing. She was an artist and she hadn't said a thing. That turkey.

"My contribution to your greatness." She handed him the sketchbook with a flourish.

It was a cartoon. A baby panda bear leaning over an artist's palette getting paint on his paws, curious. "You're good."

"So are you. And Marcus…I'm not that pretty."

"You're beautiful."

"And you've been listening to my mother too much. What did she have to say this evening about London?"

A well-done tangent, he let her get away with it. "Afternoon tea. She is very impressed."

"She gave me the recipe for scones."

"Want to try making them someday?"

"Only if you volunteer to clean up after the disaster I leave in my wake. Two hours of cleanup for one batch of cookies. They were good, but not that good. I plan to let another month go by before I consider stepping into a kitchen again. I never did get very domesticated."

"Shari, some of the people I like the most are Quinn, Lisa, and Kate. Enough said?"

"You've got a high tolerance for clutter."

"I would rather have a case solved, a bad guy caught, a standoff peacefully concluded. If the clutter bothers me before it does them, I pick it up. Besides, you're smart. You could learn."

"Like I can learn to tell directions?"

"Well—that one might take some time."

"You're being generous. I think it's an impossible cause."

"How's the speech you were working on this afternoon coming along?"

She winced. "It's my nightmare of the month. I thought I was done with fiscal policy and it's back to haunt me."

"What's the problem?"

"John's legislation hit what I call the cement wall—the opposition in the senate finance committee. It's on its way to crashing and burning. So...the cycle starts all over again." She shook her head. "It doesn't help that I don't understand John's insistence on the positions he's taken. Personally, I would change the legislation. There's a compromise sitting there to be taken, but neither side wants to be the first to move to the middle."

"So why don't you just write the speech you think should be given and see what John thinks? Your strength is persuading someone to your point of view."

"I work for him. I'm supposed to be writing his speech, not mine."

"So call it a proposal," Marcus replied. "He'll love it when he sees it."

"You've got more faith than I do."

"More confidence at least."

"Ouch. And I'd hate to let it be said that I ducked a challenge."

Shari crumpled page five of the speech, the sound sharp in the quiet kitchen, the paper yielding to the pressure of her hand as she pulled it in with her fingers and crushed it into the center of her palm. The words were too bold.

She started writing again on the next sheet of notepaper.

"What are you working on?"

"The proposal for John you talked me so sweetly into writing." She didn't bother to look up at Marcus; if she did she would never get her concentration back. It was 1 A.M. and she still had several hours of work to do.

"It's not going well?"

She grimaced. "It's going fine. I just can't see John ever moving this far from his present position."

He pulled out a chair. "May I?"

He had shown her his sketch. She passed over the text. "It's still rough," she warned, nervous.

"Relax. What I've read of your stuff is good."

He took a seat and in doing so totally distracted her. Jeans, an old sweatshirt, barefoot. She forced herself not to stare. He started reading. "Okay if I make comments?"

She nodded and he reached for his pencil.

He made a few notes in the margins.

When he finished and got up, he squeezed her shoulder lightly. "Good job. I'll be back after rounds."

She nodded and accepted the pages of the speech.

She read his comments. The one at the bottom of the page left her stunned. *Why aren't you running for office?*

She spun around only to find with frustration that he had already left.

Run for office. It was her lifelong dream. One her father had always supported for her future. It was like having someone suddenly shine a spotlight and illuminate a hope, long resting dormant.

She had to wait forty minutes for him to return. She heard him talking to Quinn in the front hall. Gathering her courage, she poured two mugs of coffee and went to join him.

"Thanks."

"All quiet?"

"All quiet," he assured.

He nodded to the living room and waited for her to have a seat before he sat down nearby.

"Why did you say that? About running for office?"

"You're a good speech writer. But you're not going to be content there forever. You were made for something more."

"I've always dreamed of being a legislator in Washington someday."

"So why aren't you? What are you waiting for?"

"You need to be married to run for Congress."

He threw back his head and laughed. "Shari, that's a cop-out. You'd make a wonderful representative. I'd vote for you. Go for it."

"It takes money."

"No. It takes friends. And those you've got." The warm smile hit her in a wave.

"You're serious."

"Yes, Shari, I am. It's a dream. I'm not in favor of seeing dreams die."

"You really think I could do it?"

"Think about it. You've got a work ethic that would put most people in the ground after a day. You know the state of Virginia; you know the issues inside out. You've got good political skills and the Rolodex to match. What do you need that you don't already have?"

She wanted to seize the suggestion, found it incredible that he was so strongly in favor of the idea. Was he that different from Sam? Or didn't he see them having a relationship beyond friendship in the future so it didn't matter what her career was? She was suddenly not certain of anything. "I'll think about it."

"Do."

She got to her feet. "You'll be up for a while?"

"Yes."

"I left the coffeepot on. I think I'm going to head to bed."

"Sweet dreams."

Shari nodded and walked toward her bedroom.

When she curled up in bed, she hugged her pillow and looked at the ceiling. Marcus had dug until he touched her heart, snugly wrapped inside her passion for work. What she did for John, what she dreamed of someday doing, it wasn't a job with her. It was how her heart beat. He had patiently found it and then watered it with a quietly written note at the bottom of a speech.

The hard part was figuring out how much of it he had done deliberately and how much of it was simply Marcus being who he was. She wanted to read into it something profound and hope it was true. Her heart was involved. She wanted this to mean something profound.

He had her heart in his hand. Did he even know that?

She loved him.

Marcus believes I can do it. The emotion was intense, the realization he was serious. To see that in his calm face, that confidence, it stunned her.

If I go for my dreams, do I lose a chance to have a future with him? He might not want a wife who is in politics. And I have to trust that someday he will change his mind and believe. I love him more than I do my dream. And I couldn't say that with Sam.

Jesus, I want a future with Marcus, and I want a political career. Are You telling me both are now possibilities on the table?

Tracking the private jet was only a matter of time and money and charm. Lucas had been a pilot since he was seventeen. He leased a piper cub and flew to New York, where he was just another pilot who liked to borrow a cup of coffee and chat. The private charter pilots and the maintenance crews liked to talk and they remembered planes like other guys remembered cars. Two weeks after Connor was arrested, Lucas had tracked the private jet the marshal had used back to Kentucky and from there west to Montana.

The chase was coming to an end. Lucas picked up the sniper rifle he had arranged to have modified, spent a day in the country sighting it, then he headed west.

Finding the plane they had used was a matter of searching the ranches in the corridor of the last known flight plan and locating the plane he sought. Most of the ranches had private airstrips, finding the right one was simply a matter of time. He found it on Wednesday, August 30.

He had changed planes, leasing from a private company the same plane the park service used to create their topographical maps. High-powered cameras mounted to the skids were recording every detail of the ranches far below. He flew high, straight, on a direct bearing to the next town, covering the airstrip and house in the morning, and that evening flew a straight return path mapping the approach roads, barns, and fence lines.

By morning the film was developed and tacked to the wall of the office he had rented. The hangar had been designed for privately flown twin-engine Cessnas, not the larger business jets, and the tail numbers were visible through the open hangar doors.

The dry summer and fall would make the trek in by foot slow but not particularly difficult. The security perimeter they had established was obvious from the air. Interesting. He studied the pictures and was pleased. This was not going to be all that easy after all. The cops guarding Shari knew what they were doing. He had always appreciated a good adversary.

He picked up the phone. "I've found her."

"The secret grand jury panel convenes on Saturday. Kill her before it convenes."

Lucas hung up the phone with a frown. Saturday. He'd just found them and they were about to abandon this place and fly back to Virginia. Wonderful. He would have preferred to have more time. Still, it could be done.

He looked at the maps. They did give him options. He would prefer to avoid that perimeter around the house. If they were going to be leaving, that meant the airstrip would be back in play.

He'd kill them at the airstrip. Kill them all so no one could interfere when he got up to walk away. He smiled. He might even borrow the plane. He could be in Canada before someone realized his witness had been killed.

TWENTY

Dawn was brightening the sky. The trees around the ranch house were silhouettes against the blue sky. Marcus leaned his sketch pad against the corral fence as he sketched the nearby stand of oak trees with color pencils.

"Aren't you cold? It's chilly out here."

He glanced to his right. Shari's hair was tousled and her eyes still sleepy. She'd come to join him for a sunrise; Marcus didn't miss the significance of that. "Good morning. Hot coffee helps."

She moved to lean against the fence beside him. "The sketch is pretty."

He was drawing the trees, determined to know each one in detail so he would know instinctively when something out there was wrong. There was no need to tell her that. "Thanks." He leaned over and softly kissed her good morning, wise enough to keep his hands full.

She leaned against him and kissed him back. "Nice."

"Hmm." She settled into silence beside him as he resumed his sketch. She seemed peaceful enough, but he noticed her hands were tight against the fence. "Bad dreams?"

"Vaguely."

"You want to talk about tomorrow and the grand jury testimony, the security arrangements we've made?"

"Not really."

She had been ducking the topic for a week. It made him uneasy, that absolute trust she was putting in him to keep her safe.

"I suppose I should go pack."

They weren't coming back here, and her disappointment with that was obvious in the way she had been dragging her feet in getting ready to leave.

"A change in location is necessary, Shari."

"I won't be seeing you as much."

"No," he said softly. He was tucking her away at Quantico, the FBI academy, for the next several weeks. She would be living in the on-site housing with the next training class. An unusual move, but it was there or a military base. It would be hard for Lucas to reach her, that had to be the deciding factor. They would drive her there each evening after her grand jury testimony, and she would be living there full time after that until Lucas was located. Marcus would be around, but it would not be the same. He didn't like the idea any more than she did.

She sighed. "What time are Dave, Kate, and Lisa arriving?"

"Shortly after 4 P.M. We'll fly out around 7 P.M." He wanted them arriving in the middle of the night.

"Okay. I'll be inside."

Marcus watched her walk back to the house. In the next twenty-four hours the danger to her life would escalate sharply. Lucas not appearing here during the last weeks had been a relief, but now it only coiled the fear Marcus felt tighter. Lucas might have chosen to spend all that time studying the courthouse, preparing to act there.

He looked back at the stand of trees, closed his drawing pad.

Jesus, I figured something out last night. He had begun to pray again early of a morning, cautiously, feeling out the words to reestablish what he had once had. It was a slow reconciliation. *The anger of being abandoned as a child—I didn't know where to direct my pain; You were near. I knew I could hurt You, and I tried my best to do so. I rejected Your comfort.*

You sent it anyway. You sent the O'Malleys. Only You could have figured out the combination that is this family. I'm coming to see that You never left me. But I've been trusting only myself for so long…

It's come down to crunch time. I need Lucas stopped. I can't do it on my own. I'm trusting You, Jesus. Not only with myself, but with Shari. Tell me what I need to do. I'm depending on You.

Marcus felt the buffeting wind as he stepped from the truck and watched the plane line up with the airstrip to land. The weather forecasters had been wrong. The storm front that had not been expected until late this evening was coming through much earlier. On the horizon the sky was dark and lightning could be seen.

Dave was the first one down the steps when the plane stopped. "We've been tracking the front with the on-board radar. We can still get out if we get the plane turned around and prepped quickly. Get Shari and Quinn and go now. If we wait, we could be stuck until late tonight, assuming we can even get out."

Marcus turned to scan the sky again. Storms, weather. Was it just fanciful thinking to consider the weather change as a show of God's hand? Shoving them out early, or telling him to wait?

Lucas saw the plane arrive. He had hiked in during the night and reached his chosen spot before dawn. The location was even better than he had hoped for: the slight rise in the land, the perspective below. He drew a bead down on the airstrip to watch this new development unfold.

He saw the men talking. In the crosshairs of the scope each man came close enough to touch. He recognized Marcus O'Malley from the newspaper photographs. The weather must have caught them by surprise.

He did not see Shari. But where Marcus was, Shari was not far away.

He felt anticipation build inside. They would be leaving before the weather closed them in. This was it. His hands settled the rifle into stillness. He mentally began adjusting for the wind and distance. The first shot would go for the cop nearest to Shari, confirm his adjustments and remove the only person who could help her. Shari Hanford would be dead before the sound of the second shot reached them.

Marcus saw lightning flash to the south. Dave was right. They needed to move now. Once the storms arrived, there was no telling how long the rain would last. And the airstrip would have to be checked afterwards for tree limbs and other blown debris. That could put them leaving well after dark. And if for some reason they couldn't fly out, they risked the downpour from the storm cutting off the road by flash floods.

But he felt...queasy...with the idea. He didn't want to move Shari out of the secure perimeter on this ranch until absolutely necessary. Arriving in Virginia early was simply too dangerous. Lucas was out there somewhere...waiting.

He shook his head. "No. We wait it out."

"You're sure?"

"Yes. I'm sure." His gut told him it was the safe thing to do. "Let's get Lisa and Kate to the house."

Lucas watched two pilots appear from the plane, start walking around doing their post-flight check. Two more passengers disembarked. The marshal talked briefly with the group. Lucas was surprised when they gathered up their belongings and moved to the waiting vehicles. They were going to the house.

They weren't leaving immediately? They had time to beat the storm front. He glanced at the darkening horizon, then back at the plane. The crew was preparing to move the plane into the hangar.

Wonderful. He was about to get wet.

Lucas withdrew a stick of gum from his pocket and unwrapped it. He could tolerate the rain even though he disliked it. He had worked in worse and it would give him good cover. It wouldn't affect a bullet. A few more hours, and this job would be over.

Shari would be dead.

He hoped she had an enjoyable last meal.

Marcus was relieved to see Kate, to hear firsthand that Jennifer was reacting well to the latest treatments, to have a chance to say thanks again to Lisa for the work she had done in the last few weeks. He led them to the house.

Kate and Shari shared a long hug. Kate turned and looked at Marcus, her arm still around Shari. "I don't know about the rest of you, but I'm hungry. Let's fix dinner and talk afterward," Kate suggested.

"What sounds good?" Marcus asked.

Kate grinned. "Pizza. We girls will make it, you three guys go talk."

Marcus looked at his two sisters, then at Shari. He sensed a girl talk conspiracy forming. "I don't know about this—"

Lisa pushed him toward the door. "Go."

Marcus went. He settled in the library with Dave and Quinn. They spent an hour reviewing the security arrangements for Shari's testimony.

"We'll keep her safe, Marcus," Dave reassured.

"Lucas is out there somewhere. He's going to have found out when and where the grand jury testimony will be by now. Is there anything we are missing?"

"We're ready, Marcus," Quinn agreed. He glanced at his watch and got to his feet. "I'll be out on the perimeter."

Marcus went to check on dinner.

He walked back toward the kitchen, following the laughter. He stopped at the door, couldn't stop a chuckle. Susan had turned the kitchen over to them; the place was a mess. There was as much sauce on Kate and Shari as there was on the pizzas.

"I thought you said you were going to make pizzas? This looks like a war zone."

"We're being...creative," Shari replied.

It was enough to set Kate off into another peal of laughter; it was obvious they had both crossed into the giggle zone where everything was funny.

Marcus smiled, for the laughter was contagious. Shari needed a little relief; it was absolutely the best thing in the world for her. He paused beside her at the counter and snitched a sample of the grated cheese. "Put green peppers on my half."

"Half?"

"I'm hungry."

There were four pizzas in the making, she scanned them. "With or without mushrooms?"

"Without." He pointed to the pepperoni pizza. "That one."

"Kate, did you leave onions off one?" Dave leaned around the doorway to ask.

She scowled—she hadn't—and she began picking them off the pizza she had just finished. "Just because you dislike kissing me with onions on your breath..."

"Your breath," he corrected with a grin.

"I hope you recognize what a sacrifice this is. I happen to like onions."

Marcus, watching the interchange, stored it away as a memory never to be lost. He liked seeing Kate happy.

"What kind of cheese do you want, Marcus?"

He glanced back at Shari. She had both provolone and mozzarella grated. He leaned over and kissed her. "Both."

"What was that for?"

"No reason." He'd just left Lisa and Kate speechless. He didn't know if Shari would appreciate him saying that. "Call us when the pizza is done."

Dinner was filled with laughter.

When it finished, they moved to the library, and the mood changed, turning somber. Marcus tugged Shari down beside him on the couch. It was still raining out, and it was time to talk about the case. "Lisa, you've got the floor. Take us through what we know."

"Do you want me to argue for the prosecution or for the defense?"

It was a telling comment. "Both," Marcus replied.

Lisa leaned back in her chair, folded her hands, and settled herself as she organized her thoughts. "On Wednesday July 5 Connor checked into the Jefferson Renaissance Hotel to hold secret merger talks under the guise of attending the judicial conference. We know he came to the conference for more sinister reasons.

"On Friday night, during the evening program, he slipped into Carl's hotel room. He shot Judge Whitmore when he came back to his room at 10:20 P.M. He tried to shoot Shari, did hit Joshua and William. He fled up the stairs to the thirteenth floor and entered room 1323. There he stripped off the hairpiece he wore and changed his suit and his shoes. "We think his planned celebratory drink turned out to be one of anger instead, for he hurled the glass—he was drinking Scotch by the way—at the wall and then had to clean up the broken glass. The guard at the fourteenth telecommunication center saw Connor at the merger discussions shortly after 11 P.M. He checked out of the hotel the next day at 10:14 A.M.

"What we have for evidence—in Carl's room: the shell casings, a thread from the shooter's suit, bloody shoe prints, the fact the shooter is left-handed. From room 1323—we have a trace of Carl's blood on the carpet, threads that match the suit, and blood on the glass slivers."

Lisa sighed. "Arguing for the defense—I can find a reasonable way to explain away all of our evidence. Without the gun, the hairpiece, the shoes, there is nothing direct. Even the DNA can be shot down because, one, there is not enough to repeat the test by the defense making it liable to challenge, and two, it doesn't say if it was Frank or Connor and that means reasonable doubt.

"The fact that Connor is clean, not even a parking ticket, and Frank is known to work for Titus and is dead makes it too easy to pin him for the murder. And Connor has an airtight alibi for when Shari was shot at the church, so that says it was Titus and Frank acting alone. Connor can argue he cut himself off from his family ages ago, and the beautiful thing is, he has."

"Nothing links Frank to Connor?"

"No."

"Can we prove it was Titus behind killing Carl?" Quinn asked.

"Not without Connor. And beyond Shari's direct testimony, we've got nothing else we can use as leverage. The case is circumstantial."

Shari sat forward on the couch, for the first time entering into the conversation. "My eyewitness testimony is the difference in this case."

"Yes."

"No wonder he wants me dead." She squeezed Marcus's hand. "When do we leave?" The rain was still coming down heavy outside the windows.

"Two hours, maybe three."

She got to her feet. "I'm going to go finish packing."

Lucas had long since accepted being cold and wet. As time passed he considered his options from all angles. He had hoped to see the rain come to an end before sunset but it showed no signs of abating. The airstrip below was deserted; the perimeter patrols around the house were doing their best to cope with the rain. And while he could wait this out, they couldn't. Shari had to be in Richmond tomorrow.

Would they decide to drive out, take a commercial flight? He had to stop her here.

He slowly rose from the ground, a dark shadow appearing where there had been nothing before.

TWENTY-ONE

Marcus leaned his shoulder against the doorpost of the guest room and watched Shari as she absentmindedly fingered a rose petal from the vase on the dresser. He tried to arrange for flowers to be brought in every week, partly because he loved to write the cards and partly because he loved to see that sparkle appear in her eyes. "You're welcome to take them with you if you like."

She turned and smiled, albeit slightly sad. "No, that's okay."

"Can I help with anything?"

She shrugged her shoulder. "I'm packed."

"Just not ready to go."

"No."

"You may get your wish. I came to tell you the storm appears to be getting worse." A rolling crack of thunder outside punctuated his words.

"I see what you mean."

"We may end up flying out at 2 A.M. I'm sorry for that. It will mean a broken night of sleep."

"Don't worry about it. I doubt I'll sleep much anyway. I'll need the distraction."

"Tomorrow is just another step toward justice. Don't be afraid of it."

"I'm not. I know you'll keep me safe."

He knew the words that would most reassure her. He meant them. "I'm also trusting Jesus to keep you safe."

She absorbed those words slowly, and then her smile blossomed. "That's progress, Marcus."

"Yes. Some." He let himself share her smile. "Ask me what I think in a month, by then it might have a little more confidence to it."

"It doesn't have to be a leap back, Marcus. Slow and steady is good too."

"Hand me your bag."

When she did, he closed his hand over hers and leaned down to gently kiss her, letting it linger. "Something to think about while you are tucked away at Quantico."

"Quinn should be back by now." Dave strode into the den where Marcus and Kate were watching the weather report. "He went out to walk the perimeter and he's not back."

Marcus instantly tensed and reached for his radio. "Quinn, come back." Only the static of the storm was heard. "Quinn."

He looked out the window to the darkness lit by the lightning.

He had made the same mistake at the church. It was a perfect night for a sniper. The house was lit up like a beacon. "Kate, kill all the lights except the living room and get everyone down in the cellar."

She was already moving, her pistol out and safety clicked off. "Where is it?"

"The breezeway built on behind the kitchen. Move aside the planters and you'll see the wooden doors of the old storm cellar. Dave, you're with me."

Marcus grabbed the dark jacket and cap still dripping from his last walk around the perimeter forty minutes ago. There were eighteen men on that perimeter. Quinn being off the air—he was down, or he was hunting. Marcus was heading toward the side door of the house, his nine-millimeter Glock in his hand, when he saw Shari in the hall walking toward him. The fear was intense. "Kate."

"She's covered. Go."

Marcus and Dave slipped out into the rain.

A cold hard-driven rain struck his face. Marcus blinked and waited for his eyes to adjust to the night. On any other night they would be patrolling with night vision goggles, but wearing them when lightning struck would do permanent eye damage. They had pulled the perimeter in to compensate. Good move or bad? It was too late to second-guess that decision.

Dave pointed west and Marcus nodded, then turned east toward the fence line where he had been sketching that morning, where Shari had joined him.

Jesus, don't let me down. I've got serious trouble here.

He ducked under the railing.

Quinn materialized beside him. "He's here. I saw him with a sniper rifle silhouette for a moment down by the hangar. He's working his way around the barn to get line of sight to the house. The perimeter is pulling back even tighter to the house."

"Good. Don't let him get past."

Quinn squeezed his shoulder and disappeared.

Shari found the sound of thunder muted by the storm cellar eerie. Marcus, Quinn, and Dave were out in this, not to mention the other men of the security detail she had come to know and like.

"Where two or three are gathered together…this counts," Kate said softly.

"Keep them safe," Shari said.

"Amen."

"What are you two talking about?" Lisa asked, curious.

"We'll explain later," Kate replied, sharing a look with Shari.

"What was that?" Shari was determined not to be the most nervous one of the three of them, but she couldn't help it. Something had just brushed by her foot.

Lisa found a flashlight on the shelf by the stairs, illuminating the dark, dry earth out of the reach of the one bare overhead bulb.

Shari took a rapid couple steps back. "That's a snake hole."

"Too big," Lisa replied, discounting that suggestion. "And not large enough for a gopher. Besides, look how dry and packed the ground is. It's abandoned."

She went poking around behind the storage shelves where boxes of canning jars were stored.

"Lisa, if we have company down here I would prefer not to know," Kate remarked.

"It's probably just a mouse," Lisa replied, tipping boxes forward to look behind them. Shari was relieved when Lisa wasn't able to find anything.

Lisa turned her attention to shining the light back in the crawl space that went under the breezeway. "Well, hello there."

She found a pair of thick tough work gloves and pulled herself partway up into the crawl space, reaching back. A moment later she wiggled back, holding something in her hands.

"Yuck," Kate said flatly.

Shari found herself looking at a mole. It was horrifyingly fascinating.

"He just came inside to get out of the rain. His tunnels must be filling up with water," Lisa said, looking at the six-inch smooth furry animal, holding him firmly. "Did you know a cat would catch him but not eat him? He's too bitter."

"I can see why," Kate replied.

"I've never had a mole before."

"You're going to keep him?" Kate asked, then shook her head. "Never mind, of course you are."

Shari found a shoebox being used to store candles and emptied it out. "Lisa, will this do?"

Marcus's sister looked at her, grateful, then carefully put the animal inside. "Thanks."

"He is kind of cute."

Lisa grinned. "I think I like you, Shari Hanford. I'm going to name him Charlie."

Thunder rumbled overhead. The humor disappeared. "I sure hope this cellar doesn't leak. That rain is pounding down."

"It's dry. Just look at the cobwebs."

Shari turned a crate over and tested it, then took a seat. "Kate, could I tell you a secret?" She had waited for just the right moment.

"Sure. I love secrets."

"Did you know Marcus hates broccoli?"

Small rivers of water were cutting into the sun-baked land of yesterday, running across Marcus's boots as he moved through the darkness. The driving rain covered the sound of his movements...and those of his adversary.

He worked his way from the house east, slipping into the trees he had sketched that morning. The branches and leaves blocked some of the rain, transforming the storm into heavy raindrops and a deafening assault of sound. It was a dangerous place to be not only because of the lightning. Lucas would have to come this way in order to get line of sight on the living room and the one remaining light on in the house.

He reached the oldest of the oak trees and put his back against it, eliminating his silhouette, listening intently. Locating a man in this...

A shot rang out.

Kate surged from her seat, heading for the steps out of the cellar. "That was a gunshot, not lightning."

Lisa grabbed her from behind.

Kate tempered her instinct to throw an elbow since it was family, tried to break free, only to have Lisa literally try to lift her off her feet. "We wait," Lisa insisted.

"That was close to the house, now let me go."

Lisa just tightened her hold. "No. I can't keep Shari safe like you can. I'm not as good a shot. Dave is fine, Kate. Dave is fine."

"You don't know that," Kate whispered, breathing hard but stopping the struggle.

"He's too stubborn to get killed."

Shari tentatively touched her arm. "Marcus and Quinn...with Dave they're practically the three musketeers. They'll cover each other's backs."

"They'll try," Kate said grimly. Lisa let her go, and she paced away from the stairs. "I hate waiting."

Lucas was picking off their perimeter guards. As a tactic, it was an effective one. Marcus's heart pounded as he ignored the radio traffic over his earpiece. Others were helping the injured man. He focused on putting himself between the shooter and the man that had gone down. The movement made him a target, but it couldn't be helped.

Lucas was close. Already south of the house.

Marcus reached the edge of the trees. Lucas could pick them off; they could also pick him off. As a plan, it left much to be desired, but it would work. At this point, that was the only thing that mattered.

He needed a place to wait out Lucas. And this wasn't it. He wanted to be situated so Lucas would have to literally go over him to get to the house.

He stepped from the tree line. Lightning struck close, hitting and exploding a tree on the ridge. Marcus dove for the ground as another shot rang out.

That one had been meant for him.

At least he now knew with reasonable certainty that Lucas too had set aside using a nightscope because of the lightning. One man injured instead of killed, an actual miss…Lucas was using the lightning to establish his shots; he would have never missed otherwise. Marcus said a silent thanks for small favors as he spit mud out of his mouth. That had been too close for comfort.

He crawled toward cover. Lucas was directly south.

A single click over the earpiece alerted him to company. He cautiously turned his head, scanning, and a shadow behind him to the right lifted a hand. Dave had joined him.

Marcus pointed to the knoll ahead, his best guess. Lucas had moved to the high ground. Dave nodded.

Eighteen minutes. Marcus had counted every second. He knew where the man was; he'd actually seen the muzzle fire of the last shot. Patience. Lucas would move to change locations or he would try to shoot again.

Stretched out on the ground with his gun sighted on the knoll, Marcus waited. Water rushed in the front of his shirt, his body acting like a dam in the way of what was becoming a river. The wind was easing up, the intense storm cell drifting east, but the rain had intensified. It pounded on his back, his jacket now a heavy weight. There was not an inch of him that was dry.

They had triangulated on Lucas, Quinn taking the left flank, Dave the right. It would be possible to flush him out if Marcus were willing to use the other agents, but it wasn't worth another injury and possibly the first death.

He'd wait.

Because he wasn't going to lose.

If he made a mistake, he was dead.

There was nothing like a foxhole to focus one's heart and mind on what really mattered.

What was really true.

Jesus, please be my Savior again. You've waited a long time. I'm back, and I'm all Yours.

He relaxed, finally at peace.

Lightning spidered overhead between the clouds. The light illuminated a man lifting from the ground. Having sketched that face so many times it took only an instant for Marcus to confirm an identity. Taking him alive wasn't even considered. Protecting a witness came first. Protecting those he loved. Marcus pulled the trigger.

The shot knocked Lucas back and down.

Shaking slightly that he'd actually caught Lucas moving, Marcus rose from the ground and tightened his grip on his weapon. He held it in both hands in a shooter's stance as he walked forward with care, expecting to have to react. He didn't trust that stillness.

Quinn joined him. Lucas had crumpled on his side. They stood in silence as rain beat down on them. Quinn knelt and closed the man's eyes. "It's a shame he ever went bad," he said heavily. "Had he worked on the right side of the law, he would have been one of the best."

"He just about got through." Marcus holstered his Glock. He bent to retrieve the sniper rifle, carefully cleared the chamber. The hollow point would have been lethal had Lucas been able to draw a bead on Shari.

Jesus, it was necessary. But I'm sorry.

Quinn accepted the rifle. "Ask Lisa to join me with her cameras. Dave and I will put together the case scene notes then get your statement. You can't help, and Shari doesn't need to see this."

Marcus knew he was right. "I'll get them. The men?"

"Brad hit in the shoulder, Gary in the arm. They'll recover."

And Lucas Saracelli was dead. Shari was safe for now. Marcus wasn't sure what to tell her. It had been necessary to kill, but it hurt. Would she understand?

Shari started at the thud from above. Kate shoved her back against the dirt wall and the cellar shelves, her pistol coming up, sighted. Four knocks, a pause, and two more came sharp against the wood, and then the large wooden doors swung open. "Don't shoot me, Kate," Dave protested. "You ladies okay down there?"

"Fine," Kate replied dryly, lowering her pistol from a direct bead on Dave's face. "But Lisa has found a new pet."

Shari shook slightly as the relief settled across her. The wait had been horrible. They stepped out of the back shadows into the light of the one bare bulb as Dave came down the six wooden stairs. Kate was now acting as if it hadn't bothered her, and Shari silently shook her head at that even as she understood it. Lisa opened the shoebox lid so Dave could glance inside. "That is not flying back on the plane with us."

"He's just scared."

"Sure."

"I think he's kind of cute," Kate commented, coming to her sister's defense.

"Cute," Dave replied, doubtful.

Lisa moved to the stairs. "What happened? Is Quinn okay? Marcus?"

"Let's talk upstairs," Dave replied. He stepped back to let them precede him.

Shari was grateful to leave behind the claustrophobic reality of being underground. She found Marcus in the kitchen, wiping his face dry. His expression was grim. "What happened?" she whispered. "Where's Quinn?"

"He's fine." Marcus held out his arm, and she accepted the silent invitation, not caring that he was dripping wet. He wrapped both arms around her, hugged her close. "Lucas is dead."

She froze. "He was here?"

Marcus rubbed her back. "Quinn spotted him when he was making the rounds."

"Who killed him? Quinn?"

"I did."

Marcus had shot someone to keep her safe. She rubbed her cheek against his wet shirt, seeking to add warmth, seeking to comfort, knowing how awful that must be to deal with, and feeling ashamed at the relief she felt. "I'm sorry you'll have to carry that."

"I promised I wouldn't let anyone hurt you."

"I'm grateful. The others? We heard shots."

"Two injured, they are going to be fine." He eased back, saw her worry. "It could have been much worse," he said softly. "Let it go."

Lisa had joined them. Marcus reached over and squeezed Lisa's shoulder. "Quinn needs your help."

"He actually asked for my help?"

"He did," Marcus confirmed, smiling slightly. "Go enjoy it."

"I will." She lifted the box in her hand. "Could you watch Charlie for me?"

"What did you find?"

"Another friend. Dave isn't so sure about letting him fly home with us though."

Marcus opened the lid to look inside, then raised one eyebrow. "Got your backpack?"

She nodded.

"Tuck the box inside. Quinn will smuggle him back for you."

"Think so?"

"Oh, I think so."

She sighed. "If he keeps this up, I may just have to change my mind about him. Then life will get boring."

Marcus took the shoebox. "Somehow I don't think that will happen."

"Let me go get to work." She kissed his cheek. "Shari, get him some coffee to warm him up. Unless you can think of a better way."

Shari blushed.

Marcus laughed and swatted Lisa's arm. "Go on. Quit embarrassing my girlfriend."

"Girlfriend?" Shari whispered as the kitchen door swung shut.

He carefully set the shoebox down on the table, his startled look confirming he hadn't meant to say it that way. "Got a problem with that?"

"Well—"

"Oh, now I'm getting that grin that spells danger. What are you thinking, minx?" He linked his hands behind her back, his hold light, his gaze frank and appreciative.

"Do cops have girlfriends who are politicians?"

"This one does."

"No, let's think about it."

"Honey, I have. And if you haven't, we've got to talk about your lack of thinking ahead. I hear it's a politician's greatest asset."

She rested her head against his chest. "Get me through this, Marcus. And you've got a girlfriend."

His hands rubbed her back and she felt the brush of a kiss on her hair. "Deal."

TWENTY-TWO

The federal courthouse in Richmond had become a secure fortress. Shari watched Connor through the one-way glass of an interview room as Dave and Quinn faced off with him one more time over the shooting. She would go before the grand jury at 1 P.M., and unless Connor plead guilty, she faced at least a year of protective custody until the trial was over.

A year would not destroy a chance at a relationship with Marcus, but it added more uncertainty than Shari could accept.

Jesus, let this end. Let there be justice now, and strong justice. Against everyone involved. Please.

She watched as a series of photos were laid down on the table. Crime scene photos. Frank. The place his body had been found. The brutal way he had been killed.

"Tell us about your father," Dave said.

Connor's glaze flickered to the photos, then back up, his face remaining impassive. "Why?" He smiled. "You'll never convict me."

It was the cool confidence in his voice that pushed Shari over the edge. Before Marcus could grab her arm and stop her she had pulled open the door to the room and stepped inside. Her color was high, her pulse up, her anger hot.

"You look surprised to see me," she remarked, seeing the startled look on Connor's face as well as on Dave and Quinn's. She planted her hands on the table and focused on Connor. "Don't worry. That big future payment you thought you would have to make will never come due. Lucas is dead. And I'll even tell you where I'm going to be from the grand jury testimony to the end of your trial. Quantico."

Dave grimaced, and Marcus took her arm. "Shari."

"No. I want him to know. I want him to try again. It will ensure he gets a death penalty when the next fool sent to kill me gets captured alive. Just try it, Connor."

Marcus pulled her from the room.

She paced, hot anger triggered at being a foot away from the man who had killed Carl and her dad burning off.

"You shouldn't have done that."

She sent Marcus a frustrated glance. "He's so confident he's going to walk."

"He won't. Your testimony along with what else we have will be enough."

Marcus looked back into the interview room, where Quinn was stepping in to take advantage of the unexpected moment.

Quinn laid down photos of Connor's brother Daniel after the execution. "You are going to join him for killing a federal judge. The only way you can escape a death penalty sentence is to plead guilty and start talking. We want to know about your father, about his involvement, about his business."

Connor moved the photos around on the table and finally picked up one. "He didn't deserve to die."

"You do."

Connor set the photo down, then looked toward the one-way glass. He looked at Quinn. "Titus ordered Frank killed."

Titus was working at his home office, very aware of the date, the time, and ruthlessly keeping himself occupied. Lucas would strike, swift, like a cobra, and the news would begin to come out in rumors—"The witness is dead, the grand jury has been postponed."

The call came an hour later than he had expected.

Titus listened to the lawyer on the phone, his expression growing cold, his fingers on his pen tightening. He didn't say anything, just hung up the phone.

Anthony had joined him.

"Connor is talking. And I won't pay for his mistakes. Kill him."

They were on the way to Quantico. Shari watched the countryside pass by along the interstate.

Marcus reached over and gripped her hand. "Relax. Frank is dead. Connor has turned against his father. We've got enough to bring down Titus. Once he's in custody the threat to you will be contained."

"I know. But I'm still stuck at Quantico until Connor and Titus go to trial. All Connor gave up was that Titus had Frank killed. He admitted nothing about Carl."

"Shari, we take it a day at a time."

She didn't know what to say. She didn't want to face a potential separation of several months.

The car phone rang. Marcus reached for it. "Yes?"

Shari looked over at him when the silence lasted. Something had happened. The distant look was there in his gaze. "How?"

She reached over and touched his knee. His hand came over and firmly grasped hers.

He didn't say anything after he hung up the phone. "Marcus?"

"Connor was just killed at the jail as he was being processed back into solitary."

She started. "He's dead?"

"It looks like an ordered hit: Titus just killed his son." Marcus leaned up to speak with the driver. "Tell our escorts to pull in tight. And get me every cop car in the area converging on us, now!"

Shari didn't think she would ever get accustomed to Quantico. After what had turned into a tense drive to reach the safety of the compound, she had found herself joined by a group of very grim bodyguards.

It was a fascinating if intimidating place. She had been there three days when she came down from her room to the cafeteria for lunch to find Marcus waiting for her. She didn't care who was watching. She wrapped him in a hug and kissed him.

He didn't let her go. "I think I'll show up for a welcome again."

"Thanks for coming."

"Feel like sleeping in your own bed tonight?"

Emotions washed over her—relief, hope, intense joy that this long nightmare was over. "You're serious?" she whispered.

"Titus has been arrested. The FBI came down on his organization like a hammer, and people beneath him are already rolling, giving evidence against him to get an easier deal themselves. There are strong rumors there is now a contract out on him. There are a lot of people in the world who fear what he might say. He'll cooperate eventually, if only to get the government's protection to prevent his associates from reaching through the prison doors to kill him."

"He's reaping what he sowed."

"Yes."

"Watch how fast I can pack."

They were on a private plane flying to meet her mom and brother who were arriving in New York an hour later.

"Who's this?" A rather beaten-up raccoon sat in one of the plane seats, a big red bow around his neck.

"Rugsby. He's about to reappear. I was dispatched to Rachel's home to retrieve him."

Shari picked up the raccoon, delighted with it. "No ransom?"

"It has to be paid next week. And you'll notice I just kidnapped you from Quantico to pay my part."

She grinned. "True. Kate mentioned there was an O'Malley dinner scheduled."

"I thought you might like to join me."

"I would."

She relaxed in her seat and watched the ground become smaller below them.

"What are you thinking about?" Marcus asked.

She looked over at him and went out on a limb. "The future."

He leaned back, folded his hands across his chest, and lazily looked back at her. "So…do you want to run for state legislator or go straight for what you really want, a congressional house seat?"

"You're determined to get me to go for it."

"It's your dream."

"You have to be married to run for congressional office," she reminded him.

He quirked a grin. "I guess that means you'll just have to marry me before the elections."

She blinked. *He just proposed.*

"I love you, minx, with all my heart."

"I love you too," she whispered back.

"I know." His warm smile curled around her heart. His foot nudged hers. "The O'Malley family thinks you should run for the open house congressional seat. Lisa wants to be your field manager; she sees it like running a military campaign. Kate will organize your volunteer staff so she can boss around Jack and Stephen, and Dave volunteered to handle transportation. Oh, and Jennifer thinks we should make the wedding be the event of the Virginia social calendar so everybody will love you, and they'll vote for you because they adore you."

His entire family was saying welcome. She loved them all. "What do you want to do?"

"Elope."

Shari laughed.

"But since the O'Malleys will never let us get away with that, a social event of the year sounds like a good second choice."

"My mom will love it."

"I know." His expression became serious. "Shari, I'm not threatened by the idea of a smart wife with great ideas and a passion for her job. You have to dream big if you're going to fit with me."

"You're serious."

"You're one of us now. So start defining your dream, and we'll help you get there. Kids, a political career—we are a family that believes in fulfilling dreams. And Shari…we don't believe in small dreams."

She knew that was true. She considered him. "What's your biggest dream?"

"I'll tell you on the honeymoon."

She blushed but didn't mind. "I'll probably convince you to sleep in." She laughed at the look he gave her. She was going to enjoy the permanence of a marriage with him. Just getting to tease him would fill her days with laughter. She picked up the aged raccoon. "I like your family."

"You're fishing for compliments. They love you."

"It's important that they feel like I'm joining your family and not taking you from it."

"They know it," Marcus reassured. "You want to surprise them at the family gathering?"

"How?"

He nodded toward Rugsby. "While he was gone, he found himself a lady and they had baby raccoons."

She burst out laughing. "He did?"

"Start thinking of names."

"I like the fact you encourage the silliness."

"It's called smart family management. The O'Malleys unoccupied just come up with trouble."

"Good try, but you're really still a kid at heart."

"Maybe true too."

She set down the raccoon, looked over at him, smiled, and came around to a subject she had meant to mention to him. "You know, I realized something the other day when I was sorting out what was in my purse."

"What's that?"

"I still have the slip of paper with the pager numbers you asked me to memorize. I never had reason to page you with my private code."

"You will in the future," Marcus noted, watching her.

"I think I'll have to. I noticed something about the private code you assigned me."

"Did you?"

"I should have noticed it before…"

He slowly smiled. "Yes, you should have."

"225-6469 spells CAL-MINX."

"Well, what do you know…" He laughed at her expression.

"I only saw it because I was bored and was doodling. You weren't going to tell me, were you?"

"Nope."

"You're terrible."

"I love you too."

They shared a smile. Shari tilted her head to one side, considering him. "I'll need a private code for you, for when I want you to call me back immediately…"

"Why do I get the feeling you thought of one?"

She had a hard time containing her joy. "484-8463."

He pulled out his phone, looked at the keypad, putting letters to the numbers. He laughed softly as he figured it out. "Minx, I like the way you think."

"Not too subtle?"

"I'll remember it," Marcus promised.

"Can you use the phone while we're flying?"

"Briefly."

She unclipped her pager from her belt to see the display. "Page me."

He smiled at her as he dialed. "Just wait until we get on the ground, Shari."

The numbers flashed on the pager.

HUG TIME.

Dear Reader,

Thank you for reading this book. I appreciate it. This was one of the most fascinating books I have written to date. I fell in love with Marcus O'Malley while writing *The Negotiator,* and I knew this man who leads the O'Malleys would have a powerful story. He blew me away with his story and surpassed my expectations. This is the book I look back on and think, I wrote that? Some stories are gifts. This was one of them.

Prayer is such a rich topic to explore, both from the viewpoint of someone strong in their faith and someone who walked away from faith years before. One has concluded prayer is answered by chance as much as by a caring God; the other believes God is answering prayer despite the fact the answers are hard to accept. But they are both struggling with the conclusions they've reached. I found myself able to defend the conclusions of each one of them. I think they both made rational decisions—yet only one of them made the right one. Understanding why was a rich journey through my own beliefs.

I have found in a lifetime of prayer that Jesus really does love me and know me, and best of all likes me. His answers eventually work out to my good. Even those I do not understand yet, I continue to trust will be good answers…

As always, I love to hear from my readers. Feel free to write me at:

Dee Henderson
c/o Multnomah Publishers, Inc.
P.O. Box 1720
Sisters, Oregon 97759

E-mail: dee@deehenderson.com
or on-line: http://www.deehenderson.com

First chapters of all my books are on-line, please stop by and check them out. Thanks again for letting me share Marcus and Shari's story,

Sincerely

Dee Henderson

book three

THE TRUTH SEEKER

*"For this is the will of my Father, that every one who sees the Son
and believes in him should have eternal life;
and I will raise him up at the last day."*

John 6:40

ONE

The fire had been alive; it had left its signature in the coiled, twisted wood, the bent metal, the heavy ash. It was a tamed beast, but still here, ready to come back to life with a nudge. Lisa O'Malley walked with great respect up the stairs following her brother Jack into the heart of the fire damage. The heavy boots he had insisted she wear were welcome as she realized it was glass crunching beneath her feet. Lightbulbs and picture frames had shattered in the heat.

The fire coat was harder to get accustomed to. The Nomex cloth was rough and it felt like thirty pounds on her back as she struggled to keep her balance. When Jack worked a fire he ran stairs wearing the coat and an air tank, carrying another forty pounds of gear. She didn't know how he did it. The man rarely showed a serious side, but it was there when he was doing the job he excelled at.

Reaching the upstairs landing, she turned her flashlight to inspect the hallway ceiling and walls. The superheated gas created by the fire had reached down five feet from the ceiling, burning into the paint and wood, marking a suicide line. Two or three feet down indicated a severe fire; five was explosive. The firemen confronting this fire had been taking their lives in their hands in facing it head-on.

"Watch your step, I don't trust this hallway. Stay close to the north wall."

Lisa returned her flashlight to the floor to pick her next steps. Jack had hesitated before letting her come up. The house was safe for now, but with the weight of walls and joists shifting to beams not designed to handle the weight, every day brought the structure closer to collapse. It had rained yesterday, making the damaged wood swell and further stressing the structure.

She was careful not to get snagged by a nail or by exposed wiring. The fire crews had pulled down part of the hallway ceiling and torn portions of the walls back to the studs in order to locate dangerous pockets of lingering heat. Six days ago this had been a two-alarm fire. In the smoldering remains, still in his bed, the body of Egan Hampton had been recovered.

She reached the back bedroom and stopped.

"An accident—" She could only shake her head in disbelief. The furniture was charred, the mattress burned down to the springs; books on the shelf were now warped spines enfolding wrinkled pages of ash; the alarm clock was a chunk of deformed plastic adhered to the bedside table; the television tube had cracked and buckled in.

The only items not burned or blackened in the room were a portion of the bedding that had been protected by Egan's body and a section of the floor rug that had been under the bed frame. The bedroom door was still on its hinges but it had burned on both sides to a fraction of its normal width.

"Like I said, it was a hot fire."

She stepped with caution inside the room, instinctively looking up to make sure she wasn't going to get hit with something. The ceiling was open in sections, revealing part of the attic, and in one place she could see all the way through to the sky.

Through the destroyed window she could see the orchard and nursery, the buildings and commercial greenhouses that comprised Nakomi Nurseries, the business Egan had built up over the years and recently passed to his nephew Walter to manage.

Jack dealt with fire every day; he knew how it moved and breathed and burned. She'd learned enough from him to understand the patterns. This looked like a flashover—everything in the room heating up, reaching burn point, and suddenly bursting into flames *en masse.* "Did the room smolder and smoke before flashover or was it a steady fire? In the police report Walter said he saw the smoke and then a flash and called 911."

"It began as a smoldering fire." Jack knelt and picked up large shards of glass from the shattered window. "Look at the smoke stain that burned into the pane of window glass."

He used the crowbar to pull off the bottom piece of the window frame casing and turned it over to show her the details. "You can tell it started as a floor fire burning upward because the fire swept across this wood and out the window. Had it initially been flames at the ceiling coming down the wall and out the window, the burning would be pitting on the top of the wood, not this charring underneath."

Daniel had done the autopsy on Egan Hampton. While smoke had killed the man—carbon monoxide had been found in his lungs indicating he'd been alive when the fire started—there was also a puzzle. He had suffered a contusion on the left temple coincident to death. It wasn't severe; the bruising had just begun to seep into the deep tissue.

The explanation could be as simple as something falling on him when the fire began, but it needed to be explained. And there was the fact he had taken what had been determined to be two sleeping pills. Within the doctor's prescribed dosage, but still a factor to be looked at. For now the autopsy results were inconclusive.

As with all cases that could go either way, it had come back to the central staff at the state crime lab for another look at the autopsy results in light of the case circumstances. Her boss had dropped the case in her lap Friday afternoon.

As a forensic pathologist the question she asked was simple to state and often maddeningly hard to answer: Was the death suspicious, warranting a murder investigation, or accidental?

Lisa loved a good puzzle, but not one that arrived to ruin a weekend. She'd read the reports yesterday, concluded only that she needed more information. "It would help if you could tell me this was an arson fire."

"It was a hot fire, but then it's been a hot, dry summer. The house has no air-conditioning, and the furniture and flooring had absorbed the afternoon heat. We found a lot of dry rot in the roof, and with this being a small back bedroom the fire was able to flashover within minutes."

"The fire started at the base of this wall?"

"As best we can tell, he fell asleep and dropped his cigar. We found the remains of one there." Jack pointed. "It hit what appears to have been a burlap bag of laundry. The fire moved across the floor, you can see the distinct burn line—" he traced it with his hand—"and eventually reached into the closet where it had an unlimited fuel load. It built in intensity and then moved back into the bedroom along the ceiling—see the bubbling in the wood? By then it was moving hot and fast."

"How long before the smoke blanket dropped low enough to kill him?"

"The fire probably took four to six minutes to get a footing. From then to a killing blanket of toxic smoke, you're talking maybe two minutes at the outside. The window was open, and the door, an unfortunate reality for him. The airflow would cause a natural eddy of smoke into that corner of the room over the bed."

She looked at the damage, now more able to understand why Mr. Hampton had not awakened. The fire Jack described would not be loud enough to wake a man sleeping heavily under the influence of two sleeping pills and building carbon monoxide. By the time the fire surged from the closet back into the room, the smoke would have been thick enough to kill.

She looked again for what might have caused the bruise. "The heat weakened and collapsed the plaster?"

"The house is old construction, they used a plaster paste over wood, and you can tell that most of it broke away. Directly above this room in the attic were cardboard boxes storing his wife's things, including clothes."

"Another fuel load."

"Yes. Once in the attic, the fire was burning on both sides of these joists."

"So falling plaster could account for the blow." Lisa walked to the remains of the bed frame and started searching the area. "Is there any evidence of a picture on the wall? Something else that might have fallen on him?"

Jack started tugging back debris.

They searched for ten minutes and found the remains of two picture frames and a shelf. The shelf would have been heavy enough, or an item on it. She felt herself relax. "One of these items is probably what caused the bruise."

"Agreed. The cat was found there." Jack pointed to the far corner of the room.

"Cat? What cat?"

"It wasn't in the notes? There should be an addendum to the fire report. Craig found it during the fire mop-up. We figured the cat was on the bed, got a face full of the smoke, retreated to escape the fire, then got trapped."

"A cat losing all of its nine lives? I thought the door was open."

"It was open when we came up the stairs fighting the fire. I suppose it's possible the force of the water pushed it open, but that would be apparent in the burn patterns."

Jack crossed over to the door and carefully swung it to take a look. "The door was open during the fire. If it were closed, this door edge around the knob and the edge back by the hinges would have been protected by the door frame, but both show serious burning."

"Then why didn't the cat bolt from the room?"

"It's hard to tell a burned cat's age, but it looked young. And a cat is not going to jump through fire at the window or past fire in the doorway. It tried to hide and the smoke eventually overcame it. We've seen it before."

"Jack?"

"Up here, Ford."

Footsteps sounded on the stairs as the detective assigned to the case came upstairs. He had been talking with Egan's nephew Walter. The house was going to have to be demolished in the next few days. Walter was in the process of recovering what essential papers he could from the downstairs office.

"Ford, do you know what happened to the cat?" Lisa asked before she realized Walter had also come upstairs with the detective.

Walter was the one to answer. "I'm sorry, I buried the cat this morning. I didn't realize it would be a problem. The crows had been attracted by the death; I found them in here." He swallowed hard. "Listen, it's in a shoe box buried at the end of the garden. It will take only a minute to get it for you."

"No," Lisa replied, stopping his retreat. "It's okay. Jack just told me it had also been killed."

"Egan liked that cat. It was from a neighbor cat's spring litter. I guess the house was lonely at night since Patricia was taken to the nursing home. He never liked pets before."

Lisa saw Walter look again toward the bed and knew it was best that they leave. She could see how hard this was on him. He was in his forties, lean, a landscaper by profession with an appearance that fit it, his jeans and gray T-shirt sweaty in the heat. At close range, the ravages of the last six days—the healing burns, the stress, the grief, and the lack of sleep—were all there to be seen on his face. He'd tried to reach his uncle but had been unable to get past the flames.

"I've got everything I need to finish up my report. We were just coming down." She was comfortable with the assessment that this had been a tragic accident. The dead cat disturbed her, but Jack was right, pets died in fires. She'd think it through again tonight, look one last time at the autopsy results, and if she didn't see anything else, she'd recommend to her boss that they sign it off as an accidental death.

Lisa was relieved. The last thing she needed was another murder investigation.

U.S. Marshal Quinn Diamond walked through the concourse at O'Hare, carrying a briefcase he hated, his cowboy boots leaving an echo behind him. His face was weathered by the sun and wind, the lines around his eyes deep. He was not a man to enjoy the crush of people, but at least Chicago was better than New York or Washington.

He had planned to take a direct flight from Washington, D.C., to Montana, spend his month of vacation at his ranch, let the physical hard work wipe away the aftereffects of two months spent tracking down who had murdered a federal judge.

Instead, he was in Chicago on very short notice. The folded newsclip in his billfold was from yesterday's *Chicago Tribune*. There was a book signing Tuesday night for a Sierra Club book entitled *A Photographic Guide to Birds in the Midwest.* The author's name—Amy Ireland Nugan.

Quinn had been checking out of the hotel in Washington when the news alert service tracked him down. It had been so long since the last lead. Was it her? Was it the Amy Ireland he had sought for so long?

He'd been able to get a few answers. She was married to a Paul Nugan. She was the right age, thirty-seven. Amy had been seventeen when she disappeared from Justin, Montana, twenty years ago.

The same day Amy had disappeared, his father had been shot in the back out on the southern range of the ranch near the bluffs.

After twenty years of searching he had finally accepted that Amy must have also died that day, but if she had instead fled and appeared sometime later in Chicago—he didn't think she would have pulled the trigger, but she might have been with someone who had.

If he could solve what had happened to Amy Ireland, maybe he could get a lead on who had killed his father.

He had almost given up hope of ever finding a trace of her. He'd eliminated dozens of Amy Irelands over the years, but this one...the sense of hope was back. It fit. Amy had been a high-school photographer with a passion for what her camera could reveal. She'd had real talent even in her teens. Quinn could easily see her making it a future career.

He had to know if this was the right Amy Ireland. And if it was, he had to be very careful not to send her running again. Practicing patience was not going to be easy.

His partner, Marcus O'Malley, would have joined him if Quinn had alerted him to the hit on the name; he was that kind of friend. But Quinn hadn't wanted to interrupt Marcus's chance to spend time with his sister who was undergoing cancer treatment at Johns Hopkins and his new fiancée, Shari. Instead, Quinn had called an old friend.

Quinn found Lincoln Beaumont waiting in the United Airlines' business lounge. If he hadn't known better, on first impression he would have assumed lawyer or investment banker, not retired U.S. Marshal and now private investigator. "Thanks for coming, Lincoln." He tipped his cowboy hat to the lady with the retired marshal. "Ma'am."

"Emily Randall; I handle Lincoln's research." She was a nice-looking lady, businesslike in her handshake, feminine in her dress, and confident in her gaze. "It's nice to meet you, Mr. Diamond."

"The pleasure's mine," Quinn replied with a smile. Lincoln had been right; she'd be perfect if it became necessary to have someone approach Amy.

The smile directed at him showed curiosity. He was accustomed to it; he made no attempt to disguise the fact he was a misplaced man in the city. Why that should draw women was a phenomenon he accepted but didn't really understand.

It didn't attract the attention of the one lady he wanted to notice him. No, he changed that. Lisa O'Malley noticed; she just found his interest uncomfortable to deal with and more often than not scowled rather than smiled when she saw him.

He was determined to get Marcus's sister to accept a dinner invitation on this trip through Chicago. She'd been ducking him long enough. He wasn't after something profound; he just wanted to change her rather mixed reaction to him and replace it with a solid friendship. He visited Chicago on a regular basis; he wanted to be able to call Lisa when he was in town and have her actually be pleased to hear from him.

Eating alone was a waste of time, so was spending his downtime at a hotel watching TV. He spent enough time with strangers. Lisa he knew, and she was the kind of friend he wanted: loyal, fun, and smart, with a stubborn streak he liked to ruffle. It was a bit like rubbing a cat's fur the wrong way. She was cute when annoyed, and calling her ma'am always got a reaction. One thing was certain: Lisa's life was never boring.

He smiled as he thought of the excuses she was likely to throw up to the invitation to dinner and unfortunately misled Ms. Randall into assuming his smile was in response to hers. Before she could say something that would put them both in a fix, he calmly turned the conversation. "Tell me what you've found out about Amy Ireland."

Her hair smelled like smoke, her jeans were going to have to be bleached to remove the ground-in ash, and she'd managed to rub the back of her neck nearly raw with the sweat and heavy pressure of the fire coat. Miserable didn't define it. Lisa paused to let Sidney out of his cage before heading to the shower. The ferret was a recent pet and one of her favorites; he scampered up her arm to push into her flyaway hair, and she sneezed. "Sorry. I'm covered in ash." She lowered him to the floor and with her foot sent a small rubber ball rolling down the hallway. Sidney gave chase and leaped to stop it.

Lisa glanced into her office as she headed to the shower and saw the answering machine blinking. Work would have paged...Jennifer. She abruptly changed course, hoping it was her sister.

It was Jennifer, and the recorded message was three hours old. Regretting having not been home to take the call, Lisa picked up the cordless phone and punched in the hospital number, hoping she wouldn't have the bad timing of catching Jen when she was sleeping. Jennifer's fiancé Tom Peterson answered, reassured her that Jennifer was awake, and passed the phone over.

"Thanks for calling back." Jen's voice was soft and Lisa had to press the phone close to hear, but compared to some days when the pain and the fatigue slurred her words, Jen sounded good.

"Hey, it's my pleasure. I had to work this afternoon or I would have called earlier. Are you having a good day?"

"I'm running a fever."

"That's excellent!" Lisa sank into the nearby chair, overjoyed. Jennifer's immune system, overrun by the cancer, was finally getting a foothold to fight back.

"I'm going to lick this yet." The optimism in Jennifer's voice throughout the weeks of hospitalization hadn't wavered, even though it was there in spite of the facts.

"You better believe it." The cancer was around Jen's spine and had touched her liver. The odds were severely against her, everyone in the O'Malley family knew that, but they also knew Jennifer had to win this fight. It was incomprehensible to imagine life without her.

Lisa rubbed her eyes and winced as the smoke residue made them burn. Staying positive was mandatory; yet it came at a cost. There was so much fear inside—she had seen too many people die. It was her profession to deal with death, but this situation was going to crumble her defenses and shatter her heart. Jennifer had to get well, she just had to.

The cancer was doing permanent damage each day it progressed, and the toxic radiation and chemotherapy being used to battle the disease were inflicting their own lasting damage. Lisa wished she had chosen pediatrics as her medical specialty like Jennifer had instead of forensic pathology so she could be less aware of the painful truth—death was coming. Unless the process could be checked, she was going to lose her best friend.

It was a struggle to force her voice to stay light. "Tom's there, so I gather you're enjoying the evening."

"You better believe it. Mushy movie, good-looking date…"

Lisa had to laugh. "Being engaged suits you."

"The wedding won't come soon enough."

Jennifer had set her heart on getting married October 22; it was looming a short five weeks away. The family had already caucused with Tom: If the O'Malleys had to arrive en masse in Baltimore and have the wedding at the hospital, they would make it happen for her. "Have Marcus and Shari arrived?"

"They got in this afternoon. Shari is a sweetheart."

"Yes, she is."

"So what were you working on this afternoon?"

"Follow-up on a fire case from last week. I dragged Jack along with me out to the scene and spent two hours climbing around in a burned-out house. It was hot, heavy, dirty work. I haven't been this beat in ages."

The doorbell rang. Lisa turned; she wasn't expecting anyone. She was tempted to ignore the doorbell, but her car was in the drive making it obvious she was home. Which local kid had she not bought candy from for the junior high band trip? She'd seen Tony and Mandy yesterday. Chad.

She reached for the spare stash of cash she kept tucked inside the baby panda cookie jar on her desk along with an assortment of hard candy and slipped the money into her pocket. The problem was that she always said yes, and all the kids knew it. And to miss someone— She'd long ago determined not to let that happen. She moved through the house, taking the phone with her.

"Kate brought me the *Chicago Tribune* and the *Sun Times*. Was it the Paretti family fire? I saw the write-up in the metro section."

"No, thank goodness." The Paretti family had died in a house fire on Monday. "This one was an old farmhouse out in Villa Grove. It looks like a dropped cigar started it." Lisa looked through the front door's security hole and flinched. "Jen, I need to call you back. Quinn's here."

"Is he?"

"He's supposed to be in Montana," Lisa said darkly. "And I've got enough ash in my hair it looks gray," she muttered, releasing the chain and turning the dead bolt, "while he looks his normal, elegant self." Her brief glance had been enough to confirm that. In the habit of cops, he was standing three feet back from the door and off to the side while he waited for her to answer the summons, his thumbs resting comfortably at the pockets of his jeans, his hands halfway to his concealed weapon.

He was tall and lean and fit and would probably live to be a centurian. From the boots to the cowboy hat to the way he walked through a crowd, he was a man who knew where he came from and was comfortable with it. She distrusted the politeness and niceness. He was Marcus's partner, and the stories she had heard about what the two of them had pulled off over the years… Appearances were deceiving with this man.

His black hair was often smashed by the cowboy hat, and the deep lines around his blue eyes showed his habit of spending his days outdoors without sunglasses. It should have made him look ruffled; instead it just added a relaxed tone to the already strong sense of presence.

She didn't like the fact that at five foot four she had to tilt her head to look up at him. His presence intimidated witnesses he was interviewing, and he worked so hard to change that perception when he was off duty that it unfortunately just made her more aware of it.

Quinn worked all over the country with her brother, and while she warily tried to keep track of him, he still caught her off guard at the most inconvenient moments.

"He's gorgeous enough to make your toes curl, and he's one fine date."

"You should know." Jennifer had dated Quinn two years ago. Last year Quinn had dated her sister Kate. Lisa had no intention of being number three. Not that she minded losing out to her sisters, but it was the principle of the thing.

There was something humiliating at being thought of as third. And any guy who dared ask out three sisters in the same family either had a lot of guts or a lot of nerve—in Quinn's case, both. She thought her answer to his last dinner invitation had been creative, eloquent, and final. She'd sent him a petrified squid.

"Smile at him. And call me back."

"Maybe," Lisa replied to her sister's laugh. She hung up and forced herself to open the door.

"Hello, Lisa." She looked confused to see him; Quinn considered it an improvement over annoyed. A wave of cold air washed out from the house as she stood in the doorway, one hand gripping the door frame and the other resting on the screen door handle. "I was in town, I thought I'd say hi," he elaborated.

"Oh. Hi."

He tipped his hat, the brim rough against his fingers, and silently laughed as he scanned and enjoyed. Freckles. Baby blue eyes. Hair so fine and thick the sun set its color and the wind defined its form, much to her dismay and his pleasure. Cut short to try and tame it, her hair now curled and bobbed as she moved.

Her voice held a touch of the full world—Quebec French, South American Spanish—the blend and tone of her voice changed with each passing year as she added traces of the people she met. She'd been in Venezuela six months ago and some inaccessible part of Africa a few months before that, absorbing the local culture and fitting herself in. He loved listening to her voice. He wanted to add to it a touch of Montana drawl. "Can I come in?"

She flushed and stepped back. "Yes. Sorry. I just got home."

Bad timing on his part. Black ash streaked her left forearm, her faded yellow shirt was sweat stained, and her jeans were grimy at the knees. There was a marked tiredness to her polite smile, and something had scraped her right cheek.

As she turned his eyes narrowed at the blisters he saw on the back of her neck. A fire scene, and for Lisa that meant victims. He couldn't get a break even when he most needed one. She was obviously not in the mood for company tonight, even though she probably needed that distraction more on this evening than most others.

"I was just talking with Jen." She lifted the phone she carried, looking awkward. "Let me hang this up. I'll just be a minute."

"Of course," he said gently. He'd seen Lisa's sister last week; the reality of that call explained part of the droop to Lisa's shoulders. The situation was a source of stress to everyone, but for Lisa... Quinn knew how close the two of them were. And with Lisa being a doctor—the placating words others said in reassurance would not help her. She understood how much the hopeful language covered grim reality.

He'd do what he could to get that stress to drain away tonight, even if he had to resort to badgering her into getting angry and letting that tension loose against him. It was one of the odd times where ruffling her into reacting would be the right thing to do.

She turned toward the hallway, and he shot out a hand to grab her arm. "Hold it, you've got more company." The animal nearly tripped her as it darted between her socked feet. It scampered across his boots and returned, intrigued by the smell.

Quinn scooped him up in a worn, calloused hand and held him at eye level, he and the animal showing equal curiosity. His smile was easy and amused. "One of your more interesting choices." He settled the animal on his shoulder and it reached up to explore his hat. "Take a shower, Lisa, clean that scrape, and I'll take you out somewhere nice to eat."

"I've got plans for tonight."

"I know. With me." He didn't ask her to extend the lie by trying to come up with what the plans were. She was a lousy liar. And since Marcus—the oldest and thus guardian of the O'Malley clan—was currently half a continent away, he was stepping in by proxy to make happen what was best for her. She needed a relaxing evening out. She started to protest and he interrupted. "Marcus and Shari have been talking about wedding plans; I thought you'd be interested."

She shot him a quelling look, annoyed that he knew details before she did, but reluctantly gave in. "Drinks are in the refrigerator; help yourself."

He turned that way, lowering the ferret to the floor, knowing better than to stay put and give Lisa a chance to get her bearings. When she dug in her heels she was a formidable opponent. "Has she fed you yet, buddy?"

TWO

Lisa rested her head against the shower door and let the cold water take the sting out of the sunburn on the back of her neck. How did she get into situations like this?

She had been planning a quiet night at home with maybe a record on the stereo and her topographical maps of the Smoky Mountains spread out on the table to plot her next vacation trek. She'd just bought the vinyl thirty-three with "Rainy Night in Georgia," "Worried Man Blues," and "Kentucky Rain" for a quarter at a garage sale yesterday morning, and it was the type of music that suited her mood for tonight; she'd enjoy the vacation planning. Instead of those evening plans—she wasn't sure what she had ended up with, other than the frustrating realization that she was being nicely manipulated.

Quinn was comfortable enough to just drop by whenever he was in town, and she had no idea why he continued to do it. It wasn't like she had sparkling, interesting conversation to offer. She got positively tongue-tied around the man. He had a free evening, and he wasn't the type of guy to spend it alone. She knew better than to think of it as a date.

It fit Quinn's pattern. Even his dates with Jennifer and Kate had been more focused on having someone to spend his time with than anything serious, the mood more laughter and teasing than romantic. But Lisa didn't fit that same mold as her sisters, and she knew she'd disappoint Quinn if he expected the same thing from her.

It went with her miserable track record that Quinn had arrived while she looked like a charcoal block. She wasn't vain about her looks; she was the middle of the O'Malley sisters in that regard and comfortable there—classical beauty was Rachel's, sultry was Kate's, Jennifer didn't count as she'd be a petite size six for her wedding—but it would be nice if Quinn didn't have a knack for catching her at her worst.

She flinched under the spray as a blister broke. The sun had done a number on her today, and Jack's air-conditioning was out in his car; the ninety-two-degree heat had wilted her. If Quinn felt the heat of the day, it wasn't obvious. His body simply absorbed the sun and turned his skin a deeper, darker tan.

It wasn't that she didn't like Quinn. Her brother's partner was…an interesting man. Tenacious in a quiet way, he had to be in his midforties and it showed in his demeanor. She'd rarely seen him be anything but relaxed, calm, and professional. But he tracked down fugitives and worked cases with a single-minded focus she rarely saw even among the cops with whom she worked.

She didn't understand the man. He owned a prosperous ranch in Montana, was obviously more comfortable on the open land than in the city, and yet he worked as a U.S. Marshal traveling the country. Whatever his history was, it was tightly held.

She knew herself very well—she just didn't want to go out with a guy where getting her heart broken was inevitable. She didn't know how to play it casual. If Quinn hadn't settled down at forty, he wasn't going to. She could get hurt letting herself get close to him.

If Kate and Jennifer weren't good enough to get him thinking about settling down, there was no way she would be. And she didn't have the ability to let people come and go from her life and not record the scars—too many people had already left.

The water slowly began to ease the ache in her muscles. She shampooed her hair for the second time.

What were they going to talk about after the first ten minutes? She washed away the soap, then realized her hair still felt rough. She reached for the shampoo to do it a third time. She knew it would just be a tangle of flyaway strands when it dried.

She hated talking about herself, and he had to have already gotten his fill of the O'Malley family gossip just by being around Marcus. The case—it was the only thing she really was comfortable talking to Quinn about. And that would make great conversation.

It didn't make sense that the cat had died.

She frowned at the thought, but because it was easier to think about work than Quinn, she let herself follow the tangent, puzzled.

The cat would have awoken early, long before the fire blocked the doorway. Either the doorway was closed so the cat couldn't get out—and Jack had said it was open—or the cat hadn't been able to wake up.

What would a sleeping pill do to a cat?

It bothered her that Egan had taken two when his doctor's notes said he was reluctant to take even one and used them only sporadically. The fire had been early in the evening. It wasn't like he had taken one, still been awake hours later, and then taken the second one. He had taken two sleeping pills, gone to bed, turned on the TV, and smoked a cigar.

She dropped the shampoo bottle.

Smoked a cigar, but the ashtrays and cigarettes were in his office and on the kitchen table. He'd been having himself a treat, a last cigar.

She swore as soap ran into her eyes, hurriedly stuck her head under the water to rinse the shampoo out, grabbed for a towel, and made the mistake of hitting the hot water on instead of off, nearly scalding herself.

It hadn't been a tragic accident. Not if he had also given his cat a sleeping pill, not wanting to die alone.

It had been a suicide.

Quinn paused by the painting on the wall by the kitchen phone, captivated by the fourteen-inch watercolor. The wildflower garden was a vibrant explosion of color around a reflective pond, the scene alive and yet at the same time tranquil. He leaned down to read the signature. A Sinclair. In the kitchen. He laughed softly at the discovery.

Lisa was so casual and careless about the art she acquired. A collector himself for decades, his mother had been a professional artist; he envied Lisa's talent to spot something excellent. She bought something because she liked it and had no concept of how good she was at making that choice. He was going to have to convince her to come wander the downtown galleries with him. He needed something for the office back at the ranch. He had found a Calvin Price sculpture in New York and needed two paintings to make the arrangement complete.

With regret that the odds of getting her to part with the watercolor were nil, he moved on to dry his hands and got down two glasses from the cabinet.

Lincoln Beaumont and Emily Randall had promised some solid answers on Amy Ireland Nugan by noon tomorrow; there was only so much background information that could be dug up on a Sunday without it being obvious they were looking. What they had found so far was inconclusive, going back only as far as New York where Amy had lived before coming to Chicago.

His father was dead; Amy Ireland was going to be at the book signing Tuesday night. A link would last forty-eight hours. Quinn didn't think Lisa would understand the favor he was paying her by being here instead of investigating tonight. He didn't plan to tell her why he had come to Chicago; it was a quiet, private search. He'd rather have Lisa irritated at him than feeling sorry for him.

He heard the water stop then a door close. Lisa was not a woman who lingered over makeup and hair—with her looks and smile she already caught plenty of attention, and her attempts to tame her hair tended to frustrate her and make the problem worse. He picked up the tall glass of cold fruit juice he'd poured for her and walked back toward the living room. She'd looked not only parched and tired but stressed. He hoped to the depths of his heart that the victim had not been a child.

He should have found something better to say. She'd looked so defensive about being caught just back from a crime scene that it had made him want to wrap her in a hug. She usually showed so much intensely focused energy that he was caught off guard by the moments that showed the other Lisa—tiny in stature, drained of energy, showing the strain of her day.

He'd seen her slogging through marshes to reach a murder victim, dealing with the remains of a lady who had died at home and not been found for a week, coping with a stabbing victim. He'd spent the last two months watching her put together the forensic evidence they needed to identify who had murdered a federal judge. She was incredibly good at her job.

But she was defensive about it because others had made her that way. It wasn't something a woman was supposed to enjoy doing. Doctors were supposed to go into the profession to heal the living, not investigate deaths. Lisa didn't enjoy what she saw on the job, but she was wise enough to be good at it. He understood Lisa well enough to know she had never chosen the easy or the traditional. She'd been going her own way for a long time. She had the strength to deal with unpleasant facts, to face them head-on and do what needed to be done. He admired that enormously.

He didn't mind her job; he liked a maverick—he was a bit of one himself. And she wouldn't be Lisa without that fascinating contradiction. She was the only lady he'd met who intrigued him more the longer he knew her. And while he didn't want her to treat him like a brother, he did wish she would relax with him like she did with her brothers.

He heard her coming, her voice pitched low, letting him know a ferret had found her. For a lady who had lizards and snakes and mice for pets, the ferret was practically conventional.

Quinn looked at her casual blue cotton shirt and clean jeans and sighed. "You want a hamburger somewhere. I was going to suggest a nice restaurant."

"We're not going out to eat." She reached for the briefcase on the floor by the couch, opened it to retrieve her phone log and her cellular phone, closed it with her left foot, then juggled the items to one hand as she dug her keys out of her pocket.

The slight distance to her voice, her attention and concentration on her own thoughts, a precision to her movements—he'd seen it before, her shift-into-work mode.

Even when relaxed she tended to be restless, spinning something in her fingers, tapping her foot, unconsciously always having energy moving. But it changed when she locked into work and her concentration centered on a puzzle, her very stillness a mark of her intense focus.

She had no idea she could be read so easily, but then he'd been studying her for a long time. At least she hadn't reached for the small black canister rolling around at the back of the briefcase. To his relief she was a woman who didn't mind fighting dirty and wasn't above taking help along if she was going somewhere she thought might be trouble.

Unfortunately, her track record with getting into trouble was well established. She was nearly as bad as her sister Kate. For years Quinn had watched Marcus quietly try to keep close tabs on the two of them. Kate, a hostage negotiator for the Chicago police department, had been known to walk into situations where a guy had a bomb; Lisa just walked into murder scenes, determined to find a killer. "Where are we going?"

"To ask a man to exhume a cat."

THREE

"I'd ask you to clarify that, but I'm afraid you mean it literally."

Lisa glanced over and found Quinn watching her with that mildly amused look he got when he was humoring her. She had to force herself not to drop her gaze. She had been relishing the fact she was squashing his dinner plans for the evening, but he was turning the tables on her. The man knew exactly what she was thinking.

"I do." She scooped up Sidney, the animal's coarse warm fur, long body, and slight musky smell familiar and comforting, and walked back to the spare bedroom to put the animal back in his cage. Sidney clasped himself around her wrist and sniffed her fingers, with reluctance returned to his home when set down, then promptly chattered as he spotted the ping-pong ball in his cage and hurried to pounce. Lisa rubbed her finger down his spine, then closed his cage door. The animal was playing from the moment he woke until he dropped asleep from exhaustion.

When she returned, Quinn hadn't moved. "Please explain."

She didn't want to share case details with him, but if they were not talking about work, she didn't know what to say. "Bring my briefcase; the case folder is inside."

"Drink this first." He held out a tall glass, one of her good company glasses with its little red rose pattern around the rim. She favored the plastic thirty-two-ounce monsters that fit her car's cup holder.

The tone in his voice said it was nonnegotiable and she was impatient to leave. She gulped the juice down, then slowed to savor the last of it. It tasted like nectar. She set the glass down on the side table atop a book club newsletter. "Okay?"

"Better." He picked up her briefcase. "Keys." He held out his hand for them and she didn't argue the point, simply handed them to him. She'd let him wrestle with the slightly off-center dead bolt.

She waited at the edge of the walkway while he locked the house. In the drive his car was parked behind hers. "I'm driving," she insisted as he handed back her keys.

"Fine, but I'm riding with you. Your word, or I won't move my car."

It wasn't beneath her to try to give him the slip, but she hadn't been intending to; she'd only thought about it. "My word," she agreed grudgingly.

It was almost 7 P.M. The sun was low in the sky but the heat was still intense, and when she unlocked her car door it hit her like a wave. She should have risked the possibility of a late afternoon summer thunderstorm and left the windows open a few inches.

Her car was a mess.

Quinn was not known for being neat. He had a wonderful lady who kept his ranch house in order, but when he traveled—there was a reason he stayed in hotels. If he saw this mess in her car, all those times she had teased him would be wasted. She had thirty seconds while he moved his car to the street.

She rapidly grabbed what she could and shoved it into two plastic sacks she found tucked between the seats: her fast-food dinner sack from yesterday, a pair of jeans that needed to be returned to the store, three coffee cups, a thermos that now had floating green stuff growing in the liquid, overdue library books, and a birthday gift bought but not wrapped that was now three days late.

She was normally so neat and organized, so proud of how she kept her house and car that she got teased about it by her family; instead of that, Quinn was going to see her after a week in which her schedule had been one of a thousand interruptions. It wasn't fair.

She popped open the trunk and dumped the sacks there.

"You didn't need to clean up for me."

She slammed the trunk closed. "Shut up, Quinn."

"Yes, ma'am."

He opened the driver's door for her. She stopped, caught by surprise, looked at him, and then eased inside with a slight smile. She should have expected it; Quinn was consistent to a fault about politeness.

He held the door for ladies, let them step inside first, insisted on carrying things and getting the car when it rained, always picked up the check, made a point of waiting for a lady to speak first. But when he did those things for her, there was an extra twinkle in his eyes; he liked doing them because he knew it would fluster her.

She found that reality amusing but would never admit how much she enjoyed the unspoken dance. She kept hoping to catch him off guard, but in the years she'd known him he always managed to keep a step ahead of her.

She started the car and turned the air-conditioning on high while he circled around the car to the passenger seat.

"Is there a baseball game on tonight?"

She flipped on the radio and punched in WGN, relieved to find his guess was right. It was a town favorite, the Chicago Cubs playing the Chicago White Sox. The familiar voice calling the play-by-play was a welcome addition; it eliminated the need for conversation. She pulled out of the subdivision and considered traffic on a Sunday evening to choose the best route northwest.

Quinn settled his hat on one knee. "Tell me about the day. I can tell it's been bad."

Just when she wanted to be annoyed with him, his voice changed and he said exactly the right thing. No wonder both Jennifer and Kate had raved about the man when they dated him. He placed a high value on listening. She let herself relax a bit. "The file is on top in the briefcase."

He retrieved it.

She looked over when it had been silent for several minutes to find him studying the photos. There was nothing gentle about his expression. She looked away, not sure what she thought of that expression and the intensity in it. He looked like what he was: a cop.

"It doesn't look like arson."

"It's a suicide, Quinn, and I missed it. There's an addendum in there on a cat that died. The bedroom door was open, and yet the cat died in that bedroom. Egan fed his cat a sleeping pill, took two himself, smoked his last cigar, and lay down to die."

She felt annoyance. "I just didn't think suicide; that was stupid. It fits this case like a glove. His wife has been moved to a nursing home, he'd passed running his business to his nephew, friends admitted he was lonely, and his cat died in a room with an open door. He killed his cat."

"If you're right, be glad he didn't show up at the nursing home and kill his wife, then himself."

"I know."

She pushed her sunglasses up and rubbed eyes still gritty from the smoke. She was botching a case right in front of him. It couldn't get worse than this.

Walter Hampton had arrived at the farmhouse before them. He was waiting beside a white-and-blue truck advertising Nakomi Nurseries. "Quinn, he's a grieving man; I'd prefer not to have him think this was a suicide until I know something definite."

"Relax, Lisa. It's your case. I'll stay in the background."

She parked behind Walter's truck. "You couldn't stay in the background even if you tried."

"I'll admit, I rarely try." He opened his door, got out, and slipped on his hat.

She had considered calling Detective Ford Prescott or Jack, but it was now after seven on Sunday evening. She was here to retrieve a cat, have a brief look around. If she found something, she could always call them back to the site.

Lisa waited for Quinn to join her before walking forward to meet Walter. She struggled to find the right words. "Mr. Hampton, thank you for coming back over to the house."

He turned his baseball hat in his hand. "Your message said it was important."

"This is awkward, but I need a favor. Would you mind exhuming the cat?"

"Of course. Let me get a shovel; it will take me twenty minutes at most. The shoe box is buried at the edge of the garden."

The lingering suspicion that it had been foul play and Walter had been involved eased even further with his immediate agreement. "Thank you. If we could borrow the key again, we'll be in the house. I need to check one last item."

"Of course." He reached into his pocket for the key and looked from her to Quinn.

She stumbled over the error; Quinn was not in the background when he was standing right beside her. "I'm sorry. Mr. Hampton, this is U.S. Marshal Quinn Diamond."

Walter dropped the key as he handed it to her, then dug it from the dirt with an apology. He nodded briefly to Quinn. "Mr. Diamond. Let me get that shovel."

She watched him walk toward the detached garage. "I feel sorry for him," she said quietly to Quinn. "This is tough."

"The guy is nervous."

"Because he dropped the key?"

"He didn't look at me once we were introduced, but given the circumstances, I don't suppose I can blame him. He knows there's something you're not saying." Quinn turned toward the car. "Get the flashlight, let's go to work."

She walked back to the car and opened the trunk. She found the flashlight in the box with the roadside flares and the jug of extra windshield wiper fluid. The flashlight gave a weak beam. She should have changed the batteries before coming.

"What are you looking for in the house?"

"I just want to see the scene again from a different viewpoint."

He walked with her up to the house and wrestled the front door unlocked.

The house groaned around them as the evening breeze picked up. The charred smell of burned wood hung heavy in the humid air. "Let's check the office area; maybe he wrote a final note," she suggested to avoid facing the upstairs for a few more minutes. She'd be surprised if there was one; statistically most suicides didn't leave one, but it was possible.

Walter had boxed what papers were salvageable from the desk. If there had been something in the office, he would have likely found it, but Lisa thumbed through the box to double-check. They spent time searching through the downstairs rooms but came up with nothing specific. There was no diary, no letter, no note left in his Bible.

"I'm going to look upstairs again," Lisa said, accepting the inevitable. Quinn joined her. The flashlight flickered as they reached the steps.

"Wait," Quinn cautioned. "I saw another flashlight in one of the desk drawers."

He disappeared back into the office.

Striking the flashlight against her palm a couple times brought the beam back. Lisa shone her flashlight back up the stairwell. She needed to see if there was any other evidence of a last evening: a favorite book, a keepsake like a picture nearby. If this was a planned suicide, Egan had probably changed his normal nightly routine in more ways than just a cigar.

A flash of movement at the top of the stairs stopped her. Something was up there. Something fell, and she heard the unmistakable bark of a squirrel. The last thing she needed was an animal disturbing the scene.

She started up the stairs. "Quinn, there's a squirrel trapped up there."

She reached the landing, choosing her steps with care. The beam illuminated the animal at the end of the hall, its golden eyes gleaming back at her. She could sense the poor thing's terror and the panic it must feel with the burned smell all around. How was she going to get it out of this house? She couldn't leave it here.

It darted toward the bedroom, and she moved to close the other doors in the hallway, eliminating other places it could run. She was aware her foot was on something soft an instant before the world moved.

The wood gave an explosive break, and she was falling into darkness.

It was pitch black. Her flashlight was gone. She was lying on her back, and she had landed on something sharp.

Lisa struggled to breathe, could feel the shock swallowing her, couldn't stop the narrowing of her vision.

She was impaled on something; it was a horrific realization. It hadn't punctured a lung, but she could feel the agonizing pain ballooning through her chest.

"Lisa! Where are you?"

The voice was edged with panic. It echoed through the clouds of billowing, choking ash settling on the remains of the collapsed stairs and flooring, settling on her face and clogging her breath, smothering her. All the annoying things she had ever thought of him she silently apologized for.

"Quinn."

He had to have exquisite hearing to catch her faint whisper; as soon as she said his name, his light moved toward her. The beam pierced the cloudy ash and struck her face, and then he was scrambling over beams and through rubble toward her. He jammed the flashlight into a crevice and pushed aside the remains of shattered flooring and part of a stair step.

In the wavering light she saw him flinch, and she tried to offer a reassuring smile. He yanked off his shirt, the buttons flying. "Hold on."

She couldn't get enough air; she had to know. "What...land on?"

He didn't answer her.

It must be bad.

She shivered and felt a warm flood rush across her hand as her vision went black.

FOUR

"Quinn, quit fussing."

"I'll fuss as long as I like. Get used to it," he retorted, his voice abrupt but not his hands. He was trying to figure out how to get Lisa out of the car without touching something that would cause her more pain, and it was proving to be an impossible problem to solve. Eight days in the hospital and about the only thing on this last Monday in October that hadn't changed was her irritation with him.

Finally accepting that there was no pain-free way to do this, he turned her legs toward the street and slid his hands under her arms. "Here we go." He eased her to her feet, holding his breath as her mouth went thin and taut. She was too stubborn to admit how bad it hurt, but her forearms rested against his chest and he braced to take her weight.

Her head bowed as she fought the pain off. He didn't catch the words she said, but he got the drift. He ran a soothing hand across her hair, silently giving her time.

"Don't you dare let the other O'Malleys see this."

"I won't."

They had a little conspiracy forming as they stood there and the other two cars pulled into her driveway behind them. A shift of his body shielded the distress she was in from her family. The ride to her home had been hard; there was no way around that. She had insisted the doctors release her today, and she was paying for it.

She wouldn't be walking anywhere very fast, anytime soon. The joist rebar had done more damage than a bullet. Two inches to the left and it would have paralyzed her, two inches higher, killed her outright. As it was she had suffered through four days in intensive care and four days on the general ward to deal with the trauma, surgery, and massive amount of blood loss. Displaced ribs were slow to heal.

The other O'Malleys saw, but they silently pretended not to.

"Okay. I can make it."

He kept a firm grip under her forearms as she straightened. Only after he was sure she was steady did he reach back into the car for her things. He handed her the cane she'd been ordered to use for the next few days.

"I am so glad to be home."

He set her suitcase on the drive. She was trying to close her left hand with its broken index finger around the cane. Watching her cautious movements made him hurt; he shifted the cane to her other hand and moved her injured hand to rest on his forearm. "Let's get you inside." One of the others would bring in the suitcase.

"Who's been taking care of my animals?"

"Kate or I have been by every day."

All of the O'Malleys with the exception of Jennifer were here, and it had taken a concerted effort from the others to get Jennifer to stay in Baltimore. She had been prepared to be on the first plane out, chemotherapy or not.

Quinn had never met a family more united than this one. The seven of them were related not by blood, but by choice. At the orphanage—Trevor House—they had made the decision to become their own family, had as adults legally changed their last names to O'Malley. Two decades later this group remained incredibly tight.

And they'd made him part of it.

He'd felt the change in the last week. They'd always made him feel welcome, but it was different now. When it came time to move Lisa home and get her settled, they had passed that assignment to him without even asking.

He was under no illusions of why. Lisa's accident and his part in it had hit this family hard. Their group reaction had come in stages. It would have been fascinating to watch if he hadn't been in the middle of it. As it was, he was simply trying to survive it.

Stage one had been direct. Jack had slugged him. A fast right cross had caught him on the jaw line and come close to rounding what had always been a rather square jaw. Quinn had found himself flat on his back in the hospital parking lot, looking up at the sky, feeling like a truck had hit him. He hadn't even seen it coming.

Quinn had shaken off the stars to find Stephen, the paramedic in the family, standing over him, yelling at Jack. Quinn had moved to touch his jaw, and Stephen had looked down and given him a blistering order not to move or he would finish what Jack had started. The dynamic duo of brothers had been mad at him for letting Lisa get hurt; they'd just differed on how to most effectively make their point.

Marcus had arrived in the middle of the exchange. The man had flown back from Baltimore and arrived to find his sister still in surgery. Quinn had stayed on the ground precisely because he was the man's partner. Marcus was the oldest O'Malley and guardian of the group, and he took Lisa's welfare personally. Marcus wouldn't just make his jaw ache, he'd break it. It wouldn't be the Christian thing for Marcus to do, but it would be the older brother thing to do. Quinn wasn't willing to find out which would win out.

They were worried; therefore, they were mad. And in the simple equation of guys looked after girls, he was responsible. They'd made their point.

Jack had cooled off first, had offered him a hand up. Quinn had warily accepted. Frankly, getting hit had helped. He'd deserved it for letting Lisa get hurt.

The brothers had accepted his apology, and the four of them had ended up pacing as a group while they struggled to wait for Lisa to get out of surgery.

Stage two had been the sisters. Jennifer, Kate, and Rachel had insisted on hearing the details of what had happened.

He'd spent over an hour on the phone with Jennifer. As a doctor she had wanted to know everything he could remember about Lisa's injuries. Kate had asked for details because as a cop she wanted to find something that would implicate someone as responsible.

Rachel had been the toughest to deal with. A trauma psychologist, she had worked her way under the "I'm fine" cloak of words to the truth. She had pulled out what it had been like from the first sound of wood collapsing, through the realization of how bad Lisa was hurt, to the desperate realization Lisa might not make it to the hospital. By the time Rachel was through with him, he'd been taken apart and put back together. Effective, but incredibly draining.

Stage three was to give him a chance to make it up to Lisa. It was the hardest to accomplish because it was self-driven. Until Lisa was back on her feet and no longer dealing with the aftereffects of the injuries, he was going to feel responsible. She'd been hurt on his watch. He should have protected her. He'd failed. He didn't need her brothers to point that fact out, or conversely, her sisters to tell him it had been an accident.

He felt responsible.

Quinn hoped getting Lisa home would turn the corner. He wanted this behind them even more than the other O'Malleys did.

While the others began to unload the flowers that had packed Lisa's hospital room, Quinn walked her slowly to the front door. He and Lisa were passed several times as they walked, Jack and Stephen joking with her about what her ferret Sidney was likely to do with the florist shop she was bringing home. Lisa joked back, but her comebacks were at a fraction of their normal speed.

Rachel held the screen door for them.

"Couch or chair?" Quinn asked Lisa quietly.

"Couch."

The strain in Lisa's single word bit. The car ride had jarred the injury and this walk was capping it off. Her back muscles were going to spasm if she didn't relax.

He grasped her elbows and eased her down.

She sucked in a deep breath. "Thanks."

Afraid she'd started to cry, he brushed back her hair and raised her chin, knowing she was going to tense on him but more petrified of the possible tears. He read the pain clouding her eyes. "What do you need?"

He'd startled her. He waited for it to pass, not moving away, and was rewarded as her eyes softened with humor for the first time in days. "New ribs. But I'll settle for something to make me forget the ones I have."

"This will do it." Rachel joined them carrying a prescription bottle. "Jennifer said this muscle relaxant would take down an elephant."

Quinn reluctantly eased back, leaving her to the care of the family descending on her. Kate came into the room bringing Sidney. The guys turned toward the kitchen debating over what to fix for dinner.

"I want a steak," Lisa interjected into the conversation.

"Not for another week, doctor's orders," Stephen called back.

"Stephen."

"Live with it. We're having fish."

Lisa made a face even as she laughed.

Quinn got himself a soft drink, took a seat across from Lisa out of the way, and settled in to just watch her. Marcus had once described Lisa as the one they had simply chosen to envelop. Having watched her family interact long enough, he now understood it.

Abandoned at birth, in seven foster homes before Trevor House, Lisa had never felt like she fit in. She'd arrived at Trevor House independent to a fault, a lizard peeking out of her backpack. The group had simply enveloped her then and they were doing it again now.

This last week he'd watched them override what was her instinct for space with a smothering presence of love. Even if she tended not to reach for it, she drew her strength from it. He was gaining a rapid education in how to deal with her that he wasn't going to forget.

She'd never been alone; Marcus had tried to make himself comfortable in the hospital chair late at night, Jack and Kate through the days, Rachel and Stephen in the evenings. Quinn had taken the predawn hours when the dreams tended to haunt her, when he didn't have to hide what he felt from the others.

She'd been hurt while with him and the guilt was heavy.

He listened to Lisa laugh as she played with Sidney, saw the strain in her face ease as the muscle relaxant kicked in, and for the first time in a week his heart settled back into a normal rhythm. He never wanted to come so close to losing her again.

He had to go all the way back to the time surrounding his father's murder to find a week more draining than this one. Physically exhausted from lack of sleep. Emotionally drained by how long and hard the battle had gone on before Lisa was out of danger. Spiritually…turmoil was a good word.

Three of the seven O'Malleys were new Christians—Jennifer, Marcus, and Kate—and their expectations for what Jesus would do to heal Lisa…their expectations were so high.

At two in the morning he'd been sitting with Kate and Marcus in the hospital cafeteria privy to a strategy session on how to get Lisa to listen to the truth. It had been uncomfortable. Quinn agreed with their objective, and at the same time felt like he was betraying Lisa by talking about her behind her back.

Kate thought it would be better to push the subject of God while Lisa was still dealing with the turmoil of almost dying and there might be a window of opportunity available. Marcus had been a little more cautious but had agreed with Kate. Quinn had tried to urge Jennifer's approach that had been so effective in reaching the two of them: a steady one that didn't push to hard.

Now Quinn was praying for wisdom. Marcus and Kate...he wouldn't want the two of them focused on him, and he was afraid that would be Lisa's initial reaction.

"You look down," Kate said softly, settling on the arm of his chair.

Trust her to get to the point. "I'm okay."

Kate borrowed his soft drink. "Your heart's been on your sleeve for a week, you might want to tuck it inside again before she realizes it," she whispered.

Quinn leaned his head back to look up at her. The lady he had dated for a few months and come to consider one of his most important friends knew him very well. He would be lying to say his emotions weren't involved; eight long days focused on Lisa had intensified everything he felt. But Kate was seeing what she wanted to see. He laughed softly and didn't have the heart to break her bubble. She was happy; she wanted Lisa to be happy. "It's noticeable?"

"But very cute."

"She's on my case for fussing."

Kate grinned. "And you do it so well. You can fuss over me if you like."

"She's already talking about when she goes back to work."

"I know. It's crazy to be going back to work so soon, but she needs it. It's a distraction."

"She's going to be hurting for months."

"Yes." She squeezed the back of his neck. "She'll recover. Did you hear from Lincoln?"

The investigation into Amy Ireland Nugan had been forced to the sidelines by circumstances, and it took a moment for him to refocus. Kate knew the history. "Lincoln got word from his contact in Canada last night. They confirmed Amy was born in Quebec, eventually moved to New York, then here. It was a different Amy Ireland."

"I'm sorry."

"So am I." There was no way to put into words what it felt like to lose another promising thread. Giving up hope of finding the man who killed his father took something of his spirit with it, and it was happening as each promising lead failed.

"It won't stay unsolved forever, Quinn. Nothing does."

He appreciated the thought. It wasn't in him to give up, but eventually he was going to have to. He had sought the truth for so long, but the deadline he had set for himself long ago was approaching. He'd have to get on with his life without the justice he needed. It was a terrible thought. He nodded toward Lisa and changed the subject. "Are you staying here tonight?"

"Yes. Craig's covering my pager."

"Thanks."

"Dave's coming over when he gets off work. You want to stay around and keep Lisa company while Dave and I go for a walk?"

"You just want to go flirt with your boyfriend."

"You got it."

"I'm glad you found him." He felt more than a minor protective interest in who Kate had in her life. Their friendship had happened more by accident than planning. The first few meals had been informal and spur of the moment—sharing a sandwich while she sat through a day-long negotiation, buying her a hot dog at a ball game, helping her haul a new couch into her apartment and sitting on the living room floor sharing a pizza before they returned the moving truck.

Quinn had found Kate to be a great friend. He'd started worrying about her like her brother Marcus did, wondering what risks she was taking in her job. It had taken only a few months of spending time with her to know it mattered to him that she eventually find the right guy to share her life with.

He'd been relieved when Dave came on the scene. The FBI agent was a guy who had already proven he'd do what it took to protect her.

"He's a good man." She ruffled the back of his hair. "Something like you."

"I'll stick around."

She glanced at her sister. "Lisa could do worse."

He took back his glass, found Kate had left him the ice, and smiled. "Don't you start. She can make up her own mind." He wanted another chance with Lisa. He was determined to get past the last eight days and back on plan. He still owed her dinner and he was determined to get an opportunity to deliver on it.

FIVE

"Quinn, you don't need to stay."

"Quit protesting; I'm not going anywhere." He turned on a table lamp and then reached back and killed the overhead light, having seen Lisa rub her forehead more than once, a telltale sign that she had a growing headache. The rest of the O'Malleys had left a short time ago; Kate and Dave were catching a private moment together watching the moon come up.

"Even if I said I was tired and I want you to go back to the hotel?"

"You've had two naps today, you're hurting because the painkiller is wearing off, and you're feeling sorry for yourself. So which do you want first? Something for the pain or a distraction?"

She frowned over at him. "I'm home; I'm fine. And you don't listen."

She wanted a fight; he smiled slightly and refused to give her one. "No, I don't."

"I wish you'd quit feeling sorry for me…or guilty."

He got to his feet. "Give me a break. You nearly got yourself killed a few feet away from me. I'm allowed." He stopped in front of her and held out both hands. "Come on. You've been sitting for an hour. If you don't get up and move, your back will lock up."

She frowned as she looked at his hands, thinking about it. He laughed and wiggled his fingers. "Come on."

Her hands slid into his and he felt how cold they were. He reassuringly grasped her hands, careful how he held her injured one, and pulled her up. As soon as she was steady, she removed her hands from his and pressed one against her left ribs.

"Aches?"

"Every time I breathe," she admitted. "Want to do me a favor?"

"If it's not going to get me into trouble with one of your brothers."

She tipped her head and smiled at him. He was a goner for that smile even if she didn't know it. "What do you need? Maybe we can just not tell them."

"I've been craving a milkshake. Kate won't tell."

Not exactly what her doctor had in mind. And she needed something hot.

"It's practically all milk," she offered.

"I don't suppose it will kill you."

"Fix it while I peek in on my pets?"

He laughed. "Sure. Go on."

"Thanks."

"You're welcome," he replied dryly. "Go."

He watched her walk slowly down the hall and enter the spare bedroom she had turned into a home for all the living things she collected. He shook his head. She was a walking contradiction—annoyed at him one minute, flashing that smile the next.

He went through the dining room to the kitchen and opened the freezer. Vanilla or chocolate? He thought about asking, then decided he might as well make his favorite. He opened the chocolate ice cream.

He fixed two milkshakes, cleaned up the counter, then dug around in the drawers for two straws. He carried the glasses with him to find Lisa. She already had a habit of forgetting to eat when she worked, and the last several days had been little more than IVs; the calories would do her good.

Quinn stopped at the doorway, watching her. She was in her element with things that crawled and swam.

The mice were awake, three adorable white and one sleek brown tumbling over the hollow climbing blocks she'd carved. Sliding aside the mesh top of the cage, Lisa took a moment to reach inside and greet them. They scampered across her palm and tickled her fingers. She refilled their water, then closed the cage lid.

"Where did you find the brown one?"

"A neighbor's pet; Scott was moving and couldn't take it with him."

She opened the jar of fish food flakes for the guppies she was raising. He had taken the time yesterday to clean the tank, change the filter, and replace the evaporated water. With close to two dozen baby guppies swimming among the upper leaves of the plants it had been an experience. He didn't think he'd accidentally killed more than a couple. As she closed the cover the fish began to grab the flakes, shaking off smaller pieces.

"Hi, Truebody." Lisa tapped on the glass of the second fish tank. The praying mantis moved up the twig it clung to toward the light. She lingered over the third large tank, talking to the iguana. Oscar was one of her favorites.

In the next cage a hamster pushed its way out of a burrow of shredded white paper. "Baby, what have they been feeding you?" The hamster had grown fat in the last ten days—very fat.

"Kate thinks she's pregnant."

"Really? Oh that will be so cool. I hope she has several." She tilted her head to look at him. "You know, you could do with a pet…"

He laughed. "On a ranch the size of mine, it has to be able to fend for itself."

"Nothing smaller than a breadbasket?"

"Not unless it can outrun a wolf."

The parrot whistled, stalking back and forth. "I haven't forgotten you, Iris," Lisa reassured. She opened the cage door and offered her hand. The bird stepped up gracefully and ducked its head as Lisa brought her out of the cage. "Did you miss me?"

The bird shook her head and fluffed her feathers.

"Yes, you did, I recognize that huff." She stroked the bird's chest and it preened and cooed back at her.

"A dangerous pet to have, given your others."

"I know. But we've got an understanding, don't we, girl? She got loose at the pet store and sort of chose me. Landed right on my shoulder."

He didn't miss the way her voice softened at that statement.

She put Iris back in her cage and folded down the cover to tuck the bird in for the night. "It looks like everyone lived through my absence."

"We tried, although I'm glad you said the grade school had taken the mole."

"Charlie was adorable."

"If you say so." He held out the second glass he carried. "One milkshake."

"Thanks." She took it, sampled it, and nodded her appreciation. "Good."

Sidney was awake and ringing the small bell attached to the top of his cage. Lisa knelt down, picked up one of the empty paper towel tubes stacked on the supply shelf, and offered it to him. The ferret stood on his back legs to grasp it and haul it back into his cage. He proceeded to push his head inside and wiggle his body through it, chattering in a high pitch as he rolled. He reappeared, grabbed it with his feet, and tumbled it around.

"He loves those things."

"Almost as much as he does things he can chase." She got to her feet. "I appreciate the time you and Kate took."

"We didn't mind. Although I'm pretty sure Kate drowned your plants."

She laughed, then groaned at the pain it caused. "It wouldn't be the first time. I need to sit down." She waved him back toward the living room. "You never did tell me what they discovered at the house."

He shortened his stride to match her slow walk, glad to see her balance was improving. "The major beam under the bedroom had cracked. When it gave way, the flooring and hallway folded and collapsed into the den. Unfortunately, you were in the hallway at the time."

"It wasn't somewhere I stepped?"

"No."

"Well at least that's nice to know." She gestured with her glass to the briefcase by the door. "Is the Hampton file Jack brought over in there?"

"Lisa."

"I want to see it, just for a minute."

He opened her briefcase and got the case file. They had autopsied the burned cat Walter Hampton had gone to retrieve. He waited until she had eased herself down on the couch. "You don't need to do this now."

"Quinn."

He reluctantly handed her the folder. She flipped through to read the lab results. He already knew them. He was prepared for the disquiet in her eyes when she finally looked over at him.

"The cat showed no signs of a sleeping pill."

"No."

"I got hurt for nothing," she said softly.

"The toxicology was run several days after the fact. It was a stretch to consider something would be found."

She shook her head. "The pill wouldn't have had time to entirely dissolve, and even crushed it would have been so concentrated it would have still been there in measurable doses, fire or not." She dropped the folder and rubbed her eyes. "I went out in the field on another of my hunches, determined to check the scene, and got myself hurt. It would be funny if this weren't what...the fifth time?"

He perched on the arm of the couch. "You wouldn't have been doing your job if you didn't pursue what was a logical question. And there's still an open question of why the cat didn't escape the room."

"As Jack says—pets die in fires. There's not enough to say it was a suicide. In a way I'm glad I was wrong; it's awful to put a family through that."

She rested her head back against the sofa, studying him. "I haven't told you thanks for what you did. I knew when I saw your face that it was pretty bad. I'm sorry; I should have told you thanks ages ago."

His hand tightened on the glass he held so he wouldn't reach out and rub her slight frown away. "You're welcome."

"I would wake up sometimes late at night and see you there beside the hospital bed praying."

He stilled. "Did you?" He'd been praying all right, scared to death the infection would spread, that the antibiotics wouldn't work, that he'd lose someone more precious to him than any lady he could remember.

"That was...nice of you."

"It's okay, Lisa. I know you don't believe." He'd watched her for years, putting together pieces and glimpses of her past, trying to understand why she appeared so indifferent when the topic of faith was mentioned. She was normally so curious about every subject under discussion. It frustrated him because he wanted to change it but couldn't figure out how.

"I think it helped."

She seemed bothered by that more than pleased, and his eyes sharpened as he searched her face, absorbing that impression, testing it. She shouldn't be reacting that way. "Well I had a vested interest," he said lightly. "Not having you around to bug me would have been a bummer."

"No, I mean it. The pain would be bad, I'd wake up and see you praying, then it would ease away before I could page a nurse for more pain medication."

"You're serious."

"Yes, I am. I nearly told Jennifer."

He reached over and wiped away a tear as it slipped from the corner of her eye and down her cheek. "Tell her. And I'll keep praying for her." It was killing him to have Jennifer sick; he could only imagine what facing that was doing to Lisa.

"Thanks." She wiped away the other threatening tears and gave a rueful smile.

He wished she believed. Jennifer did, Dave and Kate, Marcus. It brought a strength and a peace and certain knowledge of the Resurrection. Lisa didn't have that hope, and she so desperately needed it.

He'd survived the death of his father because of his faith. Without that hope… But the solution was not going to be as simple as he had thought, as simple as convincing her to come to church with them and hear the truth. There was ancient hurt there, buried deep in those blue eyes he had thought he understood.

"Did I hear you've got a scrapbook?" he asked to help her out.

"A few of them."

"Jen could use one for all the cards and gift notes she's receiving from friends and former patients. I thought of it when I saw her hospital room."

"That's a great idea."

"She'll be out of the hospital soon. She's headed toward a remission." He had to keep believing that, for Lisa's sake as much as his own. He didn't want her to have to bear the loss of Jennifer, would do anything to protect her from that if he could.

"Maybe," she said, but it was filled with doubt. She set aside her glass, and her expression lightened, became almost humorous, as she studied him. "You look exhausted."

"I always look tired," he replied, amused at the doctor's tone she reverted to on occasion with him. "Trying to sleep in the city is like sleeping in a bright noise factory."

She laughed, groaned, then frowned at him for causing it. "Do me one more favor. Go back to your hotel, dig out a bed, and sleep for twelve hours. You really do look like one of the walking dead."

"You're sure?"

"Yes."

"I'll call it a night if you promise me you won't even think about going anywhere tomorrow. If you won't give yourself a week at home, at least make it a few days before you go back to the office."

"I can sit there as well as here."

"I'm serious. It's too early. You'll just give yourself a relapse."

"I already promised Marcus I'd stay home tomorrow, make it a half day Wednesday."

"Good enough."

The patio door slid open and Dave and Kate rejoined them, Kate laughing as she tried to untangle herself from Dave's arms. "Lisa, one of your neighbors has a dog that's baying at the moon."

"That's Wilfred. He's English."

"Who, the neighbor or the dog?" Kate asked, dissolving into a fit of giggles as Dave scooped her up. "Would you put me down?"

"Not till you admit I was right."

"Lisa, tell him bats don't fly this far north. He swears one was going to land in my hair, and he had to protect me."

"Actually..." Lisa looked at Dave to get the right answer, "they do occasionally. The brown wedge-wing bat is native to Ohio and does come into Illinois."

Dave grinned over at her, then looked back at Kate. "See?"

"Oh, you—"

He stole a kiss and set her down. "I'd better get going. Lisa, it's a delight to have you home."

"Thanks, Dave."

"I'll walk out with you," Quinn decided, retrieving his hat. He didn't want to leave, but as much as he'd like to take advantage of Lisa's lowered guard and risk asking a few questions, a sense of fairness wouldn't let him do it. "Lisa—" what he would've liked to say she wasn't ready yet to hear—"take care. I'll see you later."

"Good night, Quinn."

He turned the lock on the front doorknob. "Kate?"

"I'll get the dead bolt."

He nodded his thanks and stepped out with Dave.

"A nice night," Dave commented, pulling out his keys.

"Beautiful," Quinn agreed, looking up at the full moon.

"Heading back to your hotel? Or do you want to join us down at the gym?"

The late night basketball games were a tradition when the O'Malleys were in the same city. It was a good way to deal with the stress. "Another time."

"If you change your mind, we've got the court till eleven."

Quinn unlocked the door to his rental car. What he would really like was a four-hour horseback ride checking fence line—a chance to think, let a week of stress bleed off, and figure out what to do next.

He'd pass on the basketball game; the O'Malleys were too perceptive. Marcus and Kate already knew where his interests lay, and the others would figure it out. The last thing he needed was Lisa feeling pressure from her family.

He started the car, turned on the lights, and waited for Dave to pull out. Quinn held up a hand in farewell as the car lights crossed his back window.

Dave turned left at the thoroughfare and Quinn turned right. He was staying at the Radisson Hotel downtown near the regional marshals' office. To break the absolute silence in the car, he turned on the radio, changed it to FM, and found a country station. As he glanced back up he saw headlights flash in his rearview mirror. Someone else was leaving the subdivision.

Traffic was light for a Monday evening, and out of habit he kept half his attention on the traffic behind him.

He needed gas and a newspaper. He turned off at Route 43 and pulled into a new gas and convenience store at the corner of Sherman and Waukegan. All the pumps were free and he pulled to a stop at the first. Ten minutes later, having paid for the gas and the newspaper, he walked back to his car.

As he pulled back onto the road, a dark green Plymouth pulled out from the graphics art printing business across the street. It pulled across to his lane, two cars behind.

Quinn adjusted the rearview mirror, his eyes narrowing. Once was something to note, twice unusual, three times—he reached for his cellular phone. He entered his partner's pager number, then punched in an added code unique to him. Interrupting a basketball game…

His phone rang back moments later. "Hey, Quinn, coming to the game?" Marcus was breathing hard. "Adam and I have got Stephen and Jack on the ropes. We could use your awesome defense in center."

"I've got a tail."

"Where are you?" Marcus asked, his voice instantly turning serious.

"Waukegan Road, just passing the railroad tracks. I'll be at Willow soon. I'm going to divert north on Sunset. See if you can pick him up."

"Same dark green Plymouth?"

"Hanging two back." Quinn removed his Glock and slid it under the newspaper on the seat beside him. There was a sense of cold anger settling inside. "I think he tagged me at Lisa's subdivision."

"We're moving. Stay on the phone."

When Quinn had left after a visit to the bookstore where Amy Ireland Nugan had held her signing, he had noticed the Plymouth behind him. It had been there again three days ago across from the hospital.

Lisa's subdivision.

He'd just put her in danger. "Marcus, get someone on a phone to Kate, tell her to be on her guard. Just don't let Lisa know."

"Dave just walked in, he's already calling."

Quinn turned north on Sunset and watched as the Plymouth also turned, now directly behind him. The front license plate was gone. Looking back into the car headlights there was no way to identify the driver; he couldn't tell if it was a man or woman, and he had learned the hard way not to assume.

The tail was making no attempt to keep back at a safe distance. "I'm coming up on Route 68."

"Don't risk the Edens, head east into Glencoe and come south on Green Bay Road. There'll be enough traffic we should be able to get near him. Dave and I will try to get beside and behind him."

"I'm heading for Green Bay."

Quinn wanted to slam on his brakes and catch the driver by surprise; he forced himself to be patient and wait on backup. Why a tail in Chicago? Why across from the hospital? There were always men being released from prison who would be more than happy to make trouble for him, but there had been no release bulletins mentioning cases from here.

Had something in Lincoln's investigation caught someone's attention? He didn't see what it could be. And if Lincoln had picked up a tail, he would have mentioned it.

"We're on Green Bay, coming up on Tower Road," Marcus said. "Where are you?"

"Turning on Green Bay…now," Quinn replied, using the brief moment in the turn under the streetlights to try and see the driver of the other car.

The Plymouth suddenly accelerated through the intersection and turned north.

"He broke off! He's heading north on Green Bay."

Quinn swiveled around to try and catch the license plate. "I've lost him." Traffic was too heavy to immediately U-turn.

"We're pushing to catch him."

"He'll likely be heading to the Edens."

"Dave's diverting now. I'll keep coming up Green Bay."

Quinn pulled into Tudor Court and turned back north.

They spent the next twenty minutes with the three cars crisscrossing the area looking for the Plymouth.

"Marcus, I'll meet you at the 7-Eleven on Route 68 and Pfingsten," Quinn finally called, ending the search.

"Two minutes."

Quinn parked and shut off the car but left the radio on. "Lord, what now?" he asked, seeking wisdom he didn't have. The tension was just beginning to drain away. It wasn't the danger of the threat so much as the unknown of what he was dealing with, the realization Lisa had been brought into its periphery.

He hated his job at times. It was rare to get so angry, but fatigue and frustration were combining. "Lord, I'm tired of dealing with tails and uncooperative witnesses and threats that come veiled and not so veiled. How long are You going to leave me chasing leads that go nowhere?"

His future should have been clear. Instead, he felt like he was having to live life one day at a time, constantly reacting. He had to figure out what had happened to Amy and his father. He desperately needed the closure.

"I want to go back to ranching full time, Lord." He rarely let himself admit how much internal pressure had developed. He had hoped getting back to the ranch for a month during his vacation would help ease that pressure and push off the decision for a few more months.

He returned the Glock to its holster with a sigh.

He really didn't need this happening tonight. A year ago getting tailed would have been just one more thing in life to roll with. Tonight—Quinn picked up his hat and rolled the brim in callous hands. He was going home. He was letting go. Even if it meant leaving the man who had killed his father free.

The sadness of that was overwhelming. But it was time.

Lisa. Quinn's hand tightened around the rough fabric as he frowned. She was hurt. She was going to have Kate and Marcus—for all the right reasons—pushing her out of her comfort zone. She struck him as needing a friend. And he was lousy at walking away in those circumstances.

She wouldn't be thrilled if he stuck around; he would feel guilty if he left. "Lord, I didn't need this either," Quinn muttered, checking the mirror as car headlights swept across the window. The car turned in the opposite direction; it wasn't Marcus.

He'd been a Christian a long time, but some of his friends were not Christians. It was a dichotomy he had accepted over the years as the place God had put him. He couldn't be a light among a sea of candles. It wasn't a comfortable place to rest, constantly having to tug a dark world toward God while not getting sidetracked by it.

He was forty-four. The days he wanted to hang around entirely with guys were long gone. If he had to take extra care in how he was friends with a woman, then he would find and watch that line, make that extra effort. Having friends in L.A. he could call when he was in town, someone in Dallas, someone in Chicago—they made it possible to accept the other drawbacks that came with a profession that sent him around the country.

And if over the years he'd bought more than a few wedding gifts—well at least he had the good sense to choose wonderful ladies to be his friends.

Quinn wasn't going to get romantically involved with someone he couldn't marry—he'd already had a lifetime of dreams not coming true. He wasn't about to let himself head down a road that before he took the first step he knew would not lead anywhere. Life was about choices, the toughest ones involving where he put his time.

During the last year Jennifer had come to believe, then Kate and Marcus. There was hope for Lisa. Distant, but there. She would be his friend either way—

Car headlights reflected across the mirror and this time the car pulled into the parking lot.

Marcus pulled into the parking space beside him and got out of his car to circle to the passenger side, leaning against the side of it. Quinn rolled down his window. Marcus crossed his arms across his chest as he thought about the situation, then looked over at Quinn. "Someone looking for you? Three times—he's tracking your movements. Why?"

"Your guess is as good as mine. If he was looking for a chance to deliver a message, he's already had it. And if he's watching for someone else—well he's not a professional. Have you noticed someone following you?"

"No."

"Just me. Wonderful. I didn't exactly advertise I was coming to Chicago."

"Amy Ireland?"

"Maybe, but why? It was a dead end. She's Canadian, not even the person I was looking for."

"You made the newscast when the house collapsed and Lisa was airlifted to Mercy General. Someone saw you were in town."

"It makes about as much sense as anything."

"Watch your back in the morning, and check the car before you turn the key. We'll run the release sheets in the morning, see who's out there with a grudge."

"Sorry I interrupted the game."

Marcus smiled. "Don't be. Jack looked relieved. I'll shadow you back to the hotel."

"Lisa?"

"Dave was going to swing back by. Relax. If trouble did come calling, no one would get past Kate."

"True. Still—" Quinn started the car. If it weren't for the fact he'd possibly be bringing danger back to her subdivision, he'd go watch Lisa's house for the night.

Marcus pushed away from his car. "Next time, back up into him. A car accident would be appropriate in the circumstances."

"Believe me, I was tempted."

Quinn headed back to the hotel, Marcus driving a few cars behind. Quinn slowed to pull into the hotel parking garage and Marcus lifted a hand in farewell and pulled past him. Quinn hesitated, then started circling toward the top floor. He'd seen the results of more than one car bombing in his lifetime. If he missed something during the check in the morning, better to blow up the roof than the basement.

SIX

"What time is it out there?"

Lisa reluctantly admitted the truth. "Four A.M."

Jennifer chuckled softly. "I'll send you some of my dawn. It's gorgeous. My hospital room faces east. And you were prescribed sleeping pills for a reason. Take them next time."

Lisa had lain awake long enough the shadows in the bedroom had become furniture and clutter, the open sliding doors to her closet creating the only cave of blackness left undeciphered. This Wednesday, her second morning back home, was starting much as her first: The sleep she wanted refused to come. If she tried to get up she'd wake Kate, who was sleeping in the second spare room down the hall. So she had lain here letting one sister sleep, thinking about another, until the clock finally made it unseemly early only on the East Coast.

"The last guy I saw who took sleeping pills burned alive in a fire." She didn't mean to be morbid, but Jennifer was the one person in the family who not only understood but also expected to hear the truth about what was going on.

"Doozy of a nightmare?"

"In spades." Lisa shifted uncomfortably, the two bandages hurting and the pressure on her back reigniting the sensation of fire inside her chest. "The scars are a mess. I took a shower for the first time last night; the stitches look like they were done by a guy with a fishhook, and those are just the ones I can see in the front. I don't even want to think about my back. I do a better job on a cadaver after an autopsy than he did on me."

"He was in a bit of a hurry. You were bleeding to death on him."

"Well, I hate to think what he'd have done if he had to crack my chest and go after something vital. I've already got enough displaced ribs barking at me."

"Lizzy, I saw a faxed copy of the chart. That bar hit practically everything vital there is inside you. Go swallow another painkiller."

"I already did. They make me dopey."

"The scars will heal, the bright redness will fade."

"I'm complaining." She didn't complain, not normally. She hated feeling this way.

"You're allowed." The empathy traveled a thousand miles. Lisa knew Jen was hurting too; the radiation pellets they had inserted to deal with the cancer around her spine were being removed a few at a time this week, lest they so decay the vertebra in her spine it collapsed.

"How's Quinn?"

Lisa groaned. "Sticking like a shadow."

Jen laughed. "I really like that guy."

"He's okay."

"Uh-huh. If you like handsome, sweet, thoughtful, and tough."

"Try strong-willed, stubborn..." The normal list that came so easily to mind petered off; it was habit now more than meant.

"You like him," Jen said softly.

"Yeah. Some."

The silence stretched, that of old friends and open hearts.

"Lizzy, I promise the right guy won't mind the scars."

"Tell me again why we are up at the crack of dawn?"

"I want to go to work."

Kate paused in pulling on her tennis shoes. "That's what I thought you said. I think you need to see another doctor. One to look at your head."

"I'm not spending another day stuck here bored out of my mind," Lisa replied, not feeling up to facing another sister with the truth. Kate was just annoyed because she never liked mornings; she'd get over it.

Dave had come over again last night. She'd heard Kate and Dave whispering, then heard the TV in the living room come on as they found a late movie to watch. She hadn't heard Kate turn in until well after 1 A.M. "If you want me to drive myself—"

"No. I'll take you. But couldn't you wait for something like the actual sunrise?"

"Not if I'm going to talk to Greg. He gets off at eight, and he's working the triple homicide/suicide from Pilsen. I want in."

Kate pushed fingers through her hair to straighten it, reached for her pager, and clipped it onto her belt. "You could ease back into work, you know, take it slow. Marcus will read you the riot act if you dive back in and overdo it."

Kate was right, but she wasn't going to let it change her plans. "How would you feel if someone sidelined you for part of a month?"

"Okay. Valid point. But I'm not leaving without coffee."

Shifting the cane to her other hand, Lisa turned toward the bedroom door and glanced back to grin at Kate. "It's already made. You can carry mine to the car for me."

Her sister laughed. "Head toward the car. I'll catch up."

Lisa took her at her word and walked down the hall, stopping in the dining room to dump her purse on the table. She pushed her keys into her pocket along with her staff ID, a credit card, and twenty dollars. She'd do without something to carry today.

Walking down the sloped driveway with caution, she unlocked the passenger door and slid her cane in the back, then eased herself into the car. She gingerly turned, wishing she had thought to bring out a pillow for her back. As the muscles stretched, she gritted her teeth at the pain. She stopped moving and it eased off.

Kate joined her, carrying two blue thermal travel mugs, the bases of the cups designed for the car's cup holders.

Lisa accepted hers with a thanks and wisely stayed silent as Kate got settled and started the car. Lisa didn't think her sister would appreciate an observation on how pretty the sunrise was this morning. Its beauty was hiding the coming reality; the day was predicted to be unseasonably warm, in the nineties with high humidity. It meant there would be several heat deaths today.

Kate slowed at a stop sign in the subdivision.

"Stop, Kate. That's Walter Hampton." Lisa recognized the white-and-blue truck of Nakomi Nurseries. "I want to say thanks for the flowers and the visit."

"Lisa."

"Stop."

Kate pulled to the side of the road.

The house on the corner had sold recently to a young couple from San Diego; they had moved in last month. There were several trees on a flatbed truck along with several bushes and rolls of sod. Walter was working on digging out part of a prior rock garden along with three other workers. They were obviously trying to get the most physical part of the work done and the plants in the ground before the heat of the day arrived. Lisa wasn't that surprised to see Walter out working with one of his crews; he had struck her as more of a doer than an office manager.

Lisa unbuckled her seat belt and carefully reversed her movements to get out of the car.

Walter had seen her; he set down his shovel to walk down the yard. They met halfway. "Miss O'Malley." His smile was genuinely pleased.

"It's good to see you, Walter."

"You're looking much better on your feet."

"I'm recovering fine. How's your wrist?" Walter had been walking back to the house when the beam collapsed, had helped Quinn dig her out.

He flexed it. "Almost good as new."

"I wanted to say thanks for the flowers. They were lovely. And numerous." He had sent a bouquet every day.

"I had a greenhouse full just waiting to brighten your day."

"They were appreciated. How is your family?"

"My brother Christopher is having a rough time of it, and my aunt Laura is now complaining that Egan doesn't visit her anymore. Personally, it feels good to be back at work. We're coping in our unique ways."

"I'm returning to work myself."

"I'm glad for you."

She looked over the scope of what he was undertaking, impressed. "The yard will look wonderful when it's complete."

"I hope so. It's a vision in my head at the moment; we'll see if I can make it appear."

"It looks like you got an early start."

"In this business, 4 to 6 A.M. is best; you don't want to be stuck in traffic with a couple ten-foot white birch trees." He nodded toward the car. "Heading downtown? There's construction on the Edens south of Winnetka today."

"One of the reasons for my early start."

"You'd best be heading that way then." He wiped the dirt from his hands on his jeans. "Can I give you a hand back to the car? The ground's a bit unlevel."

"I wouldn't turn one down. The cane makes me feel a bit old before my time." She walked back with him.

Lisa settled back in the car and introduced her sister. Walter nodded a greeting across to her. A final good-bye, and they pulled back onto the road. "Has that case closed?" Kate asked.

"Yes."

"It looks like the nursery does a good job, though I'm surprised to see them in your neighborhood."

"You should have seen the size of the Nakomi Nursery grounds, they must do business around the entire Chicagoland area. Walter strikes me as a hard-working guy who loves the business he's in. Expanding it would be the natural thing to do."

"For someone you've met three times, you've got a definite opinion of him."

"The flowers he sent from his greenhouses were picked on the optimal day to last as long as possible in a vase, and did you notice the patch of yard they were getting ready to sod? Someone took the time and care to leave a twelve-inch patch of grass around a wild violet in an area otherwise stripped and prepped for the sod. I have a feeling that was the work of the boss." Lisa bet the flower would be taken home and potted at the end of the day. It showed the business was more than just a job.

She reached for her coffee and wondered if she had the endurance for a half day at work. She hoped she did. She was pushing it to return to work this early, but it was the one place she could lose herself and put the accident behind her. She needed her life back.

"Have you thought any more about what we were talking about last night?"

Kate was watching the road. There was nothing offhand about the question even though Kate's body language was trying to convey that impression.

Kate had been her usual direct self last night, wanting to talk about the Bible passage in John she had been reading. Half the family had become Christians in the last three months—Jennifer, Kate, Marcus—and it was making for some sincere, heartfelt, but awkward family conversations.

Kate was passionate about her new faith. Excited. Like most new Christians, she was trying to convince everyone around her to believe too. Lisa didn't have to wonder what motivated her actions. Kate cared. Lisa couldn't fault her for that. But she wasn't interested.

In another month the excitement would fade, the subject would get dropped.

In a family with few secrets, there were still some things about her life before Trevor House that Lisa had kept private.

During her years in various foster homes she had attended Lutheran, Catholic, Presbyterian, and Baptist churches. As a child she had been exposed to religion more than most of them. A typical Sunday school teacher did not expect to get grilled on the various points of theology by a fourth grader.

They had all tried to answer her, surprised by her questions and the depth of what she wanted to know. They had all given good answers based upon what their denominations taught. Lisa's problem had been that while the answers were similar, they weren't the same.

When she had probed to ask why, each said the other perspectives were well-meaning but wrong. Trying to end the confusion had only increased it. Even as a child she had hated feeling like she was being humored. And over the years, adults tended to dismiss the confusion as just a fact of life…she had never been able to accept that.

Kate, Jennifer, and Marcus becoming active in a church hadn't been that big a deal before the accident. Lisa had listened and watched the three of them, respecting the change yet keeping her distance from the topic.

Since nearly getting killed, there was a conspiracy ongoing among the three of them to get her to believe too, and she was getting tired of it. About the only one who hadn't been pushing the subject of religion recently was Quinn. He believed, but it was different when she was with him. The few times the subject of religion had come up it hadn't felt like she had to be defensive. She frowned slightly at that thought and forced her attention back to Kate. "No, I can't say I've thought about it."

"It's important."

"I know it's important to you. And I'm happy that you've found something you and Dave can share. But it doesn't mean I have to share it too."

"Why are you so absolute in not talking about what the Bible says?"

Lisa didn't want to have this conversation. She didn't want to pit herself against Kate, against Marcus…against Jennifer. A conversation with Quinn was one thing, but family…

She understood like no one else in the family what it meant to die, to return to dust. The process began when the last breath was taken, and while she had never said as much to Kate, she knew what the Gospels, the first four books in the New Testament, said. Mark and Luke both said Jesus breathed His last; Matthew and John said Jesus gave up His spirit.

Jesus had hung on a cross for hours and died. The Bible said that explicitly. And if that was true, she knew what had happened to Him five minutes later, an hour later, three hours later, a day later. She didn't know the exact entomology of which flies lived in Palestine, but they would be cousins of those she understood very well from here. She knew the basics of Jerusalem two thousand years ago at the time of Passover: crowds, dust, heat—and flies. There would be no body left to resurrect three days later, not a body recognizable as the man Jesus.

Maybe if the Bible tried to argue He died for a few minutes, even an hour…but days—

Lisa knew from bitter experience that life ended forever with that last breath.

The old memory returned, a sharp stab, coming back in color and texture and terror. Lisa raised a shaky hand to adjust her shirt neckline. She silently cursed as she tried to shove the memory back into the past and get that floating dead face out of her mind. She was normally so careful to skirt everything that might brush against the memory, and instead she'd walked herself right into it.

She took deep breaths, slowly calming down. She'd had enough of this conversation. Kate was not one who did subtle, not unless it was on the job where she would willingly make small talk for hours if it was necessary to negotiate a peaceful conclusion to a dangerous situation.

"People don't rise from the dead," Lisa replied bluntly, knowing it would end the conversation for now. And just to make sure it stayed ended, she reached down and turned on the radio.

"It's been abysmal without you around, Lisa."

Her boss rose to greet her with a welcoming smile. Lisa walked slowly into his office, returning the smile. Ben Wilcott was in his late fifties, had overseen the state crime lab for the last eleven years. "Thanks, Ben. I almost got caught up on my reading thanks to your contributions—though I think the doctors were a little startled to see copies of the NIJ Journals and FSA Bulletins on the bedside table."

"I know how hard it is to go cold turkey from work, and I'd like your opinion on those National Institute of Justice proposed protocols."

"I took notes," Lisa replied, having anticipated the request. "And the Forensic Science Academy has another seminar scheduled on fiber collection and analysis. I think it would be a good idea to send Kim."

"I'll get it arranged. Can I get you something? Coffee? A soft drink?"

She'd worked for him too long not to know when something was coming that she wasn't going to want to hear. "I'd love something cold."

He brought her back a cold soda and one for himself, then settled in the chair beside her rather than behind the desk. "Classic looking cane."

Lisa spun its white ivory handle and burnished mahogany wood. "Stephen's contribution."

"I was surprised the doctors okayed you coming back this soon, even for desk duty."

She smiled. "They were afraid I meant it when I said I'd go sailing if they insisted I take a vacation. Seriously, I'm looking forward to being back."

"Gloria was asking about you."

She sipped at the soda, wondering where this was heading. Ben was walking one of the wooden nickels his granddaughter had given him through his fingers, and he only did that when he was thinking about something during a meeting unrelated to the topic at hand or when he was waiting for the right time to mention some news. "Is Gloria here today? I was surprised not to see her at her desk outside your office."

"Funding came through to move the police file archives into the new cold storage warehouse. She's in her element cataloging and organizing the move; making it happen has been her personal crusade."

"That's wonderful news. That funding has been held up for, what? Two years? How'd you ever get it to happen?"

"Actually, that's what I want to talk to you about."

She lowered her drink, her smile flickering.

"The new police commissioner wants a reexamination of all unsolved murders over five years old in light of new forensic techniques. I told him I'd do it..."

"...if you got funding to combine the archives."

"Exactly."

She could see a rushing train coming her way. "Ben, one of the lab guys, Peter—"

"I need more than a good technician. You spend a good portion of your days out at the crime scenes, and you've worked directly with cops, you can interpret the case notes. You're on desk duty for the next several weeks anyway, and you know better than anyone what evidence is worth the time to analyze."

"Don't do this to me."

"Sorry, it's done." He gave her a sympathetic smile. "Don't worry, it's not Siberia. And I'll owe you one when it's done."

Bribery still worked. She considered him and wondered how hard she could push it. "A new mass spectrometer?"

"I'll see what I can work into next year's budget."

Whoa. She should have thought larger; that had been a fast yes. He was serious enough about this she might have been able to wrangle another technician slot.

"You'll do it?"

She rubbed her eyes, hating this proposition with a passion, remembering her last visit to the police archives. The files were in poor shape, only a fraction of the records had been computerized, most cases had to be located from incomplete and fading handwritten indexes. And the older the case, the more disorganized the evidence. She owed Ben more than one favor, but still… "You're asking for a miracle. Those cases are cold for a reason."

"Anything you need, ask."

"A vacation is sounding better all the time—"

He laughed and got to his feet. "Thank you, Lisa. I knew I could count on you." He offered his hand to help her up.

She accepted, already dreading the next few weeks. She was getting exiled, graciously, but exiled.

"I took the liberty…you'll need a place to work. There is a lot of material." Ben's executive assistant, Gloria Fraim, pushed open the door to the task force room. Basically, it was one large open room located one floor below the laboratories. It could be configured to suit the needs of the particular situation from a large disaster to a multiagency case.

A series of worktables, a whiteboard, and a light table had been moved in. Metal shelves on rollers lined the inner wall; they were stacked with black boxes two deep. The boxes were worn and sagging, the writing on the ends barely visible because the black ink had faded.

Lisa rubbed her finger in the dust on one of the box lids. This case hadn't been worked in years. She scanned the row of boxes. "These are all the cases?"

"Sorry, only about half. We've been setting aside the unsolved murder cases as we find them." Gloria walked over to the other side of the room and pulled the blinds up on the wall of windows, letting in the sunlight. "I asked for you."

"Did you?" Lisa smiled; she should have guessed. "I don't know if I should thank you."

"Before this is over you will," Gloria promised. "You've always enjoyed a challenge. Some of these cases that haven't been solved will break your heart."

"What shape are the files in?"

"Photograph film is brittle, paper yellowing. About what I would expect. Stop by the cold storage records room in the next few days and take a look at the entire project. It's quite impressive. We're bringing over the archive files in batches, transferring the most vulnerable of the records to CD-ROM, using charcoal to deal with the odor and moisture in the paper files, indexing and computerizing the cases records."

"Massive doesn't begin to describe that project."

"We'll get it done on time, although I'm afraid you'll have to deal with the murder cases in their original shape from the police archives. We'd need to hold them up several weeks to take them through the charcoal process."

"I'll talk to Henry about the ventilation and get some air filters in here before I start opening decades worth of history. It won't be a problem."

"Is there anything else I can arrange to be brought in for you?"

Lisa looked around the room that would be her home for the next few weeks. It had the essentials: quiet and space. She smiled. "You know me, Gloria. I'm sure I'll collect things as I need them. I've just got a larger office to fill up with my toys."

They shared a laugh, for they were both pack rats. Gloria a neat packrat who knew where everything could be found; Lisa was more one to pile and make it fit. "I could use a good assistant to help get these case files entered in the NIJ database."

"Diane Peller. She's already begun working on it."

Lisa nodded. Diane was good.

"We've changed the locks on the room; you'll hold the only key."

"Thanks." It would save her having to move the files and evidence she was working on to a vault every night. "Get the log and let's review the inventory here. I'll sign off and take over chain of evidence responsibility."

Janelle Nellis, dead at age forty-two, found murdered in her garage. The case was fourteen years old. Lisa held the X-ray film up to the sunlight coming in the windows. Shot in the back from close range, one bullet hitting her left lung, the other nicking her heart. The ballistics report said it had been a .22.

Lisa sneezed and gasped as pain tore through her chest. It eased slowly and she took a cautious breath, wiping her eyes with the back of her hand.

She moved the desktop air filter closer. She had chosen one case at random to look through while she waited for Kate to arrive. After barely half a day, she was exhausted and ready to go home. She had badly misjudged how much energy she would have.

Pushing away the sense of fatigue, she spread out the dozens of crime scene photos on the table. The struggle that had occurred was obvious—part of a storage shelf in the garage had been pulled away from the wall, cardboard boxes were crushed. Janelle had tried to get away from whoever had shot her.

Her body had been found at 7 A.M. by a neighbor. She had last been seen alive at 6 P.M. the evening before leaving work at a deli shop eight blocks from her house.

"Okay, Janelle. What can you tell me?" Lisa started reading the autopsy report. It was an old College of American Pathologists format, and she had to flip through the report and the attached documents to tug out information that on current forms had their own designations. It was strange to realize just how little toxicology had been available fourteen years ago, and the radiograms she had in the medical examiner's packet were faint and minimal in number. Even in a murder case film had been deemed too expensive to do more than the basic X-rays.

Establishing time of death would be the key to solving a murder case like this and it was annoyingly broad in the autopsy report. Sometime between 10 P.M. and 4 A.M.

She frowned at that finding. A death discovered less than twenty-four hours old in an open garage on a summer night: state-of-the-art technology today could pin down time of death to within two hours using entomology evidence, temperature of the body, a careful exam of rigor formation. She read the autopsy report with care, looking for clues she could tease out of the narrative. If the doctor had made detailed notes he may have given her the evidence she needed, not realizing how significant an observation would be years later.

This wouldn't be such a bad assignment if she had chosen it for herself. This lady deserved justice. The more she read, the more interesting the case became. The bullet slugs had been recovered; she had an old evidence tag number. If she were lucky she might still be able to find them in the ballistics vault.

"So this is where you are hiding."

Quinn startled her.

"Welcome to my new office," she replied dryly, closing the file. She had a comfortable chair. She was waffling on her opinion of the rest of the assignment. "You're my ride home?"

"Yes."

Lisa saw Kate's handiwork. "I should have guessed." She gathered up the case photos and autopsy report, then returned everything to the evidence box. "Could you put this box back on the shelves with the others?"

"Sure."

He looked curious as to what she was doing in here but didn't ask. Lisa got to her feet, leaning heavily on the cane until she could straighten.

"Do you need to get anything from your office?"

"No. I'm ready to go."

She locked the doors to the room and pocketed the key. They went down to the lobby and she signed out while Quinn returned his guest ID. He held the outer door open for her.

"So how was the first day back?" he asked as they stepped into the hot afternoon sun. The only relief was the hope of rain; the sky to the west had the heavy dark look of potential thunderstorms.

"An experience." Lisa grasped the handrail, determined to walk down the stairs rather than use the ramp.

"Plan to tell me about it?"

She reached the bottom of the stairs, and they began the slow walk to the parking lot. Quinn's stride was so checked he was barely moving so as not to outdistance her. "I'm stuck in the dust bowl of history. They've got me reviewing cold cases for at least the next month." He indicated his car and opened the passenger door for her. She lowered herself carefully inside. "Thanks."

She leaned her head back and closed her eyes, relaxing into the warmth of the seat. It felt wonderful against her aching back. "This was not the day I envisioned when I left for work this morning."

He pulled into traffic and broke the silence several minutes later. "You going to kick this depression?"

She opened one eye to confirm that smile she heard. He was gorgeous when he smiled. She closed her eyes again. "Eventually. Just let me enjoy the bad mood for a while."

His chuckle warmed her heart. She needed someone who would accept with lightness what could at times be for her a slow transition away from work.

"Could I interest you in an early dinner?"

She was tempted but accepted reality. "Not today. Just home. I want a nap."

"Another time then."

She forced herself to stir. She'd be asleep if she left her eyes closed for long. "When are you heading back to Montana?"

"You don't want me to stick around?"

It had just been a question, but he had made it something more. Quinn was joking, he had to be, but she wasn't sure. "Quinn—"

"Relax. My flight is Sunday."

She grimaced; she was stumbling over her words again. "You've got a beautiful home, your ranch." She had enjoyed her one visit to his ranch even though it had been under stressful circumstances. That expanse of land gave Quinn roots, something she could admit privately that she envied. He could afford to leave the ranch for his job because he always had it there to return to.

"It's beautiful no matter what the season. Anytime you want to sell that Sinclair, let me know. I've got just the place for it."

It wasn't often she heard envy in his voice. "I picked it up by chance over lunch one day," she said with a slight smile and a small shrug.

"By chance."

"I liked it."

"Remind me to tag along when you window-shop someday."

Early dinner, stick around, tag along someday... He was definitely asking for something that she was hesitant to consider. He'd turn the force of his personality in her direction and she'd end up caring, try to please him, then manage to fail miserably at it.

"What else do you splurge on besides art? And travel? I noticed some interesting reading on your coffee table. Zimbabwe is next?"

"Only if the college anthropology team goes for a dig next year. Otherwise I'm planning to stay stateside for a while."

"Got anything planned?"

"Some serious backpack trekking. Fossil hunting. Caves. Everything I won't be doing for a while. I had tentative plans to go rock climbing next month."

"They're only postponed."

Postponed for months. Somehow she didn't think her back was going to tolerate hefting sixty pounds of tent and gear while she walked for ten days and fifty miles anytime soon.

The air conditioner ruffled her hair, sending tendrils across her face. She used both hands to push it back. She shouldn't have cut it so short; at least when it had been long she'd been able to secure it in a ponytail. Quinn adjusted the vents upward.

"Tell me about this new assignment."

Work—she could handle that topic. "Ben wants me to review the old murder cases to see what new forensic tests can do with the evidence. He's using it as a way to get funding to combine the archive files. I know it needs to be done, but..." She was whining. She shut up.

"You were hoping to get back into the field."

"Crazy, I know, but yes, I was." She bit her lip and looked at him, wondering if he would understand. "I need to. Does that make sense?"

"Sure it does. So does waiting a few weeks. Your job will still be there; it's not going to disappear while you take some time and heal." He grinned at her. "It takes longer than that to train your replacement. Consider the assignment the compliment it is. Take what they are expecting and give them back something better."

"This is your version of a pep talk?"

"Yeah."

"You need to work on it some more."

He burst out laughing.

SEVEN

Lisa loved her house, but it was testing her patience tonight. She walked on carpet squishing with water out through the back door, carrying her cellular phone. "Jack, when are you getting off duty?" She'd caught him at the fire station, relieved to find he hadn't been out on a call. She circled to the back of her house, looking at the gutters.

"Eight. Need something?"

"My gutters must be clogged. That brief rainstorm was wonderful, but it had me finding towels. My swamp is back, and this time it came in under the back door."

"Your swamp monster returns? You mean it didn't just unlock the door and wander through the house? Face it, you've got a living thing in your yard. It never dies."

"Jack." Next she was going to hear about those stupid monsters from the swamp movies he loved.

He relented and turned serious. "I'll swing by and take a look."

"I appreciate it." She'd called him because no matter how badly she disrupted his schedule, she knew he would say yes.

She walked around to the garage to see what would have to be moved in order to get the ladder out. Jack would have to do it. She did carry in the box floor fan to help dry out the carpet.

At least the water had turned only about a foot and a half of carpet into a soggy mess before she'd realized the problem and stopped the flood. An evening of moving air should go a long way to drying the carpet out, although in this heat the pad underneath might mold in even that short time.

She'd have to ask Jack if he thought the carpet should be pulled up. The idea of handing him pliers to pull up the tackstrip for the carpet made her wince. On second thought, maybe she wouldn't ask. She carried the wet towels through to the laundry room and started another load.

The three-hour nap she had taken when she got home had been wonderful; she had awoken to the sounds of thunder and rain. She'd enjoyed listening to the rain until she got up and walked down the hall.

She was going to have to get a load of dirt dumped to raise that portion of the yard so water would flow away from, not back to the house. The downspouts were set to direct the water from the roof well out into the yard, but when they clogged, she had trouble.

Surprisingly hungry, Lisa wandered into the kitchen, wishing she had gone grocery shopping. She settled for pulling out a box of Velveeta cheese, cutting off the end that had dried to toss into the trash. She made herself a toasted cheese sandwich.

She was finishing the sandwich, feeding the crusts to Sidney, when the doorbell rang. She dumped the paper plate, returned Sidney to his cage, and went to meet Jack.

He wore a blue T-shirt with a small white fire department emblem stitched above the pocket. It was the same shirt some enterprising kid at the last fire department open house had decorated with fabric paints, adding a red fire engine that looked like it had a flat tire. Jack loved the shirt. It was now too small for him; it had shrunk when washed in hot water, and the paint had begun to crack and flake off. But getting Jack to let the shirt die was impossible.

"What's this?" Lisa accepted the drink he handed her.

"A slushy. Grape. It seemed to fit."

"Jack—you had to?" His sense of humor was impossible to tame.

He tore open the wrapper on a stick of beef jerky. "I had to." He waved his dinner at her. "Show me the damage. Your brother is here to save the day."

"You'll try," Lisa agreed. "Whether you succeed—" She got an ice-cream headache drinking the Kool-Aid in crushed ice. "Come with me."

Jack followed her into the house. "Where's Sidney?"

"You can play with him later."

"Lizzy."

"Later."

"I brought him a new toy."

"Does it make noise?" Lizzy said.

"Of course."

"They do make quiet ones, you know."

"They also make earplugs." Jack bumped into her when she abruptly stopped. "What a mess."

"Tell me about it."

He gingerly walked across the wet carpet to open the back door and look at the source of the problem. "If it rains any more, you'll have a river coming in."

"I need you to look at the gutters."

"Gutters, smutters. I need a shovel so I can dig you a swimming pool. You would never have a water bill to fill it."

"Jack, you've been asking me to put in a pool for the last three years. I'm not going to do it."

"You let me build the deck."

Lisa didn't bother to point out she'd let him build it under their brother Stephen's supervision. "Lumber is not the same as concrete."

"Concrete is more fun."

"You just want to plant your hands in it and be remembered for posterity."

"A guy has to have a goal in life."

She laughed as she pointed back toward the garage. "Outside."

Twenty minutes later, Jack was on a ladder at her roofline. "Got yourself a forest up here." He turned and playfully tossed a handful of storm-stripped leaves in her direction.

His grin was infectious. "You need gloves."

"I'd just get them wet."

He leaned over to look down the length of the gutter. "Got a broom?"

"Somewhere. Hang on."

She found it where it actually belonged, hanging on the garage wall. She took it back to Jack and held it up. "Here you go."

He climbed the rest of the way onto the roof and walked along the edge with a casualness that spoke of easy comfort with both the slope and the height. "Here's your problem. Your wire end cap was knocked loose, let the drain clog." He retrieved it and cleared the drain spout to replace it. "You want to try and work on the yard next weekend? I'll be glad to heft bags of dirt around for you."

"As much as I would love to be your boss for the day, I think it's going to take more dirt than we could get down at the yard department of the Home Depot store. I think I'll give Walter—Nakomi Nurseries—a call. Since he's got a job in this neighborhood, he might be able to just bring out a truckload of dirt one afternoon and dump it."

"That would certainly solve the problem." Jack strained to reach over and clean out the turn of the guttering. "So how's Quinn?"

"What?"

"I heard you two went out to dinner."

How had that started? "The grapevine was wrong." Which surprised her because the family grapevine rarely got facts wrong. "He picked me up from work is all."

"I thought…never mind."

Her eyes narrowed. "What did Kate say?"

"Nothing."

She leaned against the ladder and jiggled it enough to make the metal ring. "Jack…don't make me want to tip this over. It would be a pain to pick up."

"You would too." He sighed. "Quinn was asking about directions to Casa Rio."

She blinked. Next time she was going to have to be more selective before she said no to dinner.

Jack tossed down more leaves. "I could be talked into taking you if you'll please lose that sad puppy dog expression."

"I haven't been to Casa Rio since my birthday."

Balanced on his heels, Jack rested his arms across his knees. "Quinn remembered it was one of your favorites. The guy has a good memory for details."

"I'm noticing."

"Why didn't you say yes?"

"Jack—"

"This is your brother asking."

"I didn't want to give him the wrong idea."

He looked stunned. "Quinn? He's not like that lowlife Kevin."

"Speaking of which—you didn't have to bust Kevin's nose."

"Sure I did. He made you cry."

"Jennifer exaggerated." She scowled. "What did he call me?"

"Lisa—"

"I know you. Kevin said something and you hauled off and hit him."

"He had it coming. And you should have dumped the guy long before."

She shifted on her feet, uncomfortable. "Probably."

His face softened. "Someday you'll have to tell me why you didn't."

She hated having perceptive brothers. "Maybe."

"Quinn is a safe date."

"This is a crazy place to be having this conversation."

He grinned. "I like it. You have to look up at me."

"Would you finish and get down here?"

He stood. "I've got time for a walk in the park if you're interested."

The subdivision had a small pond and walk path a block away. It sounded like a nice way to end the evening. "I'm interested."

Quinn squeezed into a tight parking place one block west of Dearborn and Grand and reached for his suit jacket. Lincoln's message had been urgent. He checked that the jacket covered his weapon, secured the car, pocketed his keys, and kept an eye on the crowds around him as he walked toward the gallery where Lincoln had asked to meet him.

Downtown Chicago at 9 P.M. was a busy place to be as those who lived in the city came out to enjoy the fall evening and mingled with tourists looking for the nightlife. He found himself watching traffic, looking for a dark green Plymouth. He hated mysteries, and one that tailed him was not likely to just go away and remain gone.

Dara's was one of a number of small galleries that thrived in the art culture that dominated Chicago. It was much like dozens of others he had patronized over the years, although this one tried to maintain the prestige of its heritage with its rich burgundy canopy over the entrance and its address just four blocks off the magnificent mile, even as the art it carried had become more and more modern. The reason for the black tie became obvious as he approached the gallery and saw the sidewalk podium and the assembled valets. A new show was opening tonight.

Guessing Lincoln had arranged the invitation, he gave his name to the host at the podium. He noted the quiet advance word that passed between the host and doorman. The word *buyer* had an interesting impact no matter which gallery he visited.

The opening tonight had brought out the champagne, a few art critics he recognized on sight, and a crowd that would please the owner. People were lingering as they discussed the various paintings; movement around the gallery would be a challenge.

Quinn scanned for Lincoln while also doing a quick summary of the paintings. All those in sight were oils. The painter was…intense. It wasn't displeasing to the eye with dark colors dominating the works, but the subject matter—mostly scenes of the city at night—would be an acquired taste. He settled in to move around the gallery with the pace of the crowd.

Someone else might have painted the moonlit Chicago river as romantic; this artist had instead made the black shadows in the water dominate the work. He quirked his eyebrow at the violence it suggested. It took talent to create such a subtle impression.

"Thanks for coming."

He glanced to his left to find that Lincoln had joined him. "Interesting request. I didn't know you were into art."

"I'm not," Lincoln replied dryly, making Quinn chuckle. "To your far right, a couple in their fifties talking with a vivid lady in red who is toying with a glass of white wine."

Quinn set the back of his left boot heel and turned without appearing to move. He scanned the room, passing over the threesome Lincoln had described. The lady in red was probably also in her fifties, but she wore the age very well. She was photogenic, obviously involved in the discussion, animated, captivating.

"The lady in red—Valerie Beck."

"The artist of tonight's exhibit."

"Yes."

"Her name, her work, doesn't ring a bell."

"No reason it should," Lincoln replied. "Wander to the back; there's something you should see."

"You want to give me a hint?"

"I don't want my opinion to sway yours. Go have a look."

What Lincoln was not saying mattered as much as what he was. Quinn looked one more time at the lady in red and nodded.

What had Lincoln found?

It took him several minutes to reach the archway into the next room. It was merely the middle of the gallery, another archway indicating another room. His way was blocked by a large group of guests, the critic from the *Chicago Fine Arts and Sculpture* magazine commanding a good portion of the room so he could hold court on what he thought of a retrospective painting of the Chicago World's Fair.

Quinn slid past the crowd with some reluctance. The man needed a history lesson if not an art lesson, and he was half inclined to stop and give it to him. He actually hoped the man would write the drivel he was saying in his review so the rest of Chicago could see his lack of insight. The painting was an interesting piece, not as dark as some of the other pieces. Once the group drifted on he'd have to come back and do some serious consideration—it might fit the space he had available in the ranch's dining room.

He stepped through the second archway.

Photographs, not paintings. He stopped in the doorway, absorbing the change in mood and tone of the work. There was a photojournalist quality to the subjects chosen: people dominated, events. The photographs did not have the technical expertise he would have expected from an artist of Valerie Beck's caliber.

The room had only two other guests casually perusing the pictures; there was no crowd here.

This was the work of a different artist. He searched for a title and an artist's name to confirm his hunch.

"She called that one *Endurance.*"

Valerie Beck had joined him, as vivid up close as at a distance. She was looking with great indulgence at the photo he had been examining. It captured the start of the Chicago marathon, although it was hard to place the year of the race.

"My daughter's work."

Quinn checked his discomfort and wondered where Lincoln was. He didn't know yet what he was supposed to be looking for, but it was apparently in this room. "The photographs show talent. You have reason to be proud of her, Mrs. Beck."

"This is the best she'll do, I'm afraid. My daughter was murdered a decade ago. She always wanted a showing of her work."

Violence, and something that had caught Lincoln's attention…Quinn could feel the threads crossing. "A tragedy. But this—" he looked around the room—"is an act of love."

His words brought a grateful smile in return. "I received more enjoyment out of putting together this showing than I did choosing works for my own."

He was playing this by ear, not sure what to ask. Quinn nodded to a photograph to his left. "I like this one."

"Horses. Rita did love them."

"She also had a great subject. He looks like he was a jumper."

"I believe he was. Do you collect art, Mr.—?"

"Diamond. Quinn Diamond. And yes, I've been known to buy a piece I like."

"Diamond—a lady's best friend?" She smiled at him as she touched the sleeve of his jacket. "Indulge me, Mr. Diamond, and I'll tell you about some wonderful photographs by a promising young photographer."

He returned the smile, relaxing, liking her. "I would enjoy that."

And for the next twenty minutes he did, hearing about a daughter from a mother who loved her, obviously missed her, and remained very proud of her. The word *murdered* still resonated as a harsh, discordant ending to the story, but she seemed to have moved past it enough to recover the good memories.

They had almost circled the room when he stopped in his tracks.

"My daughter. She was sixteen when that was taken."

It was a five-by-seven-inch snapshot, a casual picture, hanging low on the wall among a display of awards. Rita looked very much like a younger version of her mom even at sixteen. Rita had her arm around the shoulders of another teen, both girls holding cameras. The other girl in the picture was the very girl he had sought for so long: a smiling Amy Ireland.

"I do love this man." Lisa curled up on the couch and reached for the remote to adjust the volume. Tom Hanks and Meg Ryan were about to kiss for the first time. She snuggled the phone closer to her shoulder. "Jennifer, does Tom kiss this good?"

"Better," Jennifer replied smugly.

It was a quarter to eleven; Jennifer had called shortly after 10 P.M. to pass along word that she'd found the movie playing on the romance classics channel. It wasn't the first time they had watched a movie together long distance. Lisa was feeling quite relaxed. A muscle relaxant had ended any pain and a canister of Cheetos lay open on the table.

"Who was the last guy you kissed?" Jennifer asked.

Lisa grinned at the intrusive question. "Jack. He cleaned out my leaf-clogged gutters tonight."

"Brothers don't count."

"Well it wasn't Kevin," Lisa replied, grateful that was true. For all the mistakes she had made with Kevin, that hadn't been one of them. She was choosy about whom she kissed.

"Good. I never liked that ER doctor." The movie went to commercial. "Quinn was a good kisser, but there was an awkward height difference."

"What? You admit he has a flaw?" Lisa teased.

"He'd be just about right for you."

Lisa squirmed against the cushions, remembering the couple times he had held her as he helped her move from the car. Jen was right...his chin had brushed her hair as he held her, sent a quiver direct to her gut. If he kissed her... "I don't intend to find out."

"Why not? He's interested."

Jennifer was reading what she wanted to see. Quinn might be interested in a friendship, but nothing more. "No he isn't."

"Want to bet?"

Having already walked into a family bet once tonight compliments of Jack and his latest dare, she wasn't touching this one. "No, I don't. Besides, even if he's interested, I'm not."

She was smart enough to know there would be nothing casual about a relationship with Quinn, not on her side. She had a habit of being overly cautious and then abruptly just handing her heart over and saying here. There wasn't a safe middle, and unfortunately she hadn't chosen well the few times she had risked it in the past. She still had the child's habit of making an all-or-nothing decision.

"Quinn's not that old," Jennifer said, puzzled.

Forty-four. There were nine years between them, but Lisa had never thought his age was the problem. He wore it well. It was what it said about him that was the problem. The guy should have settled down long ago. But it would be putting down the guy to make that point, and she found herself reluctant to be critical. Knowing Quinn, there was probably a decent reason behind his unwillingness to settle down. "I don't want to live in Montana," she replied, lying through her teeth as she let herself dream a little.

"You would love it and you know it."

"Can you see me being a stay-at-home wife?" Living miles from a decent-sized town, with only Quinn and the ranch hands for company…it actually sounded wonderful. She liked the city, but she got out of it every chance she could.

"You'd have your pilot's license within six months," Jen replied. "And it would take a couple years just to identify all the wildlife that stops by. I heard Quinn saw a cougar last winter."

Lisa perked up at that news. The closest she had ever come to seeing a cougar was finding pawprints in the snow as she hiked through the mountains. "Really?"

"It came all the way down to the main barn."

"I hope he didn't kill it."

"Knowing Quinn, he probably sweet-talked it into moving on. Besides, just think of all the land you could explore. Aren't there caves on his property?"

"Several back in the bluffs."

The movie came back from commercial. Lisa was relieved. It was only a matter of time before her sister worked the conversation around to the subject of religion. Jen was only marginally more subtle about it than Kate. Religion and Quinn had become favorite conversation topics for her sisters. Talking about a guy with any of her sisters was always done at her peril. They had long memories for what she said…and what she didn't say.

"Oh, I'm going to cry. This is so sad," Jennifer said as Tom and Meg said good-bye, possibly forever. Lisa moved aside the phone as Jen blew her nose. Personally she thought the movie was a little overblown. Nobody was this romantic in real life although Marcus and Shari came close. But it never hurt to dream.

"Lincoln, what is going on?" The Italian restaurant a block east of the gallery had partially emptied, due to the late hour. Quinn ordered coffee and a sample platter of appetizers to give them an excuse to linger while they talked.

"It's Amy Ireland?"

Quinn was still trying to take in the stunning realization of what Lincoln had found. "Yes. She attended a two-week camp sponsored by the Chicago Museum of Art when she was sixteen. She must have met Rita Beck then. And since I don't remember seeing Rita on the camp roster, it explains why I missed finding the connection."

"I thought it was Amy, but I'm not exactly in a position to ask Mrs. Beck."

"Why not?"

"I'm trying to prove that Grant Danford did not murder her daughter."

Quinn winced. "The case you've been working the last two months, the guy serving a life sentence."

"Rita was twenty-five when she disappeared. Her body turned up eight years later buried on Grant Danford's estate. A witness placed Grant and Rita together the last day she was known to be alive, contradicting his statements to the police. The jury came back with a murder conviction."

"You think he's innocent?"

"His sister does; she hired me. After two months of looking at the case— I think there's a whole lot more there than what came out at the trial. Not that Grant is helping me much. The man is being a royal pain to work with, asking questions in answer to my questions instead of giving me straight answers. I've been interviewing everyone involved in the case that I can find."

Quinn considered his friend, thought about it. Lincoln chose the cases he worked these days. He wouldn't have taken this one, stayed with it this long, if he didn't have a gut instinct there was something to find. The sister probably sincerely believed Grant was innocent—and Lincoln had never been able to turn down a plea from a lady. Quinn wished him luck. Clearing a guy already in prison was a tough challenge. "Why were you at the gallery tonight?"

"Filling in background, looking for people who knew Rita."

"Seeing who came to see her pictures." If Grant really was innocent—killers tended to return to their victims, even years later.

Lincoln nodded. "Footwork. I'm doing a lot more of it now that I'm retired."

And still liking the work, Quinn could hear it in his voice. "I'm going to need to talk with Mrs. Beck at length about her daughter's friendship with Amy. And as soon as Mrs. Beck learns Amy Ireland has been missing for twenty years, it's going to bring back a lot of painful memories; she may shut me out. And she's definitely not going to want to help me if she knows the two of us are old friends and that it was you who found the connection between the girls."

"The fact Rita was missing eight years before being found might actually help you—Mrs. Beck will identify with another mom needing closure." Lincoln considered him and slid the check over. "And I won't take our disassociation in public personally, as long as you're picking up the tab when we sit down to compare notes."

Quinn picked up the bill. "You drive a hard bargain."

Lincoln smiled. "I learned from the best. Emily should also be able to help you out with the background work. She hasn't wanted to touch the Grant Danford case with a ten-foot pole; she thinks he's guilty. She'll be able to do some research for you without people connecting her to what I've been working on."

"I appreciate it. I need to find out everything I can about that summer the girls met before I talk to Mrs. Beck."

"You'll be amazed at Emily's resourcefulness."

"Can I also see the Danford files? I'll need to be prepared before I step into the minefield of how Rita died."

"Come over tomorrow, I'll show you what I have." Lincoln spun the ice in his glass. "Lisa worked the case."

Quinn set down his coffee without tasting it. "She did?"

"She was the one who excavated the grave."

EIGHT

Robin Johnson, age thirty-one, shot and killed during a convenience store robbery. The case was seven years old, unsolved. Lisa slid the first X-ray onto the light table over the special hotshot bulb that could get more light through the old film, then swung over the high intensity magnifying glass. She frowned at the fracture lines in the skull that radiated across the left parietal bone in an oblong starburst. Robin had been hit—a hard blow from something blunt, long, and heavy.

She scanned the other X-rays she had on the light table. The angle of the bullet went from the abdomen up into the chest. Robin had been knocked down and then shot? The cruelty was incredible. Lisa studied the films, absorbing everything they could tell her. There had to be something she could do with this case.

Two hundred and sixty cases. Arbitrarily, counting boxes and thumbing through the printout of unsolved murders, Lisa figured she could solve 10 percent of the open cases through a solid forensic review of the evidence. That gave her twenty-six cases going back thirty years.

She had decided to identify the most promising cases and then take them apart: send unidentified fingerprints and bullets back through the current databases; analyze the crime photos, scrutinize the autopsies; read through the police reports, case notes, and depositions looking for contradictions and assumptions; and try the latest techniques for fiber, blood, and fingerprint collection on the evidence.

It was the last Saturday in October, and while it wasn't atypical to spend part of her weekend at work, she was doing it today just so she wouldn't sit around the house and brood.

He hadn't called.

Lisa crumbled the page on her notepad when she realized she'd been doodling Quinn's name, annoyed to have him intruding again. She missed the trash can, and the page joined the half dozen other crumpled balls that had flown that way during the day. Quinn was leaving for Montana tomorrow, and he hadn't bothered to call to say good-bye.

She didn't want to admit she'd been lingering around the house the last two nights on the hopes he would drop by, making sure she had her cellular phone nearby when she was out on the hopes that he would call. She had told herself she wasn't going to care; it didn't matter…but it did.

She'd put the things he'd said and done into the expectations column, and then the days had passed and he didn't call. She rested her head in her hands. She needed to go home. Go back to bed. Admit she'd pushed way too hard on her first week back at work. The fatigue was a good part of this depression. Her body hurt. And she deserved this pity party.

She gave herself five minutes, then forced herself to detach her personal life from work and accept reality. He would have called if he'd realized it was that important to her; he hadn't meant the slight.

Go home or stay?

Stay. At least she could try to do some good here.

Work had always been the best way to get back her perspective. At least she was alive. She pushed her chair away from the light table and returned to the desk. Robin Johnson. She picked up the police report. She needed to see how far the case had gotten during the initial investigation. If they didn't have DNA available to tell them who the killer was, then what forensic evidence could do was provide that last piece of the puzzle; the investigation had to provide the framework.

The first success was going to be the hardest.

"You're working late."

Lisa blanked her expression before she looked up. Quinn. Her heart skidded to a stop somewhere around chagrined at what she'd been thinking earlier.

"Going to forgive me?"

Now she was confused. "For what?"

"Dropping off the face of the earth for a few days."

It was either a good guess or she hadn't blanked her face fast enough. "Oh, is that what you did?" She pushed out a chair with her foot in silent invitation, feeling the joy taking over and turning her day bright again just because he was there. He looked so good—a man shouldn't be able to make a gray shirt and faded jeans a fashion statement.

He pulled a white sack from his pocket and offered it across the table. "You didn't even realize I was gone." White chocolate-covered raisins, somewhat smashed. He had a habit of bringing something.

She took a handful, considered them, considered him. She gave a slight smile. "I realized."

Seated across the table, she got a chance to look at him more closely and her amusement faded. He looked tired, no…exhausted. The humor that was normally around his eyes was gone; the energy that pulled people toward him dimmed. The man looked discouraged. "You want some coffee?" she asked, feeling out the situation.

"I could use some."

She got up and took two mugs from the collection Diane had assembled and reached for the half full coffeepot. She brought the sugar bowl and a spoon back with her, knowing his preference.

"Thanks." He was silent as he drank the coffee. She wondered what was wrong.

He turned one of the photos on the table toward him. "No one solved this case?"

"Cold seven years. Somehow I don't think I'll be finding a miracle."

"She deserves one."

"Agreed. I'm just not a miracle worker, despite rumors to the contrary."

They shared a smile. "I've got faith in you." He leaned back in his seat and sighed. "I need a case. It's closed, but they said it would be somewhere in the archives Gloria is working on."

He'd come to ask a favor. She didn't know why it made her feel so good, but it did. She leaned forward and touched the keyboard, taking her laptop out of sleep mode. "Not a problem; I can access the larger database Gloria is building. Which one?"

"Rita Beck. She disappeared eleven years ago; her remains were recovered three years ago on the Danford estate. Grant Danford was convicted of the murder."

The image of bones turned chocolate brown from rich, dark topsoil clicked back into her memory in vivid detail. All the emotions she had felt at the time were coming back with intensity; Lisa tried not to flinch. "I remember the case," she said softly. "Her body was discovered buried near the stables." She pulled up the search screen and gave the case particulars. "I've got to learn to type," she muttered, punching the delete key.

Quinn laughed; it sounded a bit rusty, but it was a laugh. "I notice you're pecking with two fingers."

"And the busted finger isn't helping. Why this case?"

He hesitated. "Lincoln is working for Grant Danford's sister. He thinks there may be something to Grant's claim of innocence. And there's a possible link to a missing person's case I've been working on for a number of years. I need to see the full file."

"The district attorney made his name on that case. If he convicted an innocent man—" She frowned as the laptop went dormant and the search paused; if it locked up again she was going to resort to hitting it. Ever since she had expanded the memory, the machine had been acting up.

"Okay, here we go. Rita Beck. Box 46C2." She read the index. "It's been processed and is in the charcoal stage to remove moisture. It will be down in storage room five."

Quinn wrote down the number. "Stay. I'll have the evidence clerk get it." He disappeared before she could get to her feet.

Lisa collected Robin Johnson's case file and stored it away, hoping that Quinn would rejoin her rather than find the file he was looking for, say thanks, and sign out a copy. She really did want to help.

He came back with a sealed blue crate. She pointed to an empty table. "Let me unseal it, deal with the charcoal."

While she worked, he circled the room. Most of the open murder cases had been located, brought in, and slid onto the metal shelves. Gloria was down to locating a handful of stragglers.

The rudiments of a decent crime lab, including one very expensive microscope, had taken over the east tables. She was getting into the chase. There was a bold red *twenty-six* written on the whiteboard, and she saw him smile as he noted it.

She set out the contents of the box. "Where do you want to start?"

"I'll copy and take it with me."

She wanted to protest but bit back her words. He didn't look like he had slept much in the seventy-two hours since she had seen him last. "There's a copier next door. Stamp the pages as confidential; the evidence clerk can authorize the release."

When he came back she was shutting down her computer for the night. "When did you last eat?" She reached for her briefcase.

"I'm fine, Lisa."

"Don't bother to argue. I'm buying."

"Quinn, you're supposed to take the Do Not Disturb sign off the door occasionally so the hotel maids will clean the room."

"I'll remember—eventually." He crossed over to the room safe to store the Rita Beck files inside.

He hadn't bothered to unpack his suitcase; it sat open on the dresser, stacks of clothes spilling out. There was at least a week's worth of newspapers cluttering the table and tossed in a stack on the floor. Two Chinese carry-out cartons were balanced on the top of the wastebasket and several cellophane wrappers from peanut butter cracker packs were heaped on the bedside table next to the TV remote. His Bible, the leather cover so worn it was beginning to separate, was on the bed next to a pad of paper filled with his precisely printed handwriting.

She picked up water glasses and stacked them on the tray, swirling a finger in the ice bucket now full of room temperature water. Quinn needed someone to look after him.

"You like to sleep in the ice age?" It was all of sixty-five degrees in the room he had the thermostat turned so low.

He glanced back as he locked the safe. "This is comfortable."

"If you're an Eskimo."

He tossed his hat on the side table. It landed with a thud, sending a yellow phone message fluttering to the floor. "Let's go eat."

"After you take something for that headache."

He paused and nearly scowled, making her want to laugh. He had a thing about aspirin; he really didn't like taking them. "Yes, ma'am."

She leaned against the door to the bathroom while he rummaged through his shaving kit for the aspirin bottle. He opened the childproof cap and shook one tablet out into his palm.

"Two tablets, Quinn. One isn't even going to remove that frown let alone the pain."

"Just how much medical school did you have?"

"Enough to make it an order."

He swallowed them with a grimace and shut off the bathroom light. "Let's go eat."

"Which restaurant?"

"Sinclair's, downstairs."

It wasn't the casual restaurant she had expected; this was upper tier elegance and they were both underdressed. The room lights were dim, the music subdued, the decor rich. A group of five businessmen were finishing a late meal; two couples had tables near the windows.

"Two, Michelle, nonsmoking."

"Right this way, Mr. Diamond," the hostess replied with a welcoming smile.

That answered Lisa's question as to which restaurant Quinn normally frequented. She would have placed him at the more sports-oriented restaurant one level down, not amid this elegance. Apparently she had been wrong.

The hostess led them to a white linen covered table, two large vases of long stem roses framing the nearby window; she laid down two menus for them. Quinn held Lisa's chair for her. The hostess took their drink order and left.

Lisa glanced around before opening the menu. "This is a gorgeous restaurant."

"Peaceful," Quinn agreed. "They've got great steaks here."

"Another time for me. Unlike you, I had dinner."

Their waitress joined them a few minutes later, bringing Quinn's coffee and her ice water.

"Good evening. Would you like more time, or are you ready to order?"

Lisa closed her menu. "I'd like a bowl of French onion soup and a side salad, blue cheese dressing."

Quinn held up two fingers. "The same, Sandy." He handed the waitress the menus.

"It will be right out."

Lisa watched Quinn watch the waitress walk away. "You know her?" He'd been around Chicago enough in the last year she wouldn't be surprised if he did.

"She used to work over at the Renaissance Hotel, breakfast shift, if I remember correctly."

"You remember the waitresses."

He glanced back at her, a distinct twinkle in his eyes. "Sure. You don't?"

"I don't live on eating out."

He buttered a piece of the hot bread and offered it to her.

She accepted. "Is this called breaking bread together?"

"The Arabs say you can't fight with someone you eat with."

"Do we need to sign a peace treaty?"

"Insurance never hurts." He leaned back in his chair, stirring sugar in his coffee. "What's this I hear about Jennifer possibly getting out of the hospital?"

Lisa felt her fatigue disappear as a relieved smile took its place. "The doctors brought up the possibility this morning when the latest blood work showed marked improvement. If she gets another positive panel, she could be out of the hospital in a couple weeks."

"That's fabulous news."

"If it happens, the original wedding plans will be back on. Jen and Tom will get married in Houston near her home, so some of her pediatric patients can come."

"October 22?"

"Yes." It was Jennifer's parents' anniversary date, her way of remembering them on her special day.

"Soon."

"Not if you listen to Jennifer. She wants it tomorrow."

"Understandable. Are you going to stand up as one of her bridesmaids?"

"Yes. She's asked Kate, Rachel, and me." She'd been ducking that last dress fitting, not wanting to admit they might have to loosen the fabric of the dress so she could handle wearing it for three hours. Anything tight brought a lot of pain. If Kate was there and heard about it, Lisa would have the entire family to deal with again. She was supposed to be telling them the truth when they asked how she was feeling, and she had been doing a decent job of lying this last week.

"The wedding pictures will be lovely. A bride and three princesses," Quinn commented, and she couldn't stop the blush at that speculative gaze. "Have you decided on a wedding gift yet?"

She'd been worrying about that for weeks; gifts were not her thing and were never easy to choose. "I don't have a clue."

"We'll go shopping."

"We?"

"A really nice painting from both of us." He smiled. "Your taste, my money."

Oh, that would go over just wonderful in her family. Even if it was an interesting offer. She weighed the need against the comments that would be inevitable. "I'll buy the painting, you can buy the frame." The two were often equally expensive, and she was out of time to figure out what to get.

"Fair enough."

She was glad to see the laugh lines back around his eyes, even if it was amusement at her expense.

"Who's making the wedding arrangements for Jennifer?"

"Rachel has been coordinating the details since July, Tom and Marcus are handling the logistics." Their soup and salads arrived. "I'm surprised you didn't order a steak."

"Wait until you taste this. You made an excellent choice."

He was right; the soup was delicious.

Lisa was pleasantly surprised as the meal progressed. He was good company. Maybe it was the fact they were both coming off a stressful day that made it easier to relax; whatever the reason, she stopped trying to think before she answered a question. And if some of her answers brought a smile, it was at least as much his fault for the question as hers for the answer.

She looked at her watch as they lingered over coffee at the end of the meal and was surprised to find it was almost eleven. "It's late. I'd better head home."

"I've enjoyed the evening," Quinn replied, refilling his coffee from the carafe Sandy had brought to the table, obviously not bothered by the time. "Finish telling me about Jack. Is he going to have to move fire districts with the station house consolidations?"

"His has become one of the new hub stations. They've transferred another engine and two crews."

"How much more territory are they covering?"

"A mile and a quarter out from the station. It's dangerous."

"Budget cuts always are."

"Well it's my brother being asked to assume the risks."

"Who have you complained to?"

"Besides the fire commissioner, the mayor, and Jack's city councilman?"

"Write the newspapers next. Give them a good human interest story—sister who knows the risks is worried about her brother."

"Jack would murder me."

"Blame me."

She thought about that…Jack and Quinn…it would be about even.

He chuckled at her expression. "Remind me never to suggest something I don't mean."

"I'll think about writing the newspaper." She looked at him and slowly smiled. "Do you play the harmonica?"

"What? Where did that come from?"

"Ranch…cowboy…riding the range…playing the harmonica. Do you play?"

"I'm supposed to find the logic between that question and talking about Jack?"

"Yes. But you probably wouldn't understand. Just answer the question."

He slowly tipped back in his chair and gradually grinned. "Well, ma'am, now that I think about it—"

"You do! Oh, this is perfect. Can you teach me to play?"

"Explain first."

"Jack. He dared me to learn to play a musical instrument."

"When was this?"

"We were taking a walk the other night around the park..."

"Mistake number one."

She grinned at him for realizing it. "And we got to talking about what we hadn't done as kids because we grew up at Trevor House. Jack never got a chance to be a Boy Scout and I never took piano lessons."

"And the bet became?" He winked at her surprise. "O'Malleys. That wasn't hard to see coming."

He did know them; Marcus had walked into a few family dares over the years. "I have to learn to play a musical instrument and Jack has to do a dozen good deeds. The bet is payable by his birthday. Lose, and you're paying the other person's bills for a month—with your own money. I don't intend to lose." She couldn't afford to.

"I'll teach you to play."

"What's it going to cost me?"

He shook his head. "Uh-uh, I'm saving this one."

"Quinn."

"I'll be nice. It's me or the local piano teacher."

It wasn't that hard of a decision to make. "I can afford a harmonica."

"I've got a story I need to tell you."

It was late. Quinn had insisted on giving her a lift home, that they'd get her car the next day. Lisa turned her head against the headrest, pulled out of her quiet reverie of a relaxing evening by his words.

Secrets. How well she knew them, how well she understood that slightly different tone that came into someone's voice when the territory of such a memory was invaded. "We can take a walk around the pond, if you like."

He parked in front of her house instead of pulling into her drive. "No. I think I'd just rather sit out here if you don't mind."

The passenger door was already locked; Lisa turned to rest against it. "If you'd like. I'm comfortable."

She saw his smile in the faint light of the streetlight. "I'll make it the Cliff's Notes."

He reached over and adjusted the side mirror, killing time rather than speaking, for the street was quiet as it passed midnight. "Did Marcus ever tell you about the reason I became a marshal?"

"I once heard a rumor that it was to cover his backside," she replied, grateful it was true. She didn't have to worry as much about Marcus knowing Quinn was with him.

"That's the reason I stay a marshal," Quinn replied with a chuckle.

"Then no, I don't think I heard. Why did you?"

He hesitated over his words. She knew this man; hesitation wasn't a normal part of his makeup. She settled deeper into the seat, ignoring the sharp twinge of pain that shot across her back and curled her toes inside her tennis shoes. "We keep secrets in this family very well. Despite the grapevine, there's another, quieter code of honor none of us would ever think to break. Marcus doesn't talk about you, not the confidences…neither do Kate or Jennifer."

"I know that, Lisa. It's just been private for a very long time."

She wasn't sure she wanted to hear it. A secret shared implied a two-way street. And she didn't want to be sharing hers.

"When I was twenty-four, back from college, working at the ranch, I found buzzards circling what I thought would be a heifer who had died giving birth. What I found was my father, shot in the back. His killer has never been found."

There were no words for the grief she felt at the news. It welled up inside; she could see the scene as he would have encountered it. "It was a hot day?" she whispered.

"June 18, not a cloud in the sky. Out in the south pastureland by the bluffs."

Sandy soil, limestone based, coarse grass—it would have helped slow the ravages of decay beginning at the moment of death, but only slowed not stopped the reality. "I am so sorry."

"I became a marshal when it became obvious the case had become cold. I've been working it in my spare time ever since."

"That's why you don't spend much time at the ranch."

"I love the land and ranching as a lifestyle. I'll go back to it full-time eventually, but for now it's a reminder that there is unfinished business." He sighed. "That's the start of my story. There's more."

"I'm listening."

"A girl named Amy Ireland disappeared the same day my father was shot. She didn't live close by, but for Montana distances, her family would be considered neighbors. She was seventeen at the time. The police considered the possibility of a runaway, foul play, an accident…they worked the case for years until having to accept it also was cold."

"You think they are linked. The disappearance of Amy and the murder of your father."

"I've been working both to try to find out."

For twenty years he had been working the two cases during his off hours. She needed a better word than tenacious. *Committed.* He wasn't going to ever give up. She admired him for that. And for all the years she had known him, he had never said anything. She was disappointed in that but had to accept that her attitude toward him over the years had probably been the reason; it hadn't encouraged confiding something this critical. And then it clicked. "This has something to do with the Rita Beck file you requested."

"It does. Lincoln found a connection between Amy and Rita. They were friends when they were sixteen." He thrust his fingers through his hair. "I've spent the last three days looking at everything I know about Amy and the two-week visit she made to Chicago for an art camp. I'm more convinced than ever that the break I need might be found in their friendship—a teenage confidence, something Amy told Rita, that from the perspective of today will mean something."

"I'd like to help."

"I've been trying to avoid asking you to get involved."

That hurt. He saw it and shook his head. "Lisa, it's not personal. There's a lot that's going on unrelated to this right now, and I'd rather be cautious and limit this to Marcus, Lincoln, and myself."

Something that had him worried—something dangerous. Kate acted the same way when her gut was telling her something wasn't right. She didn't want people around. "Then why tell me now?"

"Because I need to see where Rita died. And I need you to show me."

NINE

The former Grant Danford estate was forty acres in Lake Forest, backing up into the Lake Bluff Forest Preserve and the Skokie River. Lisa was grateful she was finally able to handle a car ride without having to brace for every turn. Quinn was a safe driver, but his attention was elsewhere and he was ignoring the speed limit to instead flow with traffic. The fact he said nothing during the hour-long drive was also a good indication he had other things on his mind.

She understood the intensity that demanded a case be solved. She'd been there. She understood now what had made him the way he was: patient, steady, but tenacious. What had happened to his father was always there in the background, lingering as an unanswered question, eating at him because it remained unsolved. It had to have contributed to why he had never settled down; he'd been focused on the past, not his own future.

He had gone to church with Kate, Dave, and Marcus, then had come over to pick her up afterward. As graciously as she could she had declined his invitation last night to join them. He hadn't pushed the subject, but he'd been studying her as he asked the question, noting her reaction. And what he had seen must have bothered him for he started to ask something, then caught himself and changed the subject.

The last thing she needed was Quinn deciding to probe that subject too.

Lisa knew she'd made a tactical mistake. Kate was the heart and soul of the O'Malley family, and when she keyed in that there was something wrong, she didn't leave it. Their conversation four days ago had triggered a red flag, and Lisa knew it hadn't helped that she'd cut off a similar conversation with Jennifer; a fact that might have gotten back to Kate.

At times she hated the family dynamics. If she read them wrong, couldn't finesse a situation, more often than not it triggered an issue into a state of prominence rather than getting it buried as she hoped.

All the O'Malleys had pasts that were complex and areas of their lives before Trevor House they rarely talked about. But those zones of privacy were around things they didn't talk about easily, not around things that were hidden. And she was hiding. That had Kate worried, and it was only a matter of time before Marcus came by. He wasn't a casual guardian of the O'Malley family. He cared enormously, would want to do whatever he could to fix what was wrong.

It would hurt to push them away and hurt if she let them in. She just wanted the past to stay the past. It couldn't be fixed, she knew that, but they'd try anyway because they were O'Malleys. Because they loved her.

She'd been the focus of the family since the injury, now this…. She had to figure out a way to get their attention focused on someone else. The power of the group could be overwhelming.

What she needed was an excuse to be so busy she could honestly say she didn't have time. It had worked before; it would work again. She'd just have to figure out how to stay ahead of them for a while.

She looked at Quinn, considering the unthinkable. If she said yes to a few invitations, she wouldn't be using him exactly. It wasn't like he ever saw someone for more than a few months, and that would be enough time to get out of this family scrutiny. And if she did say yes to a couple church visits—at least it would deflect their concern and give her some space.

It was the coward's way out of the problem.

It was depressing to realize she was seriously considering it.

"Who owns the estate now?" she asked as Quinn turned into the long, winding private drive that led back to the house, grateful for the time being that she could focus on work.

"Richard and Ashley Yates. They're in Europe for a month. They weren't thrilled with the news the old murder case was being looked into again, but Lincoln convinced them that it would be best to let him do it rather than risk someone else eventually investigating who would not be as cautious about keeping it out of the press."

Quinn parked in the estate's driveway turnabout. "We're going to be meeting with the manager of the stables. When the Yates bought the estate, they also bought Grant's horses and they kept him on."

"Samuel Barber? Berry? Something like that…"

"Barberry. Good memory."

"I'm surprised he's still working. He had to have been in his seventies when I met him."

"I spoke with him briefly—Scottish?"

"Yes. He was the one who found Rita's body. They were rebuilding the stone terrace behind the stables; the land slopes to the river, and it was terraced to make room for a level exercise ring. They were replacing and leveling stones when they found her remains."

"I've read Lincoln's notes, scanned the full file early this morning." He shut off the car and removed his keys. "You excavated her grave?"

She nodded; some of the realities of her job were best left unstated. She'd been here the good part of three days, the age of the crime scene having her working with archaeologist's tools to brush away the layers of dirt from the bones.

"Good. I won't have to wonder about evidence having been missed."

Even as she absorbed that compliment, he nodded toward the briefcase in back. "Bring the file? I'll go locate Mr. Barberry."

The stables were located near the back of the estate grounds, providing easy access to riding trails that disappeared into the heavily wooded forest preserve. There was also a swimming pool, adjoining pool house, and a tennis court on the estate grounds. Lisa remembered the house as being traditional English inside—heavy fabrics, polished wood. There had been a full suit of armor guarding the hall, rather hard to miss with its invisible man holding a jousting spear and four-foot sword. Grant Danford had been a man who liked to make a statement with his surroundings.

The estate grounds had lost some of their elegance; they gave the sense of being subtly neglected. It wasn't obvious—the sculptured flowerbeds, evergreens, and white birch trees were still beautiful—but nothing had been added, everything had simply grown and it had thrown off the balance.

She carried the briefcase and delayed joining Quinn, in no hurry to step back into this case. It had been a hot summer afternoon, not unlike today, when she was called out to the scene. The police had cordoned off the area, and while they tried to maintain need-to-know on details during the early investigation, the press had already staked out the roads to the estate when she arrived. Grant Danford was a man with financial and political power and had the enemies that went with it. This case had created a firestorm of interest in the press.

For three days she had labored here at the scene, painstakingly recovering the remains. The subspecialty of forensic anthropology took years to learn all its nuances, to read everything bones could say, but her years hunting fossils and going on archaeological digs had helped hone her skills. She knew how to recover remains and read a burial site, and those were the most critical steps in the process. Burial sites were the most fragile of recovery sites for evidence even though they looked the most sturdy.

An expert from the Museum of Natural History had joined her to help with the three-dimensional grid work, the careful record of the dig. How long Rita had been dead before being buried, how and even where she had been killed—the potential evidence in the gravesite was enormous and this one had yielded all of those markers.

She had worked in focused concentration with a scribe, a photographer, and an evidence technician to document and preserve each clue uncovered. By the time the remains were lifted to the black vinyl body bag, Lisa knew Rita Beck better than most people had when she was alive.

She'd been proud of the work she had done.

And now Lincoln thought the man convicted of Rita's murder might be innocent.

She wasn't supposed to feel it was a personal slap.

It was her job to speak for the evidence. She was legally required to be impartial, to state the facts contained in the evidence, to remain silent when the evidence was silent, to be persuasive in explaining when the evidence spoke. It was not her job to speak to guilt or innocence of the person accused. Sometimes her testimony helped the prosecution, sometimes the defense.

In this case, with the media swarming around it, she had been true to that impartial mandate down to the very choice of adjectives she used. When she had given her expert opinion at trial, she had limited it carefully to what Rita's body and grave had revealed. But the defense lawyers had tried their best to shred not only her statements but her reputation. She could feel the anger building just remembering those grueling days in court.

She rubbed her forehead. She did not want to be back in this case. If Grant had been wrongly convicted, her testimony had been part of that injustice. What she had said played a large part in the conviction; the body of the victim always did. It wasn't much help to know that it had only been part of the case the jury had heard. The jury had heard a total case and rationale for the crime and convicted Grant Danford on that record. But had she missed anything? Anything that would have been exculpatory?

"Lisa."

She moved to join Quinn and Mr. Barberry; they were talking at the door to the stable. She shook hands with Mr. Barberry, not surprised that he remembered her.

"We'd like to simply look around if that's okay with you," Quinn said.

"Take your time. I'll just be puttering around here."

Quinn nodded his thanks.

They left Mr. Barberry and turned to the stone walkway that curved between the barn and the large exercise ring. The open pastureland was to the west.

Quinn paused her with a hand on her forearm. "You don't have to do this if you would prefer not to."

She wiped her expression of emotion, annoyed that she had let her disquiet with the situation show. "It's no problem."

His eyes could pierce someone's soul. "Lisa—" he hesitated, obviously choosing his words with care—"you worked this case. It was gruesome. You don't need to be involved again. I can follow Lincoln's notes on my own, ask questions if something is unclear."

"You need to understand Rita's life and death if you're going to get a handle on her friendship with Amy. Did they stay in touch after that summer camp? Did they have other common friends? Did Amy ever talk about coming back to Chicago? Is it anything more than a coincidence that two friends both disappeared years apart and one of them turned up murdered? No, Quinn. I'm staying."

She forced herself to smile. "The main reason this case is unpleasant is the memory of the publicity that surrounded it. As a crime…Quinn, working a scene this old is one of the easiest cases I can have. Time consuming, but not that hard. Bones don't have skin that feels cold and empty eyes that look back at you."

"To watch you work, it isn't obvious the victims bother you like that."

Did he think she didn't remember the faces and the crimes? They lived with her, gray, terrified ghosts, trapped in the moment of death.

"The children are the worst." She shifted the briefcase to her other hand, needing to change the subject. "It's my job, Quinn. Let me do it."

She couldn't interpret his expression, but she was very aware it had changed. She wanted to squirm under that intensity. She could feel herself being summed up, prior assumptions rethought. If this was what suspects felt… It was hard to remain quiet and not start babbling.

"You see the victims, don't you? See the struggle to stay alive through their eyes and relive with them their deaths. That's why you're so good at figuring out what happened."

"Something like that." She looked away. He was hitting too close to the truth for comfort.

She started when his hand closed over hers on the briefcase. "Who'd you see die?"

She jolted and tried to jerk away at the soft question, but he had hold of her hand and wasn't letting her move away. His expression was grim and she instinctively tensed.

"Lisa."

She wasn't going to say anything. She didn't lie…and she didn't talk about it.

"Have you told anyone? Kate, Marcus? Any of the O'Malleys?" His voice was steady, calm, but she heard beneath that the intensity and the disbelief with the realization she hadn't.

He was pushing into turf that was off limits, and she mentally recoiled, her expression turning stony and cold. She lived with that ghost and victim because she had to, but she wasn't sharing the secret…especially not with Quinn.

His hand over hers tightened and his free hand turned her face back toward him. He held her gaze with his and rubbed his thumb against her chin. There was compassion in that gaze, so deep she could drown in it if she let herself. "I'm sorry for that memory."

"Let me go," she insisted, hating him.

"When you need to talk, I'll listen."

"I won't."

He pushed back the hair blowing across her face. "You don't need to defend yourself against me. I won't use the truth against you."

"So you think."

The hot emotion in his gaze frightened her. "Don't fight me, Lisa. You'll lose."

"You want too much."

"Yes, I do. I want your trust." He released her chin and her hand, stepped back and paced away, then turned back, looking incredibly frustrated. "But you're too stubborn to realize what you need."

He was into her past, was verbally hitting her with an intensity she had always known was part of his personality. He had his bone to worry now, just like the O'Malleys had theirs, and he'd be at it ruthlessly until he had answers. He'd crush her if he invaded that concealed truth. She couldn't afford his interest but didn't know how to deflect it.

"Quit looking like that."

"How?"

"Like I stepped on some favorite pet of yours," he muttered.

"Quinn—"

"Forget it." He rejoined her and took the briefcase from her hand. "Let's get to work." He took off his hat and dropped it on her head. "And I could do without your getting a case of sunstroke."

She watched him walk away, relieved to be out of the quicksand subject but distressed at the fact he was mad at her, and worse, that he was deciding she wasn't worth the trouble.

She awkwardly adjusted the too large hat, finding that abrupt action of his disconcerting. Even when mad, he still paused to shove his hat on her head.

He opened the file and looked back at her. "Take me through what happened here."

She pushed her hands in her pockets and reluctantly walked forward to join him. It was hard to get focused on work, but he'd made the transition with a completeness that was almost ruthless. "She was found back here."

She felt nauseous. She'd been weighed and found wanting; it wasn't a new feeling, but it made her regret what she'd said. Kate wouldn't have responded that way to him, or Jennifer. He wanted her trust. She'd concede reality: She already trusted him. She just didn't want to give him what he was asking for. Her past was private, and for her sake best left alone.

The terrace was formed from a curving wall of rocks about four feet high. She walked down the five stairs to the lower level, walked north along the path, her steps slowing, and then she stopped. It was like walking back in time. She let herself remember and then realized she had been standing there silently for several moments; Quinn was patiently waiting, watching.

"They were excavating this turn in the stones, reinforcing it so they could enlarge the exercise ring in this direction. They uncovered her left foot, still wearing the remains of a blue tennis shoe. We were called out."

"What did you find?"

"She was lying face down, buried immediately behind the rocks at a depth of about two and a half feet. She would have been buried deeper than that originally; the ground along here had been washing away over the years with the heavy rains, being pulled down to the river."

She crouched down, ran her hands along the weathered, flat smooth stones, each one heavy and about ten inches deep. "When we began work, this wall of stones had a back and forth tilt, they had been undisturbed for years and had settled. It looks neat now, but then…you could see grooves where the rains had cut into the soil and torn away the packed dirt between the stones. Nothing had been disturbed since she was buried here."

She sighed, remembering. "Her hands were behind her back. There were remnants of the duct tape used to bind them still around the bones." She frowned.

"What?"

She stood, glanced back at him. "Her hands weren't just bound at the wrist. The backs of her hands were pressed together and tape also wrapped around her palms. She had two broken fingers, as if she'd been grabbed, bound in that fashion, and thrown to the ground on her back, her fingers breaking under her own body weight.

"She had a dislocated left shoulder and wrenched vertebrae in her lower back indicating a struggle, consistent with how she had been bound. No skull fractures recording a blow to the head, no nicks in bones recording a bullet. The hyoid bone in her neck had mostly decayed, but I found a pressure fracture in the left branch of the U-shape bone and a break at the forming fuseline."

"She was strangled." Quinn's voice was cold. He had a special hatred of men who used physical violence toward women; that was so clear it was painful to see.

"Or at least put in an injury-inducing choke hold," she replied quietly. "At twenty-five, the three bones in the horseshoe formation of the hyoid had just begun to fuse. The pressure fracture indicates it was serious, but was it the fatal act? She may have been suffocated or even drowned as the actual cause of death. What I do know is she was grabbed by the neck during the time of her death. But the vertebrae damage is inconclusive as to how she was held."

Quinn took a seat on the steps between the terrace levels, opened the file, and laid out the pictures, studying them again. "You have a hard job."

She didn't need his pity. "We die and we turn to dust. I just know a bit more than most people about how that actually happens."

But the pictures pulled at her. She took a seat beside him and picked up one of the gravesite photos recording the excavation. She'd been lying beside the body in the deeper side trough they had dug to create a pedestal for the skeletal remains. They had to record what they found by grid and depth, for below the body was often trapped a treasure trove of evidence.

This photo was typical: She had her gold pen clamped between her teeth and a frown of concentration on her face as she tried to retrieve a fragment of thread and a button from the dirt with a long pair of tweezers, apparently not bothered that she was stretched out inches from a skeleton. The gold pen was more than a fashion statement, blood and bacteria couldn't get into the casing; it could be wiped clean with one of the foil-wrapped medical swabs she carried by the handful in her pocket when she worked a scene.

"What other evidence did you find?"

"Her only jewelry was a ring on her right ring finger. She wore no watch. Her clothes had decayed, but there were remnants of threads from a white polyester shirt with a blue front pocket. Her jeans had decayed to the seam threads and a zipper—cotton always decays fast—and she wore blue Nike tennis shoes.

"That clothing is significant because it matched what she was last seen wearing the day she disappeared years before. The ground around her body was unusual; there was a much heavier concentration of black topsoil than was found at the same depth just a few feet away."

"Not uncommon around a stable and landscaped grounds."

"True, but it made her remains decay faster than say a clay-based shallow grave."

"She was buried here. No one would notice the turned-over dirt?"

"The month she went missing, this stone wall terrace was built. It's why the police think this spot was chosen for the grave instead of somewhere in the forest preserve—an animal might have dug up the body there. This apparently had sod laid down to the edge of the stones, making it relatively easy to conceal the site if he had the time to work and dig the grave. And back then Grant Danford did not have the full-time staff working this property."

Quinn looked around the area. "How far back does the Danford property extend?"

"Roughly to that line of trees. From there you are on forest preserve land."

"No one from the house could see here."

"And as you can see, the forest preserve trails are nearby but not in the line of sight. From evidence in the grave, the type of bug cocoons found, she had been dead for a few hours before being buried. Small bits of gravel and wood shavings found on her shoes and under her body suggest the murder occurred somewhere in the forest preserve."

"She was killed the day she went missing?"

"An assumption, but reasonable. She was wearing the same clothes."

"Statistically, killers who abduct and kill in the first hours are strangers to the victim."

"This is a case, not a statistic. Grant Danford knew Rita; they had been casually dating for six months when she disappeared. During the missing person's investigation, he told the police he hadn't seen her the day she disappeared; during the investigation of her murder, a witness was found who placed them together walking the forest preserve trails that very afternoon."

"Was he ever really a suspect when this was just a missing person's case?"

"Not really," she admitted. "He had put out a large reward for information, cooperated with the police, added his political pressure to keep the case alive. But the case eventually became cold from lack of evidence."

"The cynical interpretation being that he stayed so close to the investigation he made sure they never looked where evidence could be found."

"Yes."

"And when her body was discovered here on his property, Danford became the chief suspect if not the only one," Quinn speculated. "They never looked any further once they had a witness who contradicted his original statement to the police."

"They moved pretty fast on making the arrest."

"He was overseas when the stable manager found the body?"

"England."

"If he was guilty of the crime, why in the world did he risk leaving the body here all those years?"

"Arrogance? He thought he had gotten away with it. Fear? Why mess with something he had dodged once? The vast majority of buried murdered victims are never found. That's a statistic you know as well as I."

"A crime of passion?"

She got up, walked a few feet away before turning back to face him. She didn't like that question because of its answer. "That's what the police concluded and the DA proved to the jury's satisfaction."

His eyes narrowed. "But?"

"That never felt right, not with the bound hands. Those case notes—you'll find interviews with practically every woman Grant ever went out with. He didn't type as a guy with dark fantasies, and that's what the bound hands, the struggle suggest."

"So he was convicted because of association with the victim and location of the grave."

"And testimony of a witness. Christopher Hampton testified that he saw Grant and Rita together the afternoon she disappeared. And by the way—you met Christopher's brother the other day."

She'd caught him off guard with that observation. "Hampton? Christopher is a relation to the guy who just died in the fire?"

"Believe it or not, yes—a nephew. Christopher was actually working for Grant part-time that year at the stables, as well as working part-time for his uncle. He wanted the chance to ride regularly and this way he could afford it. Christopher said he was taking his afternoon break, walking the trail to head over and get a late lunch for the other stable hands when he saw the two of them together."

Why didn't he speak up during the original missing person's investigation?"

"During the trial he admitted he was getting lunch for the guys, but he was also meeting his bookie, paying off a gambling debt, and he didn't want his uncle to know. Blaming his boss, the guy offering the reward wouldn't be to his benefit, and the only thing he could testify to was that he saw the two of them walking on the forest preserve trail about 2 P.M. He chose to stay quiet."

"Did you believe him?"

She shrugged. "I suppose. It seemed credible."

"He bribed Grant Danford for his silence."

"What?"

"Lincoln uncovered it. Found out about the gambling problem; found out from the bookie that there was no way Christopher could pay his debt, and yet a few days later he had the whole amount in cash. And Grant as much admitted it when Lincoln pressed on the matter. Christopher demanded Grant pay up or he would go to the police. And he apparently paid him quite handsomely over the years Rita was missing."

"So Christopher told the truth at the trial—he did see them together the day she disappeared; Grant knew it and suppressed it."

"Yes."

This didn't make sense. "Why didn't Grant just say he had seen her if he's innocent like he claims?"

"His explanation—Rita had asked him not to mention she had been by; her parents wanted her focused on college, her photography, and her career, not dating a much older man. When the police first asked if he had seen her he said no, then felt like he couldn't risk changing his story later. And once he paid off Christopher—big mistake. Christopher just kept coming back for more."

"How does Grant explain her body being found on his property?"

"He blames an unknown killer," Quinn replied, his opinion of that in his voice.

"I'm surprised Lincoln took his claim of being innocent seriously. Grant was dating Rita; she was seen here the day she went missing; her body was found on his property. It doesn't leave much room to maneuver. Not to mention the fact this murder is eleven years old. New evidence is going to be hard to find."

"But why did he kill her? You said yourself a crime of passion doesn't easily fit the image of the remains. They had been going out six months, were apparently happy together even if her parents were against it. What triggers a man in a relationship to suddenly turn murderous, choke, and kill?"

She couldn't give him a good answer. "You said he's apparently hiding secrets, being uncooperative. Was there one that she found out? If not a crime of passion, then was it a crime of necessity? Does Lincoln have any ideas? Any other suspects?"

"No. Right now he's simply talking to everyone who testified at the trial." He set aside the file. "Do you think Grant Danford is guilty?"

Her answer would carry some weight with him; she didn't answer right away. She thought about that summer. So many had wanted Grant to be found guilty…but the evidence she'd testified to had been solid, and she remembered the victim. No matter how powerful the man, it was the victim she had focused on. "Yes."

Quinn thought about it, thrust his hand through his thick hair. "I tend to agree with you. The lie, the bribe—he really wanted to keep hidden that he saw her that day. That points to guilt. But Lincoln isn't so sure. I can't dismiss that. And if Grant is innocent—then someone else killed her. Someone who is still out there. What are the odds a murderer kills only once?"

What a tangled question. The only real answer was it depends. There were as many varieties of killers as there were reasons to kill. The gamut ran from domestic disturbances that got out of hand to killing someone picked out at random. She'd unfortunately seen examples of them all.

Quinn didn't wait for an answer. "I've seen enough to understand the basics of the case, what memories it's going to bring up when I talk to Mrs. Beck. It was headline news for the duration of the case, that's the biggest point I need to know. Let's call it a day."

Lisa was more than ready to agree.

He waited for her to join him on the steps, put a hand on her back to steady her. It was an impersonal gesture, done casually, but she found herself welcoming and relaxing against that touch.

He paused by the pasture fence. "Grant had a good eye for horses."

"Really?"

She leaned against the railing beside him. Quinn pointed. "The chestnut is exceptional. Not a racer, but he'd be a great saddle horse. Do you ride?"

"Enough not to fall out of the saddle."

"I'm surprised you've had a chance for even that. I've noticed in the city it takes money, access, and time."

"Right to all three."

"Maybe next time you come west there'll be time to help out your education."

"Maybe." She didn't expect to have a reason to go back to his ranch, but she wasn't going to say that, not when he was offering an olive branch back to the friendship of yesterday. She lifted off the hat and held it out to him. "Thanks for the loan."

He accepted it. "Something else we'll have to fix. You need your own."

"Yours smells like horse."

He curled the brim, his expression practically one of affection. "It's been kicked around for a few years." He slid it on, then whistled; the chestnut raised his head and came ambling over.

The horse nuzzled his shoulder, tried to knock off the hat. Quinn rubbed his muzzle. He glanced over at her and smiled. "You can pet him. He's just a big baby."

"Who's interested in knocking you over." She stroked the chestnut's shoulder, feeling the powerful muscles flex under her hand.

"But at least I can't step on him by mistake." The chestnut chose that moment to take a playful nip at Quinn's shoulder.

Lisa stepped back, laughing. "I'll stick to my pets, thanks."

"Rita loved horses."

"Did she?"

"Mrs. Beck had several of the photographs Rita took of horses on display at the gallery." Quinn's voice turned serious. "Amy loved horses too."

"That's pretty common when you're sixteen. And Amy lived on a ranch. It was probably one of the reasons the girls became friends."

He looked at her intently, telling her something with his eyes before he spoke. "I've been wondering if this was one of the places Rita took her pictures. If Rita had known about this stable when she was sixteen. If the two girls hung out here and got to know Grant Danford."

Lisa blanched. "You think there's another body here?"

"If he's guilty—kill one girl, why not two?"

"Quinn."

"There has to be a reason he killed Rita, a good solid one, not that flimsy one they sold at the trial. You said yourself it wasn't a good fit for the way the remains were found. Think about it. Assume Grant really is guilty.

"What if Amy came to Chicago again when she was seventeen? What if she had a fight with her mom, her boyfriend, just got on a bus or hitchhiked here to see the girlfriend she'd been sharing all her secrets with for a year? They returned to the old places they had enjoyed, this place being one of them.

"Amy's a runaway, needs a place to stay, and Grant's a man who is concerned about what is going on, knows them both from the year before, persuades Amy to let him help fix the mess she's gotten herself into. And when Amy disappears as suddenly as she came, Grant convinces Rita he helped Amy patch things up with her family and that she left to stay with her aunt out east for a while."

Quinn was spinning a story that was killing her with its specificity because it was only too plausible, and it was making her sick to see it.

"Only Amy never left. She's dead and her body is buried somewhere out there in the forest preserve. And years later Rita is seeing Grant, having never really lost her crush on this guy that was nice to her and helped her friend, and maybe on that fatal day they take a walk and she stumbles on something that was never supposed to see the light of day again: Amy's skeleton.

"Grant can't have that Jane Doe identified, Rita knows he was supposedly helping the runaway Amy, and he can't convince Rita to ignore it. He has to shut her permanently up. But he's also learned his lesson and he can't bury her in the forest preserve, not if he wants her to remain lost forever. So he buries her on his own estate at the one place he can dig without his staff being suspicious."

"Stop it. Okay? Just stop."

"It fits. I need to know."

She closed her eyes, then opened them to look at him with painful clarity. "We both do."

TEN

Lisa leaned against the railing on the back deck, letting the quiet of the Tuesday night settle inside and ease her tension headache. The problem with getting close to Quinn was that his burdens became her own. She wanted to be able to help him solve the mystery of who had killed his father, what had happened with Amy, but she didn't have the emotional energy to give him. Extending the job she did at work to her time off gave her no chance to unwind.

She should have taken that vacation after all. She would be so glad to have Jennifer's wedding to go to, have a four-day break, and a chance to get away from casework that was uniformly grim.

The patio door slid open; Kate stepped out and came to lean against the railing beside her.

Lisa glanced over. "Find your shoes?" Kate had moved home yesterday but as usual had left a trail of stuff behind.

Kate quirked a grin. "One of them. I must have tossed the other into that bag after all."

"I'll give you a call if I find it."

"They aren't my favorites; if they're gone I can't say I'll mind."

Kate had come over for more than just her shoes; Lisa knew that. She sipped at the glass of ice water she held, not in a hurry to break the silence. They'd been friends for over twenty years; she knew Kate. She'd get around to the point sooner or later. Beneath the calm appearance there was a fine layer of strain and tension; it showed in the small tells of the way Kate's hands gripped the railing, the way the Southern tone in her vowels had stretched out.

"You've been really down this last week since you got home. Is there anything I can do?" Kate finally asked.

"Trade jobs for a few days." Lisa's smile was tired. "I'll be okay, Kate. I'm just coming back slowly. The fatigue is hanging on with a persistence I didn't expect."

"You want to do a movie some evening? Share a laugh?"

The idea sounded like a wonderful break for both of them. "I'd enjoy that."

A shooting star descended within a ten-degree arc of the full moon. Lisa followed its trail down, wondering if the meteor had burned up in the atmosphere or would become an interesting find for some rock hound.

"I see you got the yard depression filled with dirt."

"Walter Hampton from Nakomi Nurseries brought out a load of dirt and leveled out my sinkhole. He's bringing sod tomorrow and talking about shrubs, flowers, trees—he can't stand to see a great house not landscaped properly."

Kate turned to look at her. "What?"

"I'm going to have to twist his arm to get him to give me a bill. He's kind of like Quinn, just smoothly rolls over your objections with a smile and does what he likes."

"Lizzy, Walter likes you."

"What?"

"I'm serious. The flowers on your dining table—he brought those over when he brought the load of dirt?"

She had thought it was simply a nice gesture. She'd been distracted at the time, had appreciated the gift because she loved beautiful things and it fit so easily with what she knew about him. "Yes." She rubbed her eyes, not needing this complication.

"Say a nice thank you for the flowers, chat with him while he improves your yard, and let him do what he likes. It never hurts to have a friend."

"I'm not going to bust his heart or anything?" she muttered, annoyed that Kate was right and she hadn't seen it.

"He just wants to do something nice for you. Let him. There's no obligation in that, and given how much this house means to you, spending time talking with a landscape expert would be enjoyable for both of you."

She trusted Kate's opinion. This house did mean a lot; she would love to have the yard looking really nice, and Walter did an exceptional job. Spending a couple hours talking plants and trees would be fun. "I'll do that," she agreed, glad to have the advice.

"Did you hear about Jack's first good deed?"

"Let me guess, you've been talking to Quinn."

"Guilty. He found it rather amusing that you asked him for music lessons."

Lisa wondered what else Quinn had told her and was painfully aware that if Quinn had talked out of turn, Kate was going to be chatting tonight about more than the family bet she had with Jack. Quinn wouldn't have broken her privacy; she knew him. Her voice was light when she answered; she was getting as good as Kate at masking her thoughts. "Well, it's not like any of the O'Malleys could help; none of you know how to play any instrument."

"I can whistle."

"It has to be something you use your hands to play. Jack insisted."

Kate thought for a moment. "I can hum a piece of grass held with my thumbs."

Lisa laughed. "I remember. You did get pretty good at that." Lisa relaxed. "I bought the harmonica. A good expensive plastic one. It cost me three dollars. I haven't opened the wrapper yet. So what was Jack's first good deed?"

"A roofing repair job for Tina Brown." Tina was in her sixties now, a friend of all the O'Malleys from the old neighborhood.

"Nice of him. I'm sure Tina appreciated it, and in this heat, that's a good deed he really earned."

The quiet between them returned.

"Anything else you want to talk about?" Kate asked, not probing hard, but probing nevertheless.

"Quinn's told you what's going on with Amy?"

"Yes."

"There's no way to search that forest preserve in a systematic way for remains over twenty years old without a few hundred volunteers. That's assuming, one, that Quinn's idea is right, and two, that Amy's remains are still there to be found. Grant would probably have reburied them somewhere else. And we can't get a warrant to search his former estate grounds without some solid evidence."

"So you're looking for that historical link?"

"Yes." Lisa sighed. "It's a mess, Kate. And I'm worried about Quinn, the way he's handling this turn in the case."

"He needs the case to finally break open. I'm glad you're helping him."

"Marcus is doing most of it, and Lincoln. I'm just helping sort out the information they find."

"It's costing you."

"Heavily. That gravesite excavation is still too current in my memory."

"Tell him."

"No. Quinn needs me in the loop." And even if it was in a grim way, she wanted a reason to be around him. "Quinn and Marcus are cops, not death investigators. I look for different things. Make different assumptions."

"He needs to be able to find justice."

"It's why he's never settled down."

"I think it's a major part of it."

Lisa sensed a change in the conversation leading toward a discussion of her relationship with Quinn and didn't want to deal with it tonight. "How are things going with Dave?"

Kate groaned. "He wants to go shopping for a ring."

Lisa straightened. "Really?"

"I'm not so sure I do."

"Why ever not?"

"Every page I get I can see him tense up, and we're only dating. If we were married—"

"He's not going to ask you to give up your job."

"I know that. But I feel the pressure to find something less dangerous."

"His job is not exactly a cakewalk either," Lisa pointed out.

"I'm afraid I'm going to hesitate a fraction longer than I should during a crisis because I'm thinking about the ramifications of something going wrong."

Lisa shook her head. "The last thing you do is think about the consequences to yourself before you act. Trust me on that; I've seen you respond to too many situations." She smiled and slid a hand through her hair. "You're responsible for most of my gray hairs. Having Dave in the equation isn't going to change how you react. You'll just finally have someone always around when the crisis is over. Give Dave some credit, he wouldn't be asking if he hadn't resolved the question in his own mind. Besides, I'd be more concerned with him taking a bullet than you. You've got a SWAT team keeping you company. He's the guy on the front lines."

"You did have to remind me."

"You love him."

"So much it's kind of scary."

"Let him get you a ring. You don't have to set the date for the wedding. It's probably more insurance on his side that you're not going to do something stupid like act noble and say no for his own good. Admit it, you'd change jobs before you'd give up Dave."

"True." Kate held out her left hand. "I don't want anything fancy."

Lisa laughed. "I'm quite sure to get you to say yes, Dave will let you get what you prefer."

"I know him. He'll just overcompensate for my choice when he buys the wedding ring."

"One of the perks of going out with a guy who comes from very old, very deep money."

"True."

Lisa relaxed against the railing. She couldn't feel sad that Kate and Dave were making that next step. She liked Dave. He was exactly what her sister needed, someone who would stick forever.

But as happy as she was for them, she was sad too. The exclusive group of seven was going to become ten when Jennifer and Tom, Marcus and Shari, and Kate and Dave married. It was going to change, and while she knew there would always be a place for her, after they were married she knew she'd be thinking twice before she picked up the phone to call one of them in the middle of the night. It was those little changes she dreaded.

"I've got a favor to ask," Kate said.

"Sure."

"Would you consider coming to church with us next week?"

While she had known the subject would come up again, the question came out of the blue, and Lisa wasn't ready with a graceful answer. She simply shook her head. "I'll pass."

"I wish you'd come."

"Kate—" Causing friction in the family was the last thing she wanted to do, but Kate didn't know what she was asking. And Lisa was tired, didn't want to have to deal with this.

"You'd be welcome. They're a great bunch of people. And I'd like you to meet the rest of Dave's family, his friends."

"Have a barbecue; I'll come. Dave's place has room for a small crowd."

"You can't avoid the subject of church forever."

"Why not?"

"I've never known you to form an opinion without having the facts."

"I know what I need to know."

"Scripture is true, Lisa, even though you find it hard to accept. Jesus is the Son of God, and He did rise from the dead. He is alive."

"Leave it alone. Please."

"I always thought you were open-minded enough to at least listen."

"Insults aren't going to help."

Shock crossed Kate's face, then pain. "I'm sorry. I didn't mean it that way."

"And I'm a little sensitive about the subject right now. You, Jennifer, and Marcus have been laying it on pretty thick in the last few weeks."

Kate absorbed that. "We didn't mean to. I really am sorry, for all of us."

Now she'd made a mess of it. Lisa rubbed her face. "I'm sorry too. I didn't mean to bite, but I really would like you to just drop the subject. I'm tired. I'm not going to change my mind. And I'm really not interested."

It was so obvious Kate wanted to ask why, but she stopped the question and gave a reluctant nod. "All right, Lisa." Kate's pager went off. She glanced at the number, frustrated. "This job has lousy timing. I've got to take this one." She reached into her pocket for her cellular phone and punched in the numbers with her thumb. "Yes, Jim?"

Lisa saw the shift to an impassive expression, knew whatever was going on it was serious. "I'm on my way." Kate closed her phone and sighed. "I've got to go."

Lisa reached out and hugged her, not wanting her to depart with tension between them. "Be safe, Kate."

"Always." Kate kissed her cheek. "Get some sleep."

"Lisa, where do you find these records? That sax is wailing like somebody is in mourning," Quinn asked, wondering if he could convince her to change it without admitting it was getting on his nerves. It was Friday evening, and he and Marcus were camped out at her place, going through what evidence they had been able to gather, trying to formulate their plan of attack for the next day. Lisa had insisted she wanted to help and Quinn had finally conceded the point.

He was enjoying the chance to quietly invade her space. Her ferret was draped over his knee, half asleep. They had moved from the dining room to the living room after Lincoln got paged and had to leave. It was after 9 P.M., but Lisa showed no signs of wanting to call it a night.

Sitting on the couch, using the coffee table as a work area, she didn't bother to look up from the photographs she was sorting. "I like jazz."

"Your music taste is decades old."

"Really? I figured you would have heard it when it was new." She glanced over at him and smiled as his partner chuckled. Quinn made a face back at her. The last three weeks had done some good; at least she'd started to relax with him.

It was such slow progress.

The more he knew about her, the more he wanted to know. The attraction went deeper than like, but not as strong as love; it hovered there in the middle like a balance waiting to settle. It was an incredibly dangerous edge, one he worried about privately when he prayed. He'd always been able to control his emotions and how close he got. This time events were overtaking him and he felt like he was picking his way through a minefield.

The convergence of issues had created something he had never expected. Spending time with Lisa in the investigation had opened up a look at her professional life, just as helping her out as she got over the injury had opened a window into her private life.

She was intelligent, fair, independent, kind, and above everything else, curious. But when it came to being willing to talk about things of faith, that curiosity changed to indifference. He had watched Kate try, then Marcus. Lisa had rebuffed them both.

Quinn frowned at that ugly reality, knowing something had turned off that curiosity, dreading both what it could be and how hard it was going to be to uncover. Lisa was formidable in keeping her secrets.

Of the three problems he'd faced—she wouldn't let him get close, she didn't trust him, and she didn't believe—he'd made progress on only one, and even that was fragile. She had let him closer than he expected, but she still wasn't ready to trust him, and he had gotten nowhere with the question of faith. He had the feeling getting her to trust him was going to be key to figuring out why her hackles rose so fast when Jesus was mentioned.

Lisa and her secrets—she wasn't going to give them up easily.

Neither was this case. Quinn forced himself to turn his attention from Lisa back to the work at hand. It was so frustrating. The search for information had bogged down. Grant was being uncooperative to the extreme, would answer nothing about Rita and when he had met her or if he had known Amy Ireland. It made Quinn more determined than ever to crack open what he was hiding.

Lincoln was trying to prove the man innocent; they were trying to prove him guilty of a second murder. Grant Danford was in a box squeezing so tight that it was going to eventually have to pop one way or the other. And it was actually easier to make progress on the case with all of them working together, looking at all the information gathered with different objectives.

From Amy's mother had come shoe boxes of photographs and slides Amy had taken during the two-week art camp. From Valerie Beck—told only of the search to locate Amy—had come old letters Rita had kept from friends, Rita's diaries—kept daily during her teens with sporadic entries into her twenties—and access to Rita's photographs. Rita had been intending to make photojournalism a full-time career and her film negatives were extensive going back to when she was fifteen. Lisa was trying to get them into some sort of chronological order.

Quinn watched Lisa work for a few minutes longer, then turned his attention back to Rita's diary. "What were you doing when you were sixteen?" he asked casually, curious if she'd answer.

She looked up. "What?"

"What were you doing when you were sixteen? Rita was boy and horse crazy by the sound of her diary."

"Lisa was into running track and pretending she didn't like Larry Rich," Marcus answered absently on her behalf. He was sitting on the floor using the couch as a backrest, leafing through old newspaper clippings from the initial missing person's investigation of Rita Beck.

"I was not," Lisa protested.

"Sure you were. I chaperoned that year's prom, remember?"

"I didn't go."

"You half did; you slipped out to meet Larry over at the high school gym so you could borrow his brother's motorcycle. You ended up going bowling if I remember correctly."

"Who told you that?"

"Larry. He was wise enough to ask permission before the two of you disappeared."

Quinn turned a chuckle into a cough as Lisa shoved Marcus's shoulder with her socked foot.

"Forget it, Sherlock; I'm still going to start vetting the guys in your life again."

"Kevin was a mistake, okay? I learned my lesson."

Marcus reached back and tweaked her foot. "Stephen stood there and watched Kevin's nose bleed after Jack slugged him. I was so proud of him. He asked about Jack's hand before he dealt with Kevin's broken nose."

"You should have read them both the riot act."

Marcus smiled. "I love you too. Where's that stack of letters Amy's mom sent out?"

Lisa shuffled through the box of material they had brought over to the house, found them, and handed the packet to him.

Quinn was grateful for their help, even if he did feel guilty that Marcus had chosen to stick around for the last days of his vacation to help out. It was clear just watching Marcus and Lisa together that his partner had decided to do some low-key meddling in her life.

He was relieved to see that the pain she'd been doing her best to hide appeared to be fading. She was not pausing to think before she moved as she had been; he'd only seen her reach to shield her ribs twice tonight. And that brace on her broken finger was going to be gone in another couple days if she kept fiddling with it. He wanted to reach over and still her hands as she worked at the tape holding it in place. Doctors had to be some of the worst patients there were.

Her parrot stalked along the back of the couch and stepped down onto her shoulder. Lisa absently stroked her feathers. "What's the matter, Iris? Peanuts gone?"

The parrot whistled. Lisa pulled another one from her pocket, still in its shell, and offered it. "Take it back to your perch."

Iris grasped it and flew with a rush of feathers to the perch by the patio door.

The ferret looked up, and then rolled over in Quinn's lap onto his back. Quinn obliged the silent invitation and rubbed Sidney's stomach. After a week of dropping into Lisa's home, it was obvious she'd be lost without the pets. They were part of her life. He'd remember that when her birthday rolled around.

"Who's this?" Lisa asked. "Amy took a lot of pictures of him."

Quinn accepted the photo she handed him. The teenage boy was throwing a bale of hay from the bed of a pickup truck to waiting cattle. "Amy's boyfriend at the time she disappeared. Fred Wilson. They had been going together for about two years."

"Nice-looking guy."

"Pretty devastated at her disappearance from what I remember."

"He was ruled out as a suspect?" Marcus asked, looking at the photo.

"He was rebuilding a fence with his dad the day Amy disappeared. No one was ever totally ruled out, but he's low on the list."

Marcus nodded and handed it back to Lisa.

"Did Amy have her camera with her when she disappeared?" Lisa asked.

"Good question. Yes, one of her Nikons was missing."

"Never found?"

"No."

"I wish we could find some kind of proof that she came to Chicago." She stretched carefully, taking the strain out of her back.

"If it exists, we'll find it," Quinn replied, certain of that.

The room became quiet as they worked.

"So what were you doing when you were sixteen?" Lisa casually tossed the question back at him. It caught him off guard; it was the first probe she'd made into his past. There was a wonderful irony to the fact she was asking while her brother was in the room.

"At sixteen I was doing my best to survive the rodeo circuit and seriously pursuing Ashley Blake, the soon-to-be-crowned Miss Montana."

"You didn't catch her."

"On the contrary. She made me the envy of every guy in the state for the next two years running. Then she married my best friend."

Lisa laughed. It was a good sound, with no hesitation part of it. "Why do I have a feeling you were part of that?"

"Jed's a quiet kind of guy. Ashley just needed an excuse to hang out with him."

"And it gave you cover from all the girls chasing you."

Quinn winked at her, then glanced at Marcus. "She's smart."

"No argument here."

Lisa didn't follow up on it, to his disappointment.

She looked back at her notepad and running list of issues. "How much money did Amy have access to when she disappeared?"

"Not much. Maybe thirty dollars according her mom."

"Unless she had been hoarding money for a while in preparation of leaving."

"Which is why we might be having such a hard time finding a record of her travel. If it wasn't a spur of the moment runaway, then she either got transportation arranged early or Rita made the reservations for her."

"Do we have access to Rita's accounts when she was sixteen?"

"Her mom sent over what she had, but there's not much there. No way to trace all the cash from her summer jobs. What she wasn't spending on film, she was spending on camera equipment. There's just too much money unaccounted for to tell."

Quinn turned the page in the diary. Rita's handwriting at age sixteen had been enthusiastic, the letters sweeping and the words expansive, the number of exclamation points and underlined words and sad or smiling faces making it very easy to formulate a good idea of who she was.

A happy kid.

Fights and secrets with friends, crushes, occasional comments about family, a lot of plans and dreams for her future.

She hadn't dated many of the entries and often had several that appeared to be written during the course of one day. He was in the section of the diary for the right year the girls had met. She'd spent five pages on her birthday party describing who had come and what they had said and what gifts she had received from whom, but he'd found no reference yet to the art camp or to Amy.

He turned the page and stopped at the first part of a new entry.

Horses!! Sam took me to the forest preserve over by his house to ride bikes and one of the trails goes by a big estate with its own stables. It was so cool! There were like six horses and a foal out in the pasture. Mr. Danford told me I could come back and visit if I wanted, bring my camera to take pictures of the horses. He was riding a big sorrel that was just magnificent!

"Gotcha," Quinn said quietly.

"What?"

He held out the diary to her. "Top of the left page."

She read the passage, then looked over at him. She didn't say anything for a long moment, and he understood that expression. There was sadness there. "He knew Rita when she was sixteen."

"We'll prove he knew Amy too." Quinn was convinced of it now.

ELEVEN

Lisa twirled the plastic stem of a rubber-tipped dart between her thumb and first finger and considered the now slightly smudged, red twenty-six circled on the whiteboard. She sidearmed the dart toward the board and it stuck with a squishing sound just below the six. She scowled at the miss. Her eyes were blurry from the long days spent reading and the hours at the microscope. She ignored the darts on the floor that had not stuck and scored the four inside the circle. Four out of five was an improvement.

Two weeks working in the archive files and she had zilch.

She got up from the table, glanced one last time at the case she had spread out, and paced toward the far counter and the coffeepot. It was after eight on a Wednesday night, she was getting nowhere, and if she were smart she'd call it a night and go home. In the quiet night, the empty building, it wasn't just her imagination that had the victims haunting this room, that sat at the tables before their spread-out files, looking at her and silently shaming her for not seeing the truth.

She had to stop reading Stephen King before she went to sleep. The silence was accusing.

She dumped sugar into the coffee to help kill the headache and looked around the room at all the tables. There were seventeen cases presently set out, all ones that had shown promise. When one stopped yielding ideas, she had moved on to the next. And while results were still outstanding on most of the ballistic, fingerprint, and DNA tests she had requested, the first round had come back. She had added new evidence to several cases, but overall she had moved not a single case significantly forward.

There was a knifing death, a strangled assault case, two gunshot victims, a burned Jane Doe, three victims from an armed robbery gone bad.... The tables were weighed down under tragedies.

She had to find justice for somebody.

She'd even concede, cutting that goal of twenty-six successes to two if she could just get movement somewhere.

She could open another box and start a new case, but if she couldn't solve any from the first set she had already examined, it left little hope for the others she would open.

There had to be a better way to work this problem.

"What are the odds a murderer kills only once?" The question Quinn had asked lingered like an intriguing thread. In the unlikely event that Lincoln was right and Grant Danford was innocent, then there was a killer still out there. Or if Quinn was right and Grant had killed twice, what were the odds of a third time?

Two hundred and sixty cases—two hundred and sixty different killers?

No way.

Somewhere in this room there were cases that were similar. Find the common MO and she'd find cases she could link and leverage together.

It was a good enough idea to have her setting aside the coffee and reaching into the small refrigerator for a soda instead, knowing it would keep her awake unlike the coffee, a psychological difference if not a caffeine- and sugar-driven one.

Where did she start?

Group by age of the crime? type of crime? type of victim?

She was looking for a particular man, a particular killer. He would repeat himself.

The home invasions where robberies had resulted in a homeowner being killed—she'd already seen several of them. And the shootings—several were thought to be drug-related cases; those might be linked.

She went over to the shelves with the stacks of boxes she had yet to go through. Diane had done a first pass through the boxes, finding the original case numbers and figuring out which had some information already online, getting the basics entered for the remaining cases.

She brought up the database Diane was building and saw that all two hundred and sixty case numbers had been entered, and while the case subclassification had just begun, the date, location, and original detectives working on the case had been entered.

Lisa sorted the cases by date, called up the summary report, and printed a copy. She found a red pen, pushed the metal shelves around on their wheels to scan the boxes, and located the first case on the list.

The box was heavy and slid out to land with a thud on the tile floor. She sorted through the files until she found the crime scene photos. A shooting. She noted it on the printout and closed the box, then wrestled it back onto the shelf. The second case on the list was one she had already reviewed. An assault; the lady had died two days later from a fractured skull. She scrawled that in the margin.

The third case was on the top shelf. She eased the box down to the floor, holding her breath as it tried to shift before she was braced for the weight.

Lisa could feel an odd sense of relief building. This was a puzzle she now had a way to attack. She wanted a solution to at least some of these cases; it had become a very personal challenge. The victims were tugging at her, demanding justice.

The buzzards were circling. Quinn reined in his horse at the sight, lifting his hat to shade his eyes as he looked to the south. He left his current job of moving cattle to veer off and investigate. In calving season they usually lost one or two heifers at birth and it was always a personal loss. He almost preferred losing one to the occasional wolf than losing one to birth.

He had been back from college only a few weeks and his back was sore, not yet accustomed to being back in the saddle for twelve hours a day. He rode toward the circling birds and found himself riding into darkness, the spacious landscape slowly disappearing from his peripheral view for the memories he was riding back into were black.

The bluffs were always dangerous places both to people and to cattle.

A man was on the ground, and even from a hundred yards away the red staining the back of the shirt was visible.

Dad!

Quinn choked as he woke in the hotel room to the strident sound of his beeper going off, sweating in the chilly room. The sheet was tangled in a knot around him. If he ever did marry, he'd run the risk of tossing his wife off the bed with his flailing around. The nightmare came more often now that he was actively working a lead for the case. He struggled out of the dream and back to the present, reaching for the pager that continued to sound.

He didn't recognize the number, but he couldn't ignore it. His hand reaching for the phone sent his watch and an empty water glass falling. He punched in the numbers. "What?" he growled at the intruder of his restless sleep.

"Quinn?"

"Lisa?" he queried, regretting the fact he'd barked. She'd hesitated to answer him. He turned around the alarm clock and the red lights glowed back at him. 1:42 A.M. He clicked on the bedside light. "What's wrong?" She had called him exactly once in all the years he had known her, and at this time of night…

"I can't see a clock and I'm not wearing a watch. What time is it?"

"Late. What's wrong? Where are you?"

"The office."

Some of his tension eased. Not at home with a problem, not in a car accident somewhere. But with that injury… "Are you okay?" Getting answers out of her was like pulling teeth.

"Quinn, I'm fine," she replied, her voice tinged with annoyance. "Now would you listen?"

He closed his eyes to stop his first reply. "I'm listening."

"I've found something you should see."

He waited and she didn't add anything. "Okay," he said cautiously.

"Well are you coming?"

"Now?"

"Quinn—"

"Hold it, before you get mad at me—you woke me up, Lisa. Give me a minute here. What's going on?"

There was dead silence that lingered. When she finally spoke her voice was edged with sarcasm. "Never mind. I'll call Marcus."

"Don't hang up," he ordered, half afraid she already had. He'd just blown it with her. And he deserved to. O'Malleys didn't ask questions. He'd seen Marcus catch a flight at a moment's notice when Lisa said she needed to see him, not asking why, the request itself sufficient. Lisa did not make unnecessary or trivial requests; none of the O'Malleys did. "I'll be there. Give me twenty minutes."

He held his breath until he got her terse reply. "I'll tell the security guard to expect you."

The bakery down the block from the state crime lab had its lights on, the staff beginning preparations for the dawn onslaught of customers. Quinn bought four still-warm blueberry muffins. It wasn't much of an apology, but it was something. Not hardly enough though. She'd actually called him before her family and he'd blown it. He had a headache and it was his own fault.

Quinn pulled open the door to the lab. He waited at the security desk while the downtown marshal's office confirmed his ID and the security guard cleared him, then clipped on the guest badge and headed upstairs.

The door to the task force room was closed, but light was visible beneath it. Quinn opened the door and was met with the assault of another wailing saxophone. He had to get her some better music.

Lisa was leaning over the light table, studying a set of X-rays. She had said she was okay, but it was a relief to see for himself. She had been here all day; she was still wearing the blue-and-white striped shirt he enjoyed because it set off her eyes fabulously, and her blue jeans were the well-washed pair speckled in white patches where bleach had washed out the color. He thought of them as her old comfortable favorites and knew when he saw her wearing them that she'd had something rough happen the previous day or night and had instinctively gone for comfort. "You're late," she commented, not looking up.

"Food."

She looked around, spotted the sack, and her smiled flashed immediately. "You're forgiven, and thank you. There's not even a vending machine on this floor and I'm famished." She nodded toward a desk. "There is safe."

He set down the sack and tossed his keys beside it.

"I've got four women found as skeletons across the Chicagoland area, just like Rita Beck. Only their four cases are still open."

He stopped in the act of ditching his hat. This was definitely worth being pulled out of bed in the middle of the night to hear. He dropped the hat on the desk. "Which cases?"

She gestured immediately to her right. "These four tables." The case boxes were open, the files laid out on the tables.

"Please tell me Grant Danford knew them all."

"Quinn…I just got started."

"Sorry. Tell me what you've got."

She sat down on the edge of the desk, picked up a marker, and began to add information to the rolling whiteboard she pulled over. "Martha Treemont, found in 1993, missing for six years. Heather Ashburn, found in 1995, missing for ten years. Vera Wane, found in 1998, missing two years. And Marla Sherrall, found last year, missing eight years."

"And if Grant Danford is responsible, add Rita Beck, found in 1997, missing eight years, and a suspicion of Amy Ireland, missing for twenty years."

"Yes."

"Five, possibly six cases, going back twenty years."

"That we know of."

He nodded, accepting the very valid qualification. If there was a pattern in these deaths, it was that the evidence of the murder was only uncovered years later. There would be more victims than just these five if they were linked.

He picked up one of the dropped darts from the floor, twirling it between his fingers as he looked at the dates she had written on the board. "A common MO in the victims?"

"A twenty-four-year-old architect student, a sixty-two-year-old retired widow, a forty-five-year-old former landscape nursery worker, and a thirty-two-year-old French bakery worker."

He was puzzled at that. "It doesn't fit Rita or Amy."

"Women, all single; different geographic areas, different economic statuses, a vast age range."

"Lisa, you've lost me. Having five open cases over fifteen years in this surrounding area where the female victim was buried is not surprising given the number of murders each year."

"You're right. And there are another twelve cases vaguely similar that I set aside as explainable to different factors—obvious gunshot wounds, known abusive situations, suspected family violence. But these—Quinn, I don't know how to better explain it than the fact the hair on the back of my neck stood on end when I scanned the reports. It's what isn't there. No obvious blows, gunshots, no apparent causes of death—just a skeleton appearing in the earth buried face down. Three of the four cases show hands behind the back, the other was moved before it could be noted; two of the cases show remains of duct tape."

Quinn winced. "An MO in the method but random victims."

"Exactly."

"Then let's hope it is Grant—or at least someone already behind bars." He read the names and dates, made an educated guess. "They weren't connected before because they come from different jurisdictions."

"Different jurisdictions over a long period of years, and several of the cases were not even in the computer databases until this review began."

"Where do you want me to start?"

"I need the who, what, where, and when summarized for each. I've got to get focused on the physical evidence and see how similar they really are. Quinn—"

"I know. If this is one killer, and it's not Grant, you just landed in one of the biggest, deepest messes of your life." Women were disappearing and turning up as bones years later.

She looked hesitant. "Thanks for helping. This may be a false alarm and there's nothing here. I was kind of rude about waking you up."

He reached over and slid his hand behind her neck, wanting the contact just to make his reassurance reach inside and go deeper than words. His thumb rubbed the back of her neck and she slowly relaxed under his touch.

He hated knowing he had contributed to her hesitation and wanted to ensure she didn't hesitate next time she considered calling him. "The ghosts in here are thick. If you're wrong, I'll buy you breakfast and enjoy the fact you asked for my company. If you're right—you'll be stuck with me and Lincoln like your own personal shadows. Please don't count my rather abysmal initial reaction against me. I appreciate that you called."

"Maybe next time you won't be so surprised when you hear it's me calling."

He smiled at that soft acceptance of his apology. "I found it a very nice surprise that I would like very much to have repeated."

She grasped his forearm and squeezed as she nodded.

He reluctantly lowered his hand. "Get started on the physical evidence and I'll start reviewing the files. We both know Rita Beck's case inside and out. If these have a similar feel, it will be obvious to both of us. Do you have what you need here, or do you want to go over to the cold storage evidence vaults?"

"I've got the basics here: the crime scene photographs, autopsy reports, and the X-ray slides."

"Then eat a muffin, and get to work."

She crossed over to the desk and opened the sack. "Do I have to share?"

He glanced over from the folder he had picked up and smiled at that subtle plea in her voice. "If that's dinner, then no, have all four."

"If I wasn't about to inhale this muffin I'd tell you thanks again."

"You're welcome. And you're easy to please."

She sat down holding the first muffin and spun her chair around toward the light board. "You have good taste in food, unlike Kate, who tends to get the banana nut ones."

"Good taste?"

"I'm not afraid to admit it when you're occasionally right."

"In that case, how about dinner some night and I'll show you what really good food is?"

"I like hot stuff."

"You would. I'll see what I can come up with."

"Thai is good."

"Plan to pick the restaurant too?"

She smiled. "Just broadening your palate a bit."

"You'll have to get more creative than that. I've eaten at the best ethnic neighborhood restaurants from New York to L.A."

"A challenge?"

"I can probably spring for two meals if you want to compare choices."

"Deal. I'm hungry. And I'm broke."

The admission made him laugh. "What did you buy now?"

"It's still on layaway at the gallery. I found a Krauthmerr portrait. It's fabulous. I needed a break Monday, so I took a late lunch and went browsing. The hike in my homeowner insurance payments is going to kill me but it's worth it."

She was so pleased with herself; he enjoyed enormously sharing that pleasure. "And I wonder why it is so hard to find something good when I'm at the galleries. You've been there first."

"Guilty."

He loved the fact they shared a passion for art. "Just to satisfy my curiosity, the last time I invited you to dinner—where in the world did you get that petrified squid you sent me in reply?"

Her eyes danced as she laughed. "Trade secret."

"I found it to be a very unique no."

"I'd hate to be thought of as less than original." She turned on the hotshot bulb to warm up. "If you can keep a secret, I'll show you my real treasures. They're in my office filing cabinet."

"You collect odd specimens."

"The more unusual the better. Would you hand me that red folder by your left elbow? It should be Heather Ashburn's dental records."

Quinn flipped it open, confirmed that it was, and handed the folder over.

She turned her attention back to work. Quinn watched her for a few minutes, then turned his attention to the first case and reached for the initial police report.

When he finished reading the details of the fourth case, dawn was less than an hour away. Lisa was taking measurements from a set of X-rays, jotting numbers on a pad of paper. "See anything there?"

She absently nodded as she moved the caliper. "Martha Treemont. There's a fracture in her radius as if her arm was first rotated behind her back and then struck a hard surface: The bone shattered up into the elbow joint. She put up a fight; that seems to be common to these cases."

Quinn saw her rub her eyes, and that frown was back. She had a tension headache and the way she was sitting her back was hurting too. He closed his file. "We need to visit the most recent scene. After you get some sleep."

She looked over at him and set aside what she was doing. "Marla Sherrall?"

"Yes. The way she was buried—it's Rita Beck all over again. Face down, hands behind her back, no apparent cause of death."

"Yes, it is," she admitted. "And you're right, it would be good to see the scene."

He leaned forward, rested his forearms on his knees, and studied her, something in her voice alerting him. "Lisa, what's wrong?" His voice gentled. "Did you work this case too? I didn't see your name on the reports, but I know you would have helped."

"No, I was out of the country when she was found. I did some of the lab work, helped during the analysis when the case got cold, but that's not it." She looked away from him as she got to her feet, but he could see the tension in her posture. "I once lived down the block from where she was found."

TWELVE

Marla Sherrall's body had been found here, within sight of the hummingbirds. Lisa looked around the grove of white birch and weeping willow trees, the place peaceful but forever marked by the blight of what had occurred. The public park and small pond adjoined the zoo, the land an expansion area should they need to extend the exhibit space.

"I doubt she was killed here," she said quietly, pushing aside the low-hanging limbs of the weeping willow tree to get closer to where the grave had been discovered. It was an awkward place, isolated, but remote only in that the focus was on the adjoining exhibits in the zoo to the right side of the path, and not on this stand of trees to the left.

"Agreed. But he made an effort to bring her back here."

"Location is important to him. Maybe central." She studied the damage at the base of the willow tree. Decay had rotted the tree trunk, causing sap to run out. It was too near the zoo to use pesticides to kill the beetle infestation. Park personnel had been digging out the tree when their shovel had hit Marla's left arm, breaking the radius bone.

"It reads that way, given the chance he was taking to bury her here."

She nodded even as she tried to think like the man. Why here? There was a reason. Marla had been buried near water, sometimes a significant signature. She'd been buried in her own neighborhood. Was the proximity to the zoo significant?

Knolls Park was hidden in the north section of Chicago within an easy commute to downtown. The streets were narrow; the oak trees tall, old, and overhanging the streets; most homes brick two-storied, tall, and narrow with steep roofs. The upper-middle-class community was made unique by the small zoo. It was the community's pride and joy and thrived as the local alternative to the much larger downtown zoo.

This was a community that still had local businesses in its downtown—an ice-cream shop, an upscale clothing store, a bridal shop, a gift card shop, and two local restaurants along the main street. The French bakery where Marla had worked was between the library and the bank, a fourteen-minute walk away. They had timed it to figure out if someone could have stalked her from work, caught her alone on the path, and killed her here. But the location suggested it had been a much more deliberate act, planned long before it occurred.

Lisa stood up, studying the path. The grove of trees was only about twenty feet from the back of the zoo's aviary building. Behind the fine mesh of the nearest enclosure hung a row of odd-shaped, red-based water tubes filled with sugar water, nectar to the hummingbirds that were attracted by the color. Lisa knew the zoo, knew those birds, had watched them for hours as a child. They could dart and maneuver and hover with wings moving too fast to see.

She had enjoyed the zoo. It was one of the few good memories in a cluster so sharp and painful the explosive emotions were hard to contain even after all these years. Follow the dirt footpath and the next block over was St. James Street. She forced the thought away, even as she felt the tension grip her. She'd had enough of this place. "I've seen everything I need to."

"The bakery is still in business; let's see if it's the same owner. I want to know more about Marla's boyfriend."

"No." She said it too sharply and felt his attention change from the job to her in a fraction of a second. She moderated her voice. "I don't want to talk to him, not until we review his original statements when she disappeared and when she was found again. I want to be ready to spot any inconsistencies." And she'd be very sure to have a last-minute conflict so she wouldn't be available to go along with Quinn for the interview.

He studied her, then finally nodded. "All right. We'll wait."

Lisa turned back the way they had come, relieved to get out of here.

Quinn rested one booted foot on the bench in front of the Knolls Park Bank as he ate a turkey croissant sandwich. Lisa, seated at the other end of the bench, was so tightly wound up she started every time the outside book drop for the library was used. Whatever was wrong, the longer they stayed in this neighborhood, the worse it became.

He'd insisted that they stop at the bakery so he could at least look around inside. Lisa hadn't wanted a late lunch but hadn't been able to refuse since he knew the last things she'd eaten were the blueberry muffins over ten hours ago. She was nibbling her sandwich like it was plaster paste while he'd rate his as one of the best sandwiches he'd had in a long time.

He wished she would tell him what was wrong.

He considered deliberately stalling them longer to use the situation to probe for the reason. In another situation he would have done it, even though she was a friend. Kate had been that way; he'd had to crowd her to get her to open up. Jennifer had simply called and cried, and he'd had to wait out the tears before she could tell him what had happened.

With Lisa—the silence was different. She would never allow herself to break, it was a different weight she carried, and knowing that, he wasn't sure how to proceed. He had learned a long time ago that secrets, even those made to protect someone, always over the years came back to the fact they were lies to maintain and wore a person down. She had her secret buried deep, but this place was resurrecting it.

He hated the fact she was hurting and he wasn't sure how to help.

Quinn wadded the waxed paper wrapper into a small ball and lowered his foot back to the ground, straightening. "Ready to go?"

She didn't answer for a moment, then only glanced over at him. "Yes."

He didn't like the quiet of her voice. For the first time there was an edge of defeat to it. The fact she didn't protest when he dropped his arm around her shoulders and steered her back toward the car bothered him even more. "Let's go see a movie."

She glanced over, caught by surprise, and smiled. "Sure."

She could keep her secret; he'd just have to find out the answer another way.

Under the large lighted magnifying glass, the tweezers designed to pick up a single hair looked big and clumsy. Lisa held her breath to steady her hand as she separated another thread within the edge of the duct tape taken from Rita's wrists.

Two of the four cases she had discovered had duct tape binding their hands. So had Rita's. It was improbable that the tape came from a common roll because the crimes had happened too many years apart, but if the tape matched to a common manufacturer—that would be useful knowledge. Certain brands were more common for consumer sales while others sold only through industrial channels.

Lisa carefully used the tweezers to count the threads. Forty-two threads in this tape weave. She groaned. She had hoped for fifty-four. She leaned back from the magnifying glass and closed her eyes to let them relax before she looked again at the tape.

Was it complete side to side, or had a strip of the tape been torn away? She focused again on the sides of the tape. It had been twisted around the wrist bones, and it took time to flatten it out far enough back to check the side edges. This strip of duct tape was intact. It did not match the tape from the other two cases.

Heather Ashburn and Vera Wane were linked. The duct tape in those cases had been fifty-four thread, seven millimeter, which typed it as the consumer brand of Triker Duct Tape. But Rita was forty-two thread, eight millimeter, and that made it a different brand she would have to track down.

If they couldn't find a pattern in the victims, then it became even more important to find a solid, consistent MO to the method of the crime. A difference in brand of tape was a problem.

She leaned back, rubbing the back of her neck. She did not need this.

What about Marla Sherrall? There wasn't duct tape available to help establish a common MO, but given where and how she had been found, how the excavation had been done—there had been no tape discovered but that didn't mean she hadn't been bound.

The cold storage warehouse was just that: cold. Lisa wished she had thought to grab a sweater from her office before signing through security to come over to this side of the state crime lab complex.

She walked down the tile hallway of the lower level, stopped at the third door, and unlocked it. While it had an official name nowhere near as descriptive, the room was called by those who entered here for what it was: the bone vault. The fluorescent lights overhead snapped on, bathing everything in sharp, bright light, intensifying the impact of the room. The skulls looked back at her, neatly lined up on foam circles along the shelf of the back wall—three men, two women, and two children.

It really felt like entering an open-air graveyard, one of the few places in the building where Lisa felt the silent stillness and foreverness of death. The morgue was not nearly so overpowering in its effect.

She reached for the evidence log clipboard hanging on the wall inside the doorway; glanced at the clock; wrote down the date, time, case number, the lab ID number next door where she would be working; then signed the log.

There was a long metal table in the middle of the room. She rolled it over to the storage case and started scanning for Marla Sherall's case number. Similar to an architect's storage case for blueprints, the long, flat skeleton drawers were eight inches deep, five feet long, and two feet wide. Finding the right drawer, she adjusted the metal table height and slid out the drawer onto the table.

Lisa covered the box with a lid, not for the protection of the remains but for the comfort of anyone she might pass in the hallways. She rolled the table from the room, locked the vault, and took the skeleton to the X-ray room.

"How long an exposure do you need?" Janice asked, holding the door for her to the lead-lined room.

"Let's start with ten minutes." Lisa didn't have to worry about the radiation exposure a hospital doctor would with a living patient. Ten minutes would give her any clues the bones hid deep inside.

It had been months since she had last held the bones; they were dry, and over the passage of years had lost their ivory smoothness. She carefully positioned the left hand for the first X-ray, then stepped into the adjoining room and gave Janice the all clear. The X-ray machine began to hum. Lisa watched the first X-ray film print roll from the developing machine fourteen minutes later. She had the clarity she needed. "Exposure time looks good," she confirmed.

Janice helped her set up for the left wrist picture.

An hour and forty minutes later Lisa had the images she needed. "Thanks, Janice."

"Anytime."

Lisa rolled the table with Marla's remains to the service elevator and took them to the task force room where she had set up an exam table.

She slid the X-rays onto the light table.

Was there a way to prove without the duct tape being recovered that Marla's hands had been bound the same way as Rita's? Duct tape around the wrists and also around the palms pressing the back of her hands together? It was a signature Lisa had never seen before. Finding it would be enough to link the cases.

Lisa started with the obvious break in Marla's left arm.

The radius bone had been broken by the shovel long after her death: The bone break was brittle, sharp-edged enough to leave splinters, grayish white in color after the dirt had been carefully removed.

In a living bone the edges of the break would have curls recorded in the bone layers as the pressure built and it finally snapped; the edges of the break would also have deepened in color over the years as the rest of the bones had to match the surrounding soil.

Marla's wrist bones were undamaged, but her palm—there were two breaks in the fourth and fifth metacarpal bones, the outer two bones of her palm. Even under the powerful microscope they showed no sign of healing; she'd died within hours of the breaks.

Lisa moved over to look at Marla's right hand and found a break in the outmost bone of the palm.

She leaned back in her chair, thought for a moment, then held her own hands out in front of her, considering the bones Marla had broken. When someone put her hands out to break a fall, normally one or two of the finger bones broke because they were bent back, or one or two of the wrist bones broke if she landed on the base of her palms. And if Marla had struck someone with her fist, she would have probably broken the long bones of her fingers.

To break the edge bones in her palms but not her fingers…

Lisa leaned forward and put her hands behind her back, pressing the backs of her hands together, and slowly leaned her weight back against the chair but found it impossible to shift her hands around with the backs of her hands pressed together. If Marla had been bound, thrown down to land on her back, she would have broken the small finger bones in her hands just as Rita had done.

This didn't make sense.

Lisa looked at her hands again, turning them palms up. Maybe someone had stepped on her hands? She turned to look at the X-rays only to stop midway in the turn, her thoughts taking a tangent.

She slowly nodded. Maybe.

She stood up, crossed over to the desk and put her hands behind her back as she suspected Marla's had been bound. She turned and let herself fall back against the desk, and felt the sharp sting of contact as her hands hit. It was the outer palm bones and not the finger bones, not even the wrist bones.

Rita had been pushed back and fallen to the ground. Marla had been pushed back and hit something but had been able to stay on her feet.

Lisa sighed, facing another dilemma. How did she prove that?

"Now that is a deep scowl."

Quinn turned away from the screen and the report he was trying to write, relieved to have the interruption. "Kate. Thanks for coming."

"I see you still hate paperwork."

"That's an understatement."

She entered the small room he had borrowed at the regional marshal's office and cleared a chair so she could sit down. "You called. Here I am."

He grinned; she was clearly having a good Friday off work. His call had woken her this morning, still curled up in bed at 9 A.M. While he'd been fighting paperwork all afternoon, she'd been out having fun.

He offered her the glass jar of jelly beans she was studying. "Orange still your favorites?"

She rolled the jar to keep stirring the mix as she selected a handful one at a time. "I never could figure out why they would make green. Who wants to eat green candy? They remind me of mold."

Quinn chuckled and took back the jar after she was finished; he had to agree.

"What are you working on?"

"Do you have any idea how many dark green Plymouths there are in this city, let alone the surrounding counties?"

"One at every used car lot at least. Do they still even make that color?"

"Unfortunately, yes. And checking out 826 Plymouths is impossible."

"It was probably stolen anyway," she replied cheerfully.

"Thanks for pointing that fact out." Quinn knew she was probably right even though there hadn't been a stolen car report. "I don't remember you being this perky back in the days we used to date."

"Dave took me shopping."

Quinn didn't react for a moment; he couldn't. "He took you shopping, and you liked it?"

His voice was so disbelieving she laughed. "We bought Jennifer's wedding present. She's going to love it."

"Did you?"

"It's this really great plush chair, at least a thousand colors, the most predominant one bright orange, very retro. It had to come straight out of the sixties."

"You didn't."

"She's wanted one for years. She always was a rebel under that perfect decorum."

"Kate—"

"Relax. After Dave about had a conniption fit we bought her a really nice and perfectly acceptable car. Well, we picked it out, at least. It will be delivered from a dealer in Baltimore if she's still in the hospital, or a dealer in Houston if she's home."

"You bought her a car."

"A spitfire-red Corvette. She's always wanted one of those too."

"And you'll be paying on it for the next century."

"It's on plastic. And Dave owes my debts when we get married. He can afford it."

He broke out laughing. She was serious. "Kate, you're terrible."

"I know." She ate another two of the jellybeans. "Actually, everybody but Lisa is in on it. She can't keep a secret worth squat. So we'll tell her about it five minutes before we hand Jennifer the keys."

Quinn knew better than that about the secrets but kept his own counsel. "Let me guess, you're prowling for donations."

"Always accepted."

"In that case, Lisa's broke. Put me down for both of us."

"I knew I could count on you." She stretched out in the chair, her voice turning serious. "I know it's extravagant, and most people won't understand—"

"I do. Some people talk about a trip to Hawaii for their fiftieth birthday, a cruise when they retire. Jennifer has always talked about her someday-dream of having a red convertible."

"She doesn't have a lot of somedays left."

Six months, a year... It wasn't long if the cancer couldn't be stopped. "Kate—she'll love the car. Give her a chance to enjoy her dream. She'll understand."

"I hope so." Kate slouched in the chair and crossed her ankles. "So...back to the start of this conversation. You called. What's up?"

"Your shoelaces are untied."

"What?"

He snagged her left foot and lifted it to rest against his knee so he could take care of the problem. "You need new tennis shoes." These were so beat up this one about had a hole in the sole.

"Dave's already bought me at least half a dozen different styles and colors. He just doesn't get the fact these are my lucky pair. I haven't lost a handball match against him yet while wearing these shoes."

"The first sprained ankle is going to change that."

"Not likely. They're too loose. I'd just slip out of them." She looked at the very neat knot he had tied. "Perfectionist." She crossed her feet again, then looked back at him. "Now that you tried that subtle redirect that didn't do you any good—why did you call?"

He hated the way she could read people. He had been hoping against hope that he would hear back from someone with the details he was looking for before Kate got here, but his last outstanding query had come back an hour ago. He was out of options and he needed answers.

"Has Lisa ever mentioned much about when she lived in Knolls Park?" He got straight to the point, knowing that with Kate it was best to be direct.

Lisa was going to kill him. He had wrestled over what it meant to go to her family for help—to protect Lisa's right to privacy or to break her implied trust and share her secret. He didn't have a choice. What he needed to know, not many people could deliver; he'd found that out this afternoon. But Kate could.

If she knew something and was going to cover that truth, deny it, he'd see it as a slight distance entered her gaze and she shifted subtly into work mode, concealing her thoughts. But her expression stayed open and only turned puzzled.

"I didn't know she ever had. Her foster homes were all to the south and west of Trevor House." Her expression turned to a frown as she picked up on his shift in mood. "Why are you asking?"

He would have told Marcus first, but he knew the two of them. His partner would have absorbed the news and picked up the phone to call Kate; they were that tight on what was best to do for the family. In the end, he'd made the choice to go first to Kate. Marcus had the nationwide contacts, but when it came to Chicago, Kate knew the system, knew how to find facts buried deep.

"We were working a lead, a lady named Marla Sherrall who was found buried near the zoo at Knolls Park. Lisa said she once lived a block from where Marla was found." He pushed his hand through his hair, knowing what he was about to do would have consequences. "Lisa reacted," he hesitated over how much to say, "badly to the situation."

"Quinn...keep talking," Kate said softly.

"She couldn't wait to get out of the neighborhood, she didn't want to stop and talk to people who might have known the victim, made an excuse not to enter the bakery where Marla had worked."

"She shut down."

"Hard. It took me three hours after we left the neighborhood to get her out of that quiet...*despair,* for want of a better word. I don't like it."

"She never lived at Knolls Park."

Quinn looked at her.

And the silence stretched.

Kate's eyes darkened. "I'll check," she agreed quietly. In her voice was the firsthand experience of knowing what secrets in a childhood often meant.

Quinn could only nod. If Kate found what he feared... Quinn hoped Lisa would be in a forgiving spirit when she learned what he had done.

THIRTEEN

"It's a reach."

Lisa turned at Quinn's words, frustration written all over her face, and he just waited it out. He was right, she knew it, but she didn't want to accept it. Her supposition over how Marla might have broken the bones in her hands was a very long reach. Even if true, it didn't prove her hands had been bound that way. It only was a hypothesis that fit what they hoped to find.

"It's not that far a reach." She dropped into the chair by the desk, winced at the jarring impact of the movement, and stared with frustration at the whiteboard. "And we need something to fit."

It was late Saturday, they had been debating the merits of the evidence in the four cases nonstop for the last few days. They were both tired enough it had come down to sniping at each other.

She was pushing herself too hard; he was pushing himself too hard. It wasn't worth it. For the first time Quinn was ready to admit solving something twenty years old wasn't worth what it was costing him in the present.

Lisa leaned her head against the back of her chair and looked at the map on the wall as she absently rolled her chair back and forth with her foot. "I can't believe all these dead ends. We can prove Grant knew Rita when she was sixteen—but he's already been convicted of killing her. We can't find any connection between Amy and Grant; we can't find any connection between Grant and these victims. I know all these cases are related, I can feel it, but I can prove only Heather and Vera are linked."

The map with red dots marking gravesites, blue dots marking victims' homes, and green dots where they had worked showed no discernible pattern. They were all over the Chicagoland area. Yesterday morning Lisa had proposed that maybe it was like the I-45 cases in Texas, a common interstate running within a short distance of all the sites, but there was nothing obvious on the map. No cluster of dots, no common thoroughfare.

"Go home. Get some sleep. We'll look at everything with a fresh perspective on Monday."

She turned in her chair at his words. "You want to give up."

There was accusation in her voice. She was a fierce little thing, and it pleased him, but at the same time one of them had to face reality. And in this case he appeared to be the one who had reached that conclusion first.

"I'm not saying these four cases might not be linked, I'm not even ready to rule out Grant as the guy who killed them. But I think we can rule out the idea of trying to match them to anything having to do with Amy."

He sighed when he saw her expression.

"Lisa, we may well be chasing something that is not there. Yes, Rita and Amy knew each other. But it's time to consider the reality that that may be the extent of it. They were friends when they were sixteen, kept in sporadic touch, and that is all that's there. We've found no trace that Amy ever came back to Chicago."

"Rita's diary for that period of time is missing."

"Lost, not missing," Quinn corrected. "It's frustrating because that is one thing that would rule in or out the hypothesis that Amy came here, but you have to admit, there would be other evidence too. Two weeks with four of us looking for that link and we haven't uncovered a thing. My idea is cold; I can feel it."

He had learned a long time ago how to be a pragmatist. If there was any more evidence to uncover regarding Amy, they would have found something by now. Lincoln had as much as indicated that was his conclusion over lunch but hadn't said it outright.

"You think Amy's buried somewhere out in Montana?"

"It's always been the most logical explanation for her disappearance, even if it is the most difficult to confirm."

"This is so frustrating."

"Go home. Forget about this for the rest of the weekend."

"I want to read through the Treemont case again."

"It wasn't a suggestion. I'll call Kate if you're going to be stubborn."

She scowled. "It's not nice to go behind my back."

The words stung, with an implication she wasn't aware of. "I only do it when it's necessary," he replied quietly.

Quinn walked through the front doors of the hotel into the near-empty lobby at eleven-thirty that night, tired—physically, emotionally, and spiritually. It had taken another hour to convince Lisa to go home. She would live in that lab if someone didn't take away her building keys.

Two more days, then he was going to call this search ended. Lisa needed her life back, she was working too many extra hours on a problem that was going nowhere. And he needed to release it rather than hold so tight he lost his perspective.

The day couldn't get worse than this.

Kate was sitting in a plush chair among the general seating across from the check-in counter, choosing the one chair that would put her back to the wall and watching those who entered the hotel. Tension coiled through his spine; he changed course to meet her. She got to her feet as he came over. He took one look at her expression, settled his hands gently on her forearms, and nodded toward the lounge. "You need a table or a walk?"

"Let's walk."

He wrapped his arm around her shoulders, reversed course, and pushed open the doors for them both. The night was warm but there was still a breeze. Kate shoved her hands in her pockets and they headed down the wide downtown sidewalk toward the river bridge.

"You got a page." He knew the signs. Kate could walk into tense situations and negotiate through them, apparently bored, transferring her lack of excitement to those emotionally charged scenes, calming them down, finding a resolution that was peaceful. Afterward though, all the emotions she suppressed discharged far away from work. He could see her burning through it.

"A drug warrant arrest went wrong. A cop got tangled in the middle of it, and two kids. It was a long afternoon."

He rubbed his thumb against the knot in her shoulder. "Everybody okay?"

"Yeah. I feel like punching something, but that's nothing new. The emotions will pass. I sat in the hall on the other side of a busted apartment door for six hours. Hot as blazes, I went through about a dozen water bottles, but not as bad as most cases lately."

"Keep drinking a lot of water tonight or your muscles will cramp."

"I will."

She would typically have called Marcus when she needed to unwind about a case, but she'd taken the time to track him down instead. She hadn't paged—because she knew he'd been with Lisa? The case she'd worked wasn't the reason she had come to find him.

"There was something waiting for me when I got back to the office tonight." She looked over at him. "You're not going to like this, Quinn."

They were at the river bridge. He turned her toward one of the benches where they could sit and watch the boats. Quinn braced his forearms against his knees, not looking at Kate because he had a feeling he knew what subject was coming and that his first reaction was not going to be worth seeing. "What did you find?"

"I had to call in nearly every IOU I had to find someone who could check Lisa's foster care files. If they had been court sealed like mine, I wouldn't have been able to get anywhere, but they were still available in the archives. I found a caseworker who had the clearance to look. Lisa was seven when she was placed with the Richards." Her tone of voice had reverted to fact mode, the cop was taking over, but he could feel the tension that she couldn't mask.

"They were a couple in their late thirties, had two children of their own, and cared for two foster kids. Their oldest boy Andy was two years older than Lisa. At that age Lizzy was a tomboy; she and Andy apparently got along great together, tagged around with each other from the start." Her voice went flat. "Preliminary adoption papers got filed."

Kate stopped talking. Quinn looked over and saw she was almost crying. He reached over to squeeze her hand. "What happened?"

"Andy drowned."

Quinn closed his eyes, absorbing that pain.

"A swimming pool. He hit his head doing a dive. Lisa couldn't swim. Almost drowned herself trying to help him." She scrubbed her hands down her face. "I followed up on a couple names I was given who knew what happened. I wish now I hadn't. She's going to hate me."

He rubbed her back. "No she won't. I started this. Lisa is above all else fair."

"Quinn, I found the minister of the church the family attended who did Andy's funeral, spent about an hour talking to him; he remembers them, remembers Lisa. Maybe I touched a guilty conscience, but he was pretty open once he knew who I was, why I was asking. The Richards were solid Christians; Lisa had been going with them to church, had even talked to the minister about salvation and being baptized. The Richards turned their grief over Andy toward Lisa, blamed her, sent her back into the system. She went through a couple more foster homes, then ended up at Trevor House."

He didn't say anything. It hurt too much.

"She never said anything to any of us about the Richards. I know something about the other foster families, but she never mentioned any of this. To yank preliminary adoption papers out from under a seven-year-old after she'd just watched her best friend die... I'm ready to be sick. The things I asked Lisa...I didn't know but still it's inexcusable. The comments must have cut like glass.

"The more Lisa expressed disinterest in church, the harder I pushed. Christians were the ones who had told her they loved her, gave her the most hope she'd ever had of having a family, and then tore her to shreds. She's got a right to want to have nothing to do with the subject."

"Have you told Marcus?" Quinn asked softly, hurting for Lisa, worried about Kate. She had obviously come to find him straight from learning the news. Kate's heart was to protect people, and when it was someone she cared about—this news was devastating to her.

"Not yet."

"Tell him. Lisa has lived with it for years. Let her have some room for now. And give yourself some space."

"No wonder Lisa is so convinced the Resurrection doesn't make sense, that people don't come back from the dead. She watched them do mouth-to-mouth and try to get Andy to breathe again and he never did." She pulled in a deep breath. "I'm so mad at what they did to her. As if it were her fault."

Kate wiped at tears now falling. Quinn turned her face into his shoulder, let her cry, absorbed her tears. He knew exactly what she meant.

Lisa had always longed for a place to belong, thought she'd finally found it, and tragedy had ripped it away. Even if he could understand the Richards' pain and grief, other Christians in the church had seen what was happening to Lisa, and no one had stepped forward to at least be another foster family and stop her from being sent back into the system. She'd had to deal with what happened on her own. He hated what it said. Adults should have known better.

Kate had had it no easier, but at least for her the system had been a relief, getting her out of a horrible situation. "You survived and got past the pain; Lisa will too. And this explains the independence, why she makes it so hard to get close."

"It used to hurt, at Trevor House, when Lisa would stand off to the side and decline when I'd invite her to do something. I thought she didn't like me, that it was something I had done. She'd spend her time instead with her pets, as if they were more important. And even now—she takes most of her vacations alone, trekking off into the world as if she doesn't need anybody."

"She probably tells herself that still," Quinn said quietly.

"It's not right."

"She trusts you, Kate. Even if you wonder about it, I've watched her, listened to her. She waits to see what you think before she makes major decisions. You really matter. You've stuck for twenty years. That's the best healing you could have given her. She loves you, even if she finds the words hard to say."

"I love her too." Kate looked at him. "What are we going to do?"

"Think. And do a lot of praying."

"She's gone to scientific reasons why the Bible isn't true, will argue the point from logic, rather than admit the emotional reason she's not interested. There are so many layers that would have to be stripped away just to get to this hurt."

"Jesus can heal it."

"Do you really believe she'll ever trust Him enough to risk getting close again? She started to believe once before and watched her life crumble."

"She's not a coward. And something that has to hurt this bad—she's thought about it, Kate. She's probably thought about it so much it's become a boulder in her past she can't move."

"There has to be a way to help."

"We'll find it. Go talk to Marcus. He needs to know."

Quinn paced his hotel room, picked up some of the clutter to avoid sitting down. He didn't know what to do. Yes, he did. He was just trying to talk himself out of it.

He tossed his hat on the bed, realized what he had done, and scowled. Wonderful; he'd just given himself three months of bad luck. He moved the hat to the table. The old rodeo superstition died hard. Throw a hat on a bed, the only way to get rid of the bad luck was to kick it out a door. The hat had been beat up enough as it was.

Quinn picked up the soda he'd sacrificed a dollar for at the vending machine down the hall, opened it with a snap, sat down on the edge of the bed, and pulled the pillows over to pile behind him against the headboard. He reached over and picked up the phone, punching in a number from memory. He needed to know.

It wasn't answered until the fifth ring. "H'llo."

"Lizzy, it's Quinn."

There was a momentary pause. "Hey. Hi. You told me to get some sleep. I was."

He leaned back against the headboard and smiled. "I can tell. Your words are wandering. Sorry I woke you up."

She yawned and her jaw cracked. "You're forgiven." He heard her shift the phone around. "What's up?"

She even used Kate's words. Quinn wondered if Kate realized that. Kate wondered about how close she and Lisa were, while someone else from the outside could see it so clearly. "No reason, I just wanted to hear your voice."

"Oh."

The silence lengthened. "Longer words, Lizzy. I didn't call to hear you breathe, as pleasant as that is."

"Quinn," she chided, even as she chuckled. "At least choose a topic. I seem to remember you were the one who started this conversation."

"I called to talk about the wedding," he temporized in place of what he really wanted to say.

"Did you?"

"It's next weekend."

"Please don't remind me. The last dress fitting is Monday."

She sounded worried. "What?"

"I can't wear the dress."

He thought for a moment, then winced when he understood. "Too tight?"

"Only if I want to breathe. It's not a dress that gives much leeway."

"I bet she's a brilliant seamstress."

"I hope so. But I'm not looking forward to it."

"If you need to pass on standing up at the wedding, Jennifer would be the first person to understand."

"If she can make it, I can."

"It's still on for her to get out of the hospital tomorrow afternoon?"

"If the doctors try to change their minds, she's going to leave anyway," Lisa replied, amused. "She's flying back to Houston on Monday."

"Marcus has our travel arrangements set for noon Friday."

"Good. Want to carry my luggage?"

"Do you pack like Kate or like Jennifer?" Marcus had just laughed the first time Quinn mentioned he was doing Jennifer a favor and taking her to the airport. He'd learned.

"No one travels with as much stuff as Jennifer. But I guarantee I'll have more than Kate."

"I'll handle it," Quinn promised.

"Thanks."

"I think I should wake you up more often. You're awfully polite tonight."

"I want a favor."

"Ask away."

"My first music lesson. Jack is already three good deeds up on me and I can't even get the scales to come out right."

"I forgot to warn you about one thing regarding choosing the harmonica as your instrument."

"What's that?"

"You have to be able to breathe." If she'd been able to strangle him through the phone she would have done it. "There will be time during the trip to Houston," he offered.

"Dave's flying us down?"

"Yes."

"Nice."

"It sure beats having your flight get delayed and then canceled."

"Very true."

The topic had worn down and a silence crept in. He wasn't accustomed to being the one keeping a conversation going. He turned serious. "I'm sorry I threw cold water on your idea about Marla."

"Don't be. You were right."

"If the cases are linked, something else will show up."

"Let's not talk about work. Even if that means we have to talk about the weather instead."

"The real reason I called."

"I didn't figure you woke me up to talk about the wedding."

Still he stalled but edged closer to what he wanted to ask. "When you joined the others at Trevor House, what was it like?"

She didn't answer for a long time. "Why do you want to know?"

"Something Kate once said. About hoping for a family."

"Kids who go to Trevor House are too old to find families."

"Why didn't you stay with the previous foster family? Why the transfer?"

"Mark Branton got a promotion. To take it, they had to move out of state."

"And they chose the job over you."

"It was a logical choice. Foster families are always temporary."

"Do you remember your first one?"

"Quinn, why are you asking all this?"

"I'm just trying to figure out what it might have been like growing up with so many different families."

"Do you really want to know?"

"Yes."

"I learned to make sure I cared about only what would fit in my backpack."

"I'm sorry about that."

She didn't say anything.

"Do you stay in touch with any of them?"

"No." She shifted the phone. "Most promised they would write. That would last maybe a year or until my address changed a couple times, then it would dwindle. And if you say you're sorry for me I'm going to hang up this phone."

"Can I think it?"

"Quinn, it was my life. At least it was better than Kate's."

"How did they make the decision to move you?"

"Change your line of questions already," she replied, frustrated. "I don't want to talk about this."

"It's important. How did you find out about the moves? Did you have much warning?"

"Well, I can't say I remember much about the first two," she replied with a sarcastic bite to her words. "I was a baby at the time."

"Lizzy."

"Sometimes they would tell me a few weeks before, okay? And sometimes they would just come and get me."

"In the middle of the school year."

"Quinn…101 about being a kid in foster care. You don't get a say in what happens or asked what you would like. You go where they tell you, when they tell you, and hope there's a bed for you when you arrive and you're not on a cot somewhere in some office shelter because they messed up the paperwork."

"And that's the bright side?"

"In a word, yes."

"Trevor House was a relief."

"Of course it was a relief. The only people who got tossed out of Trevor House were those picking fights on a regular basis. Otherwise you got your walking papers the day after you turned eighteen. Can we change the subject now? Please?"

"I heard you went skydiving for your eighteenth birthday."

"About broke my neck," she replied instantly. "The chute didn't open, I had to go to the reserve chute, and I came down on a roadway instead of the field where we were supposed to hit. It was a blast."

"You're serious."

"Sure. I went up again the next day."

"What do you want for your birthday next year?"

"I can't say I've thought about it. It's not exactly soon."

"Well, start thinking about it."

"Does this mean I'm getting a birthday gift from you?"

"Depends what is on your list."

"Size or price?"

"Try ease of finding it."

"In that case, I really want a wooden yo-yo. I've been looking for one for years."

He laughed. "You're serious."

"Of course I'm serious. I can do a cat's cradle better than most, and walk the dog… It's just that these plastic ones are too high tech; I want a good old-fashioned, hand-carved, perfectly balanced wooden yo-yo."

He had a feeling this was going to be a very difficult gift to find. "Have a wood preference for it?"

"Mahogany would be excellent. Or a nice cherrywood, or even a white pine."

"A wooden yo-yo. At least you're unique."

"Always. Quinn, it's almost 1 A.M. Can I go back to sleep now? Or are you going to tell me why you really called?"

He got to the point. "I know what I'd like as a return favor for the music lessons."

"What's that?"

"A promise to listen."

"About what?"

"That's a subject for a future date. I just wanted to tell you what the favor would be."

"Just listen?"

"Yes. And don't throw whatever is nearby and handy at me at the time."

"I'm not going to like the subject."

"Maybe not. Call the favor insurance."

She thought for several moments. "Okay. Now I'm curious. You've got your insurance."

"Thank you."

"You're welcome, I think."

"You can go back to sleep now."

"With pleasure. Quinn?"

"Humm?"

The pause lasted long enough he wondered if she was going to say it. "Thanks for calling."

That'ta girl. He smiled. "Good night, Lizzy."

FOURTEEN

Lisa didn't believe in the Resurrection. Quinn closed the Sunday bulletin with its order of service and creased the edge of the paper with his thumbnail. It made sense, as soon as Kate had said it, that it would be the core doubt Lisa had to overcome. He wasn't sure how to even talk about the subject with her. He just believed it was true, and possible.

If he wasn't ready for the questions, she would take him to pieces with her way of probing a subject. So where was she going to hit the hardest—the impossibility of it? the evidence supporting it? the reason the Bible said it was necessary?

How did he convince someone who dealt with death every day to accept the Resurrection?

Where did he even start the conversation? He had to figure out a place to start, find the right words.

"Lord, what words of Scripture are going to cut like a two-edged sword to the heart of the problem?" He'd been wrestling with that question and he didn't have an answer. There was a verse, a series of verses, that would be able to make the difference.

He was considering using the passage in the book of John that described how Jesus spent the days after the Resurrection before He returned to heaven. But maybe he should go more directly to the underlying problem, set aside trying to answer her questions on the Resurrection and simply let her know again that Jesus loved her.

What he wanted to do was wrap her in a hug and get her to finally believe it hadn't been her fault that Andy died. Lisa might know it in her head, but he very much doubted she had accepted that fact in her heart. She had found with the Richards that love had been contingent on her actions, and if that fact had been absorbed into who she was…

How many people had he met through the years who rejected God's unconditional love because they judged themselves guilty and not worthy of that love? Lisa needed to know that God's love was so deep it would swallow that pain from the past. She might not feel worthy of being loved like that, but she needed to accept it. She needed that kind of love to surround her: unconditional, total love. But Quinn knew the reality: Lisa had survived by being reluctant to let someone get close… She would be taking a big step to trust God. He didn't need to deal with just the Resurrection, he needed to deal with Lisa's heart.

"Lord, I'm not cut out for this. I don't have the words." He couldn't afford to fail. If Lisa let him get close, trusted him, and he fumbled the discussion it would be a house of cards falling down. He couldn't afford to fail. "If someone is going to reach Lisa's heart, it will be You. Find a way under her reserve and help her hear. I can do my best to find words, but they are going to fall flat unless You help her understand. Draw her to You, woo her in. It matters, Lord. And it feels like the right time. Lisa needs to hear the truth and understand it."

Quinn took a deep breath, then let it slowly out along with the tension. Faith was about trust. God would give him the words he needed by the time he talked with Lisa.

As the choir finished the opening song, one of the elders of the church came to the podium to give the morning welcome.

Quinn turned his bulletin over, found a blank space, and wrote down a question.

Kate was sitting beside him. "Hand this to Marcus," he whispered.

She passed it down the aisle.

His partner read the note, leaned forward to look past Kate, then nodded to confirm Jennifer was expecting everyone to join her at church the morning of the wedding.

Quinn relaxed against the padded bench. That's what he had thought. There was no way Lisa would be able to decline that invitation. If there was going to be an opening for a conversation anytime in the near future, it would come next weekend.

There was no good way to predict how Lisa would react to the situation. Indifference was the most likely. And given how intense the emotions of her past were, he hoped the service next week and the people she met were the opposite of what she remembered from her childhood. It was the intangibles that would make the difference. Who came over to say hello, how much Lisa felt welcome versus put in the spotlight. The type of music, the choice of sermon topic. So many small things would make the difference.

Lisa had resisted talking to Kate, to Marcus. He had to try. "Lord, everything needs to come together next weekend." The prayer came from the bottom of his heart and it was followed by a quiet comfort. There was real relief knowing God cared even more about the outcome than he did.

The choir director came to the podium and asked that they stand for the opening hymn. There was a rustle of people and paper as hymnbooks were opened and people found page 212.

Quinn saw Kate reach for her pager, set to vibrate; seconds later Marcus reached for his. Both immediately reacted. "Move," Marcus whispered tersely.

"What?"

"Lisa's emergency tag. Move. Now!"

Kate threw open the passenger door before Quinn had the car stopped. Lisa's car was in the driveway but she wasn't answering the phone. An ambulance should have beaten them here; Quinn prayed Lisa hadn't collapsed before she got that call made. It would be like her to call family before medical help.

Kate was the first one to reach Lisa's front door only because Marcus was defensively scanning the area as he ran. Quinn closed the distance, getting there just as Kate, finding the door locked, hurried to use her key. She was sliding the key into the lock when the door opened from the inside.

Lisa was shaking. Kate grabbed her wrist, lifted Lisa's arm around her own shoulders, and took Lisa's weight before her sister hit the floor. "You should have stayed sitting down, I've got keys."

Marcus reached around Kate to get hold of Lisa's other arm until he could get through the doorway. "How bad is the pain?"

Lizzy looked confused, her pallor sharp. The phone in the house was still ringing because Kate had not closed hers when she tossed it on the front car seat to race inside when Lisa hadn't answered.

"Get her down. I'll get medical help," Quinn ordered, fear tearing through him at that look on Lizzy's face. Had a blood clot formed and broken free? She looked like she had had a small stroke.

"I–I'm okay." She blinked trying to focus and shivered. "H–he was here."

Definitely not okay. Quinn picked up the phone and hung it up to get back dial tone, then placed the call Lisa should have made first.

Marcus shoved aside the coffee table to get it out of their way.

"Who was here, Lisa?" Kate asked, easing her down on the couch.

Lisa tried to stop the shaking of her hands by gripping one in the other. "I shouldn't have touched it, we need to get prints."

Marcus's hands cupped both sides of her face, got her to focus on him. "Lisa, what are you talking about?" he asked, calm and clear.

She struggled to explain. "It was left on the deck."

Quinn turned his startled attention toward the sliding glass doors to the back deck. The lightweight white shears had ripped, caught in the lower sliding track of the closed door. He could see a plastic glass slowly rolling back and forth on the deck pushed by the breeze. He finally connected with what she was saying, quickly gave the last of the information to the dispatcher, dropped the phone, then headed toward the deck.

He rested his hand on his sidearm as he scanned the area, then eased open the door with his elbow to keep from leaving fingerprints. He stepped outside. Lisa had been working outside. Two sprinklers were watering the new sod and a hose was soaking the base of the new elm tree. Three geranium pots and a long cactus planter were on the table. The plastic glass rolling back and forth was disconcertingly out of place.

The breeze ruffled a square of white blown into the corner of the deck.

Instinctively knowing that was what Lisa was talking about, Quinn took out his pen, capped it, and used it and the edge of a matchbook to pick up the piece of paper.

"Quinn?"

"I've found it," he called back. "Hold on."

For something written to have resulted in Lisa's reaction…he stepped inside, knowing a hard reality. This house wasn't safe. "Marcus."

His partner was already moving to pass him, Kate having eased into his place beside Lisa. "I'll search the grounds," Marcus said grimly.

"Marc—be careful!"

"I will, Lizzy."

Quinn set the piece of paper down on the dining room table, already studying it even before he read what it said: white twenty-pound paper, folded over in fourths, a streak of dirt on the side from where it had fallen. He opened the folded page using his capped pen and the salt and pepper shakers to hold down the page corners.

The words were block printed in five neat lines.

DID YOU SEE
THE HUMMINGBIRDS?
MARLA LIKED TO
WATCH THEM WHILE
SHE ATE LUNCH.

FIFTEEN

Quinn felt a chill, felt his vision narrow, and then the fury swept over him. No wonder Lizzy was spooked. "Go cover Marcus's back," he ordered Kate immediately.

She looked over at him, startled.

"Do it, Kate. I'll take care of Lisa."

"Please," Lisa urged, trying to push her that way, "he may still be here."

Kate checked her weapon. "I'm going."

Quinn took one last look at the note and left it on the table. It had already done its damage. He eased himself down on the couch beside Lisa. There was a pasty grayness to her coloring. That note had struck terror—it was probably one reason it had been left. He let his hand brush across her hair, settle gently against her face.

"The guy who killed her," Lisa whispered, "he knew we were there."

"And he knows where you live," Quinn said simply, putting the situation fully into words. He briskly rubbed her arms. She was terribly cold.

"He called."

"What?"

"The phone rang. No one was there."

"After you saw the note?"

Lisa shakily nodded.

He had to have been watching when Lisa stepped out on the deck and found the note. No wonder she hadn't picked up the phone again. Quinn wanted to help Marcus and Kate search but had to trust they wouldn't miss anything.

"Where exactly was it left?"

"Tucked under the edge of the geranium pot."

"Did you see anyone? Anything else out of place?"

"No."

"When were you last out on the deck before this?" He wanted to simply comfort but had to know the details.

"Last night, no—" She frowned, then looked at him, confused. "I also went out this morning, early, after I fed the pets. I trapped a moth that had gotten inside and I went to release it. I don't know if I would have noticed the note or not, I was thinking about other things." She took a shaky breath. "I'm sorry, I didn't mean to panic like I did. I just...couldn't think."

The investigation could wait. He cradled her head against his chest and wrapped his arms carefully around her. "Let it go." For all the investigations and cases Lisa worked, she didn't deal with the personal threats that Kate did, and this was one of the worst by what it implied. He felt her shake. He closed his eyes and just rocked her.

The glass door slid open. Marcus and Kate came inside together. Quinn looked over, and Marcus silently shook his head.

"It's on the table," Quinn said quietly.

They went to see the note. Quinn heard the quiet discussion between them, heard the phone calls they made to Kate's boss to bring in the police, to their brothers Stephen and Jack.

Kate came to join them. "She's okay," he reassured softly, seeing Kate's intense worry. "Lizzy, are you up to going with Kate? One of your flannel shirts would be a good idea. You're cold." And he had to talk to Marcus, now.

Kate understood that silent message. "Come on, sis, let's get you something warm."

Lisa leaned back.

Quinn cupped her chin, holding her gaze. "It's going to be okay. I'm going to handle it." There would be no independent Lisa walking into this one on her own and getting into trouble.

"It's all yours," she whispered.

She'd change that once she was feeling more steady, but for now it was enough. "Go with Kate," he said again and helped her stand.

Lisa swayed as she stood and had to lock her knees; Kate reached to steady her. "This is embarrassing."

"No, it's not," Kate replied. "You were much more unsteady than this after that car crash two years ago."

Lisa tried to smile as she leaned heavily against Kate and took her first steps. "You were the one driving."

"You were the one that screamed dog."

"There really was a dog; he ran away."

"I still think you made it up. You just wanted to see me drive into a ditch."

The soft debate continued as they walked slowly down the hall. Quinn watched until they were out of sight before turning to Marcus. And all the emotion suppressed in the last thirty minutes showed on his face. "I'm going to pulverize him."

"After me."

"He stuck around to watch her pick up the note, called her just after she paged you and Kate, not saying anything but delivering the message just the same." Quinn could feel the fury at that additional twist of terror the man had caused. "What are we going to do?"

"The guy that killed Marla Sherrall was here. Are we confident that's the meaning of this message?"

"It's got to be a pretty vicious joke otherwise—someone would have had to have seen us Thursday in Knolls Park, known who Lisa was, and somehow figured out where she lived. It's not like she's in the phone book to be looked up."

"The killer lives in the neighborhood, he saw you two poking around, and he followed you when you left."

"A fact that gives you a real warm fuzzy feeling inside, doesn't it?" Quinn shook his head and hoped that was actually true so they would have a place to start looking. "Conversely, he's been following us for days. If Lisa's right and these cases are tied together, then who knows when or what question we asked that caught his attention. It may extend all the way back to the visit we made to Grant Danford's estate."

"What about before that? The guy in the Plymouth?"

"Someone after me using Lisa as a convenient way to get my attention?" Quinn let the idea roll around and gel. "Yes, it's possible. The hummingbird reference—it's the first thing someone would notice about that crime scene. And the fact I haven't seen the tail recently doesn't mean he hasn't been there, biding his time. Maybe we haven't stirred up a killer, we've stirred up a guy who wants revenge." He shook his head. "I don't know which is worse."

Quinn looked around, seeing now just how poor the security was at Lisa's home. Dead bolts and locked windows wouldn't stop someone determined to enter. If he'd come after her rather than just left a note— "She can't stay here."

"I'll take her over to Kate's for a few days, and we'll be able to get her out of town this weekend for Jennifer's wedding. It will buy us some time before we have to take more drastic measures."

"Marcus, if we put too much obvious police presence on this case, whoever this is will go underground as fast as he appeared and Lisa will never be safe. We've got to find him."

"Maybe we got lucky and he left a fingerprint. Maybe we'll be able to trace the phone call. We can quietly canvas the neighborhood, see if anyone noticed a car, someone they didn't recognize in the neighborhood."

"The landscaper. Walter Hampton."

"Do you think—"

It was too obvious and Quinn didn't think it fit the man's personality, but he knew better than to make assumptions. "He's got a crew working at the house down at the corner. He's been around here to dump dirt and lay sod. He may have seen something suspicious." The sound of sirens noted the arrival of medical help and police officers.

"We get Lisa taken care of, then you and I are going to find some answers."

Egan Hampton's burned-out house was gone; in its place was now only a cleared-out empty lot. Quinn slowed as he drove past, wishing the aftereffects of what had happened could be as easily erased.

"I'm surprised the fire didn't jump to that stand of oak trees," Marcus commented, also studying the site.

"No wind. Walter was fortunate. Had the wind been from the east, the fire would have raced through the nursery."

The road turned and the now empty lot disappeared. They drove along the east edge of the orchard. The manager at the greenhouse had pointed them this direction to find Walter.

"There." Marcus saw them first.

Two men were wrestling a fifteen-foot elm tree onto a flatbed trailer using a forklift to help with the massive ball of burlap-covered roots. Both of them were straining to shift the weight toward the center of the flatbed. From the language Quinn could hear through the open car window, the man with Walter was cursing up a blue streak as the tree refused to move.

Quinn parked behind the Nakomi Nurseries' pickup truck. "It would be impolite to stand and watch them work," he noted, even as he prepared to do just that.

"Good. I'd rather be asking the questions before Walter has time to think up the wrong answers," Marcus replied, a bite to his words.

"Lisa doesn't think he's involved."

"She likes people who are nice to her pets."

Quinn, who was normally the stand-back bad guy during interviews, found himself mentally reversing roles and wondering how hard Marcus was planning to push. His partner was rolling toward a boil. "He did help save Lisa's life," Quinn noted, more curious to get Marcus's reaction than to change his mind.

"And he's done a remarkable job at weaseling himself into her life since then."

This was an O'Malley family matter, and the skepticism level anyone would have to pass was stratospherically high. For Lisa's sake, Quinn was glad.

They walked toward where the men were working.

The tree finally slid to the center of the flatbed with the use of a two-by-four fulcrum. Walter reached around the tree for the first securing line. Only when it was in place did he acknowledge their presence with a nod of greeting. "Mr. Diamond."

"Walter."

The man working with Walter ignored them, pulled tight his gloves, and started threading the first rope through the metal tie-down ring. When the rope coiled the wrong way on him, a snap of his wrist straightened it. Quinn noted the neat coil and the precision of the man's movements in tying the knots, recognized his skill with the rope.

Walter grabbed the edge of the flatbed and swung himself to the ground. He left the other man to the job and walked over to meet them. As Walter approached, Quinn double-checked his original assessment. If there had been nervousness the first time they met, there was merely interest this afternoon. Walter met his gaze straight on. "What can I do for you?"

"We have a couple questions if you have a moment."

Walter rubbed the dirt from his hands. "Glad to have a reason to take one."

"I don't believe you've met Lisa's brother. This is my partner, Marcus O'Malley."

Walter was a little slow in offering his hand. "Marshal."

It was the job that made the man nervous. Quinn tucked that observation away for later.

"I saw you finished laying the sod at Lisa's," Marcus commented, introducing himself with the question.

"I also planted a tree and a couple bushes and flowers she picked out of the catalogs." Walter glanced between them. "Sidney didn't get into that honeysuckle, did he? I knew that was going to be a risk planting it so near the back deck."

"Sidney will dig it up long before he tries to eat it," Marcus noted. "He's already started with the snapdragons."

Walter winced. "At least he's got good taste."

"When were you last at Lisa's?" Quinn asked.

"Monday? No, Tuesday afternoon. Chris and I took the new elm tree over."

"You haven't been there since?"

Walter shook his head.

"Where were you last night?"

Walter frowned at the question, started to say something but was cut off. "He was bailing me out of jail," the man kneeling on the flatbed tying down the tree retorted. "Leave the guy alone. He didn't do whatever you're probing about."

Walter's expression flashed hot with anger. "Chris, shut up."

Chris—the brother who had testified at Grant's trial, the gambler willing to ask for a bribe. Quinn pivoted and did some poking of his own. "Where were you since you got out of jail?"

"Arrest me, and we'll have a staring contest over the answer."

Walter took off his baseball cap, ran his hand through his hair, then put the cap back on. The move was more to get control of his anger than to adjust his hat. "Ignore him. My brother is in an exceptionally bad mood today." Walter looked over his shoulder. "And it started with dumping a tree on a busy freeway!"

"If you'd used a less fancy knot that would actually tighten, your precious tree would still be in one piece."

"There was nothing wrong with my knot, the problem was your driving. If you dump this one too, I'm going to take it out of your inheritance."

"As if a chunk of dirt I can't sell would matter one whit to me either way," Chris retorted, pausing to loop the extra rope around the corner post of the flatbed truck before swinging himself to the ground. Quinn's eyes narrowed. Most people would have tossed it to the ground. "I'm leaving. If you want me to help plant this tree, you'd best catch up."

"Assuming you actually get the tree there."

"Walter, you might be older, but you're no more the boss than I am." Chris pulled open the driver's door of the truck pulling the flatbed. "I won't be waiting around for you if you're late." The truck pulled out, the tree rocking against its restraints.

Quinn seized the moment. "Walter?"

He looked over and scowled. "What?"

"Where was your brother last night after you bailed him out of jail?"

He didn't like the question but took heated pleasure in answering it. "He's living in the former nursery manager's house down at the south end of the orchard. You can see it from Egan's place. I dropped him off there; as far as I know that's where he stayed."

"And this morning?"

"I am hardly my brother's keeper. He dumped the tree at 4 A.M. He finally showed up back here around 1 P.M. Not only did he cost me a landscape job I worked two years to cultivate, he destroyed a good elm tree."

"And what about you?"

He bit back a retort. "Gentlemen, I spent last night cleaning up stupidity. Chris was driving a nursery truck last night, drunk, when he was arrested. He claims to have misplaced his car, which probably means he wrecked it. I spent this morning visiting my aunt Laura, who wanted to know how come my uncle Egan hadn't brought her coffee this morning, something he hadn't done in over a decade even before his death. And then I came back here to the office about noon to find I had a customer with a hole in the ground, no tree, and unexpected guests arriving. Now I really do need to go."

"Did you see anyone when you were at Lisa's house on Tuesday?"

"Is this really necessary?"

"Yes."

He checked his impatience and thought about it. "A kid on a bike—early teens? It was a blue mountain bike with red handlebars. And there was a mom, two kids, and a poodle. The dog barked so much I heard Lisa's parrot start to mimic it. That's all that I recall. The neighborhood is quiet. Anything else?" His tone of voice suggested there had better not be.

"One last question. Have you ever done any work in Knolls Park?"

"Not in the last five years since I've been doing the scheduling."

"Before that?"

"During the life of the business? Probably. But Egan kept business records as order carbons, and it's impossible to get the simplest question answered. If you're feeling adventurous, ask Terri at the office. She can point you to the file cabinets as well as I can."

"That's all we need."

With a terse nod, Walter headed to the Nakomi truck to go after his brother.

Quinn and Marcus walked back to their car.

Quinn started the car, then pulled onto the road. "What do you think? Walter?"

"It's obvious he could have left the note, but it doesn't type: too much the older brother, in control, forces life to fit his mold. He's getting Lisa's attention the direct way, finding reasons to see her."

"Christopher."

Marcus nodded. "He would have to have seen you in Knolls Park, but assume for now that somehow he did—"

Quinn thought about it and shook his head. "Christopher's not the type to leave a note," he decided. "He's too in-your-face. He wouldn't hide behind paper."

"So what did we learn?"

"Beyond the fact the brothers hate each other? Not much."

"Still—tell Lincoln to push a little harder. He's been wanting a reason to ask some questions about Christopher ever since he learned about the bribe Grant paid him."

"Have him look up any Knolls Park records?"

"Yes. Add it to the list for Emily to sort out."

Traffic had increased as the Sunday afternoon wore on. Quinn headed toward Kate's.

Marcus broke the silence. "I don't think the note was a cruel joke, I think the note really was left by Marla's killer."

"So do I," Quinn replied grimly.

SIXTEEN

"We can rule out Grant having killed Marla."

At Lisa's voice Quinn looked up from the phone company log of calls to Lisa's home. She was tucked into one of the tall wingback chairs in Kate's apartment with a pink sweater around her shoulders, purple socks on her feet, and a quiet determination to ignore what her family suggested about lying down and trying to get some rest. He was relieved at the reappearance of that stubbornness, for it was a good indication that the shock of the morning was finally wearing off.

"Why?" he asked simply.

"He's in jail. It's obvious he couldn't have left the note or placed the call. So someone else killed Marla. Lincoln's right, and we're on the wrong trail."

"Lisa—" He didn't want to confuse the situation for her but had no choice. "It's not quite that simple. The note may simply have been a lucky guess by someone who saw us in the neighborhood." Even if he didn't think it likely, he had to make sure they didn't rule out anything.

His words caught her off guard. "A guess?"

"What was the first thing you noticed about the place where Marla was killed?"

She hesitated, then reluctantly nodded. "The hummingbirds," she whispered. She closed her eyes for a moment, then looked over at him, confused, angry, struggling not to cry from the intense frustration. "You really think this might have been a cruel joke?"

Her emotions were in such turmoil and there wasn't much he could do to help but promise it was going to go away. "We're going to figure out who it was; it just may not be a simple answer."

"What does the report show for the phone call?"

He set aside the printouts. "A cell phone."

"Nothing useful."

"What I expected," he clarified, hearing her disappointment.

Lisa tugged at the sweater, frowning at the thread she pulled by accident. "Why do you think it might have been an ugly joke?"

"Someone has been following me."

Frustration, annoyance, and fear all crossed her face. "So they go after me?"

"It got my attention," he replied dryly.

"That's why you didn't want me involved initially with the Rita Beck case."

"Yes."

"I want the details."

She had a right to them, needed to know them now. "The day you came home from the hospital I spotted him for the third time. He was tailing me as I drove back to the hotel." Quinn winced inside, realizing that if it was the guy also responsible for the note, he would have known her address for weeks. "Dave and Marcus almost got him that night. Since then—I haven't spotted him again, but a problem like that doesn't just go away. He's probably been watching me on and off ever since."

She frowned. "You were tailed long before we ever visited the Danford estate?"

"Yes."

"Quinn, which is it? Was the note left by the guy who killed Marla, who may have killed all the victims, or by someone who's been tailing you, watching where we go?"

"You're staying here until we can figure out that answer."

"You promise you'll take good care of my pets?"

"Guaranteed. I'll even give Iris her peanuts."

"I want to keep going to work."

"I'll take you, or Kate can. But until this is solved, you won't be doing any more unescorted window-shopping during your lunch hour."

She half smiled. "At least I'll save some money." The smile faded. "The note will tell us a lot. Andrew is good at the analysis. He won't miss anything. Prints, brand of paper, handwriting..."

"He's already promised to call you with updates as it's processed."

"So what are we going to do in the meantime? That's going to take days."

"Marcus had a good point. We may not know who this is, or what it is that we've done that has gotten his attention, but we've clearly succeeded. We've got his attention. So if we keep doing exactly what we have been, he'll likely come calling again. And this time there will be Lincoln, Marcus, Dave, and Kate around to help spot him."

"We keep investigating."

He nodded. "All the questions we were pursuing yesterday before this happened. Did Amy ever come to Chicago? Is Grant Danford innocent or actually guilty of killing not only Rita but others? I keep trying to track down the dark green Plymouth I saw. You keep working to connect the four cases you've found."

"I don't like the way this is escalating."

"Which is why we have to push harder and break it open. We are apparently a lot closer to the truth than we realize."

There was a rustle of sound as the front door was unlocked and opened. "Pizza's here!" Kate called.

"It's about time." Lisa set aside the book she had been paging through. "Even if a pizza from Carla's is worth the wait."

"You're hungry."

She gave a sheepish smile. "Fear does that."

Trust her to have the opposite reaction from most people. "I'm glad." He turned toward the hall. "Kate, you need a hand?"

"I've got it covered. Jack's coming, he was just parking his car." The front door opened again. "He can help."

"Sure I can. Help with what?" Jack asked.

"Drinks."

"I want one."

"Fix six. Marcus and Lincoln are joining us."

"Oh, okay. Got any fizzy water?"

"No, I don't have fizzy water. You can have lemonade."

"With pizza?" Jack asked in disbelief.

Quinn looked over at Lisa, saw her struggling to keep her laughter silent as they listened to Kate and Jack move into the kitchen.

"Jack, you're my guest. Quit complaining."

"I've got time to run to the corner store." There was the snap of a towel. "Missed," Jack said cheerfully. "Does Dave know you're practicing with that?"

There was a knock at the door. "I'll get it," Jack quickly volunteered.

The door was unlocked and pulled open. "Marcus, buddy! You stopped at the store?" There was the crinkle of paper bags.

"We did decide on pizza, yes?"

"Absolutely."

"Then Kate's cupboards need help. The jalapeño peppers are for Quinn and me. Save me a couple of those sodas."

"Marc—you're a lifesaver. Hi, Lincoln. Good to see you again."

"Jack."

There was the sound of the refrigerator freezer opening and ice being retrieved.

"Marcus—you're spoiling Jack," Kate complained.

Marcus burst out laughing. "And you're not? That pizza's got Italian sausage on it."

"Really?" Jack asked.

"It is almost your birthday," Kate conceded.

"As good an excuse as any," Jack agreed. "Hey, Lizzy, how are the music lessons coming?" he called down the hall.

She put her head in her hands.

"What else do you need, Kate?" Marcus asked.

"Plates and napkins. I think everything else is ready."

The group finally appeared in the doorway: Jack in front carrying four glasses, Kate behind him carrying three stacked pizza boxes, Marcus and Lincoln bringing up the rear with plates and towels. Quinn accepted drinks for himself and Lisa.

"Hey, kiddo." Jack sat down on the armrest of Lisa's chair.

"Jack."

He dug into his shirt pocket and handed her a small gift-wrapped package.

"What's this?"

"Open it."

She tugged at the wrapping paper. It was a small, thin, bright blue square with a grid at the top and a big red button.

"If you get another note that takes your breath away."

She pushed the button and a Halloween scream echoed through the apartment. Kate winced and Lisa laughed. "This is great."

"Jack, you've got to grow up someday," Kate noted, stopping beside him to ruffle his hair.

"Why?"

"Because you're acting like a fifth grader with your gag gifts?"

"Hey, this one was practically practical." Lisa giggled at her own pun.

"And her doctor would love me. Laughter's good medicine."

Lisa hugged him. "Thanks."

"You're very welcome."

Quinn caught Jack's gaze, prepared to be amused as Kate was but found himself instead looking at a very serious man behind the humor. He thoughtfully nodded and made a note not to get fooled again by the surface lightness. The humor was deliberate, a serious purpose behind the laughter.

"Lisa." Marcus held out a plate.

"Thanks." She accepted it and looked at the boxes being set out on the coffee table. "Kate, which one is just cheese?"

"I think I insulted Carla with your request. She gave me a lecture about the virtues of at least a vegetarian pizza."

"She'll forgive me when I call and rave about how good the pizza was."

Kate slid a thick piece from the box. "She put cheese in the crust for you."

"See? She's just protesting for the sake of it."

Quinn joined Marcus in starting on the supreme pizza.

"Kate, where's Dave?" Jack asked.

"He'll be here shortly. He was having dinner with his sister, then was going to pick up dessert on his way over."

"Cheesecake?"

"Knowing Dave, probably."

"Great."

"You just like to eat."

"Freely concede the point," Jack replied, taking his second slice of Italian sausage pizza.

"Lincoln, are you having any luck with dates I gave you?" Lisa asked.

"Where Grant Danford was on the dates the women disappeared?"

Lisa nodded.

"Emily is still working on it. He did some traveling, but proving where he was on a particular day a decade ago—not an easy proposition."

"Lisa, forget about work for a while," Marcus recommended.

"I've just got a couple questions."

Marcus tugged her purple sock. "They'll keep. Eat."

"Has anyone heard from Jennifer?" Jack asked.

Lisa perked up. "She was supposed to call after the doctor released her today."

"I talked to her this morning," Kate said. "She's going to call when she gets to the hotel."

"She should be there by now. Let's call and see."

Jack reached over and snagged Kate's phone. "What's the hotel number?"

"It's the Bismark Grand Hotel in Baltimore," Lisa replied.

Jack called information, was connected to the hotel, and asked for Tom or Jennifer. Nodding, he twisted his wrist to move the phone away to pass on the answer. "They've just checked in. He's ringing Jennifer's room."

He moved back the phone, smiling. "Jennifer? It's Jack. Want to marry me?"

Lisa giggled. Jack's opening was an old family joke.

"Oh, I don't know. We were sitting around debating if we should show up for this shindig of yours next weekend." Jack laughed. "Really? In that case I've got to be there."

"What?" Lisa whispered.

"She says I get to throw you in the hotel pool after the wedding," Jack whispered back, obviously improvising.

Lisa shoved him.

"You want to talk to Lizzy? She's acting pretty ditzy at the moment."

"Give me the phone."

"Hold on, here she is."

Jack passed the phone to Kate instead, who accepted it with a laugh. "Jen, Jack is being his normal jokester self tonight." Kate reached for another napkin. "Lisa's fine—although she had me order cheese pizza from Carla's again. How are you doing? Ready to fly home tomorrow?"

"Sure. Which ones? The true white or the cream?"

Kate turned to Marcus and mimicked writing a note. He reached behind him to the end table for her notepad. She nodded her thanks as she took it and the pen.

"What else?"

She started making a list. "Not a problem. If I don't have it, Stephen will." Kate looked over at Lisa. "Do you know if you kept one of Tina's lace handkerchiefs in your scrapbooks? Jen needs to borrow something old."

"I'm sure I did."

Kate added it to the list. "I'll bring everything," she confirmed to Jennifer.

"Dave's flying us down at noon Friday. Have you tried on the dress again?" Kate smiled. "I can't wait to see it. I'd better hand you over to Lisa now." Kate passed over the phone.

"Jen? They're ganging up on me again," Lisa protested. She listened for a moment, laughed, then settled back in the chair. "Really? I don't know." Lisa glanced over, caught Quinn's gaze. "I suppose I could ask him."

He quirked an eyebrow at her, wishing he could hear both sides of that conversation. Jen said something and Lisa dropped her eyes, actually blushed, a fact that made Quinn sit up straighter and grin as he watched Lisa.

"No." Lisa snuggled deeper into the chair and turned her attention to pulling threads from the tear in the knee of her jeans as she listened to Jennifer. "Maybe." She shook her head. "No, it should be Rachel." She made a face at the phone. "Jen—"

"Oh, all right. Hold on." She held out the phone to Quinn. "She wants to talk to you."

Quinn accepted the phone with some surprise. "Hi, Jennifer."

"I need a favor."

He knew when it was time to be cautious. "Okay."

"Lizzy."

Quinn looked over, found her watching her. "Humm."

"She's being stubborn. I want her to be my maid of honor. But she wants it to be Rachel or Kate, and they both insist it has to be the others. My wedding is going to get here before it gets settled. So I've made an executive decision. It's going to be Lizzy. But I'm not there to convince her."

"Jen."

"Come on. After all this time, don't you have a little pull? Sweet-talk her into it or something."

"Or something." Still, Quinn smiled. "I'll see what I can do."

"Thanks. So have you asked her out yet?"

"Jenny."

She laughed. "I vote with Kate. It would be good to keep you in the family."

He couldn't think of a reply.

"Are you blushing?"

"Probably." His drawl had intensified, a good indication he was.

She laughed. "Then I'll be nice and let you go. But I want you at my wedding wearing your tux and your boots. And I'm putting you in charge of Lizzy while she's here."

"Impossible, but I'll do my best."

"Thank you. Pass me to Marcus. My brother and I need to chat about this bachelor party thing. I want Tom awake at our wedding."

Quinn laughed and complied.

Marcus accepted the phone. "Hi, precious."

"What did she want?" Lisa leaned over to ask softly.
"That would be telling."
"Quinn."
He loved watching her struggle with patience. "Later."

Quinn watched Lisa stretch her hands over her head, her movements slow, then wince when she tried to straighten her arms. She hurriedly lowered her arms, taking a deep breath as she pressed her hand against her ribs. He saw it, Kate didn't. The family gathering had just broken up. Marcus, Lincoln, and Jack headed out together. Dave was still lingering. Quinn could understand that. He wasn't in a hurry to leave either.

"It's later. What did Jennifer want?"

Quinn looked at Lisa, then glanced over at Kate. "Kate, give us a minute."

Kate paused in picking up the clutter, looked at him, and stopped what she was doing. "I'll walk Dave to his car."

"Circle the block."

She grinned. "Did you hear that, Dave?"

He stepped back into the living room. "What?"

"You have to take me for a walk around the block."

Dave leaned against the doorjamb and grinned. "Really? I have to?"

Kate encircled his waist with her arm. "Yes." She glanced at Quinn. "We'll be back in half an hour?"

"Good enough."

The two of them left.

"You just tossed her out of her own apartment," Lisa remarked, stunned.

"She didn't mind," Quinn replied, amused, knowing it was true. He got up to finish the task Kate had been doing, replaced the candy dish and magazines that had been moved from the coffee table earlier, and carried the drinking glasses into the kitchen, using the time to decide what he wanted to say.

When he returned, he settled on the couch and studied her. "I'll get you out of being maid of honor if you're saying no because you can't wear the dress that long."

Lisa cringed. "That's what she asked you?"

"One of the things."

She leaned her head back against the tall wingback chair and closed her eyes. "Quinn, I don't want her to know. The last thing Jennifer needs to be doing is worrying about me."

"If you were to wear the dress for literally just the wedding ceremony?"

"Even if the seamstress could work magic tomorrow—" She shook her head. "The painkillers will help, but the maid of honor is the host of ceremonies for the reception. Even if I could change out of the dress, I'd be hurting and Jen's way too perceptive."

"Do you want to be able to say yes?"

She nodded.

"Then let me work out the logistics. I can make it happen without anyone realizing it's happening."

She looked doubtful.

"Trust me."

"Okay, I'll tell her yes."

"Let me tell her. I'll call in a few markers when I do it."

Lisa nodded. She awkwardly pushed herself out of the chair, then turned to look out the living room window. "Quinn, about the note?"

"What about it?"

"Do you think it was Marla's killer?"

"Yes." He left it simple and straightforward. It was always the better choice.

"I want to go back and look again at the scene where Marla was found."

"No."

She turned and looked at him. "It's not a light request. I need to see what I missed. It's time to ask a lot of questions."

"Lincoln and Marcus are on the case full-time now. There is no need for you to be in the mix."

"Quinn—"

"No. That's final. From both of us and your boss."

"You talked to Ben?"

"Yes. And the only way you keep working these cases is if you listen to what we're telling you. He has no desire to see you get hurt again, and Marcus and I don't want you in the way of the investigation."

"It's my job to investigate suspicious deaths."

She wasn't going back to Knolls Park until the person responsible for that note was stopped. "Whether you like it or not, you're a civilian and this is a job for a cop."

"Don't take away my ability to do my job."

"The limits are there for your own protection."

"I don't like it."

The mutiny of emotions on her face mixed together—relief not to have to face Knolls Park again, frustration that she was being ordered to stay away. Quinn kept his voice calm. "I know, but you'll keep within them anyway." He took a risk, invaded her space, settled his arms around her, and hugged her. "I don't want you thinking about any of this tonight. I want you to get some sleep."

He'd surprised her; she tensed but then he felt her relax. She moved her cheek against his chest. "Not going to call and wake me up to talk?"

She sounded disappointed. And he felt hope. "Another time."

SEVENTEEN

"They were all buried near water."

Quinn looked up from the police report on Mrs. Treemont. The whiteboard had become a grid: down the left side were the victims' names; across the top, common traits. Buried face down was marked for all of them. Tape was marked for Heather, Vera, and Rita. Lisa had added the word water at the top of the grid as a common trait.

"Rita, buried near a river. Marla, buried near a pond. Heather, buried under a fountain." She noted a *yes* in the grid boxes.

"Mrs. Treemont was found buried near her rosebushes, and Vera Wane was found next to her garage," he countered.

"We haven't visited the scenes." She put in question marks for those two names instead of a no. "The officer may not have realized the significance of location to this killer. Maybe there's water nearby and it simply isn't mentioned."

"Daylight," Quinn offered.

She wrote that as a common trait. "That has to be significant. It's not only the added risk he takes, it's the fact that it's true in all cases. He hasn't struck at night."

"What's that tell us? He works nights, so has to kill during the day?"

Lisa winced. "Or he's in a job where his boss doesn't realize he's gone."

"Lisa, we think he was watching the victims for some time before he struck, correct?"

"That would definitely appear to be the case with Marla."

"In order to take advantage of their routines, he'd have to snatch them about the same time of day he's been observing them."

She hurriedly found a piece of paper to jot down the idea.

"He watches them for several days if not weeks to learn their routine. He grabs and kills and then buries them, the location of the grave being a significant part of his MO," Quinn summarized.

"He can't be doing that with an occasional day off work. His job is taking him to his victims and putting him into their worlds."

"Exactly. A workingman killer."

"But look at the geography pattern," Lisa noted. "Who would travel that kind of range? Be able to stay in one area for a week or weeks necessary to make the selection of a victim, establish her routine, and carry out the crime?"

"A salesman would be in and out. Even repairmen would be too temporary."

"A builder," Lisa offered.

Quinn slowly nodded. "Knolls Park has been undergoing a lot of restorations over the years turning it into an upper-middle-class neighborhood. And didn't Vera have a garage built recently?"

"Where's the master list of case names? All the people the police indicated they interviewed. If we take them for all the cases, sort them together—maybe there will be a common name across all the cases."

"Give it to Diane to work up. There are a lot of names in these files."

Lisa started marking pages with Post-it notes to photocopy for Diane.

Quinn set down his pen and rested back against the chair to look at the board. "We're making progress."

"Slowly. I wish we had some indication of who left the note."

"The odds of getting prints were small. I find it more interesting that he was so bothered by what we were doing, he risked telling us he was around in exchange for scaring you. That risk doesn't make sense."

"Maybe he saw it as an opportunity to tell someone what he did. It's a nine-year-old crime. He got away with it, but no one knows."

"A killer with an ego."

"The police didn't find anything when they canvassed my neighborhood?"

"No."

"Do you think whoever did it will leave another note?"

"Doubtful. It wouldn't take much to realize you're not home."

"I miss my pets."

"I know you do. I'll take you over to the house Thursday to pack for the weekend; you can see them then." He changed the subject. "How was the dress fitting?" She'd been gone about three hours this morning. Lisa made a face. "That good, huh?"

"She'll do her best. The dress just isn't styled to allow for a lot of addition in both the front and the back."

"Still feel like you can handle it for an hour? If so, I'll talk to Jennifer tonight."

"Even if I have to turn blue, I'll handle it."

"Let's go buy her wedding gift."

"Now?"

"Yes, now. I want to stretch my legs. And I've heard you can be a very efficient shopper when you choose to be."

"Who told you that?"

"Kate."

"Quinn, I prefer to crawl along like a snail and spend hours window-shopping. Kate is the one determined to get in and out in a few minutes. Anyone who shops with her is efficient; it's a matter of survival."

"Then let's go meander through a few galleries. With you, I don't think I'll mind dawdling along."

"Was that a compliment?"

"I see I'll have to be more blunt; let's try this again. Lisa, I want a couple hours of your company. Would you like to go shopping for Jennifer's wedding gift?"

"And I'll let you buy me dinner too."

He smiled. "Will you?"

"What's your absolutely favorite Chicago steak place?"

"No question there: Weber Grill."

"I always get hungry after I spend a lot of money."

Quinn laughed as she offered a hand to pull him to his feet. "Okay, Lizzy. We'll go out to dinner after we buy her gift."

"So are you going to walk me to the door or are we going to sit out here watching the stars until the sun comes up?"

Quinn reached over and picked up Lisa's hand and rubbed his thumb across her palm. He had parked on the street just past Kate's apartment, shut off the car and turned off the lights, but the radio was still on, adding a soft backdrop of country music. "I rather like late nights with you. You stop thinking through your answers after 10 P.M."

In the dim light from the streetlights, Quinn saw her smile. "That's because I'm falling asleep, but I'm too polite to do it in front of you."

He tugged her hand. "Why don't you come here for a minute?"

"What?"

"Now you're trying to think. Quit it and just slide over here."

"Oh." She was dense at times; he chuckled as she caught up with him and blushed. She slid over toward the center of the seat.

Quinn turned her slightly so she could rest against his shoulder, and then he wrapped his arms around her. "Better." He didn't try to make it more than a comforting hug. She was shy all of a sudden and he could feel the nervousness. He lifted her hand and placed it carefully against his. "Your broken finger has almost healed." The splint had been removed and the finger taped to the one next to it for some temporary support.

"Another two weeks," Lisa agreed, beginning to relax.

"How's the ribs?"

"You've broken a few in your lifetime?"

"A few," he agreed, lowering the number. It was more like ten.

"Multiply it by a few factors to account for the surgery."

He gently rested his hand against the injury, could feel the bandage under her shirt. "Still taking pain pills?"

"They ought to rename them knockout drugs. I'm sticking to over-the-counter painkillers to the extent I can."

"I'm glad there have been no complications."

"So am I."

The quiet stretched between them. He finally broke it, deciding to risk the subject. "I've been thinking."

"Have you? I've heard that can be a dangerous thing to do."

He leaned his chin against the top of her head and felt her chuckle. "Lisa?"

"Hmm?"

"Tell me about Kevin."

She stiffened, and he tightened his hold on her hands. "Please."

"You don't want much, do you?" All the laughter had left her voice.

"I watched Marcus pace with frustration over the situation. I know you got hurt. I'd like to know what happened."

He waited.

The song on the radio changed, then played to completion. Quinn didn't interrupt the silence between them; he knew Lisa was deciding if she was going to trust him.

"He wanted me to go back to practicing real medicine so he could introduce me to his family."

Quinn intertwined his fingers with those of her good hand and stopped himself from giving his opinion of that.

She squeezed his hand. "He surprised me. I lost my ability to be eloquent. I don't think he even understands what he did."

"He may have been going out with you, but he hadn't taken the time to know you."

"And you think you do?" she asked with some skepticism and lingering hurt.

Yes, he understood her, better than she realized, but this was definitely not the time to tell her he knew about Andy. "You're going to have to trust me enough to tell me about who you saw die. Then I'll really understand. But I know you chose understanding death as one way you would cope with that memory."

"I did," she finally agreed.

Relieved to be out of that quicksand, he rubbed his chin against the top of her head. "I also know you've treated with dignity those whose deaths you've investigated. I'm proud of you for being able to do that. I see too many cops and other law enforcement personnel who don't have that grace."

"That isn't hard to do, Quinn. They have relatives and spouses and children and friends. Everyone who dies still matters."

"Can I ask you something?"

"I don't know if I like your questions."

"Would you have married Kevin had he better understood you?"

He thought she wasn't going to answer she thought about it so long. "Yes."

"Why?"

"Quinn, I was proud of him and glad to be with him. He's a good man even if he has a bit of a big ego—ER docs have that failing. I admired the job he does,

I liked the fact he was close to his family." She hesitated. "And he liked me," she added softly.

"I can understand why Jack broke his nose."

She tried to turn as she protested.

He stilled her. "No, hear me out. I said I can understand it, not that I would have necessarily done the same thing. When he took that slap at your profession, he not only took a slap at part of you, he offended the family. He should have been proud of you, instead he dismissed what you did. It was a classic case of poke one O'Malley, poke them all."

"Jack shouldn't have been that touchy."

"He's your brother, he's allowed."

She turned her head to look up at him. "What about you?"

"What about me?"

"Have you ever been close to tying the knot, so to speak?"

"No."

"Why not?"

"Finding someone who loves Montana, likes art, adores me, shares my faith, and wants to settle down is not an easy proposition."

"Why not Jennifer? or Kate?"

"Lisa, get that tone out of your voice. I did not offend your sisters. And you think Jack gets defensive about family."

"They weren't good enough for you?"

"Sheath your claws," he remarked mildly. "Jennifer didn't want to think about leaving Houston and her patients, and I can totally understand that. They are her kids. And I already knew Tom was in the picture even if Jen hadn't yet figured that fact out. Kate—she's a good friend. Being more than that was never in the cards. So ease up a bit on me."

"You shouldn't have asked me out third."

Ouch. That one hit his gut. "True." He hugged her. "I didn't mean to hurt your feelings."

"It looks bad."

"You've got a right to be annoyed," he agreed cautiously.

"If you ask out Rachel, I'll murder you in your sleep."

"Cross my heart, I will not ask out Rachel." He hadn't been able to entirely hide the laughter that shook him.

Her elbow hit his ribs. "What?"

"I already did." She stiffened like a board. "I asked her first. Rach just laughed and said ask Jennifer."

Lisa slumped as if her bones had turned to liquid. "You didn't."

"Rachel's a bit of a matchmaker."

"This is humiliating. Fourth."

"I am sorry, Lizzy. I didn't intend it to happen this way."

"Let me up, I'm going inside now."

He tightened his arms. "No."

"I can make you regret that answer," she warned.

"Not till you accept my apology."

It became a silent battle of wills. "Okay, I accept your apology," she said grudgingly.

"Thank you. And I will make it up to you."

"I don't see how," she muttered, sliding back to her side of the car and searching for the shoes she had kicked off.

Quinn knew what it felt like to be in the doghouse; the worst part of it was he deserved it. He circled the car and held open the car door for her. "Lizzy?"

"What?"

"Don't stay mad forever."

It was after midnight in Houston. Quinn reluctantly set down the phone when he saw the time. A minute later he picked it up again and placed the call. It was answered on the third ring. "Yes?" Jennifer's voice was alert, focused, very much a doctor responding to a call from her answering service.

"Jen, it's Quinn. Sorry. It's not a patient."

"Quinn." He heard her smile in the warmth that flooded her voice. "I thought we still had a deal—you don't apologize for the time you call, and I don't get on your case about your lack of sleep."

"I'm not going to get much sleep tonight, I'm afraid."

"What happened?"

"I offended Lizzy."

"Quinn?" Her voice had gone cautious. She wasn't sure which side she should support.

He rubbed the back of his neck. "I asked her out fourth. She about handed my head to me on a platter."

"Oh boy. You did make a mess of it with her, didn't you?" She thought about it for a moment. "She'll get over it."

"You didn't see her expression. She deserves to be ticked at me. What do I do?"

"Apologize. And keep doing it until she tells you to stop, then apologize some more."

"Grovel, you mean."

"Good word."

"I didn't mean to hurt her."

"Good words to start with."

Quinn eased off his left boot. "I solved your maid of honor problem."

"Did you?"

"You can have a rolling maid of honor. Rachel gets before the wedding, Lisa gets the wedding, and Kate is master of ceremonies afterward."

She laughed. "And here I thought Marcus's fiancée, Shari, was the politician in the family."

"Deal?"

"Deal. And thank you."

"My pleasure. Now that I woke you up, tell me how you're doing."

"Don't you start. I just got off the phone with Marcus an hour ago."

"We don't want you to overdo it before the big day."

"Tom is hovering too."

"Good."

"Quinn?"

"Hmm?"

"The wedding's going to be hard on Lizzy."

"I know. She's happy for you but feels like the family is changing."

"Yes. I don't want her to be sad."

"Don't worry—I won't give her a chance to be. We'll see you Friday afternoon."

"Thanks. And she will forgive you."

"I hope so."

"Good night, Quinn."

"G'night, Jen." Quinn depressed the button to hang up the phone and get back dial tone. There were reasons to appreciate the size of the O'Malley family. He called Marcus. He didn't have to wonder if his partner was still up. Marcus answered and Quinn went straight to the point. "What did you find on the second note?"

They had intentionally not told Lisa about the second note he'd discovered when he went to take care of her pets this morning. Marcus had been working on it all day while Quinn did his best to keep Lisa otherwise distracted.

Marla liked the salted pretzels best.

The paper had been soggy, the ink beginning to run. It had likely been left with the first one but not discovered because it was tucked in the seam of the garage door, which they hadn't opened yesterday.

"No prints. Same handwriting. The reference does appear to be to the vendors inside the zoo."

"It's almost like he was toying with what to say. There was no evidence of another note?"

"Given where these two were found, I'd almost bet there was a third one that blew away."

"Does this change the game plan?"

"I'm trying to get confirmation that Marla really did like to watch the hummingbirds over lunch, if anyone remembers her buying pretzels, and prove these notes were more than just good guesses."

"Lisa was asking about seeing her pets. Do we tell her about the second note?"

"Not unless we absolutely have to. How was dinner out?"

Quinn squirmed. "Fine."

"Lizzy just gave me a call."

"Did she?"

"Yes, she did. Anything you want to tell me?"

Quinn thought about that for a moment, trying to decide what Lisa would have told Marcus. "No."

The silence stretched and Quinn refused to break it even though he understood his partner very, very well. It didn't matter how deep their friendship was, Marcus was going to take Lisa's side. "You're lucky she said the same thing."

Quinn felt a distinct sense of relief. "Why did she call?"

"No reason. Which tells me there was a reason and she chickened out. Is it something I need to know about?"

"She got annoyed that I asked her out fourth."

There was an appreciable pause. "You asked out Rachel too?"

Quinn winced at the underlying tone. "There are a few things I didn't tell you."

"This situation is causing Lisa enough stress and the last thing I need is you complicating it further."

"Marcus—"

"Fix it."

"I'm trying to," he retorted, frustrated because although his partner was right, there wasn't much he could do about it at the moment.

Marcus relented a bit. "Basic lesson for dealing with Lisa? Time does not make it better."

"I'll remember that."

"And tell her we know about Andy sooner versus later. If something gets said by accident and she finds out that way—"

"I hear you." Quinn picked up his belt buckle and fingered the letters marking the third place finish in a rodeo he could only vaguely remember.

"Kate and I have been talking. Next Sunday—start with 1 Corinthians 15:35."

"I wish you'd have the conversation with Lisa."

"Sorry, buddy; Kate and I have both been striking out. This attempt is all yours. Knock down Lisa's doubts about the Resurrection, and then we can start dealing with Andy. And that had better happen soon. I do not like her hurting and hiding it."

"I dislike it more than you do."

"Loving them is tough, isn't it?"

He had been trying to avoid that word. "And here I thought I was just trying to get Lizzy to accept dinner out."

"When did she get under your skin?"

"Besides when she smiled at me while she was bleeding to death?"

"Good point."

"I think it was the purple socks. When she looks beautiful in purple socks, there's a problem." He'd given up fighting the inevitable. His emotions were involved. What could he do about it? He'd already apologized to God for letting the situation get so turned around.

He should have understood much earlier that getting to know Lisa was not going to be like getting to know Kate. With Kate it had been a good solid friendship and no draw toward something more. He'd set out to have that same friendship with Lisa and instead got caught by the undertow of emotions that came with being with her. He hadn't been ready for it.

He should have ended the evening out with her tonight long before ten o'clock. He knew it. As enjoyable as tonight had been, it put them on rocky ground. Tangling up her emotions and his when they couldn't be more than just friends was foolishness.

He was about to learn a large dose of patience.

Lisa had been resisting Kate and Marcus's attempts to talk about faith because it had come with too much pressure. He was in danger of pressuring her because he needed her to believe. It wasn't a good position to be in. Lisa would be making up her mind on her own schedule, not his.

It was probably just as well. He had to pull back because she didn't believe. It was likely saving him from a more embarrassing reality. If she already believed and he asked her out on a real date, Lisa would likely turn him down flat. He gave a rueful smile. She'd probably say no with something even more creative than a petrified squid.

"Quinn, when you talk to her, don't push her to believe because you need her to. She'll spot that motivation a mile away. This isn't about Lisa and you; it's about Lisa and God."

Quinn got the message. Hurt Lisa and a hammer was going to come down. "I won't do that to her." Those who said chivalry was dead in the modern age hadn't met Marcus.

"Thank you. Get some sleep. You're going to need it."

"Very true. Page me if you get anything on those notes."

"Deal."

Quinn hung up the phone and ran his hand through his hair. He was too old for this kind of emotional mess. He didn't mind a long wait if there was hope at the end of it. But life didn't always give him what he hoped for; he knew that more than anyone. "It would help if Lisa believed. It would help if I didn't," he said quietly to his God. He was staring at an impasse.

The yard looked gorgeous. Lisa leaned against the back deck railing, feeling relieved to be back home, if only for a short time while she packed.

"Lisa, are these two suitcases it? You've got everything else you need?"

She turned as Quinn stepped out onto the deck. "Those two cases and the garment bag. Would you read my instructions on the animals' care, see if they make sense?"

"Already scanned it. Other than warning Todd that Iris considers your finger something interesting to taste, I think you covered everything."

"Iris and Todd get along just fine. I think the problem is you're a guy who doesn't have pets, and Iris was smart enough to know that. She was just joshing you about it."

"I just think she thought my thumb was another peanut."

Lisa picked up Sidney who had come wandering over the threshold to the deck. "Can we stop by the gallery next and pick up the picture?"

"If you like."

"Might as well get all the errands done at once. Come on, Sidney, time to go back to your home. Quinn, I promised Kate a call when we were done here. I want to see this chair she bought as a wedding gift."

"Lizzy, you can't even imagine it. Any bow she uses is going to disappear."

"White?"

"Probably the only color that isn't in that chair."

EIGHTEEN

"No. Hold it like this." Quinn reached over and corrected Lisa's hold on the harmonica. "Use your left hand to move it and your right to change the air flow."

They were somewhere over the state of Missouri, flying south to Houston. It was a gorgeous day, the plane now above a bank of clouds so the sun lit a bright white blanket beneath them. Kate had just moved forward to join Dave in the cockpit. Stephen and Marcus were deep into a game of chess while Jack had settled back in his chair to take a nap.

"I can't figure out how you remember the right distance."

"Think eights. Divide the harmonica in half, divide those two pieces in half as well. That gives you the four major sections. Then think left side of a section or right, and that gives you eighths. Every sound you make is a combination of which of those sections you cover and how you breathe."

She lowered the harmonica and looked at it with frustration. "Something this simple should not be this hard to play."

"Actually, it was a good choice. It will help your lung capacity come back." He laughed at her look. "Try again. You'll get it."

She leaned back in her seat and raised the harmonica. "Maybe I should just admit defeat and tell Jack he won."

"Before your first lesson is over?"

"I didn't say I was going to, only that I should." She tried a simple scale again.

Quinn settled back in his seat, did his best to keep a straight face.

"Quit looking like that," she muttered.

"Like what?"

"Like you swallowed a lemon."

"Would you murder me if I bought earplugs?"

"Slowly," she promised.

"Breathe."

She tried again. He couldn't cover the wince. "A deeper breath and you'll get musical notes instead of a screech."

"After the wedding, we're not going to do the traditional walk down the aisle," Jennifer explained from her chair in the center aisle, where she had been orchestrating this walk-through of her wedding. "Tom and I are going to stay at the front of the chapel and greet our wheelchair-bound guests so those who need to return to the clinic can leave first and those able to stay for the reception can have some extra time to make it over to the hotel."

Quinn listened with half his attention while he watched the more interesting byplay going on between Lisa and Kate. There was an animated, whispered conversation going on between the two of them as they sat on the top step of the stage. He knew trouble when he saw it. They'd only been in Houston twenty-four hours and the two of them were conspiring to drive him crazy.

One of them, and he wasn't quite sure which, had snuck into his hotel room and unpacked for him, then stolen his hat and returned it with a garland of flowers around the brim, alternating white and yellow daisies of all things. He was sure the choice of flowers had been Kate's, but swiping his hotel room key—that had to be Lisa.

Lisa giggled.

"Lizzy, what did I just say?" Jennifer asked.

She looked over at her sister, trying to look chagrined at being caught. "The reception starts at 3 P.M. sharp. And will Stephen please stay away from the cashews until after the guests have left."

Jennifer set aside her notebook. "What are you two deciding now?"

"You don't want to know," Lisa replied cheerfully.

"What if there's a fire alarm? How do you want to manage clearing the room?"

"Jack, thank you for that delightful thought; it was farther down on my list, but we can talk about it now. There are two handicap-accessible entrances, the doors by the choir loft and those at the front of the building. Jack, can you and Stephen manage thirty special-needs guests should the need arise?"

"Quinn, Marcus, Dave, you're recruited to keep the front aisle cleared," Jack decided.

"What about the lights going out?" Marcus asked from his seat on the front pew, his arm wrapped around Shari.

"I think the more relevant question is, what if the air-conditioning goes out?" Stephen asked.

"Guys, please don't give me worst case here. Nothing bad is allowed to happen at my wedding."

"Can I light the candles?"

"No, Jack. I have responsible people to do that. And no, you are not carrying the ring either."

Quinn coughed. He had to love this family.

"Everybody know their cues?"

"We're ready, Jen," Marcus replied. "And you've still got to decide if you want to throw your bouquet here before you go to change or later over at the reception."

"Reception. And I'll stay in my wedding dress too through the end of the reception."

"No you won't." A chorus of voices all vetoed that idea.

Jen's fiancé leaned over her chair to kiss her nose. "Pictures only. Then you change and watch the happenings from a comfortable seat."

"I'm feeling fine."

"Good. This way you'll stay that way."

"I want to stand for the ceremony."

"If you cut it to twenty minutes. Move the second song up to the prelude before you come down the aisle."

"Tom."

"Live with it."

"Then you owe me another kiss." Tom complied, drawing long wolf whistles from the family. He rested his hands on her shoulders, gently tugged her wig, and studied her blush. "You look good as a blonde."

"I was thinking about wearing a purple wig for the reception. That was my patients' vote."

"Knowing you, you'd do it too."

"I still might. Rachel, did I forget anything?"

"Rice."

"Oh—very important. Jack, if you cook the rice so I get hit with white soggy stuff I'm going to make you eat it."

Jack burst out laughing. "Jen, I hadn't even thought of that one. And why are you always picking on me? You know Kate dreams most of this stuff up."

"Whitewashing my car windows this morning—are you telling me that wasn't you?"

"I claim the fifth."

"I thought you would."

"And Dave helped."

Jen looked over at Dave. "Let me guess, you were trying to keep Kate out of trouble."

"Hey, he can get into plenty of trouble on his own," Kate protested.

"I just want you all to remember I have a long memory. This might be the first O'Malley wedding, but I doubt it will be the last." Her amused threat was met with laughter.

"Marcus and Shari are next," Jack agreed.

"Only if I can't talk Kate into walking the aisle first," Dave countered.

"We're eloping," Kate replied immediately.

She was greeted with a chorus of boos. "Sorry, you get the full wedding deal," Marcus insisted on everyone's behalf. "Jen, what else?"

"Rachel has managed a minor miracle getting the reception ready at the hotel. Kate's already volunteered to do the face painting for my young guests. I need someone to blow up the balloons for the animals Shari is making."

"Dave," Kate volunteered.

"Sure, I'll do it."

"Friends from church are going to handle the cake and punch tables. Anything else I forgot?"

"Where are you going for your honeymoon?"

"You think I'd tell you guys?"

"Home."

There was a burst of laughter from the family as Jennifer and Tom contradicted each other.

"Okay, we're done here. I'll see everybody tomorrow morning for church."

Marcus got to his feet and crossed over to kiss Jen's cheek, officially breaking up the walk-through. "Take her home, Tom."

There were numerous hugs and the group began to disband.

"So where do we want to go for dinner?" Jack asked the group, turning his attention to the upcoming evening.

Quinn settled his arm around Lisa's waist, stepping in to take over. "Lisa and I are going back over to the hotel."

"We are?"

"Yes."

She was puzzled but nodded, looking over at Kate. "I guess I'll catch up with you later."

Kate looked at him, then back at Lisa. "I'll wait up for you."

Quinn winked at Kate. "We'll be late." He looked over at Marcus, got a slight nod. Earlier this afternoon the two of them had planned out the next few minutes. "Come on, Lizzy." Quinn turned her toward the side door.

"Is there a reason we're not going with the others for dinner?"

"Yes."

Lisa laughed. "Going to tell me what it is?"

"I thought I'd show you." He held the door for her.

"Where are you parked?"

Quinn nodded to the right and jiggled his keys. "Over there."

He led Lisa over to a fire-red convertible.

"Wow. Nice car." She slid into the seat as he held the door.

He walked around to the driver's side, started the car. "The keys are getting handed to Jennifer tomorrow. Tonight we're just getting her to admit she wants one so that tomorrow she won't be able to refuse the gift."

Lisa's reaction was everything he could have hoped for. He wished he had a camera. He reached over, put a finger below her chin, and gently closed her mouth.

"The family bought her a car."

"You did too. We can debate who picks up your portion of the bill later. I may take it in kind for that Sinclair watercolor."

"Quinn."

"Honey, they wanted to surprise you too. Personally, I think it worked."

"They didn't think I could keep it a secret."

"Maybe one percent of it. Hold on a minute." Quinn backed up to the canopy entrance where Jennifer and Tom had just appeared.

"Jen, what time is the service in the morning?"

"Nine o'clock." She was studying the car. "Want to give me a lift tomorrow to the reception? I can arrive in style. And I don't think Stephen and Jack could fill a convertible with balloons."

"I thought you might like it."

"Anything red is hard not to like."

"I'll give you a ride tomorrow," he agreed. "You'd best get off your feet so you'll be up to walking down the aisle tomorrow. We'll see you in the morning."

"Till tomorrow," Jennifer agreed.

Lisa waited until he pulled onto the interstate. "She's going to be so surprised."

"I already told Marcus I'd bring a Kleenex box. Knowing Jen, she'll need it."

"She's good at happy tears. She's never going to make it through the service."

"Probably not. Tom will be ready."

Lisa ran her hand over the dash. "I'm glad they chose this. She needs her dream while there is still time to enjoy it."

Quinn looked over at Lizzy, concerned.

"The remission is just that, a remission. It's going to get worse."

"Don't borrow trouble," he said gently.

"I'm trying to be realistic. I just hope she gets a decent couple months with Tom before she's back in the hospital."

"Lizzy—"

"Ignore me. I just hate the reality. She is so happy—it's not fair that she's the one who is sick."

"She's at peace with the situation even if the worst happens. So is Tom."

"Because they believe."

"Yes."

"I think that makes it worse. It's false hope."

"You're wrong."

Lisa shoved back hair that was blowing in her eyes. "You really want to debate the question of whether life after death is possible with a forensic pathologist?"

"You don't have a monopoly on the truth, you know."

"About this subject I do."

"Kate's right. You're closed minded."

"Quinn."

"I'll grant you that now is not the right moment to have this discussion, but we will have it, Lizzy."

"You're as stubborn as Kate."

"Tenacious. Especially when I'm right."

Lisa changed the subject. "Where are the speakers in the car?" She turned on the radio and turned up the volume. Quinn reached over and showed her which button changed the woofers. "Try that."

He pulled into the hotel parking lot as Lisa rummaged through the glove box. "Sunglasses, sunscreen, lip balm, hairbrush—let me guess, Rachel stocked it."

"Shari, actually."

"Did we get Jen any CDs?"

"Tom did."

Quinn circled the car to open her door. She didn't move. He chuckled. "Yes, you have to leave the car. It's not yours."

"I bought a piece of it, didn't I?"

"You just used it up on the drive here."

"Shoot. I was hoping we could go for a long drive tonight."

"You like convertibles?"

"Are you kidding? Look at this car. It's like a dream on wheels." She reluctantly got out of the car. "I want to know when I can get a matching one, only in blue. How much did this cost?"

"Honey, if you have to ask, you can't afford one."

"Well, I have to admit, the artwork will probably appreciate better."

Quinn walked with her toward the hotel lobby. "I want to talk to you about this mysterious invisible roommate I seem to have acquired."

"What now?"

"It seems someone replaced my jeans with several pairs several sizes too big."

Lisa giggled. "Did they?"

"You really are pushing it."

"I know. But you're so much fun to get."

"I was thinking you might want to turn some attention to Marcus."

"What did you have in mind?"

"If he sees me, I'm going to be toast."

"Then don't get caught," Quinn replied, amused. "Ready?"

"If you double-cross me…"

"Have a little faith. Go."

Lisa took the room key and disappeared down the hall.

Quinn stepped into the vending machine area and dug out change for a soda, killing time while he listened for the elevator. They all had rooms on the same hotel floor although they were spread out. As it had worked out, the guys were at one end of the floor, the girls at the other.

His soda was half gone when he heard the elevator doors open. He heard

Shari and Marcus talking about dinner plans. Quinn glanced at his watch, then tamped down the amusement in his expression and went to intercept them. He needed to delay Marcus for two minutes.

"Hi, Shari, Marcus. Did either of you see Lisa downstairs?"

"No."

"I've lost her—again. I'm going to have to put a bell on her. Marcus, did you talk to Tom about Kate's gift? And note, I'm using that word loosely."

"Tom's going to help us smuggle the chair into the reception while Jennifer is changing. When she comes to the reception, it will be her throne for the afternoon. I've even got the photographer in on it. He's bringing a Polaroid camera so he can take pictures of the kids sitting on her lap and hand them out on the spot."

"Great plan. Let me know how I can help. If you see Lisa, tell her I'm looking for her."

"Will do."

Quinn headed toward his room, knowing Marcus would be a couple steps behind him once Shari turned the other direction toward her room. Lisa had had six minutes. She'd requested he make sure she had five.

He paused as though he were unlocking his hotel room door, then pushed open the door, catching the piece of paper Lisa had slipped into the door frame to prevent it from locking. He stepped inside to see Lisa rush into his room from the connecting room, her hands full.

"I thought you were going to intercept him for me!"

"I did. I got you the five minutes you asked for."

"I should have asked you for ten." She collapsed into the chair by the window, out of breath and giggling.

"Did you leave him anything?"

"From his razor on down the list, he's going to have to find everything again. I never realized how many places there were to hide things in a hotel room." She twirled the toothbrush between her fingers. "Who do you think we should give his toothbrush to?"

"Shari."

"Oh, that's conniving."

"He won't suspect it."

"I wish I were going to be here when he reads the note."

"You'll have your chance. He's coming down the hall."

"Quinn! Why didn't you say so? Let's get out of here." She shoved the items she held into the dry-cleaning bag and slid it under the bed. "So where are we going?"

"First, to take a walk."

"Let me go change to comfortable shoes."

"Two minutes. I'll meet you at the elevator."

They heard the door open next door. "Bye," she whispered and cautiously opened the room door, checked the hall, and slipped out.

Quinn waited until the door closed, then tapped on the connecting door. "Marcus?"

His partner opened the door and rested his shoulder against the door frame. "She fell for it?"

"Hook, line, and sinker."

"I wonder how long it will take her to realize she just raided Dave's room, not mine."

Quinn smiled and leaned in to check the room. "She even managed to short sheet his bed? She must have been flying."

"Never let it be said Lisa didn't enjoy setting up a good joke. Go on out for the evening, just stop by my actual room when you get back. I want to see Lisa's face when she realizes her mistake."

"Glad to. Can you slip Dave's key back before he realizes they were swapped?"

"Piece of cake."

"I ate too much, laughed too hard—I can't believe how exhausted I am."

"Admit it, you had fun."

Lisa twirled her new sombrero around her fingers. "I had a wonderful time," she agreed, "and my ribs ache."

Quinn rubbed her nose. "You've acquired a sunburn in the last day."

"My freckles are going to stand out in the wedding pictures tomorrow." She dropped the hat back on her head. "What time is it?"

He checked. "Shortly after 9 P.M."

"Suppose Jen will notice if I sleep in tomorrow instead of attending the church service?"

"Lisa."

"I was just checking."

"Ready for the wedding?"

"Not really." Lisa shrugged one shoulder, her expression defensive. "It's not just me. The entire family has been trying to cram a couple years' worth of practical jokes into the last weekend the family exists as the original O'Malleys. None of us likes the idea of change. We're reverting to our childhood."

"I've noticed. You're looking at the guy who's been on the receiving end of a lot of them." He held open the hotel door for her.

"Do you think Jen's mad at us?"

"Jennifer is so happy right now she would only be offended if she didn't think you all were having fun." Quinn tugged her hand. "Come on. The reception ballroom should be all set up by now. Let's go look at the decorations."

"I want to go crash."

"Half an hour."

"If I fall asleep on my feet, I'm told I snore."

He winced. "Did I really want to know that?"

"Just telling you, in the interest of full disclosure."

The hallway to the banquet rooms and the ballroom being used for the reception was empty and quiet. Quinn opened the door and turned on the lights.

"It's beautiful," Lisa breathed. There were balloons and streamers and white tablecloths and flowers of every kind. There were tables for the cake, the punch, and the gifts. "I want Rachel to plan my wedding. She's thought of everything."

"Her wedding present to Jennifer," Quinn agreed, impressed by what he saw. Jennifer would have a good wedding. It was comforting not only to know that, but to see it.

"So much love in this room." Lisa ran her finger along the lace pattern in the tablecloth. "I think I may cry."

"You'd have to borrow a napkin, I'm afraid. Jen already used my last handkerchief."

Lisa wandered to the bay of windows. "I hope it's a sunny day tomorrow, doesn't rain."

Quinn slowly followed, watching her. "If it rains, maybe she'll get a rainbow."

"Do you think she'll like our gift?"

"The painting? She'll love it."

"What Jen would really like is for me to believe."

She said it with such sadness…her ambivalence had been hiding an internal war over what was happening. He should have realized it. "You've been thinking about it, haven't you?"

She shrugged one shoulder, traced her finger along the windowsill.

"You want to talk about it?" he asked gently.

She sat down in one of the chairs and rested her forearms against her knees as she creased the brim of the hat. "Quinn, it hurts. I don't like disagreeing with the family. They're all I've got that matter to me, and I'm in a disintegrating situation with Kate and Marcus. Now Jennifer wants to talk with me." She looked up at him, and he could see the fatigue that had reached her eyes. "Can you please get me out of church tomorrow morning?"

He had no choice but to shake his head. "I wouldn't try. It matters too much to Jennifer that you be there." It mattered too much to him.

"You know, when Kate talks about believing, she gets so excited about it. Her eyes sparkle and her voice lightens, and she looks…happy. Marcus—" she quirked a sad smile—"he wants to pray about everything now. Jennifer says everything is going to be okay, even though she's dying. It's confusing. I just want my family back the way it was."

"Lisa, look at the truth. Believing in Jesus has changed their lives for the better."

"That doesn't mean what they believe in is true." She looked up at him. "I know you believe too. I'm not trying to be insulting, but knowing their lives are happier doesn't mean much. A doctor can give a patient a placebo and have the symptoms improve. It was the patient who believed that brought the improvement, not what he believed in." She sighed. "Can you prove it to me?"

"Prove what?"

"That Jesus rose from the dead?"

He pushed his hands into his pockets and leaned against the table across from her. "Why ask me? You're convinced you already know the answer."

"Do you have to rub it in?"

"Lisa." It wasn't the right time for this. She was too tired to have a complete conversation, was asking the question for reasons that made the situation even more difficult.

He pulled over one of the chairs, spun it around, and straddled it, folding his arms across the back of the chair. He studied her face, trying to decide how to convince her that the God he served was not only alive but loved her too. "Do you really want to talk about this? I'd be happy too, for as long as you like, for as many questions as you have, but only if you really want to have the conversation. I know the pressure you're feeling. You'd rather just have it go away."

"That's not going to happen. They're family. I'm tired. If I'm wrong, convince me. If you can't..." She shook her head. "I don't want what's coming. We've always been one family, solid, together, and it feels like we're in the process of splitting in two in so many ways—the wedding, Marcus and Shari's engagement, the deep division over faith."

"You have to be willing to trust me and listen." To talk about the Resurrection and not to talk about Andy was to ignore the elephant in the room; yet he could not bring himself to try and approach that subject. "What are your questions, Lizzy?"

"I know what happens when someone dies. It isn't that easy to set aside what I know for something you are asking me to believe. The two contradict each other. How can Jesus rise from the dead? And please don't give that 'because He's God' answer I've gotten all my life. If something so profound is true, then it should have more substance beneath it than simply someone's word that it occurred. There should be something on which faith could be based rather than a 'believe because I told you to' answer. That's blind faith, and I need a rational faith."

Quinn tried to make it as concrete an answer as he could. "When a child is born, he has features of both his mother and father. The genetics of both combine to form the child, correct?"

"Yes."

"In the Bible, Jesus is called both the Son of God and the Son of Man. He has traits of both God and man. Jesus, as God, existed forever. Jesus of Nazareth, the man, had a day He came into existence...and He also had a day He died. That's the death you understand, Lisa. When He was resurrected on the third day, He was still Jesus the Son of God, He was still fully divine, but He was also what the Bible called the first resurrected human, a look at who we will also be someday in the future." She started to interrupt and he lifted a hand. "Let me finish. You asked for a rational reason. I'm giving you one. People saw Jesus after the Resurrection. He appeared to the twelve apostles, then to five hundred of his disciples."

"That's supposed to be conclusive?"

"Lisa, if someone who looked like Kate and acted like Kate tried to take Kate's place, how long do you think they could fool you? An hour? A day? How long could they fool you if you had reason to doubt it was really her?"

She conceded his point with a nod.

"Jesus still bore the wounds in His hands and side. His friends could recognize Him, so He looked the same. His voice must have sounded the same. He could eat. But His body was clearly different—He could move through a closed door, He could vanish. Men and women saw Him after the Resurrection for over a month before He ascended to heaven. They recognized the man they called Jesus. They recognized His words, His actions, His appearance. An impostor could not have fooled so many people for so many days."

"You would argue that the historical record within the Bible is sufficient proof the impossible did happen."

"Look at what the men and women who saw the resurrected Jesus went out and did. They took the Gospel to the entire Roman world. Thousands of them were killed because they chose to continue to insist what they saw was true rather than recant to the authorities. You tell me, is mass hysteria over a common event going to last for a couple thousand years? And not only last, but stay consistent across all those years as to what actually happened? Fifty years after the event, people were still standing as eyewitnesses to the fact they had seen Jesus alive and resurrected three days after He had been crucified."

"It's only recorded in the Bible."

"On the contrary, what the apostles and early Christians did is recorded by secular historians of the day. Christianity did not have an isolated, obscure beginning. It happened in the open and was recorded as people who followed Jesus literally disrupted cities with their radical message."

"You would argue that Jesus is alive now, but in a different body, not one made of dust as ours are?"

"Lisa—"

"What?"

"Please don't get upset, but Marcus wanted you to see one passage from the Bible. I wrote it down." He slid the folded page from his shirt pocket.

"You were talking about me."

"Marcus loves you. He wants to answer your questions as much if not more than I do. Please, if you're my friend, read it."

She reluctantly reached for the note.

"Your question is not unique. This comes from 1 Corinthians 15:35 on."

"Your handwriting needs work."

"So does yours. Read."

He knew what it said, understood why Marcus had felt so certain Lisa should see it. *"But some one will ask, 'How are the dead raised? With what kind of body do they come?'.... So is it with the resurrection of the dead. What is sown is perishable, what is raised is imperishable.... It is sown a physical body, it is raised a spiritual body.... The first man was from the earth, a man of dust; the second man is from heaven. As was the man of dust, so are those who are of the dust; and as is the man of heaven, so are those who are of heaven. Just as we have borne the image of the man of dust, we shall also bear the image of the man of heaven.... For the trumpet will sound, and the dead will be raised imperishable, and we shall be changed. For this perishable nature must put on the imperishable, and this mortal nature must put on immortality."*

"You believe this."

"Yes, Lizzy, I do. This world was not designed to die; sin did that. But Jesus has beaten sin, and it gave Him the right to put on the imperishable as those verses describe. I believe the Resurrection is true. Jesus is alive. That's what Kate has been trying to convince you of, Marcus and Jennifer also."

She folded the note but didn't hand it back. "I'll think about it."

"Please—think hard." He hesitated, then said what his heart demanded. "Lizzy, even if you don't believe, I will still be your friend. Nothing is going to change that. I'm loyal to my friends for a lifetime. There are no qualifications."

She just looked at him for a long time, and then the smile that could make his heart roll over appeared. She got to her feet and lightly tapped his arm with the sombrero. "You're forgiven for asking me out fourth."

She would have passed him but he snagged her hand. "Lizzy."

She stopped.

"I saved the best for last."

NINETEEN

She was going to have to tell him about Andy. Lisa rolled over on her bed with a groan, stared at the ceiling. It was 1:14 A.M. She was so tired it was making her punchy. She'd slept an hour only to have a horrible nightmare and wake shivering.

She turned on the bedside light, admitting sleep wasn't going to return soon. Quinn's Bible was on the side table. He'd handed it to her tonight and suggested she borrow it for a few days. She picked it up.

It showed its age. Quinn had carried it with him for years and it was falling apart. There were notes in the margins and verses underlined, some of them dated with cryptic notes beside them. In the front of the book were tucked a couple letters, a faded newspaper clipping—it was like glancing through a guy's version of a diary.

She was familiar with the book. She turned to the passage Marcus had noted and read it again.

She had prayed that Andy would breathe again and he hadn't. It had convinced her that Jesus could not work a miracle and bring back the dead as the Bible claimed. She'd dismissed the Resurrection.

And over the years she found it easier to ignore the subject entirely than rethink it. She'd learned at Trevor House that the only way to deal with the turmoil of the past—religion being just one issue of many—was to draw a line in time and leave the past behind.

It helped to know the Bible did try to argue that the body of dust returned to life. Not much, but it helped.

"They recognized His words, His actions, His appearance."

If Jesus was alive as Quinn and her family claimed, then His actions now should still be consistent with His behavior recorded in the Bible. He'd been a hands-on man, teaching, healing the sick.

Again she felt the same disquieting realization as when the pain had eased during her hospital stay because of Quinn's prayer. It had not been a case of her belief changing the situation for the better; it had been a case of Quinn's belief changing the situation. That required there to be someone else acting. And Quinn said it was Jesus.

Ignoring the time, she picked up the phone and punched in a room number. "Quinn?"

"Lizzy? Hi."

"Can you meet me for a walk or something?"

"Sure." She heard the concern, and he didn't even comment on the time. "Five minutes? I'll tap on your door."

"Thanks."

She staggered to her feet, moved across the room to her suitcase, and unzipped it. She pulled on a white shirt and jeans, not really caring what it was her hand found first in her suitcase; she just wanted to get out of the room for a while. She was tying her shoelaces when he tapped on her door. She slipped her room key in her pocket and went to slide open the lock. His gaze swept across her, concerned. "Bad dream?"

She nodded.

"I'm sorry about that."

"I need a walk."

"We can take care of that," he assured. She pulled her room door closed. He wrapped his arm around her shoulders and turned her toward the elevators. Lisa reached up to grasp his wrist, appreciating the company. She would have normally gone for a walk alone. This was so much better.

They walked through the lobby and outside to the gardens that landscaped the open area between the hotel and the conference center complex.

"You're going to need a jacket. I should have thought of it upstairs."

It was kind of chilly out, but she shook her head. "I'll be fine for now."

She'd never been good about sharing secrets. She didn't want to talk about Andy. She needed to, but she didn't want to see the pity that would come into Quinn's eyes. It was better all around that she not say anything.

"Has Dave forgiven me yet?"

"He thinks it was Kate. She's denying it, of course, but she doesn't have much credibility on the subject and Dave doesn't believe her."

"I think I'm relieved."

"You should be. You really did a pretty good job for five minutes."

"I can't believe you had me raid the wrong room."

"Me?"

"I think this means we're even."

He smiled. "Just about."

She leaned her head back to look at the moon. "It's not full."

"You sound disappointed."

"I am."

"It's only full one day this month." He tightened his hand. "What was the nightmare about?"

She hesitated about answering him. "Do you dream about when you found your father?"

He stopped walking. "Yes."

"I dream about Andy."

He turned her to face him, his hands settling on her shoulders. "Do you?"

She looked up, wondering why he hadn't asked the more obvious question: who was Andy? He was looking at her with that expression she'd seen once before, compassion so deep she could drown in his gaze. "I don't like the dream," she answered awkwardly, pulling back from telling him the truth.

His thumb rubbed against her jaw line. "I'm glad you asked me to join you for your walk," he answered simply. "It will make it easier to get back to sleep." He tucked her back under his arm and resumed their walk.

"How'd we end up like this for the weekend? Friends? Paired off?"

"Does there have to be a reason? I can't just enjoy your company?"

"I don't understand why."

"Are you asking something I'm too dense to figure out? It is kind of late, you know. Why do I like you?"

She shrugged.

"What's not to like?"

"I work with dead people."

He laughed. "Your job? Lizzy, I don't mind it. Although I think you do at times. That's why you didn't protest to Kevin; you just walked away hurt. Part of you thinks he's right."

"I'm getting analyzed at 2 A.M."

"I've been thinking about it a while."

"Really?"

"Don't sound so insulted. Figuring you out has been a many years puzzle."

"Am I harder to figure out than Jennifer or Kate?"

"I don't compare."

"The mark of a wise man."

"You're an O'Malley. I've learned the basics." He tipped up her chin. "I'm glad you phoned me, although I admit I'm a little surprised."

"Why?"

"Kate's next door to you. I figured you would have woken her up instead."

"Kate? You've got to be kidding. I'd rather wake up a grizzly bear."

"She's that bad?"

"Dave doesn't know what he's getting into."

"What about you? Are you a bear of a morning?"

"Why do you want to know?"

"Curiosity."

"You'll have to come up with a better reason than that."

"Prickly. It must be bad."

"I've been accused of talking in my sleep."

"Really?"

"Don't sound so amused."

"Well, Lizzy, it all depends on what you say."

"You'll forget I said that."

"I think it's kind of cute."

"It's embarrassing."

"Tell me about the dream."

He caught her off guard. "No."

"Why not?"

"None of your business."

"Lizzy, your hair's damp. I don't think that was a shower."

"I keep my room warm versus icy like yours."

"Try again," he said gently.

"So it's a bad dream. Talking about it just makes it worse."

"You're sure?"

"Very."

"You're not exactly relaxing."

"Sometimes it takes a long walk. You don't have to stay."

He ignored that suggestion. "So what do you want to talk about?"

"We don't have to talk, you know. Silence is pretty nice."

"I know. But I like to hear your voice. You're starting to get just a touch of Montana drawl in your speech."

"You're serious?"

He laughed at her alarm. "It sounds good, Lizzy."

"No offense, but everyone who meets you will remember your drawl for years. It's kind of nice on a guy, but a lady…"

"You mimic people you listen to. Don't be so bothered by something that's very unique to you."

"I wish you wouldn't have told me."

He tightened his arm around her. "Actually, your voice is one of the things I like the most about you. I wish you'd call me more often just so we could talk."

She blinked. "You do?"

"Yes."

This was embarrassing. "I don't have anything to say."

"So call me and tell me to come up with questions. I can probably keep us talking for a few hours."

"Maybe someday." When she had a lot more courage than she did tonight. They walked around the garden in silence for a time. "I would have called you even if the other O'Malleys were still awake."

His thumb slipped into the belt loop of her jeans. "Would you?" She saw his smile. She'd pleased him with that answer.

"I'm ready to go back."

"We have to?"

"We've got to be up again in a few hours," she pointed out.

"Want to share breakfast?"

"I was planning to inhale a cup of coffee on the way to church. Besides, it wouldn't be fair to get you up before the last minute. You need the sleep even worse than I do."

"Be kind. I'm not that old."

"Your bones are creaking in the night air."

"Now you're pushing it, Lizzy."

She laughed softly; it felt good to tease him.

He turned them back toward the hotel.

The lobby and hallways were empty of guests.

"Thanks for the walk," she said when Quinn stopped at the door to her room.

"It was my pleasure." He smiled. "I'm tapping on your door in exactly five hours. I want breakfast."

She pushed him toward his room. "Good night again, Quinn."

The maid of honor was not supposed to cry. Lisa tried to blink back the tears, feeling her smile quiver. Jennifer, walking down the aisle on Marcus's arm toward the front of the church, looked absolutely beautiful.

Lisa accepted the wedding bouquet from Jennifer so her sister could turn and hold hands with Tom; Lisa passed the bouquet over to Rachel.

It had been an emotional day, church had been…uncomfortable, and now this—Lisa tried to sneak her hand up to wipe her eyes and caught a smile from Jack across from her. The day couldn't be more perfect.

They had timed the wedding to be twenty minutes. Jennifer was radiant, all the fatigue of the last week's activities pushed aside for this moment. Lisa listened to the song and then the minister begin to speak while she watched Jennifer for any sign of a sway, ready to steady her if needed. It was harder for Jennifer simply to stand than it was to walk, for nerves around her spine would pinch and suddenly flare as shooting pain.

Lisa had Tom's wedding ring slipped onto her middle finger so it wouldn't slide off until it was time to hand it to Jennifer. It felt heavy on her hand. Jennifer had bought Tom a beautiful, thick gold band. Marcus was holding Jennifer's wedding ring for Tom. He'd simply slipped the ring box in his pocket, being practical about it.

When it came time to get the ring off, Lisa found her hands had swelled under the tight grip she'd had on her own bouquet. She had to twist the ring free, feeling like every person in the packed church was looking at her. One of the children giggled and Lisa had to smile. Of course it would get stuck. The ring finally slid free and she very carefully passed it to Jennifer, glad to have her one critical point in the service completed. Quinn was to her right standing behind one of the ushers, helping the guests who needed an extra hand. If she turned slightly she'd be looking at him. She was careful not to turn in that direction, afraid to catch his gaze and find him smiling at her.

The wedding ended with a song and a long kiss that had Kate and then Rachel starting to softly laugh when Tom didn't release Jennifer. Seeing the real reason and knowing Jennifer would hate to have it common knowledge, Lisa dropped her bouquet, and the children, who were close enough to the front to see Jennifer's hand now clenched white, turned instead to look at her as Lisa tried to get her dress to turn so she could bend over and pick up the bouquet. It took clenching her teeth to move that way; she intentionally managed to roll the bouquet over to one of the girls Jennifer privately called her sweetheart. With a giggle Amy leaned over in her wheelchair to help. "You drop things like I do."

She said it loud enough some of the adults in the front row had to laugh. Lisa kissed the little girl and set the bouquet in her lap. "Hold it for me, please?" she whispered.

"Sure." Amy was missing one of her front teeth, making her *s*'s whistle.

Jennifer slowly turned with her hand tucked under Tom's hand. Lisa shared a smile with her sister as the minister formally introduced the couple to the congregation.

The music began, and Lisa stepped aside as Jennifer and Tom moved to greet their special guests, starting with Amy.

Lisa watched Jennifer and found herself wanting what her sister had. Tom loved her so much. She finally felt it safe to try and wipe her eyes.

"Lizzy," Quinn's hand settled firm and warm against her shoulder, "come with me. It's safe to slip away and change."

Quinn thought it was the dress causing the threatened tears. She didn't try to correct the assumption. The pain was an ache that flared with each breath.

"This way."

He didn't try to take them through the crowds now filling the aisles, but instead moved back through the choir doors and into a hallway. "Watch your head." He ducked under the hanging streamers to slip back into the hallway where classrooms had become dressing rooms. "You want me to get Rachel or Kate?"

She eased off the wrist corsage. "Rachel."

"Two minutes."

Rachel joined her a few minutes later, laughing. "Didn't it turn out wonderful?"

"Excellent."

"Quinn said you're part of the reception surprise."

Lisa smiled. "He's keeping the plans to himself. I'm just following directions."

Rachel helped her out of the dress. Lisa breathed easier for the first time in over an hour.

"Okay?"

She nodded at Rachel rather than try to answer. She'd brought over a blue cotton blouse and jeans for the reception. Very casual, but they were doing it intentionally so Jennifer could also be talked into truly relaxing during the reception. If the fatigue she felt was anything like Jennifer's, her sister had to be exhausted. "Thanks, Rachel. Would you let Quinn know I'll meet him after I get my shoes on?"

"Sure."

Rachel slipped away. Relieved, Lisa pressed a hand against her ribs. It was definitely time for another painkiller. She swallowed it dry, making a face at the chalky taste.

"Ready to go over to the reception?" She turned too swiftly and hit the edge of the table with her hip. Quinn steadied her. "Lizzy?"

"I'm ready."

His hands settled on either side of her face and he tipped her head back, frowning. "When we get down to the reception you are sitting down." He slid his hands down to hold hers. "Between lack of sleep and painkillers, you're going to give me a headache here."

"You?" She rested her head against his chest, feeling the day catching up with her. "I'm really feeling it."

"How bad are the ribs?"

She laughed, then groaned. "Please don't make me laugh."

He carefully folded his arms around her, took her weight. "You did good today, covering for Jennifer."

"How many saw?"

"Marcus, Jack."

"Good."

"You were as beautiful up there as Jennifer was. The pictures will look lovely."

"You're being kind."

"Get me one?"

"What?"

"A picture."

"You really want one?"

"Yes. And you're fishing for more compliments." He eased back half a step. "Come on, I'll get you a seat at the reception and some punch and you can orchestrate things from the sidelines."

"My favorite job."

"Now why did I figure that might be the case?" He laughed at the face she made. "Come on, Lizzy. And you have to behave at the reception or I'm going to disown you."

TWENTY

"I wish we had long weekends away like that more often."

Lisa dropped her garment bag beside Kate's couch. "I need a week's vacation to recover from it. Weddings are exhausting." She collapsed on the couch, letting the cushions absorb her weight and support her back. Lisa watched the strands of a new cobweb sway by the overhead light and idly thought about getting up to knock it down.

"It was fun."

"I laughed more than I thought possible," Lisa agreed. "Did you see Jen's face when she realized the car keys were for her? I never knew someone could cry that much."

Kate reappeared crunching on a carrot. "I noticed she gave the keys to Tom."

"Best act of love I've ever seen. I don't think I would have given them to my husband. He might get dust on it."

"I noticed you and Quinn had a pretty good time together."

Lisa was too relaxed to mind the question. "We did."

Kate settled on the arm of the couch. "He's a nice guy."

"We haven't exactly been dating," Lisa qualified.

"Who said anything about dating?"

Lisa tucked her arm behind her head and smiled at her sister. "I know that tone of voice."

"Want some advice?"

"Not really, but I think I'm going to hear it anyway."

Kate smiled. "Don't let him get away. He makes you happy, Lizzy. That's special."

"Yes, it is." Her smile faded and she pulled over the throw pillow to cover her face, wrapped her arm around it. "Kate, what if we can't solve what happened to Quinn's dad? Will he ever want to settle down?"

"Yes, he will. And work can wait until tomorrow."

"Tomorrow is coming too soon."

"You're meeting with Lincoln in the morning?"

Lisa lowered the pillow. "Quinn was going to meet him for dinner tonight." She made a face. "I want my own bed."

"Maybe the analysis of the notes has revealed something."

"Notes? There was only one."

Kate bit her lip.

"There was more than one."

"Sorry, Lizzy. So much for keeping my mouth shut. They found it tucked in the garage door, apparently left at the same time as the note you found."

"What did it say?"

"Pretty innocuous. Something about pretzels."

"So who decided to keep me in the dark?"

"Lizzy—"

"Don't even try to weasel out of answering."

"Marcus and Quinn. They would have told you had it changed either how much was known or what should be done."

"Sure they would have."

"Please don't get mad at them."

"I'm too tired and in too good a mood to get mad." A beeper started to chirp. Lisa lifted her head. "Is that yours or mine?"

Kate went to check. "Mine. How did they know I just walked in the door?"

Lisa smiled. "Spies."

Kate called in to the dispatcher. "Where?" She scrawled down an address. "Lizzy, I've got to go. You've got apartment keys if I end up being gone a while?"

"I'm set. Want me to call Dave for you?"

"He'd just worry. But I'll call him if it looks like it will be a long deal."

"Be careful."

"Always." Kate grabbed her phone and the bottle of water she'd just opened. "See you later."

Lisa heard the door swing shut and Kate turn the dead bolt. Lisa debated whether to take a nap on the couch before she thought about dinner. She needed to unpack, and she had laundry to do if she was going to be here another week.

The wedding was over; Quinn's vacation was up in another week. The thought was depressing. She didn't want a life that simply revolved around work again.

She set aside the pillow with a sigh. It was an impossible situation.

She didn't want to do laundry. She could fix that by getting more clothes. Her new sod patch in the yard needed drenching. And she desperately wanted to see her pets.

She looked at her watch.

She'd go feed her pets. Twenty minutes at the house, she'd be back before it was dark.

She'd even leave a note for Kate.

Quinn rang the doorbell as he juggled the restaurant carryout sack. Knowing Lisa and Kate, they had found the most convenient thing for dinner, even if that turned out to be ice cream.

"Lisa, what—" Kate pulled open the door and stopped short. "Quinn."

"What's wrong?"

"She's gone out," Kate bit out. "She's late. And I'm going to kill her."

"Where?"

"I just got back from a page. She left me a note."

"Dump this on the counter." He handed over the sack and read the crumpled piece of paper. "Come on. I'll drive."

"She wanted more clothes. She could have raided my closet." Kate slammed the door behind them.

Quinn tried to lighten her tension. "Only if she's grown several inches in height since I saw her last." He held the car door for Kate.

"I can't believe she left behind my back."

"She wanted to see her pets. I should have taken her by earlier."

"Was it quiet here while we were gone?"

"Yes." He pulled into traffic. "This is not your fault, Kate."

She didn't answer him.

"How'd the page go?"

"The guy shot himself before I got there."

"I'm sorry, Kate."

"Not your fault."

"It's one reason you're angry."

"Drive faster. She said she'd be home no later than six-thirty. It's already seven."

"There could be simple explanations."

"And there could be bad ones."

He was already breaking the speed limit. He maneuvered through traffic and broke it further.

They were pulling into Lisa's subdivision twenty minutes later. "Quinn."

"I see it." There was smoke rising in the air. He could hear the fire engines rolling somewhere ahead of him in the subdivision.

"No. Oh no!"

It was Lisa's house, and there were two fire engines rolling to a stop in front of the house, men pouring off of them.

Lisa's car was in the drive. The house was fully engulfed.

"Lisa's inside!"

Jack swung the ax with every ounce of energy in his body, the muscles in his legs through his back propelling the blow. He didn't waste time on words. It was an accelerant fire unlike any he had ever seen; even the ground seemed to burn.

The shouts of men who fought the dragon were a noble chorus around him.

The second blow splintered the door at the lock; it swung open—and a wall of fire slammed out with ferocious intent. For a horrifying instant Jack was inside the fire, his face mask taking the brunt of the beast's breath; he was trapped by heat and light and angry flames.

Eighty pounds of water pressure per minute hit back; scalding steam roiled, and the flames slowly began to retreat.

One second.

Two.

Three.

They weren't getting through it fast enough.

At seven Jack surged through the doorway, not caring anymore what it was going to be like inside, stealing through the opening in the wall of flames to the left and toward the hall.

There was no way to shout, to hear Lisa against the roaring noise. She'd be down low to the floor trying to escape the smoke while trying to get toward a window…if she were able to still move. The smoke was too low, hugging near his knees. Her lungs would have already seared with the smoke, which made for an agonizing death. And the windows were the last place he wanted her moving toward—they had been laced and marked to burn. She'd reach safety only to have it denied her. And Jack knew from horrifying experience that once clothes caught fire…

He wasn't leaving her in this house.

A hand clamped down hard on his shoulder, squeezing twice, Cole signaling he'd search clockwise around the room while Jack moved counterclockwise. Jack reached up and tapped Cole's hand in agreement.

Only another firefighter would understand why they were inside an inferno when hope was so slim. The fact it was his best friend and the head of the arson group at his side—Jack was grateful. Cole was the most experienced man in the company. If there was a chance, Cole would help create it.

Which room?

Kitchen? Living room? Bedroom?

Pets.

Jack knew exactly where Lizzy would have tried to go.

And knowing that, it might just save her life.

He moved forward with Cole down the hall, judging distance by the number of steps he took, and felt for the door frame of the guest bedroom, committing himself and Cole to searching this room first, and possibly last, if the fire had its way. It was terrifying, the knowledge Lizzy could literally be lying one foot farther down the hall, and in this smoke he couldn't see her.

He was blind, and his sister was dying.

"Take out the window in the guest bedroom next!" Stephen shouted over the roaring flames. Quinn turned the long pike pole with its metal hook to break out the glass and latch around the burning windowsill. He could feel the heat blistering his face as he strained to tear out the wood, grimly ignoring the pain.

Marcus latched his fire hook around the wood to help. "Pull!"

Stephen had wisely given them a job, for neither of them could handle standing by to watch. Jack and Cole had risked their lives going inside to get Lisa. They needed a way to get her out. Quinn refused to accept the reality that he could feel, see, smell, and taste. The fire had already won. Water hissed around him as the flames roared and ate the water thrown against it.

"Lisa!" It was a shout from Kate behind him and to the right. Quinn risked seconds to look away and checked his movement midstroke. Lisa, running hard across the sidewalk from the direction of the nearby park into the street without looking, falling forward and catching herself as her feet moved from sidewalk to asphalt. Quinn dropped the fire hook and swerved sharply to cut her off.

Her eyes were wide, bright, and focused past him. "No!"

Quinn caught her, steel arms wrapping around to stop her. The force of the contact drove a bruise deep into his side.

"Jack, get out of there! Lisa's safe. She's outside!" Kate screamed over the roaring fire.

The top of Lisa's head caught Quinn under the chin sending sharp splinters of pain into his jaw and face. She was hard to hold. She'd learned to fight dirty and she wanted past him; in the adrenaline rush to reach her pets she wasn't thinking, just reacting. Those were her pets dying.

He forced her to turn away from the fire, not to watch, and felt her chest heave as she tried at the same time to breathe and speak. "Don't, Lizzy, please don't. It's already over."

He could feel it rush over her, could feel the shock break and the truth hit. Her body shuddered. She'd lost everything that mattered to her: the scrapbooks, the records, the art…and the pets. The pets she had loved were dead.

He held on because it was all he could do to help.

He could hear Jack coughing, Kate angry in her relief, and Cole ordering people back. The fire viciously roared as the roof collapsed.

It took Lisa minutes but Quinn felt the change. She stiffened as she took a deep breath. She braced and pushed herself a few inches back from his chest, stumbled, and found her footing again. She was reeling and fighting it and her eyes— His hands tightened and she tried to shake him off. "I'm okay. Go help Jack. Someone needs to help Jack."

Marcus read the situation in a glance, slid his arm around her waist, and took over. "Lizzy, you scared us, honey."

Marcus met his gaze, and Quinn understood the silent message. Quinn let his hand tighten on Lisa's shoulder. "I'll get Jack so you can see for yourself he's okay."

Lisa was sitting on the side step of the fire engine, silent, one tennis shoe off because she'd stepped on a hot ember and burned the sole. She was moving her socked foot slowly back and forth in the soot-blackened water rushing down the street toward the nearest storm drain, her gaze never leaving the dying fire. Her brother Stephen had wrapped a fire coat around her and she gripped it with both hands, pulled tight.

Quinn kept a close watch on her as he leaned against the driver's door of a squad car, waiting for a callback from the dispatcher. She was alone in her grief, her emotions hidden, her eyes dry. She'd lost what she valued, and he hated to realize how much it had to resonate with her past.

Kate sat down beside her.

Quinn watched as the two sisters sat in silence, and he prayed for Kate, that she would have the right words to say.

Instead, Kate remained silent.

And Lisa leaned her head over against Kate's shoulder and continued to watch the fire burn, the silence unbroken.

Friends. Deep, lifelong friends.

Quinn had to turn away from the sight, so much emotion inside it was going to rupture out in tears or fury.

He found himself facing a grim Marcus.

"Quinn, get her out of here."

"Stephen has already tried; she won't budge."

"No. I mean out of here. Out of town," Marcus replied tersely. "He goes from notes and phone calls to fire. He's not going to stop there."

Marcus was right. Lisa had to come first. "The ranch. She's going to need the space."

"Thank you."

"I'll keep her safe; now that it's too late."

"Quinn—we'll find him."

That wasn't even a question. He was going to hunt the guy down and rip out his heart.

"Lizzy." She was awake but looked unseeing out the plane window, her face still bearing the streaks of soot and her clothes the strong smell of smoke. Quinn tucked the blanket around her lap, then eased her head forward and replaced the jacket she'd bundled up with a pillow. He reached for her hand and closed it around a cold water bottle. "Ice water. It will help."

He loosened the cap when she tried and couldn't turn it.

He wished she'd say something, wished she'd at least cry, but instead she had pulled back into silence, turning her face away from him, watching the black night sky. Dave had chartered the flight for them so she'd have no one else to have to deal with.

Rachel had wanted to come along, and Kate, but Lisa had just shaken her head. It had hurt the others to see her pulling away from them, but Lisa hadn't seen that. She'd simply wanted to retreat on her own. And because he understood, he'd quietly suggested to her family that they give her a couple days.

He wanted so badly to reach out and pull her against him, take the pain away, but she wasn't seeking him out either, and that hurt, deep in his soul it hurt. She wasn't turning to him.

He reached over and held her hand. For the duration of the flight it remained lax within his.

TWENTY-ONE

Quinn walked down the long hardwood floor hallway in the ranch house, past the sculptures and the art, the mail on the side table and suitcases still unpacked by the door. He accepted the phone from his housekeeper. "Jack?"

"How's she doing?"

Quinn didn't have a good description. "Still in shock. Too quiet." He worried about how long it would take her to come out of it. This Lisa, so passive she followed directions without comment, was a mystery to him. He hoped that if she couldn't sleep she'd at least seek him out, rather than slip from the house to walk alone. "How are you doing? Honestly?"

Jack's voice had deepened an octave and still sounded rough, an aftereffect of all the smoke he'd inhaled. "I would not recommend running air tanks down until they start to chime. I'm thankful Cole was with me."

"It's painful, knowing the risk you took when she wasn't even inside."

"Quinn—" Jack's voice became grim—"if she had been inside, she'd have been dead. The flames were coalescing to the center of the house, the toxic smoke was as low as my knees. Every room was filled with the smoke; it was pouring through the air-conditioning vents like small chimneys."

"Arson?"

"The place was soaked in fuel oil. Poured into the ground and soaked into the wood of the patio. It went with the same ferociousness as a natural gas line break would burn."

"He wanted to kill her, not just scare her."

"He set the fire while she was out of the house; I don't think that was an accident. Marcus found a note tucked under the windshield wiper of her car. *Go away.*"

"The fire was a threat." Quinn felt sick. There was no more room to escalate but to murder. They had to find this guy. "How'd he start it?"

"Preliminary—a lighter tossed into the flower bed at the back of the house."

"No one in the neighborhood saw anything?"

"I'm sorry, Quinn. Her immediate neighbors were gone for the weekend, and the patrols that have been watching the neighborhood didn't see anything out of place. But my gut tells me he stayed. I don't think he set the fire and left the area. We're reviewing the news reporter's tape of the fire to see if there was anyone in the crowd that stands out."

"She didn't tell many people she was going to be gone or when she would return."

"He's close enough to her to know the details, either directly or second hand."

He had nowhere to direct the anger he felt. "Why didn't Lisa smell the fuel oil?"

"It's like motor oil: once it's soaked in, it's not going to be that obvious. And they were asphalting the driveway three houses down. Even I would have had a hard time separating the smell of fresh asphalt from the faint, lingering smell of fuel oil." Jack's voice turned rough. "Quinn, that note. Why does he want her gone? It has to tie to the murders you two have been investigating. Just how close are you to the truth that he would risk such a public action to slow you down?"

"I don't know. If we're staring at it already, I don't know what it is."

"Find out. Until you do, I don't know how we'll stop him."

"Was there anything salvageable?"

"Kate and I will find out tomorrow once the ruins have cooled down."

"Don't tell Lisa what you've told me."

"Not until she's ready to hear it," Jack agreed. "I'll call in the morning."

"Please do."

After he said good-bye and hung up the phone, Quinn just stood in the hall, looking unseeing at the floor, weary to the bone. It was almost dawn.

Lisa had had to start over so many times in her life. He didn't know if she had the reserves to do it again. She'd loved having roots, a place that was hers.

She'd loved that house. She'd needed that house. And now someone had taken it away. She struggled to let herself attach to people, would now add a struggle to let herself attach to another place knowing it could also get ripped away. There were only so many losses a person could take.

"Lord, I want to find whoever did this and rip away what he values most, make him feel the same hurt he inflicted." Quinn felt the ache settle back in his stomach, like a wound that wouldn't heal. He'd nearly lost her for a second time. "I'd give my right arm to know how to help her right now."

There was nothing he could do, that was the harsh part. He wished from the depths of his heart that he could share this ranch with her for more than a few days, he wished he could make her part of it and the roots of this house and land that went back not one generation but four.

"What's going to help, Lord? She's hurting. And it's breaking my heart."

Montana was doing its best to show itself at its finest. The sunset was painting the sky, the temperature was cool but comfortable, the evening breeze faint.

Lisa took a seat on the steps of the porch rather than take a chair. Quinn gave her the space, leaning against the post of the porch, watching the sunlight fade. The sounds of the night were beginning to rise: the faint sounds of cattle and horses moving around settling for the night, the quiet rising sound of insects.

As peaceful as the night was, Quinn doubted Lisa felt it. Five days. It was Saturday and she had yet to come out of the silent place where she grieved. Pets like people were mourned. Her face was drawn from lack of sleep. He couldn't get under that reserve, hadn't tried. He understood the patience of time.

His mongrel dog with the odd name of Old Blue—cattle smart, loyal to a fault—angled from coming to him to veer toward her, his tail moving slowly back and forth as he stopped near where she sat. Lisa didn't respond. The dog moved forward, nudged her hand, and rested his muzzle on her knee.

It was a silent standoff between the two of them and Quinn tensed.

Lisa finally reached forward and rubbed the dog's head.

And Quinn saw the first tear fall.

"Someone burned down my house and killed my pets."

Sitting on the porch step beside Lisa, Quinn just nodded. "I know."

She wiped her eyes with one hand, the other continuing to stroke Old Blue's head. Quinn was relieved that there was life back in her eyes, even if the emotion was primarily anger.

"Someone who had to be following us that day we visited Marla's grave. And he likes fire. We know that about him now."

"I had copies of the case files sent out." He knew the work would help, would give her a safe place to function while she dealt with the emotions.

"I want to see them."

"Let me get you something to eat first." She desperately needed some sleep too, but he knew he would get nowhere encouraging that at the moment.

"The files are in the study?"

"The white boxes stacked by the bookcases."

"I'll eat as I read."

He wrapped his hand around hers. "Please, go call the family first. It will help them—Kate, Rachel, especially Jennifer. And Marcus can fill you in on what he and Jack and Stephen have been able to find out." She'd talked to them when they called, but she'd been holding herself so far back from everyone it had made her words seem merely polite. It had been so hard on them to wait, not to fly out as the days slipped by, to give her the space she wanted.

"I'll call them."

Afraid he'd say too much if he stayed, he kissed her forehead, then got up from the porch step beside her.

"Jen, I'm sorry."

"Please quit apologizing. It's not necessary. I was absolutely sick when Marcus called to tell me the news."

Stretched out on the couch in Quinn's study, her head resting against the armrest, Lisa idly wrapped the phone cord around her finger. Her family loved her enough to forgive her for being rude. She'd pushed them away for five days and they were still there waiting for her when she came back to her senses. "Someone wanted to kill me, Jen."

"I know."

"I'm scared."

"I know that too."

Lisa reached down toward Old Blue and got her hand licked for her trouble. The dog rolled onto his side and she buried her hand in his warm fur. She had a feeling Old Blue wasn't a house dog, but Quinn had shown up with sandwiches and the dog at his heels. Lisa was pretty sure the dog was hanging out with her because of the food she'd been sharing but felt relieved to have him with her regardless.

"I miss Sidney so much. He was so special. And Iris—" She was crying again and wiped at the tears, furious with herself for having so little control, glad Quinn had given her privacy for this call.

"They'll find whoever did it."

She reached over for another Kleenex.

"You never told me why you left the house to go walk around the pond."

Lisa hesitated.

"Lizzy? You want to talk about it?"

"Quinn." She tried not to put all the confusion she felt over the man into the word, but it was there.

"I wondered," Jen said softly. "You two were pretty tight over the weekend."

"I went for a walk to try and clear my head. A lot of good that did me. If I'd been at the house, I might have been able to save my pets."

"I wish someone had been able to. I know Jack tried."

"They would have been terrified in those minutes before they died."

"I know."

Lisa forced herself away from the image that had haunted her dreams for days. "Quinn's being nice. He's hovering, kind of lost as to what he should do."

"I gathered that from the conversations I've had with him. Do you know what you want him to do?"

She wanted a hug but didn't know how to ask for one. He was kind, and there, and wanted so badly for her not to be hurting anymore. It no longer surprised her that it mattered so much to him. Under the watchfulness he showed the world, he was a man who was as protective of her as her family. "He loaned me his dog."

"Did he?"

Lisa rubbed Old Blue's ears and heard a dog's version of a sigh of pleasure. "I think he's going to want him back," she remarked regretfully.

Jen laughed.

Reality was settling in, and it left an enormous ache in her heart. "The house is gone, the art. All the scrapbooks. It shouldn't matter so much, it was just stuff." But it did. She could remember painting the rooms while Jack painted the ceilings, wallpapering the bathroom, rearranging furniture so many times Marcus wanted to strangle her when she said, "No, I like it better where it was, move it back."

All the firsts in that house—first dinner party for family, first mortgage payment, first winter snow and shoveling the drive, first flowers in the spring. It was gone, and she was going to have to start over again.

"It was home."

"It was home," Lisa agreed. The first one she'd ever really had.

"Marcus said he was dealing with the insurance guy for you?"

"I faxed him power of attorney. Stephen said he'd help me find and fix up another place."

"What's wrong with Montana?"

"Jen—"

"I know Quinn's heart. He's the right guy for you."

"You're reading too much into the situation."

"I'm not saying marry the guy tomorrow."

"Thank you for that. Would you tell me something?"

"Sure."

"Did you decide to believe because it mattered to Tom?"

"Honestly?"

"Yeah."

"It was the only reason I went to church initially because it was important to him. But I started listening, and after a while I found something there that I wanted for myself."

"What was that?"

"Forgiveness."

"The drunk driver who killed your parents."

"Living with the bitterness for so long…I just wanted to be able to forgive and let it go so I could get on with my life. But I couldn't do it for myself. I found out that Jesus could do it for me, He could help me forgive."

"You believed in Him because you needed Him."

"I trust Marcus because I need to, but also because I know he's trustworthy. Which came first?" Jen asked. "There's no easy answer, Lizzy. Jesus loves me. He's helped me forgive a man I hate, helped me into remission with the cancer, worked out things with Tom to make me the happiest I've ever been in my life. I believe in and love Jesus because He is who He is. He's worth loving. Which came first? I don't know. He's just perfect. And I know Him. That's the most peaceful reality I've ever had in my life."

"I prayed for a family and He let adoption papers get ripped away," Lisa whispered. She'd never told that to Jennifer before.

"You ended up with the O'Malleys," Jen finally said, tears choking her voice. "And you make our family complete. Maybe He knew that."

Lisa closed her eyes. She wouldn't trade the O'Malleys for anything.

"Lizzy? Risk asking Jesus for your deepest need. You'll find out He's sufficient."

"That's assuming He's alive."

"You're not even protesting anymore that the Resurrection's not possible. You already know He's alive."

Her hand stole across her ribs to touch the scar. "Maybe."

"Let's go back to talking about Quinn."

Lisa heard the smile in Jen's voice. "Are you matchmaking?"

"I'm married. You wouldn't believe how great it is. Tom is—"

"What?"

"I look into his eyes and he lets me see all the way to his heart. He trusts me to love him."

"I always knew he was special," Lisa replied, having to talk past the emotion that welled up at Jen's description.

"He's going to take me over to the clinic tomorrow and let me be a doctor again for half a day."

"Enjoy it, Jen."

"I'm going to beat this, the cancer. I know it."

"I believe you."

"No you don't, not yet, but that's okay. I understand why. I've seen the lab work too. I'm just telling you now so I can say I told you so later on."

Lisa had to laugh, and then she turned serious. "Jen, if there's anything at all that I can do to help—I don't want anything to happen to you."

"I've got too much life to enjoy before I'm ready to think about heaven. Would you be willing though to do me a favor?"

"If I can."

"I want you to be able to believe. So whatever your doubts, face them, talk to Quinn if you need to, just don't push them aside for another day."

"Why don't you ask me to do something easy?"

"Sometimes the best things are never easy, or simple."

Thinking about Quinn, Lisa had to agree. "It's late your time. I'd better let you go."

"Will you call me tomorrow?"

"Sure. I want to hear how your patients like your new doctor's chair."

"My partners cringed when I moved it into the kids' waiting room. It's fabulous. Tom bought me a Polaroid camera so I can take pictures of kids in the chair to take with them."

"Have Tom take one of you in the chair and send it to me. I can start a scrapbook with it."

Jen tried to keep her voice light but failed. "Deal."

"Jen—" Lisa found it hard to put the emotions into words. "I love you."

"I love you too. And you're making me bawl here."

Lisa wiped her eyes as they laughed together. "Do you really think he won't mind the scars?"

"Does my husband seem to care that I don't have hair?"

"Point taken. Thank you."

"I want to be your matron of honor."

"Well shoot," Lisa joked. "I kind of liked Kate's idea of eloping."

"Be really glad you're half a continent away at the moment."

"He looks really good in a tux and boots."

Old Blue rolled over under her hand. She turned to glance down at him and froze. Quinn was leaning against the study doorjamb watching her—comfortable, boots crossed, smiling. He hadn't just arrived.

"Jen, I'll call you tomorrow." She abruptly ended the conversation, hung up the phone, feeling heat rise across her face.

Quinn crossed the room and set the extra mug he carried down onto the end table. "Your style of coffee." She started to sit up only to get sidetracked when he slid his hands under her ankles and sat down at the other end of the couch, her feet in his lap. "Tux, huh?"

She pulled a pillow over to cover her hot face.

"Eavesdropping doesn't normally reveal such nice compliments."

He was laughing at her. "Quit tickling my foot."

"Honey?"

"That's not my name."

"We'll change it for a while."

"As long as I don't have to answer to it."

"I'm going to have to kiss you before long."

"That is something you had to tell me."

"Anticipation is half the enjoyment."

She lowered the pillow slightly because she just had to see his face. He was smiling at her, he was gorgeous, and… "I'd prefer it if you didn't."

His amusement turned serious and his hand rubbed her ankle. "Why not?"

"I don't kiss all that great," she muttered. He was going to anticipate it and she would just disappoint him.

His expression turned tender…and just a bit too delighted for her comfort. "Practice helps."

"You really should have let me know you were there."

"I know." He squeezed her ankle. "Lizzy?"

"What?"

"She was right, you know, about the scars. I won't mind."

"You should. They're ugly."

"I've got my own, unfortunately at about the same place too. I got gored by a bull back in my rodeo days."

She didn't say anything, couldn't.

"I got hung up and came down in front of him. He caught me between the seventh and eighth ribs, tossed me across the ring, and then nearly hooked the rodeo clowns who risked their lives to distract him."

"How bad?"

"I recovered. So will you."

She turned her foot in toward his ribs. "About there?" She'd guessed correctly. He was ticklish.

She was at a distinct disadvantage in the ensuing minutes. "Uncle! I give!" She was going to split open from laughing so hard. He finally relented and stopped tickling her feet.

She curled her toes. "Where's my sock?" She'd lost it sometime during the preceding minutes.

He closed his hand around her toes, his hand warm and solid, leaned over to pick up the sock from the floor, then paused. "Sorry, it looks like I'll have to buy you another pair."

She found the energy to raise her head from the arm of the couch. "That has got to taste horrible." Old Blue was having a good time taking the sock apart.

Quinn eased her feet aside so he could get up and rescue what was left of the sock before the dog made himself sick.

Lisa pushed herself to sit up, reached for the coffee mug he had brought her, and found it had cooled off. "Warm up the coffee, and let's get to work."

"You need some sleep first."

"Later."

He accepted the mug. "It was good to hear you laugh, Lizzy."

She smiled back at him. "It felt good. Go."

"I still think the water is significant."

"Part of his signature?"

Lisa absently nodded. She turned the page of the notepad, started thinking through another idea.

Amy. She drew a circle around the name, drew a link from that circle to Quinn's dad, and marked it with a question mark. They still didn't know for certain if Amy's disappearance the same day Quinn's father was killed were connected.

Amy had known Rita.

Lisa wrote down Rita's name and circled it, then linked Amy and Rita. She could see them now in her mind. Two teens, sixteen—camera; boy; and horse-crazy. Happy.

Amy missing; Rita dead.

The picture on the pad of paper was grim.

Grant had been convicted of killing Rita.

She added him to the page, hesitated, then dotted a line from Grant to Amy. "We have to find some way to place Amy back in Chicago."

"It's not there, Lizzy."

"I think it is. We just don't know the right question to ask." She drew a circle around the name Marla. Connected it to the circle of her house fire because of the hummingbird note—and felt the focus click in.

Egan.

She wrote the name down and just stared at the page.

It fit, but why?

That fire had been an accident; Jack didn't miss arson.

No more glimmers of an idea appeared. She shifted her attention back to Grant. Christopher had worked part-time for Grant at the stable, had black-mailed payment from him to keep quiet about Grant and Rita being together that last day, had later testified at the trial. It was enough information for her to add Christopher's name to the page and circle it.

She drew a line from Christopher to Grant, then drew another from Christopher to Rita. It was a moment of epiphany. Christopher had known Rita. It was obvious. He'd known who she was when he saw Grant and Rita together.

When had Christopher started to work for Grant? She scrambled to find the right file.

"What?"

"Just a minute."

She finally found the answer on a note Lincoln had made during his background investigation. Christopher had started to work for Grant when he was seventeen, in 1978. She was startled at that answer. He'd been working for Grant at the stables when Rita had first begun to come around at the age of sixteen.

She looked at the date, then back at her picture. Her hand shaking slightly, she drew a line from Christopher to Amy. If the girls had been hanging out at the stables, they would have certainly met a guy their own age working there.

Two teens, sixteen—camera; boy; and horse-crazy. They would have been flirting with Christopher.

The picture spoke for itself. From Grant, lines to Rita and Amy. From Christopher, lines to Rita and Amy. And Rita's body had been buried at the stable.

She felt a chill. "Quinn, what if it was Christopher who killed Rita, not Grant?" she whispered.

It fit.

Christopher had been there the day Rita went missing.

He had known Rita when she was sixteen and he was eighteen. Rita had chosen to date Grant, not him. Christopher had a temper. How many murders had she investigated over the years motivated precisely by that fact?

"Talk to me." Quinn had set aside his notes, was watching her.

"Christopher knew Rita. He was working at Grant's stables part-time when he was eighteen. He was there when Rita started coming around at age sixteen. He was there the day Rita disappeared. He had access to the site where she was buried. He had a temper. If he was jealous Rita had chosen Grant instead of him…"

"The blackmail?"

"Why not frame Grant? Extort money to keep quiet about the fact Grant and Rita had been together that day. Bury Rita somewhere that would point to Grant. Testify at the trial and put Grant at the scene. Christopher set him up."

She looked at Quinn as he thought it through. "Lincoln poking into the trial past would have spooked Christopher," Quinn said quietly.

"You said someone started following you while I was still in the hospital. This could explain that too. When you started asking about Amy and Rita…Christopher is safe as long as no one comes forward to say he and Rita knew each other for years. If Lincoln or you discovered that Christopher had as much a motive for killing Rita as Grant did…"

"Christopher knows where you live; he helped Walter plant the tree."

"Would he be the type of guy that would set a fire?"

"I think so," Quinn replied grimly. "The note. *Go away*. Someone is very desperate to see you stop probing into Rita's death…and the others'."

"We were thinking it would take a career like a builder for someone to cover the geographic area of the murders, be around long enough to learn their routines. Working for his uncle at Nakomi Nurseries, doing landscaping—Christopher would have had that flexibility."

"Lincoln has the records for the customers Nakomi Nurseries worked with in the Knolls Park area. If Christopher was in the area at the time Marla disappeared, we should be able to prove it."

"Emily has been working to figure out Grant's whereabouts on the days the women disappeared. Ask her to do the same for Christopher."

Quinn reached for the phone. "Is there any way to connect Christopher to Amy?" he asked as he dialed.

Lisa looked back at her page of circles. That two-week visit to Chicago.

She shifted around the boxes to find the pictures Amy had taken. "I need a picture of Christopher as a young man." She had met him in his late thirties at the trial, but she wasn't sure she would recognize him at age eighteen. Amy had liked to take pictures of friends, and there were several dozen people they had yet to identify in the pictures.

Quinn passed on the idea to Lincoln and they talked for a few minutes. Quinn reached over and hung up the phone. "Lincoln will find out where Christopher has been, check the Nakomi Nurseries' records."

"Let's hope he finds something."

"Lisa, it's a good idea."

"There's not enough evidence to prove anything."

"It fits. We haven't had that before. If the evidence is there, we'll find it."

"Someone burned down my house. At least this way it's one person who committed all the crimes."

"Walter said he and Christopher were working on a job a good two hours away when your house burned."

"You said yourself Walter protected Christopher over the gambling. Protecting him over a suspicious fire…"

"Walter knows more than he is saying."

"Let's find something conclusive that suggests Christopher is guilty before we accuse Walter of lying."

"Pass me Lincoln's notes."

She found them and complied.

Lisa looked at her sketch of circles. They needed to prove the motive that Christopher had not only known Rita but had possibly even dated her. "Was there anything in Rita's diary about a Chris or a Christopher?"

"I don't know that I would have recognized it as significant. You'd better review those that we have to make sure."

Lisa found the first diary.

She heard a soft rumble. She looked up and grinned. "That is your stomach growling."

"It's Old Blue's."

"Sure it is."

Quinn got to his feet. "I'll prove it to you. I'll go get a sandwich, and you can listen to Old Blue."

She chuckled. "Do that."

"You want something?"

"No. I'm fine."

She was asleep on the couch. Quinn paused in the doorway, late coming back, having been sidetracked by a conversation with his ranch manager. He moved quietly into the room. The diary was cradled against Lisa's chest with one hand, a stack of old pictures resting in her lap. Her other hand rested on Old Blue's side. His dog was sleeping too. Quinn had a feeling he'd lost his dog's loyalty forever.

He thought about moving her. Thought about it and instead just settled into the chair opposite her, resting his chin on his fist. She was gorgeous as she slept.

TWENTY-TWO

"Try this one." Lisa offered the long stick and the toasted marshmallow.

Quinn leaned forward and carefully slipped it from the stick. "It's a good thing I don't mind the taste of burned marshmallows."

"This one came out better."

"You get too impatient. Hold the stick higher and turn it more."

He licked his fingers of the sticky marshmallow.

Lisa finished eating hers. It was only a bit charred. "Want another one?"

"Sure."

She reached for the plastic bag of marshmallows, watching Quinn while she did so. Firelight flickered across his face. He was totally relaxed, resting his head back against his saddle, using it for a headrest. She liked that about him, his ability to set aside everything else going on and totally relax. They were having a campout dinner although they were only a half-hour ride from the house. Lisa had insisted that she wanted a real bed for the night so the tour he'd been giving her of the ranch had been cut short to four hours.

She rubbed the small of her back. It had been about three hours too long. Quinn had said he would show her the south part of the ranch tomorrow, but if this didn't ease off she was going to have to pass on the invitation.

"Sore?"

"You weren't supposed to notice. My tailbone hurts," she admitted.

"You need to ride more often."

"I thought you said Annie was docile. I spent the afternoon convincing the mare I did not want to canter."

"I said she wouldn't try to knock you over or toss you off. I didn't say she was dead. There's a difference."

Lisa tossed her hat at him.

He grinned as he caught it with one hand, rolled the brim with the other. "A lady should never toss her cowboy hat to a guy."

"You're kidding. Why not?"

She reached down and tugged at the laces of her left tennis shoe. She swore her feet had swollen while riding during the day. She finally just slipped the shoes off to give herself some relief.

"It's kind of like a lady giving a knight of old her colors to wear."

"Really?"

"The hard part is the guy doesn't get a choice about whether he wants to accept it or not."

She slapped his leg. "Give me back my hat."

"Nope."

He leaned his head back and used her hat to block out the moon. "You got your full moon tonight. It's bright."

"It's beautiful. Get out of the city and you can actually see the stars." She skewered two marshmallows and held them out over the fire. "Thanks for giving me an excuse to take an afternoon off."

"Even if I had to practically drag you away from the files?"

"Even if." She leaned back against her saddle and braced the long stick against her knee to keep it slowly turning over the fire. It was a beautiful expanse of open sky. A quiet Tuesday night. Still. She'd loved the day spent with Quinn. He was so comfortable here on the open land. She loved it too. She could breathe here.

The fire popped, sending sparks into the air.

"Lizzy, we need to talk."

His voice had become serious. She turned her head to look at him. "About what?"

"Andy."

She wasn't expecting it, and the memory triggered by the name stole her breath. Every muscle in her back tensed. "No."

"You have to trust me at some point."

"I don't want to talk about it," she muttered, looking back at the fire. She didn't want to share her secrets. He didn't have to know.

He sighed, set her hat on the ground beside him, and interlaced his fingers behind his head as he watched her. "I know what happened."

She turned startled eyes toward him. "What?"

"Kate found out for me."

She shoved aside the stick, dropping it into the dust, not caring, as she surged to her feet and strode away. He'd invaded her privacy, gone behind her back, told her family…he'd broken her trust.

"Don't go far," he called quietly. The fact that he made no attempt to follow drew her slowly to a halt as she reached the spot where the horses were tethered. She stopped by Annie, resting her hand on the powerful shoulder of the horse. Annie shifted and turned her head, sniffed Lisa's shirt, and butted her arm to get attention.

Quinn knew. Kate knew. Kate would have told Marcus.

Lisa closed her eyes. "How long?"

She knew he heard her. Sounds carried in this quiet, open land.

"Since before you got the hummingbird note," Quinn finally replied.

Even before she had been staying with Kate. All the late night talks they'd had—Kate had known. Her sister had been pitying her. The anger that swelled inside was incredible.

She glanced at the horizon, decided the faint area of light on the horizon had to be the ranch house, and started walking.

The coarse grass, the ground rocky in places, hurt her socked feet, but she kept walking. If she didn't see Quinn for a month she'd be happy.

She heard him coming after her and ignored him.

He held out her shoes and she took them and flung them at him.

"Would you listen?"

She kept walking.

He went back to get her shoes and brought them back again. She considered throwing them at him again, but she was beginning to limp, and it was going to be a long walk. "You can't just walk away and leave a fire burning. You told me so yourself."

He caught her arm, brought her to a stop. "True. Stay right here while I go put it out. Besides, you're going the wrong way. That light is the town, about ten miles from here, not the ranch house."

She didn't get that confused about directions.

He took her shoulders and turned her farther to the west. "Over there."

He left her there, and she turned to see him walking back to the flickering fire. She took a moment to pull on her shoes and then started walking again.

He caught up with her fifteen minutes later, leading the two horses, both now saddled.

"I don't want to ride."

"Fine. We'll walk."

He'd known something had happened at Knolls Park and he'd had to go find out. "I trusted you," she said bitterly.

"I apologize."

She nearly told him what he could do with his apology.

"You're mad because it's a painful memory."

"Painful?" She turned away, swearing, wanting to hit him. "I see him underwater, dead, floating there, his face distorted and unseeing eyes open. I was seven. And I didn't need you to know!"

"Lizzy, I'm sorry."

She stumbled on a depression in the ground and slapped his hand away when he tried to help her.

She wished he'd go away.

He walked in silence beside her for several minutes. Quinn caught her hand. "Annie knows the way home, she won't let you get lost." He handed her the reins.

She took them because he surprised her. Quinn turned away and swung up on his own horse. He held out her hat to her. "We do need to talk about it." She took the hat and didn't bother to say anything. He held something else out to her, and she silently took it as well. His handkerchief. "I'll see you back at the house." She grudgingly nodded her head.

He nudged his horse to a walk and gave her the space she wanted. And Lisa finally felt free to let the pain wash away in tears as she walked.

She needed the walk. It didn't matter that her legs burned or that her tears gave her a headache. The walk was time to think.

She missed Andy. He'd been her best friend. He had a problem with dyslexia. Since her schooling had been choppy at best, she'd been struggling to learn how to read and he understood the frustration. It had been such a happy summer. They spent it working with a tutor the Richards had hired to help them both.

Andy—glasses, lisp, and more courage than sense. They'd climbed trees, hunted frogs, dug up worms, snuck flashlights and late-night snacks, had been against the same things and for the same things. He'd been her brother in heart and spirit.

And in a blink, he was gone.

She hadn't cared when she was sent to another foster home. She'd let no one else close for years. Until Kate…she'd been the most persistent of the O'Malleys, refusing to go away; Jennifer the kindest; and Rachel…as her roommate, Rachel had just ignored that a wall existed and assumed Lisa wanted to know all the details of her day whether she asked or not.

Lisa had thought about running away from Trevor House to get away from them, had in fact tried to do it one night only to have Marcus catch her in the act and sit her down on the back step. With the conviction of a future big brother he convinced her to change her mind.

The nightmares about Andy had haunted her during those years. Rachel, sitting cross-legged on her own bed, had always been the one who would sit and talk in the middle of the night when Lisa woke shivering and angry, hating the dream and needing the light on. Rachel had covered for her so many times when the floor mom wanted to know why the light was on. It was always Rachel who said she wanted it on.

Lisa picked up a clod of dirt and crushed it in her hand. She still woke occasionally, shaken from the nightmare.

Andy should never have died.

If Jesus didn't hear a prayer said in terror, it made no sense to trust Him when times were calm. It was when the chips were down that help mattered the most.

They'd said it was her fault.

Maybe it was. She could have talked Andy out of showing off. She knew that. And she hadn't tried.

The bitterness was an old memory, deadened by time and tears. She missed Andy; it hurt to talk about him, but it was the past.

The betrayal was new.

The last thing she wanted to deal with was her family and the entire subject of Andy. She'd kept it private for years, and now, in one action, Quinn had destroyed what she had protected for so long. She closed her eyes, feeling the fatigue wash over her. There was no way to undo what he had done.

"Come here, Annie." She swung up into the saddle, let Annie take her back to the ranch house. What she would say to Quinn…she didn't know.

Quinn heard the horse coming before he saw it. He didn't move from his position by the stable door as she appeared from the darkness and came into the light. No matter what she said about her skills, Lisa rode well, was comfortable in the saddle. She came to a stop a few feet away and dismounted. The tears had flowed, then been dried. And that sight hurt.

"I'll take her," he offered quietly, holding out his hand for Annie's reins. His own horse had already been brushed down and stabled for the night.

She handed them to him. "We need to talk."

"Give me five minutes. I'll find you."

She nodded and walked toward the house.

He stabled Annie.

He found Lisa in the study, curled up in the recliner, her shoes kicked off, the late news turned on, but she wasn't paying attention to it. Her head was lying against the headrest, her eyes were closed.

Quinn sat down on the couch. "I did what I thought was best. But I never intended to hurt you."

"Of everything you could have done, going behind my back was the worst."

"I was wrong. I'm sorry."

She wearily opened her eyes. "Apology accepted. But you can't undo the results. I've got to live with them. Did you ever consider there might be a reason I didn't want the family to know?"

"I saw what the memory did to you. Burying it was not the right answer."

"Stephen's sister drowned."

The news shocked him.

"It was my choice to decide if the family knew about Andy, not yours."

The reality of good intentions…it didn't fix a serious mistake. She'd cleaned his clock, and he deserved it. "I truly am sorry, Lizzy."

"I dream about Andy. I can never remember what he looked like alive; he's always dead."

"Do you have a picture of him?"

She didn't answer right away. "In one of the scrapbooks that burned."

Quinn rested his head in his hands. "I'm going to shut my mouth now; I've done enough damage for one night."

"Quinn?"

He looked over at her.

"You did it because you cared. We're okay. I just don't want to talk about Andy. There's nothing more that needs to be said."

"There's one thing. What the Richards did was wrong."

"No it wasn't. They lost their son. Had I stayed, I would have tried to replace him…and that would have destroyed me."

There was wisdom in her quiet words.

She pushed herself to her feet and walked over to where he sat. Her fingers brushed his shoulder. "At least there are no more big secrets. Good night, Quinn."

"'Night, Lisa," he said quietly, squeezing her hand. She was wrong; there was one big secret remaining. He was falling in love with her. And it was going to be his secret for a lifetime the way things were going. She was never going to accept the Resurrection with this in her past.

Just friends. He wanted a freedom he didn't have to make it something more.

"Show me where your father was killed."

Quinn turned in the saddle to look at Lisa. After asking her to face Andy last night, he couldn't deny her right to the tough memories of his own. "Are you sure?"

"I need to see the scene. If it is somehow related to Amy…"

He nodded, accepting that it was necessary. "It's farther south."

"Quinn—"

"It's okay. I've been back here many times."

"Actually, I was going to ask if we could walk for a while."

He reined in his horse and laughed. "Sure."

She slid from the horse with a sigh of relief and rested her head against Annie's neck. Quinn frowned at the realization that this was more than just too much time in the saddle and quickly swung off his mount to join her. "Lizzy?"

"I think I'm getting motion sickness," she muttered, frustrated.

He rubbed her back. "You're serious."

"Oh yeah."

He wrapped her in his arms, hugging her, trying not to laugh because it was obvious she was feeling awful. "I am so sorry."

With her head buried against his shirt, her words were muffled. "Sure you are."

"I really am."

"Good, because you're about to get a blister in those boots."

"You don't want to head back to the house?"

She shook her head and took a step back. "I want to see the area. Marcus said it was near the bluffs?"

"Let me call my foreman, have him come out with a truck. There's no need for us to walk."

"Quinn—I'm fine. And if you're going to fuss, I'm going to get annoyed."

He moved over to his horse, opened the saddlebag, and retrieved two bottles of juice. "Okay. We'll walk." He uncapped one and handed it to her. "Let's head over to that crest. It will be downhill from there."

It was a quiet twenty-minute walk. November had arrived and the land was changing to reflect the coming winter, grass becoming dormant.

The bluffs were visible once they reached the rise in the land. Lisa stopped to look over the area. "It's an awesome vista. Water cut out the bluffs and the ravines?"

"See the streambed? This tributary runs down to the Ledds River. When the flash floods come, they tear through this land and reshape it."

"There are caves in the bluffs?"

"Dozens."

"I would love to explore them someday."

"Someday," Quinn agreed quietly. "We can walk down to the streambed. We'll have to ride from there, but it's not far."

The stream had dried to a trickle during the hot summer. They remounted the horses, crossed the stream, and Quinn led the way toward the bluffs.

"I found him here."

Lisa got down from Annie and retrieved the juice bottle. "You came from there?" She pointed back to the crest they had walked over.

"Yes."

She slowly turned in a full circle.

"He was shot in the back. From close range?"

"The sheriff figured about ten feet."

"So he knew the man who killed him, or at least had no reason to be uncomfortable at the idea of turning his back."

"Agreed."

"We're closer to the bluffs than I had assumed. Could a truck come back this far?"

"When my father was killed, the ravine we crossed had water flowing through it from a flash flood the week before. A vehicle would have had to come up from the south to reach here."

"What's out that way?"

"Besides rough terrain? About five miles of pasture, woods, and deep ravines."

She pulled out a piece of paper from her pocket and unfolded it. It was her sketch of the circled names and links they had suspected and proven. Lisa sat down on the ground and reached for her pen.

He recognized the slightly unfocused look on her face. "Have an idea?"

She nodded. "Come here."

Curious, he dismounted to join her.

"Why did someone kill your father?"

"We have no idea. Possibly because he stumbled across something he shouldn't have."

He stood at her shoulder, watched her darken the circle around Rita. "We also think she was really killed because she stumbled on proof of Amy's death."

Lisa leaned her head back against his knee, squinting against the sun as she looked up at him. "Stumbled on something." She looked down and darkened the circle around his father. And then she darkened the two lines that flowed into it. One beginning with Grant that ran through Rita to Amy to his father, and the other that began from Christopher and flowed to Rita to Amy and ended at his father. "See it?"

She looked back up at him. "If we can't prove Amy returned to Chicago, can we prove Chicago came to Amy?"

He blinked. "One of them came to Montana."

"Time for a break."

"Not yet," Lisa commented absently, reading the transcript from Grant's trial.

Quinn could have predicted that answer. He crossed over to where she sat on the couch and slid the report from her hand. "Yes, now. You said you wanted to see my old rodeo tapes." It was after 11 P.M. They'd been going through the files ever since they got back from the bluffs, and he knew she still wasn't feeling that great. She'd been sipping 7-Up all evening.

"What did Emily find out about where Grant bought his horses?"

"We just asked the question this afternoon. Give her time to find an answer."

"I know something is there."

"I think so too. And it can wait a couple hours. Come on." He pulled her to her feet and directed her toward the living room.

"So what are we watching?"

"The high school national rodeo championships."

"How'd you do?"

"Let's just say Montana sent the Lone Star State home without the trophy they dominated for a decade."

"Do I hear a bit of pride in that outcome?"

"Well deserved. I wore the bruises of victory for weeks."

She settled down at one end of the couch. "You fixed popcorn?"

"Ask nicely, and I might even share."

She picked up the bowl. "Ask nicely, and I might give the bowl back," she replied, eating her first handful.

He slid in the tape, adjusted the volume, and reached for the remote.

"So what did you compete in?"

"Bull riding, calf roping, steer wrestling. I stayed away from goat tying."

"Goat tying? They have such a thing?"

"Yep. They even give Horse of the Year awards."

Bull riding was up first. He watched her wince as the first rider appeared, survived six seconds, and was thrown off. Two rodeo clowns worked in tandem to distract the bull while the rider got out of the ring.

"Quinn. You did this for sport?"

"You spend a lot of time training before you ride one of these guys. Most injuries come from inexperienced riders making basic mistakes in balance and timing. It's a sport where errors compound quickly. In my case I simply drew a more experienced bull."

"What do you mean?"

"The bulls they use at the high school national championships are the same as the ones in the professional circuit. When you draw a new bull to the circuit, you've got a better chance of completing the ride than if you draw one with experience. I had the misfortune of drawing Taggert II. He'd been on the circuit for seven years, seen every move, learned a few of his own."

"Please don't tell me this tape has you getting hurt."

"No one gets hurt."

She watched, fascinated. "You get points for yourself and your team when you compete?"

"Yes."

Quinn didn't have to watch the tape to remember the competition. He settled back on the couch, crossed his ankles, reached over and tugged at the popcorn bowl that Lisa shared but didn't release.

Love was a bit like a wonderful piece of art. The best pieces were those that grew on him, were interesting for deeper reasons than the surface, became more beautiful the more he looked at them. Lisa was like that.

She glanced at him for a moment and blushed. "You're watching me again."

"Guilty." He loved watching her.

"It's disconcerting." She raised her hand to brush down her hair. "It makes me think I'm looking like a dust mop or something."

He laughed at the image and reached over to still her hand. "You look just fine. The sun gives you a tan and turns your hair blond."

"Streaky flyaway blond is not pretty," she muttered.

"It is if I say so."

"Flattery only works if it has an element of truth to it."

His dog came to join her.

"Why do I get the feeling I've lost my dog?"

She laughed as she offered Old Blue popcorn. "He knows a better thing when he finds it."

He took a handful of the popcorn.

"What's this?" she asked, indicating the new event on the tape.

"Calf roping. The calf breaks into the corral, the rider comes through seconds later. Lasso him, get off your horse, toss him onto his side, loop rope around his feet, then throw up your hands."

"Is it hard to do?"

"Much harder than it looks. Holding flailing legs to get the rope around fast is tough. And getting kicked in the face is more common than you'd expect."

"I don't know that I wanted to know that."

They watched the first several riders try their luck.

He saw the change in her expression, the look of distance appear. She'd just drifted away to thinking about work.

"Excuse me, Quinn." She pushed away from him, got to her feet, headed back to the office.

He thought for a moment about joining her but stayed seated. He knew how fragile ideas were until they crystallized.

He reached around for the phone. Despite his words to Lisa to be patient, he was anything but. "Marcus, how's it going?"

"The same as it was thirty minutes ago." He partner was not nearly so willing to change the focus from Grant to Christopher. "Give me another couple hours, Quinn. I'll call as soon as I find anything useful. Hold on. Lincoln just got here." His partner muffled the phone for a moment. "He's got news. Let me pass you to him."

"Quinn?"

"Hi, Lincoln."

"Does the name McLinton mean anything to you?"

Quinn's hand rubbing Old Blue went still. "Yes, it does. They own a ranch to the southeast of here."

"Grant bought three horses from a Frank McLinton over the lifetime of the stable."

"Can you get me the dates of those sales, or when he might have been out here to see the horses?"

"Emily's working on it."

Until a few days ago this was exactly the news he had hoped to hear. Now it just raised more questions. It put Grant back at the top of the list. "Any word on Christopher?"

"Not yet."

"Thanks for this. Call whenever you hear anything else."

"I will," Lincoln reassured.

Grant had come to Montana.

Quinn hung up the phone and went to find Lisa.

"Lisa."

She held up one finger, motioning for a moment of time. He crossed over to join her and see what she was studying that was causing the frown.

The excavation of Rita's grave.

She finally shook her head slightly and looked up at him. "What?"

"Grant has been to Montana. Emily found out that he bought three horses from Frank McLinton, the owner of a ranch southeast of here."

"When?"

"She's still getting dates."

Lisa leaned back against the couch, thinking about it. "Grant was out here to buy horses. That fits." She looked up at him. "How did he get the horses back to Chicago? He wouldn't have flown them back, so did McLinton deliver them or what?"

"Great question. Do you have the phone number of the stable manager? The Scotsman?"

"Samuel Barberry. It would be in Lincoln's notes."

Quinn found it and picked up the phone. It was late, something he would apologize for, but he needed the answer. It took a few minutes to describe what he needed to know.

"Normally I'd take one of the horse trailers from here and go pick up the new horse," Mr. Barberry explained. "Or if it was a horse coming from a distance, a couple of the stable hands would fly out, rent a horse trailer, and drive the animal back."

"Do you remember the horses Grant bought from Frank McLinton?"

"Sure. A nice chestnut and two bays. Greg and Danny flew out and brought two of them back, Chris went out to pick up the other."

"Christopher Hampton?"

"His brother Walter helped him drive it back. They've got distant family out that way."

"Do you remember when that was?"

"1980, '81? Somewhere around then."

"I appreciate the help, Mr. Barberry."

"Anytime."

Quinn hung up the phone.

"What?"

He looked over at Lisa and took a seat on the chair across from her. "One of the horses was driven back to Chicago by Christopher and Walter Hampton."

Her surprise at the news matched his. "Both brothers?"

"Two drivers, they must have driven straight through to Chicago. And the time is right. Grant bought the horse in either 1980 or '81."

"Amy disappeared in 1980."

He nodded. "Grant and Christopher were both here. Chicago did come to Amy."

She started tapping her pen on the table, and Quinn waited. "That tells us more than I thought we would find." She reached for one of the photographs on the table from the excavation of Rita's grave and held it out to him. "What do you see?"

It was a photograph taken looking down into the grave site. The skeleton beginning to appear was lying face down, the dirt had been brushed away so that Rita's arms and hands were uncovered. He looked back at Lisa. "What?"

"It matches what they were doing during the calf roping."

He looked back at the picture, stunned.

"It's a calf roping loop. Look at her hands. The tape first figure- eights around the wrists, then goes around the palms fast and then loops between the hands."

The silver reflection of the duct tape suddenly became the focus of what he was seeing. "Rita was killed by someone who knew how to calf rope."

"It's bigger than that. Someone who roped like that probably killed Rita, Marla, Vera, and Heather."

"Christopher."

She rubbed her arms. "I think so. And if that's true, it suggests Amy is buried somewhere around here, bound in a similar fashion," she whispered.

He absorbed that.

Lisa got to her feet and came over, closing her hands around his. "We need to go back to Chicago."

He slowly nodded. It meant Christopher had probably shot his father.

"Quinn? We'll find out the truth."

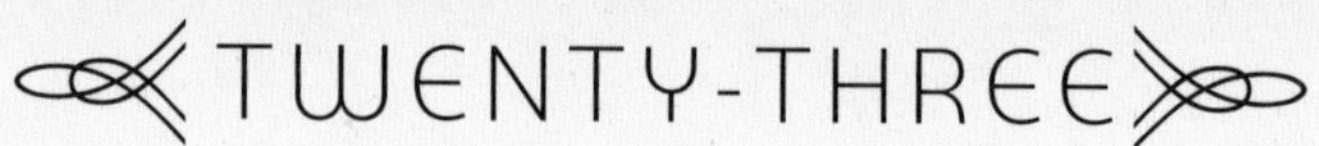

TWENTY-THREE

"Christopher did it."

"Convince me," Marcus said quietly.

Lisa scowled at her brother. She was so tired she could barely keep her eyes open, and he wanted to sit and review what she and Quinn had spent the day proving.

"Lizzy, I trust your conclusions. I just want to see how you reached them. You and Quinn are both very close to this."

She pushed back her chair and got up to walk over to the whiteboard. Marcus was right. And if she'd missed something in this list…it mattered. She'd already helped convict Grant Danford of a crime she was now arguing he did not do.

"The Plymouth clinched it."

"What? It was found?"

She nodded. "Lincoln found it this morning at a junkyard, crushed. Christopher had hauled it in. He said he'd hit a tree. It got him fifty dollars. He was the one following Quinn. As soon as we had that, the other threads started falling into place."

Marcus absorbed that, then nodded. "Go on."

She wiped the whiteboard clear to draw the circles she now knew by heart. "It's the number of links that point to Christopher, rather than any one piece."

She started with Montana. "It wasn't just Rita and Amy who were horse-crazy. So was Christopher. Quinn was the one who pointed out that to ride in the city, it takes money, access, and time. Christopher started to work for Grant Danford at the stable so he would have the ability to ride. Christopher met Rita Beck and Amy Ireland when they were at the stables taking pictures of the horses. Amy returned to Montana. A year later, Christopher went out to Montana to drive back a horse for Grant. During the time he was there, Amy disappeared and Quinn's dad was shot."

She started the list for Chicago. "Rita Beck. Christopher knew her. His testimony puts himself at the scene when she disappeared. He had access to where she was buried.

"Marla Sherrall. She was buried in the same way as Rita. Again, Christopher has put himself at the scene. He's driving the Plymouth, following us, he's the one leaving the notes about the murder, telling me to go away. He's nervous because we're investigating Rita and Amy and finding out we're investigating Marla is enough to push him into trying to stop me. He's running scared now as he feels the noose tightening."

"Why kill Marla?"

"Why he chose her? We don't know. It's the MO of the killing that makes them connected. But with Vera—the type of duct tape positively linked Vera and Heather. And we've placed Christopher knowing Vera. She worked for his uncle before she retired, knew his aunt. If she knew about the gambling—well we know Christopher had been trying to cover up that fact from his uncle."

"Martha Treemont?"

"A similar burial to the other victims, but we don't have a direct connection to Christopher. We're hoping to find it in the Nakomi Nurseries' records, that he worked a job near where she disappeared."

"Christopher burned down your house."

She nodded, hating him for that. "We think so. It's the fact Egan's house burned down. I don't think that was an accident," she said quietly. "We didn't find it, but he may have gotten away with murder. Egan didn't have to be the one who dropped the cigar. The only other person besides Christopher who might benefit from Egan's death is Walter—and that doesn't type. Walter wouldn't have risked a fire that near the nursery when a turn of the wind in the wrong direction would have sent the flames racing through the nursery grounds. The nursery is his life."

"Agreed. But Walter had to have known or at least suspected something about his brother. Lizzy, he gave Christopher an alibi for the day your house burned down."

"He's protecting the nursery, trying to be big brother. Christopher is named as a passive owner. If Christopher is proven to be the arsonist, the insurance company will come after him for the damages, and thus go after the nursery."

Marcus looked from her to Quinn.

"It's Christopher," Quinn stated. "And I want him."

Marcus nodded. "I'll get the search warrant."

"Christopher's home, vehicles, and the nursery grounds," Quinn added. "Jack thinks he can match the fuel oil if we can find him a sample of where it came from."

TWENTY-FOUR

The nursery grounds were busy on Saturday afternoon. Customer cars filled all the parking slots in front of the two long greenhouses; drivers were now parking in the grass on both sides of the road.

Quinn pushed open the nursery office door and felt a wave of slightly cooler air rush out to meet him. The front room with its open service counter, large scheduling board, and time clock was noisy with phones ringing and a fax machine active, but it was empty of customers at the moment. "Walter."

"Back again?" He tore off the fax, scanned it, and passed it to the office manager. "Write up the work order for this and check the inventory. I'll figure out which crews to assign later." Terri nodded, cast a curious glance at them, and turned toward the back office.

Walter picked up his gloves and walked around the counter. "What can I do for you?" He sounded willing to help but also looked ready to leave.

"We've got a problem."

Walter looked out the window, saw the squad cars pulling in, and stiffened. "Okay…"

"We're going to have to talk with your brother. Do you happen to know where we can find him?"

"I wish I knew. He was supposed to be working on a job at the new First Union Bank in Naperville, but he never showed. I had to send another site manager, putting the job three hours behind schedule. Why?" He groaned. "He's been gambling again, hasn't he? I knew it. What kind of trouble has he gotten into this time?"

"We'd like your permission to look around the nursery grounds while we wait on a warrant to his home."

Walter looked stunned. "What do you think he did?" He looked from one of them to the other, but they didn't answer him. "Listen, Christopher's got some problems, not the least of which is his temper, but he's an okay guy." He took a deep breath. "I own the house he's been staying in. The only thing Christopher has is a passive interest in the nursery business. As far as I'm concerned, you can look anywhere you like. I'm sure this can get resolved without going as far as a warrant."

Quinn looked at Marcus, got a slight nod. "I appreciate it. And I hope it can be resolved with a few questions. You'll be here for the next couple hours?"

"Here or up at the toolshed. I've been working on the sod baler."

"There's going to be an officer staying here at the office. Please don't move any records."

"Of course not."

"We'll be in touch."

Walter's business and home were landscaped and carefully maintained for a beautiful image. The house where Christopher was staying was the exact opposite. The yard needed mowing; weeds were growing in the cracks of the walkway from the driveway to the house.

A motorcycle was being taken apart in the front yard, a few feet off the driveway.

Despite Walter's offer, they had waited for the warrant to search the nursery grounds and Christopher's home before coming over. Quinn found the front door unlocked, knocked, and received no answer. He opened the door and stepped inside. Dumped in the hallway were two hockey sticks, a bike helmet, and a set of golf clubs. There was the faint odor of bacon grease in the air.

"Christopher? Police."

Quinn walked through the silent house.

Christopher needed a housekeeper. The place hadn't been dusted in months. The kitchen would take a few hours to clean; the dishes were piled in the sink and the counters were littered with coffee grounds and spots of jelly.

"Where do you want to start?" Marcus asked.

"I'll take the desk in the den. Why don't you take the bedroom and closets. If he's our guy, I think he'd have kept something as a memento. And if he's Lisa's firebug…well most arsonists like the paraphernalia of firemen."

Marcus headed toward the back of the house.

Quinn found the overhead light in the den had burned out and the lightbulb had not been replaced. He turned on the side table lamp.

The desk was a clutter of mail, open magazines, and jumbled newspapers; two of the drawers had caught on crumpled pages and not closed all the way.

Quinn tugged out the vinyl black cover he spotted under what appeared to be an insurance policy and found it was a month-at-a-glance calendar. It fell open at the current month. Quinn was relieved to see that Christopher apparently used it. The squares were filled with scrawled notes and times. He turned back several pages looking through the months. They'd be able to get a good idea from this who they needed to talk with to establish Christopher's whereabouts. He checked January and found it similarly marked up. Odds were good there would be a calendar from the previous year around here somewhere.

He pulled out the chair and tugged open the first drawer on the left. He found a thick brown book with its cover falling apart, held together by three rubber bands. Holding it together, he slipped off the rubber bands. It was a disorganized address book, stuffed with business cards and torn off scraps of paper with jotted phone numbers.

"Quinn."

Quinn slipped the rubber bands back in place and set the address book and calendar to one side to take with him later. He headed back through the house to join Marcus. "Find something already?"

Marcus nodded to the dresser on the far side of the room.

Quinn saw the pictures and walked forward as his jaw tightened, shocked.

Lisa paged through the printouts the office manger had run for her, looking for jobs Christopher had worked near where Vera had lived.

Walter tapped on the door. "Lisa, I've got a lead on where Christopher is, but he may not be there for long. Bring the printouts and let's drive over and get the marshals. I'd like this situation cleared up and settled. Customers are finding it rather disconcerting to see all the cop cars around."

She was surprised at Walter's suggestion but also relieved. They needed to find Christopher. She closed the printout and picked it and her notebook up. "I know it's troubling Walter, but it's necessary."

"I wish you'd just tell me what you think he did. I know Christopher. He doesn't always think before he acts, but that makes him a pain to have around, not a criminal."

Being left in the dark had to be frustrating. "It may not be that serious once we talk to him. You really think you have an idea where he is?"

"I tracked down one of his more questionable friends. Apparently there's a poker game going on this afternoon." Walter held the office door for her, and they stepped out into the bright sunlight. "We'll take the truck. Your brother said they were going over to Christopher's house."

She grabbed the door frame and pulled herself up into the truck, relieved that her back no longer barked with every move she made. The dust stirred behind them as Walter drove around the office building to the back road.

"Walter, have you ever been to Montana?" She knew the answer but wanted to hear it from him.

If he was surprised by the question, he still answered it. "A couple times over the years. We've got distant relatives out there."

"You and Christopher once drove a horse back for Grant Danford."

"Grant tell you that? We made a couple trips like that, for Grant and for his neighbor Bob Nelson. Must be twenty years ago now. What's that got to do with all this?"

Lisa took a chance and dug out the picture from her portfolio. "Do you remember ever having met this girl?"

He reached over and took the wallet-sized photo. His face went tight. "Where'd you get this?"

"You know her?"

"Sure. Christopher's got her picture on his dresser mirror."

Quinn reminded himself to breathe. There were several pictures of Amy, a couple of them taken of Christopher and Amy together. The pictures were in a small cluster near the corner of the dresser mirror, held in place by yellowing tape. "He kept the pictures of his victim."

"Quinn."

"Why else do you have twenty-year-old pictures taped to your dresser?" Quinn stepped back, clenching his fists to stop from touching the pictures. "He was involved in Amy's disappearance. He shot my father in the back."

"Maybe," Marcus said quietly.

Twenty years of looking had come down to a small collection of pictures in a run-down house in a suburb of Chicago. Rather than relief, there was intense sadness. This wasn't the vindication and justice he had sought; it was just the truth. "Where's Lisa? She needs to see this."

"At the nursery office. She was going to ask Walter about getting the customer records for the jobs Christopher worked, to see if he can be placed in the area where the women disappeared."

"It's why my brother drinks."

Walter's hands had tightened on the steering wheel. Lisa slid the photo back into her portfolio. "What do you mean?"

His expression was grim. "He was in love with her. He never got over the fact she dumped him."

"When did they meet?"

"I don't know all the details. She was here on vacation or something like that. I remember Christopher talking about her all the time. He made a big deal about getting a chance to see her when we went out to Montana to pick up a horse for Grant."

"Walter, she disappeared."

"What?"

"Twenty years ago, from her parents' ranch outside Justice, Montana."

"You're kidding."

"No."

"Christopher saw Amy that last day when we were out in Montana. We drove back home, and he never heard from her again. He started drinking heavily after that trip." Walter looked over at her, accusingly. "You're looking at Christopher, you think he's involved."

"There are some questions that need answers."

"He had nothing to do with it."

Lisa set her portfolio on the seat beside her, then turned to glance back at the *Y* in the road they had passed. "Walter, doesn't that lead around to Christopher's house?"

"Yes. But that road is blocked with sod pallets waiting to be picked up. We'll have to go around the other way."

The screen door banged shut as Marcus stepped out of the office. "Quinn, she's not here."

Quinn had pulled up outside the office, stayed in the car, his arm resting out the open driver's window, expecting Lisa to join them. "What do you mean?"

"Terri, the office manager, says Walter and Lisa were heading over to see us; they took one of the nursery pickup trucks."

That puzzled Quinn. "We should have passed them."

"Lisa may have wanted to see the cleared lot of Egan's home. They would have come around the orchard from the other direction."

"Let's go find them."

Marcus got back into the car.

Quinn drove around the greenhouses and the front of the orchard to where Egan's house had stood.

There was no sign of a Nakomi Nurseries' truck at the cleared lot. Quinn pulled in behind one of the squad cars to see if Lisa and Walter had been by.

The officer leading the group of men searching the site came over to greet them. "I was just getting ready to call you. We've found something."

Quinn got out of the car, waited for Marcus to join him, and they walked with the officer around the remaining foundation of the house. A small group of officers had assembled near the east end of what had been the garden. Someone had recently tilled under the plants and weeds, leaving the dirt evenly broken.

"There was a patch of the garden you could see had been circled around rather than tilled over. We wondered why."

It was a four-by-three-foot square of packed ground one of the officers had dug into with a shovel. He now stood a few feet away with the other officers.

Quinn accepted the collapsible shovel, carried as part of the standard equipment in the squad car trunks, and walked over to the hole.

It was the end of a cardboard box, half collapsed under the force of the shovel, less than a foot beneath the surface of the ground. Quinn pushed back more of the dirt. He used the shovel to lift back the lid, then turned his head away at the rush of an awful smell. His eyes watering, he looked at what had been found: small bits of fur still present, scorched.

A cat. Or what was left of one.

There had been a second cat caught in the fire? Why hadn't Walter said as much? He had obviously buried this one too. Quinn looked closer at the cat and frowned. This one obviously had a broken back, the front and back feet were twisted in the wrong directions.

Was this the one that had been in the bedroom, the one possibly given a sleeping pill? Sleeping under the sedation, still managing to wake to the fire, heading toward the door scared…and getting viciously kicked so it wouldn't get away.

Even if there had been no sleeping pill, this cat had obviously met a more serious fate a few minutes before the fire burned it to death.

Someone had been in the house when the fire got underway. It hadn't been an accident, a suicide…it had indeed been a murder.

"Get a small black body bag, take this in."

"You're serious?"

He gave the officer a sympathetic look; the cardboard box was not exactly in any condition to be picked up. "You'll understand why later. Just do it."

"You've got it wrong."

Lisa braced one hand on the dashboard. The truck was beginning to bounce around; Walter was going too fast for the dirt road. Seeing the tension in his face, hearing it in his voice, she chose not to comment on his driving. "How do we have it wrong?"

"Christopher didn't have anything to do with Amy's disappearance. Grant did."

Lisa felt a shiver of warning inside at the way the conversation was changing. "What do you mean?"

Walter's gaze didn't leave the road. "Grant killed Amy."

"You know this for sure?"

He nodded.

"How do you know?" Lisa whispered, watching him.

"I buried her. Or more accurately, hid her." The truck rocked as he abruptly changed roads. "Grant accused Christopher of the crime, I stupidly believed him, and I hid her body; it was the last day before we left Montana."

"Why didn't you tell someone?"

"I had disbelieved my brother. If I had bothered to check out Christopher's story before I believed Grant's accusation, I would have known Christopher couldn't have done it. Instead I assumed…and I didn't ask those questions until it was too late."

And then she understood and felt incredible dread. "Did you have reason to believe Christopher could have done it?" She hesitated but had to ask. "Had he done it before?"

Quinn turned the ignition key. "Marcus, Walter had to suspect the fire was intentionally set when he found that cat."

"He knows his brother is guilty, is trying to protect him."

"He has to know about Amy too—those pictures."

"You'd think so."

Quinn pulled back onto the road, speeding. "Lisa's with Walter."

Marcus was already reaching for the radio to check in with the officer watching Christopher's home. Lisa had not been there.

Quinn frowned. "I don't like this. She was at the office with him, left to join us, but she didn't arrive at Christopher's home or here at Egan's. Where would they go?"

"Let's check the orchard."

Quinn took that turn in the road while Marcus put out word for the other officers to systematically search the nursery grounds.

"Walter, take me back." He had just pulled out of the nursery back road onto the interstate. "We need to talk to Marcus and Quinn. It won't do you any good to warn Christopher. They'll still track him down and find him."

"I was sorry about your house, the pets. I liked the animals, especially the parrot."

"Walter." She put steel into her voice. "Stop this truck."

"You know, I should have believed him. It wasn't like the situation I walked into wasn't suspicious. Christopher and Amy had been seeing each other practically every day during our five-day visit, although she made Chris keep it quiet. She had another boyfriend from school, you know, and we were leaving as soon as Grant settled on which horse he would buy."

Walter pulled around traffic into the fast lane, heading south.

"When I walked into the bunkhouse, saw her, then found Grant suddenly behind me in the doorway… Grant laughed. I should have known then not to believe him. He was laughing about what was going to happen to Christopher."

"So you protected your brother?"

"Nothing new there. I'd been doing it for years. He was always sneaking away—gambling, partying. If my uncle had realized that…" Walter shook his head. "Christopher would have been disinherited eventually. Egan was always talking about doing it, these last few years it was a fairly constant refrain. I'm relieved that he died before he could do it."

"Walter, where are we going?"

“She’s not answering her pager.”

“Do we know for sure she’s with Walter?”

“She’s not on the nursery grounds.”

“She wouldn’t leave on her own without telling us.”

“I know. Let’s get the truck license plate. We need an APB out.” Quinn slammed the car door. “She’s got a habit of getting into trouble…but this time we let her walk right into it.”

TWENTY-FIVE

"Walter, put that down. This is crazy." Christopher had been drinking, he was showing his temper, and he was honestly confused by what was happening. So was Lisa. Petrified was the right word. The gun Walter held was ancient, a fact that worried her more than comforted. A gun not well-maintained had a habit of exploding when fired. She'd not only end up shot, she'd also probably get blinded by the flash burns.

"They know you started the fires," Walter said.

"What? I didn't set any fires."

"You left the note on Lisa's patio."

Christopher flushed. "Fine. Guilty. But what has that got to do with this?"

"You've got to leave town now, before they catch up with you."

Kate would have known what to do, would have already defused this situation. Lisa tried to intervene. "Walter—"

"Shut up. Christopher deserves a chance to get out of town. And you're going to help ensure he gets it."

"A chance because of what?" Christopher protested.

"You were following them."

"Because you told me to! You said they knew about the cash Grant paid me."

"They know you killed Egan."

"Oh, come on, Walter. You know I didn't. I had no reason to."

"He was going to disinherit you."

"Well, he was effectively going to disinherit you too by selling the nursery to pay for Aunt Laura's long-term care. And I'm not the one who considers the nursery his life."

"He wasn't going to sell the business."

"I'm not arguing with you, Walter. You just might want to rethink your assumptions," he placated. "You've been wrong about me before. You're wrong this time."

"Why did you leave the note about the hummingbirds? And the pretzels?" Lisa risked asking.

Christopher shot her a glance, looking relieved. "I was bored, okay? You and that marshal spent half the day in Knolls Park while I killed time trailing you, then sitting in my hot car watching you eat lunch. It didn't take more than a couple questions at the local bar to figure out why you were poking around that area by the pond. The note I left was one of the tamer ones I invented that afternoon. I was just twisting your tail, poking fun at your job, nothing more."

"And the phone call?"

"What phone call?"

"You called that Sunday morning when I found the note."

"Honey, thank you for the compliment, but I was drunk that morning. I dumped the tree, then I went to curse up a blue streak at the local bar before I dealt with the mess. I never called you."

Lisa understood the frustration that spoke of honesty. She believed him, but it left a quandary. Who had called? It surely hadn't been a wrong number? "Did you ever date Rita Beck?"

His startled look told her more than he realized. "What is this, memory lane?" Christopher had reason to kill Rita. He'd been dating her before she started going out with Grant.

"They're looking for you, Christopher. Come on, we're leaving," Walter insisted.

"And go where? I've done nothing wrong."

Walter raised the gun. "Get out the keys to your car. You're driving."

They had set up a command post in the nursery office, taking over the building to leverage the phones and the fax. Jack and Stephen were helping with their invaluable knowledge of the area roads, the fire department districts not just familiar to them but memorized. As Quinn argued on the phone with the state tollway officer, Marcus opened the door. "They found the truck."

Quinn hung up the phone midsentence. "Where?"

"Outside a bar in Waukegan. Cops are canvassing the area now. Let's go."

Quinn circled the counter. "Jerry, call the regional office and get us those additional resources. I don't care if you have to threaten murder, I need every available marshal out here now. Jack, Stephen—come with us." He followed Marcus outside. "Christopher?"

Marcus nodded as he opened the passenger door. "They're showing a picture around now. He was there."

"Did anyone see Lisa?"

"Not that they've found."

"The truck was left behind. Does anyone know what Christopher was driving?"

"A blue '97 Ford."

"Can the DMV find tags?"

"Already called in."

Quinn was relieved there was no sign of blood or a struggle in the cab of the truck. Lisa was keeping her wits about her.

The sun had heated the cab. The crime scene technician had just opened the door of the vehicle and the heat rolled out. Careful not to touch anything that might disturb prints, Quinn lifted out the printout from the mat on the passenger side floorboard, saw Lisa's clutch purse, and picked it up as well. Lisa couldn't have realized there was trouble when she initially got into the truck. When had that changed? She wouldn't have come here of her own free will. And she certainly would not have left here by choice.

He leaned his head against the metal door frame, sick to his stomach when he found the small black canister still in her purse. He knew she would have moved the pepper spray to her pocket had there been any way she could do so without attracting attention. "Lord, don't let her get hurt. Please don't let her take chances that are going to get her hurt." He was more worried than he knew how to put into words.

Lisa was now with Christopher.

He handed the printout to Marcus. "She was looking for evidence that Christopher had been working jobs near where the other women were killed."

"Walter knows he can no longer protect his brother."

Quinn forced himself to start thinking like the men he was after. Christopher would need to run. And Walter wanted to help him. "They're three hours ahead of us. Where are they going to go?"

"Odds would say they're trying to leave the state," Marcus agreed, "but which direction? Indiana? Wisconsin? Across to Missouri?"

Lisa was good at directions, but she was now totally lost. After the sun went down, Christopher had been taking so many turns on so many winding roads that she could no longer even figure out which direction they were going. Somewhere in the heartland of Wisconsin, far enough north that they had not passed by a town in over an hour.

The shadows of the trees they passed became orderly and evenly spaced. "Don't miss the turnoff, Christopher."

"Would you let me drive?" Christopher snarled back at Walter. He had a hangover and the two brothers had been sniping at each other during the entire drive. Christopher turned left onto a dirt road, and the jarring made Lisa clench her teeth. Wedged between the two brothers, she was getting by far the worst of the ride.

Christmas trees. Through the pounding headache she finally understood what it was she was seeing. The Wisconsin land was a Christmas tree farm.

The building that finally appeared in the light was a large equipment barn, metal sided and plain. Christopher pulled around to the side of the building. She could run, disappear into the trees. It was the first time such a moment had appeared, and she wondered if her legs would support her for the effort.

"Come on, lady." Christopher hauled her out the driver's side door, and she yelped at the surprise and the pain as she hit the steering wheel.

Walter shoved open the side door of the building. It must have been closed up for months—the air was musty, the equipment covered in a fine sheen of dust. The light Walter had turned on was a single bulb by the door. He left the overhead lights off, and the light did not penetrate past all the equipment. Did they own this place?

"Sit down."

Christopher pushed her toward a bale of straw beside what looked like a baler. She was relieved to comply. She was doing her best to read the situation and figure out what was going on with the two brothers. It was obvious Walter was trying to protect his brother, but she wasn't sure what Grant had done, what Christopher had done, and what Walter had known about.

"See if there's gas."

Christopher picked up a flashlight from the supply shelf and disappeared toward the rear of the building.

Walter paced toward the tractor and back, shifting the gun from one hand to the other. He had grown more nervous as the hours passed.

She wanted to ask him why he was doing this, what he expected to have happen, but decided silence was the best course of valor.

Christopher had admitted to being the one who was following Quinn, admitted to being the one who left the notes, but his reasons in both cases made sense: He had been bribing Grant and was worried about the investigation. She could see him getting bored watching them and doing something stupid like writing the note just to tweak her tail.

Walter believed Christopher had been responsible for the fires that had killed Egan and destroyed her home. He was trying to protect his brother but was also trying to protect his own role in Amy's disappearance.

Christopher denied setting the fires.

If Grant had been the one who killed not only Rita but also Amy, then who had killed Marla and the other ladies? She had thought it was Christopher, but if he'd left the hummingbird note not out of knowledge but as a guess…now she wasn't sure anymore. Who had really killed Marla? She had been buried in the same way as Rita; it had to be a common killer. Lisa was too confused to figure out the answers.

"There's gas," Christopher said. "Now what are we going to do?"

"We need to change vehicles."

"I am not driving all night just so we can run out of gas again in the middle of nowhere. You didn't even think to get cash before you got us into this mess."

"It's not like you gave me much of a choice. They will arrest you on sight."

"Yeah, and the three of us traveling together makes us real inconspicuous," Christopher replied. "Did you really think adding kidnapping to flight would help things out?"

She was going to have to run. These two men were on a course to implode, and she would be an albatross to be discarded along the way. The fear was making her shake.

It was late. Quinn, Marcus, Kate, Dave—they would all be looking for her and they wouldn't stop until they found her. She tried to find comfort in that, but it was hollow comfort. Had they found the truck yet? If they had, would they even be able to get a handle on where to look next?

And if they did find her while Walter was in this mood… The odds of all of them walking away unhurt weren't good. She had been sure Walter wasn't the type given to violence, but now… She had been so horribly wrong. If only she could get him to calm down and start thinking again. If the brothers did split up, the last thing she wanted was to be leaving with Christopher.

"They had to go to ground somewhere."

"Walter owns the nursery. What else does he own?" Quinn asked, staring at the maps and the dots representing reported sightings, none of them having yet panned out. There was no pattern to them, which might at least suggest a direction of travel.

"The nursery is it," Lincoln replied.

"What about Christopher? Or his uncle? Is there anything still owned by the estate while the will is in probate?" Marcus asked.

"I'll get on it," Emily replied immediately.

Quinn broke yet another pencil under the pressure of his fingers. "They haven't used credit cards, they can't go forever on the cash they had in their pockets, they had to at least buy gas even if they are avoiding a hotel room."

"It's 1 A.M. With two drivers, they could still be on the road somewhere."

"But in which direction? We're at five hundred miles now and it's enlarging with every passing hour." Quinn was scared to death at what it meant. If Lisa wasn't found within the first twenty-four hours, the odds were she would be found dead somewhere.

"Quinn, look at this." Kate nearly knocked over Jack as she hurriedly squeezed around him at the table with the maps. "Sorry." She shoved aside items on the desk to set down the crumbled printout in front of him. It was the printout Lisa had been studying. "Marla, Vera, Heather," she said grimly, flipping between pages marked in red. "Nakomi Nurseries worked jobs near them all."

"Christopher."

Kate shook her head. "Walter."

"What?"

"Not only that, there's enough evidence in here to prove Christopher was elsewhere."

Quinn felt a sense of dread. "Walter."

He inwardly shook as the implications of so many threads he had connected incorrectly registered. Multiple murders...it was all about control. Christopher didn't have the personality to try and control his surroundings. He was hot tempered, irresponsible, a drinker. Everything about Walter was about control, about shaping and ordering the world to his vision of it, driving the nursery to his vision of the business, fitting his brother into a mold. The motive didn't make sense, but the probabilities did. The problem of every investigation was the question of motive, which was answered last, if at all.

"How did we miss it?" Kate asked, her voice edged with fear.

"Worse, does Lisa realize it?" Not knowing the truth, Walter was the brother Lisa would most likely trust.

TWENTY-SIX

Marcus passed over the night binoculars. "Off to the east of the building about twenty feet."

Quinn took them and adjusted the focus. "Thank you, God," he breathed out the prayer and for the first time felt hope. They'd found the car. "Are they still there?"

"No windows, but there is a sliver of light under that side door."

The property had been in Egan's wife's name. The only good thing about the layout of the large stands of trees and expanse of the property was that they could block all exits from the property without giving away their presence. But flushing the brothers from the building without getting Lisa hurt—in a standoff the advantage would clearly lie with those inside the building.

"Let me try and talk them out, end this peacefully," Kate whispered.

Dawn was two hours away. It had been a long night searching. A confrontation after the men left the building—for all its advantages of getting them out into the open—it would also mean they were awake, looking for problems, and tightly controlling Lisa, putting her into the equation. She'd be their protection for getting out, and they would use her as their trump card. It was critical that they take her out of the equation. "No. We have to go in while we have surprise on our side." They didn't have time to wait it out.

"If that fails…"

"We won't fail," Quinn replied.

"Down on the floor! Now!"

Lisa jerked awake to a deafening concussion of noise and light so bright it blinded her. Her left wrist twisted painfully as she was yanked backward toward the bathroom door, her right ankle catching on the edge of the mower and the back of her head striking the door frame. She felt the desperation in the man holding her wrist, recognized Walter, and had no way to get traction to pull away from him.

Christopher had been near the front of the building for the night and Walter the back, neither able to stand being near the other. Men in ghostly black streaming through the blown-open doors had hit a jumble of equipment. If Walter got that door closed to the small cinder block bathroom that smelled of sour water and that spiders called home….

Her bound hands had lost their circulation. She couldn't get a grip on the now twisted duct tape that also formed a tether between her and Walter. He hadn't wanted her to be able to run while he slept, and the loop in the tape scared her to death. It wasn't neat, her hands were in front of her, but the mere fact Walter had reached for the tape told its own story. The gun Walter held caught the side of her face as he yanked her up and his arm encircled her neck. The move jerked her left arm around at a painful angle, twisted backwards so she couldn't even grasp his arm to try and get leverage to ease the stranglehold, and nearly broke her right wrist.

"Freeze!"

"Back off!"

Lisa gritted her teeth against the pain, tried to blink against the bright light in her face blinding her, had to go from memory for what was around her, stumbling back as Walter forced her to move. She felt her arm go numb as the nerves screamed.

"Let her go!"

Walter was edging around equipment moving backward toward the storage shelves. Was there an exit from the building back here? The pain was screaming and it was hard to think. If only she could fall or trip or somehow get out of the way, then they could stop Walter and this would be over.

The hold around her neck tightened.

Glass jars fell to the concrete and shattered around her feet as Walter backed into a shelf. She panicked as the overpowering smell of turpentine swallowed her senses; she tried to twist around but could feel her neck being crushed.

They shot him.

She heard it, felt the bullet hit him, and was yanked backward as he fell, his arm locked around her neck. She hit hard at an awkward angle, Walter's knee in the middle of her back. She heard her neck pop.

Around her there was a flurry of motion, voices, and hands. She couldn't respond. She couldn't breathe.

The last of her air was escaping and she couldn't draw another breath. The panic was overwhelming.

Desperate.

Panic.

She couldn't breathe.

It was no longer Walter's arm around her neck blocking her airway.

"Watch her neck."

They didn't understand, and she was desperate to make them understand, couldn't seem to move. "Lisa, hold on."

Her mouth was open, but her throat was closing. *Please, help me!*

"She's not breathing."

"Hold on, Lisa, Stephen's here. Hold on."

"She's not breathing!" *Quinn. Thank you, Quinn. Speak for me.*

Her brother Stephen appeared in her line of vision.

She could feel the calm descending, taking over the panic. The color was fading from her vision, becoming shades of gray, as her mind starved of oxygen. *Andy, oh Andy... I'm so sorry you died this way.*

"Get me an airbag and a knife. Move!"

She was going to die on her brothers. She wasn't going to be able to tell Quinn she loved him.

Her dying breath was past, her dying thought...she held tight to that final thought. There had to be a Resurrection. *Jesus, Son of God, help me.*

TWENTY-SEVEN

"Don't try to talk."

Quinn's hand was shaking as it brushed down her flyaway hair.

She had no voice even if she wanted to whisper. She could hear the whistle of air. Stephen had done a tracheotomy. Was her neck broken?

She could feel her legs and the tightening of restraints as men worked around her. It was the most blessed feeling she had ever experienced. They had removed her from the warehouse.

Quinn had never looked so good. The grayness was fading to be replaced with light, with color. The numbness in her hands was giving way to strength.

Jesus, life is so precious.

"Shh…" Quinn wiped at her tears, his distress obvious, and she had no way to tell him they were happy tears. She'd learned well from Jennifer; they were flowing. For the first time in her life, they were flowing happy tears.

She was so relieved to be alive.

Had Jesus felt like this the first time He had walked from the grave? Life was more powerful than death. She could feel it, the wonder of it, as she curled her toes just to enjoy the sensation of moving. Eternal life. The promise had an incredible meaning having now come so close as to touch it.

She'd made a mistake, drawing a line in time and dealing with her past by pushing it all away. Faith was a choice. It was a decision. It had taken years to make, but in the end it was simple. Jesus was alive. She knew more about death than anyone should. Now it was time to learn about life—the abundant life Jesus had promised. Her curiosity was full blown. And Quinn was showing her the steady way it could flourish.

She wanted to be able to hug the man and convince him to give her a kissing lesson, to swat his arm for being late to find her, to replace his intense worry with a smile. She'd risk the words now, when she could say them. She'd risk *I love you* and not worry about his reaction. He wouldn't let her down.

She blinked as the sky changed colors and realized with surprise that the dawn was grabbing the sky in a moment of time, turning it alive. She had seen it before but had never lain on her back and watched it happen. She'd missed something.

Jennifer said she liked waking early to watch the sunrise because dawn was the new day Jesus promised. A new day. A new life.

She understood now why Jennifer was so confident in spite of the circumstances. She was holding on to Jesus. And He was still healing today, bringing life, restoring hope. Jennifer needed a breath of new life and she'd sought the One who could give it. Jennifer had brought a miracle to the O'Malleys by stepping out to believe.

Sadness suddenly flooded through Lisa as her heart broke. So many years had been lost. *I'm sorry, Lord. I got so angry at Kate for bugging me about You when she was just trying to love me. Is she going to forgive me?*

It was getting hard to breathe.

Lisa tried to rein back the emotions. Now wasn't the time to give way to the emotions. Not yet. The swamping sensation across her chest was more than just emotional, it was physical. She was losing her ability to breathe.

Quinn's face reappeared, swimming across her vision. "Enough." It was a curt order, and she could hear the fear underneath it. He wiped at her tears. "Calm down, Lisa."

Lisa locked her gaze on his. *Jesus, he prayed for me in the hospital and the pain eased. I'm the one asking this time.*

Quinn suddenly leaned across her and the world filled with noise and wind. It was a sound she had heard many times in the past. At least she would be awake for this helicopter ride. Quinn leaned back and she got her first glimpse of the red and white markings on the helicopter—they'd called in one of the Chicago trauma teams.

Marcus appeared in her line of sight. His hand gripped hers. She wished she had the strength to return the grip. "Ten minutes, Lizzy, and you'll be fussed over by the experts. Stephen and Quinn are coming with you. Kate and I will meet you there. I've got to deal with Christopher first. He's got a hangover that is making getting straight answers out of him impossible."

At least Christopher was still alive. She was incredibly relieved at that. She blinked slowly to let him know she understood.

"Good girl." He looked at the paramedic. "Get her out of here."

Quinn was praying.

Lisa angled her hand on the hospital bed toward his, nudging his first finger up with hers. It was about the extent of her energy. It was such a blessing to know the man was consistent through thick and thin.

He looked up. The relief that crossed his face was incredible. "Welcome back."

She blinked slowly in reply. She was in the ICU on a trachea respirator. That fact registered slowly. She was relieved to have the help to breathe. Her stressed body hurt.

He looked so tired.

Quinn reached across her for the buzzer. She wished he hadn't done that.

He gently brushed the back of his hand against her cheek. "Everything is going to be fine, Lizzy. I promise." She held his gaze, searching to see if the reassurance was forced but found only calm confidence.

She smiled with her eyes and carefully, just a glimmer, with her mouth, for any movement that caused the trachea respirator to shift would hurt. Stephen had done a good job, but he'd been forced to work in the field, and it had been fast surgery.

Quinn smiled back. "I've been praying for you to wake up. Sorry. I know you need the sleep, but it's so good to see your pretty eyes."

That Montana drawl over tenderness...she loved listening to it.

"Lisa, I'm Dr. Paulson." She shifted just her eyes. The man was smiling at her. "You've slept away about twenty-two hours now. How are you feeling?" She decided she liked the patient voice.

She closed her eyes, then opened them. All things considered, she wasn't feeling too bad.

"The swelling has been going down since you arrived. Did you know you were allergic to turpentine?"

She wrinkled her forehead.

"That choke hold started the swelling, but the turpentine aggravated things."

No wonder she'd panicked when she smelled it. Her subconscious would have been screaming a warning as the smell enveloped her.

"Everything is going to heal just fine. You won't have more than a faint scar when this is over." He checked the monitor behind her. "You're reading at 92 percent oxygen in the blood. Would you like to try breathing on your own for a moment, get a feel for how you're doing?"

She blinked several times, and his smile widened. "I thought you might." He squeezed her hand. "I hear you make a lousy patient, wanting to play at being your own doctor, so listen carefully to the real doctor—that's me." She wanted to laugh but couldn't.

"This might make you a little dizzy," he said gently. "That's normal. The swelling is down, but it will go down a lot more in another twelve hours. It's still going to feel like you're struggling to get air. I'm going to keep you on the trach respirator until the morning regardless, so don't try to prove you're fine. I know better. Still want to try this?"

She blinked more slowly.

With a smooth movement, the doctor disconnected the respirator and covered her trachea. "Breathe for me."

It burned, her airways were so swollen, but she was able to get her first natural breath. She took another breath, as deep as she could, and felt the relief.

"Very good." He let her stay off a minute, watching the equipment behind her. "Okay, just relax." Moments later the respirator was breathing for her again.

The doctor wiped her eyes. "You held at 84 percent oxygen. By tomorrow, you'll be left with a sore throat, a headache, and my bill."

She had a comedian for a doctor. Quinn chuckled for her.

She squeezed one finger of the doctor's hand in thanks.

"Get some sleep," Dr. Paulson advised.

She had more important things to do at the moment. She turned her gaze back toward Quinn. Two minutes ago he'd looked tired, every one of his years; now…his relaxed, comfortable smile was back as he lifted her left hand and slowly entwined their fingers. "I brought you candy corn and sweet water taffy, but I had to use them to bribe the nurses so I could stay."

He was staying. She'd been afraid he would take the doctor's word as gospel and leave her to sleep.

"The family is out in the waiting room." He looked at her, his expression turning serious. "I hope you don't mind. I asked to be the one to stay."

She loved him for it. She wanted so badly to be able to talk, to share the decision she had made. It would matter to him, and she didn't want to wait until tomorrow. *Jesus, just a couple words. Please. It matters.* She struggled to form the words.

With a frown, Quinn got up and leaned over to try and hear.

"I'm sorry, Lizzy. I don't understand."

The worry in his voice… It hurt too much to try and say the words again. She closed her eyes, trying to think of something else, and felt him brush the back of his fingers across her cheek. She couldn't even turn her head to press against his hand in appreciation. It was frustrating.

She opened her eyes, locked her gaze with his, and used most of the energy she had to lift her hand. She pointed. He'd left his Bible on the table beside his chair.

"The water?"

She kept pointing.

"The card? The Bible?"

She blinked fast.

"The Bible. Okay." He reached for it and she closed her eyes, relieved. She heard him sit back down. He moved the chair closer. Now what? She opened her eyes. He solved her problem by lifting her hand and setting the Bible on the bed. The item she sought she found by touch. The folded piece of paper was still inside the front cover where she had placed it when he let her borrow the Bible. She put it in his hand and rolled his fingers around it, the paper crumbling. She smiled at him.

It was a simple message. And he'd always been a smart man. She wasn't expecting to see him blink away sudden moisture in his eyes. "It makes sense?"

She let her smile bloom not caring that it hurt. Quinn's hand had a fine tremor in it as he intertwined his fingers with hers. This time when she managed to say a couple words they were clear enough to understand. "I believe."

He laughed, squeezed her hand, leaned close, and just smiled at her. She could drown in those fascinating eyes. "I'm glad."

She had so much to say and no way to say it. About faith. Andy. What she had thought during the darkness as she waited for him to come.

He turned their joined hands and kissed the back of her hand. "Who cares if it's hardly the appropriate place," he said abruptly. "I love you. And if you walk into trouble like that again..."

Only Quinn. She looked at him and silently formed the words *I love you too.*

"You're turning into a Jennifer on me." He wiped the tears, looked frustrated when the Kleenex turned soggy before her eyes were dry, then reached over to retrieve the box. "Did you really have to spoil my big speech? I've been practicing it for weeks."

She caught his wrist, the power and strength in it impressive, wanting to laugh, yet having to settle for a gentle tug to bring him down to her.

The kiss was a brush when she wanted a real one. "Tomorrow." It was a promise. He wrapped his fingers through hers. "Be good, and I'll stay here to see the dawn with you."

She closed her eyes. This was what it felt like to be treasured. And it felt good.

"I think I kind of like you being forced to whisper for a while."

In the last three days she'd learned to be quite expressive with her body language. Lisa caught Quinn's shirt collar with her fingers and tugged him down toward her. "Hear this whispered shout. You're heading toward trouble."

He laughed softly and kissed her. She leaned into it, loving it, then she regretfully pulled back. "Don't take away my breath."

"You take away mine."

It was a lovely compliment. She had napped on the flight back to the ranch. Quinn had invited all the O'Malleys to come out for a long weekend at the ranch. Jennifer and Tom had arrived the day before. She couldn't wait to see them. She wanted to hug Jennifer.

Jesus was so good. She'd found her verse, the one she remembered from her childhood, in Psalm 18:19. It was her verse, claimed and held tight. *"He brought me forth into a broad place; he delivered me, because he delighted in me."*

She hated to memorize, and the three-by-five card had been plastered to her bathroom mirror to help her out. It was the delighted part that had thrilled her as a child, and as an adult she appreciated it even more. *Delight* was a powerful word, and yet it could barely do justice in describing the depth of emotions she felt toward God. To know He felt the same about her was priceless.

Lisa slid her hand comfortably around Quinn's forearm. "Where's my dog?"

"Your dog, huh? I thought we were going to share."

Marcus had driven down from the ranch house to meet the plane. He opened the back door of the jeep and Old Blue jumped down and shook himself. Quinn whistled, and the dog came trotting over, ignored him, and nearly knocked her over. She knelt down to return the affection.

"Traitor."

She tilted her head to look up at Quinn and laughed at his amused disgust.

She straightened and slid her arm around his waist. "We'll get you your own dog."

He tugged at a lock of her hair. "I have a feeling every animal on the ranch is going to become a pet. Just don't make a pet of my horse."

"Now that's impossible. He blows on me and I fall over."

"Lizzy, before we get up to the house: You do realize Dave is carrying an engagement ring for Kate."

She leaned against him to whisper the truth. "I talked her into saying yes."

"Did you?"

She nodded. She was proud of herself. Payback. She had owed her sister a big one, and she'd been able to deliver. Kate nervous…she hadn't known her sister had it in her to get cold feet. But she had.

It had taken just a few carefully chosen whispered words. "You were right about Jesus. I'm right about Dave. Get off the fence." Lisa was still doing a little private dancing that she'd been able to push Kate so smoothly back on track. Although it had probably helped that Kate wanted an excuse to be pushed.

"Let's go to the house." Lizzy snapped her fingers and Old Blue fell in beside her as she walked to the jeep. She wanted to see Jack.

There were now two groups within the O'Malleys—those who believed and those who didn't. It was time to close the deal with Jack, Stephen, and Rachel. It was Lisa's new mission in life. She now understood the passion that drove Kate, Marcus, and Jennifer, that burning desire to share the Good News. Lisa wanted to grab Jack's arm and drag him to church. Kate had laughed at that pronouncement and turned the tables, pulled her back, and reminded her rather bluntly how Lisa had reacted when pushed too hard. Lisa knew Jack. It would just take some creativity. Jack was a challenge. She was ready for a challenge.

Quinn paused her. "Not with Marcus. Over here." He held out keys.

"What?"

He pointed toward the hangar.

And she stopped. "You didn't have to do this," she whispered, overwhelmed.

"I know."

"Why did you?"

"It gives me pleasure."

She could barely breathe as his words settled inside. "Quinn—"

The convertible was even blue.

"It's time someone spoiled you a little." He smiled at her. "Besides, you need an excuse to visit often in the next few months." He linked his hands around her and drew her back against his chest. "Like it?"

Her thoughts couldn't keep up with her heart. A tremulous smile was the best she could manage as the emotions overwhelmed her. "Thanks."

"You're welcome." He rested his chin against her hair. "I like doing things that bring out that smile of yours. It makes my old heart feel good."

She laughed and relaxed against him, comfortable suddenly with a man who had so often confused her. "You're not that old."

"I'm ancient," he countered.

She squeezed his arm around her waist. "Lay off that malarkey. Come on, I'll let you drive me to the house." He didn't move, and she glanced back. "What?"

He smiled. "Nothing."

"Uh-huh, something. What?"

"Kate said if you let me drive it I'd know that you really loved me."

"It takes Kate to convince you I meant it?"

He kissed away her frown. "I love you, Lizzy."

"I know that. I'm holding the car keys to prove it."

He laughed. "Let's go up to the house."

TWENTY-EIGHT

"Quinn, is there a cave with water?"

The mood had become solemn the farther they rode. Finding where Amy had been buried—or as Walter had claimed, hidden—remained a mystery they had not been able to crack. The only thing that made sense was that Quinn's father had stumbled upon Walter and been shot in the back. Lisa had been back to look at the area with her family, but on this occasion she had asked only Quinn to come.

"Not that I know of."

"You said the day your father was killed that this tributary running down to the Ledds River was still filled from a flash flood the week before."

"Yes."

"Does it cut close to a cave?"

Quinn stood up in the saddle and looked around. "Farther down…see where the streambed bends? If the water had topped its banks, it would flow into the bluffs. That's how some of the deepest ravines have been cut. It's possible the water would cut into a channel near some of the caves."

"Have they been searched?"

"Those near here. There are dozens of caves in these miles of bluffs, and most of them branch off and go deep and interconnect with each other."

"Let's explore a couple of them today."

"You're up to it?"

"I'm up to it." She loved this man, and he was hurting. It was a quiet grief. She had found him on more than one occasion sitting on the back porch with Old Blue late at night. It was where he went to pray. When she'd asked what she could pray for him, Quinn had replied with one word: peace. He was searching so hard to find it. She understood. He was grieving his dad in a way he never had before. The killer had been found. Now he had to find a way to accept what had happened.

Quinn was preparing to resign from the marshal service and return here for good; she wanted to make it a clean transition for him. If she had to search these bluffs for months, she would try to find those final pieces of the puzzle. Walter had revealed enough in his words and actions that she knew it had to be possible to put the pieces together.

Walter had said Amy had been hidden. He'd used that word because it was his predominant impression twenty years later of what he'd done.

Lisa could easily imagine that day in Walter's life. Scared. Faced with the idea that Christopher had killed. Wanting to ensure that Amy was never found…

The key was the water. She was convinced of it. Every murder since then he had hidden his victims near water because water had helped him hide that first victim. She knew it from a lifetime of seeing the graves. Patterns…it was all about patterns.

He'd bound Amy's hands because he had to bring her out here, probably on a horse given the terrain. The way rigor mortis would have set in, he'd probably had to tie her body down, bind not only her hands but her legs to keep her resting across a saddle without spooking the horse. He'd buried her near water. She just had to prove it.

She shifted the reins. "Come on, Annie."

"Are the batteries in your flashlight still strong?"

"Yes." Lisa slid the flashlight strap around her wrist. Even though the reason for the exploration was grim, the cave spelunking presented just enough of a challenge behind every turn to be fun. They'd found arrowheads, places rock hounds had chipped out samples, several shed snakeskins. This would be the fourth cave.

Quinn tied the guide rope to a boulder near the entrance. "The inclines in this cave are not steep, you can walk them without a problem, but there are several dropoffs that will require a rope descent."

"I'll stay close," she reassured. He had much more experience doing this than she did.

The entrance was no more than a four-foot-high opening in the bluff. She slid inside after Quinn, had to walk half crouched for the first four feet until the cavern opened up into a six-by-seven-foot hollow. It was cool in the cave, a slight draft of air suggesting at least one of the passages led back to the surface elsewhere. The rock floor showed two small depressions still holding water. "Is that moss?"

Quinn straightened as best he could. "Yes. There must be standing water in here most of the time." His light illuminated the options. "Which way? Left or right?"

"Right."

The passage grew taller and more narrow. Quinn had to turn his shoulders to slip through the tightest places; she found it narrow but passable.

"Good choice." His voice echoed, and a few steps later she understood why. It was a massive cavern a good fifteen feet high, ten feet wide, and thirty feet long, with limestone stalactites and stalagmites from the ceiling and floor meeting each other. His light illuminated the dripping formations. "There's been water running through here."

"The colors are pretty."

"Metal deposits in the limestone."

"I wish I had my camera."

"We'll come back," he promised. "It keeps going. There's another passage ahead."

"Let's go for it."

His light cast back his shadow on the wall as he moved to the far end of the cavern and ducked to enter the next passage. "We've got our first drop."

"How far?"

"Only about seven feet, but there's water down below."

She joined him, adding her light to his. It was more of a very steep slope than a dropoff. "The water is still. It could be another shallow depression."

"Or it could be similar to a well shaft with no bottom."

"I don't think so. The passage takes a bend and keeps going." She studied it; she really wanted to go see what was around that bend. "Even if the water is deep, that ledge is wide enough for two. You can go first, check it out."

Quinn shrugged off his climbing rope and pulled on his gloves.

She knelt beside the dropoff and lit his way as he walked backward down the slope, controlling the rope to make a graceful descent.

"Okay, your turn."

Holding the rope between her hands, playing it out slowly through the metal clip and balancing her weight, she took her time, determined to move as smoothly as Quinn. An afternoon of practice had removed the rust from her skills—she enjoyed this. She landed lightly on the ledge beside him. He steadied her with a hand on her back while she secured the rope.

"Lisa."

Quinn's light reflected off something in the water. It was tucked back under a rock outcrop. "I'm going to swing over to that outcrop."

She stepped back, made sure her rope didn't cross his. "You're clear." She held her light to help him out.

Quinn swung to the other side of the standing pool, caught hold of the protruding rock. Gripping it, bracing his feet against the rock wall, he eased out more rope so he could turn, reach down into the water, and pick the object up.

He aimed his light at it, then turned his light to search the water.

"What is it?"

He slipped it into his shirt pocket, buttoned it, and looked up at the rope. With a push of his foot, he swung back across to join her. She caught his arm and steadied him.

When he had his footing, he looped the rope once to secure it. "What do you make of this?" He pulled the object from his pocket.

It was a small piece of broken glass. The one side that was not jagged was a very smooth curve of thick glass. "Not something from a pair of eyeglasses, the curve is too circular, and it's too thick."

"A camera lens," Quinn replied.

He was right. She turned the glass over in her hand, not able to determine a sense of age. The glass wiped clean under her finger.

She looked up at him and saw the change. The cop was back in front while he pushed his private emotions down. She knew him well enough to know those private emotions were going to overwhelm him.

"What's up ahead?" It was time to finish this.

Quinn squeezed her hand and turned.

He led the way around the bend, had to crouch with the lower ceiling. The passage was wide but a gash had the right side of the floor dropping away, falling into a trough, water trickling through the limestone rock slide.

Quinn shone his light along the water and rocks.

"Back up. There. Pinned between the rocks."

"I see it."

He was just able to reach it.

It was a lens cap, a piece of black plastic. Her light picked out the impression in the plastic. "Nikon." She rubbed the plastic with her thumb. "Quinn."

"I know." She heard the change in the words. He'd turned the corner, absorbed the emotion, and was taking charge. "Turn around, let's go back to the entrance. If we're going to systematically search this cavern and its passages, we need more people and a lot more equipment."

Lisa let a handful of dirt trickle through her fingers. She sat beside the small fire keeping the chill away as night came.

Kate walked over from the truck to join her, knelt to warm her hands.

Lisa appreciated her sister's silence.

They had found the truth.

It was depressing.

She was relieved it had not been Quinn who had found the remains, but rather one of the sheriff's deputies. Amy had died like the others had, strangled, buried face down, hands bound. Her dental records would confirm identity, but it was a formality. The locket she wore on the gold chain still glistened, engraved with her name.

"Grant killed Amy."

Lisa nodded and tossed a twig onto the fire to watch it be consumed. Grant had killed Amy. And Grant had blamed Christopher in order to manipulate Walter into helping bury her.

For twenty years Walter had fought the internal turmoil of trying to reconcile what he had done with his need to relive it. Lisa had seen too many murders not to understand that fatal attraction.

Walter had seen someone get away with murder, had seen Grant come back to Chicago and grow in power and money. And Lisa understood the impact of that. Grant had seemed invulnerable. While Walter's life had been anything but.

Walter—the older brother who tried to make the world work, who fought to keep his brother in line, who struggled to make the nursery business succeed—had to deal with the fact his brother gambled and drank, his uncle would sell the business out from under him. He had nothing in his life except 4 A.M. mornings and work to do.

The forensic psychologist who had the job of reconstructing Walter's motivation was puzzled by the complexity of his actions.

Lisa thought she understood the patterns. Walter had a lifelong pattern of trying to protect his brother, and in the end he had tried to frame him. It explained so much. Walter wanted out. But he had to eliminate what he was responsible for in order to get out. He couldn't just walk away.

Walter blamed Christopher—so he would frame Christopher.

Walter saw Grant as a man who had escaped justice—so he would kill Grant's girlfriend Rita and frame Grant.

Walter saw his uncle as betraying him—so he would murder him when there was no other way to stop him.

Walter saw her investigation as a threat—so he would burn down her house to force her away.

Walter acted to reexert control when he felt he had lost it. Walter murdered, hid the victims, and framed his brother for each one. For a moment in time Walter had had the control he wanted in life. He became the invincible one.

Kate reached over and stilled her hand. "It wasn't something you missed."

"Walter went to his grave taking the reasons he chose those particular women." And she'd nearly fallen for his lies. Until the end she had thought it was Christopher. She'd liked Walter. And she hadn't seen the other side of him.

"Let it go," Kate said quietly. "Even if he had explained, how much of it would be the truth, how much a lie?"

"I know. It just makes me tired."

"Walter took a lot, from Quinn in the past, from you in the present. Had he lived, it would have been hard to find sufficient justice. At least now it's over."

"Yes."

The battery-powered floodlights illuminating the cave entrance were attracting swarms of flying bugs by the time the men finally emerged from the cave carrying the body bag.

The coroner's van was opened, the body bag carefully lifted inside.

Kate went to meet Dave.

Lisa watched the men talking but chose to stay where she was. She had been in on discussions such as they were having many times in the past.

Quinn walked over to join her. He had aged during the last hours. And he had also turned the corner. The blanket of stress pressing him down for years was lifting away. In a week she bet his laughter would finally be fully alive. He crouched beside her, held out his hands to warm them.

"Her parents will be relieved to have closure," Lisa said softly.

"Yes."

The fire snapped, sending sparks into the air.

Lisa understood the silence, didn't try to break it.

"It removes a ghost."

Lisa nodded, appreciating the word he had chosen. She carried her ghosts. Quinn had carried his. That was what had changed. This had buried his ghost.

Quinn reached over and brushed back her hair. "Years ago, did you get to go to Andy's funeral?"

She shook her head.

"Would you like to have a service for him?"

It was such a simple question, and yet the comfort expressed behind it was salve over deep scars. "Quinn, I would."

"We'll have a private memorial service for Andy and my father. Finally have closure."

She wrapped her hand around his forearm and leaned her head against his shoulder. "Thank you."

They sat in silence for several minutes, watching the fire.

Quinn rubbed his thumb against her chin. "You're good for me, Lizzy."

"I know."

He chuckled and wrapped his arm around her shoulders. "Humble too."

"Somebody's got to keep you young." She gestured to the open land. "I like Montana. It kind of grows on you."

"I'm glad."

"I like your house too. Of course, that could be because I like your art collection."

He laughed, leaned over, and kissed her. "I like a lady with good taste who also tastes good."

"Horrible pun."

"It got a smile." He pulled her to her feet. "Let's go home."

"Sure."

"Want to ride double?"

"On your horse?"

"I promise Thunder will be on his best behavior."

"Quinn, he has no manners. He tried to take a nip out of my hat yesterday."

He groaned. "He didn't."

She held it out. "Look at it. You can see the teeth marks."

"Lizzy, you promised not to make a pet out of my horse."

"What?"

"He's falling in love with you."

She burst out laughing at his grim pronouncement.

"I'm serious," Quinn insisted. "What have you been feeding him?"

"I wasn't supposed to?"

"Lizzy."

"Sugar cubes. He likes them."

"You're hopeless, you know that?"

"I didn't mean to."

He wrapped his arm around her shoulders. "Sure you didn't. Please remember the cattle are sold as beef. This is a working ranch."

"Quinn—" she couldn't resist—"even the pretty little ones?"

Dear Reader,

Thank you for reading this book. I deeply appreciate it. I fell in love with Lisa O'Malley while writing *The Guardian,* and I knew her future with Quinn would make a great story. Her questions about the Resurrection were a look into the future that awaits us with Jesus.

Kate O'Malley and God's justice and mercy, Marcus O'Malley and prayer, Lisa O'Malley and the Resurrection—the stories in this series have offered me wonderfully broad canvases. I find this family fascinating. I hope you will join me for Jack's story in *The Protector*.

As always, I love to hear from my readers. Feel free to write me at:

Dee Henderson
c/o Multnomah Publishers
P.O. Box 1720
Sisters, Oregon 97759
E-mail: dee@deehenderson.com
or on-line: http://www.deehenderson.com

First chapters of all my books are on-line, please stop by and check them out. Thanks again for letting me share Lisa and Quinn's story.

Sincerely,

Dee Henderson

THE O'MALLEY SERIES

The Negotiator—**Book One:** FBI agent Dave Richman from *Danger in the Shadows* is back. He's about to meet Kate O'Malley, and his life will never be the same. She's a hostage negotiator. He protects people. Dave's about to find out that falling in love with a hostage negotiator is one thing, but keeping her safe is another!
ISBN 1-57673-819-1
Audio book also available
CD: 1-59052-101-3/Cassette: 1-59052-100-5

The Guardian—**Book Two:** A federal judge has been murdered. There is only one witness. And an assassin wants her dead. U.S. Marshal Marcus O'Malley thought he knew the risks of the assignment... He was wrong.
ISBN 1-57673-642-3
Audio book also available
CD: 1-59052-105-6/Cassette: 1-59052-104-8

The Truth Seeker—**Book Three:** Women are turning up dead. Lisa O'Malley is a forensic pathologist and mysteries are her domain. When she's investigating a crime, it means trouble is soon to follow. U.S. Marshal Quinn Diamond has found that loving her is easier than keeping her out of danger. Lisa's found the killer, and now she's missing too…
ISBN 1-57673-753-5
Audio book also available
CD: 1-59052-107-2/Cassette: 1-59052-106-4

THE O'MALLEY SERIES

The Protector—**Book Four:** Jack O'Malley is a fireman. He's fearless when it comes to facing an inferno. But when an arsonist begins targeting his district, his shift, his friends, Jack faces the ultimate challenge: protecting the lady who saw the arsonist before she pays an even higher price...
ISBN 1-57673-846-9
Audio book also available
CD: 1-59052-116-1/Cassette: 1-59052-115-3

The Healer—**Book Five:** Rachel O'Malley makes her living as a trauma psychologist, working disaster relief for the Red Cross. Her specialty is helping children. When a school shooting rips through her community, she finds herself dealing with more than just grief among the children she's trying to help. There's a secret. One of them witnessed the shooting. And the murder weapon is still missing...
ISBN 1-57673-925-2
Audio book also available
CD: 1-59052-103-X/Cassette: 1-59052-102-1

The Rescuer—**Book Six:** Stephen O'Malley is a paramedic who has been rescuing people all his life. But now he's running—from job burnout, from the grief of losing his sister, and from a God he doesn't want to trust. He's run into a mystery. Stolen jewels are turning up in unexpected places, and Meghan is caught in the middle of the trouble. Can Stephen rescue the woman he loves before catastrophe strikes?
ISBN 1-59052-073-4
Audio book also available
CD: 1-59052-114-5/Cassette: 1-59052-113-7

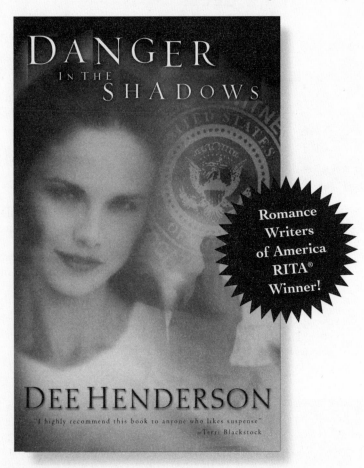

JOIN US IN AN ALL NEW DEE HENDERSON WEBSITE AT www.deefiction.com

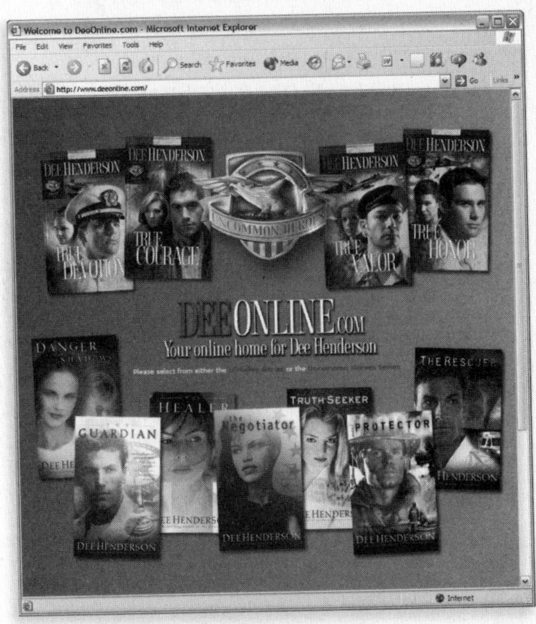

This site is packed with information, sample chapters, and consumer activities on the O'Malley and Uncommon Heroes series by Dee Henderson.

THE UNCOMMON HEROES SERIES

by Dee Henderson

TRUE DEVOTION
Uncommon Heroes series, book one
While Navy SEAL Joe Baker struggles with asking Kelly to risk loving a soldier again, Kelly's in danger from her husband's killer, and Joe may not be able to save her...
1-57673-886-8
Audio book also available
CD: 1-59052-123-4/Cassette: 1-59052-1226

TRUE VALOR
Uncommon Heroes series, book two
Gracie is a Navy pilot; Bruce works Air Force pararescue. When she is shot down behind enemy lines, Bruce has got one mission: get Gracie out alive…
1-57673-887-6
Audio book also available
CD: 1-59052-178-1/Cassette: 1-59052-177-3

TRUE HONOR
Uncommon Heroes series, book three
Navy SEAL Sam "Cougar" Houston is in love with a CIA agent. But it may be a short relationship, for terrorists have chosen their next targets, and Darcy's name is high on the list...
1-59052-043-2
Audio book also available
CD: 1-59052-118-8/Cassette: 1-59052-117-X

TRUE COURAGE
Uncommon Heroes series, book four
FBI agent Luke Falcon is hunting his extended family's kidnappers. He fears that if his family never returns, his own chance at love may vanish as well.
1-59052-082-3
Audio book also available
CD: 1-59052-121-8